THE SPIRAL ROAD

JAN
DE HARTOG

HARPER & BROTHERS

NEW YORK

THE
SPIRAL
ROAD

THE SPIRAL ROAD

CHAPTER ONE

T HE old man lifted his champagne glass, held it up against the light, and waited so long before he spoke that he startled the boy when he said, "Dear Anton Zorgdrager," so many times had he held a test tube against the light with the same gesture, to mutter, "Cloudy as hell." To the boy it made the festive table suddenly seem unreal; the well-known faces in the candlelight no longer seemed friends who had come to congratulate him on his success and wish him good luck on the eve of his departure, but episodes of his life which had come to bid him farewell before the new existence began in which they would have no part. An odd thought occurred to him: "Now I could die; this is the end of a well-rounded life."

He no longer listened to what the old man was saying at the head of the table; he scanned the double row of faces now turned away from him in gay attention, a double row of memories—this must be the way a drowning man saw his life pass in front of him once more in those last moments before death. He looked down at his champagne glass and tried to capture his reflection; the gesture, intended to break the spell, deepened it. Candlelight, wind, a shutter banging monotonously in the attic, in the shadow beside the fireplace the slow ticking of a grandfather clock. Himself a thin child on a high-backed chair at the supper table, trying to catch his reflection in a cup of tea, trying not to listen to his father talking like a dream penguin in his black coat and his white shirt front, talking against the wind and the loneliness and the sleep, "Professor I could have been . . . Fame and riches could have been mine . . . but God punisheth those He loveth: your mother had to die; I had to shoulder the cross of becoming a parson in the bleakest corner of this bleak country, so that in the end I might live like Jesus: saving souls . . ." And the child's cool reflection: liar, windbag, he talks about saving souls but doesn't leave any cheese for me.

The dislike for his father came back to him for a moment like a cold draft; it was part of the old vicarage, the foaming elms in front of the attic window, the fear of Jesus' revenge after he had secretly stuck out his tongue at Him inside his hands folded for grace. It all came back: the sadness of the lowlands, his fury as he tried to cycle against the gale along the dike to school; the false piety of the spinsters of the congregation who sat nodding while his father's voice inquired plaintively of God how many angels could take a seat on a needle's point; the smell of humid plush and stale cigar smoke in the vestry where the spinsters came to maudlin after the service, while his father changed collars and the elders sat counting the collection on the green baize table underneath the window with the fly screen. The desolation of the motherless child came back: smoking in the attic, vomiting in the old-fashioned privy afterward; shooting sparrows with a catapult on the roof; waking up sobbing from the feverish dream that his mother had put her hand on his forehead and brought him a cup of mint tea and asked what fairy tale he would like to hear and he had answered: "The Little Mermaid."

He heard laughter around him, looked up and saw Dr. Bakker beam across the festive cake, his eyes sparkling in the candlelight, a drop of wine like a ruby in his mustache. He was flushed with the drink and the heat, his lower lip glistened underneath his open mouth, he listened eagerly like a child. It was wonderful to see him like this, it chased the chill of those other memories with a wave of affection. He loved that man; God only knew how his life would have turned out without him. He remembered him as he had first seen him years ago: an untidy giant with a wild mustache, dusty animal's hair and bushy eyebrows over two sky-blue eyes that radiated friendliness. He remembered him singing on the box of his buggy and spurring on Gracie, his mean but untiring mare, with obscene noises and Indian yells as they swayed and bumped along the frozen cart tracks toward a confinement, a broken leg or a boil, the sun a disk in the mist and their faces taut in the morning air. Old Bakker had given him his goal in life: to become a doctor; for he had never once uttered the words "saving souls" and yet saved more of them than he had ever caught fish, though the one photograph in his home pictured him, grinning, with a rod and a dead pike.

He saw the still canal again, the sailing white clouds among the king-cups and the green islands of duckweed. He heard the reeds whisper again in the soft summer's breeze, and the lowing of the cow behind the dike. Dr. Bakker and he were fishing while waiting for the confinement of a farmer's wife, and while they both sat staring at the little red float, he suddenly confessed that he wanted to be a doctor. Bakker remained silent for a long time, then he said, "Could do worse. Not bad as professions go," but he hadn't managed to hide his emotion. Between them stood his midwifery bag, limp and ugly after fifteen years of almost daily use; and the very moment their float dived, the farmer shouted "Doctor!" above them, on the crown of the dike. Bakker scrambled cursing to his feet, grabbed the little case by the scruff of its neck, cried, "Keep it going, boy, I'll be back in a minute," and an hour later he giggled because he had taken the jam jar of worms with him; it had fallen over in his bag when he opened it at the bedside. In the meantime, he had saved two tiny souls by holding them upside down by their ankles and smacking their little blue buttocks until they squealed. For an hour he had sweated and slaved in his rolled-up shirt sleeves, his ears ringing with screams, yet the only thing he talked about on the way back was the pike they had missed. It was impossible not to compare that man to his father.

Yet he would never forget the trembling of the lips in his father's podgy face when he told him that he wanted to be a doctor. He had to think violent words: hypocrite, liar, to prevent himself throwing his arms around that lonely neck as he heard him stammer, "I had so hoped that you would one day follow in my footsteps; we have so many things in common. . . ." During the years that followed, his conscience stared at him with that face. He saw it in front of him in the empty sky as he cycled along the dike, every day to college and back. He saw it in the wavering candlelight as he sat doing his homework at the table; he saw it in the darkness as he lay listening to the rain in the elms outside the attic window. The only joys of those years had been the rounds with Dr. Bakker through wind and snow, fog and sun, the gazing through a microscope at the miracle of the splitting microbes in a drop of ditchwater, even the nausea when he had to hold an arm while the flashing lancet slashed a sore. And now there old Bakker sat, on the other side of the festive table, like a hand-colored woodcut with those angular shadows and black grooves in the candlelight. He had pulled a generation of toilers and shapeless women out of the clay with those big hands of his; and yet never had a thought about the simple greatness of his life. He had just been honest and common in indignation and in joy, with an instrument case like a mongrel and an umbrella like a branch and a night-shirt and nightcap and a bachelor's iron bed. Old Bakker had comforted him when his father died and he had found himself helpless with inexplicable grief; old Bakker had found a job for him in an office in town after his graduation when there was not enough money to go to the University; old Bakker had, three months later, noisily mounted the stairs of his dismal digs, flung open the door, cried, "Vivat!" thrown his arms around him and danced until they fell dizzily onto the bed. Then, panting, he told him the news: he could continue his studies after all, thanks to a relative of his in the Ministry of Health. He told him of the miracle incoherently and with tears in his eyes; the tears and the joy came back as poignantly as the smell of cabbage, the slanting gray light through the high little window, and the print of the kitten in the boot over the bed. Yes, he could become a doctor after all, and it wouldn't cost him a cent: the Dutch Government offered a scholarship every year to a limited number of young men to study medicine at the expense of the state, on condition that they signed a contract to serve ten years as a Government doctor in the Dutch East Indies after they qualified. The relative in the Ministry had promised to sneak him in for a bottle of Geneva and five hundred cigars; well, boy, how's that?! They slapped each other on the shoulders, cursed with joy, and terrified the landlady as they thundered down the stairs. They had a meal in a real man's place with wine and a pudding that was on fire and finished with coffee, brandy and black cigars. They daydreamed without stopping, about the jungle and the tigers and you watch out, boy, for those brown girls; they gave a guilder to the violinist of the trio to make him play "High in Yonder Coconut Tree" and they toasted one another, solemn with emotion, until old Bakker looked at his watch and suddenly fled, for the last train was about to leave and Mrs. Hansen's baby was expected that night. Now there he sat: listening to the speech of a Professor of Tropical Hygiene who addressed his assistant Anton Zorgdrager like a son, holding the golden lily of his champagne glass delicately by its stem. Now the grease of colored candles dripped on the icing of the cake, a fluttering ring of little flames round the legend *Cum Laude* in chocolate. The candle flames flattened and smoked; the door was opened by Trudi who carried a tray.

Trudi—fat, blowsy, giggling; during the first weeks she had seemed to be the only kindred soul in the somber teacher's home where an advertisement had landed him as a paying guest. The pompous curtains, the haughty brass, the spinsterish china in the glass cabinet—God, how lost and lonely he had felt, before Els arrived like a butterfly among the moths. The only thing he could remember of that first meeting with her was a halo of blond hair and two cornflower blue eyes, so guileless, young and gay that he had blushed with sudden shame of his pimples. It seemed incongruous that this elfin creature was the daughter of that bottle-shaped father and that mountainous mother, and the sister of those flat-chested suffragettes who talked French at table on Saturdays, German on Mondays and who, after dinner, made the Erl King gallop round the room with his child's corpse four-handed, until Trudi came in with the tea. Everything she did that first night seemed breathtakingly reckless in that haunted house, where every day was an exact replica of the previous one: 6 A.M., one—two—three—knees—bend—early-morning—P.T.; 7:30 A.M. for-what-we-are-about-to-receive-Oh-Lord-make-us-thankful-amen—breakfast; 7 P.M., Job sixteen—verses eleven to twenty—Supper; 9 P.M., did-you-read-about-that-murder—tea; 10:30 P.M., night-Mums-night-Dad-night-Anton—bed; and 1:30 A.M., the neutral swishing of Mums on the toilet. He watched her with a feeling of alarm, constantly looking from Mums to Dad to Prue to Sis to see how they reacted, but they stuck to their timetable undaunted. Dad read the newspaper through his pince-nez and glanced at the clock over it; Mums counted loops with praying lips and then continued to knit with her head in her neck and her double chin knitting too; Prue and Sis read magazines, their lips tightly shut and their knees pressed together; nobody seemed to notice that all pomposity had been chased by that guileless gaiety, that silvery laughter, that whiff of perfume, that grace and, my God! those eyes. She warmed her hands around the lamp with pink opalescent fingers; Dad continued to read although he could hardly see. She sat down on the floor with a graceful innocence, as if she were nude; Mums continued to knit although she was sitting on her wool. She asked him a hundred questions, so frank and unexpected that he blushed and blanched in turn, but let the answers slip out before he realized; Prue and Sis leafed on through *Homes and Gardens,* and only their breathing betrayed their fascination. She asked, for instance . . .

Her laughter beside him startled him out of his reverie, and he put his hand over hers with sudden tenderness. She didn't notice it; she was looking at Professor van Goor at the head of the table; the candle flames twinkled in her eyes. "I don't think I need explain how funny it was," the old man said. "My young friend will doubtless remember . . ."

Yes, as if it were yesterday. Their first meeting in the park: "Anton, what on earth are you doing here?" when he knew for certain that the shortest way to her cookery school was not through the park. The doubts, the recklessness, the cowardice, the delight and the horror of that autumn, hazy with love; their first kiss, "Don't! Don't . . ." with only their breaths in the silence and the dripping of a leaf, the fog a little rainbow round the gaslight, and behind the tree a cave of shadow reaching into the darkness. Then the steps of the park keeper slowly approaching on the gravel, the flash of the gaslight on his epaulets, his shadow swinging round the lamppost, and his steps slowly crunching away. The moving innocence of those first months secretly holding hands on the couch while the sisters made the Maiden pray; the trembling kisses in the darkened corridor, with the voices of Mums and Dad loud behind their bedroom door: "No, no, *there,* man! There it goes, near the lamp!" and then the thud of a pillow thrown at a mosquito against the ceiling. The daydreams about her as a doctor's wife underneath the waringins, in a little pavilion with a gallery and a babu and a djongos, and of how she would help during operations in a white coat and a little white cap. Then the slowly encroaching sin, the desperately fought desire, the wild embraces, the burning lips, the panting breath, but suddenly a door opening, or a cough in the hall, or Trudi with a vacuum cleaner, or "Prue! Are you upstairs?"—"Yoohoo!" The inner battle, won by day but ignominiously lost by night in unsavory nightmarish dreams; then, like an act of God: Mums' eyes, enormous and distorted behind a lorgnette, staring at an innocent little kiss underneath the coat stand as if through a magnifying glass. Dad's hoarse speech, pacing to and fro with his hands behind his back, frequently glancing at Mums, like an unsure actor at the prompt corner. Els to a boarding school! Anton ought to be ashamed of himself! Misuse of trust! Received like a son! If he weren't an orphan! Only one solution: proofs of his good intentions. Proofs by studying, by passing examinations, cum laude, magna cum laude, by serving ten years in the Dutch East Indies keeping pure, and then, finally, back to Holland, buy a practice and they would talk again. Now not another word! To bed!

Examinations . . . The first corpse, anticipated with horror, shameless and impersonal in its blue nakedness; the frozen grin of yellow teeth, the smell of Lysol, the professor snipping and cutting the colorless material like a tailor. The fear of contamination: aware of teacups and doorknobs and washing one's hands fifteen times a day; the headache that was typhoid fever, the belly-ache that was dysentery and the temperature that was lockjaw. The loneliness, the feeling of being an outcast from the community of the students, a state orphan: member of no club, no debating society, none of the beer-drinking associations with names like "The Friends of Erasmus" and "Truth Above All" in Latin; instead of that the frustration of the inferiority complex, and a strange revulsion for the other pariahs: teetotalers and nail biters with permanent colds in their noses. The embittered concentration on his work: reading, studying, taking his revenge for missed parties and masked balls to which he had not been invited by provoking compliments during public lectures. "The liver, you say, Mr. Meters? You must be feeling liverish yourself. Any of the other gentlemen? You, Mr. Zorgdrager? The gall bladder, that's right. It would seem that you are the only young man present who is aware of the fact that his pater has enrolled him in the Faculty of Medicine," and the snigger of the asses at the word "pater." And during that time, only one longing: Els; and one friend: Bert.

There she sat, as manly as her name. The sharp shadows of the candle-light underlined the earnestness of her proletarian boy's face now she was listening to the speech of the old aristocrat with unmoved mouth and eyebrows and a defiant lock of hair on her forehead. The one thing she could not control, that remained feminine despite her passionate efforts to appear sexless, was the sensitivity of her nostrils, finely chiseled and touching in their secret nervousness. And then her hands—his first memory of her was her hands.

She had been the first to make an incision during the first dissecting session. A gesture of politeness from the professor that had seemed ghoulish, and that had given the ring of pale and nauseated youths standing around the corpse a feeling of relief and superiority. She had accepted the challenge without hesitation; the lancet had trembled in her hand for only a moment before she mastered herself, relaxed her grip and made her incision: a swift curve that opened its lips at once, like a mouth. He had seen it all in that one gesture—the hesitation, the self-control, the courage—and looked up at her with a new interest. He had noticed her before because of her square shoes, shapeless skirt, boy's haircut and owlish glasses. Now he looked at her with different eyes.

When he missed a lecture and had to catch up with the dictation, he asked her for her copy. A firm handwriting that tried to be impersonal, yet the passion broke out occasionally in a flourish at the end of a word or the open arms of a capital letter. He took the exercise book back to the address written on the cover: up three bare flights of stairs, past two floors with whining children, scolding women and growling men behind closed doors. Only when he saw the astonishment on her face as she opened the door, drying her hands on an apron, did it occur to him that she might think he had come out of curiosity. She was small in her slippers, and sincerely surprised to see him. She lived with a carpenter's family, helping in the household for her keep; their first conversation was constantly interrupted by a squinting child with a rash that wanted its nose blown and a shrill woman who gave six smacks to a pair of screaming twins in five minutes. He didn't understand how she could possibly concentrate in such a bedlam; she laughed and took him with her to her study: the tropical hothouse in the Botanical Gardens, where there was never a soul about and where she sat working every day on an iron bench in the damp, hot dusk.

Only months later, after they had become friends, did she tell him something of her life, while he was hearing her lessons on the bacteriology of infectious diseases. What had been the cause of this sudden burst of confidence was difficult to say: it was a misty autumn afternoon with gossamer threads between the branches of the trees outside; the banana trees and the palms of the hothouse looked like the diorama of a tropical island underneath a steamed glass bell. After the first careless words she suddenly felt embarrassed, but she went on, avoiding his eyes as she talked, staring at a fiery red bunch of cactus flowers in the darkness as at a log fire. She told him that she had never known her parents, who were officers of the Salvation Army in a leper colony in Indonesia. She had been born there and had been taken away after three months because her mother had contracted leprosy. Up to the age of sixteen, she had been in a Salvation Army home in Rotterdam, then an uncle in the Far East had sent her money to pay for her medical studies. She told him almost nothing of her youth, but he guessed a great deal from his own experience. Her loathing for singing hymns to the accompaniment of a harmonium, her suspicion of the sincerity of the Salvationists' children as they talked about "conversion" and "salvation" without knowing sin, and made hysterical confessions of childish mischief to an audience of converted drunkards and whores. Her lifelong hankering after truth; her desperate clinging to facts, like someone drowning in a swollen river of emotions; her deification of common sense and exactitude as opposed to the Soul-saving Fount of Blood and the Mercy of the Lamb. Every night, in bed, she had read Marx's *Kapital* before going to sleep instead of the Bible; she had scolded as hotly during Communist debates as her fellow-orphans had prayed during holiness meetings and she had stood as doggedly in the sleet on the street corners with *The Daily Worker* as the others had with *The War Cry*. Two things her upbringing had imprinted upon her: the horror of poverty, the shame of illness; when it was almost dark, and all he could still see of her was her silhouette, he heard her say, "I know that I am the child of a whore and a thief, unless I believe in their rebirth in Jesus," and he realized that she had turned into a Salvationist after all, with Marx's gospel, Lenin for savior and the lancet as her sword of faith.

Now he saw her sitting there he wondered why they had never fallen in love. In the romantic candlelight she was almost beautiful, a surprising beauty, the way those modern stone monsters on the new bridges could suddenly be beautiful when a sunset gave their snouts the warmth of humanity. But the very thought made him smile. Fall in love? They knew one another too well for that. Yet, she was the only one he would really miss, he suddenly thought. It had always been a solution to any problem and any mood of senseless melancholy: to go to Bert, take off one's coat, rub one's hands, talk about films or traumatic neurosis, to have one's ears boxed with the tractor production as a decadent individualist without class consciousness; or just to smoke a cigarette in the cozy light of her little oil stove and to answer "Mmm" when she asked if the tea was sweet enough.

His first contact with the human animal was established thanks to her; an organization of Red Children had been founded, something like the Boy Scouts but proletarian and wearing sandals. He helped run a summer camp to do her a favor, and for the first time in his life he felt the devotion of jubilant paupers' children. He played at Indians, burned pancakes weeping with the smoke from wet twigs, and told Oriental lies at the campfire: stories of lion hunters and pirates and gold diggers, deliberately unproletarian and without any concrete message but that the end of every dream must consist of marrying and getting rich if it wants to satisfy even conscious workers' children.

That fortnight in the forest, so pathetically small and with every secret little path barred by the notice *Trespassers will be Prosecuted,* became a revelation as far as Bert was concerned. One evening, when it was her turn to tell a story, and all she could remember was "Tom Thumb," he sat watching her for half an hour, playing with sentimental thoughts. What a splendid woman she was, after all; what an indefatigable mother, what a simple, honest girl. But toward the end of her story she slowly changed in the dying glow of the fire. Something wild and gipsylike broke through her careful mask of laboratory worker, a fury and a tenderness that he had never suspected in her. When the children were in their tents and he saw her silhouette undress on the lantern-lit side of her tent, he felt a momentary impulse to go in, urged by the sudden thought that he had thousands of things to say to her, that they didn't know one another at all, that this night was a crossroads, the last chance to grasp something that was precious—but it flitted past so swiftly that he shrugged his shoulders and went to bed, humming, with Els's portrait underneath his pillow of rolled-up clothes. A few weeks later, during an examination, he smiled again at her masculinity, and now it was too late.

Too late, too late . . . In a few days' time, he would go on board a ship and end this life completely, like a death. The thought of the sinister completeness of these years came back with all the symptoms of a deathbed: remorse for lies, regrets for missed chances, the realization of the futility of it all; he fled by listening to old Professor van Goor, who had been addressing him all that time with his glass in his hand.

". . . so let me repeat it once more as a farewell message: your only thought during all this should be for the patient. Without the humanitarian motive as the mainspring of your ambitions, you will find in the tropics only disillusion, loneliness and moral degeneration. The examples of derailment as a consequence of an exclusively materialistic attitude have left such a clear imprint in my memory . . ."

The stolid burghers of the seventeenth century must have looked like him: a starched ruff with that goatee, lace cuffs with those patrician hands, and he could resume his place in one of the gilded frames on the wall of the bursar's office. Yet he wondered where he would have found the courage to persevere during those arid years without van Goor's inspiring idealism. The humanitarian motive of medical science vanished quickly the moment one came to know the surgeons admired as demigods for the butchers they were, and the young man who sat musing in the concert hall about the greatness of the victory over death during Beethoven's Ninth should assist at a brain operation by Ostrovsky to be cured by Polish curses, or watch the interns throw old goiters at one another like snowballs in the courtyard of the Central Hospital to be awakened from his heroic dream. What a wave of tenderness the feeling of Els's small hand under his gave him—only with sugary thoughts could he chase the memory of the screaming prostitutes who, during a public confinement between lunch and tea, shrieked to shreds the romance of Amsterdam's Old Quarter.

Thank God for Els, for her loyalty and her trust and her unquestioning faith in the nobility of his work! She had come to know him so well after all those years of writing letters with crosses and weekend kisses and cufflinks for Christmas; she sensed at once if something was worrying him. "You're a big sweet dope," she would say, her child's face so wise in the restless light of the fire that all bitterness inside him waned. "If you don't have anything to worry about, you go to the black shop and say, 'Could I have another of those little problems, miss? I've finished the last one. Yes, that one's fine.'" That was why their love had grown out of the calf stage so naturally and without drama: she needed say only a few words to chase his gloom and make him smile with a sigh at the childishness of his own worries. She listened unruffled to his stories of Ostrovsky's curses and van Goor's sneers and Groen's senile blather; she let him get rid of his pent-up confessions of powerlessness, fear, despair and pointless rage; then she would ask, for instance, what old Meesters' operation had been like. The very question was a miracle of insight, for then he saw, in his mind's eye, the whispering little old man again with his incredibly calm little hands and his serene concentration during one of the minute eye operations that had made him famous; like an old watchmaker he stitched soapsud-thin membranes with microscopic stitches of gossamer gold thread; after watching an operation by old Meesters, one could only swallow and put on one's hat and go silently outside, back into a grotesque, clumsy world.

Els was the radiant proof of how good and simple and gay ordinary things could be, if they were set aglow by the joy of a cheerful heart. True, occasionally, after a heavy week in the hospital or after a day of grim cancer operations that remained gruesome even though one got used to them, her smile by the fireside could give him a shock, a short, staggering suspicion of the validity of their simple happiness. Her guilelessness would seem childish for a second, compared to Bert's motionless white mask at the first stench of the uncovered tumor. As he kissed her forehead, he saw across the soft scented warmth of her hair Bert's face like a hallucination on the curtains: motionless, controlled but for a drop of sweat that trickled down her forehead, along her nose, until it hung sparkling, threatened to fall, and was wiped off by the impersonal glove of a theater nurse. The precipice of doubt that opened at his feet during seconds like those was so breath-taking that he closed his eyes and, with a kiss, fled in Els's childlike love from the very doubt it had brought him. Fortunately those moments were rare; he could no longer imagine life without Els. He could not understand why Bert did not collapse with exhaustion, break with exertion, cave in under the leaden weight of her grim earnestness. Els was the sun, the tingling cold of the first swim of the summer, the tea on the lawn, the weeping with laughter at the fat film comics throwing puddings in one another's faces, the sniggering at the joke page of *Weekly Life* with his stockinged feet on the arm of the sofa and yes, I'd love another marshmallow. Els was spring in the park, the puppies at the neighbor's, the blessed stillness of a kiss after a week of moaning, starched skirts rustling over inaudible footsteps and the death rattle of the dying monkeys in the Tropical Institute. Els was a sigh, a slender arm, a hand slowly closing in delight, a tremulous cry; unassailable vision of happiness in the dusk of a jungle of doubt. No black necrosis, no bloody gangrene, no smell of death or heartrending retching could assail the reality he now held caught like a bird under his hand. He looked up at her, so full of love, faint fear and desperate longing, that ... Damn! Van Goor had finished. There was applause.

He stood up. "Chief, friends ..." Damn, hoarse. "I want to thank you for this party, this ... this unforgettable farewell." A penny for Bert's thoughts. "I thank you all for your presence, that is more than just a gesture. It is a ... a symbol, the personification of everything my life has consisted of so far ..." God, what a loneliness all of a sudden, as if he were addressing crates in a cellar. "Friends, whatever the future may bring, the memory of this table, these faces, will be, to me, the essence of my life in Holland once I am far away from you all, in the Far East. ..." Far East? Green, hot, topee; he knew nothing about it, nothing at all. Might as well go to Alaska. "Professor, Dr. Bakker, Mums, Dad, Prue, Sis, Bert, Els ... Here's to you all."

He concentrated, suddenly self-conscious, on emptying his glass, and only noticed the silence as he put it down. Nobody had applauded; van Goor wiped his mustache with his napkin, old Bakker nodded at him with blinking eyes and a failing grin; Mums and Dad were still drinking, their heads back, like a duck and her drake; Bert looked at him with her operation face that suddenly irritated him; Prue nudged Sis because she had spilled wine on her blouse, and Els had tears in her eyes, the darling. God, how lovely she looked in that blue dress with the gold dust of the candlelight in her hair. . . .

He kissed her without reticence, suddenly overcome once more by that eerie feeling of finality. Then they applauded and Dad closed the meeting with a spark on his watch chain and a gleam on his bald pate. Mums said, "Coffee! Cake! Sitting room! Trudi!" He did not get another chance to think until after the coats were brought from the chilly hall and everyone left after a lot of handshaking and slamming of doors and "Good Lord, it's raining!" and disappeared into the glinting darkness of the night. While he held Bert's hand, he almost said, "I'll call in later," in a foolish impulse to talk with her about that feeling of the completed existence; but luckily she said, "Splendid evening!" with such convincing sincerity that he came to his senses with regret. When he wanted to talk to Els about it before going to bed, the sisters called down the stairs and Trudi came in for the ashtrays, so they didn't get any further than a passionate kiss and the whispered words they had spoken so often by now that they almost sounded like saying grace.

Alone in his room, irresolute with all those heavy thoughts, like suitcases he didn't know where to put down, and with the rain rustling against the window panes, he took off his shoes, his tie, and suddenly stood looking at himself in front of the mirror, his toothbrush in his hand.

Fair hair, gray eyes, an irresolute chin; a face one met everywhere, three to every streetcar. A middle-class boy about to go east; a respectable nonentity.

CHAPTER TWO

Down to Genoa the sea voyage was a pleasure. There were a few people on board, more stewards than passengers in the vast dining saloon; the more experienced travelers had taken the train, saving a week's voyage. The three other young men in Anton Zorgdrager's cabin were tenderfeet like himself, put together by a clerk who had looked at a list and picked them because of their ages. As at school, the four started by hating the sight of one another and ended by wondering what benevolent Providence had brought them together, so well did they harmonize. They discovered this after Genoa.

Until then, the ship was luxurious and grand. At the vast assembly line of dining tables the sparsely sown passengers behaved with self-conscious decorum; the funny paper hats and childish squeakers handed out to them by aristocratic Javanese to put their minds on other things than manners failed to have any effect. They continued to eat silently, listening to an old vegetarian who ate celery, and nobody blew his squeaker. There was a tall, thin woman with two old-fashioned locks of hair on her temples close to her eyes, who suddenly, one moonlit night, brought out a cello, sat down in the deserted music room and started drawing quivering curves of sadness in the silence. The four young men, who had not yet arrived at the stage of playing poker, gathered shyly in the dusk outside and Anton felt his eyes fill with tears, thinking of Els. Harry Frolick, who slept in the bunk below his and who was on his way to the island of Celebes as a junior civil servant, whispered: "Lovely touch . . . Do you know what her name is?" Anton answered: "I don't, I'm afraid, but she's good." "Perfect," Frolick said. "Listen to that glissando. She must be a pupil of Casals." Then came Genoa.

The boys had looked forward to the arrival of the other passengers, the experienced ones. They had rapidly found out that the passengers with whom they had left Amsterdam knew nothing about the Far East; they

14

were all tenderfeet like themselves. In Genoa, the true rulers of the Dutch East Indies would join them, and in their mind's eye they had seen a taciturn crowd of stern bronzed men whose eyes had the greenish hue of long years spent in the jungle. They were not at all prepared for the bewildering herd of drunks that stood bellowing on the quay, whistled on their fingers for their luggage, pulled the caps over the eyes of the Italian porters and trampled on board as soon as the gangway was out like a horde of barbarians rushing a breach in a city wall.

They were so staggering in their noisy vulgarity that the four young men retired, flabbergasted, from the bar, which had changed within a matter of minutes from a discreet retreat, ideal for a private conversation, into a speakeasy on New Year's Eve. They retired to the promenade deck, where they settled down in a clover leaf of deckchairs; but there the women came a-swarming, a herd of quacking, waddling geese, who snarled at the stewards and screeched as they pinched their fingers in the deckchairs. The four young men fell back on the music room but there, underneath the aristocratic palms, where once the tall lady's cello had sobbed in the starlit night, now a fat man with bulging cheeks and a congested neck was forcing elephantine farts out of a trombone, while a lout with prizefighter's hands pummeled the piano.

Nowhere on board the majestic liner was there one quiet spot left, and worst of all were the meals. The rowdy crowd sitting down at the long tables with the rumble of an earthquake was horrible to behold and worse to hear. The paper hats came out again and the squeakers were blown until they burst; ghouls with foot-long cigars went round popping balloons and were rewarded with shrieks of laughter; barnyard sounds of digestion rang out shamelessly, and the aristocratic Javanese servants, who had hardly moved at polite democratic requests from man to man, flew like birds at commands that a horse would have balked at.

"Never," said Witzenburg, "will we descend to that level, with God's help." He was on his way to Medan as the vicar of the Dutch Reformed Church, and was the tallest of the four, so the crown of his head touched the ceiling as he sat on Anton's bunk with his knees drawn up. Anton himself lounged on the folding stool, propped up against the washstand. It was their last redoubt, the last stand of European culture against the invading barbarians; this meeting in Cabin 410 had something solemn and inspiring about it. They realized for the first time the friendship that had unobtrusively grown between them; their peculiarities which until then had prevented their becoming more than casual acquaintances were suddenly revealed as qualities. Until then Witzenburg had seemed a prig, with his refusal to drink anything but tomato juice, to say nothing of the outsize portrait of his mother in his bunk and his tropical surplice which he aired daily on the promenade deck. Until then Enters had seemed an oaf, yawning like an invitation to swab his tonsils, perpetually hitching at his underpants; now they realized what a fine Dutch pioneer spirit was in this man, on his way to the East Indies with nothing in his pockets but the address of a twice-removed cousin who had a sugar plantation somewhere. Until then, Frolick's blue silken underwear and genteel accent had irked Anton, and the way in which he listened to Bach on the gramophone was peculiarly irritating: his fingertips touching, a little Gothic arch on which he rested his chin. Now, his profile revealed an unexpected nobility with that Adam's apple, and the way he listened to music proved to the sensitive observer that he possessed an inner ear. Now Witzenburg could practice on them to his heart's content with his hearty, down-to-earth talks about Jesus, Whom one had to see as a pal, without letting oneself be led astray by the Holy Trinity or the Immaculate Conception. Now all three of them said, "Of course," when Enters asked for the twentieth time whether they thought that somewhere in Java it would be cold enough to grow broccoli. Now it didn't matter that Frolick answered, "Thank you, remarkably civil of you," after obtaining permission to use Anton's shaving soap. Now they were united in their defense against the barbarians: four resolute, bewildered tenderfeet, or, as they were called in the Dutch Far East, "totoks." Witzenburg was right. They would never descend to that level.

But as the voyage went on they grew uncertain, for they saw before their baffled eyes the barbarians grow out of their ill-fitting suits. It was a sinister, unnatural growth: the men seemed to get portlier, less ridiculous; the women became matter-of-fact, authoritative, their rowdiness changed into gaiety and their shamelessness into an easy nonchalance. At first it seemed an optical illusion, a product of their own mood; but the barbarians' authority grew from day to day, and when they changed into white drill the battle was over. Suddenly it no longer seemed incomprehensible that this crowd ruled an empire the size of the United States, and the swift and noiseless obedience of the Javanese servants no longer seemed an incongruity. The way they flung one leg over the arm of their chair was no longer bad manners but the only way to keep cool; the beer became a necessity and the siesta sensible. When the heat of the Red Sea made the boys weep with despair, the ladies sat quietly gossiping on the promenade deck; when one of the Genoese bellowers made a little speech at table on the Queen's birthday with an ease and a wit that made Enters' mouth fall open, the Four Musketeers' self-confidence collapsed. They had to admit it: they were standing, helpless, in another world, a world in which they began by feeling ashamed, then afraid, and ended by despairing that they would ever begin to understand it. Witzenburg prayed; Enters stared; Frolick listened with hanging hands to Bach; Anton blushed when the fat trombone player asked him one night on the promenade deck: "Drink, Doc?" and stammered: "Oh . . . yes . . . rather . . . thank you . . ."

"Panas," said the man.

"Saja . . . yes," said Anton. "Very hot."

"Give me Deli any time," said the man. "Do you know where you'll be stationed yet?"

"No."

"Well, we're sure to meet again one day," the man said. "Occasionally my coolies get the plague. You might drop in then."

"I . . . I'd love to."

"Or smallpox, or cholera, or blood in their stools. Interesting job— doctor, but a bit messy. Do you play the trombone?"

"No. The piano, a little."

"Useless in the East. The ants eat them. They can gnaw on a trombone until they are black in the face."

"Yes, that's true. I never thought of that."

"Married?"

"No, engaged."

"Then take my advice, and look for a Japanese housekeeper. You can send her home when the little bride arrives."

Anton said nothing; the djongos arrived with the drinks. "The tuan first!" said the man, and then: "Cheers, Doc, and keep 'em breeding."

"Cheers," said Anton, then the drink sent a shiver down his spine. He shut his eyes with a feeling that his hair was curling and he tried, choking, not to cough; for one second Els's image danced crazily before him, then he opened his eyes again, as they were filling with tears.

"Three things you've got to know in the Far East," the man said. "To drink, to let drink and not to get drunk. You're going to a mad world,

Doc, full of madmen who want to make you mad too. Say, 'Hello, boys'
but think, 'You won't get me.' Then you'll be all right."

"How do you mean . . . ?"

But the man was no longer listening. He was gazing over the oily sea
at the scorched coast of Africa. "That's it," he said, with a sudden, startling
grimness. "Whatever happens and however hot hell may get, say 'You
won't get me.' Those are the people God looks after. Believe in God?"

"No," Anton began. "You see, theology, as I see it . . ."

"You'll soon get cured of that," the man said. "In the jungle, God takes
people who say He doesn't exist on His pitchfork and makes them squirm.
He is different in the East; in Holland you can ignore him, but in the
jungle you'll hear him humming. Another one?"

"No, thank you," said Anton, "I . . ."

"Djongos!" the man called. "Two doubles!"

An hour later Witzenburg, a hazy torso like a swimmer under water,
bent over his bunk and said: "Believe me, Zorgdrager, in temptation only
Jesus . . ." Anton said, "Phooey!" with a hiccup, and giggled, so happy was
he with the thought, "You won't get me! God is different."

He was the first on the casualty list of the Four Musketeers, the first
to discern the faint, strange smell of that hellish paradise on that other
planet: Indonesia.

«««   »»»

A week later, something else happened that gave him the feeling of
approaching another world.

He was shaving in his cabin one afternoon when there was a knock
on the door. He called: "Come in," without looking round, thinking it
was the steward, but a strange voice said: "I'm so sorry. . . ." and he saw,
in the mirror, the warty face of the ship's doctor. He knew him by sight;
during the first week of the voyage when there were no patients, they had
exchanged a few colorless remarks out of politeness. Anton would
have liked to ask him all sorts of things and talk frankly with him, but
for some reason the warts made this difficult, and later he thought:
thank God. After Genoa, the ship's doctor turned out to be a poker
specialist, who let his back be slapped by the planters he swindled, and
who listened with a religious face to hangover complaints and then
prescribed aspirin, illegibly, in powders.

Now he stood in Anton's cabin, his fat red face wet with perspiration, the warts sticking out like little islands. He wouldn't sit down, thank you, he had no time; he was on his way to a bronchitis, the whole of the first class was hawking and spitting, always the same the day after entering this Indian Ocean; he had only just popped in to ask whether his colleague would do him a favor and take a look at an old Chinese trollop, groaning with money and diabetes, who had pestered him throughout the voyage with menopause complaints for which she had him paged in the bar in the middle of the night. Now she had heard from someone or other that there was another doctor on board. "She's in the royal box, you know, suite number five. You needn't look at her urine, you could stand a spoon in it. I'm giving her insulin, according to the directions of her Dutch medico—sixteen pages of it, in Latin; in plain language it says: 'Gold mine, cash in.' "

Warty Boy had not been able to conceal his spite; Anton went to see his first private patient with the refined pleasure of a specialist who had been called in as a last hope on a desperate case. But when he was standing in front of the door of the luxury suite, he suddenly found he had his examination knees again. After he had knocked twice, the door was opened cautiously by a small Chinese amah who grinned a thin, dead smile with frightened eyes, as if she were beaten up the moment she forgot to grin. He announced himself and was admitted into a small hall. A soft shaded light shone from the ceiling, there was a smell of incense and of small dogs that he heard yapping behind a closed door. Then the dead smile of the amah reappeared, she beckoned him to enter and put a long-nailed finger to her lips in a gesture of silence.

Inside the room the light was reddish because of the curtains drawn in front of the portholes. The smell of incense was stronger. In the motionless pomp of brocade and palisanderwood an enormous body lay panting on a bed, surrounded by four downy Pekinese, like a cuckoo in a sparrow's nest. Shapeless, sweating, gigantic; the wet sheet stuck to the body with dark patches of moisture, and with star-shaped folds where the Pekinese were lying. His first reaction was a faint nausea on seeing all that flesh— arms like children, breasts like suckling pigs and a belly like a sow. But her eyes surprised him. Big, dark, melancholy; helpless grace overpowered by a Colossus of fat.

"Good morning, madam . . ."

An arm, that seemed to sit up by the side of the body in order to see who was there, beckoned him to come nearer. The amah had taken up position at the head of the bed and started cooling the body with a fan of peacocks' feathers. She waved with slow, curtsying movements, stirring the stench of sweat and incense and little dogs. He sat down on a stool by the side of the bed and could think of nothing else to do than to start timidly feeling for the pulse in the arm that had lain down again, tiredly; but it was difficult to detect the feeble throb in all this warm flabby flesh. The cabin was silent, the peacock feathers winged slowly in the dusk, the amah grinned, the body panted; he could hardly concentrate on the pulse because he was acutely conscious of those strange eyes, that went on staring at him and seemed to look straight through his thoughts with a melancholy indifference. As he sat there, trying to count a pulse he hardly felt, he suddenly had the uneasy feeling that she was making the diagnosis instead of he. He realized that no doctor could deceive her, let go of her wrist and asked: "What can I do for you, madam?"

The ghost of a smile seemed to clear for an instant the resigned sadness of those eyes; than a voice asked: "You . . . going there . . . first time?"

It was a high, soft voice, so feminine that it seemed like a fairy tale: a princess inside a pig.

"Yes, madam . . ." he answered. "I am a doctor of the Government Health Service."

"Coolies . . ." the voice said, dreamily; and then: "How long I still live?"

Anton smiled, startled. "To answer that question, I would have to make a thorough examination, madam," he said. "I gather from what my colleague told me that . . . er . . . that you have an excess of sugar."

"Sugar . . ." the voice said. "Sugar." And then, suddenly, the monster on the bed sat up, like a colossal idol, the Pekinese falling off her like rats. "Sugar!" the voice cried, shrill and desperate. "Sugar everywhere! Nothing but sugar! Sugar in China, sugar in Java, husband in sugar, children in sugar, born in sugar, lived off sugar, dead of sugar! Sugar . . . !" Then the body, exhausted, slumped back on the bed. The amah had gone on smiling and fanning as if nothing had happened. When the enormous body lay panting once more it seemed as if the whole episode had been a grotesque figment of his imagination.

But the eyes were closed now, and the face was turned away; he started his examination with a sudden feeling of superiority. He worked for over half an hour, and when he finally stood washing his hands in the perfumed bathroom, he could not help thinking what a beauty of a patient she was for a final examination. She seemed a living collection of ills; it was incredible that someone could have so much the matter with her and still be alive. When he returned, the eyes were open once more and looked at him without expression. The high voice asked, kindly, "How long?"

"That's difficult to say, madam," Anton answered. He wanted to get out as quickly as possible, breathe the clean sea air, take a stiff drink, if necessary with Warty Boy. But the eyes read his thoughts.

"I want to die in China," the voice said. "Is there still time to go to Java first?"

"How long would you have to wait for a boat in Batavia?" Anton asked.

"I can leave one week after arrival," the voice said, "or I can take the next one."

"When would that be?"

"Three weeks later."

"I'd take the first one," Anton said.

Then the eyes smiled, for the first time openly. "Thank you," the voice said. "How much do I owe you?"

"Nothing at all, madam," Anton said. "I am acting for the ship's doctor. Please settle direct with him."

The arm sat up in bed once more, the hand beckoned the amah, and the voice whispered a few soft Chinese words. The amah put the fan down on the bed, the body suddenly looked like a corpse underneath a sheet covered with a spray of palm leaves. Then the amah came back with a small gilded box, which she opened at the bedside; and the hand took something out. "Here you are," the voice said. "If you are in trouble. If you are poor. If you are desperate. Give this to first Chinese official you meet, and look: the world changes. The sun rises over sadness. I thank you."

When the amah had let him out and he stood on the deck in the hot wind, with the waves hissing below and the children on the playdeck clamoring faintly in the distance, he looked at what she had given him. A gilt-edged visiting card with a few golden Chinese characters in a vertical row in the center. He laughed; it was just like a boy's adventure story. Now he would be captured by pirates, and tied to a stake, and then this little card would save him and he would drink tea, in a blue silken gown and a hat with a button on it, with the richest mandarin in China, squatting in a pavilion by the side of a pond on which toy sailing boats cruised silently among the lotus flowers. If he were a man he would tear it up now, and chuck it overboard, and have that stiff drink with Warty Boy. But, after a short hesitation, he put it in his pocket and went to have a drink with Enters and Frolick, who were in the bar, discussing the breasts of Bali with a commercial traveler in locomotives.

Three days later, his first tropical suit went into the laundry; only after the Javanese djongos had collected it with his perambulator did he realize that he had left the little card in one of the pockets. When the suit came back the next morning, the card was gone.

«« »»

The arrival was a disappointment. He had gazed his fill at Aden, an untidy stack of colored building bricks, quivering with heat underneath a Pyrex sky. Witzenburg had marveled, in Colombo, at the blackness of the women, the whiteness of the pillars and the darkness of the eternal green. Enters had watched Sabang rise out of the horizon with its tousled forests like a mountain of broccoli. Frolick had watched the blood-drenched coast of Atjeh glide past, with his back to the sunset and a whisky glass in his hand. All four of them were much more moved by the captain's farewell dinner on the eve of their arrival than they had been by the handkerchiefs of their relatives among the seagulls in Amsterdam.

The arrival in Tandjong Priok was not Eastern at all. The ship was late arriving, they moored in darkness, surrounded by the sharp cones of floodlights shining down on barracks and warehouses that were the same the world over. As they were driven to Batavia in a taxi, Java was a lurching darkness, smelling of petrol, and in the short silence while they waited at a level crossing, they listened in vain for the soft gonging sound of the Javanese xylophone, the gamelan. There was no strange music to be heard, no scent of unknown flowers, no bright bird or giant bat caught in the beam of the headlamps.

The four of them spent the night in a Y.M.C.A. hostel where only Witzenburg had booked a room in advance. Anton had looked in vain for someone to meet him among the waving crowd on the quayside, for his orders said: "Report at once to the Head of the Service." It was dead of night, there was nobody there, he did not know where the office was— they sat glumly together in the hostel room, which was no different from the same thing in Holland, except for the mosquito netting over the bed and the lizard they found hiding behind a framed motto *He who abuses himself, insults his Creator* when Enters turned it to the wall.

Now they had arrived, they had nothing to say to each other. They silently watched Enters opening the beer bottles and the bottle of soda water for Witzenburg, who suddenly looked oddly young as he squatted on the coverless bed, sucking a pipe that might be made of chocolate. "It's funny . . ." Frolick started, then he stopped. "Plop!" said the beer bottle, and the lizard: "Tee-tjak!" It darted with short, flashing movements across the wall like a little electric toy in which the current was switched on and off. It was so silent that they could hear the foaming of the beer in the glasses; a smoldering, fatiguing silence, throbbing with the hum of myriads of mosquitoes dancing in the darkness outside. They needed a lot of beer to chase that silence away, but finally they all talked together and laughed at every joke; it was amazing how many they remembered from as far back as grammar school, about making funny noises during history and letting loose a mouse in the girls' gymnasium when they were rehearsing Greek ballet for graduation, and about the stink bomb that had exploded during Practical Physics. Frolick told a story about the girl students who all got up to leave in protest after old Professor Potjer, a notoriously dirty old man, had dwelt too insistently on the potency of the pygmy males, and how old Potjer had said, as they were about to file out: "Come, come, ladies, not so hasty. The next boat doesn't leave until a week from now." Enters told about a farmer who took away the lantern from the doctor who was delivering his wife of triplets, saying: "Damn it, they're coming for the light!" Witzenburg told about a woman who came to get a book in the public library for her husband who was ill: "Do you want a religious book?" asked the librarian, and she answered, "No, thank you, he's getting better." Anton told the story of the laboratory assistant who had dropped a basin with a typhoid culture in the market place and had started trampling on the jelly, crying, "Help, people! Help! Crush them to death!" Boy, boy, did they laugh—they wept with laughter, and when they could remember no more jokes, they started telling stories from their youth, pointless stories full of street names the others didn't know, and the silence threatened to get the upper hand again.

They battled against sleep as if they were guarding a treasure. They made plans to write to one another, and as the last bottle was opened, they promised, like trappers about to set out for the trailless forest, to hold a reunion once a year, somewhere on the globe, wherever they might be. When at last they went to bed, they wished one another good night with a strange feeling of farewell, as if only now were they really leaving Holland, forever.

Anton's room was bare and hot, exactly the same, only there was a different motto on the wall: *Tomorrow may be too late.*

Tomorrow . . . He fell on his bed without undressing, and loosened his collar. He gazed at the ceiling, his hands under his head.

Tomorrow . . . He took his wallet from his pocket. Looked at Els's letters that he knew by heart. At his passport: Zorgdrager, Anton, Physician, Distinguishing marks: None. A bill: "Whisky soda 3, beer 11, cigarettes 2 cartons" with on the back: "Handkerchiefs! Iodine! Sunglasses!" Four bits of confetti from the farewell dinner party. A visiting card with the name of a chance acquaintance. Tomorrow . . . He heard bare feet pad along the corridor, listened and fell asleep.

He half woke up in the middle of the night as a soft gonging sound penetrated to him from very far away. At first he thought it was the djongos with his little xylophone, calling the diners; he opened his eyes, made a move to get up, saw the ceiling and realized that he was in the East Indies. The East Indies . . . It was the gamelan!

He listened to the soft gonging sound, holding his breath; then he recognized the tune of Big Ben, realized it must be a clock somewhere in the building, turned over and fell asleep, with a feeling of starting a nightmare. But it did not come, that night.

«‹‹ ›››

The next morning, after a hasty breakfast, he was taken to the Head Office in a sado, a sort of buggy; and it was a drive full of surprises. After he got over his wonder at the tiny horse, he marveled at the Dutchness of an old canal with seventeenth-century gables, at the incongruity of a health service in a country where, in the center of the capital, a bathing native squatted in the river to relieve himself, while three steps away another native stooped down to drink; at the cool dignity of the government palaces; at the shabbiness of the Head Office of the best organized medical service in the world—somewhere in a back alley, dirty white, at the far end of a tunnel of solid foliage, cracked pots with dead dwarf palms lining the drive. A gray old Javanese in a gray suit led him to the end of a corridor, where he opened the door to a room with an enormous fan buzzing on the ceiling.

Anton saw a desk covered with telephones and stacks of papers, behind the desk a man in shirt sleeves, and behind the man a map of the archipelago, so big that the man seemed to be sitting on guard over it. He was an ordinary man with an ordinary voice, who welcomed Dr. Zorgdrager to the Far East; a pity that Dr. Zorgdrager hadn't come in the night before because now time was getting rather short: the boat was to leave in three hours' time. He was sorry this would not give Dr. Zorgdrager a chance to get acquainted with the Service first, and he was aware that it was unusual to send a newcomer out on an expedition before getting acclimatized first, but he was forced to improvise because the circumstances were unusual. A plague outbreak had been reported in central Borneo; the district doctor had unfortunately succumbed, Dr. Breszezinska-Jansen had taken his place four weeks ago, but he had not been heard of since so it was most urgent that someone went there at once, with sixteen tins of anti-plague vaccine. Dr. Zorgdrager would fit in nicely here; he could refuse, of course, because it was a tall order and would put him to a severe test. But on the other hand, it was a fine chance to get to know the archipelago a bit, for the route . . .

The man turned round and traced the route on the map behind him with a pointer. By mail steamer to Banjermasin: there he would hire sixteen coolies; then by coaster to Rokul, where he would commandeer four prahus; then three weeks up the river Kali-Woga to Rauwatta, where he would find, if all was well, Dr. Breszezinska-Jansen and the plague epidemic. Dr. Breszezinska-Jansen was one of the oldest doctors in the Service, the foremost leprosy specialist in the world; a newcomer could not hope to be in better hands. It wasn't much of a trip, really; things always looked much worse on paper than in reality, and if Dr. Zorgdrager managed to cope with it satisfactorily, it would of course be a splendid recommendation for someone new to the Service. He would hear all the details from Dr. Martens, Head of the Expeditionary Department; just one other thing: he should not tell the coolies that they were on their way to a plague epidemic, for then they would all beat it like bats out of hell; and that would not be funny, of course: to find oneself alone in the jungle, a couple of weeks up a river, with sixteen tins of anti-plague vaccine. Well, so long, Dr. Zorgdrager. Have a nice trip, and all the best; Dr. Martens will help you on from here.

Dr. Martens: tall, thin, sickly, dandruff on his shoulders and bags under his eyes and a croaking voice: "Well, what a job to give a totok! Brinkman has already gone west in that plague epidemic; if Brits-Jansen is still alive, you may thank your lucky stars. Do you realize? Four weeks, and not a sound—how like the old man to . . . Well, let's get cracking. Mandur! Ambulance!"

There followed an unnervingly fast drive in a clanging ambulance to a hospital like a barracks: swarms of native male nurses in white sarongs, shuffling soundlessly through the dim corridors on their bare feet with an amazing speed; the stench of closed-in heat and disinfectant; a small, swift procession of ghosts around a stretcher; then a native doctor with a white skullcap and a stethoscope around his neck like a witch doctor's amulet. "Dr. Sardjono—Dr. Zorgdrager." A handshake. Martens looked like a sweating tramp compared to the immaculate Javanese. "What was it you wanted, totok? Oh, yes; sixteen anti-plague and four P.G. They're waiting, the old man says." The witch doctor called "Mandur!" and an apelike male head nurse shuffled out of the shadows: "Saja, tuan doctor?"

"Ambil itoe ampat kaleng pest sama itoe ampat P.G."

"Baik, tuan doctor . . ."

"Sit down, colleague. Your first job in the Service?"

"Yes."

"Well, give Brits-Jansen my love, will you? Tell him that I'm keeping a real beauty of a lepra tuberosa on the ice for him. Smoke?"

Martens, hanging in a steel chair, topee on the back of his head, the reflection of the flame of his lighter glistening in the sweat on his face, asked, "How's business this morning?" Anton listened with awe to the ensuing conversation about operations, exactly the same as in the clinic in Amsterdam, only the numbers were different: in Amsterdam four per morning, here nineteen.

The mandur came trotting back from the shadow, "Tuan . . ."

"Did you put the tins in the car?"

"Saja, tuan doctor . . ."

A hurried good-by from the witch doctor: "Well, we're sure to meet again. Don't forget malaria with all that plague. If you get a chance in Banjermasin, do me a favor and say hello on my behalf to van der Waard. Will I be seeing you, Martens?"

"Yes, I'll put baby on the road first, then I'll be right round. You can start putting the ruptures aside for me."

"Well, have a nice trip, good-by. Send me a picture postcard, haha!"

Outside the sunlight hit them like a wave of hot water, and the dazzlingly white ambulance hurt the eyes. They drove back to town, far too fast, Martens at the wheel, chattering like a woman. Anton looked at impressive avenues, cool and dark underneath the crowns of the royal palms; native families walked in the shadows, in single file, the man leading. "That just goes to show you that civilization is nothing but a veneer, my boy," said Martens. "Bloody nonsense, civilization. They trot along in our European towns as if they might change back into the jungle any moment, and, let me tell you, they aren't far wrong either. I saw it happen myself, in Celebes: they started a mine, built a whole village, church, school, post office and all, then the mine turned out to be a dud and within a month the village had turned back into jungle: alang-alang in the sinks, snakes in the beds, and the church steeple looking like a bloody mangrove, flowers and—damn! Nearly hit that coolie. They always do that, the silly beggars: cross the road without looking, just like the rabbits in the Nunspeet woods. Know Nunspeet? You do! Fancy that; my father was a doctor there. Quick, tell me, what was it like when you last saw it? And Zutphen? Do you know Zutphen? Lovely town; we moved there, later. Where did you stay, in the Resting Huntsman? Ha, ha, fancy that! Does that little bookstore still exist; you know, what's his name, man with a beard, and that hat shop, Maison Fifi? And the terrace on the River of the Black Boar? That's where I kissed a girl for the first time; the girl from the library it was. The Chinese lanterns were lit and the violinist played 'Birdee tweet-tweet, give me your eggies.' And the hermit in the old disused tower—you know, where the ducks are? I remember, when I got my first slingshot. . . . Oh, here we are."

After a mad rush of collecting the expedition kit, sorting out the instrument case, fleaboots, netting, compass, maps, corned beef, sugar, field glasses, Martens panted: "For God's sake, totok, let's nip across for a quick beer before we die." In the café across the road he ran into a friend. "Well, there's Banders! Hello Banders, good old Banders, how are you, you old virgin hunter? What, who? Oh, sorry—er—er—a totok on his way to the plague. What will you have? Tell me, quickly, what do you know of Murman, who . . . No! It can't be that late!"

After yet another frantic drive in the clanging ambulance: the quayside. A screaming, crashing, splintering, steam-hissing madhouse. "Mind your head!" Whining cranes, barking klaxons, Martens cursing: "Bleeding saints, where's that ape with the tins?" At last, when Anton was on the verge of tears, they arrived on board a white ship, a bedlam of running people bellowing commands, and hoarse quarrels from ship to shore over the whining of the winches. The door to his cabin was blocked by a fat, pipe-sucking dreamer, his topee on his nose, who said, "Sorry," and stepped aside. A hurried good-by from Martens, who was cursing the native porter in a frenzy of haste, in a cabin like an oven with two bunks and a whirring ventilator: "Here, traperduli, goddamn, ajo lekas! Those tins in the bottom bunk—the chest in . . . manah itu lain lima goddamn kaleng?! Well, old boy, chin up and . . . Now where did I put my . . . Oh, here. Well, old boy, don't worry, everything will turn . . . Skrobbi, goddamn bungler, the chest up there, I said! . . . Will turn out all right; but don't forget. . . . Holy mercy, that's the siren! And I've got a whole busload of ruptures waiting for me in hospital, and . . . Well, old boy, keep smiling; and don't forget. . . . Yes! I'm coming! . . . And take good care of the P.G., for they are the most important. . . . Tabeh!"

The loneliness, all of a sudden, with sixteen tins of anti-plague and four of P.G. that were the most important, but God only knew what was inside, was a relief at first, then an oppression, and suddenly a panic as the siren howled three times and the glinting roof of the shack behind the porthole began to slide past. God Almighty, there he was: on his way to a plague epidemic three weeks up a river in the heart of Borneo, and nobody had considered it worth while to tell him how one hired coolies and commandeered prahus, or what language one should speak, or how to know where one was; only: "Don't tell the coolies you're on your way to a plague epidemic, or they'll beat it" and "If Brits-Jansen is still alive, you may thank your lucky stars."

He stumbled outside, whimpering with hysterical fear. He saw the quay, the barges, the harbor, the jetty glide past, and he was about to be sick with nerves and exhaustion when the fat pipe sucker yawned, stretched, knocked out his pipe on the rail and said: "God bless Batavia. The bloke who invented that town deserves a statue with his feet in the air."

"Yes," said Anton, bravely, and swallowed. "I'll settle for Holland any time."

"Holland?" the fat man asked. "I don't believe it exists any more. A lie my mother told me, like the stork. Tarakan?"

"No, Banjermasin."

"Business?"

"Doctor. Government Health Service."

"What? Is van der Waard going?"

"No. I'm going inland."

"I see. Something wrong in the jungle?"

"Yes."

"What is it this time?"

"Plague."

"Bulbous or lung?"

"Er—bulbous."

"Well, every man to his own taste. Speaking for myself, I get dizzy if I
see a boil. What about a drink?"

"Thank you," said Anton. "My name is Zorgdrager."

"How do you do," the fat man said. "Flabbinga. Oil. This way to the
bar."

《《《　》》》

Well, here it was: Eykman's *Vade Mecum,* become reality. Only the
nicest chapters so far, so he ought to feel delighted. This was exactly what
he had imagined so often, while lying on his back staring at the slatted
light of the street lantern on the ceiling: our hero, on an expedition into
the interior to save a grizzled old doctor trapped in the magic forest. But
God, how he longed to look at that slatted light again, instead of at
this iron ceiling dripping with moisture.

In the daytime he was all right. Then he could think about it all
dispassionately. He wrote several letters to Els, which made him feel that
everything was not so bad as it seemed, that he would pull through all
right. After all, he had been a Boy Scout. He hadn't written to Bert yet;
he had started a letter but the moment he tried to talk about what was
facing him in the objective manner they used together he found it
impossible. The only way out was to romanticize it, and that he could
do to Els. He wrote to her about his experiences in Batavia, the jolly
people he had met there, the wonderfully stimulating atmosphere of
action and realism in the Government Health Service; he told her that
the Dutch East Indies were extraordinarily like the United States of
America as far as the white population was concerned; both communities
showed an enormous hospitality and a directness in making friendships
that was heartening and virile. That first day, before leaving for Banjermasin, he had already made two friends who he was sure would

remain friends forever: a wonderful old character called Martens, and a most intelligent, sensitive Javanese chap called Sardjono. He wrote about ten pages of this, and ended with: *I have to stop now for good old Flabbinga is calling me.* Good old Flabbinga hadn't done anything of the kind. Good old Flabbinga hadn't opened his mouth since they left Batavia, except to snore and to yawn. For thirty-eight hours now he had lain blind drunk in his bunk, full of stomach rumbles.

Yes, the days were all right; it was the nights that were hell. For then, in the sweltering heat, as he lay sweating in the darkness with swelling eyes and parched lips, he saw a vision. A strange, schizophrenic vision: he saw himself as an onion, being peeled in the hands of God. It was a symbol, he couldn't make out quite what it meant, but it was sure to have some hidden sexual meaning. Yet he wasn't bothered by any sexuality at all; he simply had no room for it in his mind. All the room there was, at night, was taken up by fear and by that onion, dancing on the misty edge of the dark lake of sleep. An onion being peeled, layer after layer, until only the little white heart was left, robbed of the protective armor that twenty-eight years of careful education had put around the defenseless white manikin inside.

If only he had somebody to talk to, somebody of whom he could ask things. It would have been quite easy to start talking with the ship's officers, or with the little bow-legged planter who, every morning, stood in the early sunlight in front of his cabin with a mirror, trimming his mustache; yet he could not bring himself to do it. For everyone seemed to assume that he was a man who knew exactly what he was doing, in no need of any advice. He must look like the real thing. So much like the real thing that he did not dare open his mouth and ask: "By the way, how does one hire coolies?" for fear of making them laugh at him.

The second morning he tried again to start a letter to Bert. *"Bert, I must write to you or I'll go nuts. I am on my way to Borneo with sixteen tins anti-plague and four P.G. What the hell can P.G. be? Could you look this up for me and let me . . ."* He rubbed his eyes and dropped his pen. He must be mad. Long before she received this letter, he would have found out himself what P.G. meant.

Flabbinga gave an enormous belch in the half-open coffin of his bunk, and a furry voice asked: "What's the time?"

It gave him quite a shock. Those were the first words his cabin mate had spoken since the night the ship had left. "Eleven-thirty," he said.

Flabbinga said, "No kidding." There was a long silence, then he started snoring again.

Anton crumpled the sheet of paper to a ball and threw it out of the porthole.

«« »»

That evening Flabbinga woke up, at last. This time the day had been almost as bad as the night; although there was no sign of land on the horizon, Borneo was inexorably drawing nearer, and with it chapter eleven of Eykman's *Vade Mecum*.

Flabbinga awoke as bright as a daisy. He stuck his head with the three days' beard in the washbasin, made hearty bubbling noises, trumpeted like an elephant and started to sing. If it hadn't been nine o'clock at night, this behavior would have seemed normal; just a happy man waking up to a new day, full of vim and vigor. He sang "Tiptoe Through the Tulips with Me" and the National Anthem. Then he shaved, which shut him up for a while. After shaving he trilled "Where Sheep May Safely Graze" in a falsetto voice; then he put on white tropical drill and made for the bar.

Anton was waiting outside the cabin, and the moment the fat man appeared in the doorway, smelling of hair oil, he virtually threw himself upon him, crying: "Hello! Good morning! How do you feel?" Flabbinga asked: "Morning? I see, drunk again. I'll have to catch up with you. Come on." So both of them went to the bar.

Half an hour later, Anton couldn't understand why he hadn't thought of this before. The bar was the solution. Three whiskies, and chapter eleven looked as harmless as a child's picture book. Four whiskies, and he realized that Flabbinga was one of the funniest, most generous, most experienced pioneers of the jungle. Five whiskies, and he became a Christian; he attained more than any monk had ever attained after forty years of fasting, praying, sexual abstinence and flogging himself in his cell: he loved everybody, he was full of courage, compassion and hope. Six whiskies, and he passed out.

The night was dreamless, onionless and refreshing. He was awakened in warm, pleasant sunlight by Flabbinga singing, in French: "Je crois en toi, O maître de la nature." They had breakfast together on deck, their heads pleasantly swimming, and there was a faint nutty smell in the air, reminiscent of the tropical hothouse in the Amsterdam Botanical Gardens.

Only after breakfast, as he got up and stretched and looked ahead at the horizon, did Anton realize where the smell came from. There, blue and hazy like a mountain ridge in the distance, was Borneo.

He turned round and said to Flabbinga, with a lump in his throat: "I think that's Borneo." Flabbinga, picking his teeth, spat something out and said: "All change."

Anton swallowed, and asked in a voice that was slightly cracked: "By the way, how does one hire coolies?"

"Need coolies?" Flabbinga asked, looking up.

Anton blinked. "Yes," he said.

"How many?"

"Sixteen."

"Okay," Flabbinga said, shooting his toothpick overboard, "I'll hire sixteen coolies for you. Let's go to the bar."

They went to the bar and stayed there until the ship moored. Flabbinga drank whisky, Anton drank beer. Beer wasn't as good as whisky, but it helped to keep Eykman's *Vade Mecum* shut. Finally Flabbinga went ashore and Anton followed. Flabbinga walked with dignity, and he seemed to know where he was going. He didn't go far, just to a little wooden shack fifty yards away that had a three-ply notice board nailed next to its solitary window, saying *Harbor Master's Office*. Before entering he turned round, said to Anton: "Wait here," then he vanished.

Anton waited outside in the hot sunlight for over half an hour, while inside the little wooden shack he could hear guffaws of laughter and the clinking of glasses. When Flabbinga came out again, Eykman's *Vade Mecum* was wide open; moaning shapes covered with horrible boils were crawling in every shadow. "What coaster are you on?" Flabbinga asked, sending across the sour stench of beer.

"A ship called *Henny*," Anton answered.

Flabbinga frowned. "The *Henny*? In that case you'd better look out, for the captain is a crook. Steals the knife and fork out of your hands while you are eating."

"What about my coolies?"

"Coolies? Oh yes, coolies. Let's have a drink first."

"No," said Anton.

Flabbinga shook his head as if to clear his vision. "What d'you mean no? You asked me to do you a favor, and you're too goddamn stingy to stand me a drink."

"I'll stand you as many drinks as you like," Anton said tremulously, "but I want my coolies first."

Flabbinga shook his head again, this time in resignation. "You're hard to get on with," he said. "You're a nice man, Doctor, but you're too domineering. Take my advice and don't be domineering over here, not with the white man. I know you've got culture and I could listen to you for hours, for I've got culture myself. But believe me, it will do you no good to go about this part of the world brandishing your culture. Keep it hidden, bring it out on special occasions, choose your partners. . . ."

"For God's sake," said Anton, "let's get those coolies. Please."

"All right," said Flabbinga, "I just said it for your own good." Then he stuck two fingers in his mouth and whistled, so shrilly that Anton's ears throbbed. "Sado!" he called. There was a sound of hoofs slithering to a standstill and, as Anton turned round, he saw a miniature hansom as big as a goat cart pulled by a tiny pony, a naked native with an enormous straw hat inside. Flabbinga and he got in. The springs creaked, the pony was lifted off its feet as the cart tipped backward, then the native got out and started to lead them toward the future.

«« »»

The hiring of the coolies was the most degrading spectacle Anton had ever witnessed. It took place in a small courtyard smelling of straw and urine. If the animals in the stables had been horses or stray dogs, he would have felt like reporting this to the Society for the Prevention of Cruelty to Animals. But they were human beings, there was no society to report to. While Flabbinga was looking over the ghastly creatures like a cattle buyer, pinching their arms, opening their mouths, lifting their eyelids and their loincloths, he thought of Bert and how she would have looked if she had witnessed this. He saw her face clearly, quivering in the heat of the courtyard, and he shut his eyes.

"Okay," he heard Flabbinga say, "these will do. They're not much good but it's all he's got left. How long's your trip going to be?"

Anton opened his eyes, looked at the jagged square of blue sky above the courtyard and said: "Three weeks."

"They'll last," said Flabbinga. "This little runt is your mandur."

Anton looked down and saw a scurvy one-eyed dwarf grin at him with a gaping mouth from which two yellow teeth jutted. "He'll do the kicking," Flabbinga said. "Don't touch the bastards yourself; let him get the lice."

Anton looked at them. Fifteen indifferent skeletons with pointed knees and big mouths red from chewing sirih. "Thank you," he said. "Tell them to get my stuff off the boat and take it to the *Henny*." Flabbinga took a breath, as if to say something, then turned to the mandur and gave an order in Malay. "Ah-ee!" yelled the dwarf, and started kicking. The fifteen skeletons began to move. Anton wanted to shut his eyes again, but he went on looking. He couldn't spend three weeks with his eyes shut; the sooner he got used to it the better. When finally they had climbed back into the goat cart and were running downhill, the pony's hoofs clattering as if it had a dozen legs instead of four, Flabbinga said: "Don't be soft with those coolies, or you'll get into trouble. They don't understand anything but kicks."

"All right," said Anton.

"You should have given that order yourself," Flabbinga went on. "Don't let that little runt get the idea into his head that you are a totok. Behave as if you had planted every single tree in the goddamn jungle yourself."

"All right," said Anton.

"And don't be impressed by it," said Flabbinga. "It's just like the zoo, only bigger."

For an instant, Anton knew that this was the moment to ask something basic and important, one big question that would cover everything: the fear, the loneliness, the horror of those coolies, the nightmare of the onion peeled in the hands of God. But he couldn't put it into words. They sat silently side by side while the goat cart, bucking and swaying, rushed downhill, toward a bar.

«« »»

The coaster *Henny* was a shabby ship with two thin funnels side by side, leaning backward like the ears of an angry mare. The captain proved to be a black-haired wrestler in a dirty tropical suit, wearing a badgeless peaked cap. The ship smelled of pepper and cheese; its deck was a tangle of crates, bales, goats, screaming pigs and stacks of ropes. Captain Krasser, so Flabbinga had told him, kept two Siamese women in his quarters; he must have been right, for as Anton glanced into the chartroom he saw a lipstick on the chart. The crew seemed to consist mainly of Chinese; when the cook peeped out of the cave of his galley and grinned at him with the vacant smile of an idiot, he decided to go back ashore and buy some tins to live on during the trip. There was no cabin for him; he was supposed to sleep on a couch in the captain's cabin with a missionary on another one opposite, and the captain in the bunk: a dark hole in which green flies flitted like sparks through the slanting beams of sunlight from the portholes. "Where are you off to?" the Captain asked, when he saw him go toward the gangway.

"Ashore for a minute."

"Be back within the hour!" the Captain shouted after him. "I'm not waiting for you! This is a ship, not a bus! Bos'n! Bugger those crates off the winch! And get a move on with that yellow rabble! Kick them up their lazy arses!"

Coward, weakling . . . It was no good scolding himself. He was on his way to the last man who might, God knows, give him the password, the answer to his big question: van der Waard, the district's medico. After he had left Flabbinga sprawled over a beer-splashed table in a club called Art and Friendship, yet another layer had fallen off the onion. He knew nothing, nothing at all; he was about to be chased into the jungle like a shivering domestic animal, a Pekinese in the wilderness. He was alone now, alone with a pirate, sixteen skeletons and a missionary of whom the only thing he had seen so far was a pathetic cardboard suitcase with a bit of string around it, the luggage of a charwoman.

An onion in God's hands; he felt more helpless and more naked all the time, and the worst thing was the knowledge somewhere at the back of his mind that he would fail. He'd never make it, never; it was hopeless. Coward, coward! No good. He knew himself too well—always smaller and weaker than the others thought he was. Even Els, even Bert—he had always managed to fool them; so far he had gone through life without being unmasked. But now God's hands had finished peeling the onion, now He had him on the palm of His hand, utterly alone, and asked: "Well?"

He remembered the man with the trombone and their conversation on the Red Sea, as he walked along the low streets of Banjermasin with the jungle at the far end of every one of them. He elbowed his way through a crowd of haggling Chinese, native women carrying baskets full of cackling hens on their heads, begging urchins. Flea-busy little sados clattered through the throng, their drivers screaming "Ah-ee!"; but he didn't see them. He saw that somber planter again, gazing at the coast of

Africa. "Those who say in the jungle He does not exist He takes on His pitchfork and makes them squirm."

Over the heads of the crowd in the passar a banner swayed, stretched between two poles. *Tonight at 8:30 in the Salvation Army Hall Captain Koebeest will speak about "The Mouse and the Trap" with lantern slides. Come to Jesus! Admission—1 cent.* It was written in Dutch, Malay and Chinese, with a picture of a mouse and a big trap with a piece of red cheese in it. An arrow pointed to the cheese, and on the cheese was written: *Sin.*

No, God did not give him the chance to hide in a crowd. God had given him brains, scientific knowledge and a sense of humor; now he stood alone and had to fight it out on a river somewhere in the wilderness. He cursed God because he had put all this hokum between them; suddenly he hoped, intensely and spitefully, that one day Bert would find herself pitched on that pitchfork too, squirming and screaming for Jesus Whom she had sneered at all her life, calling Him opium for the people and Santa Claus for the slaves. God, he thought, give me one minute of true faith in the mercy of the Lamb, and I would go for that jungle like St. George for the Dragon. *Professor G. J. van der Waard, M.D.* the name plate said, on the gate of the drive. He had never thought he would be a professor. He hesitated at the gate; then he went in.

He did not quite know what to expect—he had hoped for somebody fatherly, soothing, sensible. A pale scarecrow peered through the crack of the door.

"Professor van der Waard?"

"Yes . . ."

"My name is Zorgdrager. I'm new in the Service, on my way to the interior and now . . . Now I just called to say hello, on behalf of Dr. Sardjono, Batavia."

"Fancy," said the scarecrow, suddenly hostile. "Thank you very much indeed."

"My boat leaves in half an hour," Anton said, "and I would have loved . . ."

"In that case, you'd better hurry," said the scarecrow. "Good-by." And he shut the door.

Anton stood in front of the door for a minute, during which he needed all his self-control not to kick it; then he turned round and went back, down the gravel path, cursing. Halfway to the harbor, he was suddenly overcome by a suspicion: he didn't dare! He didn't dare to talk to me; he is the district's doctor, he knows what is going on, and that I haven't the ghost of a chance of coming back alive. Yes, van der Waard had given him the password after all: death patrol. They had sent him, the totok, the tenderfoot, on a death patrol.

The thought was ridiculous. He made his own diagnosis: hysterical cowardice. But it didn't make any difference: a death patrol, that's what it was. He didn't even feel ashamed of the word that came straight out of the penny dreadfuls. During all his seven years of training, he had never received an image of the jungle strong enough to chase these visions from his boyhood: witch doctors, headhunters, crocodiles, death patrols. A death patrol, Dr. Zorgdrager; they have sent you on a death patrol.

When he arrived back at the *Henny,* he had already died and rotted, his flesh had been eaten by snakes and lizards, and his skeleton found by an expedition three years later. Els had married a dentist, Bert had become a Lesbian and his name had been entered in the ledgers of the state of the Netherlands in the column "Debit." A little boy with trachoma accosted him at the gangway, asking in a high shrill voice: "Brothel, tuan?" He looked at the child, aghast, and shook his head. As he climbed the gangway he heard the childish voice again, behind his back: "Brothel, madam?" He turned round and saw a priest in a cassock following him on board.

«« »»

The first meal on board the *Henny* he would not forget as long as he lived. For half an hour he forgot all his problems, as he sat between Captain Krasser and Father Ambrosius underneath the swinging paraffin lamp, and watched a duel between a Christian and a loud-mouthed oaf, fought out with knife and fork.

Outside, on the foredeck, the Chinese were miaowing at the moon to a flute and a lute, a monotonous tune that spiraled around one note, as if it accompanied the circling of the moths around the paraffin lamp. The lamp shed a harsh, yellow light that sparkled in the eyes of Captain Krasser, flashed on his teeth, and glistened in the sweat on the waxy forehead of Father Ambrosius.

"Missionaries!" said Captain Krasser, tearing the meat off a chicken leg with his teeth. "Hypocrites, the lot of them! You can't go anywhere, you can't enter a pub or even a brothel—there they are, sneaking about in their long skirts without feet, like steam trams fed on Bibles. The gin is still glowing in your belly, you're ready to stand your worst enemy a drink, and there they are, sweeping the floor with their broom of sin and making you cough your heart up. Sin! What the hell is sin? An invention of those hypocrites, that's all. I'm not worrying about sin, I don't put bloomers on the heathens! No!"—and he gnawed the bone, crushing it. "If I fancy a girl, I've got her pants down in five minutes. Fu Ling!"

The Chinese steward materialized like an apparition behind the curtain of mosquito netting in the doorway. "Yes, Mistel Captain Sir?"

"Three coffees with a sting."

"Yes, Mistel Captain Sir."

Gone was the ghost; Anton looked back at the priest—a fat little man with a face that did not seem to match his body. He had been sitting there for over half an hour now, unmoved under the onslaught. The captain's reserve of curses had taken Anton's breath away; he hadn't let up for more than a few seconds, and yet never repeated himself. He had challenged God in several languages, and mocked Him with gestures the shadows of which still haunted the walls. He had cursed and slavered until his moron's face glistened with sweat and grease, but not with a single frown had the father betrayed that he was disturbed or even listening.

It had started when the priest had made the sign of the Cross before the meal. It had raged like a tempest during the meal, and it finished after the meal with a thunder-and-lightning finale that made Anton's mouth sag open in horrified admiration. At the beginning of the Captain's monologue he had wondered whether it wasn't his duty as a gentleman to intervene, to come to the aid of the poor defenseless priest, but at his first word, "Captain . . ." the father had looked up, his eyes so impressive with controlled strength that it had no longer been necessary for the Captain to shout "Shut up!"

Fu Ling brought in the coffee and three glasses of brandy. The priest only drank the coffee, but the Captain had either eaten too much or was too exhausted to say anything else but "They distill it themselves, but he who drinks it is a sinner." After the coffee, he went to the bridge to take over the watch and Anton tried to start a conversation with the priest; the little man smiled, said: "I don't want to seem impolite, sir, but I'm rather tired," and lay down on his couch after praying on his knees, a spectacle at which Anton, embarrassed, tried not to look. He knew of nothing better to do than to lie down himself, and he lay listening to the caterwauling Chinese until he fell asleep.

The next day, he didn't meet the Captain or the priest until the evening meal. The Captain was either on the bridge or romping with the Siamese in his cabin, which he kept locked; the priest sat reading his breviary on the aft deck behind the emergency steering wheel, in the shadow of the awning. The ship was filled to the brim with natives and Chinese; whole families of them were camping on the deck and cooked their own meals on little fires inside perforated petrol tins, making a stench and a smoke that hung motionlessly over the ship, a cloud which sailed with it along the blue-green coast of Borneo.

Flabbinga had said that he needn't bother about his coolies until they arrived in Rokul at the mouth of the Kali-Woga; the mandur would take care of their rations and the more he left the bastards alone the better it was. Yet he couldn't resist the temptation to look for them in the crowd, squatting without any protection on the scorched deck. They were sitting, all sixteen of them in a heap, absorbed in some sort of dice game. Nobody looked up at his arrival except the mandur, who grinned and said: "Tuan." He stood looking for a while at their mysterious game, listened to their guttural noises and stepped aside when one of them spat, a red spurt of sirih juice that made a bloodstain on the deck; a black pig came by, sniffed at it, and lapped it up. It was swelteringly hot, not a breath stirred the column of stench and heat that hung overhead. He went back to the cabin, found the door open and lay down, panting, his shirt open, his arms spread, his head back. The desperation and the fear of the previous day were smothered by the heavy oily heat. He could think only of how hot it was.

When, after a short blood-red dusk, night fell over the ship like a net of stars, and the paraffin lamp in the cabin was lit again, the singing of the Chinese on the foredeck brought a strange suspense, like the overture to an opera. The priest had hardly sat down at the table in his white cassock when the Captain appeared behind the mosquito netting, and it seemed as if they hadn't been away at all. Even before sitting down, he attacked the priest with a breath-taking ferocity. The night before, he had thrown dung at the saints; this night he opened the floodgates of his scabrous mind. The obscenities that he strung together without pausing for breath would have made a drunken planter blush, but they produced no change in the imperturbable chastity of the priest's face. When the Captain at last gave up, hoarse and panting, and Fu Ling brought in the coffee and the brandy, Anton began to understand that this was more than just a one-man brawl. The miaowing of the orchestra behind the dead eyes of the portholes gave it the background of a fable. That night he looked with jealousy at the praying priest, draining cosmic strength out of the universe into himself by merely folding his hands, while he could only sit and watch.

The next day, he once more tried to talk to the priest who, he understood, was leaving the following day; this meant that that evening the last act of the drama had to take place in which sin would either triumph or break its neck. The priest was very kind but not talkative. He said that he was going back to his mission school in the jungle after his yearly leave and that he knew the Captain quite well. He had sailed with him before, a curious man.

During the hours Anton sat waiting for the evening to fall, he could not sleep as he had done the previous day. He had found a corner underneath the bridge where there was a patch of shadow and from where he had a view of the smooth, shining sea and the unchanging coast of Borneo. It seemed to be cooler, yet he could not lift his thoughts out of their lethargy. When evening fell, he did not wait for the sunset and was sitting at the table when Fu Ling came to lay it for the meal.

This is the East, he thought, as he sat watching the brown hands putting the white plates on the homely checkered oil cloth. This is the East; one more layer off the onion and perhaps I'll understand some of it, be able to get hold of it somewhere. Silly thought, while watching a Chinese laying a table underneath a paraffin lamp, after all the picturesque and impressive things that had happened during the last weeks. Yet he could not rid himself of the thought; he watched the laying of the plates and the saucers as if they were cards dealt out by a fortuneteller, to be turned over presently to reveal the secret of his future.

The priest was the next to arrive; the meal had already been served when at last the Captain appeared. He was quieter than the previous days and for a short while Anton thought that his imagination had got the better of him. Nothing would happen; the scoundrel had had enough and drank his soup noisily with his mind on it. But then Fu Ling brought in a decanter with a green liquid and five glasses, without having been asked; and after the soup plates had been taken away, the Captain said: "Father, you are going tomorrow. I don't want to put you back into the forest without a little celebration; so here's looking at you." He filled the glasses; the priest shook his head with a smile and went on eating bits of bread that he broke off the loaf with a steady hand. The Captain said: "Come on, Father, you can't refuse that! Would you like me to call in a couple of nuns to give you a heart?" When the priest did not answer, did not look up, only stopped breaking bread, the Captain clapped his hands and the two Siamese girls came in, giggling, tangled up with the mosquito netting. He greeted them with a hungry grunt as if a steaming dish had been carried in, pulled them down on his knees and fed them the green liquid. They were frightened, black-eyed girls with heavy coils of oily hair and the ingratiating coyness of pet animals that are kicked out of the way when the master is looking for his slippers. He slapped their bare shoulders, made green stains on their white sarongs with the drink, pointed at the priest and said: "Well, there he is! Come on, have a dekko at uncle! Look at Uncle Holypuss in Jesus' nightie!" They looked and giggled; after he had thrown back three glasses of the green drink he started, calmly and monotonously but with a mounting richness of detail, to tell the priest what things a healthy heathen could do with two such nice little living toys. Things they had been created for: things they clamored for; things the Bible described in such frank words that a man who knew what it was all about saw stars and balls of fire in front of his eyes. Then he tore off one of the sarongs and shouted, "Here! Here, Father! Take a bite! Go on, bitch, let him put his teeth in!" and pushed the shivering creature toward the priest, and Anton thought: now I ought to get up, now I ought to get up and knock the swine's teeth in. But he did nothing; he remained seated, toying with his fork, and noticed suddenly that there was no music tonight. Only the throbbing of the engine down below, occasionally the rattle of the rudder chain, and somewhere above a soft hissing of steam underneath the stars.

When Fu Ling came in with the coffee, the girls were naked and the lamp was smoking. The Chinese turned the wick down and dusted with his napkin the specks of soot off the oilcloth and off the priest's white shoulders. He correctly turned the coffee cups round until the handles were on the right-hand side, and the priest thanked him with a smile. Then Captain Krasser got to his feet, kicked the girls into the night and strode out, tearing the mosquito netting. The priest looked up, and his eyes met Anton's. There was nothing to be seen in them; they were calm and kind, almost childish; then a drop of perspiration ran slowly down his forehead and along the bridge of his nose. It suddenly brought a memory, and Anton recognized the expression of utter self-control on that still, masklike face.

The next morning, the priest went ashore. The ship lay with its engines stopped at the mouth of a river that was no more than a rabbit hole in the wall of the jungle. A prahu had come out of it with two natives inside, and it took the priest away. As he stood at the rail, his cassock lifted to step onto the rope ladder, the Captain said: "Hey! What about thanking me for your board and keep?" "God bless you, my son," said the priest, then he went down the ladder.

The prahu sailed away and was soon lost in the blue and the green of the sea and the jungle. Then the white speck of the cassock vanished, as the wilderness closed over it.

<<< >>>

That night during supper the Captain said nothing, and he left the table before the coffee had been served. The next night he didn't say anything either, and the morning before they were to arrive at Rokul, he still hadn't said a word. He sat naked in his bunk, beset by flies, and watched Anton packing his box.

"What are you going to do in the jungle?" he asked.

"Deliver medicine," Anton answered, without looking up.

"High up the river?"

"Three weeks."

"Have you got a guide?"

"No."

"Prahus?"

"No."

"Well," he said, getting out of his bunk. "Surely you've got a gun?"

"No," said Anton.

He shook his head and made a hissing sound. "Some people," he said, "ought to be shot." Then he got up, dressed, and went to the bridge.

While the ship was approaching another rabbit hole in the wall of the jungle, Anton wondered who the Captain considered ought to be shot. He himself? The Government Health Service? The people the gun was meant for? In that case, who were they? The coolies? The headhunters? Gorillas? Tigers? He remembered a book he had read as a boy; in it the hero, wounded in the jungle and being eaten alive by ants, had shot himself by putting his toe on the trigger.

As the anchor chain rattled out he longed for a drink, but he did not want to ask the Captain. Though he had not been able to intervene while the Captain tortured the priest, he felt that the least he could do now was to ignore him.

As soon as the anchor was down, the Captain, unasked, lined up his coolies and, ignoring his feeble protest, started examining them in such a thorough fashion that Flabbinga's cattle buyer's inspection seemed gentle in comparison. After this, he discarded three of them and shanghaied three others among the deck passengers, despite their shrill protests and the miserable wailing of their families. Then he went into his cabin, came out with a double-barreled gun, held it out to Anton and said: "Here you are."

"Pardon?"

"Here you are. A gun."

"But—but in Batavia I was told I wouldn't need any arms. . . ."

"That may be so for a man who knows where he's going, but you had better take it. Those coolies smell a totok ten miles off." He hung the gun round Anton's neck. "Bos'n! Lower the longboat!"

"But, Captain," Anton remonstrated, "I'm sure it's very kind of you, but I have to tell you that I wouldn't know how to work the damn thing."

The Captain shrugged his shoulders. "That's all right. It's for show only, and if the show isn't enough, the bang will do. Only, don't hold it in front of your belly when you fire. Hold it either alongside your hip or at your shoulder." Then he turned away.

The longboat was lowered. The coolies, kicked and screamed at by the horrible little mandur, lowered his chests and his tins into it and then filed down the rope ladder themselves. He followed them, and so did the Captain. The mooring was cast off and the boat rowed to Rokul, a miserable hamlet of heavy-roofed huts on mossy poles, standing spiderlike in the mud flats of the river's delta. In Rokul the Captain commandeered four prahus by taking them away, after shouting a few coarse words at the dark holes in the floors of the huts, out of which small brown children's faces peered like baby swallows out of a nest. Then they went to a fifth hut, into which he climbed. After he had vanished inside there were sounds of altercation, terminated by a smack that seemed to settle the argument. He came back with a trembling old man who went on sniffing and wiping his nose with the back of his hand. "The best guide there is," he said to Anton. Then he grabbed the old man by the scruff of his neck, shook him, pointed at Anton and made a little speech that sounded blood-curdling even though Anton didn't understand a word of it. "All right," he concluded. "I've told him that if he tries to run away before you arrive at your destination, you will shoot him through his stomach. It'll take him three days to die and he'll regret every minute of it."

After that, he divided the coolies into four crews, four men to each prahu, the guide in the first one, Anton and his mandur in the last. "Be careful you stay in the rear," he said. "Once they pass you downstream, you'll never catch up with them again until you're back at sea. Now those tins. They all contain the same?"

"No," said Anton. "Four of them are special."

"All right," he said, and divided them over the four boats, putting one P.G. in each. Anton wanted to keep them all in his boat but he said, "Why the hell do you think they told you to commandeer four prahus? Because if one of them capsizes, you only lose five tins. And if it's only one, you'll be lucky. Got your map and your compass?"

"Yes."

"Sit down in the stern and put the gun across your knees."

He obeyed; the Captain held the edge of the prahu until he sat. It was a portentous moment, and yet somehow ridiculous. It reminded him of the time he had hired a rowing boat in his student days to take a girl out in; the boatman had held it in exactly the same way until the giggling girl was safely seated.

"Don't drink from the river," the Captain said. "Leave that to those apes. Here . . ." He took over a small crate that Fu Ling had been carrying after him. "Don't drink more than two per day, otherwise they won't last out."

"But, Captain," Anton said. "I definitely don't want . . ."

"Shut up!" said the Captain. "I've got enough beer for an orphanage. Ah-ee!" he shouted at the guide, and the first prahu cast off. It was dragged away by the current and swung round twice before it held its course. When Anton's turn came the pirate said: "That business with the priest was personal. Forget it."

"Thank you," said Anton.

"Good luck," the pirate said, pushing the prahu off. "Don't let the jungle get you down. If you come back with those tins, I'll kick you to death."

The prahu shot, turning, into the heart of the stream.

"Don't forget to relieve yourself regularly!" the pirate shouted, his hands cupped round his mouth. "Force yourself . . ."

He didn't hear the rest. The coolies dipped their palm-leaf-shaped paddles into the water and started to swing them in a slow rhythmic movement to the tune of the mandur's plaintive chant: "Ah-ee . . . ! Ah-ee . . . !"

He waved at the pirate, small and white underneath the gigantic spider of a hut; then he looked ahead. The river looked like a creek that ended abruptly, so closely did the walls of the forest approach one another.

"Ah-ee . . . ! Ah-ee . . . !"

He was alone with the Far East.

«« »»

By day it was an adventure, by night a delirium.

By day he sailed, like Harun-al-Rashid, up a fairy-tale river, dirty, muddy and wild, with always and everywhere the eternal green, the sky a narrow blue gap high up between the crowns of the trees. Occasionally there was the sudden color of a yellow or orange cluster of flowers, or a floating island of snowed-down white blossoms, and always there was the smell of putrefaction. He let himself be rowed, reclining underneath his small awning, listening dreamily to the chanting of the mandur and the twittering of thousands of birds, that ceased only in the hottest hour of the day, when all sound seemed to be scorched away by the murderous sun.

But by night, this dream world became a nightmare. First the twittering of the birds turned into the whining of the mosquitoes, then there were cries, rustlings, splashes, shrieks and maniacal laughter. He lay, panting, under the pressure of this teeming darkness with a feeling of terror he had never known before, separated only by the gauze of his mosquito netting from the delirium of the tropical night.

During the first days he was interested, alert and full of curiosity. But the deeper they penetrated into the jungle, the slower his thoughts became, the more dulled his senses. His curiosity waned, his interest flagged, his thoughts seemed to get gluey, lethargic, until in the end he could hardly think at all. All he did was to turn over lazily in his mind some strings of words, that seemed to drift past with the current at which he gazed. "Death patrol." "Tomorrow may be too late." "Borneo, all change." "Tiptoe through the tulips with me." He hummed it, out of tune with the chanting of the mandur, then the thought flashed through his stupor: "I'm letting myself go. I ought to do something, stay awake. . . ."

But the mandur sang him back to sleep, "Ah-ee . . . Ah-ee . . ."; the birds twittered, a thousand warbling, chirping noises, one endless tremolo of twittering; the drops of the paddles drew dotted lines on the river—the river, on which they had spent only three days of the three weeks. He wanted to get a grip on himself, to get up from this paralyzing lethargy, do something, show he was the leader, but he sat motionless under his awning, making only a few movements a day: open a beer bottle, take a sip, eat a bite, wipe sweat. "Tiptoe through the tulips with me. . . ." "Ah-ee . . . Ah-ee . . ."

Sometimes, in the short coolness before sunrise, as the twittering of the birds awakened him from a heavy, exhausting sleep and he watched the pink clouds of morning mist roll slowly up the trunks of the trees, it occurred to him how disgusting it was to let himself be smothered by the jungle without so much as lifting a finger. Nothing from all those years of self-satisfied living had remained standing under the onslaught of God, Who had now pitched him on His fork and Whom he heard humming, as the man with the trombone had told him. As soon as there was no one left, no Els, no Flabbinga, not even a Captain Krasser to show off to, his knees had given way and he had collapsed with a sigh. The paddlers paddled, the birds twittered, the river flowed, relentlessly; only he remained motionless, sitting underneath his little awning, and let himself be carried, asleep, a Boy Scout in the magic forest.

In the end he did nothing at all. He moved only in his thoughts. In his thoughts he took out the wallet with Els's photograph and looked at it, but it no longer meant anything to him, just a pale face from the past. He searched for things to think about in order to remain awake. He tried to remember his life from childhood onward; this was a wonderful opportunity to look back over his life and discover the pattern of it, the thread that had led him here. But he never got beyond the dark drawing room in the vicarage, the slow ticking of the grandfather clock in the shadow next to the fireplace, his father with his white shirt front and his black coat talking, talking. "Tiptoe, tiptoe, tiptoe through the tulips with me. . . ."

He tried thinking about nice things. Things that would not change, even if he never came back, even if he were never to see that dear old world again. Els's love, Bert's friendship, his first pipe. Smoke. Crematorium. As a child he had imagined what his own funeral would be like; how he would stand among the mourners around the grave and look at the faces of those who remained behind. He had imagined the solemn words spoken, the sad songs sung, the thuds of the spadefuls of earth thrown onto the coffin. Now, suddenly, this dream seemed to turn into reality. It seemed as if the real Anton Zorgdrager had secretly sneaked out of the sweating body underneath the awning in the prahu and floated upward, up, up, like a child's balloon, tied to the sleeper in the gliding square of shadow by a gossamer thread. He saw, more clearly than by opening his eyes and looking ahead, the small procession of the four narrow prahus creep slowly through a crack in a continent of green. It was such a harmless and uninteresting spectacle that he watched it as a fisherman might watch some blades of grass drift past, without looking away from his float. They drifted on, and on—only by using all his strength could he haul back that thread, slowly, cautiously, until at last he was back in his hot body, and smacked his lips, and opened his eyes, and awakened to the cradle song of the mandur and the birds.

"Ah-ee . . . Ah-ee . . ."

As he groped for a beer bottle he started to hum: "Tiptoe, tiptoe through the tulips . . ."

Hopeless. The jungle had obliterated him. Dr. Zorgdrager was no more; he had returned to the womb of time, to the world as it was before the advent of man.

"Ah-ee . . . Ah-ee . . ."

He fell asleep again.

«« »»

By the time they reached the rapids, he had become a sleepwalker.

He did what the mandur told him to do, without thinking. He got out of the boat clumsily, watched with dull eyes the coolies drag the prahus through the foaming turbulence of angry water, stepped from stone to stone with unconscious sureness: a sleepwalker.

The only straw to which his will to live still clung was: twenty tins.

Twenty tins, sixteen anti-plague and four P.G. The P.G. are the most important; if anything should happen to the P.G. I'll have to swim after them and drown. Each time the prahus were dragged through rapids by the slithering, panting coolies, he counted them: sixteen anti-plague, four P.G., with occasionally a sneer at himself, because he still had to cling onto something extraneous. Inside himself nothing was left, not a hope, not a feeling of shame, not a memory, not a regret. If anything should happen to those twenty tins, his life would be in danger; if they should get lost, he would be dead. Those tins were the last positive element; everything else had become pointless in the unchanging green abundance of the jungle. Every day was exactly the same as the one before; the aspect of the river banks never varied. Each morning it seemed as if during the night they had floated back to the point from which they had set out the previous day, like damned souls who had to make the same voyage over and over again, for all eternity, without ever arriving anywhere.

One hot afternoon, after he had thrown a beer bottle overboard and followed the bobbing speck with his eyes as it was swiftly carried away by the current, the hallucination that had recurred every day suddenly turned round. The real Anton Zorgdrager no longer floated over the jungle, connected with the body underneath the awning by the gossamer thread; suddenly the real Anton Zorgdrager was sitting in the prahu, and the sleeping body was drifting away with the beer bottle, home.

Home! It was like a blow on a gong, a sudden, violent awakening. He was lost! He would vanish in that jungle like a ghost! He had only one chance left to save his life: go home!

The beer bottle got smaller, vanished from sight, but it took the thread with it, pulling him back to the world, to life, home. The wish to turn back was stronger than the sleep; that night he lay awake with staring eyes and throbbing temples in the darkness, listening to the zooming of the mosquitoes, the gurgling of the stream, the insane cacophony of the jungle. He made plans, saw feverish visions of the end if he did not turn round now to flee: climbing plants would sneak up his body, growing with soft, groping tendrils, creeping round his neck, weaving a paralyzing net around the white manikin, the heart of the onion, now bared at last, the last of its layers gone. Then even the last certainty left him. If anything should now happen to those twenty tins, he would shout with joy, turn round and flash back with the stream, back like the beer bottle,

Anton's body, swirling home, turning and bobbing, tugging at the thread that was getting thinner, weaker, until it would snap.

He knew, somewhere at the edge of his consciousness, that the only real danger was in himself. He knew the symptoms as a schoolchild its multiplication tables. He knew it was claustrophobia, the madness of the jungle, the lone man's last enemy. But knowing it did not help. He was powerless in the grip of the wilderness. Even though he knew what he was dying of, he was dying all the same.

The next day, another day, ghostly repetition of the one that had gone before, of all the ones that had gone before, the mandur began to sing, "Ah-ee . . . Ah-ee . . ." once more. He folded his hands around the cap of a beer bottle, closed his eyes and prayed, "God, God, dear God, give me a sign, let it be a sign, save me, save me, make it a sign. . . ." Then he threw up the cap with his eyes closed, and thought, "If it falls the right way up, it means: go home; the wrong way up: carry on." He opened his eyes and looked. It was lying the right way up. Go home, God said. He threw once more—carry on. Once again—go home. Then he threw the cap overboard, feeling lost. He had spoiled the significance of the sign because he had had no faith. Now it no longer meant anything.

The thread stretched longer and longer. He lay underneath his awning and let himself be carried as if on a stretcher: too cowardly, too weak to escape.

"Ah-ee . . . Ah-ee . . ."

He tiptoed through the tulips toward death.

«« »»

The thread that connected the phantom with the body could hardly be felt any more, when the rapids that seemed to come back every day were suddenly different.

He was standing on a stone in white foaming water, the coolies were dragging the prahus across; the mandur shouted and the guide shouted; then, suddenly, the voices fell silent and the men stood motionless, looking at something that changed the world.

In the small stillness behind a rock lay a decomposed body, half under water. Two thin arms pointed at the sky, and the current made rings round two drawn-up knees. The head was submerged; its hair floated on the water like weeds. But it was not death that made them all stare at the body with horrified eyes; it was the boils on the arms, as big as fists, and black. It was the plague.

One of the prahus shot back, some coolies jumped inside, others were dragged off their feet clutching the gunwales; the current dragged the prahu downstream, home.

And then the thread snapped. He suddenly stood bolt upright, the water foaming round his legs, and cried: "Stop! Stop, goddamn you!" The other prahus started to rumble down the rocks of the rapids, all the coolies tried to flee in a panic of fear; he took down his gun, put it against his shoulder, and fired. The shot barked, muffled by the thunder of the water; the butt hit his shoulder; wood splintered off the stern of the second prahu; the coolies ducked. He fired again; the smell of the explosive blew past him; then the mandur started to scream, to shake his fists at the coolies, to kick them; he drove them back, up the rapids. They strained, moaning, in the ropes and dragged the remaining prahus into the next stretch of the river. In the distance the fugitive vanished: one tin of P.G., four anti-plague, and the guide, the only man who knew the way to Rauwatta.

"Mandur!"

The mandur came splashing toward him, bowing. "Saja, tuan besar . . ."

"Pick up that chest; put it ashore."

"Saja, tuan besar . . ."

The mandur obeyed and splashed ahead of him to the bank, headless underneath the medicine chest. He put it down respectfully. Nobody moved, but all of them were watching, as Tuan Doctor opened the chest, took out a chromium box, a bottle, a pack of cotton wool. Then he fetched a tin out of the nearest prahu, cut it open and took out a stack of small wooden boxes containing phials.

Intramuscular, four cc. He gave twelve injections to twelve trembling creatures, after having first given himself a shot in the arm to show them that he wasn't going to murder them. They didn't resist, they made no sound; they just trembled like frightened children. Then he put his instruments away, closed the chest again and said to the mandur: "Now nobody need be afraid any more; none of you will get the plague. I am taking the first boat with the map; you take the last one. Anyone who makes a move that looks like running away will be shot. Translate that."

The mandur started to talk to the coolies. He could not understand what the man was saying, so he did not stay to listen, but went back to his prahu. As he turned round he saw, casually, that they were looking at him with a respect that no one had ever shown him before. But it did not give him any satisfaction, it did not even surprise him; he just registered it and thought: "Good. We have got twelve days to go; those injections will take effect ten days from now, so when we arrive they'll be immune."

He didn't give a thought to the miracle that had happened. A new man had been born in the jungle: Dr. Zorgdrager of the Government Health Service. The boy, the coward, the traveler without destination had vanished the moment chapter eleven of Eykman's *Vade Mecum* had become a reality.

"Ah-ee!" he cried.

The coolies jumped into the boats, grabbed their paddles, pushed off and chanted after him. His prahu shot ahead, leading the convoy. He spread out the map in front of him and put the compass on top of it. They might get lost a hundred times, but don't worry, Dr. Brits-Jansen, I'll find you even if it takes a year.

"Ah-ee . . ." the mandur chanted. "Ah-ee . . ."

That awning was wrong. They should see him in the bright sunlight, from morning till evening, looking round with his gun ready, without a moment's inattentiveness. He took it down.

"Ah-ee . . . Ah-ee . . ."

The birds twittered; the water of the rapids foamed around the small stillness where the body lay, its arms stretched toward the sun. The prahus sailed away and were soon lost in the green and the blue of the jungle and the sky. Then the white speck of the topee vanished, as the wilderness closed over it.

CHAPTER THREE

Tʜᴇ first white man to sail up the Kali-Woga as far as Rauwatta was Dr. Breszezinska-Jansen, the Nestor of the Government Health Service.

Thirty years ago, an urgent telegram had ordered him to proceed at once to Tarakan, to the palace of the Governor of Borneo. Sultan Rahula Rattan Rauwari was dying—an enlightened ruler, a staunch ally of the government, the only Dyak chief who had been to Holland and even spoke Dutch—this man should be kept alive at all costs.

A very important mission, the Governor had said, a great chance for the new Government Health Service to prove its mettle. Brits-Jansen, deeply impressed, had left at once, traveled three weeks up the river, dragging an instrument case and a medicine chest with a cure for every ailment known to man, to arrive, after a nightmarish trek through mosquitoes, rapids and crocodiles, in Rauwatta: desolate breeding ground of plague and malaria on the mud banks of the Kali-Woga.

He was welcomed by the village elders and led in silent reverence to the Sultan's palace where, in the red dusk of smoking torches, the first thing he discerned was a billiard table, green and ugly, its legs standing in coconut shells filled with water to keep the ants at bay. On the walls hung the dried heads of the Sultan's late enemies, and in their midst the enlargement of a photograph in a gilt frame full of curlicues, showing a sly little native in frock coat and top hat beaming with pride on a swivel chair in the main cigar store in Amsterdam, surrounded by the pale noncommittal faces of the shop assistants. That native was Sultan Rahula Rattan Rauwari, enlightened ruler of a territory three times the size of Holland, with a population of three thousand.

Malodorous girls lifted a mosquito curtain behind the billiard table; there, in a dark room smelling like a goat sty, he found an ornate Victorian bed; on that bed, the royal patient lay in a coma, thin, tiny and impressive in his motionless suffering. The girls cautiously lowered the mosquito curtain again behind the giant doctor with the terrible beard; Brits-Jansen sat down on the edge of the bed, that sagged with a twang of springs, and from the startled glance the patient shot him he concluded that the coma was not a deep one. The Sultan moaned; his fingers twitched and he swallowed with a choking sound, but the man who could fool Brits-Jansen with a faked illness had still to be born. While examining the childish body he asked himself what purpose an Enlightened Ruler could have in pretending to be ill. When he completed his examination he still did not know the answer.

"Tell what matter Sultan. . . ." the patient whispered. "Tell what illness Sultan suffers. . . ."

Brits-Jansen slapped the little man's buttocks, answered: "Nothing," and got to his feet. "You'd better get up, sire," he concluded. "You're as healthy as a pig."

For one speechless second, the Sultan gaped at him, flabbergasted by such disrespect, then his sly little eyes filled with fury and he whispered: "Doctor worst doctor Sultan ever seen. Doctor eye and mind of sappo-lidi."

"Possibly," Brits-Jansen answered. "I may have the eye and the mind of a fly swatter, but I'm the best billiard player in the Far East."

That was too much, even for a Sultan, especially for a Sultan. Rahula Rattan Rauwari rose in his bed like a cobra, with the murder of twenty headhunting generations blazing from his black eyes, and hissed: "Sappo-lidi! Sodom man! We shall play! Sultan shall play Sappo-lidi till he is slain!"

"All right," Brits-Jansen answered. "But on one condition: if I win, Sultan is cured forever."

"And if Sappo-lidi loses?" the Sultan asked, slyly.

"Then I'll retire from the Service," Brits-Jansen said, "and nurse Sultan until the hour of my death, as his private doctor."

The Sultan got out of bed without a word. He lifted the mosquito netting and went toward the billiard table. The malodorous girls, frightened out of their wits, took flight as if they had seen an apparition. After Sultan Rahula Rattan Rauwari had chalked his cue, made his first shot, and scored twenty, eyes were peering through all the cracks in the bamboo walls and a silence reigned in the jungle as if an act of God were taking place.

They played on until the red sun rose out of the rolling clouds of the morning mist and the birds started twittering in the trees; the Sultan played like a demon, but Brits-Jansen played as only one man could play east of Singapore: Dr. Breszezinska-Jansen of the G.H.S. That morning, after he had won with an astronomical score and made the Sultan weep with rage, he put his cue in a corner and made a tour of the kampong. The inhabitants fled from him in panic—women, dogs, chickens, yelling children; he walked through a deserted village of age-old huts built on the rotting foundations of even older ones, and he saw why the Sultan had been ill. The miserable huts surrounded the gaudy palace like so many memorials to exploitation and slavery; the sly little despot obviously never showed himself to his victims and fooled them with frequent sick-beds so as to give them hope that he would soon die anyhow. The billiard table alone was a monument to a demigod: it must have cost scores of lives to drag the unwieldy thing across all those rapids between Rokul and Rauwatta.

Brits-Jansen had never occupied himself with politics, and held no respect for the politics of others; the government might consider this slavetrader to be an enlightened ruler who had to be placated for the sake of peace in the interior; he thought differently, and decided to teach him a lesson. He knew that the magic power of the demigod would be finished as soon as his subjects were shown a real god compared to whom their Sultan was a midget; the deserted streets of the kampong were already a good sign, but the Sultan's people had to be shown a miracle if he wanted to pull out the teeth of the monster in the palace effectively. He decided that an official dinner should take place in his honor, when he would show Sultan Rahula Rattan Rauwari a miracle that had left even the Governor General agape with astonishment.

The Sultan haughtily agreed to his proposal, and ordered that a feast to celebrate his recovery should be served that night in the village square, in front of the palace. During the whole of that day the village was full of the crackling of fire, the hissing of boiling water and the smells of cooking. When darkness fell, a table stood in the flickering torchlight, laden with enough food for a dozen people. Piles of fruit, stewed, boiled, and fried; fish, chicken, eels as thick as a man's arm, and a whole billy goat, filled with eggs. His own contribution was a pint of gin, his month's ration.

Hours beforehand, the square was packed with silent, staring villagers. When the Sultan finally appeared, he was in full court dress; the only things alive in his doll-like pomp were his eyes, taking in the villagers, the table and the waiting giant in a roving glance. When their eyes met, Brits-Jansen saw the Sultan realized that they were about to fight another duel, this time for something more important than a lifelong deathbed.

Brits-Jansen gave the Sultan a perfunctory bow, and did not deign to look at him again. He rubbed his hands like a man who has a good appetite, and sat down opposite the Sultan, facing the crowd. He rolled up his shirt sleeves despite the mosquitoes, poured out a full beaker of gin for the Sultan and half a beaker for himself, said, "Sire, here's mud in your eye," threw back the drink, licked his lips, slammed down the beaker and started eating. He had the impression that even the animals of the jungle were peering at him from the smoky darkness behind the torches, but he did not look up and started eating as only one man could eat east of Singapore: Dr. Breszezinska-Jansen, G.H.S. The Sultan, after his first sip of gin, closed his eyes and remained motionless; then he shot his opponent a glance of such hatred that Brits-Jansen was delighted. But Rahula Rattan Rauwari took up the challenge, and drained the beaker in one gulp, choking, but without a tremor of his hand.

The banquet lasted until the small hours. During all that time, not a word was said and not a finger moved in the crowd squatting in the square. It was much more of a battle than Brits-Jansen had expected it to be; he had to gorge himself in order to keep ahead of the Sultan, and the world had been slowly distorted into a whirlpool of darkness full of comets when, at last, Rahula Rattan Rauwari turned turtle—after three beakers of gin, four fish, eighteen eggs, a leg of billy goat and two chickens. The Sultan's defeat was impressive. After half an hour of agonizing efforts to remain upright, he slowly sagged sideways, and slumped to the ground without uttering a sound, majestically silent until the end.

When the demigod fell off his throne, the crowd in the square retired in horror to the very edge of the torchlight; but when the god went on eating as if nothing had happened, they stealthily crept nearer again: small, big-eyed women with babies on their backs, earnest little men who forgot to chew their sirih, tiny children, helpless in the grip of curiosity, who only dared peep over their fathers' shoulders. Never in his life had Brits-Jansen been so drunk, never had he eaten such a disgusting amount of indigestible food, never had he felt so close to a stroke. Yet he went on eating—fruit, fish, eggs, chicken and billy goat—until he knew: one more bite and I'll burst, and my breath will catch fire from all those dancing torches. It would have been better to go on a little while longer; the triumph would not be complete until he had entirely cleared the table, but, alas, he was only human.

Then—as he sat swaying on his stool, gasping for breath, shaken by hiccups: a white monster with a purple face and bloodshot eyes—he performed the final miracle, the Horrible Deed, that would be whispered down from generation to generation in the Borneo jungle until Judgment Day. He wiped the grease off his mouth with his beard, shoved his topee on the back of his head, looked, for the first time, at the mesmerized crowd with a glassy stare; then he took his upper jaw out of his mouth and smacked it on the table. One second later, the square was empty of villagers; they were swept into the jungle as by the blast from a bomb.

How he managed to get to his feet he could never remember; he woke up in the Sultan's bed, crawling with fleas. His head hammered and he reeled with nausea, yet he managed to make a tour through the kampong, ignoring the panic he provoked. When he returned to the palace, followed by hundreds of invisible eyes, he had not seen a single native for more than half a second, and he knew that his work was done. That night the Sultan, tottering and ill, accompanied him to his prahu. As they bowed to one another in dignified farewell, Brits-Jansen was certain that the Sultan would remain healthy and enlightened until his death, for fear that Sappo-lidi might come back; but he knew also that His Highness would spend the rest of his life brooding on a means to get even with him.

Thirty years passed before Dr. Breszezinska-Jansen sailed up the Kali-Woga again, with Ruawatta as his destination. Between the two expeditions lay a life that had become a legend in the Far East. The fat, impertinent young man who had been paddled to the deathbed of the Sultan by five slaves had become the foremost leprosy specialist in the world; the stunt with the dentures had become one of the classic stories told in the clubs and the passangrahans of the archipelago, and the jungle, that had once seemed so menacing and unconquerable, had become as familiar to him as the maze in the Royal Gardens to the head keeper.

The second expedition was really a holiday trip. When he had heard that Brinkman had fallen ill in a plague outbreak in Rauwatta, he had volunteered to go, but not for the sake of Brinkman. He had gone because of the Sultan, the billiard table, and the place where his fame had started thirty years ago; it was a pilgrimage to his youth. He was inoculated with anti-plague vaccine and, considering the gravity of the occasion, left rather hastily, with only six native male nurses, plenty of vaccine for the patients but only a quarter of a tin of P.G. He cursed his carelessness when he discovered this, one day up the river, and thought of turning round, but decided they would probably send a second expedition after him which was sure to have plenty of P.G. Then he settled down to three weeks of glorious rest; twenty days of sleep, shooting crocodiles and eating bananas and then a game of billiards with the Sultan. He hardly thought of Brinkman, dying in the wilderness, and not at all of the plague, which he had managed to tame to such an extent during these thirty years that it virtually bolted the moment it saw his beard, like the Dyaks.

As his small convoy crawled slowly up the river and he sat lolling underneath the awning, cradled by the nostalgic chant of his mandur, he tried to recall the first expedition, and it gradually came back to him. The first thing he remembered was the fear; he remembered it so vividly that it almost became real once more. Then he started to recognize the bends in the river, the rapids, the twittering birds of dawn and dusk, and the chattering monkeys following them along the river banks. Nothing seemed to have changed in those thirty years, not a tree, not a leaf; everything had remained unchanged for tens of thousands of years. The thirty years of Dr. Breszezinska-Jansen, the leprosy specialist, first seemed to be reduced to ten, then to one, and finally to nothing: a dream, from which he was now awakening. He had never been away from this forest, he had only dozed for a minute on the river. The hallucination was strong, but no stronger than was to be expected. The jungle went after souls, not lives—for thirty years he had taught this to his assistants, when they were new to the East. It was one of those platitudes one is inclined to forget are truths, too often repeated. It was nice, in a way, to experience that this truth still held, even though more so than he had bargained for. It was like making a culture of some interesting germ on his arm; but this time he had no secret fear that the culture might get out of control. He knew the jungle well enough to know exactly how far he could go in conjuring up the fat, sweating youngster he had once been, to discover that nothing had changed but that he had become a fat, sweating old man.

The great thing about the jungle was that one should never rely on logic within its green magic circle. The one thing that counted was vitality, the superiority of the lion tamer. One had to remain utterly sure of oneself; whatever threatened that self-confidence, whether it was a bad conscience, a hangover or just simply fatigue, it had to be crushed with merciless animal force, and that was a battle of life and death. He won the battle by cursing the coolies with a thundering voice, shooting at the crocodiles with a barrage of badly aimed shots, and an occasional stone hurled at the screaming monkeys in the trees; but it cost him his holiday. He had to fight as doggedly to arrive in Rauwatta as he had thirty years before, and now he was thirty years older. The giant who finally set foot ashore in the plague-stricken village felt like a dwarf compared to the trees; when he realized that he was no longer measuring himself against the people around him but against the jungle itself, like any totok who had never seen a waringin tree in his life, he knew that he had not defeated the wilderness yet. Rauwatta also looked entirely unchanged; the mud flats, the huts, the gaudy palace, everything was exactly the same as it had been thirty years ago. When the village elders met him on the river bank, he expected to be taken to the palace again, the billiard table, the Sultan's deathbed and the malodorous girls. But after his first step ashore, things turned out to be very different indeed.

It was almost dark when he arrived, and the first difference he noticed was the smell of the plague, which cured him at once. The village was surrounded by a ring of little flames: the witch doctors' torches, magic circle against the black death. Within this circle, hundreds of natives lay dying, many more than he had expected; most of these people must be strangers who had come out of the jungle hoping to be cured by the Sultan's magicians. Moaning and wailing troubled the silence, together with the buzzing of the mosquitoes that swarmed around the torches in thick clouds. In the glinting darkness of the river the crocodiles lay leering, a ring of motionless pairs of red eyes, just above the surface, luminous like glowworms. The village was a chaos of dying, dead and lunatics; heaps of corpses were stacked in the streets between the huts, and in the village square the witch doctors danced with their bewildered patients around a huge fire made of animal sacrifices.

It was a spectacle that struck even Brits-Jansen with a momentary feeling of horror; but as it liberated him from the spell of the jungle he welcomed it. He made the village elders announce his arrival to the Sultan, and sent his mandur as a representative to the Master of Ceremonies to ask for an audience at ten o'clock. That gave him three hours to clean this pigsty and bring a bit of order into the witch's cauldron in the village square.

He started work. To begin with, he chased the quacks from the square with bellowed commands and a shot in the air, the echoes of which rolled like thunder down the dark chasm of the river; then he ordered the boats to be burnt. As the panicking villagers tried to flee to their prahus, they found the river bank cordoned off by six armed male nurses, and they saw in front of their baffled eyes all their boats, even the ones in which the giant had arrived from the forest, dragged ashore and thrown into the fire of the sacrifices. After all communication with the outer world had thus been cut off, the invaders, in white coats, wearing high rubber boots and long gloves as a protection against the fleas, started to rake the corpses together and throw them into the fire too. The natives, completely dazed and unable to understand any of these magical actions, continued their interrupted tribal dance, this time around the fire in which their prahus were being consumed with explosions of cracking wood, and their dead reduced to ashes with a sickening stench of roasting. The stench grew, remained suspended between the trees, became more pungent and more oppressive, until finally they seemed to be dancing in a ghastly kitchen.

In the meantime, Brits-Jansen had cleared the ground for the first stage of the battle. He had ascertained that Brinkman was dead and buried; he had localized the epidemic by burning the boats; he had burnt the corpses. The next step would be to split up the village into sectors for the healthy, the ill and the dying, to rope off a doctors' camp, to build a hospital, living quarters and a laboratory within the fence, and to dig an anti-flea moat around it. It was a bad epidemic, but no worse than previous ones he had coped with elsewhere. The position of the village was ideal for isolation, the Sultan too weak to be an obstruction—although he had sent word via the Master of Ceremonies that he would be unable to receive Tuan Doctor until eleven-fifteen the next morning. It was a deliberate insult, but understandable. If he had observed court ritual himself he would not have started cleaning up the place before seeing the old man and getting his formal permission. Even this omission had a purpose however: to make it quite clear right from the beginning who was in command.

Everything seemed innocent and normal. He could find no reason at all for the alarming fact that, while watching the fire in the village square, he suddenly found himself humming "Auld Lang Syne."

He had as much musical sense as a monkey, would not have known the difference between the "Marseillaise" and "God Save the King"; the only music his head had ever harbored was "Auld Lang Syne." He had hummed it for the first time, all alone, one New Year's morning in New York, thirty-two years ago. The night before, he had celebrated the New Year with the crowd in Times Square, picked up a girl with a halo of gay innocence with whom he had fallen in love at sight, and she had been lured away from him by a pimp with a little mustache, in whose eyes he had seen at a glance that he had syphilis. For the first time in his life one of his brilliant diagnoses, which were the wonder of his professors, had not made him happy. The rest of the night he had wandered about the streets, making drunken plans.

The next morning, as he stood shaving in his hotel room, he had heard himself hum "Auld Lang Syne," the tune he had been taught by the bellowing crowd the night before, and he had suddenly realized that he was capable of murder. He had stood quite still for a minute, a double razor between him and his reflection; then he had wiped the razor clean and started shaving the other cheek, humming: "We'll take a cup of kindness yet, For auld lang syne." That moment of self-revelation was the reason for his decision to leave at once. Three days later he had been on his way to Batavia, one of the first officers in the foreign legion of the Government Health Service: a fat, impertinent young man with a three-ply instrument chest without instruments, one pair of socks, a pocket comb, a nail brush for his dentures (even then) and a topee from a pawnshop, who possessed only one talent: a gift for diagnosis that was almost genius, and only one merit: that he had not murdered a pimp, thanks to a Scottish New Year song.

During the thirty-two years that had passed since that morning he had occasionally found himself humming the tune, and it had always been just in time to prevent himself from committing an irrevocable mistake. It was uncanny—as if a guardian angel warned him at the last moment by humming that tune into his ear. The last time it had happened he was leaning over a woman, his syringe ready for the injection, about to murder someone after all, though this time it would have been for love. The moment came back to him with uncanny clarity, as he stood looking at the funeral pyre in the village square of Rauwatta: the little white room, the bed in its tent of mosquito netting, the sickly sweet smell of leprosy, the mutilated body on the white sheet. He had just finished examining her, as he had examined her hundreds of times, but instead of straightening up with a sigh and patting her on the shoulder, he had edged slowly away from her with a sudden secretiveness, for the blind, mute body on the bed could follow his movements by listening. He had gone to the washbasin; he had cautiously broken the phial, filled the syringe, squirted out the air, holding the needle against the light of the oil lamp, humming "Should auld acquaintance be forgot, and never brought to mind . . ." Then he had fallen silent. His eyes, squinting at the tiny fountain squirting out of the needle, had slowly focused beyond it, on the cross on the white wall, the only decoration in the room. For the first time he had realized that the cross was not a decoration, but the symbol of the life he was about to extinguish. It was the credo of the mutilated body on the bed, to whom nothing now remained of the days when she had been a beautiful woman, except her faith, which was more than he had ever possessed himself. He had stood there for a long while, the syringe against the light, staring at the cross on the wall; then he had started to hum again, louder this time, to hide from the listening body in the mosquito tent the sounds of the syringe being opened and emptied in the washbasin, the opening and shutting of the chromium box, the snap of the lock on his instrument bag. "We'll take a cup of kindness yet . . ."; he had gone back into the night without bidding her good-by, shutting the door softly behind him. The white buildings of the leper colony had shimmered like ivory in the moonlight, and echoed the sound of his footsteps as he crossed the courtyard to his laboratory. In his laboratory he had not put on the light; he had slumped down at his work bench, his head in his hands, and wept among the bottles and the test tubes, that timidly reflected the moonlight.

Why had he hummed that tune now, tonight? He was old enough to have realized long ago that chance plays only a small part in a man's life. Every thought and every action obeyed a law of cause and effect; the fact that he had hummed the tune while looking at a funeral pyre in Rauwatta was the effect of a cause that he now tried to hunt down doggedly, but in vain.

His mandur had put up a temporary shelter of palm leaves on the edge of the village, after having burnt down a square of grass and dug a flea moat around it. He undressed by the light of a storm lantern, lay down on his camp bed and tried to sleep, but the stench of Lysol, burnt grass and roasting kept him awake. Also, his thoughts would not rest; they kept going back to "Auld Lang Syne" and Betsy, the woman he had almost murdered. He had not thought about Betsy for over a month now; that was of course the reason why he had felt so good. He wondered how she was, and how Willem was, nursing her with his unfailing love and devotion. As he went on tossing on his bed, getting hotter and hotter, there came a moment when he cursed the day he had met those two; but instantly he mumbled: "Nonsense, of course I don't mean that. Nonsense!" as if he were addressing God, who had listened, frowning, to his thoughts. And God was right—if he hadn't met them he would most certainly have gone to hell. Well, let's say, a different kind of hell. For, now he was back in his thoughts at Betsy, the dominating element of his life, he was not so sure if it would not have been better to have gone to that other hell, the one of the godless, the drunks, the killers. He had been unhappy before he met her, he had known moments of black despair in those first years in the jungle, but gin had always helped and so had the company of his fellow doomed. What rabble they had been, those first doctors of the G.H.S.; what a soulless scoundrel he had been himself. During those first years, the Service had consisted entirely of the medical outlaws of the world: adventurers, abortionists, bigamists. A pack of wolves they had been, all of them with the same goal: a private practice in Java or Deli with white patients. They had operated on the natives without anesthetics, burned down kampongs out of laziness, bellowed with laughter at obscene jokes while their dying patients lay moaning on the brink of the lamplight, around which they sat playing poker for pints of gin. He tried to remember their faces, but it was difficult because the beards had made them all look alike. They were all dead now; Habermann of cholera in Celebes, years ago; Mecure knifed by a Balinese, running amok; Gunther of lung plague in Sumatra; Van Dam of delirium tremens in Batavia. He tried to remember his own face as it had been then, the face he had seen in the fly-blown mirrors of many passangrahans, the small hostels built in the jungle for the army officers, tax collectors and oil prospectors who trekked to the interior. All he could remember was that his beard had been fair then, instead of gray, and brown around the mouth because of his cigars; and he remembered the eyes he had looked at; sometimes with a feeling of alarm and despair. They were the eyes of a sadist who treated all natives as if they were monkeys in a laboratory, and who had used his gift of diagnosis only to impress his superiors or to gratify himself. For it had amused him, for some obscure and scabrous reason, to see the fear of death in horrified eyes, when after a few casual questions and a swift examination he pronounced the death sentence, which he should have kept to himself as it had never done any patient any good. Suppose he had gone on like that? Suppose he had never broken through the undergrowth with his horse that night in Java, when he had got lost on his way to the next passangrahan? His life would not have been so very different, only shorter probably; he would have gone the way of the others and killed himself, either by carelessness, or drink, or by challenging the passivity of the natives too far and getting himself knifed by a madman in a blind paroxysm of revolt.

As he broke through the undergrowth he saw an open space in the jungle, a fire in the center. Dark shapes crawled around in it, moaning, and even before he came near enough to distinguish them, he recognized the sickly sweet smell. He spurred on his horse to cross the clearing; a chorus of wailings answered the hoof beats, mutilated arms stretched out to him, and all around him ghostly faces grimaced, calling from horrible mouths. He cursed, drove his horse toward the fire, to force it over; then he stopped. A woman in white had suddenly risen behind the flames. A white woman. Next to her was a man in white, kneeling by the side of a monster. The woman was very beautiful; her eyes looked at him kindly. "What are you doing here?" he asked, roughly, to defend himself against those eyes.

"Helping," the woman answered. She had a hoarse, low voice. Her companion stood up too, a man with sloping shoulders and a tired face, holding a mass of dirty bandages.

"Are you out of your minds?" he cried. "Do you know what you are doing?"

"Of course," the woman said. The man smiled and said nothing. The horse neighed, and from all sides mutilated bodies came crawling near in the flickering firelight. "Who has given you permission?" he shouted. His horse reared. "Don't you know leprosy is infectious? What precautions have you taken?"

"None," the woman said. "God protects us."

"Is that so?" he asked mockingly, suddenly sure of himself, for he had seen her hands. "Then let me tell you that your God has made a mug of you, for you have it, my dear." He said it with a wide, fatherly smile. But as he stared intently into her eyes, waiting for the fear he knew so well and that never failed to appear, his smile slowly disappeared, and he was overcome by a growing amazement, an incredulity, that became a feeling of emptiness. For she went on looking at him calmly, without batting an eyelid, and the kindness in her eyes deepened to pity. Never before had anyone looked at him like that, with such compassion; yet he was convinced she could not have known the truth, so slight were the signs of the white death.

"Yes . . ." he said, a last defense against the void growing inside him, "you have leprosy!" He pointed at the lepers, crawling nearer. "You'll be like them! God knows how long it will take before He puts an end to you: maybe thirty years!"

When she still gave no sign of terror, still looked at him with that terrible, tender strength, he dismounted, turned her toward the fire, took her hands, opened them, closed them, looked up, and asked, "Who are you?" The man answered, "Salvationists," and his voice broke on the word.

A hand pulled at his trouser leg; he saw the stump of an arm creep up her skirt; without a word he turned away, to remount and flee back into the night. But the feeling of emptiness made him feel so lost and helpless that he turned round again, and went back to the woman who had bent down once more over the most horrible suffering in the world. He stood watching her for a long time, but she did not look up. Then he took a bandage out of a basket standing by the fire, and started a new, bewildering life by bandaging some fingerless hand.

Often during the years that followed, he asked himself: what exactly happened that night? Something had happened, because he had been unable to take up his old life again. He gave up drinking and playing poker; he went through a change of morals that made the others first gape in surprise and then bellow with laughter; they called it a grotesque conversion. He alone knew that it was not a conversion at all, but something else, something to do with her, not with God or his soul. He was unable to leave her; something drew him back to her that was stronger than his sense of shame, his urge for freedom and self-preservation. He worked, pleaded, intrigued, fought for them with much more doggedness than he had ever fought for his own sake. He pestered the Head of the Service and the government relentlessly, trying to get a sanatorium for their patients; at last, after more than a year, the harassed authorities granted them an old military hospital somewhere in the mountains in Java, a scandalous place, two centuries old, that had been a fortress, a prison and an army hospital, but abandoned by the army because the prisoners went mad and the patients died of a mysterious fever. The clubs and the passangrahans buzzed with funny stories about Brits-Jansen the Holy Roller, the Latter-day Saint; Habermann sent him a rosary with a phallic symbol instead of a cross; Gunther wrote him a letter full of drunken obscenities; the four others invited him to their yearly reunion in Batavia, and instead of rijst-tafel with beer they served him holy wafers with jam, and communion wine. It dawned on him that he had been granted the hospital as a practical joke, and he felt like exterminating all the bastards that called themselves the Army Medical Corps. Everybody was waiting for the wonderful moment when Brits-Jansen, who had crashed through the sinners' bench when kneeling down and who took his teeth out to pray, would go for the C.O. Java with his double-barreled gun. But Willem and Betsy were so happy with their Black Hole of Calcutta, the temple God had given them in His mercy, that he turned his back on the bastards and tried to share in the happy enthusiasm of his two friends. They started by hoisting the Dutch flag in the courtyard to express their thanks to the government, then they held a prayer meeting in the punishment hall, where so far only screams and curses had rung out with the swishing of birches. He feared the worst, yet helped them to fit out their hospital. He saw to it that they got instruments, drugs, beds, kitchen utensils, male nurses, patients. He took off his topee at the first holiness meeting, hummed tunelessly with their odd, happy songs, and suddenly stopped humming for the calm question in his thoughts: what the hell am I doing here? Then he shrugged his shoulders and hummed on.

The impossible succeeded. The fortress, that for two hundred years had been a monument to human cruelty, became the first leper colony in the archipelago, a model of its kind. Once they could do without him a feeling of resentment had grown inside him: they ought to be damned grateful for everything he had done for them, and, quite frankly, he was getting a bit sick of Jesus and their irritating cheerfulness. Then he learned that they had a child of sixteen months, that it had been three months old when they were forced to send it away, after he had told her she had leprosy. She mentioned it casually, while the orchestra of lepers was playing for the funeral of a limbless trunk called Pa-Kromo. It was a girl, she said: Bertha. She was now in a Salvation Army home in Holland, and they would probably never see her again. Then the trumpets blared the triumphantly unharmonious final chord of "When the roll is called up yonder" and the trumpeters, pressing down the stops with sticks because their fingers had become too short, had tears in their eyes at their own beautiful sound.

He did not breathe a word to them about it, but that day he started his battle with God. God, Who had promised to protect His servants, and Who had smitten with leprosy the most wonderful woman in the world. He specialized in leprosy with a vindictiveness that gave him, within a year, the reputation of a maniac all over the archipelago. He hunted lepers everywhere, traveled for weeks to look at a special case; he sent his colleagues begging letters, beseeching them to collect all interesting specimens they could find and keep them until he arrived. He fitted out a laboratory within the walls of the fortress, and every day, every hour he could spare from his heavy duties, he worked there, mumbling, sweating, a staggering giant in the harsh glare of hissing Primus lamps, until he fell asleep at the breakfast table and snored during grace. Every leave he got, sometimes just a single night as he was passing through, he wrestled there with God like Jacob in the desert. But at the end of each year he had to look back on a series of lost battles, and add another defeat to her case history.

During the first years of this gigantic duel, he sometimes asked himself whether it was love that had made him attack leprosy with such ferocity; whether he had challenged God only out of frustrated desire. But if this was love, it was different from what he had always known it to be, for the thought of holding her in his arms was unbearable, and made him hide his face in his hands with shame. Women to him were a luxury, like expensive beer or a really good game of billiards. He had a woman occasionally, but they were mostly one-night affairs; at last he got stuck with a fat half-caste called Poppy, who owned a boardinghouse in Surabaya and terrorized him by threatening suicide if he left her. She often thought he would, for when he came to see her he put his stockinged feet on the table, his beard a matted tangle on his open shirt, drank beer, and stared right through her as if he were alone in the room. But she need not worry; he would never leave her; he liked her. Every time she tried to hang herself or swallowed a tube of sleeping tablets, he chucked the rope out of the window or made her vomit, mumbling the same endearments he grunted to Bambo, her monkey, as it sat picking the rice out of his beard after dinner.

Breszezinska-Jansen, the foremost leprosy specialist—it was nobody's business that he was battling with God for a mutilated woman lying in a mosquito tent somewhere on a mountain on an island called Java. The Head of the Service, who had once been his assistant, sometimes asked him why he refused promotion, why he insisted on wasting his time as a volunteer for expeditions against plague, dysentery and cholera in outlying parts of the jungle where a young nonentity might have done just as well. Then he would laugh and shrug his shoulders, and his embarrassment would be hidden by his beard. For who would understand that he was on a life-long pilgrimage in search of someone he knew he would never find, and yet went on expecting with foolish hope at each bend of the road? Someone—saint, hermit or lunatic—who would know the answer to this question: How was it that in a room on a mountain in Java, a blind, mutilated woman could lie dying in a blaze of glory, while he, the giant, slowly sank into a morass of despair?

«‹‹ ›››

The next morning, he was up at sunrise. His plan of campaign was simple and he was certain of the outcome; the only depressing element in the situation was the lack of P.G. He would have to get this campaign over very quickly indeed.

The splitting up of the village into sectors of dying, ill and healthy was basically a simple operation; a trained dog could have done it. But as always the emotional element was his main obstacle; the natives stuck together in family groups. To split them up was unnerving, for the dying wept without a sound or laughed madly in their fever, the ill tried to flee on all fours, and the healthy shrieked, yammered, beat their chests and pulled their hair out; to a native the family is the last straw to cling to in a catastrophe.

He had witnessed those heartrending scenes of separation many times and he had never got used to them. There was only one solution to make it easier for everybody; Habermann had discovered it twenty-eight years ago, in Celebes. Give the lot of them two shots of P.G. and they let themselves be separated like lambs. But he had no P.G.; all he had left was about 400 cc. of it, and that dose he intended to eke out for his own use. So the separations had to be carried out without the aid of science, and it was a nasty job. He was glad when, after three hours of screams, tears and futile fights, he could leave the rest to his mandur and the male nurses; for it was nearly eleven o'clock, and he had a date with the Sultan.

He went to his tent to change his clothes; he could not go and see the

Sultan in flea boots and rubber gloves, his white coat splashed with blood and mud. But after he had taken off his gloves and opened the chest in which his white drill was packed, a thought struck him. He remembered waking up the morning after the banquet, thirty years ago, in the Sultan's bed; the most memorable thing about the Sultan's bed was that it had been alive with fleas. Small wonder; many more generations of fleas than of men must have bred and lived in the palace. And it would not surprise him if the whole building was just a roof on a vast, intricate fortress of zigzagging tunnels: rats. Plague had come to Rauwatta before; it was the only spot in Borneo where plague occurred; it might well be that the explanation was an enormous colony of rats, living underneath the palace. In that case he would have to go very easy with the Sultan this morning, and placate him as much as he could; for if his conclusion about the rats was right, there was only one solution if he wanted to finish off the plague in Rauwatta once and for all: he would have to burn down the village and blow up the palace.

So he did not change after all. He only put on a clean white coat. When he presented himself at the palace gate he was struck by an eerie atmosphere. He had to wait a long time before anyone answered his calls; there was something strange going on here. In the end, tired shuffling steps dragged themselves across the courtyard and the gate was opened, after some clumsy fumbling with the locks and chains, by an invisible hand. As the gate swung open, creaking on wooden hinges, and he entered the courtyard, he saw still bodies lying everywhere in sleeping positions. No wonder he had felt uneasy; everybody he passed on his way to the Sultan was dead. The man who had opened the gate was the Master of Ceremonies himself. The Master of Ceremonies tottered and giggled like a drunk; once the Master of Ceremonies lay down, he would never get up again. Something had to be done about this palace, and quickly.

By the time he arrived in the billiard room, he was in no mood for joking. While crossing the courtyard and following the stumbling Master of Ceremonies along the pitch-dark corridor, he had decided to placate the Sultan in the most elementary way. In his mind he had unpacked his chest and looked for something he could offer him, after a bit of salesmanship, in exchange for his palace. All he could find was an electric vibromasseur, an impressive instrument with a rubber flange, that, when plugged in and applied to the stomach, sent one into screams of giggles, but which was reputedly the best slimming device ever invented. Poppy had made him buy it, one morning when he had a hangover; she had said that he felt dizzy because he was too fat. He had bought the thing after she had threatened to kill herself if he didn't; now he was stuck with it; but maybe God had made him buy it for this very occasion, in His mysterious, impenetrable way.

When he entered the dark room, the Sultan was playing billiards, an old dwarf with a cue. Time had certainly taken its toll on him; his face looked like an old apple, mummified in a draughty loft. Either Rahula Rattan Rauwari had shrunk with the passing of the years, or he himself had grown, which seemed unlikely. He had grown only in cimcumference, whereas the Sultan had diminished in stature, for he could barely peep over the billiard table any more. Perhaps someone since their last meeting had broken his legs.

"I see you, sire," Brits-Jansen said, bowing with a rustle of starched linen, and a plopping sound as he bent his hip boots.

The Sultan did not look up. He peered along his cue, one eye shut, remained frozen for nearly a minute, then the cue flashed like the tongue of a snake, a white ball with a big blue spot whirled across the table, hit first the red and then the other white one. Both vanished into the bags at the corners, then the spotted ball rolled slowly back toward the Sultan, like a rolling eye, until it came to rest in exactly the same spot from where he had shot it. Brits-Jansen raised his eyebrows and whistled. "Hot shot, sire," he said, with genuine admiration. "Let's have a game tonight."

Only then the Sultan looked up. His black eyes looked his visitor over, slowly, from the boots upward, until their eyes met. Brits-Jansen's smile became formal, then vanished altogether. He didn't like the look the Sultan gave him; it set an alarm bell ringing somewhere.

"I see you, Sappo-lidi," the Sultan said, softly.

Brits-Jansen did not lose any time beating about the bush. "Sire," he said, "if you want to stay alive, you're in for a move. I won't trouble you with details, but the black sickness is carried by fleas, and the fleas are carried by rats. If you want me to kill the black sickness, I'll have to kill the rats first, then the fleas. You've got a lot of both."

The Sultan lowered his eyelids, a proud demonstration of modesty. "Sultan has lot of everything," he said.

"Except subjects," Brits-Jansen added, "and at this rate Sultan won't have any left at all a moon from now. What would Sultan be without subjects?"

Rahula Rattan Rauwari raised his snakelike eyelids again, looked at his guest with an absent-minded gaze, and answered: "Sultan would be happy. Sultan not like subjects; Sultan like billiards and Her Majesty Queen."

"That, I am sure, is mutual," Brits-Jansen said, as a sudden brilliant idea crossed his mind. "I am sure that Her Majesty the Queen would be delighted to meet Sultan again and talk about old times. Would Sultan be agreeable to that?"

Rahula Rattan Rauwari stood thinking for a long time, holding his cue, an old dwarf with a lance; then he answered: "No."

"Come, come," said Brits-Jansen, "you don't mean that. Think of all the wonderful things you could do in Holland. Have yourself photographed in that cigar store again, go up and down in the elevator again in Hotel Paulez, all day long, as you did last time. And Her Majesty the Queen is an old woman now, like the Sultan. You certainly would have lots . . ."

"Sultan not old woman!" the little man hissed, with unexpected fury. "Sultan sodom old Queen! Sultan only likes billiards."

"Well," Brits-Jansen went on, lamely, "in that case, Holland is the place. I know of a club in Holland where there are fifty billiard tables, side by side . . ."

"Sultan not want fifty billiard tables," the little man said, deliberately. "Sultan likes only one table—this one."

Brits-Jansen sighed, shoved back his topee and scratched his head. "All right," he said, "if that's the way you want it, sire, you leave me no choice. I've come to tell you that you'll have to be out of this palace by tomorrow night."

"Why?" asked the Sultan, quietly.

"Because I'm going to blow it up," Brits-Jansen said.

"Aah . . . ?" said the Sultan, a long, melodious sound of mock wonder. "Perhaps Sappo-lidi also going to catch moon? Pick stars from river and feed them to big god-crocodile, yes?"

"No good baby-talking to me, sire," Brits-Jansen said, with a beginning of exasperation. "I hate to remind you, but I represent your government. Your government tells you with my voice that you'll have to be out of your palace by tomorrow night, or I'll have to blow it up with you inside. Is that clear?"

Then the Sultan smiled. It was a disturbing smile, for he had no teeth left and his pink tongue lived inside the leathery cave of his mouth like a shellfish. "Quite clear," he said, with a disturbing imitation of coyness. "Sappo-lidi: cuckoo!" At this, he made a weird little gesture with an old hand by the side of his temple; then he added, soothingly, as to a child, "Let's play little game. Yes?"

Brits-Jansen did some rapid thinking. The old man was too cunning by half. Of course, he couldn't blow up the palace without the Sultan's permission, and the Sultan knew it. He had never cared about the red tape the Government had tried to tie him up in for thirty years, but there were limits. If this creature should ever get back to civilization and whisper the information into the Governor's ear that his village had been ransacked and his palace blown up by Dr. Breszezinska-Jansen against his will, there would be trouble. To a colonial official's mind, it was quite acceptable that Sultan Rahula Rattan Rauwari should perish with his entire population in an outbreak of the plague; that his life could be saved by blowing up his palace was beyond their comprehension. The Netherlands authorities ruled over the Dutch East Indies as the humble servants of its people; they didn't go about blowing up palaces and burning kampongs—he had heard that tune miaowed before. What now? Somehow he would have to trick the old man into giving his permission. He needed time for thought, so he said: "Tonight, sire, I'll be delighted to give you a game; now I have other things to do. Would you allow my men to come into your palace and take out the corpses, please?"

"No," said the Sultan, "Sultan will not, Sultan wants to keep corpses and weep over old friends."

You old bastard, Brits-Jansen thought, but he smiled the beaming smile of the humble civil servant and said: "Just as you wish, sire. I only wanted to protect you against the black sickness." The smile had come the readier, because a splendid solution had struck him. With all those corpses lying about, Sultan Rahula Rattan Rauwari would probably be a corpse himself within the next ten days.

As if the old man had read his thoughts, he smiled in return. "Sultan not afraid of black sickness," he said, "Sultan immature."

"Is that so?" Brits-Jansen said, baffled for the first time. "In that case: so long, sire. See you tonight." He turned round and strode out, authoritatively, through the wrong doorway, suppressed a cry when he saw a dead child's body with a bloated belly lying on the vast Victorian bed. Then he realized that it was a lute, went back into the billiard room, said to the Sultan, who was peering once more along his cue, "The word is 'immune,'" and walked out.

The sunlight hit him like the flash of an explosion. He had to stand still for a while, slowly opening his eyes, to get accustomed to the glare. As he stood there, the smell of the corpses sickened him. He wondered how the Sultan could stand it. He considered, for a mad moment, the possibility that the old man had some anti-plague vaccine hidden away. But he dismissed the thought with a shrug; anti-plague vaccine only lasted a couple of months in this climate. As he opened the gate and stepped into the village square, he was fighting a short inward battle with his civil servant's conscience. He ought to give Sultan Rahula Rattan Rauwari an anti-plague injection. During the first ten days it gave a greater susceptibility. No civil servant on God's earth could blame him for giving Sultan Rahula Rattan Rauwari an anti-plague injection; it was the responsible thing to do. There were other possibilities, and he considered them as he walked toward the doctors' camp. He could give him an intravenous anti-plague injection, which was the surest way of killing anybody. Suddenly he was struck by the violence of the solutions he was considering. It was like killing a sparrow with a blunderbuss. Never before had he thought so long and so emotionally about the passive resistance of a native ruler. In any other circumstance, he would have simply sent in his male nurses with the order to carry the Sultan out by his arms and legs, and signed the man's certificate of insanity in the presence of two witnesses. So he came to the surprising conclusion that he must be fond of the old man; under normal circumstances it would never have occurred to him.

As he sat down to the frugal lunch his mandur had prepared, he took his three cc. of P.G. absent-mindedly. He thought about friendship and what it meant to old people; he concluded that it was a matter of time, the result of a process of elimination. The Sultan and he were the only ones still alive from those old, wild days; they had been enemies for so long that now they had become fond of one another. To old people, it was the relationship itself that mattered, not its nature. When his coffee was served, he drank it noisily, deep in nostalgic thoughts; and when he sucked the drops out of his mustache, he had found the solution to the problem of the palace. He would play billiards with Rahula Rattan Rauwari with the palace as a stake, win, clean out the plague, and take the old man home.

After he had lain down for his nap and closed his eyes, his thoughts became vague and silly. He would take the Sultan with him on his expeditions, as Poppy took her monkey shopping. They would take a small-size billiard table with them, with folding legs, like a camp table. Or an even smaller one, as big as a tray, with ping-pong balls. Then he pictured to himself the smallest billiard table in the world: as big as a matchbox, with rabbit shot for balls and toothpicks for cues. While they played, kneeling with their heads close together like two children peering at a miniature tortoise, he fell asleep.

«« »»

He arrived back at the palace that night well rested, washed from head to foot, dressed in crackling white and feeling on top of the world. That afternoon, his men had finished dividing the natives over the sectors and he had injected anti-plague into the healthy ones. Now his coolies were busy building the laboratory, a bit of nonsense really, but it was always better to have a close look at the nature of a local plague germ. That was how great discoveries were made. If Eykman hadn't sat staring at his chickens pecking at rice, for days on end, he would never have found the cure for beri-beri.

He had sent his mandur into the sector of the dying to collect some nice fat fleas and tomorrow he would start staring at them as Eykman had stared at his chickens. Two of his male nurses were Javanese medical students: it was mainly for their benefit that he had ordered the laboratory to be built. He liked Javanese students; they were calm, intelligent and discreet. He hated the pale, emotional boys sent over from Europe to pester him with lectures expanding the theories of his worst enemies, and with lengthy confessions about their sexual life. They all ended by growing out of their suits, getting transferred to hospital service in Java or Sumatra, earning money on the side by pinching the buttocks of planters' wives and prescribing hormones. The fact that he was thinking about his pet aversion, totoks, on his way to the Sultan, was a sure sign that he was in good form. He was looking forward to the game of billiards, and proud of the solution he had found.

"I see you, sire," he said jauntily as he entered the vault, where the

Sultan stood waiting behind the billiard table amidst the dried heads of former opponents and the smoking torches.

"I see you, Sappo-lidi," the Sultan said.

"Yes," said Brits-Jansen, taking off his topee and hanging it on one of the heads. "Let's face it. We see one another through and through." Then he rubbed his gloved hands; he wasn't going to take those gloves off, even if it cost him a few points. Then he put his proposition to the Sultan.

He had been prepared for a struggle, but the old man simply said, "I agree. If Sappo-lidi wins, palace: bang. Affoo." And with that word, which thirty years ago he had defined as "A vous," the game started.

After his first shot, with which he scored nothing, he realized that the gloves made delicate playing impossible. The cue squeaked between his rubber fingers and the ball behaved oddly: it darted off at an unexpected angle. While the Sultan was quietly piling up points with a series of master strokes that made him frown with wonder and whistle with polite admiration, he fought an inward battle which ended with his taking off the gloves. It was essential that he should win this game. The fate of Rauwatta depended on it.

During the first hour of the match, he still thought piously of the fate of Rauwatta. After that he forgot about Rauwatta and thought of winning only. For that little runt, that old monkey from the jungle, went quietly on performing miracles on the green baize, while he himself played like a drunken farmer in a poolroom. God knew what was the matter with those balls; they seemed to have stopped obeying the laws of physics and darted about in a crazy pattern, as if under the spell of black magic. It was infuriating, it was more than that, it was a tragedy. Never in his life had he played so badly, and never had he played against an opponent of such dazzling skill.

He called to aid all his ruses and tricks, his shrewdest stratagems. He sweated, panted, cursed in his beard, leaned backward over the table, the cue behind him, leaned over the edge with one leg stuck out, the cue perpendicular, his beard touching the baize. He lost the buttons of his coat, his rubber boots filled with perspiration. In the end, he forgot all about the fleas, ripped open his collar, growled, took aim, blinded by sweat, stabbed; the ball swirled halfway across the table, made a little jump, and missed once more. He shook his cue at the ceiling, then put it down with a crash. The old dwarf, saintly and unruffled, stood chalking his cue with a soft, squeaking sound. Only then, while glaring at his tiny opponent, did Brits-Jansen realize that this was the revenge. For thirty years Sultan Rahula Rattan Rauwari had practiced billiards every day, waiting for Sappo-lidi's return in order to get even with him: this was the return match for the slap on the buttocks, the fat boy's arrogance, the banquet.

They played on until the dawn. By then, Brits-Jansen had not a single button left on his coat, one of his boots had sagged down to his calf, his beard dripped with perspiration, his eyes were bloodshot with rage, and the words he used would have made the mouth of Captain Krasser of the *Henny* fall open in admiration. When at last the match ended, after the Sultan had won his thirty-eighth game, Sappo-lidi roared, broke his cue across his knee, and threw the two halves at the mocking heads on the wall.

"Tea?" the Sultan asked, his head on one side.

Brits-Jansen glowered at him; his huge hands opened and shut; then he said: "God knows I'm a man of my word, but today, at twelve noon sharp, I'm going to blow up this palace and this goddamn table with it."

"Why table?" the Sultan asked, politely amazed.

"Because it's full of rats!" Brits-Jansen shouted, and then he was overcome by shame. He wiped his brow with the sleeve of his coat that was already soaked and said, "All right, tea."

The Sultan clapped his hands, then started putting the cues and the balls away while he waited for the slave to appear. He put everything away neatly, but by the time he had finished no slave had come. It gave Brits-Jansen a small satisfaction. He clapped his hands himself; the claps rang out like pistol shots in the echoing vault; they would have waked up the heaviest sleeper. As still no one appeared, he said, pleased: "All right, no tea."

The Sultan said nothing.

"Well now," Brits-Jansen went on, "you have had your little moment, now let's talk like adults. If I tell you that it is necessary to set fire to the palace if we want to defeat the black sickness, do you believe me?"

"Oh yes," said the Sultan.

"All right, then. When?"

The Sultan smiled and shook his head. "Never," he said. "Black sickness been here many times. It will pass."

Brits-Jansen said: "Listen, sire. Let's get this straight. I don't care a damn whether you die of the plague, old age or murder. If you make it impossible for me to do my job properly by refusing to let me get at the heart of the black sickness underneath this very floor, I'll call it a day and go home."

"In what?" the Sultan asked, smiling.

"Well, in my bo . . ." His mouth remained open as it dawned on him, at last, why he had heard himself hum "Auld Lang Syne" as he stood looking at the funeral pyre in the village square of Rauwatta. The Javanese students, whom he had ordered to burn the boats, had burnt all of them.

Sultan Rahula Rattan Rauwari smiled, triumphantly. "Sappo-lidi no go home," he said; "Sultan lonely; Sultan play billiards with Sappo-lidi forever, all day, until last darkness."

"Like hell you will," Brits-Jansen said; but he felt suddenly tired, an old man.

«« »»

It was three o'clock in the morning, but the lamp in the doctors' tent was still burning. At his camp table, Dr. Breszezinska-Jansen, G.H.S., sat writing; an empty tin of P.G. lay on the floor. He wrote, *Recent experience has suggested to me a necessary addition to Chapter 11, paragraph 1, page 289, third line from the bottom, in Eykman's* Vade Mecum. *The paragraph in question runs: "As a first measure to localize an epidemic, all communications should be blockaded or, if possible, cut off. In the case of communication by water, all prahus and rafts should be destroyed by fire." I suggest the addition of the words: "except one."*

Then he picked up the tin of P.G. and shook it above his beaker; as nothing came out, he cursed and threw it through the opening into the night, forgetting about the mosquito curtain. The tin came back with a clatter and he kicked it underneath the bunk. Then he wrote, on a page torn out of his journal: *My dear van der Waard. Owing to an accident, I have lost my own prahu after having burnt the others to localize the outbreak which, by the way, is a fairly innocent one. As I expect to have finished with it in about two weeks' time, you would oblige me if you could send some boats to fetch me, with reasonable speed, or I'll sit here on the bank of this river twiddling my toes for months, waiting for that donkey in Batavia to wake up to the fact that I am missing. If you could send some P.G. with the convoy, this would be greatly appreciated. How are the butterflies? Yours ever, Jansen.*

He called, "Mandur!" folded the letter and wrote the address on the outside in three languages, with the addition *Urgent and Secret*. The mandur appeared and bowed, unsteady with sleep. "Pick out your best man and have him carry this through the forest to Rokul," Brits-Jansen said. "Saja tuan besar," said the mandur. Then, at last, the lamp in the doctors' tent went out.

The first thing the doctor saw the next morning was the mandur's best man: trussed like a pig, hanging from a stake, carried by two of the Sultan's warriors. So that was that.

«« »»

Later he would write to Els: . . . *and then, after twenty-three days, we arrived in Rauwatta. The river bank was black with shouting Dyaks and a white giant came to the forefront and shouted, "Shoot at them! They are mataglap!" Of course I did not land*. He would omit to add that he had not landed only because he had not known that natives, when beckoning someone, make the gesture used by the white man to chase someone away.

Hundreds of natives stood dancing up and down on the river's edge, shouting, shaking their fists, jumping with excitement. He lay, undecided, in midstream with his small fleet, surrounded by a mass of floating tree trunks.

During the twelve days that had passed since the discovery of the corpse in the rapids, he had never lost his self-confidence. He had led his expedition through the jungle with steel-jawed grimness, his gun at the ready, his topee on the back of his head. He had shouted commands, shared out rations, driven his coolies without ever wondering that Anton Zorgdrager, who had prayed for a sign with his hands folded around the cap of a beer bottle, should be doing all this without a moment of hesitation or weakness. He had not worried about the future, for the future was fixed in his mind. He had seen his arrival a hundred times in his imagination. An open space in the jungle, a river bank strewn with corpses. He would stand up in his prahu and be paddled ashore. Kampong dogs would bark; monkeys scream and whistle in the trees; but there would be no one else to welcome him. He would step ashore with his gun under his arm, his topee on the back of his head, and without so much as a glance at the corpses, he would enter the kampong, deserted like a churchyard. In front of the doctors' camp, a dead male nurse would lie, a syringe fallen from his hand. Out of a tent a white-haired, emaciated creature would stagger, tears streaming down his hollow cheeks; then he would salute, hold out his hand and ask, calmly: "Dr. Breszezinska-Jansen, I presume?"

Now the great moment had come, the reward for his superhuman performance, and not only were there no corpses on the river bank, not only was the Dr. Livingstone of his daydreams a healthy-looking fat man, angrily shouting on the shore, but, to crown it all, he made a fool of himself by giving a girlish scream as the tree trunk he pushed with his gun jumped with a splash, and snapped at him with huge jaws full of teeth. "Shoot!" the fat man shouted. "Shoot, damn you, or they'll pinch your boats!" He took hold of himself, though he was badly rattled; he aimed over the heads of the crowd, and pulled the trigger. There was only a click. He had forgotten to reload this morning, after shooting like a bored boy with a catapult at two jabbering monkeys dangling in a tree. He reloaded with trembling fingers, cursing under his breath, then he fired a shot standing up in the unstable prahu, which heeled at the kick and almost toppled him backward among the crocodiles. The crowd fled, and at last he could go ashore.

The effect of his shot on the natives gave him back some of his self-confidence. He shoved the topee onto the back of his head, waved at the fat man, a wave of equality; the prow of his boat ran aground and he stepped off it. The fat man shouted, "Careful!" but it was too late; he had already made the step and sank up to his waist in the mud.

He laughed it off, hysterical with shock, while the fat man, cursing, pulled him ashore with his gun. As he finally stood on dry land, the lower half of his body pitch black and dripping, he saluted and said, "Dr. Breszezinska-Jansen, I—I suppose?"

"Who did you expect?" the fat man asked. "The Queen of Sheba? Have you got P.G. with you?"

"Yes," said Anton. "My name is Zorgdrager and I . . ."

"Fine!" the fat man cried, and slapped him on the shoulder with a force that made him drop his gun. "Where is it?"

He picked up his gun mechanically, turned round and called: "Mandur! A tin of P.G.!"

The mandur picked up one of the precious tins for which he had risked his life at every rapids, and as the native hesitated, afraid of the mud, he called: "Throw me a rope!" wanting to pull the boat ashore. But the fat man shouted: "Throw the tin!"

The mandur threw the tin. Anton's heart missed a beat as he saw it sail, glinting, through the sunlight. The fat man caught it nimbly, broke the seal, screwed off the cap and filled it to the brim with a colorless liquid. He threw the cap back in his beard, smacked his lips, sighed, and poured out another cap. Then he noticed Anton, staring at him, and said: "Want one?"

"What—er—what kind of medicine is it?" Anton asked, casually.

The fat man frowned and answered: "Medicine? What do you mean? This is gin."

Anton repeated, mechanically: "Gin."

"P.G.!" the fat man said. "Pure gin. Here," and he held out the cap toward him.

Then it happened. The catastrophe, which he would try to live down for the rest of his life. It would come back in his memory as a sign on the wall in moments of self-assurance; it would unnerve him whenever he saw someone else making a fool of himself.

Dr. Zorgdrager, G.H.S., burst into tears.

«« »»

For one alarming second, Brits-Jansen thought that the jungle had got the better of him after all and that he was delirious. For there stood, between a kampong full of plague and a river full of crocodiles, a young man, black with mud up to his waist, the price ticket still attached to the collar of his tropical shirt, bawling his head off.

But then he realized, with a feeling of relief, that it must be a totok who had just gone through his baptism of fire, and whose knees had given way when he heard that some of his precious tins were filled with gin. He stood a moment embarrassed, scratching his head, then he patted the boy's shoulder awkwardly, ordered his mandur to unload the tins, put a guard of coolies at the prahus under the command of one of the students, and took the sniffling boy with him to his tent. There he set him on a stool, lit the Primus, put the kettle on, got out mugs and condensed milk, filled his pipe and sat down on his camp bed, to have a look at the child.

For a child it was. They seemed to get younger all the time. Of course cruel-eyed little Kramer had kicked him straight into the jungle, without any transition. It was one of his idiosyncrasies that served no purpose but to turn the doctor at the receiving end into a wet nurse. Kramer had sent him a totok before, in New Guinea. What was his name again? He couldn't remember. Fat, red hair, freckles, and the photograph of an even fatter girl in his wallet which he had shown him the very first night saying, "But for her . . ."

Yes, sure enough, this one too was wearing an engagement ring. If lost, address of owner inside. He was in for another set of evenings of interminable stories about Kitty, or Mary; snapshots of Mary on a horse, Mary on the beach, Mary cut in half in order to take in the dog, Mary as a smudge because the camera had moved. "Ah, but for her . . ." When you met them two years later, they had forgotten all about her. Damn little Kramer! Now someone would keep the lamp burning again for hours because he sat writing to "My sweet only darling," or "My baby, baby, honey lamb." Again someone would cry out in the laboratory, "God! I've thrown out the wrong urine!" because he had been humming a dance tune while working the centrifuge and that had set him dreaming of honey bleeding lamb again. And then, after a fortnight's clumsiness, snoring and body odor, the question: "Doctor, are you asleep?" He would grunt: "Yes," but the voice would continue: "May I ask you a question?" He would answer "No," but he might just as well have said: "Birmingham" or "Cuckoo," for all the difference it made. The voice would inexorably ask: "Do you think I'm suited to this work?" He always answered that question with the "No" it deserved.

The kettle started to boil and the boy, who sat staring gloomily at his feet, his head in his hands, looked up at the sound. He must have been a long way away—three guesses where. It was a mean trick on his part, but he could not resist saying: "Bet you a tin of P.G. that I know whom you are thinking of," with a honeyed voice, a fatherly smile in his beard.

"Pardon?" the boy asked.

"Show her to me," he said, and the boy's mouth fell open. He sat gaping at him for a moment, then he put a muddy hand in his hip pocket, took out a wallet, hesitated, and pulled a photograph out of it.

He took it, looked with feigned interest at the fair-haired child with the toothpaste smile, nodded, grunted his approval, and asked, "How old is she?" the standard question. After the boy had answered: "Twenty-three," he hesitated whether he would try for another tin of P.G., but decided to be sensible and not stake his prize. A few seconds later, he regretted it bitterly, for after he had mumbled: "Quite a girl," and handed the photograph back, the boy sighed and said, "Yes . . . but for her . . ."

The water boiled; Brits-Jansen muttered, "Damn," and made the tea.

CHAPTER FOUR

Aɴᴛoɴ, after his arrival, behaved with great dignity but took care not to talk to anybody unless it was unavoidable.

He put on this act mainly for the benefit of the male nurses. There were two Javanese students among them, who had made this expedition in their vacation and now were late returning to their university in Bandung. They called him respectfully "Doctor" but he was conscious of the faint amusement in their eyes. They had seen him sink in the mud, drop his gun, burst into tears and finally, at dusk, wash his trousers in the river, afraid of the crocodiles. If they were at all as he had been himself in his student days, they were now calling him by some unflattering nickname.

The Javanese students might be taken in by his stern behavior, eventually; Dr. Breszezinska-Jansen was not susceptible to it. He was not susceptible to him at all. He treated him as one would treat a neighbor's dog: kindly, but only for the neighbor's sake. The depressing thing about Dr. Breszezinska-Jansen was that one could not imagine, even in one's wildest dreams, ever becoming like him. He was not only of a different generation, he seemed to belong to a different race of men. He must be over sixty, but he had the vitality of a bull, the stamina of a camel, and a personality so grotesque, and at the same time so uncomplicated, that he would have made Freud and his pupils tear up their notes and send him to a zoo.

Dr. Breszezinska-Jansen had told him that the epidemic was over; there were a few stragglers, but the main bulk were dead, buried and done with. The drawback was, so Dr. Breszezinska-Jansen said, that the plague was sure to come back unless the rats were exterminated. Dr. Breszezinska-Jansen had waited for nearly a month now because he did not want to act hastily. After all, a jungle doctor was a bit of a missionary. But now, said Dr. Breszezinska-Jansen, he had made up his mind: the rats would have to be exterminated, which meant burning the village and blowing up the palace. All this Dr. Breszezinska-Jansen told while sipping his tea, as if he were discussing the potato crop. So far, so good. Dr. Breszezinska-Jansen's missionary considerations had seemed real and impressively human. Then they went to the palace with electric torches, clad in rubber boots, white coats and arm-long gloves against the fleas, to look for rats.

To look for rats in itself was alarming enough; to look for rats in an Eastern palace made one feel even more apprehensive; to look for rats in an Eastern palace ravaged by plague made one give oneself a secret injection, swallow precautionary pills, gargle behind the tent, drink four caps of P.G. and check up on one's rubber armor twice during the short, hot walk through the scorching sunlight to the palace gates.

Anton had a mental picture of the inside of an Oriental palace; it came from a silent German film called *The Indian Tomb* which he had seen with another called *The Chained Woman* at the Elephant Bioscope in Amsterdam when he was fifteen. He had seen it three times, each time entering the musty little cinema with his heart in his mouth because the picture was banned to those under eighteen. The accompanying music was played by a spectacled old woman at a piano and a violinist, who also struck cymbals during battles and played a harmonium when somebody died.

As they stood waiting in front of the palace gates, Anton remembered the violin's tremolo and the nervous tinkling of the piano which had expressed suspense. Then the cymbals clashed, and the gate was opened, on creaking wooden hinges. He saw a deserted courtyard, surrounded by a sagging verandah with deckchairs, the seats of most of which were torn. There was not a single statue, nor a mythical animal in sight. The gate was opened by a dirty old native who said: "I see you, Sappo-lidi." Brits-Jansen answered: "I see you, sire," and this was the only indication Anton got that the dirty old man must be the Sultan himself, unless Brits-Jansen was jocular with the servants. In any case, Brits-Jansen did not take the trouble to introduce him, nor did the dirty old native express any interest in his person. He might not have been there at all; it gave him the feeling of a child taken into a dark museum: too afraid of losing his elders to look at the pictures.

They entered a pitch-dark corridor, which smelled so strong that he was nearly sick, then they arrived in a dark room, lit by torches, the walls of which were decorated with clay heads. In the center of the room stood a billiard table. "Okay," said Brits-Jansen. "Let's get cracking," and he switched on his electric torch. Anton switched on his electric torch also. It shone on the wall and he nearly dropped it, for the head grinning at him with glass eyes was not made of clay. He was so fascinated and horrified by the head that he slowly moved the yellow circle of light on to the next one, and the next, while behind him Dr. Breszezinska-Jansen was saying: "We just want to have a look under your floors, sire. We may have to rip some of the boards up. Don't you worry, it's just a matter of . . ."

The voice suddenly stopped and, for some reason, the silence that followed was so alarming that Anton looked round. He saw Doctor Jansen standing at the billiard table, his electric torch shining down on the baize. He was inspecting the baize, rubbing it with his fingers, then he put his gloved hand inside his coat, fumbled in a pocket, took out a pair of steel-rimmed glasses, which he put on with an angry knitting gesture, and said: "You goddamned, double-crossing runt! You cheating old bastard! You—" He went on for the better part of a minute, slowly crowding in on the dirty old native, who backed around the billiard table. Then, suddenly, Anton was dragged into the bewildering scene by the doctor, who cried: "You there! Totok, come here! Tell me, what do you see here?" pointing at the billiard table with an accusing finger. Anton swallowed, and said, at a loss, "Well—er—a billiard table, sir."

Dr. Breszezinska-Jansen slapped his forehead with his gloved hand and cried: "God! The ass! Look at the baize! What do you see on the baize?" Anton stepped forward, looked, blinked because of the sweat that was running into his eyes, then he said, "Moth holes, sir."

Dr. Breszezinska-Jansen let out a huge, greedy roar. "Aha!" he roared. "Moth holes! Do you hear, sire? Moth holes!" By then, the dirty old native was flattened, his back against the billiard table, by Dr. Breszezinska-Jansen, who lifted his gloved hand to slap the old man. Anton shut his eyes; but the slap never came. He heard the doctor's voice say: "All right. This settles it. This afternoon, after my nap, I'll finish with the black sickness, sire. And if you want to do me a favor, stay here!" Then there was a silence, heavy footsteps, and the voice said: "Come on, totok." They went out again into the hot sunlight, leaving the old native standing at the billiard table rubbing his back.

From that moment onward, the missionary element in Dr. Breszezinska-Jansen's character waned. All the way back to the camp he muttered under his breath; Anton understood only an odd word here and there, but it was obvious that the doctor was not aglow with the Christian spirit. Back in the tent, while taking off their anti-flea armor, the doctor said: "Lesson Number One—never trust a native! Lesson Number Two—never trust yourself! To think—" Then he suddenly noticed Anton, and shouted: "What are you doing in here?! Go and change outside! When I get back to Batavia, I'll have a hearty word with that megalomaniac; I'm sick of him sending me pipsqueaks to clutter up the place!" The latter part of his monologue Anton heard outside, and the worst part of it was that the two Javanese students heard it too.

"May I inquire what you gentlemen are doing here?" Anton asked, his African explorer's voice trembling with suppressed rage. "If I'm not mistaken, you were supposed to classify specimens of the patients' feces in the laboratory?"

One of them answered, respectfully: "We have finished, doctor."

Anton said: "Oh," and took off his boots.

«« »»

That afternoon, after a thorough preparation, Dr. Breszezinska-Jansen burned down the village of Rauwatta. His thorough preparation was to say to his assistant, "Chase every living soul out of the village," and to go to bed.

Anton, after a moment's hesitation, decided to follow suit. He called the two Javanese students, said, "Chase every living soul out of the village," and went to bed as well.

As he lifted the flap of the tent, Dr. Breszezinska-Jansen was already lying in state on his camp bed, his huge hands folded on his stomach, his beard sticking up. Anton tiptoed to his own bed and lay down on it, producing a series of creaks. The imperial corpse on the other side of the table asked, without opening its eyes, "What are you doing here?"

Anton answered, lightly, "I'm having my siesta."

The table seemed to shake at the blast, as Dr. Breszezinska-Jansen bellowed, "You are *what*?!"

With a feeling as if he were applying the muzzle of a gun to his temple, Anton answered, calmly: "My siesta."

Now either the world would come to an end, or he would have won a battle. There was a moment of suspense, then a heavy creaking as Dr.

Brits-Jansen rose on his elbows on his bed. "Are you trying to tell me," he asked, almost sweetly, "that you are evading an order?"

Anton did not move. He looked at the ceiling of the tent and heard himself say, in a calm, clipped voice: "I decided, sir, that as I have never before emptied a village of its inhabitants, it would be wiser to leave the job to those who have that experience, instead of making a fool of myself. I have received a training as a doctor, not as an invading Hun."

He did not look aside, but he interpreted the ensuing silence as bafflement. Then he heard a deep sigh, a heavy creaking and the word "Poof." He lay waiting for more and was not disappointed.

"I suggest," said Dr. Breszezinska-Jansen, in a calmer voice than he himself could ever hope to call to his command, "that you get up now, put on your little hat, go outside and carry out my order. You may delegate it to anyone you like, as long as you realize that it is you who are responsible. I suppose I can't keep you from being lazy, but I can keep you from being lazy lying down. Will you now get up, please?"

Anton knew it was a mistake, but some force stronger than his will made him lie silent. Then the tent seemed to blow up, beds, table, clothing and all, as Dr. Brits-Jansen bellowed: "*Get out!!*"

As Anton stood in the blazing sunlight, literally with his pants down, he looked around for the Javanese students. Owing to some miracle, they were not there; the only one there was his mandur, who grinned and said, "Tuan." Anton acknowledged his greeting with a nod, buckled his belt and said, "Follow me."

As he left the doctors' camp he heard disturbing sounds coming from the village: screaming voices, dogs barking, and, somewhere, a cock madly greeting the dawn. He discovered the cock on the roof of the first hut. It was being pursued by an old woman, trying to climb after it; she must have received the order to remove her belongings and her livestock. Then he saw in the distance a crowd of people brandishing sticks, obviously involved in a scuffle; he hesitated, wanted to turn back, then remembered his prestige and said to the mandur, "Get my gun."

"Saja tuan," the mandur said, and hurried back to the camp.

Anton stood watching the distant brawl, trying to roll a cigarette, a trick Flabbinga had taught him but which only occasionally succeeded. It did not succeed this time. When the mandur came back with his gun he stuck between his lips a little paper trumpet which, as he lit it, went up in a sheet of flame. At that moment, the older one of the Javanese students ran across his field of vision. He called, "You there!"

The Javanese stopped and said, politely, "Yes, sir?"

"How far have you got with the evacuation?"

"We're just starting, sir."

"Just starting?" he asked, raising his eyebrows. "What have you been doing all this time?"

"Talking to the villagers, sir," the Javanese answered, with the ghost of a smile.

Anton said, "I see," with the sudden suspicion that, after the way his cigarette had behaved, he might not have any eyebrows left to raise. He added, lamely, "Okay, but get a move on."

The Javanese said, "Yes, sir," and hurried away.

As he penetrated deeper into the kampong, he found complete confusion. Bands of shouting, stumbling natives ran in and out of the jungle, carrying armfuls of dead branches; weeping women trooped out, driving pathetic little herds of bleating goats and squealing black pigs; children carried by their legs flapping chickens, which made the most unnerving noise of all. Inside the miserable huts, frantic people tried to stick their ground, barricading their doorways, brandishing pitchforks and sticks. Mothers tried to hide their screaming babies, fathers slapped them, and as the search party of male nurses went from hut to hut, the screams, wailings, cackles, bleatings, barks and the squeals of pigs multiplied until the whole thing became one vast madhouse.

If he had been facing this alone, Anton would not have known where to begin. But after an hour or so, he began to discover some system in the chaos. The village was slowly but surely evacuated, and around it, on the jungle's edge, a huge barricade of dead wood was being stacked by the coolies, soon joined by some male villagers. When he arrived at the palace, fighting his way with the butt of his gun through a herd of goats with long black udders, driven by a small child and a dangerous-looking dog, he saw that the barricade of dry wood went right round the palace and down to the river. He stood looking at the palace, wondering where the Sultan was, when he heard running steps behind him. It was the Javanese student, who said: "All set, doctor."

"Nobody left in the huts?" he asked.

"I don't think so."

"You don't think so? What if there is?" He tried to ask it sternly, but his voice sounded alarmed.

"I don't think we need worry about that," said the Javanese. "When they see that we are setting fire to the kampong, they'll soon move out."

Anton searched for something else to ask, then the Javanese said, "I've lined up the rat beaters, doctor."

Anton said, "Good. I'll call Dr. Jansen." He went back to the camp, through the deserted village, wondering what rat beaters were.

As he entered the tent Dr. Breszezinska-Jansen was lying exactly as before: his hands folded on his stomach, his beard stuck up, only now his face was covered with a handkerchief. Anton asked: "Sir?"

The handkerchief moved, as the sleeper let out a sigh. "What is it?" the voice asked.

"We're ready, sir."

"All right," said the voice, but the body remained motionless. "Light it."

"Pardon?"

"Set fire to the village!"

"Very good, sir. Only . . . I don't think the Sultan is out yet, sir."

There was a silence, then the voice asked: "What are you standing there for?"

"Nothing, sir," Anton said. "I—er—I just wanted to tell you that the rat beaters are standing by."

"Is that so?" the voice said. Then, after another silence, "What are rat beaters?"

In a flash, Anton saw it all. Those goddamned Javanese students had got him at last. Controlling his fury, he decided he had better own up. "Frankly, sir," he answered, "I don't know."

"All right," said the voice. "I suppose I'd better come along."

The bed creaked as the body rose. Anton, remembering the remark about pipsqueaks, went outside to wait.

Dr. Breszezinska-Jansen appeared after a lot of throat clearing, spitting, muttering, and an occasional curse when he hit something while dressing and made the tent shudder. As he ducked out of the tent, he lost his topee and Anton knew with a dawning familiarity that he would be held responsible for it. "What the hell are you loitering here for?" the doctor asked, after he had picked up his topee.

"You told me to wait, sir."

"I did nothing of the kind! I said I was coming. I'll warn you when I'm getting amnesia."

"Yes, sir."

"What d'you mean, Yessir? Run along and join the rat beaters."

Anton went back to the village, in search of the Javanese students. As he approached the barricade of dry wood, he saw a row of men lined up along it, armed with sticks. By the time he had found the Javanese students, who rose respectfully as they saw him coming, he had seen about two hundred men with sticks and he was no longer sure who had taken him for a ride: the students or the doctor. So, instead of the tirade he had been preparing, he said to them: "All right, light it."

The elder of the Javanese said: "Yes, doctor," cupped his hands round his mouth and gave a sort of hunting call. The answer was a huge wave of cheering, the coolies threw burning clumps of grass into the barricade, and a crackling of fire grew rapidly as red flames licked up the wood. Then, with a suddenness that took Anton aback, he saw the whole of the barricade burst into flames.

The roofs of the huts nearest to the barricade caught fire first; after that, the flames jumped from roof to roof with incredible speed. When the first hut collapsed in a fountain of sparks, all the roofs were burning. The sound and the heat were tremendous; the men with the sticks had to retire step by step until they were nearly hidden in the jungle. When the doors of the huts began to burn, belching smoke, the rats appeared. They ran across the open spaces, first in pairs, then in hordes, then they joined into a solid mass and made for the barricade. The men raised their sticks and shouted and began to beat the ground, an unnerving drumming, which Anton felt creep up his legs from the soles of his feet. The rats swung round and ran back into the village; a few seconds later a great shouting and drumming sounded in the distance. Anton was waiting for the rats to appear, when he heard a voice say: "Well, this ought to do it." He looked round and saw Dr. Brits-Jansen standing behind him, weirdly lit by the flames.

"Yes, sir," he said.

"Seen the Sultan anywhere?" Brits-Jansen asked, casually.

"No, sir," Anton answered.

Brits-Jansen shrugged his shoulders and wandered off, a shambling white shape in the firelight.

<<< >>>

When darkness fell, Rauwatta had turned into a black open space in the forest, in which, here and there, a dark red glow still brooded. The small fires that were left threw an eerie light, in which the stooping silhouettes of natives could be seen, rummaging among the charred remains of their huts. Where the palace had stood, a lone, fat silhouette was wandering about, poking in the ashes with a stick

Anton stood watching it for a while, with satisfaction. Then he said to the Javanese student who had come with him: "Take a look at the mandurs doling out the rations and report to the tent." The Javanese student said, "Yes, doctor."

Strolling back to camp through the smoke and the stench, Anton felt fine. Rat beaters did exist; Brits-Jansen was looking for the Sultan; all was well. Approaching the camp, he saw from afar that the lamp in the tent was lit. It stood like a luminous cube between the dark silhouettes of the hospital and the laboratory. He wondered who had lit the lamp, as everyone was busy sorting out and feeding the shelterless population.

As he entered the tent, he saw, sitting stiffly on the stool at the other side of the table, a creature so incongruous that it took him some time to believe his eyes: a very old native in top hat, old-fashioned frock coat, striped trousers and white spats over cracked patent-leather shoes. The frock coat was shiny with age and covered with medals. The apparition said, sepulchrally: "I see you, tuan totok." Only then did Anton recognize him. He cleared his throat and said: "I see you—er—sir."

He wanted to go and tell Brits-Jansen, but then he thought it would do him no harm to poke about in the ashes a little longer. "Can I make you some tea, sir?" he asked.

The Sultan said, "Yes."

Anton filled the kettle, lit the Primus, got the mugs ready and sat down, thinking of the silhouette stumbling among the charred remains of the palace, burning its feet. Then the Sultan's hand, resting on the table, caught his eye. He frowned sharply and looked up at the Sultan's eyes. They were hardly eyes, just two little slits in a head of old cracked clay. He didn't quite know what gave him the idea, but he suddenly saw, clearly in his mind's eye, the colored illustration in chapter seven of Eykman's *Vade Mecum*, the illustration of a hand. Then he shrugged his shoulders and thought: if so, Brits-Jansen of all people will have noticed it. Considering this, he gave the Sultan Brits-Jansen's mug.

After trying to start a teatime conversation several times without success, he felt that he really ought to go and tell his chief. He excused himself, got up and walked back to the village, whistling.

As he stepped over the remains of the palace walls, he felt the heat increase underneath his feet until he could hardly stand it. Brits-Jansen had certainly been punished for his sins. He stood, sweating and disheveled, in the center of the ruins with his stick and welcomed his assistant with a growl that boded ill. Before he could come out with one of his niceties, Anton said: "Sorry to trouble you, sir, but I thought I had better tell you that the Sultan is waiting."

"Waiting—where?" Brits-Jansen asked, with almost religious awe.

"In the tent, sir," Anton answered.

Brits-Jansen took it like a man. He must have swallowed several times before he said: "I see." Then he made a move as if to throw his stick away, but, glancing sideways at his assistant, obviously thought better of it. He walked slowly toward the former village square, still prodding. "How did you find him?" he asked.

"He was sitting there when I got back," Anton answered. "In top hat and frock coat, so I thought I'd better make him some tea."

Brits-Jansen stood still with his stick. Then he said, once more: "I see."

"I wouldn't have done so, of course," Anton went on, "if I had known he was a leper. I noticed only after I had given him your mug."

He waited for the squall of wrath to hit him. But Dr. Breszezinska-Jansen merely said: "I see."

Anton did not know whether he was relieved or disappointed when the squall burst after all. "*What* did you say?" Brits-Jansen bellowed.

"Your . . . your mug . . ."

"By all the bloody, burning saints!" the giant shouted. "This is the limit!" Then he threw his stick away, brought his nose very close to Anton's and said: "Look, boy, dear boy: I have let you get away with everything. I've let you jump in the mud, sob on my shoulder, drink my P.G., squander my toilet paper, pester me with honey lamb, play with my patients, burn my village—but one thing I will not let you do: diagnose leprosy! Understand? You may diagnose fallen arches, colds in the head, menopause, dandruff, schizophrenia, you may diagnose anything you like on my patients, *except leprosy*. Is that clear?"

Anton answered calmly, "Yes, sir." As Brits-Jansen waddled away across the hot ashes he stared after him, loathing his guts. So far he had been impressed by the man, and his anger at the insults he had to swallow had been softened by admiration. Now the old man had gone too far, and he would be damned if he would stand for it. He knew he was still a totok, making a fool of himself at every opportunity, but, after all, he was no longer a student.

In the knowledge that his relationship with Dr. Brits-Jansen and his jungle had entered upon a new stage, he sauntered back to the camp in silence.

«‹« »››

As Brits-Jansen made his way, spluttering, to the tent where Sultan Rahula Rattan Rauwari had sprung yet another surprise on him, he was consumed by an unholy rage. He was at war with everything, everybody—the jungle, the village, the plague, the Sultan—but most of all with the Government Health Service, that triple-damned organization of fools, bureaucrats and nincompoops, which had grown like a rash of poison ivy over the grave of the heroes who founded it. Oh, for Habermann, Gunther, Mercure and van Dam, those old pioneers of his youth! He knew they were scoundrels, but, God, what doctors they had been! All of them had had a streak of genius, much more impressive than Eykman's card-index mind. If only they had been teetotalers and vegetarians, the Eykman Institute in Batavia would now be called the Habermann Institute, or the Mercure Foundation, and there would be a Van Dam's Home for Children. Gone were those days, gone forever. He could have strangled that boy. A leper, indeed! It was not so much the clumsiness of the remark he objected to, it was the lack of the most elementary respect for achievement. He had never taken any particular pride in it, but the fact remained that he was the foremost leprosy specialist in the world. No one of his own generation would ever have dreamed of diagnosing tuberculosis in the presence of Pasteur, or syphilis under the nose of Ehrlich. But these windbags, these clumsy louts that were piped into the jungle from some monstrous pasteurization factory in the Motherland, made him feel sick at heart. He was too old now to blame God, or Life; he blamed that little pissed-up megalomaniac, now sitting in the chair where once Eykman and Van Tricht had sat: Dr. Kramer, Head of the Service. Little Piet Kramer had been his assistant fifteen years ago, so help him, and he had been one of the worst. He had had no medical intuition whatever and had sat staring at him across their camp table in the jungle listening to his priceless dissertations about leprosy with a vacant stare of complete idiocy, like a goat. And now that abomination, that puny runt ruled the empire Habermann, Mercure, Gunther, van Dam and he had founded. When he entered the camp, he had made up his mind. He would go back to Batavia and shoot him.

When he lifted the flap of the tent, he was bristling with guns like a battleship, ready to smite the Sultan with a broadside of curses that would make His Highness explode in smoke and sink. The Sultan sat waiting for him, dressed like an undertaker, and on the table were a teapot and a mug: his mug. He thought of picking up the boy's bed and flinging it out, then he decided to keep calm and dignified and have the totok told by his mandur that Dr. Breszezinska-Jansen preferred him to sleep in a hammock outside, in the trees with the monkeys, where he belonged. He sat down and said: "I see you, sire."

The Sultan showed him the miracle of deep-sea life by grinning with his mouth open. "I see you, Sappo-lidi," he said. "Nice tea."

Then, suddenly, he saw the old leathery hand lying on the table, and an awful precipice of dark emptiness seemed to open at his feet. He shook his head, like a lion stung by an assegai; then he stared, took out his spectacles, put them on his nose. The Sultan's hand, enlarged, floated between the white clouds of the teapot and the mug. He took the hand in his, and looked at the nails. Then he felt like getting up quietly, taking his gun, going outside into the darkness and shooting himself instead of Piet Kramer, for the boy had been right. The Sultan was a leper.

But all he did was to take off his spectacles, breathe on them, wipe them with his beard and put them away. The precipice slowly closed and became a morass, the morass of the future. He was an old man now, dragging a senile body toward the end of the road. He looked at his old friend across the table and said: "Well, here we are. We're old now."

"Yes," said the Sultan, gaily.

"How old are you, sire?" he asked.

The Sultan straightened, proudly, and answered: "Three hundred and sixty-five."

Brits-Jansen stared at him, feeling lonely. "Is that so?" he said. "Any tea left?"

The Sultan said: "No."

"Want some more?"

The Sultan said: "Yes."

Yet, as he put the kettle on and lit the Primus, the sun seemed to rise hesitantly once more over the morass of the future. Suddenly there seemed to be hope somewhere. In the back of his mind there had been a deep, hidden worry: what to do with the old Sultan once his village and his palace had been turned into ashes. It was the Governor's headache really, but despite all the pranks the old bastard had played on him, he still could not help thinking of Rahula Rattan Rauwari as a friend. Now, a wonderful solution presented itself: he would take him to Man-Pu-Ko-Chu, Willem's leper colony in Java. There he would get a little pavilion all to himself and be taught how to sing, to play the trombone, or to beat a kettle drum in honor of the Lord. He would be allowed to play billiards as much as he liked. He could even marry once more if he wanted to. In the evenings he would sit on the cool verandah on the ramparts and look at the sunset and play halma with the King of Rakka, who had been in there for twenty years now, or with that little half-caste countess, Madame de la Maison Rouge, who after seven years still said each evening that it was chilly tonight, as a pretext for hiding her hands under her shawl. He would be allowed to play pranks on everybody and cheat at bridge like the very devil, for everything would be forgiven during evening prayers. Lord, what a wonderful solution! And what a satisfying prospect, to be able to play a return game so soon, on a billiard table without moth holes in the baize this time, and not by torchlight in the heart of a plague epidemic.

As he poured the boiling water into the teapot, the future was bathed in sunlight. Looking at the old head with the top hat across the table, he realized that his ghost would have haunted him for the rest of his life, if this solution had not presented itself. For outside Man-Pu-Ko-Chu, that mountain of dreams, Sultan Rahula Rattan Rauwari would have become a sad monkey in an old people's zoo, a Dyak without his jungle. He woke up to the cruelty of the picture he had given the old Sultan of the future, when he had tried to swindle the permission out of him to burn his palace. He had talked about the Queen and the elevators in Hotel Paulez and revived in the old man's memory the image he had kept from his visit to Holland as a young man: a vast green nursery under sailing clouds. There he sat, grinning at him with his brilliant little rat's eyes, waiting to be taken to Rokul, Banjermasin, Batavia, and then in a big white ship across the big blue sea to that small green land, where he would sit in a merry-go-round again with the little white princess, in full court dress, and have himself photographed among the cigars, and play billiards and drink gin with the old Queen, until he would die blissfully among the waving weeds of delirium tremens.

Then he thought about the boy. The boy had seen that the Sultan had leprosy, in the way he himself had seen it twenty-six years ago on Betsy's hands. It was no mean feat of diagnosis, even granting that he himself was myopic now and had until now only seen the Sultan's hands by torchlight. The boy, who had no practical experience of leprosy, must have a damned good eye.

Yet, as he sat sipping his hot tea, staring at the lamp, he couldn't bring himself to do the decent thing. If he were a man worthy of his age, he would call the boy in now, say: "Sorry I let myself go. You were right," and hold out his hand. But he knew that he would not let go of the hand, and start kicking. Why? Why this violent reaction? The boy must be a symbol to him of his own lost youth, his lost eyesight, his once-resilient arteries, the daybreak of his genius, now fading into dusk. He knew it, but he could not help himself. He understood now why native tyrants in the hour of their death had their wives, their children and their court slaughtered and their palaces set on fire. The thought of leaving the world he had built in the hands of another was unbearable. Yet, if he was quite honest, the thought of a successor had occasionally crossed his mind. After all, however personal the spur to his work on leprosy had been, mankind had benefited. With things as they were now his discoveries and conclusions, the results of his countless experiments scattered over stacks of illegible notes, would vanish at his death without a trace. For more than twenty years he had been compiling material for a standard work: *Elephantiasis Graecorum,* but no one except he himself would ever be able to sort out that material and organize it into a book. He even doubted whether, at his age, he himself could still do it. His squirrel's hoard had become so vast by now that only a young mind could blow away the cobwebs, chase the mice, and separate the good from the bad. Each note, each case history meant, to him, a face, some mumbled words, the smell of some corner of the jungle. When, occasionally, he had tried to classify the reports of his earliest cases, he had always found himself reminiscing about old friends, old voices, as if he were sitting beside a trunk full of old snapshots. He had to face it: he needed a successor, and he hated him before even knowing his identity. Perhaps he had always secretly suspected, as each new adolescent's face bobbed toward him in the twilight of the jungle, that here came the lout who would receive the fruits of his life for nothing.

Well, maybe this was the moment at last. Maybe he had to hand over his sword now, and resign himself to the short dusk of dotage. He tried to remember the boy's name, turned round to look for it on his box. Zorgdrager.

No, he would be damned! He was not going to be sentimental over this! He would keep an eye on that boy, submit him to tests of fire and water, chase him up the trees, drag him through the mire, trample on him like an elephant, shake him like a gorilla, give him the worst life any totok ever lived in the wilderness, and only if he came out of that with all his wits about him would he slam the crown on his head and say: "Right! Now take over."

As he sat sipping his tea noisily, he forgot about the Sultan, and started to plan the Crown Prince's purgatory.

«« »»

When the expedition left Rauwatta, a problem of space arose, for, as Dr. Breszezinska-Jansen had burnt his boats, Anton's three prahus had to carry the members and the luggage of the previous expedition as well. This would have been easier if the Sultan had not insisted on a prahu to himself. For some reason obscure to his assistant, Dr. Jansen had given in to this preposterous request, and so Sultan Rahula Rattan Rauwari had a boat to himself. He sat bolt upright in it, without an awning, his top hat on his head, and he did not move a finger. The others, packed tightly together in their boats, felt as if they were taking back with them a grisly doll. The Sultan's black clothes absorbed the heat of the sun until his top hat set the air spiraling around it, like a stove; when his prahu came alongside before passing some rapids, Anton could literally feel the heat he was radiating. The Sultan was the only one who remained in his boat while it was being dragged through the rapids by the panting coolies; and by so doing he made their job ten times more difficult. The coolies, who seemed to accept his attitude as normal, began by dragging the other boats roughly across the rocks, in order to devote all their attention to the royal yacht, which they nursed across as if it were a giant egg. They slithered, lost their balance, fell in the water, grazed their shins, but scrambled back to their feet with such devotion that their indifferent laziness toward the white members of the expedition became an insult.

Yet Brits-Jansen soon joined them in their hero worship. During the first days, he claimed all the attention of his fellow travelers for himself. He bathed at least twice a day, stark naked. He threw himself in the water with a hearty splash and a double fan of spray, in which the sun made a rainbow. Then, perpendicular like a floating bottle, he swam ten strokes, trumpeting so loudly that the birds swarmed out of the trees. After that he climbed back into the prahu, a hairy toad, and those inside the boat were forced to do some nervous balancing to prevent it turning turtle. During this performance, the three prahus formed a triangle around him and those who carried guns kept them pointed at the water, watching out for crocodiles. During the siesta he snored so persistently and with such commanding resonance that his mandur hardly dared to raise his voice above it to chant the rhythm, and Anton caught himself lying motionless in the most uncomfortable position, too intimidated by the authoritative sawing to make a move.

It was Brits-Jansen himself who upset the balance of power. When, on the morning of the third day, the royal prahu got stuck halfway down some rapids because the coolies simply were not strong enough, Brits-Jansen came to their aid. Instead of forcing the Sultan to get out at last, he dragged the boat across the rocks single-handed, with such impetuosity that the Sultan's top hat and frock coat were sprinkled with diamonds of flashing drops. This did much harm to his prestige. The mandur no longer chanted in a muted voice when he lay sleeping, but began to follow the snores with his chant, to the delight of the coolies; and during the daily swimming session the natives formed the triangle of boats with obvious signs of impatience.

Anton noticed all this with interest, but the giant himself seemed to notice nothing. He was as happy as a child, bellowed old-fashioned music-hall songs, laughed uproariously at his own jokes, at which only the Javanese students smiled, and he committed the same mistake at every rapids. At the third rapids on the sixth day, when the Sultan's prahu got stuck again in a whirlpool of foaming water, Brits-Jansen again waded enthusiastically to its aid across the slippery rocks. He put the rope, at which the coolies had been tugging for over a quarter of an hour, around his left arm, shouted, *"One—two—heave!"* and fell headlong into the water, as the rope broke. He caused some dismay, for the current dragged him off at great speed; Anton kicked his coolies, who had sat gazing at the spectacle as if it were enacted for their benefit, and his prahu shot after the bobbing head. Dr. Jansen was dragged on board, and he nearly drowned them all because he insisted on grabbing his topee as it came swirling past with the speed of a train.

The only ones who remained unruffled were the Sultan and Brits-Jansen himself. The former was, after half an hour of abject self-sacrifice on the part of his coolies, dragged through the rapids without moving a finger; the latter undressed for the third time that day until he was sitting huge, naked and steaming underneath the awning, with a great display of hair and a locket at the back of his neck that had turned round while he was stripping off his wet clothes.

He wrung out his clothes with a squelching sound and hung them out to dry. Then he fished a wallet out of a breast pocket of his shirt, emptied the water out of it and spread out its contents on the floor of the prahu, between his legs: letters, a piece of comb, a nail file, a small key and a snapshot. He turned over the letters several times to dry them on both sides. When they were nearly dry, he put on his spectacles, which accentuated his nakedness, and started to read them. Then he shrugged his shoulders, tore them up and threw them overboard. He picked up the little key, looked at it with a frown, turned it over, shrugged his shoulders and threw it overboard. He was in doubt about the nail file; for a moment it seemed he was going to throw that overboard too, but he started to clean his nails with it, first those of his fingers, then those on his toes. When he had finished he washed the nail file in the river, shrugged his shoulders and threw it overboard. He put the piece of comb back in the wallet without looking at it. The only thing remaining was the snapshot.

It had been lying face downward and he turned it over, shaking his head as he looked at it with a sentimental expression. He looked at it over his spectacles, through his spectacles, then he took his spectacles off, and put the snapshot between his thighs, the right way up. Anton, who was sitting opposite him with his knees drawn up, could not help glancing at the snapshot despite its embarrassing position. He saw the much-thumbed picture of a girl with two braids of hair, a high forehead and serious eyes. It instantly struck him as familiar, yet it took some time before he replaced the braids with a mannish haircut and cried: "That's Bert!" and stretched out his hand toward it, but Brits-Jansen snatched it away. When he looked up, he was startled by the expression on the man's face. It was as though he had caught him in a shameful act.

Minutes later, to break the embarrassing silence, Brits-Jansen asked, in

an artificial voice: "Remind you of someone?" and Anton answered, with
equal casualness: "Yes, a girl friend of mine."

"Girl friend?" Brits-Jansen exclaimed, indignantly. "This child is as
pure as—as I! I mean: the driven snow."

"I'm sorry," said Anton, feeling the blood rush to his cheeks. "I meant
—a fellow student. She was my best friend, I—I never thought of her as
anything else."

"Is that so?" Brits-Jansen said. "Fancy." Then he took down his shirt
and trousers, dry by now, rolled them into a pillow and lay down. He
winced as he felt the locket, pulled it round his neck, then he folded his
hands behind his head, scratched his right shin with his left foot, stretched
his legs with a sigh and appeared to fall asleep. After a long silence, during
which his belly swayed with the rolling of the prahu, he asked, without
looking up: "What's the name of your friend?"

"Bert," answered Anton. "Bert Waterreus."

Brits-Jansen said nothing, and seemed to fall asleep again. But he did
not snore, and Anton sat listening to the chanting of the mandur, while
the small fleet drifted swiftly down the river, toward the sea.

«« »»

Now he had told that boy everything—everything; and it seemed as if
the night were hollow with loneliness, a boundless world full of hard,
cold stars, in which he had lost something very dear, forever.

Everything—even the thoughts that were so deeply hidden inside him
that he had hardly been conscious of their existence. Like a simpleton he
had lain there mumbling at the sky: Dr. Breszezinska-Jansen, the big
bad wolf of the jungle, in a singlet in his prahu, revealing the pathetic
secret of his life. It was the fault of the night and of the Sultan, who had
now made the second of his two daily movements: he had lain down.

The prahus had been dragged halfway up the shore, side by side. The
crocodile fires on the river bank made a small red twilight over the far
ends of the boats. In the prahus, like dead in their coffins, lay the Sultan,
the boy and he, covered by the shrouds of their mosquito netting.

It had started with a hollow feeling in his stomach. He could not sleep
and he knew the boy was awake too. As long as it had been daylight he
had managed to behave casually. After feigning sleep for an hour that
afternoon, he had sat up with a realistic yawn, stretched, smacked his lips,
blinked, looked over the edge of the prahu and asked: "Where are we?"

The boy had answered: "Here, sir," and shown him a map, pointing at some bend in the river with a grimy finger. Luckily he recognized the three hanging trees they had just passed, so he had been able to say, "No, sir, here! Mark it!" Then he had yawned again, hoisted himself to his feet, surveyed his fleet, a naked admiral, put on his trousers and shirt, and tied the ropes of his sandals, his foot on the edge of the prahu. It had all been natural and convincing.

But then that wallet lay there, and he had been forced to put it back in his pocket. Although he had done so unobtrusively, he had seen the boy watching him, and he had realized that he would have to talk about it, sooner or later.

He had spent the rest of the day trying to decide how he would go about it. In the end, the desire to talk became so strong that he had gone to bed early, in order to compel the boy to lie down early too. He could not wait to start talking; after lighting a cigar he lay gazing at the stars in excited anticipation. He wanted to know everything: how the boy had come to know her, how long he had known her, what she looked like now, if she was a good doctor, if she was healthy—and then, casually, toward the end: whether she had ever talked about him.

But he got off on the wrong foot. As he lay smoking in his boat it occurred to him that his going to bed so early must give the impression that he wanted to avoid conversation. The heavy, zooming silence, after the coolies had washed their rice tins in the river and squatted down by their fires to sleep, became so oppressive that he asked: "Zorgdrager, are you asleep?"

"No, sir," the voice from the other prahu answered, so patiently that he cursed under his breath. Under normal circumstances, the boy should have put that question to him, to be followed by: "May I ask you a question?" and "Do you think I'm suited to this work?"

He lay silent for a while, getting more and more unsure of himself, knowing that he would have to say something in order to justify his question. Then, suddenly, prompted by some devil, he asked: "How old is she now?"

The voice in the darkness answered, politely, "Twenty-six, sir."

It came as a blow. He had fallen into the trap he had sprung on so many totoks with such gratifying results.

It was preposterous, his lying there whispering in the darkness, with palpitations about the snapshot of a child whom he had never set eyes on in his life, but whom he had come to consider as his own. In the most stark and dangerous moments in the jungle, he had escaped from reality by daydreaming about her. How he would return to Holland after being pensioned off; how he would have gout and take the waters in some spa in Germany, with a casino and warm soda water and a string quartet; how she would push him in a bath chair underneath the linden trees, chatting about the weather and the hotel and the wicked prices. He would be wearing a straw hat and blue spectacles, she a white dress, and she would carry a book about skin diseases from which to read to him. The evening air would be full of the sweet fragrance of linden blossoms, and the tweet-tweet of late birds would be loud in the silence. On many occasions he had conjured up those daydreams; he remembered the occasions clearly. During the big cholera epidemic in Java twenty-three years ago, the child had only been three then. During an outbreak of lung plague in the Atjeh Mountains, when whole kampongs had been wiped out within a week, and two coolies had stood on the bumper of his car with pitchforks to clear the corpses from his way. Sentimental bachelor's daydreams—she would have a little basket with a thermos flask, and when it became chilly in the evening, she would pour out hot grog for him. He would say: "Come, child, put on your coat"; she would answer: "No, uncle, honestly, I'm simply boiling"; but he would insist: "Don't be stubborn. Put it on before you catch your death of cold." Then she would put her coat round her shoulders, and he would take off his blue spectacles, and she would ask: "Comfy?" and he would answer, "Lovely," and she would say, "Honestly?" with a tender smile, and tuck in his gouty foot with the rug. Then they would sit for a while watching the other guests limping underneath the trees or loitering on the benches around the bandstand, where the band of the Imperial Grenadiers would finish the evening concert with an over-ture. And then it would start to rain. As she hurriedly pushed him back to the hotel, big drops drumming on his straw hat, he would feel guilty for the way he had chained her to him, this lovely gay young creature to an old grumbling colonial. In the hotel, as she unwrapped his wet rug, he would say: "I feel guilty. I, a sick old man, you . . ." She would retort: "If you start fishing again, I'll put you to bed." But he would go on, "All these hours you're wasting on me you could have spent with a nice boy." She would exclaim: "Heavens! What would I do with a boy?" and he would answer, soothingly: "Well, play croquet."

Ass, senile idiot, dirty old dreamer, no better than a white slave trader!

He had never seen the child; she could hardly crawl, she was still toothless, standing in her play pen bawling because of a wet diaper when he had already bought her to drive him around in his old age, a virginal rickshaw coolie. He had gloated over her letters, which the two innocent parents in their leprosy hell had given him to read with pride. He had read them, lying on his bed, grinning like a cradle snatcher.

God bless Dady and Mummy love from Bertie—two lines of childish scrawl and a row of x's for kisses.

Dear Father and Mother, How are you? I am well—four lines of a rounded schoolgirl's hand and *Your loving Bertha* underlined with a ruler.

Dear Parents, Please find enclosed my report that I hope will please you; the percentage for History is not quite my fault. . . .—three pages out of an exercise book, *Bert* with a flourish, and a P.S. about pocket money.

My dear people, I have hesitated for a long time before writing this letter, but I feel that I cannot keep it to myself any longer. To take the bull by the horns . . .—five pages of blue paper, at the end of which she finally took the bull by the horns by saying that everyone was the master of his own destiny.

That was the letter he had wanted to copy, but they had not given him the chance to do so. They wanted him to advise them. He had, the monstrous hypocrite, sat thinking for a long time, scratching his beard, reading that letter again and again, while the two poor parents sat looking at him, holding their breath, waiting for his decision. For, in the course of the years, he had become a second father to that ghost child whom none of them knew. They had waited before answering her letters until he had read them and expressed his opinion. Now, at last, he held in his hands the reward for twenty years of scheming: that wonderful, revolutionary, merciless letter from a child whose mind he had poisoned, drop by drop, and who now wrote to those two innocent Christians that she did not want to join the Salvation Army; she wanted to be a doctor.

A doctor! While he had pretended to be considering earnestly what advice to give them in their predicament, he had learned the letter by heart; then he had said: "Well—I think that everyone is the master of his own destiny. It is her life, not ours." Those two noble souls had mastered their disappointment bravely. "But . . . but what are we to do about the money?" Willem had asked. "We can't possibly . . ." And then he had said: "Oh, don't worry about that. I haven't a soul in the world of my own, and I'm earning more money than I need. I'll be happy to . . ." It became the only occasion on which they had nearly quarreled. No! They would not accept that, never! He had already done too much for them! Never, never in a hundred years . . .

Toward daybreak they had written, with his assistance, the reply that was torn up five times before at last it was ready without corrections or blots: Uncle Brits, the colony's doctor, had offered to pay for her studies on one condition: that she would pay back every cent he spent on her as soon as she had a practice and an income of her own. It had been their condition. He had taken the letter with him, to post it as he went down the mountain; halfway down, he had stopped the car and scribbled on the back: *In this letter you'll read about some money that you are supposed to pay back. I don't want it back myself; if ever you should ever earn enough to repay it and you can't think of anything better to do, give it to the Salvation Army. But you will send your uncle a photograph of yourself, won't you?*

He did not receive the snapshot until six months later. It had followed him via many outposts to catch up with him at last in a lunatic asylum in the upper Digul where smallpox had broken out. He had opened the envelope at night, alone at the night nurse's table at the crossing of the corridors, and while the lunatics rattled their doors, screaming and banging, he had stared, as at a hallucination, at the face on the snapshot—the face of the woman who had changed his life more than twenty years before. Those were the eyes he had always remembered, even though now they were sightless, and there was the same, unforgettable smile, which he had believed gone from the earth forever.

During the years that followed, he had slowly weaned the unsuspecting parents from their correspondence, by dictating questions about her studies without letting them tell her who had formulated them. In her answers, she replied in such esoteric medical terms that Willem had said: "I think you had better read this to Betsy, brother. I can't pronounce it." He wanted to make good and inspired her father to put some questions on social and religious matters. At first, she had replied curtly and shyly, but gradually more frankly, until in the end the parents had wept with happiness because, although she never mentioned God, it was quite clear that she adhered to all the principles of the Salvation Army. She wrote about clinics and communal schools, about equality for all and the distribution of wealth. Those letters had given him the satisfaction of a man who had sacrificed himself for his neighbor, and so he could dictate with a clean conscience in the next letter, *And then, dear child, we would be so happy if you could tell us your opinion of Lecoeur's inaugural oration on female frigidity,* after which the father wrote, without so much as a comma between the two phrases, *your mother and I are so grateful for everything God lets us hear from you in His Mercy.*

For years he had talked to that daughter, whispered with her, argued with her, laughed with her; she had become as familiar to him as the wart on his hand—but never, in all those years, had he mentioned her to anyone else. Nobody had known of his dreams about the bath chair, the string quartet that played "Last Rose of Summer," the little terrace underneath the blossoming linden trees, the iron table with the thermos flask, the spectacle case, the evening paper and Eykman's *Vade Mecum,* like a still life of happiness; her hand resting lightly on his, her knitting like a kitten on her lap. Without that dream he would never have survived the loneliness, the pointlessness, the doubt.

And now, in one silly monologue underneath the stars, he had given away his secret; she would never be entirely his own again. Afterward, he could not quite remember what exactly he had told the boy. He had wanted to stop, dismayed, but then a cautious question would come at him from out of the starry night, and like a patient on a psychoanalyst's couch he chattered, miserable, delighted, about that clever, sweet, tender, wonderful angel—Bertha.

«« »»

The blue mist was turning pink and the birds began to rummage in the trees when Anton heard the voice ask: "And—er—did she ever talk about me?"

He knew then that the climax had come of this strange night, during which he had heard a childlike poet dream aloud about a girl who had absolutely nothing in common with the hard, unsentimental Bert he knew as his own sister.

When this odd conversation started, he had tried to stop Brits-Jansen talking, for it had been horribly embarrassing. Then the gruff voice had started to conjure up a creature that became more and more fantastic, and he had become interested as a doctor. This was very strange indeed; how on earth was it possible that a man of sixty, whom he had come to know as a tyrant on the one hand and a brilliant physician on the other, could harbor such puerile fantasies? Then it had slowly dawned on him that he was listening to the daydream of a gigantic adolescent, a boy whose soul had remained untouched and undeveloped since the moment the wilderness had closed over him.

The night was hot and oppressive. The noises from the jungle and the river sounded romantic now they had lost the terror with which they had inspired him when making this voyage alone. Like the prince in a fairy tale, he had discovered a sleeping giant in the magic forest, touched him, and caused him to wake up in a world that was thirty years older than when he had fallen asleep.

But gradually his amazement and fascination changed into uneasiness. What was he to do? Any moment the voice might ask him: "Now tell me: What's she like? What does she do? and then he would have to choose. Must he leave this big child his illusion, or open his eyes to the truth?

Now Brits-Jansen asked whether she had ever talked about him. No, never. "An uncle in the Far East sent me money to pay for my studies." It had sounded as if she had shrugged her shoulders while saying it, but he had not been sure in the darkness of the tropical hothouse. The image of her silhouette came back to him with vividness, and he suddenly realized how similar the circumstances of the two conversations were. The moist heat, the darkness, the smell of hot earth, and that sudden, uncomfortable intimacy which prompted the thought: tomorrow we'll be sorry, tomorrow we'll hate one another for this.

It was this memory that made him decide, and answer: "Oh yes. She talked about you quite often."

"Is that so?" the voice in the darkness said. "Well, I'm—I'm not surprised."

<<< >>>

He hardly dared to go on yet he asked, his heart audible in his breath: "And—er—what does she call me?"

"Uncle," the boy's voice in the darkness answered, after a silence.

"Is that so? . . . Uncle who?"

There was another silence, in which he held his breath; then the voice said: "Uncle Leprosy."

The stars, at which he had been gazing fixedly all this time, started to flash with tears. He had imagined many names by which she would call him, in that dream of the bath chair and the string quartet, but never one so moving, fitting in so well with his picture of them underneath the linden trees in that happy land of dreams.

<<< >>>

Rokul, October 3

Dear Bert, I've only got a few minutes to write you this letter because he is drinking with the Captain and he may be back any minute. We have just come out of the jungle, your uncle and I, after dealing with a plague outbreak three weeks up the river. A lot of things have happened since my last postcard from Aden; I'll write you at length later. Just now I have an urgent request: owing to circumstances beyond my control, I have been forced to think of a name by which you are supposed to have referred to Dr. Breszezinska-Jansen, who happens to be my chief. I had to think fast; I remembered you talking about an uncle, and on the spur of the moment I couldn't think of anything better than "Uncle Leprosy." You'll probably be sick at this, but, believe me, it was not my fault and the name seems to satisfy the person in question. So, for heaven's sake, if you should ever write to him or he should write to you, don't let me down. I'll have to explain all this, I know, but we have known one another long enough for you to trust me, I hope. As it happens, he is the foremost authority on leprosy in the world. That was what gave me the idea.

Love, in haste,
Anton

<<< >>>

Banjermasin, October 9

My dear Bertha, You may be surprised at getting this postcard from me. It shows a kraton much like the one I burnt down with your friend Zorgdrager. We had a very pleasant time meeting and doing so. He is an intelligent young man who will go far, and now I know that he is your friend I will keep a special eye on him. He has told me lots about you and I was very pleased to hear you are growing up to be such a nice person. Your parents will be pleased at this too. I am taking him along with me to see them because we have to deliver a Sultan. The only thing that worries me is your health. Do not work too hard and do not go out too late with too few clothes on. Youth is apt to forget the climate in its enthusiasm for balls, parties, etc. I could go on like this and will soon but must stop now because of space. Yours, Uncle Leprosy.

CHAPTER FIVE

THEY came out of the jungle in the afternoon of the sixteenth day after their departure from Rauwatta; as the small fleet sailed triumphantly into the open, even the coolies cheered as they saw the vast glinting expanse of ocean; every man felt that he was lucky to come back alive. Every man except the Sultan, that is, who remained motionless and indifferent until the moment he had to get up in order to climb the rope ladder onto the deck of the *Henny*.

The *Henny* was lying at anchor in the muddy delta of the Kali-Woga and, seeing the rusty ship with its angry mare's ears, Brits-Jansen jumped up. Good old Krasser! That was a stroke of luck! They had been prepared to wait for days, perhaps weeks, in the mud and fish stench of Rokul. Now, they could go straight home. Brits-Jansen stood upright, waving his topee, the back of his shirt and the seat of his trousers jellying in the wind. As they approached, he yodeled: "*Henny,* ahoy! Come on out, you old pirate!" A voice through a megaphone answered, "I see you, Fatso! Why didn't you get the plague?" As they came alongside and Brits-Jansen clawed his way up the rope ladder, the voice through the megaphone called down, alarmingly close: "Hullo, wet pants!"

It took Anton a moment before he realized that he was being addressed. Offended, he returned the greeting, mumbling: "'Bonjour, Captain." Only half an hour later, after the luggage had been stowed on deck and his box taken to the couch in the Captain's cabin, the real portent of that greeting penetrated to him. He had stamped out an epidemic that was menacing the whole island; even Captain Krasser himself might have died, choking, his body covered with black sores, but for him, and the word with which he was rewarded was "wet pants."

Vanity, vanity, all is vanity. What the hell was he doing here? He knew he was being childish, that it was part of his reaction to the excessive strain to which he had been submitted, yet he was unable to forget the name

106

Captain Krasser had given him. From that moment he regarded the world with suspicion, and this suspicion was more than justified. Not a shimmer was to be left of the halo with which he had adorned himself. Everything that happened after his arrival on board the *Henny* seemed to be aimed at waking him up from a romantic dream. Everything that had seemed impressive, frightening or mysterious during the past weeks had been so only in his own imagination.

To start with: Captain Krasser. In his memory a black pirate, a grandiose agnostic. In Brits-Jansen's shadow, a pathetic half-wit haunted by the notion that he had once committed a mortal sin and consequently would go to hell at his death, unless he could prove that God did not exist and that hell was an invention of the priests. Brits-Jansen told Anton that he had known Captain Krasser for years and tried, once, to give him an unshakable proof that God did not exist. He had made the trip to Tarakan in the company of a choleric planter with high blood pressure. They had talked about God at table, and Brits-Jansen had said: "This is easy." He had asked the planter to take out his watch and to repeat after him: "God, if Thou exist, strike me dead within a minute." Captain Krasser had sat waiting with pounding heart, his mouth open, and so, Brits-Jansen realized too late, had the planter, who after a minute had a stroke. Pity, Brits-Jansen said, for now Captain Krasser was one of the most religious men in the Far East.

Then: Professor van der Waard, the district's doctor in Banjermasin. In Anton's memory, a sinister scarecrow who had not dared talk to him because he had known the trip to Rauwatta was a death patrol. With van der Waard had started the anxiety neurosis that had nearly cost him his life, until, in the nick of time, he had come across the first plague victim at the rapids. When Brits-Jansen suggested they have a drink with good old van der Waard, he refused, and when Brits-Jansen asked, amazed, "Why?" he told him what had happened. Brits-Jansen laughed until the tears ran into his beard; that Sardjono! Then he told a story about the fifth of December, some years ago, when old van der Waard was in Batavia to address the doctors of the Service at their annual meeting, in a long rambling speech trying to prove that dysentery was carried by butterflies. As it was Santa Claus Eve, the night on which the Dutch send one another presents and play practical jokes, Sardjono had suggested they play a prank on the head of the Service. The Javanese persuaded old van der Waard to let himself be shut in a trunk filled with feathers and confetti, with a hook on the inside so that he could open it. The others were to carry it into the dining room in Dr. Piet Kramer's residence. Van der Waard would wait until the dinner was under way, then jump out of the trunk crying: "Santa Claus!" snowing the room under with feathers and confetti. They closed the trunk, but secretly carried it instead into the Governor General's palace, where they put it down in the dining room as a gift from the Government Health Service, and hastily made their escape. That night the Governor was to give an official dinner to the Ambassador of Annam. They never heard the end of the story; only one thing was certain: van der Waard, who was the gentlest soul alive, said he would murder Sardjono with his bare hands the next time he set eyes on him.

Anton went to have a drink with van der Waard after all, and found him to be a shy, absent-minded old scientist who played ping-pong with the wall for a partner and who had a bookcase which held such books as: *Gone with the Wind, One Thousand Tips for the Home Handyman* and *No One Is Lonely*. The remainder comprised a bound collection of *The Lancet* and the French *Illustration*. If only he had seen this bookcase before sailing up the river, Anton reflected, what a difference it would have made.

The last illusion left to him concerned his return to Batavia. Surely he would be invited to dine with the Head of the Service, and even if that were expecting too much, at least receive some admiring words of praise. But when they stood at last in front of the desk covered with telephones in the room with the map on the wall and the fan on the ceiling, the man in shirt sleeves said: "Oh, there you are. Splendid. I didn't think you'd make that coaster, but now you're here, that's fine. Your boat leaves in three days' time."

"Is that so?" Brits-Jansen said. "What is it this time?"

"Cholera in Celebes," said the man in shirt sleeves. "Martens has all the details. Have a good trip." To Anton he said: "You'll report tomorrow morning at nine sharp at the Central Hospital, to start your training."

Brits-Jansen, already at the door and with his hand on the knob, turned round and said: "He'll do nothing of the kind. I'm taking him with me, and I'll make you pay me for training him."

"I'm afraid there is no question of that," the man in shirt sleeves said calmly. "He has to go through his hospital training in Java first. Those are the regulations."

"Is that so?" Brits-Jansen answered. "Allow me to remind you, Piet Kramer, that *I* was the one who built your hospitals and that it was my

friend *van Dam,* old enough to be your father, who wrote those regulations before he died of delirium tremens. This boy is coming with me
because I'm not going to Celebes without an assistant, I don't want any
other assistant but him, and if you carry on in that tone, I'm afraid I'll have
to speak my mind to you."

"Before we start losing our tempers," the man in shirt sleeves said
patiently, "I'd like to have a word with you in private."

"If you want privacy," Brits-Jansen said, "take me into the Gobi Desert.
I'll be damned if I'll lower my voice to please an upstart who climbed into
his seat by stepping on my toes, whom I suckled as he lay writhing with
fever in the jungle. . . ."

"Succored" the other corrected him, unruffled, and to Anton he said,
"Would you mind?"

"Succored?" Brits-Jansen said. "You pompous megalomaniac! If ever
there was a sucker, it is me! I . . ."

Anton went out and slammed the door. In the cool corridor he shut
his eyes and thought, "Vanity of vanities, all is vanity," while behind
the closed door Dr. Breszezinska-Jansen was bellowing his mind. He
thought of walking calmly out of the building to the nearest travel agency,
and calmly ordering a passage to Amsterdam, single, third class. They
would declare him bankrupt, try him for breach of contract and put him
in prison, but he didn't care. It was a matter of saving his soul. Who the
hell did they think they were, haggling about him as if he were up for sale
in a slave market? Oh, for an evening with Bert, sitting on the floor and
smoking endless cigarettes. Oh, for the smell of the oil stove and the
beastly tea she made. Only Bert could help him to sort out the tangle of
his thoughts, his wishes. Something was wrong, terribly wrong, but he was
too emotionally affected, too disillusioned and upset to work it out himself.
Behind the door a furious row was raging that seemed to be working its
way up to physical violence. Then, suddenly, the door opened and Brits-
Jansen came out, beaming, a big cigar in his mouth. "Okay," he said.
"You're coming with me. Now we're going to have curried chicken in
the Hotel des Indes."

"No, we're not," said Anton.

"Huh? Why not?"

"I don't care for curried chicken, I don't care for the Government Health
Service either, and I'm not sure that I care to come to Celebes with you."

Brits-Jansen raised a huge forefinger to his lips, said: "Ssh!" and thumbed at the door. Then he whispered, audibly enough to be heard in the office: "If he hears that, I'll have to start all over again. Come on! Come on!" He grabbed Anton by a sleeve, and pulled him out of the building.

Outside Anton angrily jerked himself free and said, "I'm afraid I must have given you the wrong impression, Dr. Jansen. I prefer to do my hospital service first. As a matter of fact, after the way you treated me in the jungle, I—I have no respect for you." It was out before he could stop it; such a childish thing to say that he felt like running away like a schoolboy who has thrown a stone at a window. But Brits-Jansen said, quietly, "Of course you haven't," and then, with his big nose and his beery breath nauseatingly near once more, he added, "That, sir, was my intention."

Anton turned round and walked away. He walked into the town, calm and composed, impressed by his own composure. As he sauntered in the hot shadows of the royal palms that lined the central square, he repeated: "Vanity, vanity, all is vanity." Everything: his job, his ambitions, his philosophy, his life. The whole Anton Zorgdrager was vanity—not a talented, sensitive boy, who could be courageous when his fear left him no other way out. Oh, no. A living instrument that the state had bought on a hire-purchase scheme. Take Brinkman. "Broken? Pity, get another one." And the other one had been delivered promptly: Zorgdrager, A., untested. Now he had been tested. All in one piece? Fine: Celebes, cholera. Have a good trip! What was the point of ideals, illusions, dreams of the future? All it led up to was *One Thousand Tips for the Home Handyman* or a molehill underneath a coconut tree with a wooden cross on it, or—a dazzling exception that happened once in fifty years—a bloated belly and a beard and daydreams about a nauseating marshmallow sweetheart, but then everybody raved about your genius. What a character was Brits-Jansen! Foremost leprosy specialist in the world! And there he went, with his sagging trousers and his locket, on his way to curried chicken in the Hotel des Indes like a child on its way to an ice cream, clutching a penny. And that after stamping out a plague outbreak that would have filled the newspapers in Europe for weeks.

Was that a life worth living? Was that a goal to strive for? Nice legs, that girl on the bicycle. Girl! That was his only difference with an instrument: instruments didn't make love. Why shouldn't he prove to himself that he wasn't an instrument? Els. Yes, damnit: Els. Beautiful letters he would write to her. How many times had he thought during the trip: I must remember this for my next letter to Els?

Letters . . . He suddenly remembered that, when he had entered the Head Office, the old hall porter had handed him some letters which he had forgotten in the excitement. He took them out of his breast pocket. *Dr. A. Zorgdrager, % Head Office, Government Health Service, Batavia, Netherlands East Indies.* Nice, rounded handwriting. Her father had paid a lot of money for it, and for English, French, German, Greek, Latin, Mathematics, Physics, Physical Training, Ballet, Elocution. Fat lot of good these would do her, once she was caged up in Banjermasin. *No One Is Lonely.* Or would you rather play a game of ping-pong? No thank you, I think I'll read the *Illustration. My darling Anton, my dearest dearest sweetheart, I have just received your letter from Sabang. Wonderful! I couldn't help reading passages from it to Professor van Goor, who happened to be here having tea with Daddy. When I read him your description of the examination you gave that poor Chinese lady, he said "Clever boy. You are a very lucky young lady!" Then Daddy and he had a long argument about your telling her the truth when she asked you how long she still had to live; Daddy said he would much rather know, but Professor van Goor looked grave and said he would write to you about it. Professor van Goor . . .*

The hell! The hell with van Goor, Daddy and your silly letters; I want to go to bed with you and if you don't hurry up, I'll find someone else. He ought to be ashamed of himself. . . . "Take a Japanese housekeeper," the man with the trombone had said. "You can send her home when the little bride turns up."

The man with the trombone . . . "In the jungle you hear Him humming." The jungle. Back to the jungle! Back to the tea kettle, the stench of Lysol, the helpless patients. Perhaps it was not such a bad idea after all to stay with Brits-Jansen for a while. He was sure that, back in the jungle, everything would make sense again. As far into the jungle as possible, away from the world, reality, and Els's letters—alone with her photograph, his daydreams, the Els he would conjure up in his imagination, unhampered by her handwriting, her innocence, her girlish vivacity, her prejudices. . . . There went that girl with the short skirt on the bicycle again. If she came past a third time he would grab her and tear her off. After all, he was Dr. Zorgdrager, home from the plague, on his way to the cholera. Tomorrow might be too late.

The memory of the motto in the hostel brought home to him more clearly what was wrong. A lifetime separated him from the boy who had fallen asleep that first night in Batavia, full of apprehension. Now he was no longer apprehensive; nothing could be worse than Rauwatta. He felt a sudden nostalgia for Rauwatta, and he realized how much he had missed by thinking all the time on that river: "Next week, day after tomorrow, we'll be in Rokul, then Banjermasin, Batavia . . ." Well, here was Batavia, and what a triumph! Praise? The only thing lacking was that the bureaucrat behind the desk should have forgotten his name.

He sat down on a bench beside an elderly gentleman with a straw hat, who was doodling in the sand between his feet with a parasol. While the old gentleman hummed an old man's tune, he read Els's letters, all five of them. When finally he leaned back and stuffed them into his breast pocket, he felt afraid. Those letters had been written to a fiancé who had died on the River Kali-Woga, six days west of Rokul. He had read them with an increasing feeling of discomfort, almost pity, as if they were letters addressed to a colleague who had been killed in action, and he were detailed to tell the wife that her husband had died a hero's death. On the other side of the square fluttered the skirt of the girl on the bicycle. He hesitated for a moment whether to wait until she came round once more, or to go away. He went away.

As he wandered through the avenues, he felt lonelier and lonelier. In the end, he felt so lonely that he asked the way to the Hotel des Indes. He found Brits-Jansen, alone at a little marble table with a glass of beer on it, reading a newspaper through his steel-rimmed spectacles, looking like a tramp among the smart colonial crowd. "Ha!" Brits-Jansen said, looking up. "There you are! I've ordered for you. Did you read about that train accident in Holland? Terrible business. Two dead. Waiter!"

The headwaiter approached with an air of condescension. "You wish to begin now, sir? Or are you waiting for the other gentlemen?"

Anton's illusion flickered for the last time. The Head of the Service was joining them! . . .

"No, that's all right," Brits-Jansen said. "One portion is for this gentleman; I'm the other three."

≪≪ ≫≫

Vanity of vanities . . . He let himself sink deeper and deeper into that paralyzing realization of relativity and pointlessness, with a luxurious feeling of doom.

It was not difficult to remain somber and aloof. After their meal, they met a couple of colleagues in the lobby. They were sitting at an Arabian card table, scratching their heads and gazing at the chandelier, trying to think of a word to rhyme with "us" because they were composing a poem. It was to accompany a bouquet they were sending to old Rekers, who was at last marrying his Indo mistress. The only word they could think of was "pus," which was unsuitable. Brits-Jansen, after introducing Anton in a perfunctory way, suggested "walrus," which meant that the next line had to begin with "said." There followed a long drunken discussion as to whether one could break lines and still call it poetry. Meanwhile Anton looked at his two fellow tramps with philosophical melancholy. One of them, he gathered, was the resident physician in the Detention Camp of Lampong, where his main function seemed to be to count the strokes of the birch and call a halt when blood was drawn. The other, a kind of Cro-Magnon man, whose body hair came up round his neck to his ears like a sweater, was called Bevers; he was inspection doctor on Route No. 9, which was along the north coast of New Guinea. They were gay, boyish and very drunk, and with Brits-Jansen's assistance the poem was quickly reduced to its essence of four-letter words. Well, there was his future. There, but for the grace of God, sat Anton Zorgdrager; and God's grace lay solely in the fact that he was still young. Ten years from now he would be sitting there, stringing obscenities under the baffled eyes of some other totok, now playing hockey on some soggy field in Holland and dreaming in his bed about his future as a doctor. Doctor? . . .

Vanity of vanities . . . On the night table in his hotel room he found a Bible, put there by the courtesy of the Dutch Reformed Mission, who had pasted on the fly leaf the motto: *You are wrong, Friend! Jesus IS attractive.* He re-read the somber, impressive opening of Ecclesiastes and reveled in it. Here was the truth, the truth on mankind; whether Jesus were attractive or not, He had arrived three thousand years too late. The Ecclesiastes had already said the last word that was to be said about human life on this planet: "I said of laughter, It is mad: and of mirth, What doeth it?" There was the truth about the three doctors, composing their valentine.

The next morning they got the Sultan out of hospital. He was accompanied by a bevy of native male nurses in white gowns and looked like a Negro Baptist taking his flock to the river. Brits-Jansen had wangled an ambulance out of Martens to take the royal patient to the leper colony.

The Sultan took off his top hat and his spats; he put the spats inside the top hat, handed it to an abjectly submissive mandur and lay down on the bed. The mandur put the top hat underneath the bed and retired, bowing. He went on bowing until he had shut the doors, then he straightened up and said irreverently to Brits-Jansen: "Okay, tuan. Peep-peep!" Brits-Jansen asked: "What the hell d'you mean?" The mandur grinned and said: "Train. Guard whistle: Peep-peep. Train leave." Brits-Jansen snorted and said, "All right, totok, let's go. We'll have to pass by the stores first."

At the stores, they were given two crates of medicine and bandages for the colony, and one crate of beer for the trip. The crates were shoved in alongside the Sultan's bed, this time by European nurses. One of them asked: "Who's the corpse, doc?" Brits-Jansen said: "None of your business. Where's my beer?" The nurse brought the beer, handed him a bottle opener, cast a last look at the Sultan, said: "If he isn't, he certainly smells like one. Enjoy your trip, doc, and don't forget to hold those bottles away from your face when you open them, what with the heat and the shaking." Brits-Jansen, with an ominous display of patience, said: "Look, dear boy: I've drunk beer in the tropics before. Why don't you go home and be a comedian?" The nurse slammed the door and said: "Okay, doc, take it away." For the first half hour of the trip, Brits-Jansen talked about male nurses.

After they had passed the outskirts and set out on the straight shadow-checkered road, Anton mused about Ecclesiastes again as he looked at the countryside. This had been a jungle once; now it had all the outward signs of a rich, civilized country. "I made me great works; I builded me houses; I planted me vineyards: I made me gardens and orchards . . . all was vanity." Then Brits-Jansen started to tell him about Man-Pu-Ko-Chu, the leper colony which they would reach by nightfall.

It had been a fortress in the time of the East Indian Company, then a prison, then an army hospital and now it belonged to the Salvation Army. He told gruesome stories of sieges, during which the early settlers of the East Indian Company, who were all convicts, had eaten one another and gone mad with religious mania. The time it had been a prison had been a time of even worse horrors: gruesome stories about epidemics, torture, madness, mutiny—the roofs aflame, screams and moans in the night, bodies falling off the walls, a hundred strokes of the birch as the lightest form of punishment. It had become a haunted ruin by the time it was turned into a hospital: blood-curdling screams rang out in empty wards, doors were slammed, invisible hands snatched crockery from the trays and smashed it against the wall; in the end nurses and patients had fled, back into the valley. After that it had been empty for years, forgotten, to be recalled some years later when a murder was committed by a mad planter, who assaulted two native women working in their paddy fields, chased them across the drawbridge, through the hollow, echoing corridors and the dark vaults of the empty rooms, drove them into a corner of the courtyard where he had butchered them in a fashion that was described in detail by the papers and discussed anatomically in the clubs. In the end, the C.O. Java had made a gift of it to the Salvation Army as a leper colony. He had intended it as a crude joke, but the Christians had entered singing, with their lepers. They had hoisted the flag of the Cross on the tower and the Dutch flag in the courtyard, and now the building sat on the bare mountain with its plump body and the red comb of its roof like a hen among a cluster of small yellow pavilions where the lepers lived. "Yes," Brits-Jansen said, "it's a nice sight to see that little flag from afar against the blue sky. It does something to you. It's beautiful, I suppose, in a moral way. In Holland you've come across the Salvation Army, I suppose?"

Anton said he had, remembering fat old women with hats like upturned baskets on their heads, trying to sell him *The War Cry*, and the Salvation Army band that had played in the park on Sundays, background music to the kisses and fumblings of the couples among the rhododendrons.

"What did you think of them?" Brits-Jansen asked.

It took an effort not to answer: vanity of vanities. He said: "Splendid people, I suppose."

"You wait," said Brits-Jansen. "Here you'll see them at the front, and let me tell you: they're fighting."

When they arrived at the foot of the mountain, it was nearly dark; the castle high up against the pale-blue sky seemed part of the mountain's ridge. The drive up the hairpin road took an hour; when they reached the drawbridge, it was pitch dark. Anton followed Brits-Jansen across the empty, echoing moat, then a door knocker hammered on a studded gate. A ghost in white let them in, through a small door that opened unexpectedly at the side. A swinging lantern beside two white legs guided them through a porchway to a door covered with a mosquito netting. Inside, an oil lamp was burning. The voice of their invisible guide said: "Dr. Jansen, Captain," and a hand lifted the curtain. Anton followed Brits-Jansen into a small office, like a cell, with high stone walls and a white ceiling. Behind a rough wooden table a man stood up, an old man with white hair and a tired face.

"Good evening, brother," a voice said.

Anton shook the hand held out to him, and suddenly the bitterness and doubt he had defended so manfully against the temptations of the world had vanished. For the eyes of Bert's father chased the doubts of Ecclesiastes with the light of the early Christians. They made Anton suddenly feel ashamed.

«« »»

Anton knew, in a detached fashion, that leprosy was a horrible disease, but he only realized to what extent when he joined the inmates of Man-Pu-Ko-Chu for their evening meal. He saw, at a long table in candle-light, the colored illustrations of Kuenecke's *Lepra und Ihre Nebener-scheinungen* come to life. As he entered the dining room with Bert's father and Brits-Jansen, it looked like a medieval mural of human misery and suffering. The décor was romantic, with its huge archways, its old brick wall, its long refectory table on which stood a row of seven-armed candelabras, that made the shadows of the mutilated sway and switch grotesquely among the mottoes painted on the wall: *"Come Unto Me, All Ye That Are Heavy Laden," "Where Two or Three Are Gathered Together In My Name, There Am I in the Midst of Them,"* and, above an empty chair at the head of the table, *"God Is Love."*

Bert's father went to the chair and sat down in it, his two guests on either side. Then he looked down the table with a smile.

Ever since he had set eyes on him in the office, Anton had hardly been able to look away. There was not much resemblance between him and his daughter; it was not his face that fascinated him anyhow. It was his eyes. A white force seemed to radiate from them, something infinitely kind, wise and ruthless at the same time. Never before had Anton been so fascinated by human eyes. He tried, while looking at them in the candle-light, to formulate what it was that made them so extraordinary. But he could not find the words for it; he only knew that he was in the presence of someone who had attained such a degree of humanity that Brits-Jansen and certainly he himself were Stone Age men in comparison. Yet, behind the radiance of those eyes, there lurked something troubling. Anton felt, as he sat looking at the wonderful old man in the romantic light, that an image from the misty maze of the past was trying to force itself on his consciousness. Then the old man said: "Let us pray."

Anton was about to fold his hands and close his eyes when he saw, to his alarm, everybody around the long table get off their seats and kneel. Even Brits-Jansen sank below the surface until only his head was visible. The spectacle was suddenly so hilarious that Anton hastily followed suit and hid his face in his hands; the pious look on Brits-Jansen's face was too much for him. He was irritated with his own irreverence, and when the old man's voice began the Lord's Prayer, he was impressed by the solemnity and dignity of the words he had so often mumbled in his youth, while picking his nose or peering with one eye at the soup. He glanced at the old man's face and then, suddenly, the association hit him.

It was so utterly unexpected, and so ludicrous, that he took his hands from his face and stared at the old man, his eyes wide open. Suddenly, he remembered clearly and unromantically a nervous old gentleman with a goatee, standing in front of an auditorium full of students. At the little table on the platform Professor Brouwer, a neurologist, was seated, fat and sweating. It was August, the high windows were open, from outside the noise of streetcars and bicycle bells came. "This patient," Brouwer was saying, "will illustrate my thesis that treatment with hormone preparations has to be handled with great care. The patient is sixty-five years old, a bank clerk, a decent, law-abiding citizen, is happily married, has a number of children, et cetera. Inflammation of the prostate became acute five months ago. Instead of having him operated upon, his doctor decided that he should be given hormone treatment. The inflammation subsided and urinary complaints ceased, but the psychological effect of the hormone cure was disastrous. The patient changed from a normal, decent, clean-living citizen into an erotomaniac. His entire life became centered around sex. He was arrested a fortnight ago in the Central Park in this city while indulging in exhibitionist practices. I was called in as an expert at the inquiry, and I'm happy to say that I was able to convince the court that his satyriasis was uniquely caused by"—here, fat Brouwer's voice hesitated deliberately—"incompetent medical treatment." Anton remembered clearly his shocked thought: poor doctor.

And now, in the midst of a prayer that for the first time in his life seemed to mean something, the old gentleman with the goatee forced himself back on him. For the face of Bert's father, now it was no longer guarded by those impressive eyes, bore exactly the same expression of

horror and utter fatigue that he had seen in the face of the old exhibitionist. When, after the "Amen," everyone got up again and the clear strength
of the old Salvationist's eyes faced him once more, it seemed to have been a
hallucination, a reaction of his own recalcitrant youth. But the association
haunted him the rest of the meal, until he dismissed it forcibly and concentrated on the conversation between Brits-Jansen and the old man.
They were talking about patients, medicine, finances, and about the
Sultan. The Sultan would get Baronne de la Maison Rouge's pavilion.
"She isn't dead, is she?" Brits-Jansen asked, startled. "Yes," said the old
man. "She was promoted to glory the week before last." Anton concentrated intently upon his food.

He had managed to forget all about the gentleman with the goatee
and to convince himself that it was nonsense, when, after the final grace
had been spoken, there was a great rumbling of chairs and the lepers
started to file out. Over the noise, he heard Brits-Jansen ask Bert's
father: "How's the trouble?" and Bert's father answer: "Splendid. Vloemans is giving me an injection every night." Anton opened his mouth
to ask, alarmed; "What kind of injection?" when he heard Brits-Jansen
ask, more clearly this time as the noise died down: "And how is she?"
Bert's father sighed and answered: "Far away." Brits-Jansen said: "I'll
go and have a look," and his face was so grave that Anton said nothing.

As Brits-Jansen walked off, the old man put his arm around Anton's
shoulders and said: "I hear you are a friend of my daughter's. You'll
understand that I want to ask you all sorts of things about her. Do you
mind?"

"Not at all," Anton answered.

"Let me look at you first," the old man said, kindly. He took Anton by
the shoulders and turned him toward the light. Under the scrutiny of
those amazing eyes, Anton felt suddenly ashamed of his diagnosis. It
was all nonsense. This man was high above the dark, hot valley of carnal
temptations. The old man smiled, but his eyes were serious. "Very nice,"
he said. "I didn't know my daughter had such nice friends. Good." Then
he dropped his hands and said: "Let's go and see my wife. You know
about her, I suppose?"

"Yes," said Anton.

They walked beside the empty table toward the door, their steps echoing. "Don't be alarmed by what you see," the old man said, kindly. "If it

bothers you, don't look. She hears every word, only she can't speak and she can't see. But she'll be happy with anything you care to tell us."

"I'll be delighted," said Anton.

They went through the door into the hollow darkness of the porchway. It was cold. Anton felt that his shirt was drenched with perspiration. He followed the old man across the courtyard; the sky above was ablaze with stars. Never had he seen them so dazzlingly clear, and he remembered that the building was eight thousand feet up. Across the courtyard were a lighted window and a doorway. The old man lifted a mosquito curtain and said: "Go in, please," in a subdued voice.

Anton took off his topee, his damp forehead suddenly cold; then he stooped to enter. As he straightened, he saw Brits-Jansen bending over a bed, inside a mosquito tent. He was in a small white room with no decoration but a black cross on the wall. From the ceiling hung an oil lamp, turned low. There were two chairs; Bert's father touched his arm and indicated one of them. Anton sat down, his topee on his knees.

There was a long silence, in which he listened to Brits-Jansen, breathing and muttering as he moved. He looked down at his hands and began to notice something strange about this room. It gave him an extraordinary feeling of peace.

Brits-Jansen stood up and closed the mosquito netting round the bed; then he went out without looking at either of them. The old man said, his voice soft and kind: "Here is the boy who knows Bertha, Betsy." He said it to the lamp. "I brought him here to tell us about her." He turned to Anton. "You don't know what an occasion this is for us," he said, smiling. "We have never met anyone who has seen her since she went away. Tell us, is she happy?"

The peace that radiated from the bed behind the mosquito netting enabled Anton to answer without embarrassment, "Oh yes. She has a natural gaiety, and a wonderful sense of humor. She never loses her sense of proportion. That is what, to my mind, makes her so valuable a person."

"And what does she look like?" the old man asked. "Could you describe her?"

"She's rather small," Anton answered, staring at the white wall, trying to picture Bert. "As we walked together through the corridors of the hospital, I could read the numbers on the doors over her head. She has dark blond hair, cut like a boy's and she is—well—she's got a nice figure.

I like her hands best, I think—capable and competent, yet sensitive hands. The hands of a doctor. She is, by the way, a wonderful doctor—a much better one than I am, because somehow she cares more about the patients than she does about her own career, if you see what I mean."

He looked at the old man, and was startled by the tremulous sound of his voice as he answered: "Yes, we do."

"Well," he continued, trying to conjure up Bert once more on the white wall, "she's got a rather stern, but at the same time very feminine mouth. But I think that the most striking thing about her is her eyes. She has the most wonderful eyes I've ever seen."

He looked at the old man once more, surprised by his own words. He had never thought about Bert's eyes in those terms before. Then he looked hastily away, for he saw the old man was crying.

He talked to them for a long time, answering many questions, but the peace he had felt was gone. For when he saw Bert's father's eyes dimmed with tears, the memory of the old gentleman with the goatee forced itself upon him once more. He was certain now that, unwittingly, he had stumbled upon a dark tragedy.

<<< >>>

Anton was to spend the night in the room of one of the colony's doctors. Bert's father took him there.

It was on the other side of the courtyard, in one of the outbuildings. As they approached, he saw through the window a young man sitting at a table in candlelight, writing; a glass of milk was standing beside his papers.

"Would you mind waiting out here for just a second?" the old man asked him. "Dr. Vloemans has to give me an injection. It won't take a moment."

"By all means," said Anton, and he lit a cigarette, a thing he had been longing to do for the last hour. Listening to the mumble of voices behind the mosquito netting in the window, and the small tinkle of metal on glass, he thought about Bert. How much happier and more at peace with herself she would be if she were able to visit her parents and see them and their work. He decided to write her a long letter and tell her about the colony. It was very important that she should know. He turned round and glanced through the window and saw the young man

give Bert's father an intramuscular injection of about two c.c. He tried
to decipher the printing on the box of phials, open on the table, but it
was too far away. Then the old Salvationist came out again, wished
him good night and God's blessing, and vanished in the darkness.

Anton stood looking after him, listening to his receding steps, and only
when he had seen him reappear and vanish once more in the lighted
archway of the porch did he turn round and enter the hot little room
he was to share with the unknown young man.

The young man was putting away the box and the syringe in a cupboard between two iron bedsteads. He looked round, said, "Ah, welcome,
Brother—I mean—Colleague. Do sit down." Then he closed the cupboard,
turned the key and put it in a pocket of his neat white trousers; a
peaked cap with the Salvation Army ribbon hung on a hook on the
wall. It gave the room the aspect of a customs barracks in some Central
American country. He came toward Anton, held out a fleshy white hand
and said: "My name is Vloemans. I'm head of the research department, after Dr. Breszezinska-Jansen, that is. His assistant you might say.
Well, perhaps not quite his assistant, but his help."

Anton said: "Zorgdrager," deciding that the young man had a truth
complex. He was stocky, his hair was cut in orphanage style and his
blue eyes were slightly protuberant, as were his thick wet lips. "I hope
you don't mind my sleeping here?" Anton continued. "I don't think
I snore."

"Well, neither do I," said the young man gaily. "That is to say, I
don't think I do. No one ever told me."

Anton said "Quite," and felt like a drink.

There was a short silence in which the young man breathed. Then he
asked: "Are you interested in leprosy?"

"I think it's fascinating."

"Oh, it's the most wonderful disease, you know, to work upon I mean.
Very, very foxy. It's a wonderful way of feeling that there is a point
to life."

"Is that so?" Anton heard himself say, remembering Brits-Jansen too
late. "I think I'd prefer looking for the point to life without getting
leprosy."

The young man's protruding eyes grew bigger and his wet lips parted
in bafflement, then he said, "Oh, ha, ha! I didn't mean that. I meant:

it gives a wonderful point to one's life to see all these people suffering, and to work, not only for their spiritual, but also for their physical salvation."

Anton suppressed an answer and said: "Quite."

As if the young man divined his thoughts he smiled uncertainly, scratched his head and picked up a couple of X-ray films that were on the table. "These might interest you," he said.

"I saw you give Captain Waterreus an injection," Anton said, ignoring the films. "Hormone stuff?"

"Yes," the young man answered, surprised. "Has Dr. Jansen told you?"

"He hasn't, but I happened to overhear a conversation from which I gathered that the Captain was a prostate sufferer."

"He is," said the young man. "Thank Heaven we have this Exaltine, a wonderful preparation. He was pretty far gone, but the results are remarkable."

"Is that so?"

"Remarkable. The thing is entirely under control."

"No ill effects?"

"How do you mean?"

"I came across a case once in which a hormone cure had a disastrous effect. Very rare, luckily, but I just happened to think of it."

"What effect, for goodness' sake?"

"Erotomania."

The young Salvationist's face changed. The protruding eyes stared at him first in amazement, then in disgust. He proffered the X-rays once more and said in a clipped voice: "I'm sure these will interest you. The Eykman Institute . . ."

Anton refused to be put off. "Does this information give you a new factor in your diagnosis?" he asked.

"My dear colleague," the young man said, with dignity, "we do not believe in saints, but if we did Captain Waterreus would be one of them. He is the greatest Christian I know; such an effect of an injection on him is entirely and utterly out of the question."

Anton shrugged his shoulders and answered, "Just as you like. It was my duty to give you this information." After that he mumbled: "Excuse me," and went outside, where he lit another cigarette.

He leaned against the wall and looked at the dimly lit porchway in which Bert's father had disappeared. Behind the mosquito netting he heard the young man mutter "O Lord," then there was a short silence and the sound of a glass being put back on the table. A chair scraped; when Anton looked round he expected to see him sitting at his table once more. But he discovered him on his knees by the chair, praying.

There was only one thing to be done. If his diagnosis were correct, Bert's father was going through tortures which were unimaginable, and here was he, a representative of his daughter, who could put an end to that suffering with a few simple words. He inhaled deeply, then he dropped his cigarette, crushed it with his foot, and crossed the courtyard. As he entered the porchway, his steps echoed and he walked on tiptoe. He reached the office window, and saw the old man sitting at his desk, his hands folded and his head bent, praying.

He looked at him for a while, then he turned round and went back to the door of his room, across the gulf of darkness that was the courtyard.

There was no moon that night, the white buildings of Man-Pu-Ko-Chu shimmered faintly in the light of the stars.

CHAPTER SIX

AFTER he had been given his injection, Willem Waterreus went back to his office, as he had done every night for over a year now.

Man can inure himself to anything, even to torture; a year ago, he had thought he could not bear it: to spend every night awake until the dawn, then to fall asleep in his chair or on the hard bench behind the table, but only for an hour before the bell tolled for morning prayers.

In the course of that year, the terror he went through every night had gradually changed into a cold disgust. Disgust with himself, the world and in the end, at the deepest state of his damnation, disgust with God. He had prayed, sung psalms, beaten the wall with his folded hands until his knuckles bled; he had done everything a man who had been God's friend for forty years could think of; but his supplications had gone unanswered. God had cast him out forever; the man who now wandered through Man-Pu-Ko-Chu like a ghost was no longer alive, was worse than dead, was a man without God.

After he lit the lamp in the office he was overcome with dizziness, famished by his year-long sleeplessness, and the fear that he had felt when the boy talked about Bertie's eyes returned, the fear of being caught unawares by an emotion against which he knew himself defenseless. He sat down hastily, and stared at the lamp. Two moths were circling around it. As he sat staring at them, they slowly blurred to a circle, the ring around Saturn. Saturn, a red ball, glowed in a blue darkness that became black, terrifying.

He shivered; it woke him up. He rubbed his smarting eyes. The battle had started once more, the battle with the devil. So far he had managed to keep the devil at bay as long as he stayed awake; but he knew that soon he would no longer be able to, even then. That knowledge brought a despair so deep that he remained indifferent under it, numbed by an excess of pain, like the lepers in the last stage, like Betsy, who would ere long enter the glory of God's eternity, "Captain B. Wilders Waterreus promoted to Glory" *The War Cry* would read. Thirty years they had served together in God's Army; now, at the end of the road, she was to be promoted and he would be damned. He accepted it, with indifference, as he sat staring at Saturn, red and round in the darkening dusk. The ring round Saturn slowly slanted; the red ball in the darkness became a face. A boy's face in a white halo. "The most beautiful eyes I ever saw," the boy said; he woke up with a start.

The lamp smoked. He got to his feet and turned down the wick. The moths were still circling; he gazed at them, his face close to the heat, until sweat stung his eyes and woke him up once more. He went to the cupboard to look for a weapon against sleep.

He squatted in front of the open cupboard, and looked at the pile of books with dismay. He had spelled out every one of them many times, now they could no longer help him, not even *Broken Pottery*, which had been the last to fail him. The bottom book had no title on its back. He lifted the pile, and read: *Our Holiday*. It was their photograph album. He had not dared look at it since his purgatory started, for fear of being weakened by the past. Now it no longer mattered.

He took it out of the cupboard, put it down on the table and looked at the worn cover of imitation leather. *Our Holiday:* the gilt lettering was almost gone. He had bought it for Betsy in Batavia twenty years ago. She had unwrapped it on the table in the white room. "Oh, Willem, how beautiful!" The memory of her bandaged hands made him open the album. A little red louse fled off the first page and hid in the back.

The first photograph was so faded that the face of the boy was unrecognizable. He was leaning with his elbow on a little pillar in front of the painted backdrop of a forest, his feet crossed, a bowler hat set jauntily on his forehead. But even if the picture had not faded with the years, it would have been difficult to recognize him; Captain Waterreus, Commanding Officer of the leper colony Man-Pu-Ko-Chu, was very different from the twenty-three-year-old boy who had himself photographed as an act of bravado, before vanishing with the money of his employers.

Three long minutes he had to stand motionless, staring at the uplifted finger of the photographer, who held the little rubber ball of the shutter in the other hand. While his cheeks went numb with smiling, he thought: "Tomorrow I'll be in England. . . . Tomorrow I'll be in England. . . . The whole of Holland will be looking for me, my name will be in all the papers, but no one will find me, for tomorrow I'll be in England. . . ."

"Perfect!" said the photographer, and he let go of the little ball, which sucked in the air with a sound like a kiss. "A perfect photograph, sir. I wish all my clients could keep as still as you did, sir."

"Easiest thing in the world," he said, and was startled by a click in his elbow as he straightened his arm. "Question of self-control."

"How true, sir, how true!" the photographer cried. "But in these times of speed and stress, very few men . . . Excuse me, after you." He lifted the red curtain with the gilt tassels to let him pass. The shop was dark after the glare from the lamps in the studio. The glass plate on the counter glinted like the glass lid of a coffin. He started to whistle, but checked himself at once, for that was a mistake. Six more hours before the boat sailed; if he gave himself away during those six hours by nervousness or fear, he deserved no better than to be put in prison for twelve years. Twelve years was what the accountant of a sawmill in Rotterdam had got for the same thing, despite a family of four children as an extenuating circumstance.

"In a week's time, sir," the photographer said, as he tore a receipt off a pad with a flourish. "Seven days, sir, and your photograph will be ready. That will be three guilders and fifty cents."

His face stiffened. He had only two guilders in small change, and ten banknotes of a hundred, one of which he had planned to change in the station where it would pass unnoticed. "Is that necessary?" he asked, and he was alarmed to hear how unnatural his voice sounded.

"I beg your pardon?" The photographer looked up, his head on one side, like a bird.

He coughed. "I am not in the habit of paying for anything before I receive it," he answered, forgetting about his voice, for his legs had suddenly started to tremble. Whatever had given him the crazy idea of having himself photographed? He must have been mad.

"As you prefer," the photographer said peevishly. "Name and address, please?"

His alarm turned into panic. He had to call on his last remnants of common sense to keep himself from running out of the shop. If he did, the photographer would run after him, people in the street would notice, a policeman . . .

"Well?" The photographer no longer looked at him like a bird but like an old woman. If he did not answer at once . . .

"The name is Waterreus," he said, and had to cough again. "But I must say . . ."

"Initials?" the photographer asked, writing.

"W."

"Address?"

"New King's Road."

"Number?"

"Eighteen." He felt sweat prickle under his hair.

"References?" The photographer now looked at him like a policeman.

"Trippema and Company . . ." It was out before he could help it, but he was too panic-stricken by now to think clearly.

"The undertakers?"

"Yes."

"Are you in their employ?"

His panic suddenly turned into fury. "That will do!" he snarled.

"Sorry, sir," the photographer said, a bird once more. "You mentioned Trippema and Company as a reference, hence my question. Perhaps you will be good enough to—sign?" The man turned the paper round with a swift gesture that seemed intended to startle him. He felt sick when he signed his name; the photographer's hand stood at the head of the paper, its fingers spread like little white legs to steady it.

When at last he was set free, he stumbled into the street, ready to lash out with his cane at the first person to touch him. While he stood waiting for the horse tram, in the rain, he looked over his shoulder and saw the photographer stare at him over a black curtain in the shop window, like a head on a plate. He looked the other way, and saw a policeman approaching. He wiped the sweat off his face, but while doing so he realized: wrong! It was too cold to perspire, for someone with a clean conscience. He hastily put his handkerchief away, too hastily. He heard steps halt behind him, glanced over his shoulder and saw the policeman. Until the tram arrived he stood motionless, obsessed by the fear that the policeman behind him could see the trembling of his legs.

Finally the tram appeared, a swaying red box underneath the trees, and stopped at his request. He stumbled as he got on; as he sat down he saw the policeman had got on too, and was looking at him. They were the only passengers.

Never before had he known such fear. He decided to get out at the next stop, knowing it was wrong, but he dared not stay there. The tram stopped; as he got to his feet, a girl with a big hat got in, so he sat down again. He would wait one more stop, for now there was someone he could look at; so far, there had only been his reflection in the window. The girl was panting; she must have been running. She rummaged in her handbag, her face hidden by the brim of her hat. She brought out a purse, shook her umbrella, and looked up.

When he saw her eyes, his panic vanished as if by a miracle. They were large, blue, and gave him a weird feeling of security, that became joy as she turned her head away, frowning. The fact that she objected to his scrutiny made him happy, a foolish relief. He crossed his legs, put his hands on the knob of his cane and relaxed to have a good look at her. She was about twenty, and obviously wearing her Sunday best. She had a small suitcase with her so she must be going to the station too. The ostrich feather was too big for her hat, and her eyes were too big for her face. He smiled at his panic of a moment ago; the police had certainly not been called in yet, and before the photographer could do anything he would be out of town. In four hours' time he would be in Rotterdam and tomorrow in England. Why should the photographer have upset him so? That effeminate, mincing manikin. He would never see a cent for his photograph, and it served him right.

Suddenly the girl, irked by his staring, got up, gathered her umbrella, bag and suitcase together and went out to the front platform, opening the door with difficulty. Fear attacked him again with such violence that before he knew what he was doing, he got up and followed her.

As he grabbed strap after strap in the swaying tram, he realized that the policeman was watching and might well come after him, for this was importuning a woman. But he reached the front platform without a hand touching his shoulder or a voice calling after him. He shut the sliding door, leaned against it, next to the girl, and the feeling of security returned. He relaxed again, took off his hat and wiped his forehead. She turned away from him angrily, the ostrich feather fluttering in the wind.

It was bad weather to stand out on the platform. Yet apart from the driver, the girl and himself there were an old gentleman with a gray bowler hat, its front dark with rain, and a drunkard who stood smiling with his eyes closed and his cap in his hand. At the next stop, another passenger jumped on, a fair-haired boy in a blue suit, with two brass letters S on the collar of his jacket. The drunkard stared at the letters, blinked, stared again, pointed with an unsteady finger and said: "Steamship." The gentleman with the bowler hat glanced at him and instantly looked away, but in doing so, he had joined in. The drunkard nudged him, pointed, and said: "Sunstroke." The gentleman dusted his sleeve and muttered: "Stupid," but the drunkard shook his head, nudged him once more, pointed and said: "Seasick." The gentleman, angered, turned to the boy and asked: "Would you be good enough to tell this person what your letters stand for, sir?" The boy answered, "God is love."

Only the drunkard was not surprised. He nodded, sighed, started to make the sign of the Cross, saw his cap pass in front of his eyes, and wiped his forehead with it instead. The girl's face lost its primness, and even the old gentleman could not suppress a smile.

"They really mean 'Saved Sinner,'" the boy said, "or, in French, 'Soldat du Salut.' They are the letters of the Salvation Army."

"The—er—what army?" the gentleman asked, intrigued.

"The Salvation Army," the boy answered. "God's Army against sin. Yes, I am a convert, and the peace and happiness I have found are so miraculous that I want to pass them on to as many others as possible."

The boy had looked round while speaking and noticed him, leaning against the door with a white, drawn face. "And you, brother?" he asked. "Have you been converted yet?"

The question startled him. "What do you mean?" he asked, hoarsely.

"Haven't you prayed to God to protect you yet?" the boy asked, looking at him as if he saw something in his face that saddened him.

He managed to control himself sufficiently to be flippant. "No," he answered. "So far I'm not that much of a sinner." He laughed, and looked hopefully at the girl, but she had turned her head away. Her feather fluttered once more in the wind.

"One always thinks that," the boy said. "Be careful, brother. Before you know, you may be too much of one."

Suddenly he felt like striking the boy. He stared at him with hatred.

"And why," he asked, "do you pick on me for your nonsense?"

"Your face, perhaps," the boy answered frankly. "You have the eyes of a sinner."

He wanted to lash out at him, but the driver called, "Central Station! All change!"

The blue boy was the first to get off; then the old gentleman, cautiously;

then the girl. She jumped off the platform with her umbrella and her suit-case, and ran; all that was to save him from perdition fled with her, among the hansoms and the carts, toward the entrance of the station.

He leaped down and ran after her, stumbling; in the booking hall he lost sight of her; then he saw her pass through the gate toward the plat-forms, so she must already have a ticket. He followed her, though he had no ticket and would draw attention to himself in Rotterdam because he would have to pay there. But she was more important. She was more im-portant than anything else in the world; if she were gone, he would no longer be able to master his fear. He knew that to chase a totally strange woman was both foolish and dangerous, but he was helpless in the spell of the panic that dragged him mercilessly after her.

The platform, where a train was about to leave, was so crowded that he lost sight of her once more. People hung out of the windows, calling, kissing, waving; women towed whining children through the crowd; porters drove trolleys with luggage along the edge of the platform, clang-ing their bells; the station master's cap was a spot of vivid red under-neath the gray vault of the roof. He ran along the train, frantic, looking in all the compartments; then a whistle throbbed. A big sound of farewell came from the crowd; the train started to move. He stood on the edge of the platform in despair, watched windows and faces moving past him, then suddenly he saw her, behind a first-class window. She instantly looked away, but he pushed the wavers aside, and ran with the moving train. Voices called to him, a man with a peaked cap tried to bar his way, but he grabbed hold of the door handle and jumped onto the running board. He wrenched open the door, climbed inside and slumped, panting, into the seat opposite her. He was not in the least impressed by the fury in her eyes, for they were the most beautiful eyes he had ever seen.

"Shameless!" she said, trembling with rage. "Shocking! To chase a lady like a—like a . . ."

Then she jumped, with the agility of a ferret, at the communication cord. After that, everything happened so quickly that it seemed all one movement. He grabbed her, crying, "No. . . !" dragged her down from the red chain; she fought, kicked, waved her umbrella, tried to grab the chain with its crook, then the train went round a bend, they lost their balance and he fell onto the seat, on top of her. Her hat with the ostrich feather fell to the ground, the hat pins pulled her hair loose and made her seem naked. A wild excitement overcame him, and he crushed her mouth with his. She fought desperately, hammered on his back with her fists, scratched his face; he heard her moan under his kiss as if she screamed, but he smothered all sounds and all movements with a force to which, nearly suffocated, she finally surrendered. Her arm sagged sideways, her fist opened to a small limp hand; he got to his feet in the sudden fear that she had lost consciousness. She lay rumpled on the cushions, her eyes closed, her mouth half open; only her panting breath betrayed that she had not fainted. She opened her eyes and looked at him. It was a strange look, impersonal; her eyes suddenly seemed even larger, but lifeless, the eyes of a doll. She shut them, opened them again; the similarity to a doll was so strong that he stared at her in alarm. Then, slowly, she focused her eyes on him, and an expression of amazement came over her face. She licked her lips; and then she smiled.

Her smile provoked such surprise and such tenderness in him that he stammered, "Darling, angel, sweetheart, darling," stroking her hair, her face, her neck, her breasts. He felt the warmth of her body through the silk of her blouse; the desire that had overwhelmed him in their embrace swept over him again. He opened her blouse with trembling fingers, pulled it aside, down, baring her shoulder, her left breast; the desire rose inside him, seething, but at the same time a disgust, a horrified knowledge of perdition; he bent over her to kiss her breast, white and round, but as he closed his eyes for the kiss and felt the warmth of her skin approach his lips, a ring started to circle around the white roundness of her breast; it slowly turned yellow, then red; the ring became two dots, circling; he opened his eyes wider, with a burning pain, until he recognized the lamp with the two swirling moths, and returned to reality, gasping, like a diver who had reached the surface at last. But it was the numbness of his hands that really woke him up.

He had folded his hands so tightly in his sleep that all feeling had gone from his fingers. He gingerly pulled them apart; he shook his hands to restore the circulation; then he drummed clumsily on the table. Only when his fingers came alive again as he sat rubbing them did he realize what had happened, how closely the devil had approached him again during those few minutes of defenselessness. It did not dismay him, it left him indifferent. After all these nights in hell, he was used to the monotony of the torture. Every time he woke up it would be worse. It would go on until the morning mist, shrouding the pavilions and the red brick wash house in the courtyard, turned red with a new day. The red mist would billow behind the mosquito curtain like smoke, and he would finally close his eyes over that vision of hell. But until then he would only doze, waking up with a start many times, fighting an ever bitterer battle with the devil for every awakening. Whatever book he opened, whatever thought entered his mind, the devil twisted everything into sin after he closed his eyes.

This had only been a skirmish; sometimes at dead of night it seemed to take hours. He had not prayed yet, although his hands had been folded when he woke up. He had not yet sung psalms, not yet washed in the little red brick building to cleanse himself, naked and alone in the hot darkness, pouring over himself the tepid water that brought no solace to his burning body, his hammering head. It would end with a prayer in the darkness, with ghosts and apparitions whispering in his prayer, devilish monsters climbing up the rope of the bucket in the well, demons dancing in the steam of the spilt water on the hot ground, vampires winging through the empty sockets of the little windows, brushing his feverish skin. Oh, what was the use? The night was long enough without his thinking about what was going to happen before he thanked God in the morning prayer for saving his soul from evil once more.

A moth had spun its cocoon between the next two pages of the album; they came apart with a soft silky sound as he separated them. He had to hold the book at an angle to recognize the image on the next photograph; the lamplight was reflected by a little square of tin full of brown smudges that had once been a beach, a beach with three shadows: a man, a woman and a donkey. Time had darkened that clear sunny day to a dark brown twilight, and changed into desert ghosts the woman, the donkey, the man holding the reins. Forty years were stretched out to twenty centuries on the rack of life—they had been photographed as Willem Waterreus and Betsy the Doll after a week of ecstasy and sin; now he saw them again they had turned into Joseph and Mary, on their flight to Egypt.

The photographer had been a sickly little man, looking like a trunk on crutches with the thin legs of his camera stuck in the sand and his head hidden underneath a black cloth. She had been afraid that the donkey would move while the photograph was being taken, but the donkey had stood still with its head down and its eyes closed and their shoes hanging from its neck, asleep. He had to beat it to life, after the head of the photographer had appeared from underneath the black cloth, his eyes blinking in the sunlight, to say that the photo would be ready in half an hour, with a whiff of gin through the smell of the sea.

"Shall we take the donkey back, or go on?" he asked.

She laughed with a flash of white teeth from above and said: "Go on!"

"It's a bit too crowded for my liking over there . . ."

"Then let's go to the Silent Beach."

"But, darling, that's very far away. And the sun will go down in about an hour's time."

"Please, let's go!" she said, her head on one side, her small face so innocent underneath the huge feathered hat that he pulled the donkey round, laughing, and smacked its bony flank with the flat of his hand. "Giddup! Giddup, donkey!"

As the donkey began to trot through the dry sand, their shadows started to glide alongside them, sharp like silhouettes. The shadow of the donkey looked like a camel, her hat with the ostrich feather the plumed beret of a Moorish horseman, his own shadow a slave plodding through the sand. As they moved along in silence, his thoughts started wandering back among the wonders of the past days. A lifetime seemed to separate him from the morning he had stood in front of the coffin with the glass lid in the photographer's shop; the thing he remembered most clearly was the hand standing at the top of the paper as he signed, the fingers like little white legs. The image came back to him with such vividness that he was overcome by a sudden dreamer's fear: that he would wake up presently, that all the joy and ecstasy of these seven days would vanish like a bubble, that he would have to take up life again standing at the counter, signing his name. He looked up at her, and a sadness rose slowly inside him, half memory, half presentiment. He knew suddenly that their shadows had glided along with them like this before, side by side, across the sand, and that they were riding toward a dark future. But as he looked up at her and saw her against the blue of the sky, gazing ahead at the horizon, his apprehension was swept away by a wave of happiness, swelling and sinking in a sigh, a wordless prayer.

"What are you thinking?" he asked. His voice sounded far away, as if it came from the sea, beyond the hissing foam on the beach, the rumbling surf on the distant banks.

She took a long time to answer. It seemed as if she had not heard him; her eyes went on gazing at the horizon. "I wish we could ride like this forever," she said at last. It sounded earnest, the earnestness of a child that says she wants to grow up and be a saint.

"Whatever makes you say that?" he asked, alarmed, fearing that she too might have sensed the darkness of the future.

"I love you," she said.

It was the first time she had said that, after all those nights, those embraces, those kisses in the train, the sand dunes, the hotel. Kisses like floes of timelessness in the dark wintry river of fate that bore them along, kisses in dusk and sunlight, in the slatted half light of the Venetian blinds as they lay naked on the bed in the afternoon, tigered by sunlight and shadow; kisses, still as death, as they lay locked in the gaslight, stark marble statues on the tombstone of their bed. It was their first moment of tenderness, of love—it should have delighted him, he ought to have kissed her foot, dangling beside him on the dusty flank of the donkey; but he said nothing, he did nothing. They plodded on through a great, silent loneliness.

When they had gone so far that they seemed to have penetrated to the very heart of the loneliness, she said: "Let's stop here." It was at the foot of a gorse-covered dune; a narrow path led through the shrubs and the hard grass toward a tuft of gorse in the blue sky. The wreck of a boat lay half buried in the sand, its ribs bleached by the sea and the sun, like a skeleton by the side of a desert road. He lifted her out of the saddle and put her down. She seemed smaller than ever because her feet sank away, her skirt dragged through the sand. With her big feathered hat she looked like a child that had dressed up to play pirates; she climbed halfway up the sand dune, and called: "Come on! I've found a lovely spot!"

He tied the donkey's reins to one of the ribs of the wreck and followed her, happy and gay again, for, after seeing her so small in that vast loneliness, he felt older than she, stronger, wiser, a man.

She disappeared over the edge; when he arrived at the top, he discovered her, smiling rapturously, in a small hollow among the wind-blown gorse and dry grass, in which sand rustled. She looked so proud of her discovery that he knelt beside her and kissed her. Her lips were hot and dry from the sun.

"Let's lie down . . ." she said, her eyes still closed after his kiss, in that strange hoarse whisper that always gave him a shiver of desire.

"But the sand . . ." he said; "our clothes . . ."

She began to unbutton her clothes without opening her eyes; when she stood up to step out of her skirts she saw that he had not moved. "Come on," she said. "There's nobody here. It is too far away."

He undressed, and hung his clothes with hers in the shrubs. Then he looked round, and laughed, for she was sitting in the sand with nothing on but her hat. It made her look so much like a child playing pirates that, for the first time, he lay down beside her without touching her.

He lay on his back, his hands under his head, and looked up at the sky. The sun was so low now that before long they would be able to look straight at it and watch it go down. On the horizon, mist banks were forming, thin brush strokes of silvery white. He felt the warmth her body radiated, but this time it did not excite him. All was still and peaceful, and he suddenly felt like confessing everything, everything. But there was nothing left to tell her; she knew all about his theft, his flight. On the very first night, as they lay on the wide bed in the hotel room with the distant thunder of the surf behind the Venetian blinds, he had confessed everything: that he had put the money of Trippema and Company in his pocket instead of taking it to the bank, that he had been in a complete panic when they met, and that she had saved him. She could denounce him if she liked; he didn't care any more now he had met her.

They had been the first moments of peace after the weird journey, the dreamlike drive in a hansom to the hotel where she had booked a room for her week's holiday. She was governess with a brewer's family in Amsterdam, she told him. This one week was her only holiday in a year. She told long stories about the brewer's children, Fee, Stans, Kee and Pien, about Babby the cook and "Froufrou," as the brewer called his hoglike wife. Froufrou had breakfast in bed every day, and every time the curtains were drawn back in the morning the fat woman said she hadn't closed an eye, whereas every night the brewer took his pillow and his blankets to the sitting room, to sleep on the sofa, far from the snoring of his little Froufrou, his Sugarbunny, his delicious Toffeekins.

The pink figurines from her world of antimacassars, silk petticoats and high-buttoned shoes became more real to him than the black shadows from his own existence. The tall thin Mr. Trippema, whose hands he had never seen because he always wore black gloves. The six black mutes: Piet, Karel, Piet, Abel, Hendrik and Piet, who took the cigars out of their mouths and put them in their top hats on entering the house of a deceased, to put them back in their mouths the moment the weeping family moved off to the mourning room in the churchyard, where coffee and cheese rolls awaited them. The thin, snappy Carla, secretary of the management, who wrote out the accounts on black-edged paper and whom, in despair, he had almost come to desire in that twilit world of body snatchers until he had surprised her one morning in front of the mirror, pressing out the blackheads on her forehead with a key.

Yes, he had confessed everything, that very first night. He had told her about his childhood in the orphanage, that school for thieves where he had been forced to steal hunks of bread and raw bacon out of the kitchen in order to stay alive; about his boyhood in the day school in the former isolation hospital, where moisture glistened on the walls and which smelled of mold and wet paper; about his scholarship to high school, where he was taught astronomy and bookkeeping because he had such a good mind and behaved so well; about his apprenticeship with an organ builder, for whom he had swept wood shavings and had gilded fat angels blowing trumpets until he was fired because he had surprised his employer in the loft with Clotilde, the half-witted maid, behind the silver forest of the Voces Caelestes. He had even told her his secret dreams of expeditions to the tropics and naked brown women and bananas and whips and gold and rum, dreams he had invented when he could not sleep because his landlady lay coughing behind the wooden partition between their attic rooms, waking up the sparrows in the eaves.

She had listened in silence, and seemed not at all bothered by his crime. She only asked, in a businesslike manner, what the amount was, and when he answered: "One thousand guilders," she whistled. The whistle startled him; a shrill, two-toned whistle from the underworld. He sat up on his elbow and looked down at her, small and white in the gaslight; her eyes shone with a strange brilliance. "Do you think the amount matters?" he asked, chilled by a sudden loneliness. She smiled, shook her head and answered: "No, baby," then she put her arms around his neck and pulled him down into a kiss that banished all thought.

Later, somewhere on the beach, idly throwing pebbles at an empty grenadine bottle, they talked about the future. After her holiday she would return to Amsterdam, and he would go to England. He would write first: Miss Betsy Wilders, c/o Kiosk, Station Square. She refused to give him her address and he could understand that; she might get into trouble once the police were after him. When he was settled in England and earning money, she would come over and they would get married. At least, that was his idea; she made no comment. "First see you get there," she said. "You're in for a lot of trouble with the rams in Rotterdam."

He asked who the rams were; she hesitated a second and then answered: "Oh, just a nickname for the harbor police."

He wanted to ask more, but she suddenly jumped up: there was a sand flea in her clothes. "Oh, oh, Wim! Help! Oh—it tickles! Wim!" They climbed a sand dune, panting, stumbling, to take the sand flea out of her underclothes; they could not do that on the beach; there were too many people there. And now they were lying like that once more: on their backs in the sand, in a hollow among the shrubs; but the peace they had found on that previous occasion only after they had long forgotten the sand flea had now descended upon them without their having touched one another. For the first time, they were lying side by side looking at the sky as if they had been married for years.

"What are you thinking?" he asked for the second time, and again it seemed as if his voice came from afar, out of the rustling of the sand in the hard grass, the sighing of the wind in the shrubs.

"That man," she answered, after a silence.

"Which man?"

"The one on the platform of the horse tram. With the letters."

"Why?"

"Just like that."

For a while they lay looking silently at the sky.

"Do you believe in God?" he asked.

"No" she said, instantly. "I hate him."

"Why? Were you taught religion?"

"Yes," she said. "I scrubbed stairs in a convent."

It was the first time she had talked about her youth. He had often tried to make her tell him about it, after he himself had been whispering for hours during their white nights. He tried to think of a casual question that would lead her on, without arousing her suspicions; but she went on of her own accord.

"I always prayed for a hat with a feather and a carriage," she said. "I believed in prayer as a child."

"I prayed for cheese," he said, "or, for a while, sausage. I was always hungry."

"So was I," she said. "But I was too proud to tell that to the saints, for the nuns said that the saints had always been hungry themselves. I should pray for a pure heart, they said, but as there was nothing the matter with my heart, I prayed for a hat with an ostrich feather and a carriage. I saw a child who had those things drive through the park every day as I went to fetch bread for the nuns with a wheelbarrow."

"And then?" he asked softly.

"Then one day the carriage stopped in front of the convent. The child and I were girls by then. I recognized her at once, when I had to get off my knees and pick up my bucket to let her pass. She was taking the veil; an hour later she was scrubbing too. The carriage drove away."

"And then?"

"Then I didn't believe any more."

"Why not?"

"I don't know. I hate him. I wish that one day I could lay my hands on him."

"On whom?"

"God."

He laughed because he thought it was a joke, but when she went on her voice was almost angry. "I wouldn't laugh if I were you," she said. "If that man hadn't gone for you on that tram, you would never have got me."

"What do you mean?" he asked, suddenly jealous because he believed that she had fallen for his looks and his strength.

"When that man went for you with God," she said, "I suddenly no longer thought of you as a dog."

"A what?"

"All men are dogs. They all run after you with their tongues hanging out, and they all have . . ."

"What?"

"Nothing," she said, and gently put her hands on his thigh.

It startled him, because he had been looking at the sun, red and round now, with the strange fear he had felt during their walk along the beach creeping over him again. The sun rested on a thin streak of mist on the horizon. They had lain like this before, long ago.

"Do you know why I love you?" she asked.

"No," he said.

"Because I am the first woman you've been nice to, this way."

"What makes you think that?" he asked, with a return of his jealousy. "I've slept with women before, if that's what you mean."

"Don't lie," she said kindly. "I'm the first one, and that's why I love you. Before you go away, I wanted you to know. I love you—you are the first man I have ever loved."

"Why are you talking like that?" he asked, instead of the brave and angry things he intended to say. He asked it because of the approaching darkness, which he would see if he looked away from the red disk of the sun. It had now sagged through the streak of mist.

"Darling," she said. "Oh, darling," and he felt her warmth rise beside him. "Darling . . . Come . . ." She wanted to turn him round toward her; her hands were hot on his hips.

"No," he said. "No, angel, don't. I want . . ." He could not say what he wanted. There was no time. She wanted to pull him away from the sun, the red disk, with the girdle of mist.

"Come, darling," she whispered. "Come, my love. It's for the last time. . . ."

"No, no," he said, pushing her hands away, "no, dearest, no, no, I must . . ."

He saw her silhouette rise beside him, beside the red ball with the ring around it, floating in space. He must not look away from that ball, or he would be lost. "Darling," he whispered, "I love you, I love you, but go away, let me go, I don't want to lose you, I can't do without you, help me, help, I . . ." He felt her breath on his chest. She bent over him, threw one leg across him; her hands groped up his body toward his shoulders, his neck; he wrestled desperately, wildly, as she had wrestled in the train; but he was helpless because something inside him betrayed him, a weakness that let him be pulled away from that ball, that ball in its girdle of mist, now looming red and round over the silhouette of her naked body, like Saturn in its ring.

Saturn! While she lowered herself on top of him, the ring round Saturn began to turn, faster, to swirl, faster, faster, to spin, faster, faster, faster, until at last, with a cry of pain that awoke him, it exploded into two moths, circling round the lamp.

Saliva dripped on his hand as he lifted it to rub his eyes. He wiped his mouth with his sleeve; his clothes stuck to his body. When he got up to go to the cupboard he had to support himself on the table. The moths circled around his head, faster, faster, blended into hundreds, thousands of moths, a ring, a streak of mist that reddened as the sun sank deeper. "Yes,

yes . . ." she panted; he tore himself free with a cry of disgust and tried to reach the cupboard, but she clung to his legs. He had to drag her with him, step by step, steps in a morass; "God, God! My God!"

He woke up once more at the sound of his own voice, the voice of a drowning man. God held out his hand to him; he grabbed the Bible off the shelf. The inkwell fell with a crash and a tinkling of glass; but he could do nothing about it. He could only wade back to the table, panting, praying; when at last he gripped the hard edge of the table, the Bible nearly slipped out of his hands, and he cried, terrified: "God! God . . ." He held on to it, and heaved it onto the table, onto the album with the glinting square of the photograph. He opened the Bible at the ribbon marker and read: *Psalm 102—A prayer of the afflicted, when he is overwhelmed, and poureth out his complaint before the Lord—Hear my Prayer, Oh Lord, and let my cry come unto thee! I call, Oh Lord, but there is no answer, no answer. I call, I call, but there is nothing, the wilderness, I call, oh, darling, darling, but no answer, Betsy, angel, Betsy, Betsy, answer, but there was nothing but the wind and the sand. Betsy! Betsy! Where are you! But only the wind, and the roaring of the surf on the banks.*

His clothes still hung in the shrubs, hers were gone. The sun must have gone down long ago. He shivered with cold as he stood in the wind on the edge of the darkness. He could barely discern the wreck of the boat on the beach, but he saw that the donkey was gone; the ribs of the wreck stood out in the night, a black skeleton.

He dressed hurriedly; as he ran down the slope, his shoes filled with sand. He took them off when he reached the hard beach and ran in his bare feet. Twice he lost his hat; the third time he left it where it fell. Sometimes he called: "Betsy! Betsy!" as he ran. When he had to stop for breath he stammered, panting, "Betsy, why did you do it, Betsy, darling, why did you do this to me? . . ."

The night porter in the hotel knew only that the lady had left two hours before with her luggage in a cab. He didn't know which cab. There had been plenty in the square, but now they had all gone home, and there would not be another train before the morning. Yes, it was more than an hour's walk to the station.

He started to run through the night; at first, he counted his steps; a hundred fast, a hundred slow; but the straight dark road underneath the trees soon turned into a tunnel, full of fears. He ran faster to get to the end; but there was no end, the tunnel went on, straight into the darkness. After a while, he no longer knew whether he was falling or fleeing, or running straight ahead or in a circle; he stood still, and sat down by the roadside.

The grass was wet with dew; mist rose in ghostly wraiths from the ditches behind the trees; something rustled in the reeds, and he heard a splash.

He thought: "I'm being followed!" sprang to his feet and rushed on, headlong into the darkness. His feet burned inside his sandy shoes, sand chafed his loins, but he ran on, flailing his arms, gasping for breath, haunted by the echoing reports of his steps in the vault underneath the trees.

When, suddenly, the trees stopped and he stumbled into a black void without landmark, he collapsed in the wet grass by the side of the road. His body was shaken by hysterical sobs of exhaustion and panic, and it was a long time before he could think coherently.

At last he calmed down and became conscious once more of the world around him. It was a still, ghostly world of drifting whorls of fog, slowly twisting in the darkness. There was no sound other than his sobbing breath, his pounding heart, and no thought other than the word: madness, madness, madness, everything he was doing now, everything he was about to do, madness. Only now that she had left him did he realize how utterly he had surrendered himself to her; to find her again was the only thing that mattered, even if it meant the end of him.

The rest of his journey was like a dream; he moved, bodiless, through the dawn with no words in his thoughts, only images. He traversed streets and squares, the station hall, the platform, without hesitation or thought of danger, until he sat in a train once more. The secret hope that he might be arrested and put in prison and freed of the responsibility for his future gave him a dazed courage. But no one arrested him; no one looked at him twice.

In Amsterdam he noted down the addresses of all the brewers he could find in the directory in the hall of the station. There were nine of them. It was evening when the seventh door was opened by a fat maid who he knew must be the cook she had talked about, even before she nodded and answered: "Oh yes, she did work here, but that was more than a year ago." She said it in a whisper, looking over her shoulder at a closed door down the hall. The information did not startle him; he was so tired by now that nothing mattered. When the maid told him that she did not know where the girl was now, as if she did not care to know, the door at the other end of the hall was suddenly opened and a woman in a pink housecoat came out, asking who was there. When she heard the name Miss Betsy, she screamed: "Dodo! Doddy!" and leaned against the doorpost for support. A bald man came out with a newspaper, asking: "What is it this time?" When he heard the name "Betsy" he lost his temper. He shouted, shook his fist and called him names, but he mentioned the name of a tavern: The Broken Heart.

It was night when he finally penetrated into the inner darkness of Amsterdam's worst quarter. Never before had he dared to go so far because of the stories he had heard of murder and assault. When he reached the edge of the quarter, he found two policemen standing underneath a gas lamp at the entrance of the first narrow alley. One asked, "Where are you going?" and he answered, "I'm looking for my girl." The policemen looked at each other and the first one asked: "Your girl? Where does she live?" When he answered: "At The Broken Heart," they laughed. "Ah," the second one said. "One of those." He asked the way and they told him; but he lost it almost at once.

The district was silent and dark. Shadows skulked along the walls, faces peered out of broken windows; sometimes a door opened somewhere and let out a wave of drunken laughter. When finally he found the tavern The Broken Heart, it looked closed. A rusty sign hung over the door, creaking in the wind; on it was painted a red heart split in two, from which sprang a little green devil lifting a glass. Behind the door he heard piano music; as he opened it, it let out a cloud of tobacco smoke. He stood blinking in the doorway; the smoke-filled room was full of dark bodies that shuffled round in pairs, sideways like crabs, dancing to the tune of a piano that stood against the wall, playing without a player. A big pale hand on a poster over it pointed at him with a forefinger like a pole; around it was painted the legend *You are drinking Heineken's beer for your health.*

A few bodies stood at the bar with their backs to the hand. A woman in a red jumper decapitated foaming glasses with a skimmer and shoved them across the counter. When he asked for Miss Betsy Wilders, she pushed a glass toward him and said: "Never heard of her."

"Betsy," he said, "Betsy Wilders." He emptied the glass and the woman shoved another one across to him.

"Big eyes?" a man beside him asked, without looking round.

"Yes," he said. "Very big. Betsy Wilders."

"Betsy the Doll," said the man.

"No," he said. "Betsy Wilders."

"Betsy the Doll," said the man. "Big eyes. If you put her on her back, she shuts them. But she doesn't say 'Mamma.' "

He wanted to hit the man but he was too tired. He put his hand on his arm instead. "Betsy," he said. "Where is Betsy?"

"On the streets," the woman in the red jumper said. "She may be here any moment. What's it for? A bill?"

"Yes," he said. "Yes, a bill. She'll have to pay. God, will she have to pay."

"Here," said the woman. "Have another one."

As he stretched out his hand for a fresh glass, the man beside him held him back, and said: "Don't. Don't drink any more of that stuff, or you'll start fighting."

"Why should I?" he asked.

"Don't," said the man. "If you drink any more the little devil will slip out."

"What devil?" he said. "I don't see any devil."

"Here," said the man, pointing with a black fingernail at the concave golden mirror of the beer glass. "Look," he said. "There he is. That little man. That's the devil."

"I don't see any little man," he said. "I only see myself," and he drank.

"That's it," said the man. "That's it. Yourself. God, my head aches."

"Here," said the woman. "Have another. She'll be home any minute. Take your hand away, Lammy."

The finger went away. "God," the man said. "I'm like a pelican of the wilderness. I am like an owl of the desert."

"Yes," he said. "That's how I feel. Is there no one here to help me?"

"I watch," said the man, "a sparrow, alone upon the housetop."

He tried to get away from the counter, but everybody laughed and the piano stood shaking against the wall, tinkling without a player. He wanted to get away from the future, a big hand, pointing at him. *You are drinking Heineken's beer,* said the future, *for your health.* Then the red woman said, "Here's someone to see you, Betsy." The future said, "God!"

Silence fell. It was as if the world were holding its breath, while the curtain slowly rose for the opera *The Broken Heart.* Betsy stood motionless in the center of the stage, surrounded by a chorus of swaying crabs, softly singing; God, invisible, played the piano. She stood ready to sing her aria, the hat with the ostrich feather on the back of her head, her eyes wide, like a doll's. "Go away," she sang, after God had played the overture, and the swaying crabs had hummed sadly. "Go away! How dare you!" Then he knew that he must sing, but he had forgotten the tune. "Betsy," he stammered, "Betsy, dearest"; the crabs hummed, swaying. "Go away! Go away!" Betsy sang with a wide gesture, the feather on her hat waving. "Go away! Must I have you thrown out?" "Betsy," he stammered, tears trembling on his cheeks. "Betsy, dearest, I beg you, I beseech you, protect me, save me, I'll do anything you want, I'll say honestly that you are my first, I'll steal a carriage for you, I won't ask you what dogs have . . ." "Go away!" Betsy screamed. "Get out! I'll have you arrested! I'll have the police on you!" "Betsy!" he cried, "for the love of God . . ." and then she struck him in the face.

For one second, the cloud of drunkenness lifted. For one second he saw her sharply and clearly, and she was terrible to behold. "God!" she sneered, with a hatred that pierced his heart. Then she spat in his face, turned round and went out through a door.

He went after her, spittle and tears dripping down his face. He thrust aside the bodies that tried to bar his way. He tore open the door she had shut behind her, looked up a steep flight of stairs, and saw her from below. He saw the inside of her petticoat, her naked thighs over the black stockings, as she kicked at him with the sharp heel of her buttoned shoe. She kicked his head, his shoulders, his chin; but the desire that inflamed him as he saw those bare thighs made him insensitive to pain, fear, despair. He grabbed her skirt and pulled; she clutched the banister, screaming. He felt hands at his back, tugging at him; he heard her skirt tear, and as he fell backward he uncovered her body up to her waist.

The sight of her flesh made him crazy, a mad strength shot into his arms, his legs; he fought, kicked, struck out; he saw her flee up the stairs and he tore himself free, roaring, "Whore! Here, you! Whore! Bitch! I'll teach you! I'll teach you!" He stumbled up the stairs, grabbed her ankle, fell, but held on to her; she hung, stretched out, her hands clasping the uprights of the banister of the landing, kicking with her free leg; screaming, "Help! Girls! Help! Help!"

Doors flew open on the landing. Half-naked women sprang out, grabbed her wrists, her arms, pulled, pulled; the sight of their naked bodies, their loose hair, their breasts dazed him for a second, and in that moment they tore her free. Hands had grabbed hold of his jacket once more from behind, but they could not hold him; he sprang up the stairs. She stood behind the naked women, panting, her blouse torn, her hair disheveled, a red weal across her face as from the lash of a whip. She was blinded by hatred and tears. "Get him!" she screamed. "Get him! Teach him! He's a milksop! He's a green! Teach him! Teach him!"

The women threw themselves upon him, a hot sweaty softness that pushed him down, made his knees give way, forced him onto the floor, and then they tore off his clothes. He wanted to fight, but the naked warm softness of the female bodies did what the hands on the staircase had failed to do. One sat on his head; he bit at the skin of her thigh but could not get at it; he felt his strength, his will ooze out of him as their hands began to grope over his chest, his belly. Sour beer gushed out of his mouth, and he slowly sank down into damnation. "Betsy," he groaned, "Betsy, Betsy," and then, while the devil groped for the most secret parts of his body, a voice came out of the darkness.

"I watch," said the voice, "I watch."

"O God," he moaned, "save me, save me."

"*I watch,* said the voice, echoing. "*I watch.*"

He opened his eyes and saw a little red louse walk across the hand that lay on the floor beside his head. The devil pulled at him, pulled, but more weakly.

"*I watch,*" said the voice, "*and am as a sparrow alone upon the housetop.*"

The floor became lighter, white, with black cracks between the planks. The red louse scurried away between two black lines. Then the lines broke up into words.

I am like a pelican of the wilderness: I am like an owl of the desert.

He pulled his hand away.

For I have eaten ashes like bread, and mingled my drink with weeping.

He lifted his head; the little red louse fell off the Bible and fled into the back of the album. The moths still circled around the lamp, their shadows wheeling on the wall.

He read the psalm in wordless humility, for greater than his fear of the torture that was to come was his gratitude for the moment of tranquillity God had granted him in His mercy.

But Thou, O Lord, shalt endure for ever and thy remembrance until all generations. Thou shalt arise, and have mercy upon Zion: for the time to favour her, yea, the set time, is come.

Suddenly he saw, out of the corner of his eye, something white move in the dark square of the window. He looked up and the white thing disappeared. It was a face. He swallowed, but did not move.

Thy years are throughout all generations. Of old hast thou laid the foundation of the earth: and the heavens are the work of thy hands. They shall perish, but thou shalt endure: yea, all of them shall wax old like a garment. . . . But thou . . .

Stealthy steps tiptoed away outside, and vanished in the silence. Fear crept over him; but he pushed the Bible off the album and turned another page. He listened, the page in his hand, for he heard a soft rustling sound, a small clattering that he could not place. Fear froze his body, cold sweat broke out on his forehead. He listened for a long time; then he realized that the sound came from below. He looked down and saw the half-turned page tremble in his hand; a corner of the piece of tin on which the picture of the beach was printed had come loose and rattled against the paper with a faint metallic sound. He turned the page and looked at the other side.

A big photograph of a group of people standing, sitting and squatting in three rows; the faces at the edges of the photograph were distorted by the old-fashioned lens. Behind them, between two heads wearing paper hats and streamers around their necks, a finger pointed at him: *You are drinking Heineken's beer. . . .* The bodies of Jet, Slinky Lou and Lammy Shoo covered the rest. In the foreground sat a boy with drunkard's eyes and a downy beard, holding a slate in front of him; on it was chalked: *Happy New Year at The Broken Heart—Everything Paid.* It was the slate on which Jet recorded her customers' debts and which had been wiped clean because it was New Year's Eve. The boy looked quite innocent, almost pathetic; nobody suspected that inside his coat was hidden the knife with which he was going to kill Betsy the Doll.

Betsy sat in the center of the group, in the armchair that had been carried out of Jet's parlor for the occasion by Lammy and Lou. Her hat was tilted backward by the high back of the chair. She sat there smiling, small, proud and powerful. In the big mirror behind her he could see the reflection of the lens, looking over her shoulder like a glass eye. On the photograph the lens was too small to show what he had seen from his place in the foreground; all the people of The Broken Heart caught in the big glass eye, a small group of black puppets, distorted like the little devil in the beer glass.

He had to sit still for a long time, and he felt a malicious joy grow inside him as he stared at the eye that kept them prisoners, all of them, with their paper hats, their squeakers, their dreams and their sorrows, caught in a web of red streamers woven by the spider of sin. He grinned at the eye, the eye of the Old Year, that gazed at them with a look of disgust before it closed forever. He pressed the knife under his coat with a feeling of bliss, and while the photographer slowly counted under his black cloth he laughed soundlessly at the thought: now she's drunk, presently she'll go upstairs, she'll undress in the gaslight and look at herself in front of the mirror, and then, slowly, the curtains will be opened —by me. His hands began to tremble at the thought; he tried to steady them for otherwise the letters on the slate would be blurred on the photograph, but it was a trembling of happiness, that he controlled with reluctance.

He tried to divert his thoughts by staring at the puppets in the glass eye of the Old Year. Jet, the owner of The Broken Heart; Lammy, her old slave who got drunk every night, but nobody knew how; Slinky Lou, the blind pickpocket with the upturned eyes; Bonny, Lola, Sjaan and Mensje, the four girls; Sander the Ripper, the most dangerous inmate of The Broken Heart, who talked about the human body as a butcher about the carcass of a pig. Sander was a great craftsman in the art of murdering someone without a sound; he had drawn him out cautiously, little by little, ever since the night when Betsy had been drunk and chased him with glassy doll's eyes, naked, holding a feather duster between her thighs, hiccupping: "I'm the devil, eek! Eek! I'm the devil! I'm the devil, dusting God!"

He had fled to the attic, sobbing; she had been too drunk to follow him up the ladder. Lammy Shoo sat squatting on his rags in the attic, sewing a button on his trousers by the light of a candle, a tailor in hell. When he fell on his own heap of rags, weeping with fear and drunkenness and misery, Lammy comforted him. "Patience, little one," Lammy said. "Patience, my soft little beard. A year from now she'll have started to rot, and she'll fall into your arms of her own accord, like an apple in paradise. Yea," he said, biting the thread. "Tomorrow thou shalt be in paradise with her."

Tomorrow . . . His hands started to tremble violently, and the smile on his face became a grimace as he tried to control it. Tomorrow they would be in paradise, happy and without memories. They would float side by side along the long, white beach of heaven, wading through clouds, soft as foam, and their shadows would glide beside them. The vision brought peace, and a great feeling of security; and the key to it was hidden in his coat. Tonight he would turn that key, in the small red lock under her left breast.

"A woman?" Sander the Ripper had asked, peering along the edge of his knife with one eye shut. "A woman is a different proposition," and he made the knife hiss again on the grindstone that he pedaled round with a dancing leg. "First, it depends on whether she's big or small." He was forced to shout to make himself heard because of the shrieking of the knife on the stone and the squeaking of the pedal.

He had already learned a lot during the mornings in the cellar with Sander. They had almost become friends, although Sander was a powerful man and he himself only Silly Willem, the half-wit of The Broken Heart. Sander was flattered by his reverent curiosity about his craft; and although he had started by saying, "None of your business, Silly. Get on with your shoes," he had started to talk to him all the same. It had become a full training in the art of murder by knife; now they had arrived at the women. "Let's start with the small ones," Sander said, bending the blade on the stone until it squealed. "The small ones are the easiest." He tried the cutting edge on his thumbnail, shook his head and the knife squealed again on the stone. "First, never take them sitting down. Always standing up, preferably walking, and always from behind; but you know that by now. It's the same as with small men: knife in the right hand, pointing inward, blade along your arm, close in from behind, throw your left arm around her neck, your right leg around hers, pull back, and she'll arch backward." He turned the knife round, smeared saliva on the other side and bending it made it squeal again. "She must bend backward, or else she'll scream. Put your knife in underneath the left breast, and stab upward. If possible, run her against a wall to ram the knife home, but be careful you don't catch your fingers. The trouble is the corsets; you have to hold the blade flat to slip it in between the ribs, and the bleeding corset bones run up and down. If it's a big woman you'll have to use your knee. Instead of putting your left arm round her neck, you put your left hand on her mouth. Instead of your right leg around hers, you put your left knee in the small of her back. The best thing is to catch her on the edge of a pavement and jam her feet, otherwise she'll kick her legs up and then you're in trouble, you might as well try to rope a steer. . . . Tomorrow I'll tell you . . ."

Tomorrow . . . Tomorrow I'll be in paradise with her. Now she was drunk, soon she would go upstairs, take off her clothes, look at herself in the mirror, and then the curtains would slowly open, and she would look up, thinking it was the draft. But she would be mistaken, as the others had been, all of them. Slinky Lou was mistaken in thinking that Silly Willem did not know where the money was hidden that he had stolen from his pocket the first night. Jet was mistaken in thinking that she had chained Silly Willem to her counter forever by making him drunk each time he rebelled or tried to escape. Lammy Shoo was mistaken in thinking that one day Silly Willem would give in to him, if he went on stroking him in the darkness after the candle had been snuffed out. Bonny, Mensje, Lola and Sjaan were mistaken in thinking that they could go on kicking and scolding Silly Willem when he came in to make their beds, to get their skirts for ironing, or to pick up their shoes and draw back their curtains in the gray morning. Sander the Ripper was mistaken in thinking that Silly Willem was just a doting half-wit who would never remember a word of what he told him. Betsy the Doll was mistaken in thinking that she could forever look straight through him with her big eyes, without a flicker of recognition, when they met on the landing or in the taproom. She was mistaken, oh, how mistaken, in thinking that she would be beautiful forever, a white, soft doll.

Tomorrow the doll would be broken; tomorrow their souls would be in paradise together, wading through the long white clouds; tomorrow the girls would scream when they found the doll lying broken on the bed, its dead eyes half open, a small red keyhole underneath its left breast. The blood would drip off the bed onto the floor, making a puddle of red beer; the skimmer would be lying in the beer, with on its handle the imprint of a hand. The hand of God.

The thought made him conscious once more of the pointing forefinger behind his back, from which he could never escape. Twice he had thrown his glass at it, when the devil in the golden beer glass had driven him rabid. The finger went on pointing; the crabs went on dancing; the glasses foamed; God, invisible, played the piano. But this time everything would be different. This time the world would explode in a red cloud as he hurled his beer glass at the pointing hand; this time the doll would sag in his arms, without a cry or a sigh, for he would make her arch backward, her neck in the vise of his arm, her back bent on his hip; her breath would squeal like Sander's knives when he stabbed, upward, the blade flat, and rammed her against the mirror without catching his fingers. The mirror would break, glass would shatter among her bottles, her combs, her trinkets; the big eyes would turn upward, and the doll would sag in his arms, red sawdust spilling from the slit in the silk of her skin. He smiled at the big glass eye of the lens, still staring at them all impassively; then a voice said: "Perfect!" and the rubber ball of the shutter sucked in the air with the sound of a kiss. There was a sudden noise of laughter and voices around him, chairs and tables were dragged across the floor; but, although he still sat smiling with the slate in front of him, his happiness was shattered. For the moment the glass eye of the Old Year closed, in that very moment of utter certainty, the hand on the wall behind him pointed over his shoulder and he recognized the camera, the photographer underneath his black cloth, the hand squeezing the rubber ball. It was another camera, another hand, another photographer; but God said, "Look, Silly Willem! Look, rotten apple in paradise! Where have you seen this before? And what were you thinking then? 'Tomorrow, tomorrow I'll be in England!' And did you bring it off, that time?"

"No! No!" he cried. "Let me go!"

"Easy does it, Silly," Sander said, good-naturedly. "I only wanted to wake you up, boy. Come on, get a move on. We're putting the tables back."

He looked up at the broad face, his eyes blurred with tears, and slouched over to the counter. He could never bring it off, never, he would drown in a sea of beer and his skeleton would sink into the sand, a wreck on the long, white beach.

No! He didn't want that! He didn't want to be doped by Jet, robbed by Slinky Lou, petted by Lammy Shoo in the twilight of the loft! He wanted to take up the knife, against God; but God hurled him against the counter and Jet said: "Hey! Hey! Easy! You wait your turn!"

He waited, panting, for his beer, his hands clawing the cold rail, his knees trembling with cowardice. He was going to call the devil to his aid, the devil in the beer glass; he would help him take up the knife against God's hand, now pointing at him in the mirror behind the bottles. Jet came between him and the mirror and gave him his first glass. "No monkey business tonight, Silly," she said, "even if it is New Year's Eve. If you start throwing glasses again, you'll be locked in the cellar."

"Aw, come off it, Jet," Sander said, beside him. "Let the boy have his bit of fun, once a year."

"It's all right for you to talk," Jet said. "They're not your glasses."

"We won't throw anything tonight," Sander said, "will we, Silly? Tonight we're going to be good and enjoy ourselves, aren't we?"

"Yes, yes, Sander!" he said eagerly. "Will you stand me a drink for New Year's Eve? Please, Sander! Think of all the times I've put water in your grindstone for you."

"Listen to him," Sander said, grinning. "If they all were as silly as he is, this would be a different world. All right, Jet. Give him a brown."

"No," he said hastily. "A light one, Jet. Not a brown."

"Why?" asked Sander. "If I stand you a drink, it'll be a good one."

But he begged so earnestly that Sander shrugged his shoulders and said: "All right, Jet. Let the fool have his own way."

"Mind what you're doing," Jet said. "He gets drunk on that stuff. I know him."

"Let him," Sander said. "If he starts throwing glasses, chalk them up to me. Cheers, Silly! Happy New Year!"

They drank; he shivered as the cold beer went down his throat, and for a few rapturous seconds he forgot everything. "Good old Silly," Sander said kindly, and slapped him on the shoulder. Something fell to the floor with a clatter. Sander said, "Well, I'll be damned!" and stooped. Only then did he realize that the knife had fallen out of his coat.

Sander picked it up; he did not dare look. He stood waiting, tense with fear.

"But that's my Clara!" Sander cried. "Where did you get her?"

His voice was still kind but he did not dare look at him directly, he looked at him in the mirror.

"Well?" Sander asked. "Speak up! You've seen me looking for her everywhere. Where did you get her? When?"

Then, for the first time, the pointing hand behind his back protected him. It directed a thought into his panicking brain, and made him say, coolly, "I found her this morning. I wanted to give her back to you then but there were too many people about." His voice sounded alien to him.

"Where was she?" Sander asked, with a beginning of uncertainty.

"Underneath the grindstone," he answered. "I'd put her away now, if I were you. Too many eyes."

Sander grunted, and slid Clara up his sleeve. It was his favorite knife, a thin stiletto that he would talk to caressingly as he sharpened it. "I can't understand it," he said. "Underneath the grindstone? I could have sworn . . ."

"Hush!" his alien voice said. "Better give her back to me. Quick! I'll keep her for you till tomorrow."

"You're crazy," Sander said. "You with a knife? Much too dangerous."

"Have some sense and give her to me," he said, urgently, as amazed at the authority in his voice as Sander was. "You'll get drunk presently and start showing her off, or hurt somebody with her. Hand her over."

"What about you?" Sander asked, defensively. "You'll be throwing glasses!"

"I'll stay sober," he whispered. "Let me have her, quick, before you have an accident."

Then the miracle happened. Sander gave Clara back to him, and he put her back casually inside his coat. "What about buying me another one?" he asked, still in that strange voice. "You certainly owe me something."

Sander grunted but stood him one. "Silly, they call him!" he muttered, shaking his head. "I'll be damned."

From that moment, everything was different. The hand took control of him and drove him before it, ignoring his fears and his cowardice. It drove him along the trail that he had been preparing for weeks. He drank three more glasses of beer, without looking at the little devil. The little devil was powerless, a figment of Lammy Shoo's alcoholic imagination. Never had he been so sure of himself; he looked at his hands in amazement, turned them over, shook his head; they did not tremble at all. He glanced at Sander, at Lammy, at Jet, but they were ignoring him as usual. When he moved away from the counter, he felt a twinge of the old fear, but he took a step although the terrified drunkard inside him whined: "No! No! Don't! You're drunk, you'll spoil everything, you can't. . . ." But he moved on through the dancers, to the table where she sat. Her hat hung on one ear; she was shaking with drunken laughter, her neck red under the white powder. She was him coming, pointed, cried, "Cuckoo!" and burst into screams of laughter again. The drunkard inside him writhed in unbearable sorrow, but he sneered at him and at all the weaklings around him. Someone threw a red streamer over his shoulder;

it hit the wall behind her and floated down across her hat. For a moment they were linked by a red paper corkscrew; then a dancing couple passed between them and broke it. She screamed as the paper pulled at her hat, then she embraced a man with a pig's mask beside her. "Good-by, Betsy," he said. Then he turned round, went to the door of the staircase, opened it, shut it, and stood alone in the darkness.

At the bottom of the stairs, he leaned for a moment against the wall. Then the finger, pointing at the back of his neck, prodded him on and he climbed the stairs, without a sound. On the landing he stood still and listened. Not a sound came from the rooms; the music and the laughter sounded far away. When he opened the door to her room, the hinges squeaked and the nape of his neck tingled. Then he smelled her perfume. It startled him; so far he had only seen her room through the keyhole. It was as if she were in the room, enlarged a hundred times. The whole room was she; he stood on her soft flesh, walked across it to the window. The light from the street lamp on the corner, shining on the ceiling like moonlight, was reflected by the mirror and by the bottles on her dressing table. He looked round, moving only his eyes. The bed was a white island in the dusk; the lamp a white ball between the two hanging silver disks of the gas tap.

He drew the curtain, set a chair underneath the lamp, took a box of matches from his pocket, struck one, waited until the little flame burned steadily, climbed onto the chair, pulled one of the silver disks; the gas hissed and he lit the lamp. The white ball began to glow and filled the room with a cold light; the silver disks glinted.

He blew out the match, put it back in the box, put the box back in his pocket, stepped down, put the chair in front of the table and disappeared behind the curtain. He could see the chair through a crack between the curtains. He put his hand inside his coat, took out the knife, put it with its blade upward along his arm, stood motionless for a time, then he ripped open the curtain with his left hand, sprang at the chair, flung his arm round its back, his leg round the legs, pulled it backward, and stabbed. The point of the knife hit the wood with a sharp, dry sound. He had to use strength to pull it out.

He put the chair back in front of the table, a little more to the left, went back behind the curtains, peered at the chair for a long time, ripped, sprang, gripped, stabbed; the knife struck home. He pulled it out, turned the chair round and looked at the holes. They were so close together, one beside the other, that he could loosen the splinter between them with his nail.

He put the knife back under his coat, put the chair back against the wall, went back to the curtain. He drew it aside; then he saw that a drawer in her table was open. He pulled it out.

Handkerchiefs, curlers, a round box that spilled powder, a card of hairpins, a glass brooch.

He opened all the drawers in the table. Outside, squeakers began to squeal in the alley, firecrackers barked between the houses, ships' sirens boomed in the distance, the carillon of the church began to chime. Midnight, the New Year. In the last drawer was a small bag. He opened it and found a square piece of tin inside.

The sea, a beach, two people and a sleeping donkey with their shoes around its neck.

Silence fell outside. A squeaker went on blaring for a while, voices laughed, a door was shut; then a door was opened below, and unsteady steps mounted the stairs. He dropped the tin on the table, and vanished swiftly behind the curtain.

She was singing as she opened the door, and stopped as she saw the light. She was startled, but too drunk to think clearly, as he had foreseen. She shut the door and started to sing again as she crossed the room toward the table. Her hat hung down her back, her blouse was torn, her hair tousled. "Ta-ta," she cooed with a silly smile, and she waved at her reflection in the mirror. "Ta-ta, li'l Betsy." She belched, stood still for a moment with her cheeks blown out, then she let the air out with a sigh, turned round and vanished from sight.

He heard her humming as she undressed but he did not see her; through the keyhole he had seen more. He recognized the rustle of silk as she dropped her petticoat, the soft snaps as she unhooked her corset, the creaking of the springs as she sat down on the edge of the bed, the thud and roll of her shoes as she kicked them off. After that her steps were inaudible, and she hummed no longer; suddenly she stood in front of the mirror, naked.

She was white and silky. Her small breasts rose as she put her hands behind her head to take out her combs; they were young and defenseless. He looked, in the mirror, at the spot beneath her left breast where he would stab, and pulled the knife slowly out of his coat. She put down the first comb on the glass table top; the click rang out loud in the silence.

Suddenly she stood still, her right hand outstretched, and listened. The knife was halfway out of his coat.

Both of them stood motionless, then she picked up the photograph. She had not been listening, but looking at it. She turned it over, looked up at herself in the mirror, frowning, then she looked at the photograph once more, shrugged her shoulders, and threw it, with the bag, into the drawer. When she pushed it shut the knife was out of his coat.

She took out the last comb and shook her head to loosen her hair. As she stretched out her hand toward the brush, he ripped open the curtain, sprang, grabbed, pulled, and stood still. He had seen something move out of the corner of his eye. He looked up, and saw their reflection in the mirror. The chair had been dark; now her white body in the mirror had distracted him. She stood pressed against him, her legs in the vise of his knee, her belly soft and shining, her breasts almost vanished, so tautly was she arched backward. The blade of the knife, sleek and glinting, was poised for the kill. It would sink into her without resistance.

He felt so calm that he was astonished by the look on his face in the mirror. It was the face of a terrified child. He looked down at her face, on his shoulder. Her head was pulled far back; he could see into her nostrils and into her open mouth, where a quivering tongue lay cowering. Her eyes stared glassily at the ceiling. As he stood looking down at her, she began to tremble. It started in her calves, crept up her thighs, until her whole body trembled. He lifted her head with his shoulder to look at her eyes.

Until then, he had been completely calm. But now he saw a little puppet in her eyes, like the reflection in a beer glass, and he began to tremble too. He felt his strength slowly drain out of his arms, his legs. It was drained toward his loins, and an icy fear crept over him. His heart began to pound; the grip around the knife wavered; the vise of his arm around her neck slackened; his hand went limp; his trembling finger tips touched her skin, the world exploded in a red cloud and he kissed her.

The kiss was terrible with delight; but he pressed her tighter and tighter against him, for the pointing hand was rising behind him once more. Her face went blue, her eyes glazed over; then he released her mouth and smelled the devil, and as he looked into her eyes, he saw him: the little devil from the beer glass. He roared with anguish and fury, and hurled her away from him. She crashed against the bed, fell backward onto it; her spread-eagled defenselessness made him reel with desire. He ripped off his clothes, tearing them; she tried to crawl away across the bed, groping blindly; then the pointing hand behind him opened and closed round his neck. He tried to escape by fighting with his clothes, kicking off his trousers, but the hand closed round his neck mercilessly. He screamed, "No! No!"; she jabbered with terror; then the hand lifted him off his feet and hurled him on top of her with the force that created the world. His loins burst open, and moaning with pain and delight, he felt his life gush out of him. The hand lifted both of them up, in their last embrace, and hurled them into eternal darkness.

Eternal, eternal; eternally they fell entwined in their last embrace into eternal darkness. Then a tiny star twinkled far away, a pinpoint in the darkness.

They fell toward it, eternally, a fall of eternal damnation.

The star grew bigger, brighter, hotter, until it blinded them and scorched them; then they crashed into it, and were torn apart in a flame of pain, into two suns, circling around the star.

Two planets, circling around the sun.

Two moons, circling around a planet.

Two moths, circling around a lamp.

He knew: if I can stop now, if I can hold on to this lamp, these moths, I will be saved, but he could not. The circling of the moths around the lamp became slower and slower until they came to a standstill on either side of a white ball, and he recognized the two silver disks that glinted in the gaslight.

He raised himself, and looked down at her. She lay motionless on the bed, a stillness that was worse than death. For instead of the Doll, he had murdered Betsy; there was nothing left of her now but a whore's body, stunned and drunk. Her eyes, gazing at him with a glassy stare as he put on his clothes, were soulless; when he picked up the knife she uttered a guttural sound of fear, pain, or drunkenness, he did not know which and did not care. He was overcome by indifference.

The indifference numbed everything. He put the knife in his coat indifferently, and went to the door, indifferent to the drunken waving of her arms. He closed the door behind him without looking back.

On the landing he lit the candle that was put there for late visitors. He entered the taproom and lifted the candle to look around. He saw a chaos of spilt beer, overturned chairs, empty bottles and soggy streamers and in the mirror a child holding a light over its head. The hand pointed indifferently from the wall, the piano underneath it grinned with yellow teeth in the candlelight. It was silent but for the sound of beer dripping off the counter into a puddle on the floor. It sounded like the ticking of a clock, a clock without hands in a darkness that no passage of time could now alter.

As he went down the steps to the cellar, to put back the knife underneath the grindstone, the light of his candle was reflected for a moment behind a low doorway through which he had never ventured, and which let to a vault where the vats were stored. The doorway was screened by the rags of old cobwebs that moved in the draft. He made a few steps toward it, and heard a furtive rustle among the vats. He struck the cobwebs aside and lifted his candle. The light shone onto a huddled shape with glistening eyes and a dead candle; Lammy Shoo, cowering between two vats, hiding a bottle behind his back. Lammy saw the knife glint in the darkness and began to lisp in terror. "Don't, sweetie . . ." he whispered. "Don't, sweetheart. I'll give you everything, everything I've got. . . ." He stretched out a trembling hand and offered him the bottle, whispering, "Gin, real gin. Nobody knows about it. I've drilled a hole in a vat in the corner. Nobody else can get at it for I'm thinner than any of them; here, here, you have it. Here, take it. Drink your fill, sweetie, and don't hurt Lammy. Lammy is old. Too old to hurt."

He understood now how Lammy had managed to get drunk every night without drinking in the taproom, but it left him indifferent. He took the bottle and drank, his head back, candle grease dripping on his hand; then he gave Lammy back his bottle and together they went up to the loft, where he fell asleep at once without thoughts, without regrets, a sailing away on a still, dark sea, with Lammy babbling on the receding shore.

From then onward, he stayed out of sight. He went down no more in the morning to polish the boots and listen to the squealing of Sander's knives. He no longer shuffled around in the rooms on the landing to make the beds, iron the skirts or mend the trinkets that had been smashed during the night. He did not even go down to the taproom any more, to drink and explode in fits of drunken rage. He lay all day long on his rags in the attic, underneath the pointed catafalque of the roof, like a corpse, listening to the faraway sounds in the house below. Sometimes he heard the piano tinkle and he hummed with it, "Daisy, Daisy, give me your answer, do."

He needed the daytime to sleep off the effects of the gin he drank from

Lammy's bottle at night. At night he almost came to life; after darkness had fallen he slunk down the ladder, down the stairs, out into the alley, and vanished, scurrying, in the crowd of silent shadows. Occasionally he stood still on a bridge to gaze down at the black water of the canal, humming "Daisy, Daisy"; when steps approached, he fled into the shadow of the trees lining the canal. He had little to eat, only what Lammy brought him or what he found at the foot of the trees: hunks of bread in wet newspaper, sniffed at by scavenging dogs who fled at his snarl. Nobody knew that he still lived in The Broken Heart. Lammy had told them he had gone out on New Year's Eve never to return; no one ever came up to the loft.

Only once was he seen, by a new girl who suddenly opened the door of the room where Sjaan used to sleep. She stared at him with a hand at her throat, and screamed; he vanished swiftly in the dark well of the stairs. He stood still in the empty taproom, his head on one side, listening.

"I saw a man!" a new voice called. "Somebody went down the stairs!"

"You're crazy," Lola's voice said. "Go back to bed."

Then another door opened and he heard Betsy's voice, asking, "What's the matter?"

"Nothing," said Lola's voice, "The new one says she saw a man. Let's shut up, or Jet'll come out."

"A man?" she asked, and something in her voice stirred a chord inside him but he shrugged it off.

"Ah!" said Lola. "Somebody thinks her boy friend is back again." And she slammed her door.

He wanted to go out into the street but the stairs creaked and he saw a light coming down. He hid quickly behind the piano and saw her enter, a candle in her hand. She wore a white nightdress, that was transparent as she turned round and put herself between him and the light. He saw the silhouette of her legs in the long white skirt. He heard her ask, "Anyone there?" She looked behind the counter, with the candle, and under the tables, but she did not look behind the piano. Then she went back upstairs, lifting up the front of her skirt. She did not put herself between him and the light again.

Lammy Shoo talked about her sometimes, but he never listened. He was too lazy to listen or to think; the only thing that made him restless was to be kept waiting for the bottle. He quarreled with Lammy because the old man tried to fool him by bringing up a smaller bottle after a while;

Lammy swore that it was the same and started to weep, crying that God was his witness that it was the same bottle that he had been using for three months now. He could not be bothered to remain angry so he told Lammy that he was forgiven; yet it was indeed a very small bottle, and his thirst finally drove him down to the cellar to fill it again himself, but he could not get between the vats, he was not nearly as thin as Lammy yet. It gave Lammy power, but Lammy was loyal. He was always on time, and although he often wept, and sweated a great deal as the nights grew hotter, he was a nice little man whom he could look upon with affection, once he was drunk.

One night, he was awakened by a scream from the house below. Somewhere downstairs a door slammed and a loud voice started cursing. It was Sander's. Then there was a sound of blows and something heavy rumbled down the stairs; the weak wailing that followed was drowned by slamming doors, running feet, voices; twice a woman screamed. He lay listening with his heart in his mouth, forgetting his thirst. The house remained restless all night long; steps and voices came and went; then the sound of horses' hoofs and a rattle of wheels approached in the alley and stopped in front of the house. After a short interval, the wheels rattled away and the hoofbeats receded into the distance. Then, at last, the house fell silent. When, after hours of waiting, Lammy had still not arrived, he crept stealthily down the ladder, down the stairs, into the taproom. The street lamp shone through the windows; at the foot of the stairs was a dark patch. He bent over it, saw that the floor was wet, knelt, sniffed at it, and felt like weeping, for it was gin. Lammy had broken the bottle.

The craving for drink burned in his guts; he crept down the stairs to the cellar. When he stood in front of the vats, he lit the stump of candle, full of pious, tearful thoughts, for the pointing hand loomed in the darkness behind him once more. He knew he was too fat to get between the vats, but the hand drove him into the gap. He discovered that it had become wider, and he covered his mouth to stifle his sobs, sobs of weakness and gratitude.

He crawled between the vats, found his way blocked by the wall, but discovered a narrow passage that led along it into the darkness behind. He crawled on, sideways, gasping for breath after each vat, for he had to flatten his chest to get past. Once he heard a rustle and saw a small shadow flit along the wall. There were many rats in the cellar, Lammy had told him, but they were harmless. After a long struggle, he reached the vat in the far corner. He inspected it by the flickering light of the candle and discovered a tiny plug in the bottom of the lid. He pulled out the plug; a thin silver jet spurted out and hit the floor with a soft splashing sound. Then it stopped. Despair struck him; the vat must be empty. Then he discovered another plug in the top of the lid; when he took it out the thin jet spurted from below once more. He put his finger on the bottom hole; as he had no bottle with him he lowered himself, sideways, to drink. His clothes tore and he felt a sharp pain, but the little hole was so close to his mouth by then that he hardly noticed it. At last he lay on the floor, on his side, his mouth at the hole; then he took his finger away. He had to swallow very quickly in order not to spill any, and he hit upon the idea of putting his finger on the hole after each mouthful. So he settled down to drink at his ease, and soon a golden peace slowly pervaded his body from his stomach, until his whole being seemed to be humming, singing, "Daisy, Daisy, this is a wonderful world." When at last he put the plug back, he felt proud of his self-control, and he lay smiling underneath the vats for a long time, gazing along the floor. The floor was a narrow, flat darkness around the golden lights of the candle flame. Little stars moved in the darkness, in pairs; one pair ran straight at him, shied away, and a small dark shape swung through the light. He knew it was a rat, and it spoiled his feeling of well-being. He struggled to his feet with difficulty, and it took him a long time to get back in the open again, but he felt in no hurry and deliciously drowsy. For the first time he had drunk enough to gratify his craving, and it made him feel completely happy.

That night he did not go out into the street; he was too tired. The next night, he could not be bothered either. The following night he re-mained on the floor behind the vats, and whistled softly at the rats between his teeth. To see them scatter and scurry was such a fascinating sight that he could not tear himself away. Then he saw the day break underneath the vats, and he had to hurry back to the attic before anyone stirred.

On the fourth night he felt really hungry, and he knew that drink alone would not satisfy him this time. He missed the hunks of bread he had scavenged during his nightly wanderings along the canals; perhaps it was just his imagination, perhaps he did not really need bread, but the vision of it was tantalizing: it lay, a fresh golden loaf, with a crisp brown crust, on a clean newspaper. The hunger became so strong that he decided to go out into the street that night. But once that decision was made, he started to visualize all the things he would have to do: go down the stairs, crawl behind the vats, drink, crawl back, go out into the streets, look for bread, come back, climb up to the loft. It seemed a long, exhausting business, and he tried to simplify it. At first he could not see how he could possibly leave any of it out; then the notion struck him that there was no need to stay in the attic, now Lammy Shoo was gone. He might as well take his rags down to the cellar and put them behind the vats, underneath the hole. That was not only simpler, it was safer; no one would ever find him there; and even if they spotted him, only a child could get between the vats. He would kill the child so he took Clara with him. He had been planning to put her back underneath the grindstone, until the night of Lammy's scream and Sander's curses; then he had decided to keep her. Sander would never do to him what he had done to Lammy, for he would put his left hand on his mouth, his left hip in the small of his back, jam his feet, pull him backward and stab him, the blade flat because of the corset.

When at last the moment came for him to go downstairs, he was too tired to carry his bed. He took only Clara, who was very light and beautiful to look at by candlelight. He looked forward to admiring Clara by candlelight, silver and gold: he looked forward to all the daydreams she would bring into that secret, warm little world of his. That night he did not go out into the streets either, for the hunger lessened after he had drunk a little and he felt so safe and happy in his snug little hiding place that it seemed a pity to go away. He saw the dawn break underneath the vats and heard the steps of an early riser pass overhead, in the taproom. They sounded much closer than he had expected. He heard Sander come downstairs and the grindstone began to squeak; when he heard a knife squeal the sound made him smile with a wonderful feeling of security and secrecy. Many other steps came and went in the cellar that morning but he heard them only vaguely. At nightfall, the piano began to hammer out overhead: "Daisy, Daisy"; it was not beautiful, far too noisy and near. After he had drunk a few mouthfuls, it sounded better.

That night he stayed indoors again, for he had realized something else: there was no need to go out into the streets for bread; the kitchen was close by. After everyone had gone to bed, he sneaked up to the kitchen, opened some cupboards, found bread and cheese that looked very appetizing and devoured a lot of both. He also found a cucumber and bit off the end, but he soon regretted it for it made him feel sick and he had to throw up behind the vats. After he had lain down and drunk a little, he felt much better, and he decided never to eat cucumber again. He would eat nothing for a while to give his stomach a rest. During the night, he heard the rats fight over his vomit and it made him smile. He had not been sick for nothing; this was a wonderful world.

A few nights later he felt hungry once more, and went back to the kitchen. As he tiptoed toward the cupboard there was a hard click and a terrible pain in his foot. He screamed and lashed out wildly, thinking it was Sander; but there was nobody. As he limped back to the door, something clattered along the flagstones. He lit a candle and saw he was dragging a rat trap, which had broken his shoe. He prized it loose and crawled back hurriedly behind the vats, whimpering. He had to drink a lot before the pain eased, and he decided never to go back to the kitchen.

A few nights later he felt hungry again, and went out into the street. As he pulled the front door shut behind him, he heard the snap of the lock, turned round like lightning, but it was too late. The door was shut, and he had no key. Previously he had always gone out with Lammy, who had one. He had often waited for Lammy when they had lost one another, but he had forgotten that.

He lost his temper and kicked the door; he stopped when he saw a light appear behind the window; a candle, a face and a white skirt came down the stairs. He was curious to see who it was, but the candle flame lit up the wall and suddenly the hand pointed at him. It so petrified him with terror that he forgot the candle flame until it had come very close, and a face came between him and the hand. He looked at the face, lit from below, and saw it was she. Two little candle flames twinkled in her eyes, and she had paper curlers on her head that looked like white butterflies. Then she moved, and the hand pointed at him over her shoulder. He heard her call, "Who's there?" faintly, as if she were calling him across a dark canal. He hesitated over what to do: let her open the door and slip past her, or turn round and run away from the hand; then her eyes suddenly widened and she screamed, "*Wim!*"

For a second he stood paralyzed, the name stuck in his heart like a knife, thrown by the hand. Then she opened the door, letting out the hand, and he fled. "*Wim!*" she cried after him, "*Wim!*"; two knives that were hurled at his back by the hand; then he was safely round the corner, panting, sick with terror and weakness. He leaned against the wall, his eyes closed; but then steps came running, and he saw the hand coming for him with wide-spread fingers. He screamed and rushed blindly into the darkness, his fists pressed on Clara, who wanted to fight, stab upward, ram against the wall, but he knew she was powerless against the hand. "*Wim!*"; the knife hit him between the shoulder blades; he rushed on in such a panic that he only saw the water as the rail struck him in the stomach like a sledge hammer. He broke over the rail, numbed with pain and shock.

Clara had saved him; without her in his pocket he would have broken his back. He hung limply over the rail of the bridge, and looked down into the black mirror of the canal. The trees lay reflected like ostrich feathers; between them he saw a white face. The face terrified him; he could not see who it was, but the finger in the nape of his neck pressed him slowly forward, toward it; then he vomited. The drink gushed, stinking, out of his mouth and splashed into the water, taking with it his last hopes of peace, happiness and golden dreams; when he opened his eyes again, the face was broken up into fragments that bobbed on widening rings on the water. The rings slowly smoothed out, the face was pieced together once more, and he saw it was not a face but the hand. He jumped and ran on again, fleeing from the hand; he ran through alleys, archways, streets, across squares and bridges, until he was trapped unawares in a courtyard and collapsed underneath a cart. He crouched there, coughing, choking, staring at the archway through which he had come; if he looked away from the archway, he would be grabbed by the hand that stood outside in the alley, pressed against the wall, waiting for him. He sat motionless for a long time; then sweat from his forehead dripped into his eyes and blinded him. He collapsed with a sob, his hands over his eye.

When he woke up, he felt very cold, very weak, and knew he had reached the end of his road. It was morning, a stark gray light showed up the wheels of the cart between which he cowered, the cobbles of the courtyard. He crawled from underneath the cart on hands and feet, and felt he had no strength left in his body. He looked at his clothes, and saw they were rags. He looked at his hands, wasted and dirty. He fingered his face, and felt the skull underneath the sick, thin skin, worn through at the cheekbones. He looked around him and saw he was standing in the yard of a bakery. On the yellow cart was painted in red letters the word BREAD. He swallowed, but he knew he could not eat, his stomach was too weak. He looked through the archway; a window of a house stared at him. He moved aside, for no one must see him. If he were seen, they would call the police, who would lock him up because of his clothes and his face, and then he would be forced to live on, locked up in a cage, with his memories.

Memories. He covered his face with his hands, in an effort to hide from the horror of that word. But he could not escape from the past by hiding his eyes with the cowardice of a drunkard. Now he was sober, he knew that there was only one way out: to drag himself to the water and drown. But as he stumbled to the archway, he realized that it was too late. There would be people on the streets and beside the canal. He would have to wait until the evening, slink along the walls in the darkness, wait in a doorway until there was no one about, then tiptoe to the canal and lower himself in without a sound, then let go, his feet together, his hands above his head. That way he would sink swiftly, for he would not struggle now that he was sober. He was more sober now than he had been since the day he stole the money from Trippema and Company.

He looked for a place to hide in until nightfall. In the corner of the yard was a flight of steps, white with flour. Underneath he saw a square door with a little barred window, a cellar. He would hide in the cellar.

He crept over to the steps, opened the door, and found a dank hole with straw on the floor and a chain. A dog kennel. He hesitated, then he heard footsteps in the alley, crawled in and pulled the door shut behind him. The kennel stank of excrement and sour straw; he had to keep his face close to the bars of the little window to breathe. Any minute now the baker would come with his dog; perhaps that was him coming now. But the footsteps passed by outside the archway, and then a carillon started to chime nearby. When it finished its tune he counted the slow strokes of the clock, echoing over the roofs. Eight. The baker was late. He was certain to bring a dog; he needed one in this quarter or his cart would be looted whenever he turned his back.

Every time steps approached, he expected it to be the baker, and he did not quite know what to do if it were until he remembered the knife. That was it: he would first kill the dog and then run. If the baker ran after him and overtook him, he would grab him, throw his arm around his neck, his legs around . . . He covered his face with his hands. He did not want to think any more, or remember. He prayed to God to send the baker; but God set the churchbells tolling at half past nine. Then he realized that the baker would not come that day, that he would be locked up with his memories for twelve hours. It was Sunday.

When, that night, darkness fell, a shadow slunk through the archway into the alley. The alley led to a narrow street where there were lanterns and people. From a lighted doorway came the sound of music, and people were going in: vagabonds, tramps, night wanderers attracted by the light. He waited for the last one to shuffle inside and the door to close, so that he could get past unnoticed; but the door remained open and the music went on playing; it was a violin. Then voices started to sing behind the lighted doorway: "Daisy, Daisy," the voices sang, "give me your answer, do."

The minutes of waiting exhausted him. The water was not far, but a giddy weakness overcame him and for the first time he was afraid that he would not make it. He groped his way along the house fronts, supporting himself at doorposts and window-ledges, then he stumbled to a standstill. He could not go on, he was too weak. The realization maddened him, but his fury could not spur him on; it only made him bare his teeth, the snarl of a dying animal. The singing behind the lighted doorway across the street was louder now. *"Daisy, Daisy, give me your answer, do."* He managed to drag himself one window further; it took his last vestige of strength. He would collapse and lie here until the police found him. He would have to live his life a thousand times over in the purgatory of a cell, the way he had done that day in the dog's kennel. Then the smell of coffee wafted across from the lighted doorway.

The smell gave him back some strength, a last craving. He saw the coffee float in the darkness: a steaming white bowl. He dragged himself across the street; when he reached the doorway the smell was so tempting that he stumbled inside. The heat in the room was dizzying; he slumped onto a bench and looked around. He saw a woman going from bench to bench with a tray full of bowls like the one he had seen in his imagination: steaming, white. His craving for coffee became so strong that he wanted to call her over, but he had no voice left.

Then the woman saw him. He sat alone on the last bench; the other rows were full of tramps drinking, the white bowls at their mouths, their heads back.

The woman made her way toward him, but one of the others distracted her attention. Again he wanted to call, but a voice had started talking in the distance. At last the woman came, and held out a bowl toward him over the heads. He had no eyes for her smile, only for the bowl, white and steaming. He grabbed it with both hands; it was so heavy that he spilled some, and tears came into his eyes. He steadied the bowl against his chest; then he sipped.

After the first sip he knew: I am saved. When I have drunk this, I'll be strong enough to reach the water. He felt a deep gratitude toward the woman, who stood watching him. He looked up at her over the edge of the bowl and saw something glint on her collar. It was a brass S. Only then did he realize that it was not "Daisy, Daisy" that the voices had been singing, but "Jesus, Jesus" to the same tune. He slowly looked round at the platform at the far end of the room, on which a boy stood talking.

He recognized him instantly. He would have known him anywhere, even without the double S on the collar of his blue suit. While sipping his coffee in small, cautious mouthfuls he stared at him, sipping mouthfuls of hot, sweet hatred. The boy had not changed since that morning on the horse tram, when he had said, "You have the face of a sinner." He had not hit him then; he had gone on to the station, on to a life of dissipation, hunger and drunkenness—now he faced the blue boy once more, the boy who had stood waiting all that time, waiting for him to hit him. All the love, horror, misery and pain had been a waste, a pointless detour; he was back at the blue boy once more, only much weaker, too weak to hit him.

The hatred became so intense that he started to tremble again, squandering the precious strength he needed to reach the water. He knew he should go now, now; but the hatred slowly uncoiled inside him as he stared at the boy, until his whole body was shaking. The boy was saying the same things to the tramps that he had said to the five people on the platform of the horse tram. He heard the same words: God, Love, Protection, Sin— and he felt, with terror, the pointing hand approach the nape of his neck once more.

He knew what he was doing. He knew that he was delivering himself to the life-long torture of a prison cell, but he pulled Clara from his coat, took her by the tip, and lifted his arm. Then the hatred for the blue boy became so consuming that he no longer realized the madness of his act, he only felt the hand approaching the nape of his neck and he lifted his arm. The hatred hissed from his mouth; then the hand touched him. He sprang up, and hurled the knife. It flashed through the gaslight, struck the boy across the face and fell to the floor with a clatter.

For a second he stood still. The boy stood still. Nothing moved in the stillness but the blood that ran down the boy's face from a cut on his temple. Then the boy said: "Thank you, brother. That was the hand of God."

People jumped up everywhere. There were hurrying footsteps, cries, the rumble of benches. Hands grabbed him, but he felt nothing, saw nothing. He was sitting on the bench with his head in his hands, vomiting between his feet.

A woman's voice called; the hands released him. Silence fell. It lasted so long that he looked up. The blue boy was sitting beside him, a blood-soaked handkerchief around his head. He recognized him with regret; he had hoped it would be a policeman. He rested, his head in his hands once more, saw the mess between his broken shoes, and shut his eyes.

"Can I help you?" the boy beside him asked.

He was too tired to express the hatred that flickered inside him. He kept his eyes closed and waited for the policeman.

"If you could make a wish now," the boy asked, "what would it be?"

He was too tired even to snarl. He waited for the policeman.

"I am certain that God would grant that wish," the boy said, "but you'll have to say it aloud."

Then he could not help saying, "Dead." He wished it so fervently that he blurted it out in spite of himself.

"You wish you were dead?" the boy asked.

"Yes," he said.

"Why?"

He looked up, incredulous. The boy must be very stupid. He met the boy's eyes and they looked at him in a strange way. It was not curiosity, nor kindness. It was not even pity. It was something new; but he was too tired to go on looking. He closed his eyes, once more rested his head in his hands, for it was heavy. "When is he coming?" he asked.

"Who?" asked the boy.

"The policeman."

"No policeman is coming," the boy said.

He looked up, alarmed. "Why not?" he asked, quaveringly. "You mustn't tease me."

The boy went on looking at him with that strange expression. "If you really want to die," he said, "how can I help you?"

He did not answer. He wished the boy would shut up. He tried to shut his ears to his voice, but he was too near. Then, tired, he said, "Take me to it."

"What?" the boy asked.

"The water."

The boy put a hand on his shoulder. "Brother," he said, with such compassion in his voice that it made him tremble. "Brother."

The hand on his shoulder was not heavy, but it frightened him, for the compassion that came through it brought tears to his eyes.

"I wish I could take it all away from you," the boy said. "I would, if I could."

"Shut up," he said.

"There's only one who can," the boy said, "and that is Jesus."

He suddenly hardened. Jesus did not exist. The boy was mad. That was what he had seen in his eyes: madness.

"I can take you to Jesus," the boy said, "and ask Him to take it all away from you. But you must help."

He did not answer. He suddenly felt a terrible craving for a drink. That was it! Drink! "I want a drink," he said. "Give me a drink, please, sir, give me a drink!"

"What would you rather do?" the boy asked. "Drink or die?"

He hesitated, then he said, "Die." Who knows, the madman might take him to the water if he could convince him it was the only solution. He had turned pale under that red handkerchief; he must be losing a lot of blood, for it dripped down his cheek onto the S on his collar. "If I can convince you that I must die, will you help me?" he asked. "I can prove it to you, I can."

"If you can really prove it," said the boy, "I'll do anything you want."

"Take me to the water?"

"Yes."

"Push me in? Push me back if I come up? Hold me under till I stay down?"

"Yes," said the boy.

"And you won't call a policeman? You'll wait till I've drowned and then go away?"

"Yes," said the boy.

"Swear it."

"I swear it," said the boy. "So help me God."

"I want to die," he began, "because . . ." and then suddenly he realized what it was he saw in the boy's eyes. It was love.

It took him so completely unawares that he wavered, stammered, and burst into sobs. He broke down for the first time since he had gone under; even that day, staring through the bars of the dog's kennel, he had not shed a tear. But now all the misery and the failure of his life rose up behind him, a white-crested wave of tears, storming at him from the darkness, ready to smother him; but it was not a wave, it was hand. He fell on his knees, hid his face in the boy's lap and cried, "Jesus, Jesus, save me! Dear God, mercy, mercy!"

And then the hand which had driven him to drink, hounded him through the nightmare of his delirium and hurled him to hell, suddenly halted behind him and opened into a gesture of blessing. A ghost, laden with sin, stood up out of his body and stumbled away into the darkness, moaning, until all was still and white around the sobbing boy between the benches.

But the ghost stumbled on, groping along the walls of Man-Pu-Ko-Chu, as the sinner had groped his way toward the canal. When he stumbled out of the porchway, toward the wash house, forty years had gone up in smoke; the miracle of that night in the first hall of the Salvation Army seemed to have been a pious legend. Instead of going in through the lighted doorway, he had groped on along the walls of the dark city, year after lightless year, to end up as an old man at the black water toward which he had set out forty years ago.

He lit the candle, as he had done for so many nights, to try once more in its timid light to cleanse himself and to pray for an angel in his terrible need. He undressed with the clumsy movements of a drunkard, his shadow reeling on the wall; then he put the candle on the edge of the well. He stood naked in the wash house, his hands on the edge of the well, and looked down at the black water. The candle flame flickered, and he saw a face below, as he had seen it from that bridge.

A drop of sweat fell from his forehead. It fell for a long time, then it hit the water and the face moved. It quivered, distorted, then became still again. A second drop fell, distorted the face; this time it looked as if hands were growing from it, reaching for the rope of the bucket. The hands closed round the rope and began to pull up a white body, lifting its shoulders out of the water. He wanted to flee, to close his eyes, but the hallucination kept him in its spell. A third drop fell, hit the water; the hands slithered down the rope, the body sank back into the water, but the head remained. Its eyes died, its nostrils rotted away, its ears vanished, its cheeks became gutted with gruesome pits, its mouth was eaten away to a lascivious grimace. He cried out, and staggered back from the well, for he had seen Betsy as she was now. "Oh, God!" he cried. "Save me, save me!"

But there was no answer. No still white hand rose behind him to bless him with peace. A giant bat flew hooting past the window. In the dark eaves small animals stirred.

"Save me," he prayed, "save me, O Lord, save me!" He cringed in despair, for in the red darkness behind his eyelids the devil was remolding the head into a new face, a face so terrible with temptation that he cowered against the wall, his hands over his face, praying, "Save me, save me, save me," very softly, for she must not hear it, she must not find out how weak he was, how defenseless against her passion.

"Come on!" she cried. "Look, you sky pilot! Open your eyes, little Jesus! Come on, look! Look at me!"

"Save me," he prayed, "save me, save me," but her fingers closed round his wrists and pulled his hands away. "Coward!" she whispered, her breath hot on his face. "You slimy little traitor! Open your eyes! Look!"

Then God heard his prayer, and a still strength flowed into him. He opened his eyes and said, "Yes, Betsy."

She stood over him, her eyes flashing in the gaslight, her hair loose, her naked body glistening with sweat. The heat in the little room was unbearable, the stove purred; her eyes bored into his with a hellish strength. Her face was white and hard; her breasts were white and hard; her thighs were white and hard; she stood over him like a devil hewn in marble. "So!" she said, "now you'll answer me!"

"Yes, Betsy," he said. "God bless you."

"Shut up!" she screamed, and struck his face again, so fiercely this time that his head hit the wall. "Answer! Why wouldn't you look? Why didn't you say 'Hello, darling'?"

"I couldn't, Betsy," he said. "God knows, I couldn't."

"Keep God out of this!" she cried. "You can fool the others, but not me. Out with it! Why couldn't you look at me? Why did you look away, you pious little sneak?"

"I couldn't, Betsy," he said.

"Why not? Don't you want to know me any more? Are you too good for me, now you've got a peaked cap on?"

"No, Betsy," he said. "I just couldn't."

"Have you got another girl?"

"No, Betsy," he said. "I've got no one except Jesus."

"Shut up! Shut up! Shut up!" she screamed, and slapped his face left and right until his ears rang and his cheeks tingled. Save me, he prayed, save me, save me, I can't hold out any longer, I want to grab her, hit her. . . .

"Where have you been all this time?" she asked, suddenly so quietly that he opened his eyes with a feeling of relief. She still stood over him and her eyes were as devilish as before, but no longer flashed with fury. They had become dreamy and gentle, the eyes of a malicious woman. He saw how bad she was, how obscene, and yet he knew that he would always, always love her, even if she were to turn into the devil himself. "Yes, Betsy," he said.

"Don't be silly," she said, smiling. "You look at me as if I were Sander. I won't touch you again, don't be afraid. I don't hit men who won't hit back. You can take it easy, Jesus." She stood up, went to the bed and lay down, the way she had been lying when he came in. He realized now that he had walked into a trap. It had all been a hoax: Lola, stumbling into the Salvation Army post when he was alone there, calling, "An accident, an accident! Soldiers, help! An accident!" Jet, crying, "A nigger has stabbed Betsy! Quick! Quick!" as he ran into the taproom of The Broken Heart, followed by Lola.

He heard a furtive noise behind the door; somebody was listening. Perhaps Sander, perhaps the girls; perhaps all of them were listening on the landing to Betsy the Doll raping Silly Willem, who had come back as a sky pilot, wearing a peaked cap.

"I am sorry I hit you," she said, lying on her back on the bed, her hands under her head. "I didn't mean to. I'm sorry."

"That's all right," he said. "It doesn't matter. I love you, Betsy."

"I love you too," she said. "Do you know that?"

"No," he said.

"Then why do you think I went to collect that photograph of yours in the bowler hat, for three guilders fifty? I even went all the way to the seaside to find the little man and collect that other photograph of the two of us on the beach. One guilder twenty, plus the trip there and back.

Why do you think I ran after you on my bare feet that night you banged on the door—or don't you remember that?"

"Yes," he said, "I do."

"I screamed, 'Wim, Wim, Wim!' but you wouldn't look round. Were you already afraid of me then?"

"In a different way," he said. "If I had turned round then, I might have murdered you."

"Since that night I've let no other man touch me," she said. "Did you know that?"

"No," he said.

"They don't call me Betsy the Doll any more, but Betsy the Teaser. Everybody knows that I'm waiting for you, and that I'll only let them kiss me. Jet wants to throw me out, but I've hung on because of you, so that you would know where to find me. In the daytime I work in a laundry. Do you believe that?"

"Yes," he said.

"Here," she said, stretching out her hands. "Look at these if you don't believe me. Just look."

"I believe you, Betsy," he said.

"Go on, look," she said. "I won't touch you, honestly. Just look at my hands. Look how red they are."

He looked at her hands. "Yes," he said. "I see." She was lying, small and naked, on the white bed. She could have been a child, but for her eyes. They were deep blue now, and very drowsy. He was afraid of them.

"Come and sit beside me," she said. "I won't do anything."

He sat down beside her; the springs of the bed creaked, and he thought of the night he had stood behind the curtain.

"I love you," she said. "I love you so much that I don't mind sharing you with Jesus. Do you know that?" Her voice sounded innocent and sincere, but her eyes looked at him in a way that made him tremble. God, he thought, not that. I beseech you, God, not that.

"You still look as if you were afraid," she said. "I'm not doing anything, am I? Or are you afraid of yourself?"

"Yes," he said.

"Why? If you love me it's no sin, is it? Or is it?"

"No, Betsy," he said. "Not that."

"Then what?" she asked. "Is it a sin that I love you? Won't Jesus allow us to love one another?"

"Not that," he said. "Not that."

She looked at him, intently, without moving. It was incredible that so frail a girl could be so strong that she dared to challenge God. In the sand dunes she had lain just like this. "I wish I could lay my hands on Him one day," she had said. Now she had.

"Have you ever thought about that night?" she asked.

He knew at once which night she meant. "Yes," he said.

"Often?"

"Yes."

"So have I. If I hadn't felt the point of that knife I might never have found out that I couldn't do without you. I wanted to do without you. I wanted you to go and kill yourself."

"I know," he said. "I almost did."

"I saw that," she said, "the night you banged on the door. I wanted to save you, but Jesus has beaten me to it." Her eyes were now terrible with tenderness. "And now? Have you come back to convert us?" she asked.

"No," he said.

"Why else?"

"To help. To help and . . ."

"Silly boy," she said. "As if I didn't know why."

He looked at her with a silent prayer, for her eyes were now stronger than his.

"You've come back because of me," she said, "and I've waited for you. Here I am, yours alone. Kiss me."

"No," he said. "Not that."

"Kiss me, kiss me," she said.

"No, no," he said. "No, Betsy, I beseech you. . . ."

Her arms came up, slowly. "Yes," she said. "Yes, yes, yes."

He hid his face in his hands and felt her grope through his prayer. Her hands were light and soft and small, a child's. He should not hide his face, for then he forgot her eyes, and her eyes were the only things that betrayed her. She hung around his neck, her head back, her mouth open for his kiss. Her hair hung down on the pillow, and her eyes were almost closed, but he knew that she was peering at him through the lashes.

"It will be a terrible fight, Betsy," he said, "but God will win."

"Kiss me," she said. "Kiss me, darling, darling, kiss me."

"I'll pray for you," he said, "every night, every day. I'll pray that God may break your heart; for you are bad, Betsy, and very strong."

"I can't stand it any longer!" she cried. "Come, come! I'm going mad!"

"I have not come to convert you," he said, "for that I can't do. Only you can do that, if God wills it."

"God!" she sneered. "Has he got a beard?"

"I'll pray, Betsy," he said. "I'll pray, and God will win."

"I'm praying too," she said, her head still back, her mouth open for his kiss. "I pray to you, I adore you, without you I'll kill myself."

"All right," he said. "Kill yourself, Betsy. God will win."

"I'll go on the streets again," she said. "I'll take other men to bed with me, tonight, tonight!"

"No," he said, "not that."

"Tonight!" she said. "The first man I meet I'll take to bed with me. I'll be drunk, blind drunk with misery, and I'll let him undress me."

"I could strangle you now, Betsy," he said. "I could beat you to death; but God bless you, God will win."

When she pulled herself up toward his mouth, he loosened her hands and that was difficult, for she was stronger than she had ever been; her naked body trembled with strength. As her hands slipped she bit at him, but her teeth snapped like a dog's. Then she opened her eyes, and she no longer concealed anything; she was a naked angel of hate.

"I love you, Betsy," he said. "God bless you."

Their eyes fought it out, while their bodies remained motionless; then she spat in his face and fell back on the bed, sobbing.

She was so pathetic in her defeat, so small, so helpless, that he leaned against the door after shutting it behind him, for he had almost, almost kissed her then.

There was no one on the landing; there was no one on the stairs either. In the taproom the blue boy was sitting at a table, underneath the hand of Heineken's beer.

"Hullo," said the boy.

"Hullo," he said.

They went out together, back to the post, where Sister Agnes was making cocoa for the meeting that night, stirring a pan on the pot-bellied stove. He wept as they knelt between the benches to pray; the boy put his hand on his shoulder, and it seemed as if nothing had changed in that year, except that he knew now that God would win.

Children's voices jeered outside, firecrackers fell between the benches, burned and banged, but God would win.

Raucous men's voices shouted curses through the broken window; whores screamed obscenities in the doorway; bottles and stones crashed onto the platform; but God would win.

Hooligans crowded into the hall, smashed the chairs, kicked the sinners' bench to firewood, flung boiling chocolate at the praying sky pilot, everywhere was the splintering noise of destruction, but God would win.

Drunken viragos ran like furies through the fog, shrieking derision at the three fools of Christ, who went out to help where no help was wanted, to succor the sick who spat at them, while the carts of the devil rattled through the alleys, laden with sloshing vats, but God would win.

For the message of liberation for those enslaved by the devil and of forgiveness for those who had committed a mortal sin was blown across the country with the smoke of persecution; crowds of converts fell in behind the flag of the Cross and went back into the dark dungeons of their past with the torch of mercy, to make the hallelujah echo in a labyrinth where no man who had not been born there himself could find his way; God would win!

The flag of the Cross fluttered higher every day; from every smoking wreckage, every torn-up tent, every splintered barge the converts arose, singing, cheering, partisans of God, whose song of battle made the empty churches echo and rattled the windows of the taverns; God would win!

Brewers and church councils conspired against the obsessed, who threatened to overthrow the social order by driving criminals from the brothels and beer houses into the church; preaching clergymen shook their fists at the sky, calling down damnation on the heads of the heretics, the antichrists, the red beasts from the Revelation; but God would win!

Pimps, thieves, trollops and drunkards joined the Salvation Army, and marched through the land, singing, as they pulled in God's nets; the members of the established church took over the sins the converts had cast off and robbed, burned, destroyed, violated, tortured children, set fire to haystacks, mutilated sheep, trampled crops and jeered at the meek, but God would win!

General Booth, prophet of the oppressed, sent his daughter and her husband to Holland to take over command of the Salvation Army; the massed brass bands of the Army marched triumphantly through the alleys, banging and clashing, for now the hour of that last fortress had struck; now God would win!

And then, when God's victory was in sight, the blow fell. The General's daughter and her husband turned traitors: they secretly joined the followers of an evangelist in America who claimed that he was the reincarnation of the Prophet Elijah. The couple left the country at dead of night, leaving a letter in which they called the message of the Salvation Army a heresy.

Lieutenant Willem Waterreus and the blue boy were far away, in the provinces; the news of the disaster was brought to them by a drenched soldier, who had cycled through the rainswept night and arrived covered with mud, a messenger of doom. The Commanders had deserted, mutiny had broken out among the troops in Amsterdam, terrible scenes were taking place in the red district, where the furies danced, naked to the waist, to waltzes played by a brass band of deserters in the alleys, with masks on their faces and streamers round their necks. The fate of the Army in Holland was in the balance; if the mutiny in the red district wasn't quelled before sunrise it would mean the end.

But God would win, even if the devil danced on the barricades; the blue boy and he rode to Amsterdam on a tandem, through the smoking darkness of a downpour that sewed heaven and earth together with a billowing curtain. They rode, without stopping, for nine hours, and arrived at dawn; the blue boy stumbled into the ruins that were left of the post, knelt between the wreckage of the benches and fell asleep praying, in the rain; but Lieutenant Waterreus went to The Broken Heart, lucid with exhaustion, obsessed by one relentless, hammering thought: *"God will win!"*

As he tore open the door everyone looked up. She was sitting on the table in front of the mirror, her head tilted, the feather broken, her hair loose, her breasts bared, soggy streamers round her neck, and her eyes flashed with triumph. For around her lolled and hiccupped the deserters from Christ's Army with donkeys' ears, pigs' heads, cardboard noses and funny hats, singing "Daisy, Daisy, give me your answer, do." When the door crashed against the wall, they stopped singing and gaped at him from the tangle of streamers, the brass embrace of their tubas. She took the beer bottle from her mouth and stared at him too with glassy eyes.

"Back to the post, brothers," he said, without looking at them, for his eyes held hers with such power that she sobered under the impact of his white rage. "Back to your duty, soldiers," he said, quietly and without raising his voice. "We serve God and His Son, not a couple from England. Go back to the post, and pray that our True General in heaven will not damn you for your sins."

Nobody moved; the tuba player hiccupped, beer splashed in the coils of his instrument. He looked at him and said: "Come on, sergeant"; and the tuba player got up and staggered outside, for his eyes were terrible to see.

Then she screamed, a scream of hatred, and hurled the bottle at him. It struck him in the face, he staggered under the blow, and a shock of rage shot through his arms into his fists. For one second God and the devil fought the final battle over his soul, his life; then he opened his eyes. Blood was running from his nose, over his mouth, down his chin; it dripped onto the brass S on his collar, and he said, with deep gratitude, "Thank you, Betsy. That was the hand of God."

But she didn't lower her eyes as he had done when he heard the same words said to him. She looked at him unflinchingly, and said: "No, Jesus, you won't get *me!*" Then she jumped off the table and swept out with such impressive dignity that it seemed as if she had not drunk a drop that night. He went back to the post, awed by her grandiose wickedness; but God would win.

Then came the night when a woman screamed in the mist that had risen from the canals after a day of stifling heat. Many people heard it; they pushed up their windows and leaned out, calling to one another in the mist; but no one went out into the street to investigate, except the soldiers from the Salvation Army post. It had been the scream of a woman in mortal terror; the soldiers ran along the canal, calling, thinking someone must have fallen into the water, but none of those who leaned from their windows had heard a splash. Then steps came running out of an alley and someone shouted a word that made the windows come rattling down and the doors slam shut. The word was "leper."

The soldiers ran after the man who had called, all except Lieutenant Waterreus, for he heard someone approaching along the alley, someone weakly singing.

The singing was more frightening than the screaming of the woman had been. As it drew nearer, he became afraid; when he saw it everything in him wanted to flee, screaming as the woman had done. But God would win; whatever it might be that now staggered toward him out of the mist, singing, he would face it in Christ's name.

He looked straight at it and said: "God bless you." He did not know whether it was a man or a woman, so much had its face been ravaged by the disease. It was a leper, drunk, brandishing a bottle. It lashed out at him with the bottle as he came near, but the gesture was too much for it. It fell on the cobbles; the bottle emptied with a gurgling sound. Then it lay still like something fallen from a cart.

He thought it must be an old woman, for the rags that covered the lower part of the body looked like a skirt. He knew by hearsay that in some cellars and attics of the district lepers were hiding, but he had never seen one before. He did not dare look at the body for long, for he knew that if he did his strength would give way. He bent over it, closed his eyes, and lifted it up in his arms.

It was very light, but the stench was so terrible that he would need the strength of an archangel to carry it to the hospital. But God would win; he started to walk slowly through a deserted city as in a dream.

As he entered the alley of The Broken Heart people, who had watched him coming from afar, fled away at his approach. A child stumbled and fell; he waited until someone had snatched it away before he moved on. The moment of waiting had made him feel faint; he knew he could not go much further, but God would win, God would win, although this was worse than anything he had ever known. He advanced a few steps past the spot where the child had fallen, and saw a shadow standing in the fog, barring his way. The shadow did not move as he approached; it seemed petrified by what it saw. It stood facing him, motionlessly, like Lot's wife. He waited for it to step aside; when it did not he whispered, "Get away, away; this is a leper," but the shadow did not move. He staggered, prayed; God would win, God would . . . Then he collapsed.

O God, he prayed, God, God, send your angel. . . .

Then the angel put a hand on his shoulder, helped him rise and took the body from his arms; only as she moved away did he see who it was. He called, "Betsy! Betsy, don't! Betsy!" but she did not look round; she went slowly into the mist with her hideous burden. He stumbled after her, tried to take the body from her arms, but she walked on without a word, looking straight ahead, carrying the leper.

She carried it further than he could ever have done, right into the courtyard of the hospital. Nurses in white came out, and fled back indoors.

They stood waiting in the mist for a long time, then three men in white arrived with a trolley. She laid the leper down on the trolley, and it was wheeled away. One of the men beckoned them to follow him. He wore a white cap; a white mask covered the lower part of his face. They followed him into the hospital that was high and dark. The man called others, and they surrounded them like a guard; a door was opened for them; the man said: "Take off your clothes and throw them in the hole in the floor." Then the door was closed behind them with a sound of bolts, and they stood face to face in a cellar.

A white vapor started to rise around them, as if they had taken the mist with them. The vapor rose in clouds and made them cough. Then she took off her hat with the ostrich feather and threw it into a hole in the floor, a grave in the stones. She unbuttoned her dress, coughing. He undressed also. When at last they were naked and leaned against the wall, side by side, she looked up at him in a way she had never looked at him before. Her eyes were changed. They were very light, the purest eyes he had ever seen.

"Now I'll never be able to kiss you again," she said.

He thought she meant because of the leper.

"I knew it would be like this," she said, "if ever He got hold of me. If I were to kiss you again after all this, all would have been for nothing."

Then he understood what she meant and it was as if God struck him down, now that He had triumphed at last. "Oh, darling," he said, "darling, darling . . ." But she vanished slowly in the mist, she seemed to evaporate before his eyes like a ghost. He wanted to touch her, but there was nothing. He groped vainly in the mist that grew darker, bluer; he called her name but there was no answer. When he knelt on the flagstones, he felt the coldness of the wall against his bare side. Wings palpitated among the eaves, he took his hands from his eyes and saw the candle flame flutter on the edge of the well, in the fog that descended on Man-Pu-Ko-Chu every morning before sunrise, billowing out of the valleys like smoke. He stared at the candle flame with feverish eyes, listening. In the fog a red glow dawned, like a distant fire. It reddened the clouds that were billowing, downy and wavelike toward the darkness, red clouds over a field. He stood listening, his head on one side, holding his breath, but he heard nothing. There was only the distant crackling of the fire and the moaning of the wounded boy beside him on the ground.

"I hear nothing," he said.

She did not answer; she looked as if she were standing at the edge
of eternal darkness in her dusty uniform and her soldier's hat, a sentry at
the edge of the world. She tried to peer through the red smoke, her hand
over her eyes. "Hello!" she called with a long-drawn-out note. "Anybody
there?" But there was no answer, not even an echo from space. She
looked round; her eyes glinted in the glow of the fire. "Yet I'm certain I
heard . . ." She saw in his eyes that he had seen something behind her,
and she turned round. In the distance something was approaching, something white, above the ground mist of the smoke.

It seemed to float disembodied in the night: a white face. Smoke billowed red behind the vision; it threw a high shadow onto the clouds. It
was a tall man in a black cassock with white bands hanging from the
neck, slowly approaching from eternal darkness, an angel of death.

"Who are you?" she called in a clear voice, without a trace of the fear
he knew she must feel, for she had never asked anyone who he was before;
she had alway seen for herself.

The black shape did not answer. It was a tall man in clerical robes; he
looked at the burning house behind them, at the wounded boy, at them, his
eyes red in his white face, like the eyes of a dog in the sunset.

"Could you please call a doctor?" she asked. "There is someone
wounded."

The black figure directed his gaze at her for the first time and said,
"No."

"Could you show me the way, then?" she asked. "We must get a doctor."
"No."

"Are you the clergyman here?"
"Yes."

"Did you tell the farmers to shoot at us?"
"Yes."

"To set the farm on fire? To kill the cattle?"
"Yes," said the black figure.

She looked at him long and intently and then she asked: "Why,
brother?"

He heard a great compassion in her voice that surprised him. He had
often been afraid of her courage; never before had he heard this compassion
in her voice. He had been afraid when she put on her uniform for the
first time and walked through the alleys, carrying a board on two poles
saying, *I am the happy Betsy.* All the thugs and the trollops of the alleys

danced screaming around her, throwing filth and stones at her, ripped
off her hat, pulled her hair, tore her clothes, but she walked on, the board
lifted over her head, and lured the screaming mob into the little hall. He
had been afraid during her first sermon when she stood underneath the
beams, her eyes flashing in the glaring light, utterly alone in the face of a
hallful of roaring brutes who shouted obscenities, spat at her, taunted her
with lewd noises. He had been afraid when she silenced them with a
gesture of great strength and said to them, "Now you are laughing, boys,
but wait till God gets you. I've had most of you in my arms, I know how
black your bodies are; one day God will have you in His arms and see
how black your souls are, and what then, boys? What then? Do you
think you'll be able to say then 'Bye, God, see you later,' as you said to me?"
It was a language that made the Salvationists on the platform stare at one
another, blanching; it in no way resembled the meek message of love they
had preached for so long with such undaunted cheerfulness; it was the
language of a prophet; it silenced one hundred jeering men and made
them forget to chew their tobacco. She spoke for more than an hour;
during that hour, the ramparts between the Old and the New Testament
were breached and taken by storm by an angel of wrath, and through the
warbling of the flutes and the strumming of the harps of passive humility
blared the trumpets of Jericho. Until then, the Salvationists had tried to
convert the hordes of sin with the dove that was the Son; she unleashed
the eagle that was the Father, the Lord of Hosts, the Caster of Mountains
and Baler of Oceans, Whose glory is written on the bridles of stallions. Her
first convert was Sander. He jumped to his feet, stumbled to the front,
and crashed on his knees in the conversion seat like a poleaxed ox. "Goddamn you, Jesus, help me!" he cried; and she said, "Take your quid out
of your mouth, you are addressing the Light of the World."
    The soldiers sat staring in speechless horror at this language of the
galleys, but it was the beginning of a triumphant march that soon
reached the fury of a revolution. She assailed the devil with pitch and
boiling lead, broke the centuries-old siege of sin, liberated the doomed
and debased; she battled with flashing eyes and flying hair, lifting the
flaming sword of her faith over her head with both hands, and slamming
it down with the strength of the Judges. Two women brought the Light
to the dark alleys of Amsterdam: Sister Agnes, the gentle one, who nursed
the sick and the children and slaved for the old and the helpless with the
patience of a saint; she was given the name of "The Angel Adjutant"; the

other was Soldier Wilders, "The Tigress," who once was known as "Betsy the Doll," and who now stood facing a black preacher whose congregation had broken up the first Salvationists' meeting in his parish with fire, shot at them from the darkness with sawed-off guns, and wounded the fair-haired boy. The murderers and fire raisers had trooped off singing in the night, and now all she said was, "Why, brother?" with a compassion that was more impressive than her courage. For the first time in his life he felt a respect for her that was greater than love.

But the black preacher was not moved. He looked down at her stonily and replied, "Because you are children of Belial, prophets of the devil, trying to entice the damned with false promises of grace."

"Didn't Jesus preach grace for the damned?" she asked.

"Jesus was too broadminded sometimes," said the man. "I am a servant of the Father, the Lord of Hosts, the King of Kings, and my curse be upon you. I curse you, woman, and call upon you eternal damnation."

"Curses will not lead you to heaven," she said.

"Heaven!" the black preacher cried, his voice strident with righteousness. "Who told you, poor fool, that either you or I shall inherit the kingdom of God?"

"Jesus did," she answered. "To-day shalt thou be with me in paradise."

When he heard her say this, he closed his eyes. Her voice and that of the black preacher faded away in a deepening silence as if they were drifting away from him. "I say unto you," the black preacher cried, "that you are hagglers in the face of God, trying to barter good deeds for eternal salvation. Only those who obey God's commandments in full acceptance of predestination, only those who perform good deeds knowing that they may be eternally and irrevocably damned, do truly serve my God."

"I serve a God of love," she said, far away. The black preacher's answer echoed in a hollow emptiness: "I serve a terrible God."

He saw a fluttering light, a candle flame in a blue dusk, and tightened his grip on the hand of the wounded boy. But he seemed to be sinking slowly into a pit of loneliness, an utter desolation. Animals rustled in the darkness, a kalong circled round the waringin, the kampong lay listening to its plaintive call. Outside the mosquito curtain day was breaking in a blue misty dawn. The loneliness became so bleak that tears came to his eyes, and he lay silently crying. During the day he could hide it from himself; as soon as it was light and they awoke and knelt together in prayer, he would forget his suffering by bending over the greater suffering of the lepers. After another day of nursing the sick he would feel deeply thankful that his own grief enabled him to understand many things in others; but now, after months of selfless work among the outcasts of the earth, he knew that leprosy was not the worst, as he had once thought. The worst was loneliness.

When she came toward him that night in Holland in the little hall where they had taken the Salvationists' oath together; when she said, "Willem, I want to go to the Indies, I am no longer needed here," he said, "Ah?" with deep dejection, for he had hoped against hope that one day they might find their way back to human love. Then she said, "The Commander says that, being a woman, I cannot go alone. Will you marry me?" He answered, "Yes, Betsy." She put her hand on his and said, "Dear Willem." So they sat for a long time, at the table in the kitchen, underneath the oil lamp. They did not speak, they did not look at one another; they just sat like that, her hand on his; and what he had felt then as a sadness had now turned into a torment. Again her hand covered his, but now she slept; he lay in the darkness, alone with his thoughts. He had never foreseen that God would punish him for his sins in this way; they had been married for over a year, and never once in all those months, those weeks, those hours had they touched one another except like this. Every night they lay side by side on their camp beds in the kampong of the lepers, man and wife, but between them lay a sword. On their arrival in Batavia they had sent a telegram to General Booth: *Standing by for the fight, your first soldiers in the Far East. Await your orders, Lieutenants W. Waterreus and B. Waterreus-Wilders,* and the answer had come: *Look for the worst, Booth.* What they found was worse than they had ever imagined, but when the night covered the horrors of the day and they lay side by side, hand in hand, he listened to her even breathing and was alone with the worst. Suddenly her voice came out of the darkness.

"Are you awake—Willem?"

He gazed at the blue square of the doorway, swallowed, and answered, "Yes."

"Are you crying?"

"No," he said, "no."

But she said, "You mustn't lie, Willem. I love you."

"Oh, Betsy!" he cried and he could not keep the sob out of his voice. Her hand moved and he heard her bed creak softly. Then he felt his bed move and her hand on his hair. "I know, darling," she whispered, with a small warmth in his ear. "I know, I know. I've known all along. I feel exactly the same, you see."

"Oh, Betsy."

"I love you, I love you so much that I don't know what to do about it. All the lepers in the world wouldn't be enough. . . ."

"Don't," he said, "don't."

"I must!" she whispered, desperately, "I can't keep it to myself any longer. I can't, I . . . I don't think I am really converted."

"Dearest . . ." he said, startled at first, then almost laughing; but she continued, urgently, "I have never been able to forget you, never; when you were living in The Broken Heart, when you were gone, when you joined the Salvation Army; God only knows what I did to get you back for myself, myself alone. God only knows. But when you came in that night and I threw that bottle at your head, I did it because I knew then that I would never have you back for myself alone, never, and when I saw you carry that sick woman, I . . . I wasn't converted—no, no, Willem! Let me say it, let me say it quickly, while it is still dark, I . . . I've never been really truly completely converted. I've been fighting God all the time, in secret, because I thought: one day I'll have him back for myself alone, one day he'll give me all the love he's now squandering on others, who have nothing to do with him, who . . . Please, Willem! Willem, let me tell it, I . . . When we came out to the Indies, I was a coward, I shouldn't have come to the Indies, I should . . . I don't know. I don't know what I was going to say. I—I suddenly have the feeling as if it wasn't true, as if nothing was true, as if . . . oh, Willem, Willem, every night, for over a year now, I've longed for you, yearned for you, every night, but I know, I *know* that after one kiss all would have been for nothing, that everything I am trying to forget every day, day after day, would come back all at once. If you were to take me in your arms now, my darling, darling, darling, I . . . I'd let all the lepers go to hell, I . . ." She fell silent, so suddenly that he held his breath; for he sensed that she was listening, alarmed, with all the fibers of her body taut. She lay motionless beside him on the bed, then she slowly started to tremble. "What . . ." he whispered, but she put her hand on his and he stopped. They lay like this for a time, hardly breathing, listening, but he could hear nothing. At last he could bear it no longer and whispered, "What is it?" It sounded like a shout in the tense silence.

"I thought I heard something go past outside."

"What?"

"A horse."

"A horse . . . ? There are no horses here."

"No," she whispered. "I must have imagined it."

They lay silent for a while, staring at the square of the door that had grown lighter. He had so many things to say that he found it dffiicult to know where to began. Finally he said, "Dearest, I think that we . . ."

But she was gone.

All that had happened in the wash house in Man-Pu-Ko-Chu was that the square of the doorway had grown lighter in the darkness. Soon it would be morning.

He saw himself get up—a naked old man supporting himself on the edge of the well as he groped for his clothes. He saw how thin he was, an emaciated old body in the candlelight. He saw himself gather his clothes together, put on his trousers; he saw how he had to support himself once more on the edge of the well. Then he saw himself bend over the edge, his thin arms spread out, his shoulders high and pointed, and he realized that he was about to open his eyes and stare into the well once more. A terrible anguish overcame him, for he knew that something would happen if he were to look into that well once more. He tried to pull himself away, but he could not; he was bodiless. He wanted to shout; but he had no voice. A very high shrill sound throbbed in the silence, like a tautening high chord, tauter, tauter—the chord snapped and tore the silence with a shriek: "*Amok!*"

He jumped up, the end of the bandage slipped from his hands like a blood-soaked streamer, fluttered in the wind. They all looked up—the lepers, the animals, Betsy herself, who knelt in the center of the clearing in the jungle, a white figure of mercy among the dark prostrate bodies.

The shriek came tearing out of the forest; birds billowed out of the foliage, branches cracked, dry leaves came rustling down, then the devil burst forth from the undergrowth with a flash of sunlight on a kris. The crazed leper sprang among the bodies, his kris flashed, stabbed, flashed and stabbed. Then hell broke loose. The lepers, until that moment a crawling, moaning mass, arose like one roaring monster. Panic lashed them to their feet and into the forest, shrieking, trampling, fighting, all sound mingled into one drawn-out soaring scream; then the madman, slavering, panting, splashed with the blood of his insane butchery, disfigured by the suppurant sores of his gruesome disease, stood still. He had flailed and hacked about him in the weak mass of the fleeing bodies; now he stood still, the dripping kris in his fist, his head low, his legs spread, his muscles tensed for the leap. She stood, small and white, facing him. Behind her cowered the little flock of those who could not crawl away on the stumps of their mutilated limbs, wailing helplessly in the face of approaching death. She had stood like this many times, alone opposite a drunken brawler that six men had not been able to hold, to master him with a look; but now she was lost. This was no drunkard from the slums; this was a demon from the jungle, so tortured by leprosy and thirst and the flies in his wounds that he had broken loose in an orgy of demented slaughter. All the fury of a senselessly tortured humanity stood facing her, with bloody foam on his lips, and the eyes of the devil. They stood for a moment transfixed: she, the leper and he, only the bandage fluttered in the wind. Then she stretched out her hand toward the kris, but the leper sprang loose from the spell of her eyes. Instead of coming to her aid, he fell with a cry of horror on his knees, his hands in front of his face. He wanted to pray, to get up and fight; he lay as if paralyzed, breathing the sickly smell of the bandage, feeling the burning heat of the sun on his hands. Suddenly his hands grew cooler, and he took them slowly from his face. The first thing he saw was the shadow which lay cast over him, the shadow of an angel with a sword. Then he looked up, slowly. He saw her shoes, the blood on her white skirt, the kris in her hand, her torn blouse, her hair, hanging loose over her bare shoulder; then he saw her neck, where a small pulse throbbed under the red imprint of a hand; he saw her mouth, soft and open; and then he saw her eyes.

He did not see the leper lying on the ground behind her, his arms wide like a distorted cross; he did not see the others that came crawling, limping and stumbling back from the wilderness. All he saw was her eyes, wide and astonished in her small white face against the sky. They were the eyes of a baffled child.

He took her back to the kampong, to their cabin underneath the waringin, with his arm round her shoulders. As he took the kris out of her hand, opening her fingers cautiously, he saw a red scratch, that went from her wrist across the back of her hand to the little ring he had bought for her when they were married. He undressed her in the hot little room, threw the clothes on a fire outside; meanwhile she did not speak, her face remained unchanged, she still seemed to be staring at something that she did not understand. He threw the kris into the fire, then he brought water and Lysol, and washed her. All the time she went on staring at the doorway, that grew darker as the fire started to smoke. The smoke filled the little room with thin gray veils; when he had washed her, she stood in a blue mist that billowed low on the ground. Then, suddenly, her eyes narrowed in understanding and all childishness vanished from her face before a great, human fear. He wanted to go toward her but she lifted her hand; he listened with her, staring into the fog, in speechless apprehension.

A knocking sound approached in the silence, a thudding, a drumming, it came crashing toward them, right across the wilderness; she threw her arms round his neck, pressed herself against him, crying with fear; and, while a horse and rider thundered by through the darkness, they sank down in a kiss.

A bell tolled, somewhere in the silence, one metallic stroke. She moved her head with her eyes closed, from side to side, from side to side, but the unbearable delight had turned into unbearable pain, as the bell struck. He stood up, wanted to shake her, to wake her up, but a hand touched his shoulder. "You'd better go now," said a woman's voice. "Go now, it won't be long." He looked at the woman imploring, for he wanted to stay; they couldn't send him away now, he wanted to be with her in these moments of ultimate pain, or he would forever be haunted by the vision of her face, distorted in agony, rolling from side to side, from side to side with her eyes closed. Then the doctor came and agreed that he had better go now, the room was too small for the three of them. He went outside with despair in his heart; in the doorway, he turned round once more and saw her head move in the halo of her hair on the pillow, from side to side, from side to side, in unbearable pain; then the sister closed the door. He stood in a white passage with a flickering candle flame over the door at the far end; behind the net curtains in the windows zoomed the mosquitoes. As he stood there, he knew that if he lost her he would die. The thought of her death was terrible, much more real than after her struggle with the leper when they had known the fear of the disease every night. Then a thin crying began to squeal in the silence behind the door, a small, angry bleating that became louder as the door was opened by the doctor. "Congratulations!" he said. "You have a daughter."

The bell tolled for a second time, the clanging sound quivered in the stillness. "Not so loud!" she whispered. "Tell Ahmed not to ring the bell so loud! He'll wake her up." He laughed, put his arm round her shoulders and said, "Dearest, a bell is a bell, you either ring it or you don't, you cannot ring it softly." She stood up beside the cradle, closed the lace curtain over it, and laughed too. He kissed her, and wanted to lead her away, but before they went out she opened the lace curtain once more and rearranged the little pillow; the slanting sunlight through the Venetian blinds sparked on her little ring. He followed her with his eyes when she crossed the courtyard in the sunlight, books under her arm, on her way to the Sunday school: a slender white figure with a black shadow, walking across the square of brown earth played bare by the children of the lepers in their first colony.

The bell struck for the third time, shrilly, a crack in the glass dome of silence. Even before she stood up by the fire with that old terror in her eyes, he recognized the sound, galloping toward them from the darkness. She stood up behind the flames as if she were rising from them, and her eyes were those of a martyr at the stake. Then the horse broke through the undergrowth, and the thudding of its hoofs became soft and slow among the lepers. As the horse's shiny brown chest flecked with foam loomed behind the fire, her eyes changed. She faced the rider the way she had faced the crazed leper, but the tenderness that motherhood had brought her shone from her eyes like a gentle light. She looked at the horseman with the strength and the love of twenty centuries of Christianity behind her.

It was a big man with a wild beard and the eyes of a butcher. "What are you doing here?" he asked, roughly.

"Helping," she answered. Her voice was hoarse and low, in a way he had never heard it. He stood up, holding a mass of dirty bandages.

"Are you out of your minds?" the man cried. "Do you know what you are doing?"

"Of course," she said. The man looked at him and his eyes were so merciless that all he could do was smile.

The horse neighed, and from all sides the mutilated bodies of the lepers came crawling near in the flickering firelight. "Who has given you permission?" the man shouted. His horse reared. "Don't you know leprosy is infectious? What precautions have you taken?"

"None," she said. "God protects us." He moved over behind her, put his hand on her shoulder, unnoticed by the man on the horse. A great peace radiated from her, and he knew that God was with her.

"Is that so?" the man asked, mockingly, staring at her hands. "Then let me tell you that your God has made a mug of you, for you have got it, my dear." He said it smilingly, but as he looked up from her hands at her eyes, his smile disappeared. "Yes," he continued, "you have leprosy! You'll be like they are! God knows how long it will take before He puts an end to you: maybe thirty years!"

When she still gave no sign of terror, but went on looking at him with that tender strength, the man dismounted, turned her toward the fire, took her hands, opened them, closed them, looked up. He said, "Who are you?"

As she did not answer, he said, "Salvationists," and his voice broke on the word.

The bell tolled a fourth time, with a harsh sound of despair; "Dearest!" he whispered, pressing her against him, "Don't look, dearest, don't look. . . ." She obeyed, and averted her eyes from the doctor who was bending over the cradle, whispering soothing words as he groped behind the curtain. She looked up at him; when he saw her eyes he pressed her head against his shoulder and whispered, "Dearest, dearest, dearest"; he could not think of anything else to say at the thin crying of the child, as it was taken out of the cradle, covered with a shawl and carried out. The doctor came back and put his hands on their shoulders and said that it was God's will, that it was for the good of the child, that they would see her again once she was a nice big girl, a real daughter; but he went on whispering, secretly, "Dearest, dearest, dearest . . ." until the thin crying had vanished in the silence. Then she sobbed, and he stroked her hair and went on whispering, while outside the wheels of a carriage rattled away.

The bell screeched, a shriek of unbearable torture, and she sank out of his arms. He fell on his knees by her; she rolled her head from side to side with her eyes closed, from side to side, from side to side, in the halo of her hair, spread out on the pillow. "Dearest," he cried, and shook her, but she did not answer. She rolled her head from side to side, from side to side, in agony; then he heard her voice, still and quiet, as from a great height.

"Brothers and sisters, fellow lepers," the voice said, "now God in His Mercy has given us a fortress in which to plant the banner of our love, I realize what a blessing it is that I may share your suffering."

The bell shrieked once more, and he shook her again and called, imploringly, "Dearest! Dearest . . ." but she did not answer. Her head rolled from side to side; from side to side in the halo of her hair, and he could do nothing, nothing at all to ease her suffering. At the same time he heard her voice, clear and gay, saying, "Brothers and sisters, fellow cripples, now I may face you this Christmas, marked in the same way as you are, I am filled with deep gratitude. For God has given us such joy, such hope, such fellowship together, that our radiance at this very moment shines like a beacon of hope for those still suffering in darkness."

The bell shrieked for the third time, filling the world with quivering rings of pain; "Dearest, dearest, dearest," he stammered, but she did not hear him any more, she did not feel his hands stroking her head, longing to share her torture. She heard nothing, she felt nothing, she rolled her head from side to side, from side to side with her eyes closed, while her voice said, higher and more joyful than before, "Brothers and sisters, fellow blind; now we are kneeling together once more at the manger of the Child, I cannot say anything, I cannot think of any prayer, only of a song of praise to the God of Love, who shines in our darkness with a light and a peace that pass all understanding."

The bell shrieked for the fourth time, and while her head rolled slower and slower, and he could find no words to think or to say, her voice whispered haltingly in a deep silence: "Brothers—sisters—paralyzed . . ." It stopped, and he held his breath; then it went on: "The moment—is not far off—when I—when I can no longer—speak to you—but my last—message . . ." She halted once more, and this time the silence lasted for so long that the world seemed to hold its breath, waiting for her last words. "God . . ." she whispered, "God is . . . God is Love."

The bell shrieked, shrieked; but her head moved no longer in the halo of her hair. She lay still, her eyes closed, her head on one side, as if she were listening.

He heard slow hoofbeats approach in the silence, and lifted his head to see who was coming. A white light drew near out of the red fog in which they were lying, and when it came closer, he saw that the light was seated on a white horse. Behind it came three more horses. A red horse, with the black preacher as its rider, who looked at him with merciless eyes in a white face. A black horse, with the crazed leper as a rider, who stared at him with mad eyes in a disfigured face. A gray horse, with the wild, bearded man as its rider, who bent his head as he looked at him, and tears rolled into his beard. Then the light dismounted from the white horse and lifted her up. He wanted to hold on to her, to pull her back in his embrace, back into the torture, the delight; he wanted to keep her for himself, whatever the price might be she would have to pay for it, for if she went away his life would turn to ashes. But the light took her, and lifted her onto the white horse. She was small in the light, a child with loose hair and closed eyes in a small white face. "Dearest!" he cried, but she did not answer. When the horses started to move away in the fog and the light drew away from him and the bell shrieked with despair, he slumped to the ground, sobbing, his hands over his face, for now there was no one left in this darkness, the eternal darkness of damnation, of loneliness.

Then an angel put his hand on his shoulder and said, "Captain."

"Oh, dearest, dearest," he wailed, "dearest, dearest."

"Captain Waterreus," said the angel, softly and urgently.

But he could not lift himself out of the despair. He shook his head, sobbing.

"Captain Waterreus, I can help you," the angel said. He raised his head and saw a white young man standing in the red mist, that billowed low over the ground, the smoke of purgatory. He stared at him, his face wet with tears, and stretched out his hands toward him, for he wanted to go home now. "Who . . . who are you . . . ?" he asked, still shaken by sobs.

"Anton," said the angel. "Anton Zorgdrager, Bert's friend."

"Ah," he said, "ah," and reality whipped him awake with the lashes of the bell.

"Come, Captain," said the boy. "Get up. I can help you."

"No," he said. "No, no, dear boy. Nobody can."

"Come," said the boy, gently helping him to his feet. "I can help you, believe me."

And then he dressed in the morning mist of a new day, while outside the bell went on tolling, calling the lepers to prayer.

When he came out of the wash house he looked up and saw the flag fluttering over the white buildings of Man-Pu-Ko-Chu in the first light of the sun. There were no clouds that morning; the sky was empty and blue. They crossed the courtyard, and vanished in the porchway. The sun struck golden sickles into the fog, and the shrouds sank slowly off the building, last sheaves of the night.

CHAPTER SEVEN

AFTER Anton had returned the previous night to the outbuilding where he was to sleep, he lit one more cigarette before going in, leaned against the wall and looked up at the stars. They were bigger and brighter than he had ever seen them and he forgot about the old man as he tried to identify the constellations. Then he dropped his cigarette, crushed it with his foot, turned to go in, and was suddenly struck by a memory. He was standing in a forest one starry night just like this, his foot on a discarded cigarette stub, about to turn away from the lantern-lit side of the tent on which Bert's silhouette was undressing. He shrugged his shoulders, as he had done then, and lifted the mosquito curtain to enter as he had then lifted the flap of his tent.

Doctor Vloemans lay naked on his bed, reading by the light of a candle that stood on a night table between the beds. He glistened with sweat in the golden light; the shadow of his book lay across his body. He looked up as Anton entered, but said nothing until he too lay on his bed, staring at the ceiling, where cobwebs billowed slowly in the draft. Then he said, "I am sorry, Zorgdrager, you were right."

"I beg your pardon?" Anton asked, gazing at Bert's silhouette among the cobwebs.

"The association shocked me, probably because I had never heard of such a possibility. Of course that was silly."

"I wouldn't let it worry you," Anton said, wanting to be alone with his vision. "I may be mistaken."

"No," said Vloemans "I'm sure you are not."

"Ah?"

"He has been talking about insomnia for some time, and at our purification meetings there were strange things in his prayers. . . ."

Anton listened, staring at the ceiling, and as the slow, precise voice of the young Salvationist unfolded his story, strange images came and went among the cobwebs. White shapes knelt in the hall with the texts on the wall, praying aloud with disturbing honesty, confessing sins that seemed ridiculous in their innocence; then the calm voice of the old Commander: "Deliver us from evil, O Lord, deliver us from the devil in the night." A lonely ghost roamed the ramparts in the moonlight; sounds of wailing were wafted across the courtyard by the night wind, breathlessly overheard by the lepers in their pavilions, the doctors on their iron beds. Fearsome cries seemed to emanate from the porchway, ceasing the moment anyone approached, and the lepers started to whisper about phantoms; for although they were converted, they still believed in hantus and guna-guna. Nobody ever mentioned it openly, but sometimes, in a delirium, patients whispered about the ghost from the well and prayed, panting, for the protection of Nonna Betsy, the only one who could protect them against the devil.

When Vloemans mentioned the woman in the mosquito tent in the white room, Anton nearly told him that he knew her daughter, for Bert's face was very clear on the ceiling. But he said nothing, and listened to the Salvationist, naked and steaming on the other bed, as he told him the story of her mother. Vloemans had known her when only her hands and feet were affected; he told of her physical decay and her spiritual triumph like a disciple in a fisherman's hut on the shore of the Dead Sea. Two thousand years seemed telescoped into one moment: the cobwebs billowed like the shadows of nets; the naked boy on the bed lay listening in awe, a young pagan from the mountains, to one of the first twelve Christians who had given him shelter for the night on his way to Damascus. "Although now she is no more than a dying trunk, without any means of communication with us, nobody can forget for a moment that she is there. The natives among the patients have started to worship her as if she were a spirit and there is nothing we can do about it. They believe in her omnipresence, they think she sees everything. To them, the shrouded bed in the white room is the Tabernacle in the Holy of Holies, and the Captain the High Priest . . .

And then, suddenly, the Salvationist fell asleep in the middle of his story. Anton lay listening to his regular breathing for a while, then he got up, dressed and went outside. The night was transparent with stars; the courtyard looked like a lake with its white cliffs and its caverns of darkness. He needed courage to detach himself from the shadow of the outbuildings, and to cross that lake, lonely as a boat in the starlight, toward the cave of the porchway. Inside the porchway the yellow light from the office window shone on the opposite wall. He entered stealthily on tiptoe; gravel crunched under his feet. He crept along close to the wall until he stood by the window, then, summoning his courage, he looked in.

The old man sat at the table, exactly as he had been sitting before. Moths swarmed around the lamp, their shadows wheeled across the wall. He wanted to enter, but the old man's stillness prevented him. He sat looking at a photograph album and seemed to have stopped dead in the act of turning a page. They both remained motionless for what seemed a long time, then the old man looked up. It was no more than a glance, but the expression in his eyes was so forbidding that Anton wavered, and turned back. He went quickly out of the porchway, crossed the courtyard, back to the warm safety of the room where the still burning candle watched over the sleeping Salvationist.

He undressed once more, lay down again, lit a cigarette at the candle flame, blew a cloud of smoke at the ceiling and saw the webs billow in the draft. The image of Bert forced itself upon him with unexpected vividness; he took his wallet from under his pillow and started to reread Els's letters.

Oh sweetheart, lover, if only you knew how I am longing for you every moment, every hour of the day and the night. . . .

He fell asleep, and was suddenly waked up. He sat upright in the chilly dawn and listened, staring at the doorway, behind which mist rolled like smoke. He did not know what had wakened him; it must have been a sound. All was silent, but for Vloemans' breathing. He shivered and warmed his shoulders with his hands, his arms crossed on his chest. As he touched his right shoulder, he knew what had wakened him. A hand had touched his shoulder.

He realized it without alarm; only the thought that it might have been a snake made him jump out of bed. There was no snake, only Els's letters, scattered on the floor. Then, somewhere in the mist, a bell began to toll.

When he went outside, the mist was cool and red. Halfway to the porchway, alone in a red world, he heard a voice, calling. It came from a small stone building, a wash house. "Dearest, dearest," the voice wailed. "Dearest, dearest."

On the floor of the wash house he found Bert's father, naked and in a delirium. He bent over him with great compassion but at the same time a feeling of power and said, "Captain . . ." as he put his hand on his shoulder.

«« »»

As Anton supported the old man back to his office, it seemed as if, at every step, strength came back into the tortured body. The man who had been so pathetic in the wash house was impressive once more when he arrived at the porchway.

In the office, the lamp was still burning, blue in the light of the morning. The old man picked up the little Bible that lay on the photograph album, took his uniform cap off a hook near the door and, before going out, put his hand on Anton's shoulder. "Thank you again," he said, smiling, and his eyes were as indomitable as they had been the previous day. "I'd like to talk to you, sir," Anton said. "I know that I can help you."

The old man looked at him, searchingly, then he said, "Very well. I shall be back in a few minutes after morning prayers." Then he went out with steady steps.

Anton stayed behind in the office and lit a cigarette. He felt pleased with himself, almost proud. The physical side of this case was so simple that it hardly needed a second thought; the spiritual side was more complicated. One thing was obvious: the old man's martyrdom had been unimaginable, and he had emerged victorious. It disturbed him profoundly to find himself forced to admit that these people had a strength and a control over their instincts that were undeniable. The dying woman in the white room, and the old man he had seen stagger out of purgatory were not pious comedians, as his father had been. Among the Christians of his youth, he had never observed anything but hypocrisy, hysteria, and auto-suggestion. The Salvation Army in Holland had seemed ludicrous. But Bert's parents were different; they had reached a level of humanity that he deeply envied. But even as his mind admired them, and felt that he should aspire to attain the same impressive heights, his body revolted. His body wanted to savor the adventure of life to the full, and did not at all feel like renouncing its pleasures. Even his mind realized that he would never be a Salvationist, for he would have to give up such things as smoking, alcohol and women. The women were easy. He loved only Els and did not feel sufficiently interested in sex to experiment outside. Alcohol was a bit more difficult, but he could do without it at a pinch. Smoking, however, was impossible to give up. He had tried it several times, before examinations, when he had gone as far as flushing his remaining cigarettes down the lavatory, only to go out half an hour later to buy a new pack because the constant consciousness of not smoking prevented his concentrating on his work. When he realized that he had somehow managed to identify a state of holiness with giving up smoking, he shrugged his shoulders, lit another cigarette and started to leaf through the photograph album lying open on the table. And then, suddenly, Bert's face looked at him.

She was sitting in the center of a group of people in costumes and paper hats, her shoulders covered with a tangle of streamers. Someone in the foreground showed a slate with the legend *Happy New Year at The Broken Heart—Everything Paid*. For a moment he thought it was indeed Bert, dressed up, wearing a hat with an ostrich feather, in the midst of a group of drunken students at a masked New Year's Eve ball. But the photograph was old and the costumes were genuine; he turned the pages of the album and saw Bert grow old before his eyes.

First she stood, young and earnest, in a uniform beside a male Salvationist whom he hardly recognized. Their hands were joined together and they stood underneath a curious flag; from the flowers around them in buckets and jars, it was obvious that this was their wedding.

Then she waved, in a faded snapshot, from the deck of an old-fashioned steamer with again the Salvationist at her side.

Then she stood, dressed in white, alone in a group of squatting lepers, her face set with controlled revulsion.

Then she laughed, young and girlish once more, holding a baby with a miniature old man's face, its eyes crossly closed against the sun.

Then she sat, smiling but with frightened eyes, between Brits-Jansen with a black beard and Willem Waterreus, her arm in a white sling.

Then she sat in an armchair in harsh sunlight, her smile young and gay once more; when he looked closely he saw that it was a wheel chair.

Then another group photograph: four rows of lepers with, in their midst, Brits-Jansen and Captain Waterreus. Between them sat a white figure with a large white hat, her face hidden by a veil; at her feet knelt two children holding a blackboard, decorated with flowers, on which was written: *Long live our Dear Commanders. Banjak Untung, 12½ years.*

It seemed as if the mysterious figure in white formed a link between two different lives of the same person, for Bert started once more as a child. Bert in the play pen, Bert on a rocking horse, Bert at the Christmas manger, Bert on a tricycle. She had curls, she had plaits, she had boy's hair, and then she stood in the center of a self-conscious crowd of pimply youths in whose midst Professor van Goor beamed victoriously at the camera. It had been their first year's photograph; he took the album to the window to find himself in the crowd. He saw his face at once, for over his head, almost hidden in the back row, a small cross was drawn. He could not resist prizing the photograph out, to see what was written on the back. Turning it over, he read, in Bert's unemotional handwriting: *X is "He."*

It caught him completely unawares, and he had not recovered from his surprise when the photograph was snatched from his hand. He turned round, startled, and saw it was Brits-Jansen, wearing a white coat over his naked body, hanging open and revealing a belly covered with black hair. On his head he wore a white Salvation Army cap, from which hung a handkerchief down the back of his neck, as a protection against the sun; over its peak was written, in red pencil, *Hands off! Dr. Jansen.*

"Is this you?" Brits-Jansen asked, frowning at the half-hidden head.

"Yes," said Anton.

"You look like a village idiot," Brits-Jansen said, with unexpected venom. "How anyone could fall in love with that is beyond my comprehension."

"In love?" Anton asked, bewildered. "I'm engaged to someone else."

"Is that so?" Brits-Jansen said, glowering at him from underneath that cap; then he handed the photograph back and went on: "What's this nonsense about the injections? Vloemans jumped on my bed at the crack of dawn to tell me some fable about hormones and satyrs. What the hell do you think you are playing at?"

His animosity broke the spell of the cap. "I am sorry, sir," said Anton, more sharply than he intended, "but your hormone cure hasn't done the patient much good. I don't think you could have given a man like that anything more cruel than hormone injections."

"Is that so?" Brits-Jansen asked, with grotesque surprise. "And what, if I may make so bold, gives you occasion to speak in this extraordinary fashion, young man?"

Then Anton could no longer restrain himself. He gave him his diagnosis of the case in terms that cut like the lashes of a whip. He did not intend to hurt him, he liked Brits-Jansen and needed his friendship more than ever now, but his remark about Bert had stung. He was sorry when he saw horror dawn in Brits-Jansen's eyes at the realization of the ravages he had caused in the soul of his old friend. He suddenly looked tired and old, and so defenseless that the words *Hands off! Dr. Jansen* seemed a warning, written on his cap by God.

"I—I'm sorry," Anton said. "The association forced itself on me as I sat looking at him last night, but of course I'll have to talk to him before I can be sure. I'm sorry; I think I may have been more violent than I intended."

But Brits-Jansen was no longer listening. He shoved the cap on the back of his head and rubbed his eyes. "Well, well," he said. "I must be getting old." Then he patted Anton's shoulder, absent-mindedly, muttered, "Nice work, young man," and shuffled out. In the doorway, he stopped, his back to the room, and his change of mood was so mastodontian that Anton braced himself, even before he turned round. "This is the second time you've pulled a fast one on me," he growled. "Come here, dear boy."

Anton came.

Brits-Jansen took him by the chin, turned his face toward the light and looked into his eyes with disturbing intensity.

"What—what is the matter?" Anton asked.

"Nothing," he said, carnivorously. "Nothing at all, boy," and then, suddenly, he gave him a playful stab in the stomach. Anton uttered a feminine squeak that was thoroughly humiliating, and was about to punch his nose, when Bert's father stood in the doorway.

«« »»

At morning prayers he had begged for strength, for what lay waiting for him was worse than anything he had gone through in his nights of torture. But he had felt no response, no comfort in his prayer. The state of grace he had tried to cling to so desperately during all those nights had now been taken away from him forever. Now he would appear before the judges sent by God: the two doctors who had discovered his secret. The old one, representative of his life; the young one, representative of his child.

As he thought of Bertie a pain burned inside him, so deep that he spoke the "Amen" hurriedly, turned away, and went toward the office. Never before had he realized his state of damnation so acutely. He entered the porchway without a prayer; for the first time he knew that he was unworthy of the miracle of grace. Now he understood the full meaning of the words: "The Lord gave, and the Lord hath taken away; blessed be the name of the Lord." On this edge of his life, on the threshold of eternal damnation, the words resounded in his soul, a last call of farewell. Before I lose my soul, O God, before I lose my humanity in torture, I thank Thee for this life. I thank Thee, I thank Thee. Praised be Thy name.

The two doctors looked round as he entered, and for one moment his composure almost gave way. But he kept a hold on himself, drawing on his strength, disciplined by thirty-five years of obedience. He took off his cap and said, "Good morning."

"Sit down, Willem," the old doctor said.

The loneliness without God was a cold despair. He heard their voices as he went to the table, but he did not hear what they were saying. He did not look at them; he looked at his hands, folded on the table, and remembered all the prayers that God in his loving-kindness had heard during those forty years. I thank Thee, O Lord God, my God. Praised be Thy name.

"No, no," the old doctor said. "You discovered it, you tell him. Go ahead."

This was worse that he had dared to foresee; but I thank Thee, my God, our God. Praised be Thy name.

"Captain," the boy said. "Dr. Jansen and I think we know why you haven't had a good night's rest for months now. But I'll have to ask you a few questions before we can be absolutely certain."

He sounded calm and composed when he said, after a great effort, "Yes, brother."

"Do you remember when you had your first nightmare?" the boy asked, so young, so blank, so innocent. He was suddenly overwhelmed by a yearning for life. "Yes, brother," he said.

"When was that?"

"A year ago."

"Had you ever had this—this particular type of nightmare before?"

He hesitated, then he answered, "No." But was it true? He no longer knew. It now seemed as if his hallucinations of the past year were the unborn sins of a lifetime, all the dreams forgotten on awakening.

"One more question!" The boy's voice was strained with a young excitement. "Think well before you answer, because it is very important. Did anything unusual happen to you, say, the week before your first nightmare? I mean: anything exceptional, something that had never happened to you before?"

The boy's excitement made him want to cry out, I don't know, I don't know, leave me alone; he could bear this no longer. But he composed himself, and searched his memory for that first night of temptation and the days that had preceded it. Surely it had been the night of that happy day when the medicine for his complaint had proved to be effective. He had fallen asleep with a jubilant prayer of gratitude; he had waked up . . .

"It was the night . . ." he began, but his voice cracked, his throat was dry.

"Yes?" said the boy, leaning forward.

"The night after the injections took effect." He could say no more, and he covered his face with his hands. This was the end, the end. O God, dear God, let this be the end. Amen.

"Captain," the boy's voice said, "I think I can assure you now that your ordeal is over. Doctor Jansen and I are convinced that your nightmares were a direct result of the injections."

He looked up. The boy's eyes were blue and very young. What was it he had said?

"Your nightmares will stop shortly after the injections cease," the boy went on. "Just as they started after the injections began. The only thing is: an operation will be necessary. Tonight we'll give you a sedative, and you'll sleep better than you've done for a year. Tomorrow, we'll talk about the operation, which had better take place as soon as possible. But have a good night's rest first—you certainly need it."

The truth slowly dawned on him. He realized, with a feeling as if something were about to break inside him, that this was grace, that God was about to descend into his heart once more. Then he felt a hand on his shoulder and, looking up, he saw the old doctor. "I am sorry, Willem," he said. "You must have suffered as much as she did. And she must have been the only one to know."

Then God opened his eyes. He stood up, reverently, went outside, crossed the courtyard, and opened the door of her room. When he heard her breathing halt in expectancy, he broke down. He fell on his knees, his head on the edge of her bed, and sobbed, for he had understood at last.

She had known everything; what had saved him was the vigilance of her prayer, the shield of her love. The sleeper on the Mount of Olives had been he.

«« »»

After old Willem had left, like a man in a dream, Brits-Jansen took the boy with him to his laboratory, a small building overlooking the valley and the blue mountains beyond, a wonderful view, but the window-panes were of frosted glass.

It was not one of those laboratories that invite a man to sit down and start working; it forced a man to sit down and shut his eyes in despair. The boy's face was amusing to watch as he cast his first glance round the alchemist's den where the standard work on leprosy was born. Outside, while he was trying several keys before he realized that the door was open, the boy had stood reverently waiting, topee in hand; once he had crossed the threshold, his disillusionment became comical. The astonished look he gave him seemed to ask, "What has happened here?"

He grinned in his beard, said: "Sit down, make yourself comfortable," and went to fish a bottle of beer out of the cooling tank and two cups without handles from underneath the sink. He took off his cap, found a cigarette inside, broke it in half and shared it with the boy. When they sat side by side, with the soft hissing of the beer in their fists, he said: "Listen, I want to talk to you. To start with, let's see who you are. You are an irritating adolescent, who has no idea as yet of what life is about. But you have one thing in your favor compared to other assistants I've had: you have chosen the right profession. Do I make myself clear?"

"No," said the boy.

"Good," he said. "Drink your beer before it gets hot."

They drank their beer.

"I mean: your diagnostics," he went on, after having sucked his mustache dry. "Diagnostics as taught in the universities is an intellectual trick of observation, combination and deduction; every idiot can be taught that. I am talking about real diagnostics, which is a combination of intuition and association. You've been too quick for me twice now, and this morning I suddenly woke up to the fact that your knowledge does not justify your arriving at those two diagnoses in the academic way. So I'm going to put you a question. How did you arrive at the association between the old exhibitionist you saw years ago and Captain Waterreus?"

"I don't know."

"You don't know? Well once I looked at his face as a doctor and not just as a friend, I knew at once what was the matter with him too."

The boy was silent for a while as if he had some difficulty swallowing this. Then he asked: "How did you know?"

He pushed the empty cup away and answered: "I saw it."

"I'm afraid that's difficult to believe," the boy said, "considering there was nothing to see."

"There was nothing to see on the hands of the Sultan either, for any normal person, yet you saw it. How do you think you discovered Willem Waterreus's erotomania if you didn't see it?"

The boy did not answer.

"I'll tell you why you sit there sulking now," he said with satisfaction. "You want to pride yourself on your knowledge, like all the other idiots. You think you made those two diagnoses because you are a wizard at the parlor game of diagnostics, but you know in your heart that it is a gift that may enable you to become a good doctor one day, if you do what I tell you. I am going to tell you now. But I warn you: it's not going to be pleasant."

The heat began to get the better of the boy; drops of perspiration glistened on his forehead and his nose was getting pale.

"Do you want to hear it?" he asked. "Or would you rather I left you in peace?"

"I—I—don't quite understand," the boy answered, stupidly.

"You are faced by a choice. A gift like yours can be a curse or a blessing; it depends on your outlook on life. I'm not airing pious slogans; I'm speaking from experience. I discovered the same gift in myself when I was about your age, and the consequences will be the same for you as they were for me. But I had nobody to give me advice, and that has cost me years of my life. I'll warn you once more: the advice I must give you is not pleasant. If you are still in the stage when happiness in life is identical with fun, I'll shut up and you may have some years left before you discover it for yourself. So make up your mind."

The boy looked so stupid that it was obvious he wanted to avoid the issue. It delighted him, for if the boy had said: "Please, doctor, do tell me!" he would have doubted the accuracy of his diagnosis. "All right," he said, "I'll tell you."

"I'm sorry, sir," the boy said, "I've got a bit of a headache, and . . ."

"No, damn you!" he cried and he had to restrain himself from hugging him. "Now you shall listen! Beer!"

He fished another bottle out of the tank; as he filled the cups, he said, "That gift of ours, as I said, can be a curse or a blessing. It is, theoretically, within our own power to turn it into either. But we, with our vitality, can only hope for a compromise. We can, at least, be aware of the dualism and this awareness will make us feel miserable when we are using the gift destructively or nauseated when we use it creatively. Between the two, we'll have somehow to eke out our uneasy existence. Have you any idea what I am talking about?"

"No," said the boy. "None whatever." He was beginning to get angry, splendid.

"All right," he continued. "I'll explain it to you. That gift of ours is, on a modest scale, supernormal. It is the sort of clairvoyance that is quite common among primitive people. All so-called witch doctors work with the same force as you and I, but their factual knowledge is so small that they are the inferiors of the trained mechanics delivered by our universities. A combination of the two makes the real doctor. If we want to be doctors in that sense, we must know to start with what our secret gift is, then stimulate it, give it a chance to expand. This means, I'm sorry to say, weeding out most of the things that make life agreeable. The gift is stifled by eating meat, by sexual intercourse, by stimulants like alcohol, tobacco, even coffee and tea; it is encouraged by the sublimation of all physical desires. It is an instinctive faculty, that is dependent on our moral condition, and as such it is essentially human. It increases as our humanity increases; it diminishes when we gratify our animal urges. Can you follow me?"

"I suppose so," said the boy. "But all this has nothing to do with me, I'm afraid."

"Is that so?" he said, kindly. "In that case, I'd better prove it to you, hadn't I? You have a girl in Holland."

"So what?"

"Did you sleep with her?"

"Pardon?"

"Did you have regular sexual intercourse with your whatever she is, fiancée? Yes or no?"

"I'm sorry, but I can't help wondering . . ."

"Did you?"

"I don't see the use of this question, sir," the boy said, pompously.

"All right," he said, emptying his cup, "I'll put it differently. Did you ever make one of these diagnoses in Holland? Or only since you entered the jungle? Give me an honest answer. It's important."

The boy thought and answered, "I think the Sultan was the first time this—er—happened to me."

"There you are!" he said. "You did sleep with your girl, my friend. Regularly." He sent the cup crashing under the sink with delight. "Did you eat meat in Holland?"

"Of course."

"There you are; you may remember that in the jungle we were vegetarians. I suppose you never even noticed."

"Well . . ."

"You mustn't misunderstand me," he continued, stretching his legs, settling deeper into his deckchair and putting his feet on the microscope box. "So far we have only defined the principle of the thing. Sexual intercourse and the eating of meat are less stifling to the gift than their counterparts on the spiritual plane: doctoring as a means of self-gratification, and regarding the patient as an experimental rabbit. I discovered my gift fairly early in my life because I had little sexual intercourse at the time and the only meat I had was an occasional horse steak. I was as poor as a church mouse. I led a monk's life as a student, not out of preference but by compulsion, and lo and behold: I began to dazzle my superiors with brilliant flashes of diagnostics. I became a professors' pet, a wonder boy, and what was worse, I took it to be my intelligence. I became assistant to a fashionable surgeon, Weerman; I don't know whether you've ever heard of him; and then I got into trouble. For if I were shown a patient who was fatally ill, I saw it at once, and told him so. Weerman had to make a living as a surgeon, so he usually disagreed with me and assured the patient that an operation might still save him. Then, one day, he diagnosed a case as peritonitis and I knew it was an abdominal cancer. I told him; he agreed it was possible, but started by whisking out the appendix. Then he waited three months, and whisked out three inches of the small intestine; when he was about to operate for the third time, I told him what I thought of him, and left Holland in a blaze of self-esteem. I arrived in Batavia, started leading a pig's life, and lo and behold: no more brilliant diagnoses. Then I set out on an expedition into the jungle, no woman in sight, lived off the land as a compulsory vegetarian and back it came. I looked straight through the natives who appeared in front of my folding table, as if I was a walking X-ray apparatus. But the gift was dangerous, because there was no creative impulse in me, no compassion, no humility. It became destructive and there, my boy, you have the secret. Black and white magic are not two different faculties. They use the same power, destructively or creatively. The important thing is: it is the same power. It took me a long time before I realized this; it made me waste years of my life. That can't happen to you now."

"Why not?" asked the boy astonished.

"Because of this conversation," he said. "It will stay in your memory, however hard you may try to forget it. I know that the parents' example cannot prevent their children sinning; but at least the children know what sin is, which is more than their parents knew. Now when your moment comes to choose between good and evil, you'll know. And if I'm still alive, come to me at once. I may be able to help you avoid wasting time."

"Wasting time doing what?" the boy asked.

"You haven't found a goal yet," he said. "You should specialize as quickly as possible. Start forcing your intuitive and your associative powers into creative activity. You have no time to lose."

The boy looked at him, almost in awe. His self-assurance had gone; he had become exactly what he had planned: a sorcerer's apprentice. "I—I honestly wouldn't know what to specialize in," he said.

He needed all his self-control not to provide the answer. He should leave the boy the illusion that he had made up his own mind. He had to be cunning now; infinitely cunning and subtle. "Well," he said, "it's difficult to advise you without knowing a bit more about you. How did you come to be a doctor? What are the things and the people that influenced you? Tell me some more about yourself. Your life, I mean."

"My life seems very unimportant these days," the boy said. "Just now I'm preoccupied by other things."

"For instance?"

The boy looked up at him with a shy smile. "Nothing," he said. "Silly things."

He remembered the photograph that he had taken out of his hand that morning, and was overcome by a vague feeling of alarm, "Is it about those two girls?" he asked.

"In a way," said the boy. "I have just realized that during these few months in the jungle I have become a lot older. More than that, I seem to be in the process of becoming someone different. I'm afraid that we might grow away from each other if she does not come over soon."

"Which she? So far, I have seen two."

"My fiancée, of course."

"You aren't afraid of growing away from the other one?"

"Oh no," the boy said, laughing. "That's different."

"Why?"

"Well . . . I don't know. It just is. We know each other so well, that . . . I can't grow away from her because I am not in love with her."

It was so obvious that to leave him with his delusion was a crime. If honey lamb were to come over there would be a disaster. The boy should be told, by a man with authority, that honey lamb might be wonderful in bed, but she would be hell in the jungle, and that he should marry the other one. The feeling of alarm deepened. The jealousy he had felt that morning like a wave of sickness when he read what was written on the photograph came back. It was crazy, disgusting—how could he even consider being jealous of a boy who was unconsciously in love with a child he himself had never set eyes on? A child that could be his granddaughter, that he had distorted into a preposterous fairy in his dreams? He forced himself to face reality; the research on leprosy had to go on, his life's work had to be saved, and there was only one possible successor at hand: this moonsick cretin, who had just one twist in his personality that made him preferable to all the others—he was a born doctor. Why, why, why did it have to be this one, of all the totoks he had nursed for over thirty years?

"Er . . ." he began, and cleared his throat, alarmed by the extraordinarily high pitch of his voice. "Er . . ." too low this time. What the devil was the matter with him? "Tell me something about them," he said gruffly, "if you are looking for my advice."

"Advice, sir? On what?"

"Which of the two to choose."

"But that's nonsense!" the boy exclaimed, laughing. "There is no question of choice. Els is my future wife. I love her. I adore her. Bert is only a . . . well . . . a friend."

"Is that so?" he croaked. But that was the last twitch of slain adolescent within him. He went on, briskly, "All right. Tell me about your life. Start when you were a child."

"Well," said the boy, "I was born in a small village, in Zeeland, where my father was a clergyman. My mother died when I was five and my father and I didn't get on very well. The house was very gloomy. My room was in the attic. . . ."

He looked at the talking boy, and his attention was led astray by the memory of all the youths who had at one time or another told him the story of their lives. It was disturbing and at the same time comforting to realize that all those stories were virtually identical. Every totok was born only when he woke up in the jungle; all that had gone before was but a dream, and if they didn't wake up then, they just never would, and would spend the rest of their lives sleepwalking. Then suddenly, a name caught his attention: Bert. A door opened, letting out a smell of Brussels sprouts and the shrill screaming of a child. "I've come to bring you your exercise book." Botanical Gardens: tropical hothouse; iron bench in the humid dusk; a cluster of cactus flowers like a log fire. "I know that I am the child of a whore and a thief, unless I believe in their rebirth in Jesus. . . ."

"I beg your pardon?"

The boy looked up, far away. "Sir?"

"She didn't say that, surely?"

"Pardon?"

"That thing about being a child of a thingummy and a whatsisname?"

"Yes. I remember it distinctly; it was a wonderful moment. I mean: it was a wonderful thing for a girl to say, to a boy she hardly knew."

"Is that so? Well, I wouldn't know. I'm the child of a whore and a timber merchant myself, and I don't go around doling out that information."

The boy said: "No, er—I see."

He realized that he could not just leave it at that. "My father once went to Poland to buy timber in his young days," he said. "He met a young tart there and made me. She walked all the way to Holland, put me on his doorstep and took the train back. Hence the 'Breszezinska' that was her name. He was saddled with me, and never quite got round to realizing that I was not responsible. Only when I was big enough to break his neck did he stick on the 'Jansen.' There was nothing bad about him, really; he just never got over the unfairness of the whole thing."

"I see," the boy said, embarrassed. That was the amazing thing; they all talked their heads off about their own lives, but two words about his own and they sat wriggling their ears with embarrassment.

"All right," he said. "I suppose she just is a frank sort of person."

"Yes," said the boy. "A bit aggressively so, like all Communists."

He cried, "What?" It was out before he knew, and it startled the boy into shyness.

"Yes . . ." he said, with an uncertain smile. "Didn't you know?"

It took him some time before he could answer casually, "Of course." But although, after that, he did his best, the boy talked no more about his life.

«« »»

Well, there it was, and he had better face it, well, with a sense of humor. Sense of humor after all was sense of proportion. A young woman in Holland whom he had dreamed of as a Cinderella was a rabid revolutionary with square shoes, close-cropped hair, a man's suit and nails bitten to the quick. So what? He had been a fool; the boy had the talent to become a doctor; that was all, full stop. God Almighty! There he was: sixty-two years old, three hundred and forty pounds without a stitch, a beard like a charcoal burner, gnarled toes, hairy stomach and a couple of buttocks like a gnu; he could hardly expect a girl of twenty something to swoon in ecstasy at that picture on the ceiling. And as the girl: pointed ears, sharp nose, flabby breasts and bowlegs, and if she was a Communist one thing was certain: she never washed her derrière. So what the hell! Ah, if only Habermann had been alive, he would have told him this and they would have fallen on each other's necks weeping with laughter after the fifth or sixth glass had produced its magical effect of elevation. They would have looked down at the hairy old bull and the bowlegged young heifer with helpless amusement from their alcoholic height, and the whole episode would have lost its sting. But Habermann was dead, and so were Mercure, van Dam and Gunther, and with them his youth, and his sense of humor. Yes, he had to face it: his dream of twenty years lay smashed to pieces. In his innocence and his puerile romanticism, he had paid for the education of a Communist. There was a moral somewhere, but the hell with it. He felt lonely.

He went to visit the Sultan in his new little pavilion and took him to the recreation hall for a game of billiards. The Sultan played so badly in the brilliant light and on the smooth baize that after a quarter of an hour and a smothering score he felt better. The Sultan took the whole thing in his stride; he behaved as if the colony had been built three hundred years ago in preparation for his visit. What a healthy nature that man had, what a wonderful balance of instinct and intelligence! As they stood chalking their cues with sparrowlike sounds, he said, "No girls here, sire.

Won't that bother you?" The Sultan pocketed the chalk for what reason he could not imagine, and replied: "Afoo." No conversation here; East is East and West is West. He wondered whether in the hereafter old friends would meet again; it would be nice. The hereafter was getting interesting, in a gradual way.

Toward nightfall the boy appeared among the harsh white cones of the Primus lamps in the games room, looking for him; a worried young Dante in hell. He was visibly disturbed by the mutilated players; he still had a lot to learn. Then he spotted him and came toward him at a trot. "Sorry to bother you, sir," he said, breathlessly, "but Captain Waterreus wants to talk to us." He was about to say, "Captain Waterreus can wait," then he remembered. Outside the magic cones of light, life lay waiting, with its doubts, its darkness, its Salvationists with satyriasis, its young Communist females and its graying beard. "All right," he said, "I'll be right along." Then he turned to the Sultan and said, "I'm sorry, sire, we'll have to continue this some other time. You weren't lucky tonight, were you? What about putting some moths in?"

The Sultan smiled, an oyster feeding. "Good-by," he said, "Sappo-lidi."

As they entered the darkness he was as blind as a bat, after the light of the Primus lamps, and he put his arm around the boy's shoulders. The boy felt thin and fragile, the brittleness of youth. Pointless thought: I could pick him up now, topee, pipe, veldt boots and all, and chuck him over the edge into the valley. Life was a delicate, complicated business. He needed a drink.

"I'm sorry I went on for so long this afternoon," the boy said. "I must have bored you to distraction."

He patted his shoulder.

As they entered the office, Willem looked up from his little Bible. He saw at a glance that Willem had been drinking God again. There was a light in his eyes that was impressive and exasperating. Willem's still white strength prevented intimacy; one didn't make friends with the Morning Star. "All right, Willem, my boy," he said with heartiness. "Out with it."

Willem smiled, an apologetic smile of terrifying strength. "I've been thinking about that operation," he said; "I would have to go to Batavia for it, I suppose?"

"Yes," he answered. "It isn't much of an operation, but I would be taking too many risks in the slaughterhouse here."

"How long would I be away?"

He shrugged. "Three weeks, if all goes well." Pity the Salvation Army was on the wagon.

"In that case," said Willem, "I think I prefer to go on with the injections. I can't possibly leave Betsy for that long."

He looked up sharply. The old man's eyes shone clear in the lamplight. Some man, Willem. God, this was really something. "Just as you like," he said.

There was a silence, in which he felt suddenly hopeful in a vague way, hopeful about himself, mankind, the future of the world. Then the boy's voice tore the silence, shrilly. "I—I'm sorry, captain, but I think this is shocking! Yes, shocking! Good night!"

Before they had quite registered what had happened, the mosquito curtain in the doorway was swinging. The boy had run out into the night.

«««   »»»

Don't eat meat! The whole disgusting hypocrisy of those old lechers was expressed in those three words. "Don't eat meat!" Anton shouted, all by himself in the night and his anger was echoed by the silent buildings in the starlight. How was it possible that during twenty-four hours he had been taken in by those two! That afternoon, in Brits-Jansen's laboratory, he had sat, deeply impressed, with his hands folded, virtually with a veil and daisies in his hair, as if he were being initiated into some weird druids' brotherhood, but now, after the old Salvationist had pulled the rabbit out of his hat, he had suddenly waked up to reality once more. Don't eat meat! And that from the mouth of the most notorious glutton in the Far East! The fact that he had not burst into helpess laughter at those ludicrous words proved that he had been mesmerized by the old windbag.

He crossed the courtyard with hard steps, his fists in the pockets of his trousers, and leaned over the low wall that skirted the colony. For the first time he sensed something oppressive, unhealthy in the atmosphere. There was a lie hidden somewhere, at the very heart of all this self-sacrifice, sublimation and goodness. It just was not possible that a man who had gone through hell every night for over a year should calmly renounce his liberation from torture because he did not want to leave his sick wife, considering that the wife had been ill for thirty years and might well live on for another ten. It stopped being human greatness and became abnormal, a pathological case. Perhaps the old hypocrite could convince himself that his decision was a noble sacrifice; no doctor would ever believe it. The old man must have secretly reveled in those nightmares; from the darkness of the valley memories rushed back at him of the lectures on psychiatry he had followed for a year. The genial old professor's merciless analyses of the visions of martyrs, the temptations of saints, the exaltations of nuns, drunk with love for Jesus. His anger grew into hatred, for he felt robbed of something precious, an ideal, a hope.

But even as he thought all this, part of his trained mind remained clinical. His reaction was grossly emotional; it meant that he was no longer capable of understanding the Captain's humanity. Until then, he had been intellectually capable of admiring the old man's sublimation, although emotionally he had not felt that admiration. Now his skepticism found itself justified, and triumphed. Just now, there was nothing he wanted more than a hot bath of sin. He wanted women, whisky, opium, an accordion and hoarse, lewd songs. He wanted to visit one of those houses so luridly and invitingly depicted at the side of the Broad Road on the poster in his father's Sunday school. Against the black cross on the white wall and the eyes of Bert's father there was only one antidote: black net stockings, petticoats like tossing roses, the hiss of a soda syphon, the smell of scent. What he had mentioned to Brits-Jansen this afternoon was an alarming fact: he was growing older so fast that if Els did not join him now, they would get hopelessly estranged. More than that: if she did not come soon, he would betray her. He did not yet know with whom, or where, or how, but he would; and the whole thing would then become so messy, so sordid that he would have no other choice than to break off their engagement. He wished, fervently, that he could talk it over with Bert. She was the only one who could give him clear unsentimental advice, for she saw life clearly and unsentimentally. To think that the old ghoul had wanted to sell her to him as a bride that afternoon! He hadn't said so in so many words but it had been blatantly obvious and small wonder. It would suit him fine, the old lecher, to have his little marzipan popsy brought over at his assistant's expense, so that he might put a fatherly arm round her shoulders, squint down her dress, and talk about the sexual abstinence essential to the development of the gift of clairvoyance. He'd see him in hell first.

His face was so angry when he lifted the mosquito curtain and entered the little room that Dr. Vloemans, who was pulling hairs out of his throat with a pair of tweezers in front of a mirror, turned round in alarm. "Good evening," he said tentatively.

"Hullo."

"Something wrong?"

"Not a goddamn thing."

That shut him up. He frowned, and went on making little peaks of skin on his neck as he tweaked out the hairs.

"Got pen and paper here?"

"Pardon?"

"Pen and paper. You know: to write with."

"You mean a letter?"

"Indeed."

The young Salvationist opened the iron cupboard and took out a pen, a bottle of ink, a sheet of paper and an envelope.

"If you could spare some more stationery, I would be very grateful. I've got a couple of letters to write and they're going to be long ones."

Dr. Vloemans complied; as he handed him the paper, he said: "I have been thinking about these injections."

"Stop thinking, carry on as before."

"No! . . ."

"Yes."

"No operation?"

"Check."

Dr. Vloemans sighed, shook his head, went back to the mirror and looked at himself gloomily.

Anton said: "Thanks for all this. See you later," and went back into the night.

He wandered about the colony with his stationery, his pen and his bottle of ink, looking for a quiet spot in which to write his letters. But wherever he went, people were praying, singing hymns, playing halma or, as in the case of Brits-Jansen's laboratory, giant bats were wheeling and swooping around the verandah and made him flee, gnomelike, knees bent, stationery and ink bottle on his head, victim of the Victorian delusion that bats go for human hair.

There was only one place left: the Captain's office. He hesitated, but as it was the only solution, he boldly entered the porchway and went toward the lighted window of the office. He would have to apologize sooner or later; he might as well do so now and get it over with. But outside the door he froze, his heart in his mouth, for from the office came a wail of such agony that he nearly turned and fled. Then the doctor in him got the upper hand; he hurried inside, thinking of morphine injections, to find Brits-Jansen sprawled in the chair in front of the Captain's table, his beard dented on his chest, snoring. The Captain sat reading his Bible.

As he stood in the doorway, Brits-Jansen's snoring reached a crisis that ended in a choking fit. Then the sleeper looked up, practically eyeless, smacked his lips, said, "Yes, yes," and started from the bottom of a new spiral of snores. The Captain looked at him with a twinkle in his eyes. "Good evening," he said as if to a deaf mute. Anton laughed awkwardly and said, in a half whisper: "I'm sorry I made an ass of myself just now." He was painfully aware of the inadequacy of his apology, and furious with Brits-Jansen for forcing him to whisper, which made the whole thing ludicrous. The Captain put his hand behind his ear and asked, "Pardon?" which made him answer, in a cowardly fashion, "Would you mind if I sat here to write a letter?"

"Not at all," the Captain said, obviously relieved. "Dr. Jansen was kind enough to sit up with me to stop me falling asleep."

"I see," said Anton.

At that moment, Brits-Jansen choked again. The chair creaked as his huge body stiffened, and he moved his arm in a paddling fashion, like a dreaming dog. Then he started anew, without having reached consciousness. Anton took a stool over to the table and put down his stationery. The Captain made room for it, pushing aside a pen tray and a dog-eared book of which Anton surreptitiously read the title: *Broken Pottery.*

As he sat with a blank sheet of paper in front of him he hesitated about whom he should write to first. He felt like writing Els a long intimate love letter, but he was conscious of Bert's father looking at him and decided that it was neither the time nor the place. All right, Bert first. He listened for a while to Brits-Jansen's snoring, then he wrote: *Dear Bert.*

He looked up at the lamp, trying to formulate the first sentence. A moth was circling round it, its shadow wheeled on the walls. Bert's father sat watching him; it made him feel so uncomfortable that he returned the look and smiled. The old man's eyes were purer than ever, a quiet gaze of such perception that he felt for one uneasy moment as if his thoughts were being read even before he had formulated them. "I'm writing to Bert," he said.

"Have you seen her last photograph?"

"No, I don't think so."

The old man cautiously pushed back his chair, tiptoed to the cupboard, opened the door, and as the hinges squeaked, he looked round, alarmed. Anton, in an uprush of atheism, kicked the bottom of Brits-Jansen's chair and called, "Hey!" Brits-Jansen roared, lashed out, and Anton grabbed the ink bottle only in the nick of time.

"What—what's the matter?" Brits-Jansen asked. "What's the time?"

Anton said, "It's all right, but you were snoring."

"I was what?"

"Snoring."

Brits-Jansen said, "Is that so?" and had settled down to sleep again when it suddenly penetrated to him that the chair behind the table was empty. He jumped and cried, "Where is he?"

Bert's father appeared in the lamplight with a white envelope and said, "I'm here. Everything is all right. You have your nap."

Brits-Jansen grunted, "Nap? Nonsense, I'm as clean as a whistle—I mean—I'm sitting up with you. What are you doing?"

Bert's father said, like a patient nurse, "I am reading and our young friend is writing letters."

Brits-Jansen looked from one to the other gloomily, as if those two activities depressed him. Then he shook his head, yawned, stretched on the creaking chair and fell asleep once more. Bert's father handed Anton the photograph, after rubbing it on his sleeve.

Bert looked at him sternly, with a stiff mouth and a frown. The photographer had made a kind of sunrise behind her in an effort to lend feminine softness to her hair; the result gave the impression that she was startled by an explosion behind her.

"Don't you think it's very good?" her father asked, again in a hushed voice, for Brits-Jansen was snoring once more.

"Very good. An excellent likeness," Anton answered. He again felt that it was very important he should write to her about her parents; "I'll write to her now," he said.

"We'll put her here," said the old man, and he propped up the photograph against the ink pot. "It is amazing," he mused, looking at her. "She is just like her mother was at that age."

All Anton could think of to say was, "Was she—her mother, I mean—in the Army at her age?"

The old man shook his head, without looking at him. "No," he said. Then he opened his book, and started reading.

As I stood looking at the stars over your parents' colony tonight, Anton wrote, *I thought of you. I have been thinking of you a great deal lately; I don't know how you feel about it, but I would give anything in the world for one of our old talks. . . .*

In Holland it must be around five o'clock in the afternoon now. She would just about have finished her work in the laboratory, cleared her desk, taken off her white coat, put on her mackintosh and said to her assistant, "Don't touch the microscope, Harmsen. I haven't finished yet." Harmsen would say, "All right, doctor." She would say, "Well, good night," and Harmsen would reply, "Good night, doctor. Have a nice evening." She would go down the long echoless corridor, down the rubber-treaded stairs, buckling the belt of her raincoat as she went. She would wish the hall porter good night; he would say, "Dirty weather, doctor. Want a taxi?" She would say, "Don't be silly," take her rumpled beret out of the pocket of her coat, pull it over her head like a sock, turn up her coat collar and step into the driving rain. Then . . . He woke up from his reverie as he caught sight of her photograph staring disdainfully from the ink pot. He looked at Brits-Jansen slumped in his chair; at her father, reading. He wrote on.

I felt this particularly after I met your father. He is a wonderful man, tremendously strong, very sincere, a prostate sufferer who has been treated by your uncle with hormone injections. These have been interrupted because they had an upsetting effect. Well, hell, you know what I mean, no use being genteel with you. The injections gave him a staggering satyriasis which he coped with by not sleeping at all for several months. The most fascinating aspect of this case is that here was a man approaching saintliness, who suddenly saw the fruits of a lifetime of self-denial and spiritual sublimation exploded by a simple injection. If only we could find an injection that would achieve the opposite. . . .

When he had written that, he suddenly felt as if he were waking up out of a dream. Suddenly he saw the lamp, her photograph, the table, the two old men, the mosquito curtain, the whitewashed walls with a supernormal clarity. For one second, it seemed as if all his senses were heightened, as if he had opened a door to another world, and stood overlooking a vast geometrical landscape in brilliant sunlight with straight roads that converged at the horizon. It lasted only a moment, but his hand trembled with excitement as he wrote:

Wait a minute! We have got something here! If I can break up a state of holiness by an injection, why shouldn't I be able to bring it about the same way? If I can turn a saint into a sinner by applying a chemical, why not a sinner into a saint? Good Lord, Bert, this opens a perspective that takes my breath away. Biologically, there must be a serum of conversion possible. Think of the possibilities! Man, at present tied helplessly onto the wild horse of his instincts, would be able to swing round and turn into its rider. This, of course, is the ultimate goal of all religious and political movements; but instead of trying to batter this notion into man's mind, we would make him master of his fate by an injection! This very day I have been knocking my brains out, trying to think of something to specialize in. I have thought of psychiatry, polio, cancer, even leprosy, bless your uncle's heart, but this is it! I am going to interview every single Christian missionary, every parson, every convert, I can lay hands on. I'm going to make case histories of them. I'm going to situate the moment of their conversion, take blood tests, analyze their urine, make cardiograms. In short, I am going to take St. Paul apart to see what biological or chemical difference there is between him and Saul. The preparation with which they treated your father and sent him down to hell is aptly called "Exaltine." My goal is anti-Exaltine which will capture in a phial of 2 c.c. the Blood of the Lamb, the Fount of Grace, Jesus, Saint John and Pastor Witzenburg. Bert, my old comrade, we may well be on the brink of a discovery that would suddenly make sense of our bewildered childhood and our rudderless youth. The hell with our Bible-fed consciences, our eternal feeling of guilt, our reverence for your father and his white witch doctor's clairvoyance; if I can make a sinner out of a saint by sticking a needle into his buttock and spurting a colorless liquid into his muscle, I must logically be capable of reversing the process. . . .

The moths circled, the pen scratched. Brits-Jansen snored, while Willem Waterreus sat reading the pages as they were put aside in front of him.

«« »»

When Willem Waterreus stood at the foot of the flagpole at sunrise between the old doctor and the boy, he knew.

He knew that his child was a Communist and that she and the boy were about to take up the same battle with God that Betsy and he had once undertaken. There was nothing he could do to help them, nothing at all. Each generation in its turn had to battle with God all over again for the grace of His mercy; whatever knowledge man might inherit as he crossed the shadow line between innocence and sin, it was of no avail in his fight for his salvation. There was no help in his parents' experience, example, admonition: but there might be some help, like the feeble light of a failing star, in his aging parents' prayer.

He opened his Bible at random, looked around him at the white crowd of lepers in the light of the morning, and read: *If ye then be risen with Christ, seek those things which are above, where Christ sitteth on the right hand of God. Set your affection on things above, not on things on the earth. For ye are dead, and your life is hid with Christ in God.*

He looked up at the flag, hanging limply in the morning sky, and folded his hands, but as he was about to start his prayer, his viewpoint was, for one strange and bodiless moment, breathtakingly inverted. He saw, from a great height, the fortress, the courtyard, the lepers, and the three small figures at the foot of the flagpole, gathered together in His name. He felt an immense joy surrounding him in the sky, and heard a tremendous, jubilant humming, as if the stars and the planets had voices, too vast for man to hear.

Then, as he shook his head in mortal awe, he was back at the foot of the flagpole, between his two friends, among his lepers, across the courtyard from her room.

He prayed from a great peace, for whatever might happen to those he loved, God loved them even more.

CHAPTER EIGHT

Before Brits-Jansen and Anton left for Celebes to cope with the outbreak of cholera, Anton went to see a notary in Batavia to have the documents drawn up that would enable Els to come over as a married woman. A Dutch girl could marry in Amsterdam by proxy and sail to the East as a matron without her husband having taken part in the ceremony; it was a custom left over from the pioneer days when the voyage between Holland and the Dutch East Indies took months. The notary, a solemn little man, said he would see to everything; all Dr. Zorgdrager need do was to sign some papers. It was, indeed, all; when Anton returned to Batavia, Els had married him by proxy in Amsterdam. He had been represented at the ceremony by Professor van Goor, who wore a glove on his right hand, which had given the ceremony its name of "gloved wedding." A photograph, taken of the couple among the flowers and the wedding guests, was sent by airmail to Batavia, where it startled Anton a good deal. Van Goor stood in the center of a cowed group with his head back, chest covered with medals and his flat feet in spats at an angle of ninety degrees, holding by the hand an apparition in veils, like a medium with a spirit he had evoked. Bert's head was among the row in the background, and she looked skeptical. When he saw the photograph, Anton was more impressed with the irrevocability of his act than he had been on signing the papers.

When he went to the Head Office, in the company of Brits-Jansen, he heard that their boat would leave the next afternoon at three, destination Deli, where they were to cut a sanitary road round the Atjeh highlands to isolate the lung plague. Dr. Kramer did not mention Anton's hospital service again. He just said, "Hear your wife's coming," and Anton said, "Yes." Brits-Jansen said, "Show him the photograph," at which Anton turned round and walked out.

On second thought, however, it was a lucky circumstance that their next destination should be Sumatra, for it gave Anton a chance to go and meet Els in Sabang. Surely he would find a means of nipping across from Camp Lung Plague for a day or two to welcome her. But it did not work out that way. To start with, the weekly steamer from Amsterdam passed by Sabang this time, because smallpox had been reported on a ship bringing pilgrims back from Mecca and the port was placed under quarantine. Anton had to do some eel-like maneuvering to remain out of the clutches of Sabang's district doctor, who was calling up all government doctors on vacation in the cool mountains nearby. Had this happened four months before, he would have offered himself to the district doctor with shining eyes, saluting at his topee, but the training Brits-Jansen had given him was beginning to bear fruit. He vanished back into the jungle with half a tin of P.G. from the stores, before the mandur woke up to the fact that he was a tuan deserter.

The boat was to unload the passengers for Atjeh in Labuan Redjo, known as "The Bachelor's Paradise." It was a small port, notorious for its unhealthy climate and its riotous parties given by the planters from the surrounding plantations, who all rushed to the coast twice a year, like lemmings, driven by a communal urge for gaiety. One legend said that the director of the Grand Hotel had fitted out his rooms with bullet-proof windows, that the beds were bolted to the floor and that the statues on the marble staircase were neuters. Anton, who felt a bit guilty after slipping through the fingers of Sabang's district doctor, sent a message to Brits-Jansen by jungle telegraph to say that he was to be found in Labuan Redjo if he was wanted, a nicety that he came to regret bitterly later.

He arrived in the bachelor's paradise after a gut-shaking trip in a native bus in which he shared the front seat reserved for whites with a white goat. The town was somnolent and prim like a Dutch provincial village. The heat was terrible; a few stupefied natives in white peaked caps and little else were making ritual movements with rakes on the hard green lawns, and among the vivid splashes of exotic flowers. At the intersection of Main Street and Queen Wilhelmina Avenue, a policeman underneath an egg-colored parasol regulated the traffic of a street vendor pushing a cart with papajahs and a woman driving three ducks. When the native bus came steaming down Queen Wilhelmina Avenue, it was stopped by his white baton until the three ducks and the vendor had passed, then he blew a whistle and sent the native bus steaming and cackling on with a sweeping gesture. Somewhere church bells chimed "Abide with Me."

The Grand Hotel was a gloomy building, deserted but for a native behind the reception desk in the hall who, when addressed, proved to be asleep with his eyes open, like a crocodile. When Anton asked whether he could have a room, the native opened a ledger full of blank pages and said he would have to ask the manager. Anton slumped into an easy chair, which let out a sigh as he sank, and waited. A tall man appeared, gave a stifled cry, darted across the hall, slapped his shoulder and said, "No! It can't be true!" Anton stared at the man in alarm until suddenly he recognized Witzenburg, the tall one of the Four Musketeers of his outward voyage. He thought Witzenburg had exchanged religion for hotel management; but then a fat little man popped out of a door, welcomed him to Labuan Redjo and said he could have the bridal suite. Witzenburg cried, indignantly, that he had been promised the bridal suite. "That's all right, Your Reverence," the manager said. "This hotel has nothing but bridal suites." Witzenburg gaped at this, and the manager said, "Well now, what about a drink?" After he had gone to rouse the barman with the order for a double Scotch and a tomato juice, Witzenburg started breathing down Anton's shirt again, slapping his shoulders, grabbing hold of the nape of his neck and virtually kissing him, so delighted he was to meet good old Zorgdrager so unexpectedly and both of them waiting for their little wives. Fancy, fancy. Reel wasn't his little wife yet; they would be married in Medan where he was now the resident clergyman. They had not been married by glove because Reel was traveling in the company of her parents. Reel was short for Aurelia and she was the daughter of . . . Well, he shouldn't, but, well, old Zorgdrager would certainly promise not to breathe a word about it to anybody, wouldn't he? Anton reassured him, waiting for the whisky. Then Witzenburg, practically on his lap, whispered: "Dr. Boosmans." Anton, feeling that something was expected of him, said, "Is that so?" and at that moment, as if it has been a magic formula, there was a great crashing of swing doors, a heavy breathing, and there stood Brits-Jansen: sweat-stained, a rucksack on his back, followed by a porter carrying a cage with a cockatoo. The cockatoo, the moment it entered the coolness of the hall, started to scream and to bang its wings against the bars of the cage, making such a racket that the manager flashed into the hall from the bar as if shot out of a gun. Dr. Jansen had come as a surprise.

After the cockatoo, yelling blue murder, had been carried off to yet another bridal suite, peace descended and Anton introduced the two gentlemen with a feeling of disaster. Witzenburg, who had sat smiling a bit uncertainly, asked Dr. Jansen what he would like to drink; when Brits-Jansen thanked him and asked for three beers Witzenburg took it like a man, and then, because Dr. Jansen was Zorgdrager's best friend, he saw no reason why Dr. Jansen should not be let into the secret, on condition that Dr. Jansen promised on his word of honor as an officer, not to breathe a word about it to anyone. Dr. Jansen raised his eyebrows and asked, "What's happened?" Anton replied hurriedly, "The reverend is going to be married." Brits-Jansen lowered his eyebrows and said, "Is that so?" while Anton trod on Witzenburg's foot as if it were a brake. But Witzenburg did not heed the warning. He looked around the hall with a conspiratory glance, before he whispered, "To the daughter of Dr. Boosmans."

"Ah?" said Brits-Jansen. "Who is Dr. Boosmans?"

Witzenburg gaped at him. "You don't know who Dr. Boosmans is?" he asked incredulously. "Surely you're joking?"

"I'm sorry," said Brits-Jansen, "but I'm straight from the jungle. Is he to take Piet Kramer's place?"

"Piet who?" Witzenburg asked.

"Kramer. The Head of the Service. Didn't you say he was a doctor?"

"No, no," said Witzenburg, "he's a doctor of philosophy. He is about to take"—he looked around the hall once more—"Dr. Zoot's place."

Brits-Jansen turned to Anton and asked, "Is this on the level, or are you boys pulling my leg?"

Witzenburg, piqued, said, "Dr. Zoot is the present Minister of Colonies. Dr. Boosmans, my future father-in-law, will take his place."

Brits-Jansen made a polite face and said, "Attaboy." The beer arrived with the whisky and the tomato juice. Brits-Jansen raised a foaming glass, said, "Well, reverend, here's looking at you," and drank the glass straight off with the sound of an emptying bathtub.

Anton felt that Witzenburg should be humored a little; after all it was no mean feat for a clergyman from the backwoods to capture a Cabinet Minister's daughter. He was entitled to a triumphal entry. "Is he an interesting man, this Dr. Boosmans?" he asked. "To be a Minister of Colonies is quite a tall order."

Brits-Jansen snorted, but Anton mesmerized Witzenburg with a stare of sincere interest. "Brilliantly intelligent," Witzenburg said. "An encyclopedic mind. A power of absorption which is quite staggering."

"Well, that's something," Brits-Jansen said. "Djongos!"

"Tell me some more about your father-in-law," Anton insisted. "Is he coming for a tour of inspection or something?"

Witzenburg brightened and his face assumed its look of secrecy once more. "Papa is traveling incognito. You see, officially, he's just bringing Reel."

"He is bringing what?" Brits-Jansen asked.

Anton said, "Ah, I get it. Officially he's a chaperon but, in actual fact, he's coming to spy out the land."

Witzenburg nodded. "That's it," he said, "hence the secrecy."

Brits-Jansen took a breath to say something, but the djongos arrived with a new round of ammunition. He grabbed his fourth glass of beer, lifted it and opened his mouth for a toast, but Anton quickly rose to his feet, saying, "I think I'll just stroll over to the harbor master's office to see when the boat arrives." Witzenburg jumped up and said, "Wizard idea! I'm coming with you." Brits-Jansen looked at them with hurt eyes, "Give me a chance to drink my beer," he said. "Don't hurry," Anton said. "We'll be back in a minute." As they edged away toward the swing doors, Brits-Jansen did a variety turn with his three glasses and stampeded after them. Witzenburg whispered, "Who is he?" and Anton answered irreverently, "God."

As they strolled through the hot sunlight to the harbor, the traffic policemen tried to stop them with his white baton at the crossing of Main Street and Queen Wilhelmina Avenue but Brits-Jansen said, "Don't be silly, boy," and left him with his mouth open, while the tires of the native bus returning to the jungle screamed on the hot asphalt.

The harbor master's office was made of corrugated iron and looked like a modern stove. It felt like one when they entered; the heat inside was infernal, the harbor master behind his warped desk looked like a madman. He was being shouted at by a red-faced, bull-necked major of the military police, who told him, without mincing his words, that not a soul was to go aboard the steamer before he had made his arrest. Witzenburg, alarmed, said in his mellow parson's voice, "Sorry to interrupt, major, but . . ." The major turned at the sound, fixed him with a stare of bloodshot eyes, and rasped out, "Who are you?"

"Dr. Zorgdrager and I," Witzenburg replied placatingly, "are expecting our brides. My name is Witzenburg. I'm resident clergyman in Medan. We'd hoped . . ."

But the major shook his head. "No one is going to set foot on that ship until my men have nabbed the bugger and clapped him in irons. Do you know what he is?"

"A Cabinet Minister?" Brits-Jansen ventured. Anton dug him in the ribs; Witzenburg nearly passed out.

But the major, immune to innuendo, continued, "A killer! He slaughtered a girl in Rotterdam. . . ." Brits-Jansen put a hand on his shoulder. "Surely," he said, "if one had a special pass, one could go on board? If, for instance, this gentleman here were going to meet . . ."

Anton was about to cut in and, had he been able to do so, all might have been well. But Witzenburg cried, "No! No! You promised! You gave me your word of honor as an officer that you would not divulge . . ."

A moronic slyness woke up in the major's bloodshot eyes. "Divulge what?" he asked, his steaming face very close to Witzenburg's. Anton made a last effort to save the situation, saying, "Nothing, major, nothing. As I was saying . . ." But the major barked, "Shurrup!" out of the side of his mouth, keeping his eyes on Witzenburg, who slowly backed to the wall of the office, crowded by the major's bulk and breath. "Divulge what?" the major asked menacingly. "Who is on board that ship?"

Witzenburg opened his mouth to say something, but, backing away, burned his hands on the iron wall. He gave a cry, jumped, and blurted out, "Dr. Boosmans." The major put the arm of Judas round Witzenburg's shoulders, and asked, gently, "And who is that, boy?" Then Brits-Jansen's innocent voice rang out, "His Excellency the Minister of Colonies, incognito. How's that for a slap in the puss, you big ham?"

For one second the situation remained stationary, then the major jumped to the telephone, rattled the hook, and shouted, "Give me the Commissioner! Quick! The Commissioner! Service call! Urgent!" Witzenburg rushed across to him, took his arm, started pleading, but the major had turned into a ball of fire. "Jimmy? Is that you, Jimmy?—Shut up, reverend, leave me alone!—Who? No, not you, you goddamn ass! I've got a reverend here, who has given me some information that . . ." Witzenburg, panic-stricken, tried to cover the mouthpiece with his hand, and when pushed away, started pulling at the cord, but already the major had bellowed, "The Minister of Colonies incognito! Yes! Arriving in three hours' time! You bet we'll give him a reception! Trying to creep

up on us! Let's sound the tocsin, alert every white man in the district. . . ."
They were outside by then, Anton with his arm round Witzenburg's
shoulders, Brits-Jansen fanning his chest with his topee.

They lost valuable time strolling around the lawns and the flower beds,
reassuring Witzenburg that everything would be all right. They should
have taken counter-measures at once. When they arrived in the hotel, the
manager met them, sweating and excited, to tell them that he was very
sorry but there had been a slight error. Dr. Jansen could not have a bridal
suite unless he was willing to share it with two other gentlemen because
all the rooms in the hotel had been booked and he was desperate for beds.
When Brits-Jansen asked angrily, "Booked by whom?" the manager
answered, "By the reception committee." When they telephoned for
flowers for the girls, both florists answered that they were very sorry but
all available flowers had been sold to the reception committee. When
they went to see the local tailor to hire lounge suits for the wedding dinner
that night, the Chinese answered, "Solly, tuan doctol. All pakki-brani
been hiled by leception committee." And they could not book a table in
the dining room either; no private dinners would be served that night,
the hotel was closed, all tables were being put end to end in preparation
for an official dinner, organized by the reception committee.

Witzenburg wept, sitting on a bench among the lawns, where native
military police armed to the teeth were busy cutting all the flowers with
their klewangs, to load them by the armful into a black Maria waiting
at the curb. Anton patted Witzenburg's shoulder, Brits-Jansen cursed in
a voice like a foghorn and said that he would chase that goddamn major
through the town, if needs be into the very jungle, and give him an
enema of bicarbonate of soda that would keep the bastard running until
the dawn. He said this only to cheer up Witzenburg, but it had the opposite effect. Witzenburg's mouth started to tremble, and when a convoy
of three military lorries, sirens screaming, skidded past, loaded with
planters, he gave a choking sob and hid his face in his hands. Brits-Jansen
patted his knee and said, "Come on, reverend. Let's go back to that harbor
master and see what we can do."

When they arrived at the quayside, they found an upheaval. Scores of
native military police formed a cordon around a motley crowd of angry
whites, in the midst of whom the major, hatless, stood on a crate,
haranguing them, but only an occasional word rose above the hubbub.
"Minister," "Reception," "National Anthem." Another convoy of lorries

arrived, packed to the brim with delighted employees from the plantations; and then came those who had climbed high enough on the social
ladder to possess a private means of conveyance. They came down enthusiastically to the quayside in sados, four-in-hands, and old Buicks hissing
like steam engines; a fat man on a motorbike swooped down from the
direction of the lighthouse. The new arrivals cheered the major and sang,
"For He's a Jolly Good Fellow." The major, whose military lack of
intelligence made him blind to the obvious, allowed himself to be lifted
onto the shoulders of two burly planters to make his speech. "Gentlemen!"
the major bellowed, his face beaming, "we are here! to welcome! the
future Minister! of Colonies! Ouch! Damn!" While the crowd cheered,
the major wriggled on the shoulders of the planters, one of whom had
burnt the seat of his trousers with a cigar. The major bellowed, "Silence!"
and when he could not defeat the cheering, he screamed at an Atjeh
sergeant, "Fire!" The sergeant ordered a platoon of military police to
fire a volley over the heads of the crowd. It became as quiet as was possible
on a quayside where several hundred gentlemen, fresh from the jungle,
found themselves packed together at the hottest hour of the day. The
major continued his speech, shouting: "Who is about! to arrive! with
the steamer! in cognito!"

The "in cognito" delighted the planters so much that they hit upon the
idea of jumping up and down on the wooden quay in unison, which
brought the harbor master out of his iron shed at a run. The major continued, "The Minister! supposes! that he will arrive unnoticed! but!"—
here he made a dramatic pause, and had everyone's attention because they
thought he was about to die of a stroke—"but this shall not be so!"

"No!!" the planters roared, and started to jump up and down once
more, singing rival songs of which "Holland, Dear Holland" emerged
victorious. The major, unaware of the fact that his back had been
decorated with a four-letter word, burnt into his tunic by a cigar, had
no voice left. He produced a series of croaks, understandable only to
his mother; one of the planters serving as his pedestal shouted, "Boys!"
and was rewarded with instant silence. "The Chink is bringing lounge
suits," the planter said; "twenty-five of us are going to dress up in the
harbor master's office to make up a committee; the rest will form a background and sing the National Anthem when the Minister arrives. Who's
got a piano?" Several gentlemen shouted that they had; the major started
quacking again and produced the word "band." The planter shouted,

"Never mind, boys, the police band will accompany us, and tonight a free dinner will be laid on for everybody at the Grand Hotel." The cheering produced by this information was so sincere and prolonged that the harbor master ran out of his office again, waving his arms, as the quay started creaking and swaying.

They hung about on the jetty for hours. Brits-Jansen found friends among the crowd, the friends produced other friends; in the end Anton found himself, about to faint with heat, supporting a virtually unconscious Witzenburg and listening to Brits-Jansen as he told two shriveled archaeologists how he had dug up an urn in the jungle while flattening a hillock for his sanitary road, a beautiful urn, which must be at least ten thousand years old, just the right size for his teeth. The archaeologists got very excited about this and Brits-Jansen promised to show it to them that night during dinner.

When, at last, twenty-five scarecrows emerged from the harbor master's office dressed in lounge suits, they were given a riotous reception. The police band arrived in a lorry, took up position, and the major, once more in possession of his voice, climbed onto his crate again. "Gentlemen!" he shouted. "Line up two deep!" The gentlemen complied. The major, encouraged by the semblance of order he had thus created, made a speech in which he explained, fairly lucidly, what was about to happen. His Excellency, the future Minister of Colonies, was about to arrive for a secret tour of inspection. His Excellency seemed to surmise that the Dutch East Indies were peopled with half-wits who couldn't recognize a Minister when they saw one. He was to be given a reception that he would not forget until his dying day, but it had to be serious, purposeful and well-organized, so the following plan had been made among the gentlemen: there was only one who knew His Excellency by sight, his future son-in-law, Dr. Witzenburg, who would take up position at the steps of the jetty and welcome his parent with a kiss. At this, Witzenburg cried, "No!" but he was silenced by hissing and cries of "Shame!" and "Judas!" The reception, the major cried, would begin by the singing of the National Anthem to the accompaniment of the military band. Then the major, in his capacity as president of the reception committee, would make a short speech of welcome, after which the Minister and his spouse were to be taken in triumphal procession to the hotel, where a banquet was to be held in their honor. In the hotel—and the major had to bellow again— there would be a ball to follow the dinner but—and here his bellowing was forced into screaming—*the gentlemen were expected to behave in an orderly and dignified fashion, until the Minister and his spouse had been put to bed.*

This wording of the end of the program caused such varied comments that it seemed for a moment as if the major's plan of campaign were about to be defeated by the very enthusiasm of his troops. But he managed to keep them under control; when the steamer finally appeared at the entrance of the bay, the jetty was lined by two solid rows of pigeon-chested civilians, staring with unsmiling eyes at the twenty-five village idiots who by then had nearly died in their black morning suits. The major was standing at the head of the steps in the company of the miserable Witzenburg and a native toddler kidnaped by his sergeant to present His Excellency with a bunch of flowers on behalf of the population.

When the steamer dropped anchor in the harbor, the waving crowd which lined its decks got no response. Anton did not look for Els among them. He would have given anything in the world to be back in the wilderness instead of standing here among this sweating herd of cretins, who were sure to cause a disaster before nightfall. Even Brits-Jansen had deserted him in spirit; he seemed to have taken pleasure in the situation, and the moment Brits-Jansen began to take pleasure in something he became more dangerous than three hundred planters.

Anton stood in the scorching sunlight with his eyes closed for so long, dreaming of the jungle, that he started violently when the police band struck up the National Anthem with a roll of drums and a clash of cymbals. The planters began to bellow in confusion, and a shiver ran down his spine. He opened his eyes and saw, standing at the jetty steps, a thin little man in a new tropical suit, between a fat woman in a white dress and a hatchet-faced flapper in one of those dresses that changes color. Witzenburg had obviously just delivered his Judas kiss; the thin gentleman stood rubbing his cheek, while the toddler stuck up his floral tribute to the fat woman as if he were feeding a horse. The major, with the word on his back, shouted, "Your Excellency, madame and young lady, the Netherlands East Indies bid you welcome! Fire!"

The fat woman grabbed her ducking husband's arm, as the platoon of military police fired a volley over their heads.

«« »»

When Anton found Els, it was too late. As soon as the Minister and his family had been led to a planter's Buick which had been decorated with bunting, all the men were rounded up by the major and his sergeant and compelled to march behind the slowly moving Ministerial car, which was preceded by the clashing, blaring and squealing band. The road to the hotel was lined with natives, clapping their hands delightedly; the Minister thought the applause was for him, and waved shyly with his topee; but it was meant for the band.

On the steps of the hotel, the Minister was welcomed by the manager who presented him with a bottle of whisky, adorned by a bow of ribbon. He had obviously not counted on the ladies, for he had nudged a djongos standing behind him as they got out of the car and the djongos returned with two bouquets still dripping.

The dining room of the hotel had been changed into a banqueting hall gay with flags, flowers and Chinese lanterns. On the long table in the center busy hands had spelled out, *Welcome Your Excellency* in moss; the centerpiece was a suckling pig surrounded by flowers, an orange in its mouth, parsley behind its ears, staring at the head of the table with carnations for eyes. The major, aided by the manager, made the seating arrangements; the lower classes, rounded up because of the color of their skins, were put at the far end of the table out of earshot of His Excellency's wife. The major sat between His Excellency and his wife, who had Brits-Jansen on her other side; next to him sat Els, and beside Els, Witzenburg.

It had all been a miserable muddle. Witzenburg and Anton had finally managed to reach the major and coax him into having Els paged; the major had mixed up the brides, so Anton sat next to Hatchet-face, on the other side of His Excellency. To see Els sitting there, pale and fragile in a pink fluffy dress, her blond hair shining like a halo, was more than Anton could bear. He smiled, nodded, made silly little gestures, while his eyes filled with unreasonable tears. There she was at last, at last—with her smile and her big blue eyes, a lily of the valley in the jungle, his Els, his love, his wife. For the first time, he realized that something big and irrevocable had taken place when he signed his name in the notary's office two months ago. The slender, lovely creature across the table was his life's companion. Until death did them part, she would be his, and he would be hers; they would be together all the time, day and night.

The thought of that night made him look away and put an end to the nods, the winks, the swallowings, the grins with which he had been greeting her behind the artificial sunset of Miss Boosmans' dress. For the first time, he noticed Witzenburg, looking like a man who had committed a murder in his sleep, and he shot a stealthy glance at Miss Boosmans' profile. It was aquiline and intimidating, her hard little eyes kept Witzenburg transfixed with a snakelike stare. It seemed unwise to address her before she had drawn all the blood from his face, so Anton looked round at the other guests.

The Minister, bewildered but dignified, gazed down the alley of candle-light at the pig with the carnation eyes. His plate was flanked by two miniature flags, which Anton had noticed that morning on the harbor master's desk. His spouse looked like her daughter, only fatter; Brits-Jansen sat talking to her delightedly, his hairy hand on her arm to hold her attention. The major, ablaze with pride and high spirits, was poised to make his speech, waiting until the native servants had doled out the first round of gin and orange. The manager obviously had chosen this beverage for its national color, disregarding its potency. It was indeed a pretty sight to see the double row of orange glasses converging into the far distance, two dotted lines of patriotism. The Chinese lanterns shed a romantic light, the candle flames danced gaily, like rippled moonlight on a river; it seemed natural that the felicity in the atmosphere should give birth to song. The lower classes, beating the table with their empty glasses, started the National Anthem, and the major hastily rose. There were no policemen to fire volleys this time; he had to do it all with his voice, and the range was hazardous. "Gentlemen!" he bellowed, as if on the parade ground. "*Gentlemen!*" and as silence fell, he added, flutelike, "Ladies, and Your Excellency! I cannot tell you how proud and happy this our simple township feels now you are treading it with your vener-venereal feet." Nobody knew what on earth he had wanted to say but, after a startled silence, he was rewarded with such a roar of applause and cheers that he stood rapping the table for the better part of a minute before he could make himself heard once more. But whatever he might have had in mind to say, every word he uttered as from that moment was doomed. "The joy in our hearts when we heard of your arrival"—prolonged applause—"was only equaled by our eagerness to welcome you in this beautiful . . ." —cheers and counter-cheers—"beautiful, and prosperous corner of the Empire"—shouts from the lower end of the table, "Long live the Emperor! Hail Caesar! Bumps-a-daisy!"—"It has always been one of the pillars of our community that rulers and rulèd . . ."—shouts from close quarters,

"Roulette! Shut up! Look on your back, major! Djongos! Gin!"—" . . . can sit together in a common spirit of relaxative gaiety and . . ."

That was the end. The rest of the major's swan song was drowned by such a gale of whistles and cheers that, after a heroic battle, he shook the minister by the hand, sweating and defeated, sat down, beckoned the manager and ordered the first course to be served.

The first course was noisy, but still human. Conversation was possible, even though it had to be shouted; Anton addressed Miss Boosmans by saying, "They may sound a bit riotous but they are really delighted, you know," at which Miss Boosmans looked daggers at him and asked, "Did Mr. Witzenburg announce our arrival?" Anton, caught unawares, stuttered, "No—no, no—not at all. Someone must have—er—radioed." Miss Boosmans seemed to stare into his very soul, to find a void. She pursed her lips and looked back at Witzenburg who, stung by her stare, took his glass and drank it straight off.

The second course was the national dish: rijst-tafel, which consisted of hills of rice and about three dozen spices, all of them gaily colored and lethal. The Minister, served first, helped himself to fatal quantities of the gay colors; the lower classes at the far end of the table were attracted by the gay colors in a different way. One guest started to rub his neighbor's face with tomato ketchup, which was the signal for uninhibited fun. Within five minutes, one of them was being chased around the table, bombarded by snowballs of rice, amid screams of raucous laughter. The major stood up and sallied valiantly into the heart of the rising, thus exposing the word on his back.

This was the moment when the Minister's mood changed. Until then, he had been watching the proceedings with a waning expression of bewilderment, and paternal leniency. When he saw the word on the major's back his pallid face flushed with anger, he glowered at the crowd, shot a glance at his wife, took a spoonful of sambal deng-deng, rose bodily from his chair, spewing sambal deng-deng all over the table. This was taken by the crowd to be the official opening to the evening. Brits-Jansen roared, "Attaboy!' slapping Mrs. Boosmans' fleshy shoulder. The Minister was bombarded with rice and someone struck up "For He's a Jolly Good Fellow." Anton, sensing the impending disaster, got up, went over to Els, who sat shielding her eyes with her hands, shouted into her ear, "Come on, sweetie, let's beat it!" It was a sensible decision but he had waited too long. When Els got to her feet, Brits-Jansen spotted her, roared, "Hail to the bride!" and before Anton could intervene, he had lifted her up and put her onto the table. The cheers that greeted her were terrifying. She stood for a moment petrified, then she fled away from the monster with the beard toward the pig with the carnations, knocking over candlesticks as she ran. Anton jumped onto the table and ran after her, cheered by the crowd; he caught her in his arms at a point where two tables joined. Under their combined weight the two tables reared and they vanished in the gap amid a landslide of crockery, candlesticks, bowls of rice, plates of spices and bottles of beer. Anton saw the pig with the carnation eyes slide toward them with gathering speed; he shielded Els's fragile, trembling body and was violently hit by the dish in the small of his back. Flushed with rage, he struggled to his feet, one arm around Els, grabbed the pig by a hind leg with his free hand, aimed at Brits-Jansen, who sat bellowing with laughter, flung the pig at him, but the jelly made it slip from his hand. The Minister's wife uttered a shriek as the cold little corpse struck her in the bosom. The Minister jumped onto his chair, berserk with fury, and shrieked, "Arrest him! Arrest that man! I order his arrest!" The major, tomato-streaked, disheveled, his eyes bloodshot and his hair full of rice, waded toward Anton through the debris. Anton picked up Els in his arms and fled. The planters cheered and whistled, tripped up the major, and picked up the corners of the tablecloth. At Brits-Jansen's yodeled commands, he was flung aloft, bounced, then the cloth tore and he crashed into the wreckage below. The manager, an old hand at riots, put a record on the gramophone and while the dining room turned into pandemonium, a colossal negroid voice started to moo: "Ah love you, mah baby, ah do."

The rest of the evening was like the last hours of Pompeii. The walls of the hotel stood firm, but that was all. When Anton and Els finally managed to reach their bridal suite, the hall was filled with bedclothes, pillows and the wrecks of beds among which drunkards lolled, brandishing bottles, splashed with tomato juice like blood. Brits-Jansen had been led away handcuffed, helpless with laughter, between two military police, bayonets fixed. The Minister and his family had vanished, leaving nothing but a baffling souvenir, a dress that changed color, among the wreckage of the hall.

<<< >>>

By some miracle, their room had escaped destruction. When they entered it, they found a haven of sanity, order and luxury. Even Els's suitcase was there, already unpacked. The twin beds were uncovered, the sheets neatly turned back and across one of them was draped a nightdress. As they stood looking at this with a beginning of hope, a voice shrieked from the bathroom: "Attaboy." Anton opened the door and found the parrot, obviously left by Brits-Jansen as a surprise gift. As he picked up the cage, he unleashed a demon inside, that flapped its wings, screeching, and pecked at his hand. He carried it through the bedroom to the French windows; when he opened them to put it out on the balcony, Els cried, "No!" with such despair in her voice that he turned round. She stood looking at him with horrified eyes, her hair disheveled and snowy with rice, her fluffy dress torn and wilted; she looked a picture of terror with her stark-white face and those wide blue eyes.

"What's the matter, dear?" he asked, alarmed.

She swallowed. "You mustn't do that," she said, hoarsely.

"What?"

"Throw it out of the window."

He laughed, relieved. "But, sweetie," he said, "there's a balcony out there. I just wanted to put it out in the open, that's all."

"Attaboy!" the parrot shrieked.

His smile stiffened as he turned round and put the cage gently on the balcony. He wondered why Brits-Jansen had been arrested and whether he should do something about it, but he decided it served him right. So he shut the French windows, which set the parrot off on a new series of screams, went across to Els, put an arm round her shoulders and said, smiling, "Darling, I am sorry about this evening. I needn't tell you that it wasn't my fault. It just so happened that this goddamn idiot was on board your ship."

"How can you say such a thing?" she asked. "They are the nicest people on earth. Mrs. Boosmans was a real angel to me when I was seasick."

"Well," he said with a slight edge to his voice, "I'm sorry I threw a pig at her. What about having a bath and going to bed?"

She hesitated, looked round in a hunted way, then she smiled and said, "All right. Shall I take the bathroom first?"

His irritation deepened. "What do you mean, first? You behave as if . . . I'm sorry. I'm all haywire myself. I love you, by the way."

She smiled. "I love you too," she said. And then she laughed.

"What's the matter?"

"Just look at yourself. In the mirror."

He looked and saw a mad Indian covered with warpaint. There was a scratch on his cheek, blood had dripped down and coagulated. He could not remember cutting himself; it must have happened when they fell between the tables. To a young bride he must be an alarming sight. "Jesus," he said, and then, "I'm sorry. These planters are the lowest form of human life, once they start drinking."

"Your chief didn't do badly either," she said, still smiling. "It's a miracle that he didn't give Mrs. Boosmans a hemorrhage when he slapped her back."

"Oh, he's all right," he said with a return of irritation. "He has the soul of a child and a heart of gold."

She kissed him lightly, said, "All right," and flitted into the bathroom. Outside the parrot was still shrieking.

He heard her run the bath, stood a moment in doubt, feeling suddenly very tired, then he started to take off his torn and dirty clothes. When he was undressed he fished a crumpled pack of cigarettes out of his breast pocket, soggy with gelatine, but found no matches. Her bag was lying on the dressing table, he opened it, rummaged among its contents, found a lighter, lit his cigarette, dropped the lighter back into the bag, and his eye was caught by his name, in Bert's handwriting. As he took the envelope out, he saw that it was more than a letter, it was a package. Inside he found a thick wad of thin paper, covered with typescript, without spacing.

Dear A. Here is my belated but also more elaborate reaction to your suggestions about the relationship between conversion and hormones. Indeed, a fascinating field for research. I shall be delighted to explore it with you. Before we set out, however, let us define . . .

He lay reading on the bed, ash from his cigarette dropped on his singlet, but he did not notice. Bert was a genius, a wonder girl; he laughed out loud at her lucid and brilliant analyses of his notes. He vaguely heard a voice say, "Anton. . . ?" softly and tentatively, and answered without looking up: "Coming, sweetie, just a sec . . ." He had not noticed her come in wearing the nightdress she had specially chosen for the occasion in the most expensive shop in Amsterdam and protected during that voyage round half the globe against nature and her own curiosity; he had not noticed that she had been away nearly half an hour, preparing herself for the night, hoping he would not get impatient or fall asleep. He did not see her go to the window, peer out through the Venetian blinds, he did not hear the rattle as she drew her finger down the slats. He did not see her light a cigarette, did not hear the clatter of the lighter, dropped onto the glass top of the bedside table. He did not notice how she sat down on the window seat, her knees drawn up, and tried to fight back her tears by peering through the blinds again. Outside the party was petering out in drunken snatches of song; underneath their balcony someone was sick with such abandon that she fled to bed. There was no blanket, only a sheet, and a hard roll. She lay staring at the ceiling, saw a black insect scurry across it that had at least seven legs, and hid her head under the sheet.

The only one who was really and sincerely happy that night, was Brits-Jansen. For in the cell in the police station he had been welcomed by a pygmy from the New Guinea jungle, who had been captured by a circus, escaped in Labuan Redjo, been knocked down by a car and arrested for drunkenness, because no one could understand a word he said. Brits-Jansen could, and they spent a delightful night, smoking and gossiping, while in the cell next to theirs the murderer from Rotterdam lay sadly humming "Trees," until he fell asleep.

CHAPTER NINE

THE *hope that everything will turn out all right in the end is slowly dying. . . .* Only after she had written it down did she realize how true it was.

The day before, she had started writing a résumé of what had happened during the past three months. Their honeymoon in the mountains; the boardinghouse "Senang" in Batavia, where they lived while waiting for a bungalow of their own; now she had arrived at the first night in the new house, which she had so fervently hoped would change everything, but she had been mistaken once more.

She had been mistaken many times. Her first mistake had been to suppress the vague feeling of danger she had had when he wrote asking her to come over. They had known one another for so long, they loved one another so devotedly, he was such an open book to her. . . . He was no open book. He was a book that, after she had opened it with difficulty, turned out to be written in a foreign language.

It had started with their wedding night. She knew it was not his fault that her arrival had been such an abysmal failure, and for three months she had glossed it over. But now she knew: it had not been the ghastly party, the vandalism of those brutes that had shocked her so deeply— it had been the way he had assaulted her, once he had finished reading that letter.

That had been the moment, the fatal, crucial moment, and she admitted it now. So far all she had dared write in her diary was, *Our first embrace was a surprise for which I was totally unprepared and so it did not quite live up to my expectations.*

Her expectations . . . All those months while she waited and hoped and daydreamed, she had wandered about her provincial town like a sleepwalker in the solemn, childish knowledge of being faithful. She had dreamed by night and relived by day their tender embraces, their whispered words, their butterfly-like kisses, their gentle caresses, their yearning looks full of shy desire. Daydreaming after his departure, she had felt like a nun, protecting the candle flame of her love from the wind.

The little flame had withstood the loneliness and the waiting; it had withstood even the gale in the Bay of Biscay when she had been so horribly seasick that she wished she had never set eyes on him at all. It had even withstood her flirtation with the wireless operator, who had been so correct and so understanding in the romantic light of the Chinese lanterns on the promenade deck, but who had suddenly kissed her after the Captain's ball. This had shaken her so much that she had reacted as if she had had lots of experience. He had taken her for a tough girl who needed to be wooed masterfully, and started rattling at the door of her cabin and slipping notes underneath it. It had withstood even her complete concentration on defending herself against George during that last week, a dreamlike, self-contained experience between two worlds, but it had been extinguished by the lurid thunderstorm of Anton's brutal lust.

That first time she had managed to explain it away: he had been dead tired, emotionally upset by her arrival, he had drunk too much, he was so sensitive that he had acted like a brute out of excessive shyness. But the following night, the same thing had happened. They had had a busy day, packing and traveling in a broiling heat, riding on ponies up a winding trail, past precipices and thundering cataracts that sounded like express trains in the darkness below. They arrived at last, dizzy with the thin air, at a hotel on the mountain top: oddly luxurious and civilized in that stark desolation, a Plaza on the moon. The meal was romantic, with candles and champagne; an orchestra played Indian music and Anton looked very handsome, tanned and manly, in his white dinner jacket. He smoked a pipe on the verandah when they had their coffee after the meal, and it suited him. They danced, and for half an hour she felt free and happy and a bit drunk; just like Holland in a dream, without her parents waiting, without watching the clock, without gossiping acquaintances staring at them with beady eyes. They sat sipping liqueurs until the small hours and talked about old times. When finally they went up to their room, she was dead tired and rather tight, nicely so, sleepy and peaceful. She only did her teeth and her face and washed her hands, she was so tired; as she entered the bedroom in her nightdress, she found him, fully dressed, hunting mosquitoes with a fly swatter. He turned round as she came in, and stood still, the fly swatter in his hand, looking at her with a strange fixed stare that she seemed to remember from a nightmare. Then he said hoarsely, "That's a lovely nightdress—lovely," dropped the fly swatter, and came slowly toward her like a murderer in a film. She felt herself freeze in alarm. She wanted to flee, to cry out, but that stare mesmerized her and, when his face came close to hers, she closed her eyes and he took that for surrender. It was the same as it had been the previous night; and she did not want to recall the details even now. It had been too horrible, too full of disgust and pain. She wept quietly, when at last he left her lying on the bed; he, in a ghastly misunderstanding, took it for the effect of too great a delight. He lit a cigarette and talked for hours about his work and the jungle and that wonderful man, that lump of gold, Dr. Brits-Jansen; she realized as he sat talking, numbed with shame and exhaustion, that she did not understand his work at all, that she saw the jungle he loved as a dark, terrifying wilderness full of insects, wild beasts and the stench of rotting vegetation; whereas that wonderful man, that lump of gold, was the monstrous brute who had beaten Mrs. Boosmans and lifted her herself up like a slave for sale during that orgy. When she heard him say, "Brits-Jansen is one of the shyest men I've ever met, with the heart of a bird," she shivered and prayed inwardly to God to liberate her. If Anton, her Anton, the sweet, gentle boy with whom she had fallen in love, credited that monster with the heart of a bird—then what was in store for her? God, dear God, what was in store for her?

She knew the answer now: hell. A hell of unbridled, merciless lust. A man bewitched into a muscular, bronzed leopard, who pounced upon her without warning, dragged her to his lair, tore her clothes off and dug his teeth into her shoulder, until she screamed and struggled and kicked, making him drunk with savage desire. When all was over she would get up, swaying, and strip the case off the pillow to soak it in the washbasin for fear the native servants would see the stains of tears and blood. Her dreams, her expectations, her certainties were destroyed so utterly that she was afraid of going mad. She paced up and down for whole afternoons on end in their small sitting room with the clock, the newspaper rack and the cocktail cabinet, the cocktail cabinet, the newspaper rack and the clock. The clock, the newspaper-rack . . . God, help, help! She moaned, her fists on her forehead, her eyes closed, her elbows on the sideboard—God, God, help.

The silence remained without answer. Outside a street vendor chanted: "Papaja, bultzak!" Cook in the kitchen hummed tunelessly; the neighbors' radio syncopated Chopin. She pressed her thumbs in her ears and, in the throbbing red silence, two words pulsated with the pumping of her blood: "No child—no child—no child." That was the thought, the only thought that saved her from total collapse: no child—dear merciful God; in Christ's name, no child. That was the only thing she could do; he could rape her and torture her until she passed out—but no child, no child.

She did not quite know how to go about it. In Holland, the question had never arisen; he had been so gentle and sensitive and cautious. At last she overcame her shame and talked about it to Jane Frenssen, an assistant in the Salemba laboratory, the only young matron she had met who had not repelled her by coarseness, callousness toward the native servants, chain smoking or shameless drinking as the others had done. Jane Frenssen was fat, sturdy and easy-going, but she was still a woman. The others were no longer women: shrill, repulsive screamers, sexless but for a scarlet mouth and hairless legs, deflowered by that beautiful jungle, those wonderful lumps of gold with their birds' hearts. Jane Frenssen was lucky; she was strong. "Oh," she said, "you'll have to get used to it, duckie," after she had hinted shyly that Anton occasionally was, well, how shall I say, a bit overexcited, passionately, I mean. "The temperature puts the men in heat," Jane said with embarrassing frankness, understanding her at once. "The temperature and the spices and the drink— doesn't mean a thing; when they start exaggerating, you give them a slap with a wet towel and it'll pass. But take care that you, for your part, don't exaggerate either—things are too easy for them over here. Before you know what's happened, they're in bed with someone else and what good does that do? So—think of old Confucius: 'If rape is inevitable, lie back and enjoy it,' and you'll be surprised how true that is, once you've got rid of your Dutch inhibitions. Another drink?"

"No, thank you."

"If you ask me, you're too pusillanimous," Jane said. "In the East, there's no better defense than attack."

She had another drink, on second thought, and after a while it gave her the courage to start on the subject of contraceptives, in the frank, manly, Far East style. Jane asked: "Surely your husband knows how to go about that? Good Lord, he's a doctor!" But she answered that she'd rather take care of it herself. In the end Jane promised, after some embarrassing questions, that Frans, her husband, would mix something for her in the lab—of course she wouldn't tell him for whom it was meant. God, this wasn't the first time. She must understand, however, that it was only a preventative and useless once the thing was a fait accompli.

When finally she returned home with a splitting headache, she found a note from Anton saying that he had unexpectedly been put on night duty so he would not be back that night; never had a message made her so happy in this world of terror and wilderness. She sat up all night, enjoying the luxury of being alone, drinking black coffee to ward off sleep so as not to miss a minute of this unexpected holiday. Toward dawn, when it became cooler, her headache subsided and her thoughts became clearer. Her intelligence arose once more from the jungle of emotions and fears and, for half an hour, she knew the old delight of being herself: Els van Duin, daughter of the Latin professor at Erasmus College, the girl engaged to that doctor in the Dutch East Indies. It was as if she woke up from a nightmare; she felt free, independent and deliciously unpredictable once more, the tender and feminine Els with whom Anton had fallen in love. She even rediscovered a trace of love for Anton in herself, while thinking of him as he had looked with his pipe on the verandah of the hotel in the mountains. She asked herself, honestly and objectively, what it was that had changed everything, bewitched everything, until she seemed to live in a haunted world full of smothered screams, the rustling of wings against dark wire netting, hot groping hands in the night and flashing white fangs. Was it Anton's fault? Was it hers?

Of course, the sexual side was not the most important thing in marriage, but was it her fault that it preoccupied her so completely? Why could she not bring herself to discuss it with Anton? Why did she not tell him the truth, frankly? He loved her!

Did he? He said so all the time. But then why could she not reach him at all? Why did she not understand a word of what he said, why could she not follow the train of his thoughts, why could they not laugh at the same things any more, why was he so delighted with every letter Bert sent him, why was he talking all the time about the jungle or Bert? It seemed as if those two became one in her imagination: Bert and the jungle. The jungle . . . She would never understand it. That morning, sitting up in bed in the serene, cool stillness of the dawn, she realized it. He had written to her: the Far East is another planet. She had laughed at it tenderly, with a feeling of fond superiority. He was still such a boy, such a romantic. How could anything be another planet to her as long as he was there? Now she knew he had been right: it was indeed another planet. An impenetrable, unconquerable wilderness to which man had to adjust himself or perish. Anton had adjusted himself; the jungle had absorbed him and changed him until he had become unrecognizable. There was only one thing to be done: she must try to adjust herself too. She must fight with all her strength against her panic, her lethargy, her feeling of being a stranger at a new school. Now she should try to put herself in the place of Anton, who was not having an easy time either. She knew, more from his moods than from what he said, that he was not happy in his hospital service, that he longed to be back in the jungle just as she longed to be back in Holland. Both of them were strangers at a new school. She should try to help him instead of being frightened and unhappy. She fell asleep at last with a feeling of peace.

Everything went well the next day, exceptionally well. Anton came home in the morning and went to bed dead tired; she had the day to herself and the detachment of that lovely night remained with her. In the afternoon, she brought him tea in bed. He was sweet and sleepy and, for the first time, they laughed together because of the djongos who could not be taught to turn on the lights when showing guests into a dark sitting room. During the meal, they laughed and chatted and forgot they were married; when they settled down in the cozy light of the orange table lamp for coffee he told her, casually, that he was to leave in two days' time for Sumatra, a special assignment. He would be away four or five weeks.

Twenty-four hours earlier, she would have heard this with a feeling of immense relief; now it was almost a disappointment, as if a chance to show him what she could do were taken away from her. "What kind of assignment?" she asked, and he answered: "Oh, something in the jungle. I'm going to see Brits-Jansen." He said it casually.

She did not understand herself at all, but that night she was suddenly very provocative. Only the night before, she had known but one wish: that he should leave her in peace; now she wanted him to fondle and caress her and was taken aback when, for the first time, he was indifferent. He was very tired, he had to finish an urgent report and the following night they would have the Frenssens for dinner, so he would not have a chance to work then. She went to bed alone, slowly and thoughtfully; when he finally came, late because he had slept nearly all day, she was still awake. But he said: "Sleep well, sweetie. God, I'm tired," and was asleep within three minutes.

She lay for a long time staring in the darkness, suddenly jealous of Bert. For she knew, without reason but with absolute certainty, that "the urgent report" had been a letter to Bert. Bert and the jungle had defeated her first efforts at adjustment. The following night, the Frenssens came to dinner and after they had gone, a quarrel broke out because of the Chinese djongos who had borrowed glasses and cutlery from the neighbors' djongos, so the Frenssens had eaten with their own knives and forks. He thought it was very funny; she was terribly angry, for somehow the cutlery and the glasses were a symbol to her of all the unspoken reproaches and recriminations she had been piling up. He had looked at her coldly, said: "All right. Fire him if it makes you happy. Good night," and walked out of the door. She wanted to cry, "Darling!" but could not bring herself to do so. Instead, she slammed the door behind him and the newspaper rack fell off the wall. She burst into tears, kicked the rack across the room, and then crawled on all fours under the table to pick it up. Then suddenly, she sat down at the table with her box of stationery and started a letter. *Dear George* . . .

She sat writing feverishly for over an hour, forgetting it had been meant as a letter to someone; when finally she went to bed, Anton was asleep. She put on the light over the washbasin, made a lot of noise with the taps, slammed down the tooth glass, gargled, coughed, sighed, but his breathing remained regular. When she finally lay down beside him, his back was turned toward her and she had to suppress a malicious desire to kick him. She sighed again, louder than before, said, "Phew!" flung off the sheet and then settled down in such a way that he bounced. But his breathing continued evenly. She fell asleep in a haze of self-pity and bewilderment.

When he went away the next morning, everything was nice and normal. They both were sorry and did not want to make the first move and the result was a sudden tenderness in their farewell, like a soldier who was off to the war and his wife who was very brave about it. She waved until he turned the corner, then she took out her diary, feeling quite contented, and suddenly found herself writing, *The hope is slowly dying.* . . .

She wrote no further. She never wanted to see this diary again. Nonsense, nonsense, she should do something, put her mind on other things. Clean the house, for instance, or sew on all the name tapes. Instead, she opened the drawer of his bedside table, and found a pile of letters bound with an elastic band. The envelopes were smudged and the edges worn. They were her own letters, which he had carried with him like a talisman on every expedition into the jungle. Now he had left once more on an expedition, the first since their marriage, and he had left her letters behind.

She scolded herself for her silliness, thought of explanations that all sounded sensible: he had forgotten them in his haste, he did not need them any more now he had her—but she started to search the room. She opened all the drawers, searched his desk, the pockets of his suits—she searched for hours and did not find them. He had taken Bert's letters with him, instead of hers.

That night, she thought for the first time of the possibility of writing to Bert herself.

《《《 》》》

Two nights before his departure, Anton had found on his arrival in the doctor's office a memo: *Dr. Zorgdrager is requested to report to Dr. Kramer's office at 7 a.m. sharp tomorrow morning.* He had no idea what it was about, but if it meant a dressing down, he deserved it.

That night, sitting behind his tidy steel desk, his feet on the window sill, blowing smoke at the mosquito curtain behind which myriads of insects were swirling, he tried to formulate for himself the reasons why his work in Batavia had been so bad.

Well, there wasn't much of a mystery there: the jungle had spoiled him. Brits-Jansen had not taught him the necessary respect for the hierarchy of the Government Health Service that was observed in Batavia; in the jungle, he had known of only one authority: Brits-Jansen, and one superior: Dr. Kramer. In Batavia he found that he had scores of superiors, to all of whom he had to show a carefully graded respect. He remembered nurses telling him about the hierarchy in the Amsterdam University Hospital; he himself had never been bothered by matrons, assistant matrons, under matrons, assistant under matrons, theater sisters, staff nurses, assistant staff nurses and the rest. In Batavia, the Central Hospital was alive with assistants, assistants' assistants and under assistants' assistants. There were those at the top of the ladder, who had a car, six servants and a private office at the Salemba laboratory or the Eykman Institute, where they worked in a blaze of glory from two till five in the afternoon.

To those he was expected to kowtow in deference to their role in protecting the Dutch East Indies from certain diseases. After some irrevelant and risky research, he discovered that one of them had been inquiring for years into the mysteries of the common cold; another into something obscure that looked like chilblains; the only pundit lacking was a specialist in frostbite. Their assistants and their assistants' assistants formed the rest of the palace guard that had its headquarters in the Central Hospital. The hospital itself was very efficient, but its white staff behaved with a cool impersonal callousness, demonstrated in such subleties as addressing the patients by their numbers. Brits-Jansen and he, while cleaning up their epidemics in the jungle, had certainly not been sentimentalists toward their brown-skinned brothers and sisters of the Equator, but they had at least shown some acknowledgment of their humanity and some concern for their suffering. The young doctors who had arrived after him and gone straight from the boat into hospital service in Batavia had no such sentiments. Their conception of the Far East was not that of a different planet; all they knew of it was the Central Hospital and the club, and the Central Hospital meant something halfway between the poor ward of the University Clinic in Amsterdam and the monkey pens in the Institute for Tropical Diseases. They considered him as belonging to a lower order because he had been on jungle duty; in their world a jungle assignment was a form of punishment for unsatisfactory work in Batavia.

All this, however, was not enough to explain his inner decline. Batavia and its stifling atmosphere of bureaucracy would be easy enough to shake off, once back in the jungle; something inside him had changed, that might not be so easy to redress. His diagnostics were abominable: that strange, exciting lucidity which had enabled him to see leprosy on the Sultan's hand and erotomania on the face of Bert's father had vanished completely. If Brits-Jansen was right, his marriage was to blame.

It had come as a complete surprise, the way in which Els had unleashed all his latent passion. Before her arrival, he had hardly been bothered by sex. He had been too busy and there had been little temptation. But during the months of abstinence in the jungle, he had piled up a vitality that, once released, swept him clean off his feet and came to dominate his life entirely. When he looked at the clock in the hospital or in the laboratory, it was to determine the time that separated him from the satisfaction his body craved; the drink, the rijst-tafel, love and sleep. When he came home, he could not look at Els without desiring her, and because there were few things they could talk about without uncovering the abyss that separated their worlds, he often took her in his arms to forget her in her very embrace. That was the most alarming thing about his passion: it was not Els, not one woman he caressed and kissed, it was something vague, deeply indecent: the female. His Christian background and up-bringing manifested themselves; physical love was sinful and he recognized its sinfulness most of all in the fact that he used Els to gratify the desire that other women, all women, had aroused in him. Luckily, she was not conscious of this. She was perhaps a little overcome by his passion, occasionally she seemed rather passive; but he had no means of judging that this was not the way it should be, for she was the only woman to whom he had ever made love.

He did not dare picture to himself what their marriage would look like without the physical element. Their embraces carried them over stretches of spiritual emptiness that would otherwise make their life together unbearable. For what he had suspected had proved to be true: the boy with whom Els had fallen in love had died on the Kali-Woga. Now she was married to someone else, in whom she tried desperately to rediscover the man she had loved. Things they had talked about in the past no longer interested him; his work did not interest her. Things they had laughed at with that wonderful feeling of conspiracy in Holland now seemed silly and childish to him, whereas jokes he brought home from the hospital and the laboratory left her with a forced smile on her lips. He had hoped that she would find some life of her own, but she had made no contact with neighbors or friends. Her Dutch provincialism seemed to harden instead of adapting itself to the colonial style of living; she addressed the servants with such unworldly formulas as "Would you mind awfully bringing in the tea?" and "Oh thank you, how kind of you," which left them gaping after her. It was obvious that things could not continue as they were; already she was getting pale and drawn; somehow she must learn how to adapt herself or she would wilt away.

He decided that the perfect excuse for the mediocrity of his work, which he had to justify at seven o'clock to Dr. Kramer, was that he was worried about his wife's health. On his way to the Head Office he rehearsed a sincere little speech, to be spoken softly with hands tightly folded on the edge of the desk and slightly haunted eyes. "You see, doctor, I'm afraid that the tropics have a bad effect on her. I can't tell you how worried I am. Maybe I should take her to the mountains, or something." Kramer might send another doctor to give her a checkup, but he would cross that bridge when he came to it.

When he entered the office with the fan, the huge map on the wall and the desk with the telephones, Dr. Kramer, writing, said, "Sit down," without looking up. He sat down and waited for five minutes, staring at the scribbling man in shirt sleeves—five minutes during which he was reduced from a self-satisfied, fattening civil servant to the nervous totok he had been on the day of his arrival. When Dr. Kramer put down his pen at last and looked across at him, he knew that he had better forget the story of his wife feeling poorly, or there would be trouble.

"Sorry to keep you waiting," Dr. Kramer said, "but the whole thing has come as a surprise to me as well. You leave tomorrow at 6:10 A.M. with the steamer *Rensselaer* for Medan. There you'll report to the resident's office, where you'll meet the Governor General of French Indo-China, General Doumic, whom you are to accompany with two of his aids to Langsa. There you will charter sufficient porters to carry the General, his aids and his luggage by palanquin to Camp Lung Plague, Dr. Breszezinska-Jansen. The C.O. Atjeh will provide you with a bodyguard of military police, so you'll have no responsibility for the safety of the expedition. You'll just act as a guide. In Camp Lung Plague General Doumic wants to have a look at the spot where that archaeological find has been dug up. Once he has seen that, you'll escort him back and return him to the resident in Medan. Here are your orders," and he handed him the paper on which he had been writing.

"Archaeological find?" Anton asked.

Dr. Kramer looked at him without expression and said flatly, "It appears that Dr. Jansen has dug up an urn which is thirty thousand years old, and he committed the error of handing it to some archaeologists in Labuan Redjo. As a result, Dr. Breszezinska-Jansen is now considered to be one of the world's foremost specialists on the origins of man."

"You don't mean that thing he keeps his teeth in?"

"I have not been advised of that detail," Dr. Kramer said unsmilingly. "I should, however, like to know exactly what happened in Labuan Redjo. You were there, I gather?"

"You mean—the reception?"

"I mean the orgy at the Grand Hotel in Labuan Redjo, the assault on the Minister of Colonies, the beating-up of his wife and the rape of his daughter."

"No," Anton said, aghast. "Was she . . . ?"

"Let's say: her ill-timed seduction," Dr. Kramer corrected flatly as before. "I put these questions to you because I have been advised that you took part in the proceedings in so far that you struck Mrs. Boosmans with a dead pig."

"It was all the result of a well-meant improvisation, sir. We heard at the last moment that His Excellency was arriving and—er—well, the festivities got a bit out of hand."

"I want a full report of the occurrence," Dr. Kramer said, "and I'll thank you to refrain from cheap wit while writing it. It will have to be sent on to The Hague."

"But I was only an onlooker," Anton ventured lamely.

"Did you throw that pig, or did you not?" Dr. Kramer asked. "That is the question."

"I did, sir."

"In that case, I expect a full explanation of your action, and a comprehensive report of the events leading up to it. I don't know whether it escaped you, but Dr. Breszezinska-Jansen was arrested that night, charged with breach of the peace; his name has now arrived in The Hague and consequently the Service is involved."

"Have you asked him for a report?"

"I have," Dr. Kramer said coldly, "and as you are going to see Dr. Breszezinska-Jansen, I suggest that you both take the necessary pains to verify that your two interpretations conform. I may be holding this office for another ten years, and I do not want to be pestered until I'm pensioned off by recurrent inquiries from the Ministry of Colonies about a dead pig thrown at a Minister's wife. This kind of thing has a tendency to become chronic unless nipped in the bud; so don't think I am amused, please. I am not amused by the rest of the reports I receive about you either."

"I beg your pardon?"

"Your work in Batavia is bad. You are lazy, show a lack of interest and a good deal of self-satisfaction. Why?

The "self-satisfaction" gave Anton the courage to say, "I don't agree with the last definition, sir. 'Lack of self-confidence' would be more correct."

"Why?"

"I feel out of place here."

"Then where do you feel in place? Holland?"

"The jungle."

"Why?"

"That is hard to say. . . ."

"In that case, you are talking nonsense."

"I don't think it is, sir, only the reasons are pretty complicated. One of them is that I liked my work with Dr. Jansen very much because . . . because Dr. Jansen had confidence in me."

"Dr. Jansen's confidence is flattering but meaningless. He has confidence in anyone who knows how to handle him, and he who cannot do so is a bad doctor."

"I believe that Dr. Jansen's appreciation is founded on other considerations."

"For instance?"

"My diagnostics."

"Your diagnostics in Java, if I'm to believe the reports, are remarkable for their ineptitude."

"Not in the jungle."

"Supposing I accept your statement, how do you explain it?"

Anton looked up and saw the calm gaze of Dr. Kramer's eyes looking straight through him. To that man, human beings did not exist, only cases. Here was Zorgdrager, A., a case of mental collapse. What interested him was the causes of that collapse, for reasons of expediency, not out of human compassion. "I'd like to get back on jungle duty, sir," he said, dully.

"If I were to transfer you back to jungle duty, what would be your wife's attitude?"

He had forgotten about Els. "Oh, she won't mind," he said.

"I see." When Dr. Kramer said that, Anton realized that the whole failure of his marriage had been diagnosed. He suddenly hated the little man, for it was the first time that he saw it as a failure himself.

"All right," Dr. Kramer said. "I'll keep you listed for a jungle assignment but this doesn't mean that you can go on neglecting your work in Batavia. Unless it improves by one hundred per cent, I'll have to think of another way of filling your ten years' contract. You know the prison camp in Lampong?"

"I've heard of it. . . ."

"There is a vacancy as prison doctor. Good morning. Have a good trip."

When Anton closed the door behind him, he felt sick. Lampong—

counting the strokes of the birch, to stop the punishment when blood was drawn—to end up there with a young wife meant to turn her into a nervous wreck. Only when he was outside and was walking down the lane with the potted dwarf palms did he realize that he was on his way to Brits-Jansen. Nobody was looking and he jumped with joy. "Chin up, Dr. Jansen," he muttered in delighted memory of his first voyage. "I'll find you, if it takes a year. . . ." But his gaiety turned into grimness as he realized that the trip ahead of him was going to be another trial. In the jungle itself he would find out the truth of his rash contention that in the wilderness he was a better man.

He did not touch Els before he left, not even in his thoughts. She went on waving until he had turned the corner and it was a strangely sad moment, like a farewell, but then the prospect of the expedition gave him a new resilience, a new hope. He looked at Batavia once more with pity: an ant heap of vanity. He saw himself: fat voluptuary with smarmed-down hair and a weak chin, on his way back to the wilderness, the purifying maze of God.

"Dr. Zorgdrager, G.H.S.," he told the purser.

The purser saluted and said, "Cabin twenty, doctor. Your luggage is on board."

"Luggage?"

"Two tins of the Government Health Service."

"Are they marked?"

"Certainly, doctor," the purser said, with the layman's respect for the medical profession. "Medicine, I believe: P.G."

"I see," Anton said. "That's all right."

"Is it against cholera, doctor?" the purser asked.

"No," said Anton, "against sin."

The purser did not understand, but he laughed all the same. The doctor went down the corridor humming, looking for cabin twenty, a muscular young man with untidy hair and the eyes of a detective; it was a pity those people were so taciturn, their stories must be fascinating.

"Cabin sixteen, Your Excellency," he said. "Your luggage is on board."

"Everything is there, I hope?" the Contrôleur asked.

"Certainly, Your Excellency," the purser replied, with a bow that some-how managed to be deprecatory. "Your gin is there too,"

Anton heard this, and he grinned. Life got its taste back. When he had found his cabin, he threw his topee on the upper bunk, propped his feet up on the washstand, put the ashtray on the floor by his side and started to reread her latest letter, that had arrived this morning and that so far he had only glanced at.

Dear Comrade, Brother in the Wilderness ...
He did not notice the boat leaving.

«« »»

The document that an exhausted native messenger handed to Dr. Breszezinska-Jansen after a seven days' marathon run through the jungle was written on official paper, sealed with five different stamps, bore two signatures, three sets of initials, and ran:

The Governor of Atjeh and dependencies advises Dr. Breszezinska-Jansen that His Excellency, the General Alexandre Marie Jésus Doumic, Governor General of French Indo-China, at present a guest of His Excellency the Governor-General of the Netherlands East Indies, has expressed the wish to honor with a personal visit the site where the prehistoric excavations are in progress.

When he read that far he already felt like tearing up the paper and trampling on it like an enraged elephant. There he was, in his sixth month in the jungle, cutting a road through the wilderness that would safeguard Atjeh and its dependencies from the perennial menace of the lung plague, and the Governor of that fortunate district was laboring under the delusion that he was busy with prehistoric excavations! It was one more proof that the whole world seemed to be playing a practical joke on him. He read on, breathing heavily through his nose. An awed silence reigned in the jungle; the coolies stood staring at him from a distance; the panting messenger surreptitiously backed away.

His Excellency the Governor General has, in granting this request, ordered his resident for Atjeh and its dependencies to accord the General Doumic every help and assistance so as to facilitate his journey. It is in conformity with this order that the resident hereby requests Dr. Breszezinska-Jansen to take the necessary action so as to assure the General Doumic and his retinue of a reception in accordance with his rank and status. The General will be escorted by two aides of French nationality, one guide of Netherlands nationality, the Major Stuyts of the Royal Police, a police escort of ten, and a number of native bearers.

The Major Stuyts of the Royal Military Police? If that were the bullfrog from Labuan Redjo, he would shoot him. He now breathed so heavily that he drowned the panting of the messenger.

The arrival of the General Doumic at the site of the excavations may be expected one week after reception of this communication, the bearer of which has the order to deliver to Dr. Breszezinska-Jansen one metal chest marked D.O.G. 55-6744, Medan, containing festive decorations, supplementary rations and spirits and a program for the reception prepared by the public relations office in Batavia.

He glowered at the chest with eyes that were bloodshot with anger, alcohol and malaria; the messenger backed further away, as if he felt the heat of that glare. The chest was sealed and addressed to *"Dr. Breszezinska-Jansen, Royal Archaeological Society."* He aimed a kick at it, but remembered in time that he was wearing rope sandals, so he only snarled at the chest, and read on.

His Excellency the Governor would be pleased if, during the visit of the General Doumic, Dr. Breszezinska-Jansen were to make a further prehistoric discovery.

That did it: he burst into satanic laughter. He laughed so uproariously, so uncontrollably, that the coolies fled into the jungle, thinking tuan besar had gone mataglap. The messenger scurried away from the whinnying giant as he threw the document into the air, with a cry of "Whoopee!" and collapsed on the chest, sobbing, his head in his hands. The mandurs rounded up the coolies and drove them silently back to their work on the road. The messenger vanished and, for a few minutes, the central clearing of the camp was empty. Then the mosquito curtain of the doctor's tent was lifted and a pygmy peeped, blinking sleepily. The pygmy came out, wearing a penis sheath with a bright red plume. He waddled toward the giant on short bowlegs and examined the chest, his hands on his knees.

Brits-Jansen looked up as the pygmy pushed against his thigh, and he stood up, sighing, a broken man. The pygmy heaved the chest open with difficulty; when the contents were disclosed, he stood staring at them with a look of incredulity that changed into delight, cried, "Tuan!" and then started to pull out bunting, flags, streamers, squeakers, paper hats—a fantastic carnival of color in the jungle. Brits-Jansen stared at him, then he turned away and left the dwarf alone in the clearing, cooing and chortling, wrapping himself in bunting, waving flags, trying on paper hats and blowing squeakers, thin incongruous sounds in the humming silence of the wilderness. At the entrance to his tent he looked back once more, and saw the dwarf unroll a portrait of Her Majesty twice his size, spread it out on the ground and examined it from the feet up, his hands on his knees once more. He looked ludicrous, farcical; yet that pygmy was the sanest fruit the evening in Labuan Redjo had borne, even though his very name was crazy. It had been written on a label attached to the string of beads around his waist: *Stegomyia Fasciata, Presbyterian, age unknown, height 3 feet 11 inches.* Obviously, some unknown joker of the Government Health Service had passed that way. Stegomyia fasciata was the Latin name for the yellow fever mosquito.

He had forgotten all about the urn he had given to the two little archaeologists, when he received a solemn letter from the Royal Archaeological Society in which he was advised of his nomination as honorary member of that institution in recognition of his discovery of the oldest urn in the archipelago. The letter closed with the request that he should send on to the society's headquarters in Batavia all pottery, skeletons, tools and other prehistoric finds he might have unearthed, or should unearth in the future. He received the letter in Surabaya, during one of his rare visits to Poppy. It arrived by special delivery in the middle of an almighty row between Poppy and him over the pygmy, who had been pestering Bambo the chimpanzee. Poppy had said she did not want the dirty little man in her house, he had asked what about that dirty little monkey, she had answered, "He isn't dirty because I wash him regularly and that's more than you do," he had screamed, "God Almighty!" and at that moment like an answer from on high, the chimpanzee had crashed down with the drawing-room curtain, pulling the rod with him, which had struck the pygmy over the bridge of the nose and set him shrieking. He had taken the water jug, hurled it at the tangle of curtain, monkey, woman, rod and dwarf, and just as the thing exploded against the wall with a shower of earthenware and water, the postman had appeared in the doorway, grinning, singing, "Lettah, tuan." When Poppy heard that he had been nominated something honorary, it appeased her at once and made her rather girlish, tucking up curls at the back of her head. So he had accepted, but added a rider to his letter saying that he did not know anything about archaeology and had no intention of paying a subscription.

This was but the beginning, the seemingly harmless starting point of a mystification that within a week took on grotesque proportions. The press got hold of the news of his nomination, journalists wanted to interview him and, when he threw them out, they composed long articles describing "Dr. Breszezinska-Jansen, the famous archaeologist" with a richness of detail in which the malicious anecdotes about his person circulating in the club were easily recognizable. A foreign press agency took up the juicy material of the gigantic lumberjack who had once quelled a revolution in Borneo by taking out his dentures; his name was proclaimed all over the Pacific and he was referred to as the world-famous archaeologist who burrowed for years in the darkness of the jungle until finally his efforts to locate the cradle of mankind were crowned with success. Only one paper put up a feeble plea for truth as it said, "Dr. Breszezinska-Jansen, former physician."

The articles provoked a veritable avalanche of correspondence. Half-wits, maniacs, crooks and retired colonels fired a barrage at him of brochures, letters, parcels containing dung, photographs of pigs' bones dug up in their back yards and plaster casts of old spittoons found by maiden aunts while weeding. He fled to Batavia, but even there his mail caught up with him; when he received the invitation to make a lecture tour in America, he ran for shelter back into the jungle.

In Camp Lung Plague, protected from the civilized world by a trackless forest full of snakes and elephants, he at last calmed down sufficiently to see that none of this would have happened if he had stayed quietly where he was, instead of going to surprise the boy in Labuan Redjo. Not only would he have remained sane, he would not have received Piet Kramer's communication, which nearly gave him an apoplectic fit. *Dear Colleague,* the little runt had had the cheek to write. *I would appreciate it if you could spare a moment from your many prehistoric activities to let me know by return the exact reasons, properly tabulated, for your assault on Mrs. Boosmans-Halma on the evening of the 14th ultimo. Your answers to the following are also requested: (a) Who or what caused His Excellency the Minister of Colonies to be attacked, undressed and covered with tomato ketchup and where are his spectacles? (b) Who or what took liberties with Miss Boosmans, his daughter? After answering the above questions, the replies to which are requested by The Hague, you might care to reply to this one: (c) What were you doing in the prison of Labuan Redjo on two consecutive days when your report, which I have just received, situated you in Camp Lung Plague? I wish to stipulate that, while I do not object to your taking leave for short periods at your own discretion,*

I must insist that the reports you send to me justify keeping you on the payroll of the Government Health Service and not that of the Ministry of Mythology. Your request for a supplementary ration of P.G., owing to the extreme hardship of your present assignment, is granted but the cost thereof will be deducted from your contribution to the superannuation scheme as it seems apparent that you will not benefit from the latter at this rate. Cordially yours, P. J. Kramer, Administrator.

The ridiculous dwarf came into the tent grinning with filed-off teeth, wearing a paper hat, the French flag round his stomach and Her Majesty rolled up in his arms. He felt the urge to kick the creature out, hat and all; but the filed-off grin mellowed him and he suddenly realized that the dwarf was doomed by the same curse as himself: lifelong ridiculousness. It seemed inconceivable that inside this misshapen creature, this crude joke of God, was hidden a heart the size of a child's fist and a soul as big as his own. When the pygmy polished his boots, wrestling with the gigantic calves, he looked like a monkey; but when at night he sat gazing at the oil lamp, his chin resting on his little hands, his eyes full of mysterious thoughts, he was the confirmation of the answer Willem Waterreus had given to his question as to whether one could see God: "I see Him in the eyes of my neighbor."

Stegomyia had come in with a piece of paper he had found in the chest. He took it and read with a deep, wordless dejection:

Program for the Reception of His Excellency the Governor General of French Indo-China, the General Doumic, as proposed by the Public Relations Office, Batavia:

  a. The decoration of the camp with the enclosed material;
  b. The singing of the "Marseillaise" by the natives on the arrival of the General (Malay translation enclosed);
  c. A festive meal, for which the following ingredients are enclosed: One dozen tins of mock turtle soup, one dozen tins of sliced orange (it is suggested that these be utilized in a French dish, e.g., "canard à l'orange"), 6 tins of suet pudding . . ."

He let the paper fall from his limp hand, looked across at the pygmy and said, "Gin."

Two hours later he was awakened by his mandur, who shook him excitedly. "Tuan, tuan!" He opened his eyes, asked, alarmed, "What the hell. . . ?" and the mandur stammered, "Over there . . . little hill . . . dig, dig, tuan . . . Body! Much much old!"

He got up, full of dark apprehension, and trotted to where his coolies were digging. It was a hillock, like the one in which they had found the urn; but this time they had uncovered something that made him grab his hair.

In a caved-in little vault lay an age-old skeleton, older than he had ever seen. Tens of thousands of years it must have lain there, until the picks and the shovels of his coolies had brought it to light. It lay there quite peacefully, its skeleton arms crossed on its chest, the head loose with a gaping grin, and surrounding it, were dozens, scores . . . He counted, in a breathless silence, and arrived at a total of sixty-seven urns.

«« »»

Anton had expected the Frenchman to be a haughty, thin aristocrat in a uniform with decorations; le Général Doumic proved to be a charming old gentleman with a white goatee and sly little eyes, wearing an untidy shantung suit. He was accompanied by two aides-de-camp, a tall one and a short one, who seemed to have no other function than to announce with sheepish laughter the moments when Anton was to smile at the old gentleman's far too rapidly babbled jokes.

Their meeting in the resident's office had not been encouraging, as the Dutch portentousness had been crushing. But in the train to Langsa the General asked him to stop calling him Excellency and also his guide patter about the countryside, and to tell him something about this Doctor Briszousa-Hanson. Anton inquired cautiously whether he had already been given any information; the General smiled and the two gentlemen guffawed; ever since the General had expressed the wish to go and see the site of the excavation the Dutch officials had talked about nobody else. The Governor General himself had advised him against the trip, at first with vague stories about the unreliability of the Atjehs and the danger of the route, but in the end with the confession that the Atjehs were lambs compared to the doctor in the jungle, who had written to the Head of the Medical Service that if anyone else approached him with the word "urn" he would be shot and his vitals sent to Batavia in a basket. Everyone to whom the General had spoken afterward had contributed another tale of horror about the monster with the beard; he was now as curious to see the excavator as he was to see his excavations. He had been told only yesterday that Doctor Hanson was not a professional archaeologist but a medical man, and he understood that Doctor Sockdragère had been his assistant for some time, so now he expected to be told the whole truth. How much truth was there, for instance, in the story that Doctor Hansom had chased a Cabinet Minister's wife stark naked through a hotel in Labuan Redjo, while her daughter was being violated by his pygmy batman? Anton rushed to the aid of Brits-Jansen's reputation with stories of their expeditions against plague and cholera, his crusade against leprosy and his work for the Salvation Army. It sounded rather stilted in French, but the General was impressed. He listened slyly, an old shrewd mouse, while the other two gentlemen read newspapers.

In Langsa, Anton discovered to his relief that the major who was to command their escort of military police was not the ass from Labuan Redjo, but a wiry old colonial in an open-necked shirt with white hair on his chest who knew the Atjeh jungle like the back of his hand. As it turned out, it was fortunate he was there, for Anton would have lost his way many a time, so thoroughly had the jungle effaced all trails during his few months of absence. Once they had advanced half a day beyond the edge of the last plantation, the major discreetly took the lead. They advanced slowly, a cumbersome procession of swaying palanquins, stumbling porters and watchful soldiers behind the small band of screaming, hacking coolies who cleared the trail, chasing the snakes with their unearthly shrieks. Only on the sixth day did Anton realize where they were, for then he spotted the first telephone pole of the line that linked Camp Lung Plague with the nearest kampong. There were many mysterious telephone lines in the wilderness, left over from forgotten expeditions by geologists and oil prospectors; but only Brits-Jansen's poles had beer bottles for insulators.

On the eve of their arrival, something happened that seemed to be a prelude to Anton's reunion with Brits-Jansen, the teacher, not the legendary clown. It took place in the passangrahan of a little kampong in the mountains, miles away from civilization, where they made their halt on the evening of the fifth day. The passangrahan was a dilapidated bungalow on poles with five empty rooms; travelers were expected to provide their own food and bedding. A couple of girls, wide-eyed, slender creatures with the figures and grace of kraton dancers, made the beds for the company and opened their luggage for them. Night was falling, the camp was full of the flickering of fires and smells of cooking; the omnipresence of the virgin wilderness was so impressive in the darkness that everyone spoke quietly, even the major. Anton was dog-tired and lay on his bed with his eyes closed to rest before the meal, while one of the silent girls unpacked his bag with a rustle of linen and the soft shuffle of sandals on the wooden floor. He smelled the vague, sweet scent of hair oil, and was nearly asleep when he heard her ask, "Tuan?" He opened his eyes and saw her holding up his slippers questioningly. He grunted, nodded and closed his eyes once more. She pulled off his boots. They did not come off easily, for his feet were hot and swollen after the day's march. He opened his eyes again and looked at her and she smiled shyly. At that moment he knew that she had tuberculosis. He could not see it, nor hear it in her breathing, for it was invisible and inaudible; yet he knew. He made her lie down and sounded her chest; she submitted to his examination unprotestingly, like a good-natured animal. He found proofs that the disease was in its earliest stages. In Java, he would have diagnosed bronchitis; now he knew better.

Only then did he realize that his purification by the wilderness had started once more. He did not quite know whether to be alarmed or delighted; he went to bed early that night; on his way to his room he remembered that long conversation he had had with Brits-Jansen. Don't eat meat! Sexual abstinence! It had made him furious; now it made him humble. He heard Brits-Jansen's heavy voice again in the zooming silence of that laboratory. "When your moment comes to choose between good and evil, you'll know." Now, in the jungle night, it became a warning, an omen. He stooped on entering his room, lit a candle and took his Bible out of his pack; when he opened the mosquito curtain, he found a naked girl on his bed.

He stared at her in surprise, and she giggled. It was not the one who had taken off his boots, but another whom he vaguely remembered having smiled at him as he sat by the fire.

"What are you doing there?" he asked, stupidly.

"Waiting for the tuan," the girl said, her eyes glistening in the candle-light, and she giggled again.

He handed her her sarong that lay at the foot of the bed and said, "Tuan tired. Tuan sleep."

She did not pout, she did not try to stay, she obediently slipped into her sarong, "Sleep nice, tuan," she whispered before she slipped out of the door, like a shadow. He undressed; when he lay down, the smell of hair oil was stifling.

Why had he sent her away? Nothing in him, not a thought, not a shimmer of desire had reacted to the sight of that graceful golden little body, nestling like an adolescent's daydream in the small tent of the bed. Why? He decided that it had been the surprise of seeing her there, for he felt almost sorry now. He knew that in some passangrahans in the jungle, mainly in the Menangkabau district, the native girls assumed it to be a normal part of their duties to entertain the travelers, but it had never happened to him before. Why hadn't he let her stay? Because of Els? Els. It was the first time he had thought of her since his departure, and he felt ashamed at this discovery. She seemed to be further away from him than ever, further even than when she had still been a dream in far-off Holland. With a weird desire for self-torture, he suddenly started unraveling in his thoughts the alarming mystery of his marriage. It was going wrong. Nonsense! It was only natural that the first months were difficult for her as well as for him. It was the same with every marriage. Was it? He did not believe a word of it. He knew that if he had chased that girl away because of Els, it was not because his love for her made him immune to anyone else, but to enable him to put the blame on her if their marriage went wrong. Only if he had been an example of consistency could he say, "I have done what I could." He analyzed his own feelings so thoroughly that, in the end, he asked himself, in all seriousness, whether it would not have been a greater proof of his love for Els if he had betrayed her with that girl after all. He shrugged his shoulders, opened his Bible at random, and read the story of the dumb spirit cast out by Jesus as told by Saint Mark. Where the disciples had failed to exorcise the devil out of the moonsick child, Jesus succeeded. The disciples asked him, "Why could not we cast him out?" And Jesus said to them "This kind can come forth by nothing, but by prayer and fasting."

Prayer and fasting. It was the same as Brits-Jansen had said; that had proved itself a couple of hours before. He sat upright in his bed, read and reread the chapter and, in the end, he brought out Bert's letters, because he remembered that she had written about it somewhere. When he found it, he read on for hours, until at last he fell asleep—a restless sleeper, tossing in the dawn.

«« »»

When the column, after a journey of six days through the jungle, arrived in Camp Lung Plague, a surprise awaited them. Anton, at the head of the procession with the major and the screaming coolies, broke through the undergrowth and found himself at the edge of a clearing in the center of which a tableau was grouped, a village pageant in the heart of the wilderness.

A group of figures stood frozen in unnatural position underneath a ceiling of bunting, strung between the huts. Brits-Jansen was the central figure, wearing a paper hat and an orange sash. At his feet crouched a pygmy, wearing a pink cardboard nose and a tricolored hat. Around them the coolies were also wearing paper hats, with paper French flags in their hands. The moment the column entered the clearing, the group burst into song; only after a considerable time did Anton realize that it was a Malayan translation of the Marseillaise.

General Doumic listened to it with magnificent self-control; then he was welcomed by Dr. Breszezinska-Jansen in a speech in French, read from a typewritten sheet of paper, which was totally unintelligible. The speech obviously led up to the invitation to partake of a banquet that stood prepared in the background. When the visitors hesitantly shuffled toward the low tables underneath the bunting, Brits-Jansen caught his assistant's eye, but Anton hurried past him to the tables, where there were enough food and drink for a regiment. The General, undisturbed, instantly sat down, tied a napkin round his neck and looked around him, smiling.

Brits-Jansen stood at the head of the table, took another piece of paper from his pocket, lifted a beaker filled to the brim with P.G. and read aloud, "*Sur tous les amis de la France, vivent les Indes, santé.*" The General sipped at his beaker, put it down with his eyes closed, then got up on his thin legs to make the return toast. His speech was so witty, fast and flowery that Brits-Jansen sat looking at him with his mouth open. He ended by assuring "*le célèbre, le fameux, l'illustre Docteur Breszousi-Jansim*" that only now, after meeting him, could he die in peace. Brits-Jansen took him at his word by serving him a huge helping of rijst-tafel and a coconut shell full of beer and proffering the lethal collection of gaily colored spices with convincing innocence. The General, however, was experienced and the dinner got into its stride. Brits-Jansen and he discovered a common language in pidgin English and started telling jokes that caused guffaws of laughter and mutual back slapping. The aides unthawed and began to whisper to each other; Anton gave a sigh of relief and started to tackle the food.

He had been lulled into a feeling of security when suddenly, as the banquet was in full swing, Brits-Jansen's mandur came running from the wilderness calling, "Tuan! Tuan!" Anton looked up in alarm, for it was a complete stage voice; when the mandur fell in the dust at his master's feet and cried, "Tuan! Something found! Old, old, very old. Come quickly, tuan! Hurry lekas!" his heart sank. He stared fixedly at his plate and heard Brits-Jansen cry, dramatically, "No! Not true!" The mandur answered, "Saja tuan besar. Body, oh, oh, old! Pertjoema, lalala, loh!" Brits-Jansen rose to his feet, cried, "Awas!" with outflung arm, and followed his mandur. The General jumped up, electrified with excitement, and hurried after them, the napkin still around his neck. The two aides got up as well and Anton followed them, gloomily.

He found a crowd gathered round a hillock at the edge of the jungle road. The coolies had laid bare a small cave, from which stuck a foot covered with turf and dust. It was the oldest foot Anton had ever seen, and his suspicion waned. Whatever Brits-Jansen was up to, that foot was real. Brits-Jansen, grotesque in his outfit, ordered his mandur to get the delicate instruments and two coolies came running with a crate full of forks and spoons. These were distributed among the guests and Brits-Jansen said, "Gentlemen, here we go. Gently, gently now! Don't scratch away more than a few particles at a time!" The guests, kneeling, started to scratch.

It took three hours. After three hours of breathless scratching, on their knees in the dust, like children in a sand pit, they laid bare the skeleton of the oldest Pithecanthropus erectus found in the archipelago; a historic occasion, marred only by the fact that the skeleton's thorax was stuffed with the French flag.

«« »»

Had Brits-Jansen known that the boy was to accompany that foreigner, he would not have pulled his elaborate joke. He would have taken the strangers' invasion in his stride, let them play to their hearts' content in the sandpit with their little buckets and spades, while he himself would have retired for a heart-to-heart talk with the boy, who by now must be the only human being on the globe who did not see him as a comic character. The thing he yearned for more than anything else was a long, passionate conversation about leprosy.

The conversation took place when the Frenchman and his lackeys had gone to bed in the guest tent, after bidding him an icy good night. The major and his army had rolled themselves up to snore in the tropical night; the bunting had been taken down, the tables cleared, Stegomyia had taken off his cardboard nose and his own orange sash, and the tea kettle started to sing at last on the Primus. He sighed happily when finally they sat facing each other with their feet up, while Stegomyia clattered and tinkled with cups and spoons in the shadow of the tabletop. Once the tea mugs stood steaming between them and the pygmy had retired to his nest of rags on top of the empty P.G. tins, there was a really homey atmosphere underneath the oil lamp with the communal tobacco pot between them, and the stories came out as artlessly as pigeons after a thunderstorm. He started himself with a complete confession of the shame of his archaeologists' humbug, and now the boy sat listening to him with undaunted reverence, it became almost amusing as a story. When he had finished, the boy shrugged his shoulders and said, "Well, the asses haven't got the faintest idea of the importance of your work. And that, I suppose, could be taken as a compliment."

The boy was right, absolutely right; and he was glad that he felt not a trace of drowsiness when the boy in his turn started talking. He began by saying that, since their last meeting, he had discovered that sexual activity and physical gratification did indeed harm scientific concentration. In Java he had been a bungler; but yesterday he had once more made the sort of diagnosis he had been able to make before. And why? Then he told the story of his marriage. The embraces, the spiritual loneliness, the physical exhaustion, the complete lack of interest for the subject in which he was specializing, except when he received a letter from Bert.

The subject in which he was specializing? He suddenly realized how closely the boy's fate was linked with his. If the boy refused to touch leprosy, it would be sadder than all the newspaper articles, excavations and archaeological swindles. He asked him, with feigned nonchalance, what exactly was the subject he was specializing in? And when the boy told him, he could have dragged him across the table and kissed him with delight, for it was nonsense. Nonsense, complete gaseous nonsense, kindergarten babble about sin and hormones and the millennium and the serum of conversion. Serum of conversion! He could have hugged him. Why not Life's Elixir, or the Philosopher's Stone? His relief must have been obvious, for the boy asked suspiciously, "Do you think I'm onto something or—er—do you think it is a wild-goose chase?" He thought for a long time, hiding his grin with his hand, then he said, "Very interesting. A bit esoteric, perhaps. I should like to know a little more about it. Have you done any research yet? Questioned converts? Analyzed their answers? Started a card index?"

"No," the boy replied, somberly. "That's just it. Since Els arrived, I haven't been able to concentrate, except for a few hours when I wrote about it to Bert."

"Is that so?" He put his question casually. "You wouldn't happen to have any of her letters with you, would you?"

"Yes," said the boy, hesitantly. "I could give you some to read, if you like."

"Oh, you might as well give me what you have," he said. "The night is long and I still sleep very badly." The boy looked up with raised eyebrows and he added hastily, "It started only recently. Worry, I suppose. So you'd better go and get them. You yourself must be dog-tired."

The boy got up, a trifle reluctantly, went out and returned a few moments later with a folder. He had expected letters; when he opened the folder, he found a set of brochures. He accepted them with a grunt, and heard no more of what the boy said before he turned in.

Dear Comrade and Colleague, Letter No. 7 delighted me with its romanticism and so I hope you won't think me schoolmarmish if I start at once by pointing out some glaring errors in your reasoning. You are such an inveterate Protestant that you cannot help becoming emotional the moment some magic word like "sin" or "grace" crops up. So let us start by weeding out the fetishes. . . .

He read for hours, motionless, a monster with iron spectacles in the flat cone of the oil light. He did not notice that his pipe went out, he did not notice that Stegomyia woke up and went outside, rustled to the shrubs, came back, and stared at him over the table top with a sleepy old man's face. When the dwarf asked, "Tea?" he answered, without looking up, "No, beer," and did not notice how the little creature pulled a beer bottle out of the chest, climbed onto a stool to get one of the mugs that hung from hooks on the tent pole, wrenched open the bottle and filled the mug with a soft hissing sound, lifting the bottle with both hands. He did not notice that the mug was put down in front of him, that Stegomyia, after staring at him for a while over the table top, went back to his nest, scratched himself, smacked his lips, sighed, and fell asleep. He drank his beer without noticing and sucked the drops out of his mustache without lifting his eyes from the page.

When he finished reading, the lamp was nearly empty. He blew it out and lit a candle. He sat staring at the little dancing flame for some time, his elbows on the table, slowly scratching his beard; then he turned back to the first letter and started to read them again.

He read on until the dawn; then he fell asleep with his head on his arms. The boy woke him up, saying that it was time for breakfast, for the party was leaving within the hour.

Stegomyia started cooking breakfast, and he did not mention the letters at all. The boy said, "I wish I could come and have a talk with you sometimes. It would make all the difference."

"Well, that's easy," he answered.

"How do you mean? This case was an exception. Kramer won't let me leave that hospital a second time."

"Oh, yes he will. He'll let you go as soon and as often as you like, if only you do what I tell you."

The boy looked up incredulously, but with a glimmer of hope in his childish eyes. He unfolded his plan as if it were only meant to fool Piet Kramer. If the boy were a member of his team for leprosy research, he would be called to investigate all cases of leprosy reported to the Central Hospital. Then he would be able to say occasionally to the Head of Service, "I've got a special case here which I should like to discuss with Dr. Jansen. Could that be arranged, please?"

It was not a bad plan at all, and the boy was enthusiastic. The innocence with which he walked into the trap was touching. He had been afraid that the trap would be too obvious, but the boy shook him warmly by the hand and said, "Thank you, sir, thank you. This is a wonderful solution."

"Don't be silly," he grunted. "I'm only too glad to help you out. The only thing is: you'd better investigate some cases of leprosy and write me about them and have some photos made and that kind of thing, or Kramer will get wise to you. If you were to make a serious thing of it, I could speak to him myself, which might be even better, but I don't want to burden you with something that doesn't interest you so . . ."

"No, no," the boy said hastily. "I'd love to! It suits me fine! I'm tremendously interested in your work, I'll be delighted to."

"You mustn't overdo it," he said magnanimously. "Don't forget you're specializing already. I think your serum of conversion is fascinating."

The boy's face fell. "Oh, I don't know about that," he said. "I've still got a long way to go."

He smiled paternally and said, "I'm sure that leprosy will help you with your own research. I really do think you've got something there."

Stegomyia made a big pot of coffee and fried a dozen eggs. Breakfast was a cheerful meal and when, in the end, they said good-by in front of the stony-faced guests of honor, all seemed to bode well. The porters lifted the palanquins onto their shoulders, and the major was about to order the procession forward. Then, suddenly, the boy remembered the folder and called, "Doctor, my letters!" He said, "Yes, damn!" hurried back to the tent, grabbed the folder, galloped breathlessly to the head of the column with stabs in his belly, handed the folder, panting, to the boy and then some devlish impulse made him say, "Here are your love letters, son. Have a good trip."

The expression on the boy's face made him realize that he had gone too far. "Hey!" he said, lifting his hand to make amends; but the boy cried, "Mandur! Awas!" The major called, "Forward march!" And the caravan lumbered forward into the wilderness. The boy did not look round to wave.

He went back to his tent, furious. Stegomyia saw him coming and asked, "Beer?" He felt like kicking the little runt, but saw his devoted eyes and said with a sigh, "No, tea."

In the distance, the yells of the coolies chasing snakes drew away, the woodpecker-like tapping of their klewangs faded, and, presently, there was nothing left but the birds.

«« »»

Anton could not forget Brits-Jansen's last remark. It occupied his thoughts for the rest of the day, as he tried to discover within himself how much truth there was in it. Before he had arrived at a conclusion, they reached the passangrahan where, last time, the girl had waited in his bed. As they set eating around the fire, he tried vainly to distinguish her among the silhouettes that stood staring at the white men, a motionless ring of spectators beyond the glow of the fire. He only found her after he had lit his candle and pulled the mosquito netting aside. There she lay, giggling.

This time he did not send her away. His introspection of that other night seemed to have undermined his resolve. As he took her in his arms and kissed her with a feeling of plunging into darkness, he remembered the argument that, by betraying Els, he took upon himself part of the guilt for the failure of their marriage.

The girl stayed the whole night, and never before had he known such exaltation, such complete self-liberation as in her embrace. His love-making with Els suddenly seemed infantile, a poor imitation. In the arms of this creature, invisible in the darkness but for the flash of white teeth or the gleam of a dark eye, he felt for the first time like a man, master of creation, warrior, lover, the greatest lover in the world.

Only toward daybreak, in the strange timeless peace of complete relaxation, did they talk. And it was as if he talked for the first time with the wilderness, that he had never before approached so closely. Hers was the voice of the forest, the mountains, the rivers glinting in the dawn, of God, humming in the jungle. Never before had he felt such deep, wordless piety as after committing this first big sin of his life. The wilderness lay in his arms, a featherweight on his shoulder, the soft warmth of a curl on his cheek, a scent of hair oil as if they were lying in a bed of flowers. He gently caressed the arm across his chest and he felt a tenderness, a love that he had never experienced before. Els had no idea of what a man could give, or a woman, for that matter. He suddenly felt hatred for that white body, her hard legs, her cold mouth, flat chest and pinched loins full of sawdust. He hurriedly tried to conjure up her sweetness, her girlish frankness, her wit, but found nothing but sentimentality, infantilism and lack of imagination. He tried to recapture the memory of their love, their passion, but it was unmasked as childish curiosity, the aping of adults, clumsy, sweaty kissings and pantings in the dark. It was as if the devil, after drugging him with the scent of flowers, paralyzing him with satiation, suddenly ripped aside the curtains that hid his darkest thoughts, his deepest secrets. He lay, motionless and wide-eyed with horror in the darkness that was slowly reddening in the sunrise, and saw himself, as on a stage, thrashing Els with a whip, kicking her soft belly, dragging her by her hair across the floor, beating her, strangling her, killing her, a murder of slavering, gnawing hatred. All demoniacal powers from the deepest dungeons of his subconscious had been unleashed, and charged him with such vicious fury that his muscles quivered with tension. Yet his hand went on gently stroking the arm of the girl across his chest; his tenderness was undisturbed by this tidal wave of fury but mysteriously intensified. He stroked her so softly, so cautiously, with such infinite gentleness that he fell asleep.

When the birds woke him and he became conscious of the sound of steps in the other rooms, she was gone. Only the scent of blossoms remained, faint, elusive, a memory already fading. As he got out of bed, he found the folder with Bert's letters on the floor and he remembered dropping it after opening the mosquito curtain. Bert. He no longer racked his brains to find out whether they were writing love letters or not. He did not care; he was a man, leading a caravan of stumbling tourists, a pioneer with but one mistress: the wilderness. During the rest of the trip, he felt a nostalgic longing for her body, her voice, her scent. The thought of turning round and going back haunted him as they drew away from the camp. He wanted to flee from what was waiting for him: the white suits, the stench of petrol, the hard sunlight in callous streets, the shrill female laughter and the hoarse male cocktail quack, the white body and its hard legs, that fish mouth, those cow's eyes. . . . Thank God for the major.

The major talked without respite about Atjeh, the mountains, the rivers he had explored, the battles fought in the jungle; the kind man probably went on talking deliberately in order to prevent his turning back. Once he had boarded the steamer to Batavia, he was grateful to him.

For, on the boat, protected by three miles of water, a glass of whisky and correct white drill, he stared musingly back at the forest, a hazy blue wall on the horizon, and drew up his balance sheet. All right, he had betrayed his wife. Every man did that at some time or another; if he went about it in an adult way it might even improve their relationship. It might bring the gentleness of guilt into the unbearable superiority with which he had regarded and treated her so far. Those hysterical thoughts about her as a white fish or a cow were absolute nonsense, and had to be rooted out. The sooner he forgot that little native the better; now was the time to think about leprosy and his plans for the future.

He came to feel so sure of himself that he wrote his report to the Head of the Service with a mixture of bureaucratic pomposity and pioneer's heartiness. But the morning the boat arrived in Batavia, she was not among the crowd on the quayside. Well, that was only natural; she could not know when he was arriving for the simple reason that he had not written to her. During the whole trip, he had sent her only one picture postcard, from Medan on his way to Langsa: *The Mansion of the Tengkoe Besar* with, on its back, *Hurried greetings, Love, A.* As he turned into their street, he felt his knees weaken and his mouth was dry. As he entered the front garden, his eyelids began to quiver with nerves. But when he set eyes on her, it was different from anything he had imagined.

She came to meet him on the verandah, and looked healthy and young, so gay and happy that she gave him a shock. For he suddenly realized, for the first time, that he was about to make another human being unhappy for the rest of her life, and that he could do nothing about it, absolutely nothing, and that the only way out was to forget her in her arms.

But even that did not succeed. For although she responded to his first kiss more passionately than ever before, she suddenly seemed to go limp in his embrace and turned into what he had tried to forget ever since he had left the wilderness: a cold body, a chilly mouth, a fish, that filled him with loathing and revulsion.

«« »»

At the very moment that she felt something inside her respond to his kiss for the first time since their marriage, in that very moment of utter defenselessness and surrender, she felt all warmth, all feeling drained out of her until she lay cold and soulless in his arms. She did not know why, but something had broken the spell, and chilled her to indifference; the only reason she could think of was Bert. Her hopelessness, her numb speechless wish to be dead, changed under his wet kisses into a staring hatred. Unreasonable seething hatred for Bert, the whore, the intellectual slut, who had enticed him away from her with those sly, pious letters, her catlike purring about "science" and "research," who had been lying in bed with them like a paper ghost since the very first night. All her good intentions, all her laboriously acquired wisdom, all the serenity of her thirty-six chaste days and nights evaporated in steam under the blast of that hatred; when at last she was rid of his weight and could move and breathe freely again, she felt her legs tremble, her mouth tighten, her cheeks tauten, her eyes burn with the heat of that hatred. He lit a cigarette, made a joke, was childishly happy in his ignorance; he took her staggering to be God-knows-what, satisfaction or love or the dizziness of delight but not for what it was: the stumbling with hatred. He would never notice, never, never; but that slut would, that trollop, that . . .

After he had gone to the Head Office to hand in his report, she wrote a letter to Bert. She was calm, almost unnaturally so. *Dear Bert,* followed by some babble about the East and the lovely time they were having and the charming people and the sweet little house and their young happiness;

and then, casually: *I know what a great liking you have for Anton and that you wish him the best; I don't suppose it's necessary to make myself any clearer when I now ask you not to write him any more. The only danger that our marriage is exposed to is an attachment* . . . She crossed out the last line. It meant she would have to copy the letter, but never mind. The important thing was that one sentence. It had to contain everything, and yet she should not humiliate herself. *The only danger our marriage runs* . . . She crossed it out angrily. She sat thinking for a long time, gnawing her pen, gazing at the paper rack. The *Java Courant*, the *Deli News, The Lancet.* . . .*You probably do not realize what you are doing, but your long letters and his long replies make it very difficult for me to* . . . She crossed it out.

When, half an hour later, he came whistling up the garden path, she had still not found the sentence. In desperation, she wrote hastily, *For God's sake, Bert, don't write to him any more. I am so ashamed, but I am really desperate. For God's sake* . . . Then she heard his step on the verandah, slipped the letter into a drawer, smoothed her hair, pulled up her smile and said, "Hello, darling—that was quick work."

"Yes," he said, and kissed her. "But then, I had someone very nice to come home to. Dinner ready?"

"Yes, sweetheart. What about a drink first?"

"Oh, yes, I'm dying for one."

"What shall it be? Sherry?"

"Yes, wonderful. Although, no, I'd rather you had that. I know you love it and the bottle is nearly finished. I'll have a gin and lime."

"All right, darling. The djongos has just got in a new bottle of lime, so . . ."

"Angel."

"Sweetheart. Here you are. Now don't spill any on my table, there's a darling. Cheerio."

"Cheers."

The djongos brought the *Java Courant,* and they shared it until dinner was served, occasionally smiling at each other over the top of their page.

Darkness fell quickly after a hot day; they ate by candlelight and neither of them felt like going to the cinema or to the Frenssens' afterward, although they had neglected them rather of late. That evening they both felt like staying cozily at home together, after all that loneliness.

He picked up the newspaper again and settled down by the orange table lamp in his stockinged feet, one leg over the arm of his chair; she picked up her embroidery. It was quiet, the servants had left, the soft melodious gonging of a gamelan drifted quivering through the night. Behind the mosquito curtain the gnats were zooming; through the curtain the scent of night blossoms was wafted in by the soft evening breeze. She listened to the sounds of the Far East, so peaceful and purring in the background. Tomorrow, after he had left for the office, she would write that letter to Bert. That trollop, that . . . But it did not work any more. She could no longer hate Bert, and, for some reason, that made her feel lost. As long as she had hated Bert, there had at least been something, somebody to blame, something to get hold of . . . Now tears welled up in her eyes, under the gonging of the gamelan and the zooming of the mosquitoes and the scent of blossoms from the darkness, and she realized that there was nothing to hate, nobody to blame. The gamelan made her feel so weak with its floating singsong that when he started to snore it came as a relief.

She looked up from her sewing; a cold tear ran down her nose, and she wiped it away with the back of her hand. She looked across at him: asleep, head back, mouth open, one leg over the arm of his chair, the newspaper on his lap underneath his half-open hand. The table lamp shed a soft, orange light.

Well, there he sat: Anton Zorgdrager, her husband, still almost a boy. The sight of him sitting there called forth a wave of homesickness, the yearning to throw her arms round his neck, to kiss him, stroke his hair, whisper, "Darling, darling, I love you, I love you so much," her eyes shut, cheek to cheek, her lips feeling the small warmth of his ear. What was there about that boy, snoring with his mouth open, that had delivered her so completely into his power? For although life with him was a terrible disillusion, a bad dream—life without him would be unbearable. That much she had realized during the month he had been away: she loved him, loved him, loved him forever, and God help her.

While she sat staring at him, motionless in the soft sonorous rings of the gamelan slowly widening in the stillness, a realization dawned on her.

The gamelan seemed to hum it, the mosquitoes seemed to zoom it, he himself seemed to say it with the soft grunting of his snores. A gust of wind rustled through the waringin and seemed to wash the answer toward her with the surf of its sound. But only as she smelled the scent of flowers

wafted through the doorway by the night breeze did she register what
it had been. A smell. She had smelled something on him. A scent.

She swallowed with sudden fear, a weird, wordless panic. The gamelan
resumed its humming, the wind rustled away in the tree, the mosquitoes
took up their zooming dance once more, all that was left from that
moment of clairvoyance was a word.

Wilderness. Wilderness.

Then she knew. He had betrayed her with the wilderness.

CHAPTER TEN

WILLEM WATERREUS had tried to prepare himself for it for years. Countless times he had gone through it in his imagination; now the time had come it was completely different. Betsy was dying, and there was no holiness, no reverence for the descent of God; only the death rattle of a monstrously mutilated body, decomposing even before it had expelled its soul.

That night he was awakened by a panting from the white bed; he disentangled himself with difficulty from the jungle creepers of sleep and went to her. "Betsy?" he asked. "Dearest?" Her breath answered no longer. She was unconscious.

He went to call Vloemans, who came running back with him to her bedside, losing a slipper in the porchway. When they entered the white room the stench of leprosy had grown stronger; that was a second sign. Betsy was dying; even before Vloemans whispered it, he knew. No more than twenty-four hours, and she would be promoted to glory.

Glory? During that year of devilish nights, he had lost something: the childlike guilelessness with which he had once trusted in God's watchful benevolence. He had not lost God, he had come to see Him differently. No longer the good, mild Father watching over Salvationists and sparrows, counting hairs on the heads of mankind, but a primeval light, creator of the cosmos, further away from the dying little body on the white bed than the furthest star. There was nothing in the universe to shed any light in this night of loneliness, only that dismembered trunk, that memory of Betsy, and now she was dying. "Promoted to glory," Vloemans whispered piously, and he answered, "Thank you, brother." A chill of loneliness went through him at the sight of that young face, those sleepy boy's eyes. Not that he despised Vloemans; he was a nice sincere boy, who now went back to his iron bed to fall asleep once more in his eternal dusk. Promoted to glory. Her breath rattled, halted, stumbled on toward her journey's end.

The coldness came with the morning. He prayed, kneeling on the cold tiles; a dull prayer without response, full of whispering voices. Instead of the white silence in which God listened to him, his closed eyes saw the black void of the universe, the solar systems beyond solar systems, the spiral nebulae of universes beyond the universe, all that world-large vortex of darkness, in which God was lost beyond billions of light years of loneliness.

He got up guiltily and went outside, onto the ramparts. The guilt he felt was real, for it was the smell of her that had chased him away. Instead of staying with her in this ultimate hour, instead of helping her and watching beside her until eternity took her from him, he had slunk away because she stank.

Promoted to glory. The dawn changed the rolling clouds in the valley below into billowing smoke. It seemed as if the stench had followed him onto the ramparts. He knelt once more, praying to be liberated from that horror, that decomposition of his love; then the morning bell tolled. He went down to the courtyard and prayed for the lepers, and that prayer was the first that got a response. He himself might move in a loneliness without answer—the moment he prayed for compassion to that primeval light beyond the horizon of the universe, on behalf of the mutilated and the defeated on this Mount of Golgotha, a great consolation flowed through him to those others, leaving him behind colder and lonelier than ever.

He made his rounds through the wards, laughed with the patients, admired the children's paint boxes and their multicolored sunsets; when he came back to his office before entering the white room once more, a letter lay on the table. A letter from Bertie.

He asked himself whether perhaps he did not want to be liberated, whether he held on to that loneliness out of an instinct of self-preservation, for he left her letter unopened. He went back into the porchway, to the white room, with a sudden feeling of urgency. It was a new thought; perhaps this numbing of his feelings was a protection against too great a grief; perhaps God's silence was an act of mercy. He had not opened that letter because he had felt something quaver within him; for one split second, he had realized what would happen to him if he let himself be weakened by grief.

The stench was unchanged, her breath croaked in the silence. Twenty more hours to go. He had instructed Vloemans to cable Dr. Jansen; only if he were in Java could he arrive in time. The breathing behind the mosquito curtain broke with a sob; he sat motionless, breathless, until she stumbled on, panting, toward her journey's end.

Betsy was dying. The notion of what this meant began to dawn on him, but before it was too late, the coldness and the loneliness closed round him once more. God in His mercy banished him to the outer darkness of His creation, to shield him from a grief that he would be unable to bear.

It was silent in the colony that day; everybody knew what was happening in the white room in the porchway.

Nonna Betsy, the saint of Man-Pu-Ko-Chu, was about to be promoted to glory.

«« »»

Come at once Betsy dying Waterreus.

"Yes," said Anton, "I know who that is. It's the wife of the commander of Man-Pu-Ko-Chu. Friends of Dr. Jansen's."

"Leprosy?" the man in shirt sleeves asked.

"Yes, last stage."

Dr. Kramer put out his hand and Anton gave him back the telegram. The fan whirred at the ceiling. Kramer reread the message, turned the telegram around and said, "All right. As he's a thousand miles away, you'd better go. Have you got a car?"

"Yes, sir."

"Forty-eight hours, and I won't want a report."

Anton drove off at once, without telling Els that he would not be home that night. Sardjono would give her the message; he had met him in the corridor as he left the chief's office.

It was not only concern for Bert's father that made him hurry like this. He hoped that perhaps the old Salvationist would be able to explain the reason for Bert's last letter. *Dear Anton, I am sorry but for various reasons I have decided we must not write to each other for some time to come. I trust that you will respect this decision for the sake of our friendship. Yours, B.*

His first reaction had been an unexpected jealousy. She had fallen in love with somebody and now, with typical thoroughness, she cut off their friendship at its roots. After a moment he realized how silly this reaction was, yet it prevented his talking it over with Els, which would have been a natural thing to do. He wrote Bert a letter that minced no words, scolding her in a clinical fashion, but she did not answer. Then he wrote a second letter, full of apologies and sentimentality and old memories ending with, *Come on, old girl, don't let's be silly. After all, we've gone through so much together that there is no reason why you shouldn't tell me honestly what has happened. What is it?*

No answer.

Dear Bert, This is the third and last time that I ask you calmly but firmly, what the hell . . .

No answer.

Bert! If you don't answer this letter either, I shall assume that we are now enemies. . . .

No answer.

And now he was on his way to the only person who might, perhaps, explain the mystery. During his six hours' journey into the mountains he thought up a number of openings, as if it were a game of chess.

"Well, Captain, heard anything of your daughter lately?" Bad.

"I haven't heard anything from Bert for a long time. Nothing wrong I hope?" Weak, but better.

"Oh, by the way, there's something I'd like to ask you. As you probably know, Bert and I have been carrying on a fairly regular correspondence for some time, and a couple of months ago, out of the blue, she wrote me a letter . . ."

The gray road, shimmering with heat like water, wound its way up the red mountain with uniform hairpin bends. It became cooler as he climbed, and the thin mountain air seemed to clarify his thoughts. He began to recapture some of the peace and the confidence with which he had left the colony last time, master of his fate, knight of science. A tired resignation seemed to calm his seething thoughts. For the first time, he thought of Bert as a dear friend he had lost. For the first time, it penetrated the magic circle of his egotism that he was on his way to her dying mother, to that old man with his white eyes and his exhausted face whose grief must make his own puerile worries seem shameful. In leaving the valley, he left behind more than the broiling heat and the blinding maze of light and shadow; he left the animal short-sightedness which so far had made him focus all his attention on his own sorrows and his childish preoccupations. He realized how he had been walking through the hospital of late: like a keeper in a zoo. How he had behaved with Els: like a spoiled child. When he caught sight of the fortress in the hard blue sky above him, he stopped the car to look; but when he thought that he felt her radiation he shrugged his shoulders. He should go there with the firm resolve not to romanticize any experience that might await him; it was nonsense that he should feel any spiritual radiation at the mere sight of the colony from below. All he had just done was to realize clearly for the first time that he was on his way to the deathbed of a human being who had reached the highest peaks of sublimation and was about to be dissolved in God.

From that moment he thought no more about himself. When he arrived at the drawbridge of Man-Pu-Ko-Chu, crossed it with his steps echoing in the empty moat and let the knocker fall, he was more adult than he had been at any time since he had left this place of renunciation a year ago.

The small door beside the gateway creaked open, a white shadow bade him enter and led him through the hollow silence of the porchway to the office, where at the table underneath the oil lamp the old Salvationist sat reading his Bible as if nothing were changed. The eyes that looked up at him were as penetrating as ever, and the voice that said, "Thank you for coming, brother," as steady. The old man led him silently to the door of the white room and opened it; after he had taken off his sun helmet and entered, something was changed after all.

The stench of leprosy that he remembered from his previous visit had increased to such an extent that it was now overpowering, but it evaporated at the shock of the mysterious force that radiated from the mosquito tent. It had increased a hundredfold. Last time, he had been able to analyze away the impression that a white energy radiated from that bed; he had explained it as autosuggestion caused by months in the jungle, the atmospheric preparations and the conversation in the office before being admitted to the Holy of Holies. But now, straight out of the sunlight, the selfishness and the paganism of desire, he could no longer deny it.

The deathbed of Bert's mother was the still center of a cyclone of cosmic force.

<<< >>>

As Willem Waterreus lifted the mosquito curtain and showed the boy the remains of her body in all their gruesome desecration, he saw the boy flinch and regretted sending that telegram. He could have known that Dr. Jansen would be away; this boy was too young to help. It was God's wish that he should hand over Betsy to Him as he had received her: alone.

The boy did not examine her. He barely dared approach her in his awe. When, finally, he looked up at him, his eyes were so helpless and bewildered that he smiled and closed the curtain without asking any questions at all. He called Vloemans and asked him to take the boy away.

But as he sat down in his office to read on in his Bible, he saw a shadow darken the doorway, looked up and there was the boy, pale and determined. He asked what he wanted and the boy answered, "I'd like to stay with you, if I may." He was so moving to see, helpless with all his good intentions, that he answered, "That is very kind of you," and read on without having sent him away.

From then on, the boy followed him wherever he went: even into the room, where he remained standing inside the door, his head bowed, his helmet in his hands. After the boy had trailed him all the afternoon and part of the evening, he began to realize that the very irritation his presence caused was a protection. God in His wisdom that passed all understanding had sent a guardian angel into his lonely night. As long as the boy was there, he could not give way to fear or grief. He had to remain calm and controlled, without bitterness, without a tear.

Her last hours before daybreak were unearthly. After the evening meal, he went back to her bedside, the boy took up his post beside the door. They watched by her for hours. At four o'clock in the morning, the boy sat down on the floor and fell asleep, his head on his chest; his breath became slow and regular, while hers grew fainter. Half an hour before sunrise, the boy's breath was alone.

He did not pray. He got up, opened the mosquito curtain, looked down on her body, a small dark shape in the red light of the dawn, then he turned to the boy, still sitting on the floor by the door, and said, "It is finished." His voice was calm. The boy stood up, wanted to take his hand, but hesitated. He stretched out his hand, to help him; the boy took it and said, "My deepest sympathy, Captain." He said, "Thank you," and went outside.

The courtyard was full of people, silent in the sunrise. They must have been standing there all night. A voice started to sing, "O perfect life of love! All, all is finished now," and they all took up the hymn. Vloemans went into the room and came back to say that burial should not be delayed for more than twenty-four hours. He said that it would take place at sunset that day.

Nobody else came near her. He washed her and watched by her for the rest of the day; the boy stayed outside the door all the time. An hour before sunset, two lepers brought the coffin, a square box of white wood like many he had buried before. The boy came forward to help, but he lifted her in his arms, laid her in the coffin and closed the lid. He turned the screws himself while the boy stood watching him, then he went to the washroom, where the boy's shadow waited in front of the door. Afterward he went to change in his office; the boy's silhouette stood waiting behind the curtain.

A quarter of an hour before sunset, four lepers came to carry her away. All the inhabitants of the colony followed, and stood around the grave in the churchyard outside the ramparts, where the small white crosses were turning orange in the light of the setting sun. He read a passage from the Bible and said a prayer in an unwavering voice, then she was lowered into the grave, while the lepers sang. He threw the first spadeful of earth onto her coffin, turned round to go back to his place, and saw that the boy had been standing behind him all the time. He spoke a few words about her example, her promotion, heaven; then he returned to the office to wait until the lepers had finished cleaning the room. He opened his Bible once more to the last page of the Revelation and read the passage he had read at her grave, *"And there shall be no night there; and they need no candle, neither light of the sun; for the Lord God giveth them light."*

Then he closed his eyes behind his hands and felt cold tears well up. He heard a soft clatter; when he looked up he saw the boy lighting the lamp. The yellow light grew and lit up Bert's letter standing against the inkwell. He felt such gratitude for the boy's faithful presence that he handed him the unopened letter as if to replace the words he could not bring himself to say. As the boy opened the letter, he wiped his eyes.

The boy read in silence, then he folded the letter, put it back in the envelope, stood the envelope against the inkwell, picked up his helmet, and they shook hands silently. Then the boy went out; he heard his steps echo in the porchway, the creaking of the door, the sound of a car engine that quickly vanished. He closed the Bible, blew out the lamp, crossed the porchway and entered her room.

The mosquito tent had been taken down and another mattress had been put on the bed, covered with a clean white sheet. The room smelled of disinfectant. He undressed by candlelight, knelt by the side of the bed, prayed the Lord's Prayer, and lay down. The candle flame made dancing shadows on the wall.

And there shall be no night there; and they need no candle, neither light of the sun; for the Lord God giveth them light.

When he had extinguished the candle and lay staring in the darkness, he saw her. She stood, a faint light, at the foot of the bed and inclined her head. It was only a moment, the darkness closed again almost at once, but he had seen her clearly. A sudden warmth came back to him, a weakness that made the tears run down his face in the darkness; but it was neither grief nor despair. It was the knowledge that she, freed of her body and the battle for her soul, had come back to him at last—a spark of God's light, an angel from eternity, a watcher until death. She had confirmed her last words: God is Love. Now she would be with him always.

He fell into a deep dreamless sleep with a feeling of great gratitude.

«« »»

Els woke up because the front door slammed. She sat up in bed and listened; when Anton came in, she turned on the light in a sudden fear, and saw at once that he had found out.

During all those months of subterfuge and insincere sweetness, she had found herself wishing more and more that he would discover she had written to Bert. Often she had been on the verge of telling him herself; now it was too late.

For one second he stood, tense and pale, in the doorway and stared at her with eyes so desperate in that stark white face that a wave of wretched love welled up inside her, and she would have stretched out her arms toward him if he had not come toward her. He said, "What possessed you to write . . ." Then his voice broke, tears sprang into his eyes; why it was she did not understand, whether it was his fury, shame, or desperate grief, but, as he started to weep, his hand flew up and he struck her hard across her face.

She cried out in fright and pain; he threw himself on her, beat her, pummeled her, punched her with his fists. She screamed, kicked, tried desperately to defend herself, and when he suddenly, without warning, tore her nightdress off her body, she lay for a second paralyzed with shock, for she had not expected him, she had not made any preparations for his embrace, if she did not hold him off now, anything might happen.

But it was too late. Not only did he hold her down with such strength that it was impossible to shake him off, but a weird weakness surged up within her. A paralyzing numbness, creeping up her legs, her arms; a giddy feeling of lightness, of rising, weightless, out of the violence of the struggle, swaying, swinging as she rose, like a bird winging up in spirals toward the sun. Fear made her open her eyes and stare straight into the harsh light of the lamp and scream, but it came out as a plaintive cry. He hurt her terribly, with an unbridled violence, a vicious beastly fury that she had never experienced before; fear, horror, giddiness and delight merged into a red swirling darkness, in which she floated and sank, wheeled and glided, was drawn up and dragged down, until in the end, with a choking scream of ecstasy, she burst asunder into a weak mass without a body, without feeling, without thoughts and dizzied down into a red darkness; but the darkness slowly cleared, became pink, light blue, gray, an endless sky of spotless gray, in which she floated down, down in a tumbling cloud of thousands of downy feathers, a winged bird, spiraling down to the sea.

How long she had been lying there she did not know. When she opened her eyes in the daylight, she lay across the bed, in a tangle of torn sheets and the rags of her nightdress. As she lifted herself onto her elbows, she sank back moaning, because of a stabbing pain in her shoulder. Her knees were stiff, her side ached. She got up, holding onto the foot of the bed, stumbled to the mirror, slumped on the stool and looked at herself. There were black marks on her arms, under her ear was blood, her scalp hurt as if she had combed her hair the wrong way, yet there was a strange glow inside her, a sleepy warmth that radiated through her body right to her finger tips. There she sat, raped and beaten, shamelessly yearning for his return, to beat her black and blue once more, to kick her once more and to scratch her and pull the hairs out of her head, if that was the price for that strange elation, that giddy spiraling between sky and sea, light and darkness, blue and red. She had never, not even with as much as a thought or an unformulated hope, expected this to be hidden behind the embarrassing business of bare bodies and fumblings and blind kisses after the light had been switched off. Good heavens; she had to support herself on the stool in another wave of giddiness. What had happened to her? Where was Anton? What was the time? Would the neighbors have heard? The servants? She shook her head to free herself of that fuzziness. What could it be? Exhaustion or shock or nervousness, God knows what. Come on, Els, get a move on, girl; wash, dress, breakfast.

But as she got up, she groaned and sat down again, shivering with a sudden chill. She slowly rubbed her arm, looked slowly round the room, as if seeing it for the first time. Then she dressed, with long motionless periods in front of the mirror, looking at her mouth, at her chin, at her forehead, at her nose, from eye to eye, to turn away with a shrug of her shoulders and to look for her sandals under the bed, buttoning her dress with her free hand. But behind everything was only one thought: what, in God's name, had happened?

The clock in the dining room struck eight.

«‹« ›»›

On he fled, on, on—out of Batavia, through Meester Cornelis, on to Bekasi; pursued by that one, desperate question: what, in God's name, had happened? How could he have debased himself so deeply, forgotten himself so utterly, thrown himself in one suicidal leap from the highest peaks of human sublimation into the deepest pit of bestial frenzy within six insane hours?

It was as if the Almighty had just wanted to bring home to him the triviality of his conflicts by confronting him with the most impressive death he had ever witnessed, before handing him the letter with the answer to the question that had haunted him for months. When he had read the line it did not shock him, he was so far away, at that moment, from the valley and its red desires.

I have nothing new to tell you about our friend Zorgdrager; at his wife's request we stopped corresponding some time ago.

So Els had written to Bert. If he had bothered to identify himself with her for a moment, instead of staring at his own navel exclusively, he would have arrived at that conclusion himself. It was obvious.

After the burial, in his state of half sleep, his first reaction had been one of deep compassion for Els. How ashamed she must have felt, how desperate, to humiliate herself and write to Bert. He had shaken hands with the Captain, gone out, got into his car, and halfway down the mountain he had stopped. He sat looking at the sunrise, thinking about Els, without anger or hatred, still with that compassion as a great feeling of tenderness and pity within him. As the sun rose, he started his car again and continued his descent with the plan to go to her as quickly as possible, to wake her up with a kiss and say, "Darling, why didn't you tell me?" and that would be the beginning of a new life. In a reckless moment, he had taken someone else's future happiness into his hands; now he had to do his duty by her without looking back. He must divide his life between her and his work, devote himself to her well-being and to his career as a doctor in equal parts. In that way, there would be no time left for conflicts.

While the car, with whining engine, slowly crawled down the gray creeper of the road into the red smoky valley that grew steadily hotter, he thought about their case clinically, wondering why it had developed in this way. He concluded that all passions, which in Holland were latent and harmless, were forced into a malignant growth in the incubator of the tropics. He himself was an example: in Holland he had been a shy and hesitant lover; here he was an obsessed voluptuary. In Holland he had been an indifferent physician, no worse and no better than scores of others; here he had become a lazy idler with flashes of genius only in the jungle. Els was an example too: in Holland a sweet, devoted home-bird, here a jealous virago. In Holland a pleasant mistress without much imagination or emotion, here a cold creature without a spark of love or tenderness, a chilly white leech, a clammy . . .

He came to with a start, taken unawares by the hatred that had suddenly flared up again. He must never allow himself to think like that again! If he wanted to save their marriage, he should on no account let himself be caught by the spell of the valley once more. He tried to divert his thoughts by applying his new theory to people he knew, and found it proved in every case. They all showed the same picture: what in Holland had been an unobtrusive weed burst forth in the Far East with an explosive growth that smothered the prim little garden of their souls within a matter of months, transforming them into a steaming jungle. Dear, sweet, faithful Els, that darling, girlish madcap who would never have harmed a fly, had turned into a vampire, sucking his blood. . . .

He hooted the klaxon, although there was nobody on the road, in a pathetic effort to chase away the demons dancing in the smoky dusk, and changed into third. The car leaped forward, the tires screamed on the bends. He managed to dispel the demons by driving at ninety in the long winding tunnel underneath the palms, endangering the lives of the rice pickers who, at that hour of the day, were crossing the road in droves on the way to their sawahs, their brown bodies barely visible in the dusk. He managed to recapture his faith in his own strength, his self-control; he believed once more that after this night of holiness everything would be different.

He still believed it when he stopped the car and got out; he even believed it when he opened the door to the bedroom. But when he saw her, he staggered under the sudden onslaught of such surging fury that all he could say was "What possessed you to write . . ." Then the beast of prey burst through his sanctimonious self-confidence, and what he had seen as a lurid nightmare that night in the passangrahan turned into reality. He saw himself beat Els, kick her, drag her by the hair screaming across the bed, punch her, bite her, beat and strangle her in a murder of slavering hatred. He saw it, as if he were standing outside himself; but it was no longer a figment of his imagination, it was irrevocable reality.

Only when she lost consciousness with a moaning cry did he get up and look down at her, sober with fear. For one second he thought he had murdered her; when he examined her, trembling, he realized that it was only a faint. She could wake up any moment.

But she should not lay eyes on him again, ever. He must flee, as far and as fast as he could. After what had happened there was no hope left for them; she would never forgive him. He ran outside, jumped into his car, and drove off with such speed that a mudguard scraped the gate.

That was two hours ago—and still he raced on, hurtling through the green tunnels of the avenues, roaring along the glaring white ribbon of the road to Bekasi; then the engine after a few coughing fits, stopped. He had run out of gas.

Half an hour later, another car passed. In that half hour, sitting on the fender with his head in his hands, he had recovered his composure. The other car was driven by a fat man with too small a topee and too big a cigar, a commercial traveler. He towed the car to the petrol station outside Meester Cornelis. When he drove off, he waved and called, "Tabeh, doc! Happy days!"

The native attendant of the petrol station silently filled the tank, silently accepted the money and silently stuck the tip in his headband; he started the car once more and drove straight to the Head Office.

Dr. Kramer received him with a frown that seemed benevolent, and agreed to let him go to Camp Lung Plague without any probing questions. He seemed to accept that an emergency had arisen in the colony following Betsy's death, and that Brits-Jansen should be fetched forthwith. All he said was, "You want to specialize in the disease, I take it? Well, all right, but when you come back, we'll have to have a serious talk. This time I'll want a full report. Good-by—Hey! Your helmet!—Good-by."

Only as the pierhead of Tandjong Priok sank out of sight did he realize that he had not eaten for twenty-four hours. He ordered a cold meal on deck; a strange claustrophobic fear kept him from going down into the dining room. When he had eaten and lit a cigarette, dusk was falling over the sea. A fiery feathery cloud flared out of the sunset, like a trumpet.

He who says in Holland He doesn't exist . . .

He disappeared slowly in the light, a black shape in the darkness of the boat deck; lonely traveler toward the wilderness, pilgrim to the Promised Land.

<<< >>>

All that day she lived in a dreamy drowsiness, the warmth of a wonderful memory. She did the accounts, ordered her shopping, telephoned to the house painters about redoing the front porch; but every five minutes she glanced at the clock, the hands of which seemed to crawl on sleepily, heavy with lassitude. By eleven o'clock she had already laid the table for lunch; when he had not come back at three o'clock she ate alone. She was not worried; he had stayed away before without warning and she discovered that she even preferred it this way, today. It would be nicer, much more exciting, if today he came home very late, just before supper.

She began to lay the supper table at four o'clock. She decorated it with flowers, prepared a light, gay meal; her inner contentment induced her to tell the djongos to get a bottle of champagne as if she were expecting a lover.

A lover—her husband. Never before had she felt such tenderness, such yearning for him as she did now; everything seemed changed. The house seemed changed, the view of the courtyard and the trees seemed changed, the table lamp and even the newspaper rack seemed changed: intimate, happy. Her happiness grew with the lengthening of the shadows in the afternoon; it turned into a strange piety. For the first time she felt as if she could pray, thank God for life, love, the earth, the sun, the green shadow of the trees, the scent of the blossoms, the wilderness. She no longer felt the wilderness to be an enemy; she suddenly seemed to be akin to that gentle growth, that cherishing warmth, those dappled secrets of light and shade, of life and death, of love.

Love, love, love—she hummed as she went round the house, rearranging the flowers on the table; she smiled as she leafed through her diary. *The hope is slowly dying* . . . She could kiss that page now, to comfort the Els of yesterday in her adolescent despair. The hope was no longer dying; it had materialized—so completely, so overwhelmingly that she started again to float through the rooms of the house, with graceful dancing steps, swirling, humming, "I love you, my baby, I love you," to realize only as she sat down on the banister of the front porch that it was the tune the Negro voice on the amplifier had mooed, that evening in Labuan Redjo. She laughed and gazed, humming, at the skinny white hen scratching angrily in the black earth of the courtyard. "I kiss you, my baby, I kiss you. . . ." What a child she had been that first night, what a moving, helpless child without any notion of what love really meant, what it meant to have a man, a man. . . . "I love you, my baby. . . ." The postman arrived, gliding behind the hedge on his bicycle. He swerved into the courtyard, put his bicycle against the balustrade and handed her a telegram.

Called away unexpectedly to Sumatra letter follows. A.

She should have been disappointed, she should have come tumbling down out of her floating contentment. But although she thought it was a pity and wondered what could be the matter, the core of her happiness remained intact. It was a core of tender warmth; a small, red secret of intimacy. She ate alone, by candlelight, after rain had started to fall outside, the first shower of the monsoon. It was a still, intimate celebration, with the gentle joy of wine sparkling in her glass and a smell of flowers and rain. The stillness was full of whispers and the rustlings of drops in the foliage of the trees; it drowned the zooming of the mosquitoes and the distant murmur of the town; it spun a cocoon of contentment around her. She missed him with a lighthearted, almost gratified yearning, as if the essence of him were with her all the same. She lifted the wineglass in the candlelight, and smiled at the darkness beyond: a silent toast to the rain, the wind, the night. "To the wilderness," she thought, the words a tune in her thoughts, then she drank.

The djongos moved silently from the darkness into the light; for the first time there was some sympathy between them, almost understanding. After the meal he brought her coffee, and the evening paper. The rain was still whispering behind the mosquito curtain, the scent of wet earth mingled with the smell of the coffee, and she shivered with sensual contentment. She asked the djongos to bring her wrap and told him he could go to bed. She looked at the paper absently, smoking a cigarette; when she put the paper down and stubbed out the cigarette, a small plaintive feeling brushed her. She realized, with a distant alarm, like summer lightning, that if he were now to come home unexpectedly she would be almost disappointed. He was no longer the center of her contentment; he had even stopped being part of it; he had retired slowly from her small private world of rain and candlelight and idle humming—"I love you, my baby, I love you"—until he was lost in the wind, the night, the wilderness.

Later that night, there was one eerie, distressing moment. It was when she lifted her nightdress to get into bed. At that moment it seemed as if he brushed her, a ghost, a draft of longing and loneliness, and she thought, "Anton! God—Anton . . ." But it was the wind; it billowed the mosquito curtain at the windows, and made the candle flame flicker. She settled into bed, and from the small tent of the sheet she lay looking at the ceiling and the waving shadow of a spider's web.

Strange—if he did not come now, tonight, she would no longer long for his kiss. She drifted further and further away from that unearthly experience of giddy delight; she even began to feel a little afraid of it in her memory, as if she had almost drowned. She tried deliberately to yearn for him by thinking, "Come, come, oh, come; if you don't come, we'll lose it," but he drew further away, further, further; his waving hand faded with the shadow of the spider's web as the candle flame slowly diminished. That night she dreamed that she was pouring out wine for him and that he asked, "Did you shut the icebox?" without noticing the fat white hen that was pecking at the capital letters of the newspaper on the table. It looked up and scurried away as the postman came gliding along behind the hedge, and handed her a postcard with the picture of a burning candle. She was astonished that it should be Christmas already and she woke up with relief.

The letter he had promised her did not come. She waited for it every morning, every afternoon, every evening, for a fortnight. The postman brought only letters from home, telephone bills and *The Lancet*.

«« »»

Brits-Jansen thought he was seeing ghosts when suddenly, from the forest, the boy emerged—pale, unshaven, with feverish eyes, his clothes torn, brandishing a parang as if it were a sword. He had been brushing his dentures over a canvas bucket in the shadow of the tent, and when he saw the boy stagger into the clearing, drop the parang and rub his forehead with the back of his hand as if he were about to collapse, he cried in alarm, "Gweat Fcott!" stuffed his dentures back into his mouth without rinsing them, and stumbled toward the boy, holding up his trousers, for he had taken off his braces in the heat.

The boy pulled himself together when he felt his arm around him, smiled wanly and said, "Hello, doctor." Then he disengaged himself and walked, dragging his feet, to the stool in the shade of the tent.

Stegomyia peeped from underneath the flap like an old woman, avid for gossip, and ducked as Brits-Jansen shouted, "P.G.!" The boy sat down with his head in his hands and several things were evident before he had even opened his mouth. In the first place he must have gone without food for several days, in the second place he had traveled without luggage except a small mailbag from Head Office, and in the third place he must have made the journey without a guide, or lost the man on the way, for he had come out of the jungle alone. As he drank the gin the dwarf handed him, he shivered, took a long breath, grinned shyly and said, "Well, I must say I'm glad to be here."

"Where the hell is your guide?"

"Didn't bring one."

"Are you trying to tell me that you came alone all the way from the coast?"

The boy nodded and drank.

"And why, if I may ask?"

"There was no guide and I was in a hurry."

"Why?"

"The mail."

"You're lying. You know very well that I don't care a damn about the mail. What's happened?"

"Oh, various things," the boy said evasively and he realized that he would not get any more out of him until he had been fed and given a chance to wash and sleep. The next morning he would be ready to talk, not before.

He gave Stegomyia, who stood staring at the boy with open mouth and a gin tin under his arm, a kick that made him squeal and run and he threw a number of orders after him like stones: heat soup, make bed, clean clothes, traperduli! Half an hour later, the boy sat facing him across the table, smoking a pipe. He had gulped down his soup, devoured a tin of corned beef and was now washing down the remnants of a box of Swiss cheese with gulps of warm beer, between puffs. His pupils were less dilated than when he arrived but not quite normal yet. He had made it by the skin of his teeth; one more day in the jungle and he would have gone mataglap. He wondered why, for the journey in itself was not enough to have put him in that condition.

"When did you last sleep?"

"Three days ago."

"Here—have a swig of this." He shoved a capful of gin toward him. "Beer will make you sick. It's too hot."

The boy emptied the cap as if it contained water. Another quarter of an hour and he would crash off that seat, to remain unconscious for hours.

"All right, out with it."

The boy looked at him, with small eyes that turned cunning, and said, "Nothing."

But now he had had enough; his fist crashed on the table as he shouted, "What has happened?"

The boy choked on a mouthful of gin, coughed, and answered, gasping, "Bet . . . Betsy Waterreus is dead."

"Oh," he said.

"I'm sorry," said the boy.

Then he told of how she had died, how he had watched over her with Willem during her last hours, to fall silent with embarrassment as he saw tears roll into his beard. He did not mind; they knew each other well enough by now. He was grateful to the boy for walking all those miles through the forest without a guide to bring him the news. If he had read it in a letter, it would have been worse. So Betsy was dead.

He had expected it for so long that it almost came as a relief, the end of that dull sorrow of her tortured body, her halting breath. His sadness was so deep, so overpowering, that he felt like slapping the boy on the shoulder with despair and gratitude, but when he looked up, he saw that he had fallen asleep, his head on his arms. He went round the table, lifted him off the seat and carried him to bed. As he stood looking down at him, he had a sudden impulse to stroke his hair. It made him feel like a spinster beside the cot of a sleeping child, and he cursed himself as he went out.

He walked into the forest, taking his gun to give his going a semblance of purpose. He looked up the trunk of a giant tree, straight and massive like the pillar of a cathedral, but putting his head back did not stop the tears, so he let them run, leaning against the tree, his head in the crook of his arm. Instead of bringing him relief, it made him feel worse; but he did not know how to stop. Then something tugged at his trouser leg. He knew at once that it was Stegomyia, before he heard the little voice, like that of a tame crow, ask, "Tea?" As he did not reply, "Beer?" As he still did not reply, but went on sobbing helplessly, the dwarf's small hands tugged at his coat, at the gun, and then, with a thunderclap that seemed to explode in front of his face, the gun went off. It shook him so badly and his head ached so much with the explosion that he only realized how violently he stood cursing when he saw the dwarf plunge into the under- growth, his hands over his head, like a diving swimmer. He went on bellowing blood-curdling curses in the echoing vaults of the forest until, at last, he could discern the echo and concluded with a sigh that his eardrums had survived.

The shot had broken his crying fit, and it seemed to have blown the foam off his grief. When he returned to the camp and saw the coolies gape at him, half hidden in the jungle, he called the mandur and gave him an order, to prove to his men that he had not gone mad. He threw the gun into the tent, cried, "Stegomyia! Stegomyia Fasciata! Well, God Almighty . . ." Then he discovered the dwarf hiding behind his back, turning as he turned. The spectacle was so disarming that he said, "Tea," to put the little creature at his ease; as he looked through his mail he found a medal from the French Government, and gave it to the dwarf as a consolation. Stegomyia at first did not dare approach him, but as he dangled the silver bauble on its purple ribbon in front of the little man's eyes, they became beady. He could not resist the temptation any longer, jumped at the *Palmes de l'Académie,* snatched the medal from his hand and attached it to his sole adornment, the string of beads around his belly. The rest of the mail was wastepaper; all letters with the word *"Archaeologist"* on the envelope went under the table unopened, the rest he read as far as the word *"archaeologist,"* and that took care of the lot. Not a word from Willem, nor from Bertie, not even an order from Headquarters, just a medal from the French Government and twenty-seven letters about urns.

Night was falling; he sat somberly staring at the fire; the darkness in the forest fell as quickly as if a trapdoor were closed in the ceiling of a dungeon. The coolies were preparing their meal over fires in the clearing; the smells of herbs and high meat drifted over with the acrid stench of smoke. Stegomyia, with his glistening medal flashing in the firelight, scrambled to and fro, bringing him tea, five fried bananas, a large omelet with mushrooms and ginger pancakes as dessert; he ate the lot mechanically. The flames of the coolie fires flickered on the crouching bodies, as they had flickered on the bodies of the lepers that night he first set eyes on her. Death came closer every night; thirty years had gone like a sigh, now she was gone, and the sun was setting. He must go and see Willem and visit her grave. He must also write to Bertie.

He wrote to her that same night, when everyone was asleep and the forest had started its midnight cacophony. The boy lay snoring on the camp bed; the dwarf babbled in his dreams; the yellow cone of the lamplight shone on the ink pot, his hands and the page from the logbook on which he wrote:

Dear Girl. It is very sad. But think of me. I have tried to save her for thirty years. I did not succeed. If heaven exists, she will be there now for she was an exceptional person. If there is no heaven she is alive in our thoughts. I shall buy her the best stone I can find at the Chinese. But the best monument to her goodness will lie under my stone one day. For without her I would have gone to hell. If you should ever do one tenth of what she has done for other people you will be an exceptional person too. I hope so. Much love, Yours, Uncle Leprosy.

He did not reread the letter but folded it with his eyes closed and stuck it in an official envelope. He crossed out the printed address, *On Her Majesty's Service, Government Health Service, To the Head of Service, Batavia,* and wrote hers between the lines. Then he took off his hat, stuck the letter inside the band, blew out the lamp and went to bed.

The wilderness was full of noise: creaking, rustling, sometimes a cry or a laugh. The mosquitoes swarmed, billowing clouds of sound behind the netting.

Betsy was dead.

«« »»

Brits-Jansen had finished packing and was about to leave for Batavia when the boy awoke; when he heard that he would have Camp Lung Plague to himself for at least six weeks, he nearly had a fit and stammered, "No, no, not that!" He was obviously in a bad state of jitters.

He proceeded to give the boy a piece of his mind. This shirking of responsibility had to stop. If he ever wanted to stand on his own feet, he had to take the plunge sometime and put his shoulder to the wheel. The boy, bewildered by the onslaught of mixed metaphors, did not rally to the call of duty, but started to blurt out some sordid nonsense about women instead. He refused to listen.

He told Stegomyia to fill his thermos flask with tea, called the mandur, ordered his porters to be ready in five minutes and turned to the boy for a last admonition. But he sat there so miserably, so hopelessly, that he asked, "But what's got into you?"

He got his money's worth. Once started, the boy rambled on for over an hour. He needed all his wits about him to make sense out of it all, but when the boy at last fell silent, exhausted, a number of things had emerged. He was terrified of Piet Kramer because his work in Batavia had been bad; his work had been bad because he lived with honey lamb like cat and dog and at the same time bled himself white in carnal pastimes, that were remarkable in their joylessness. Bertie had stopped writing to him at the request of honey lamb, whom he had betrayed once with a girl in a nearby kampong, and the bomb had exploded because, in a paroxysm of rage, despair and exasperation, he had given honey lamb what sounded like a very good time.

The boy obviously needed a father and he decided to put things right for him in Batavia on his way through. After all, it was partly his fault that the boy had plunged into that marriage, and it was bad for his work on leprosy if his home life was unsatisfactory. If honey lamb could not be made to see that her husband was married to leprosy in the first place, she had better go back to Holland and capture a dentist.

The visit to Mrs. Zorgdrager came at the top of his list of things to do in Batavia. Piet Kramer, cigars, underwear and a new pair of spectacles could come later. But even before he arrived in Batavia there were some minor things to be arranged. The boy was in such a state that he would certainly fret himself to a standstill if he were left to his own resources; he decided to get hold of the girl in the passangrahan that he had mentioned, and pack her off to him on his way to the coast. Those native girls could be trusted to cure the worst introvert in no time; between Stegomyia, the girl and the mandur, no one could wish for a better sanatorium than Camp Lung Plague in the Atjeh jungle. He handed the logbook, the gin and his gun to the mandur together with the plan of the road, to be passed on to the young tuan who had fallen asleep once more in the meantime. Then he bellowed the coolies of his caravan to life and entered the jungle.

They arrived in the kampong toward nightfall. He let the girls make his bed in the passangrahan, but when he pulled aside the mosquito curtain in anticipation his face fell. Whether it was fear of his bulk or his authority, he was in no position to judge; on the other hand she might have been delayed. When, however, after an hour of angry waiting no little silhouette had appeared on the curtain, he shouted for the head of the village and ordered him to round up all girls below twenty and herd them into the room next to his. It took some time, screams, smacks and angry protests; then the man appeared, grinning, at his bedside to report that his orders had been obeyed.

He went into the other room in his big, bare feet, surveyed the score of wide-eyed does, tremulously huddled together, took a ten-cent piece out of the breast pocket of his shirt, held it up in the candlelight, and asked, "Who looked after the young tuan doctor, who came a month ago with a little old man with a white beard and a funny speech?" He made the ten-cent piece glint enticingly and one of them stood up. He chased the rest of them out of the room, and put her at her ease. He was too old, she need not worry. It was about the young tuan, seriously ill in the forest and in need of a nurse. He would be back in six weeks' time; if the young tuan were cured on his return, he'd give her a guilder, if he were not, he'd cut her open. She assured him passionately that the young tuan would be a new man unless he sent her away; he assured her that there was no question of his sending her away if she gave him the letter he would write now. He scribbled a note, addressed it to *Doctor Zorgdrager, Camp L.P. Atjeh, G.H.S.* On the back, he wrote: *Please give*

the man who brings this ten cents and a kick in the pants. There are
quite enough idlers hanging around as it is, don't let him put himself
on the payroll. Then he sent the girl out into the night with a paternal
smack on her shapely bottom, went back to his bed and fell asleep at once.

A week later he arrived in Tandjong Priok, at nightfall. It was too late
to go to see Piet Kramer so he decided to strike the iron while it was hot
and go to pay his respects to honey lamb. He spent some time looking for
the house; when at last he climbed the front steps to the verandah it was
pitch dark. Through the mosquito screen of a lighted window, he saw her
sitting at the table, dining alone by candlelight. He coughed, knocked on
some woodwork and shouted, "Hello!" She seemed startled for some
reason, and did not answer; to put her at ease, he intoned quietly, "Don't
be afraid. This is a friend." She called, "Chun Chan!" ringing a handbell
at the same time, and a Chinese houseboy hurtled into the room, eyes
popping. She whispered to him and pointed at the verandah; the boy, as
he had expected, took the candle with him, leaving her in total darkness.
The boy's eyes widened even more when he saw him loom in the candlelight and he stammered, "What's the matter, please?" He took the candle
from him and, after trying three doors, entered the dining room, the
Chinese quacking at his heels. As he came in, she rose to her feet with an
unwelcoming look which he ignored when he saw her hair. It might be the
sheen of the candlelight, but he was sure she was pregnant. At first it
disturbed him; then he realized that it would miraculously arrange everything. For to pack her off to Holland while giving her the illusion that
she went of her own accord would be child's play. He had to be infinitely
sly now; not force matters, but put the words into her own mouth in a
fatherly fashion.

He took off his battered felt hat with an old-world gesture and said,
with a slight bow from the hips, "I think you may remember me. I am Dr.
Jansen, your husband's friend." She invited him insincerely to sit down
at the table with her, and he accepted gracefully. While the djongos, his
eyes still popping, watched all the food in the house disappear, he put her
at her ease by flattering her about her brilliant husband, and his natural
penchant for leprosy. He told her a series of falsehoods about the adven-
tures they had had together, and the laurels they had earned; then, with
an agility that impressed him in spite of himself, he continued, "His only
worry is that you have been looking a bit under the weather of late.

I told him, of course, that all young fathers imagine that; but maybe he's got something there. How do you feel?"

The casual "young father" was a gem, a master stroke, but she did not let herself be caught. She said, "Thank you, I feel fine," and when he scratched his beard, thinking up another ruse, she rose unexpectedly and announced she was going to bed, because she had a headache; if he wanted anything else, would he please ring the djongos; there was a bed in her husband's study, if he wanted to stay the night. Before he had managed to hoist himself out of his chair for a bow and a flowery good night, she was gone.

He called the djongos, asked for something to drink, drank some beer and a bottle of white wine, staring thoughtfully at a newspaper rack without newspapers and a portrait of the boy that looked exceptionally stupid, in a topee and collar, against a background of photographer's palms.

The next morning she did not appear; the djongos challenged him with a breakfast for ten people and lost. When he arrived at the Head Office, Piet Kramer was in conference but prestige demanded that he ignore the fact and he gate-crashed a meeting of three Foreign Office officials, crying, "Hiya, Piet! How's the hormone swindle?" Piet Kramer went white with rage, and the officials took flight; the moment they were gone, he bellowed all protests back into Piet Kramer's throat by starting, "And now, my friend, I've had enough! In what condition do you think I saw arrive in my camp the best assistant in the Service? A genius of diagnostics? A paragon in leprosy? Let me tell you . . ." and he told him, cutting a swath for his story through Piet Kramer's furious protestations by merely raising his voice. When, in the end, he had the stage to himself, he felt a lot better, for Piet Kramer had sunk back in his chair, breaking a pencil, and he knew the boy was his for life, even before the rabid little runt had cried, "All right! Take him! Skin him! Broil him! Do with him whatever you like, but get the hell out of here!"

But he had not finished yet. He changed his tone, pulled out the vox humana, and proceeded to tell Piet Kramer the boy's history. Piet Kramer slapped his forehead and cried, "I know, I know it backward, what the hell do you think I'm doing here?" He resisted the temptation to tell him, and concluded: "There's one thing you obviously don't know: his wife is pregnant. So here's your chance to pack her off, and set the boy back to work." When Piet Kramer asked him why the hell he should interfere in anyone's private life, he told him. If the Service wanted its money's worth in the case of this boy, it had to rid him of that girl. Not forever, mark you, just until the boy had found his feet. He had the makings of an excellent jungle doctor and should be sent out on his own now, preferably with a totok for an assistant. Once his wife was in Holland, all would be fine. Every man in the jungle should have a wife to write home to. If she stayed, however, she would not only force him to remain in Batavia, where he was useless, but drive him nuts into the bargain.

Piet Kramer, taking refuge in sarcasm, asked what had given him the idea that the Government Health Service was a marriage guidance bureau, but he was obviously impressed. In the end, realizing that he could be human without harming the Service, he rang for Doctor Sardjono and ordered him to make an appointment with Mrs. Zorgdrager for a medical examination, and to establish whether the government would be justified in sending her back to Holland. Then it was time for lunch and they ate together in Des Indes, a nice meal full of jokes and reminiscences. The moment Piet Kramer got out of that office, he was not a bad little chap at all.

That same afternoon he left for Man-Pu-Ko-Chu, and his visit there was much more upsetting than he had foreseen. When at last he stood, helmet in hand, at the foot of that little grave outside the walls of the fortress, a small cross in the field of white crosses underneath the vast sky full of ragged monsoon clouds, it was as if time had released him, as if he had lived toward this moment, and as if the rest of his life would be nothing but a going away from this moment, backward into the future. Willem and he exchanged barely a word; they stood silently side by side at her grave, ate silently side by side at the long table with the lepers, shook hands silently before going to bed, and lay silently staring in the darkness, listening to the distant thunder on the mountains.

It was not until two days later, as they went back to the world, that they talked about her. Willem went with him to Batavia for his operation, that could take place now she was gone. The old man was calm and relaxed; it seemed as if this first journey into the world after twenty years of isolation had put her out of his thoughts, but that was not so. All the way to Batavia he only talked of her, ignoring the cars, the airplanes, the metallized roads and the fuel stations that must be new to him. Then, suddenly, Willem told him that after her death he had realized that she was not gone. On the contrary: she was with them both, all the time, he knew that. He listened with an uneasy feeling: was the old man having hallucinations once more? He did not like that story of her standing at the foot of the bed, smiling consolingly; yet the man by his side spoke so calmly about it and seemed so well balanced, that he almost began to believe it.

That night, in an interne's room in the hospital, he turned out the light in fearful anticipation, angry with himself for his childishness, yet overcome with awe. But although he lay there breathlessly, thinking about her, conjuring her up in his imagination, even, after half an hour of waiting, whispering her name, nothing happened. No angel appeared at the foot of his bed, no unearthly feeling of consolation blessed him from the darkness, no ghostly hand touched his forehead as a sign that his whisper had been heard. Whatever Willem might have experienced after she had left them, he had no part of it. To him, who had tried his life long to defend her body against the white death, she was lost forever, leaving nothing behind but one small white cross among many in a field, on a mountain amidst the shattered mirror of the paddy fields of Java.

He only remembered the boy and Bert after he had operated on her father, taken the boat to Medan, the train to Langsa, and saw in Langsa station the announcement of a play to be performed by the local dramatic society, called *Love Letters*. He went to see it, had supper with the actors afterward, demonstrated how the upper jaw of his dentures covered a beer mat, won a bet by eating a twenty-course meal and received amidst applause a china Dutch tile with the legend, *Providence often grants trousers to those who have no behind*. The next morning, he disappeared into the jungle, a lonely man who could think of only one reason for his existence: that he had saved a boy, from a labyrinth of love, for leprosy. When, soon, that boy stood on his own feet and took over his work, he might as well be dead.

Only then did he realize that, although his expedition to Batavia had been an unqualified success, all he had done was to dig his own grave. As he was carried through the wilderness, somberly listening to the chant of the coolies hacking their way home, he wondered what God had against him.

«« »»»

Els was packing her last suitcase in the bedroom when Chun Chan came in to tell her that "an old officel" wanted to see her. Her first impulse was to have the old officer chased off the premises; after having received two of Anton's emissaries, she felt she had had enough.

The first had been that alarming brute with the beard who had lifted her onto the table in Labuan Redjo. He had broken into her home like a burglar, ransacked the icebox, eliminated her stock of beer and spirits, hiccuped and belched like a pig, looking each time as if it were the first time in his life; but worst of all he had made the clumsiest of allusions to her pregnancy, which so far she had not revealed to anyone. There was only one explanation for the dirty giant's remark: Anton must have discussed with him the possibility that their last love-making might have had consequences. The fact that he should have done so turned him, suddenly, into an enemy.

If only he had written to her, one line, if only he had sent her a telegram or even a picture with just his name, she would have forgiven him. But not a word, not a sign—only those strange sinister men, sneaking in from the darkness.

The second was a native. He arrived, like the giant, one evening during a thunderstorm. She sat, heroically reading the newspaper, closing her eyes each time lightning twitched behind the mosquito curtain and the night staggered under the crashing thunder claps; suddenly she saw in a flash of lightning a man standing on the verandah. She leaped out of her chair, stumbled into the corridor, shouting, "Chun Chan! Cook! Babu! Help!" All the panic of her loneliness and the thunder and the lightning had broken loose in her cries. Chun Chan came running, his slippers slapping; she panted, "A man! A man on the—verandah . . ." As he hurried out, she cried, helpless sobs in the surf of the thunder. He came back with a dark stranger who, headless in his white drill, loomed in the doorway, like a ghost. "Dottel Saldjono, njonja besar," Chun Chan said; as he passed her on his way back to the kitchen, she whispered, "Stay behind the door."

She lit the lamp, and found the stranger to be a smiling Javanese, whose eyes were violent in the orange light. He was polite and charming, but the look that he ran down her figure chilled her. The thunder, the wind and the rain were so violent that she heard only part of what the Javanese had to say. She gathered that he was a colleague of her husband's and that for some reason that she did not understand, and did not care to understand either, he wanted to examine her. Her fear gave way to indignation; when the Javanese stood up and asked her where the bedroom was, she cried, "Chun Chan!" and the Chinese sprang into the room like a jack-in-the-box, his teeth bared, with a spinach knife. The Javanese, unruffled, lifted his eyebrows and looked at her in polite amazement. She said, "Show this gentleman the door," turned away and sat down again, picking up the newspaper. She kept her eyes riveted on the printed page as she listened with high-beating heart to Chun Chan's voice that said, "This way, please, dottel," to the momentary silence, to the stranger's footsteps and the shuffle of Chun Chan's slippers in the corridor. When the outside door closed, she just managed to control herself sufficiently to pick up the telephone and call Jane Frenssen. A croaking voice answered as the thunder crashed, and she shouted, "Jane, Jane, this is Els, Els Zorgdrager! I know it is terrible weather, but could you please, please, come over?"

"Now?" the voice croaked.

"Yes," she answered, hoarse with the effort to keep back her tears. "At once, Jane, please, please!"

"All right, I'll be over," the voice answered; she put the phone down, tottered back to her chair, and broke down at last.

Jane arrived, drenched, found her incoherent with sobs and put her to bed. Then Jane took off her wet clothes and got into bed beside her, with a towel round her head to dry her hair, smoking a cigarette. Jane remained reasonable and imperturbable as ever; she just smoked and listened with an occasional grunt to her breathless story of Anton's strange behavior and sudden disappearance and those lugubrious men and her condition and the thunder and her loneliness. Then Jane said, "All right, I see it all." She stubbed out her cigarette and continued, "Come on. Put on some clothes. I'll borrow a shirt and a pair of trousers of your husband's and out we go."

"We! Where?" she asked, still shaking.

"You're coming back with me," Jane answered. "Do you think I'd leave you here, all by yourself in this weather, and in that state? Chinese!" she called. "Djongos!"

Chun Chan, outside, answered at once, "Saja, njonja dottel;" he must have been listening.

"Njonja's coming with me," Jane cried. "Bring a suitcase."

That was the end. At that moment, her life changed irrevocably, for after Jane had taken her home in her car, and put her to bed with a double whisky, she called their physician and took him in to her. He examined her gravely, then he said, "Young lady, I'm not happy about you." She asked, bravely, her lips trembling, "Is there something wrong?" The doctor, after a moment's hesitation, answered, "I'm afraid you'll have to choose between your baby and staying here." As she did not understand he concluded, "If you want a healthy child, you should go back to Holland as soon as possible."

Holland. It was as if, with that one word, the last gossamer thread that still joined Anton and her together broke.

Holland. The word brought a strange eerie peace—as if a power outside herself had taken over the guidance of her life. Never before had she dared to admit, even to herself, how terribly nostalgic she was for Holland, ever since she had first set foot in this beastly country. Now, the moment the doctor said that, a load was taken from her, a nightmare. For while Jane and the doctor sat talking, and she went drowsy with the effects of the whisky, she suddenly saw an image, so clearly that the whole of the Far East was wiped out: the image of a sand pit with a lopsided doll's pram, her earliest memory.

With that memory she started her homeward voyage, back to peace, to security, to Holland. It was the first memory of many: a vase with tulips on the windowsill; the carillon of a church tower starting to play, sowing pigeons out of its belfry; the bouncing of the doorbell in the passage after the postman had rung. The memories accompanied her all day long, more as moods than images; they slowly exorcised the reality of the monsoon, the oppressive heat, the twitching lightning, the thunder crashing in the night. It was as if, now that she expected a child, Holland had come toward her to protect her from the wilderness, with tranquil thoughts of long ago, of home. Seagulls in the park; the steam from the tea kettle freezing into flowers on the window pane; the smell of a freshly ironed apron. Those thoughts brought one overpowering sensation: a feeling of security. She was safe, at last, in the fortress Holland, safe behind the dikes of her memories that made reality seem indifferent and harmless.

Jane Frenssen could not understand it; nobody could understand it. Everybody babbled, prated, held forth at her, mothered, gossiped, smothered her with advice. She smiled and kept silent. Jane was flabbergasted when she told her very calmly, while arranging flowers on the sitting-room table after she had returned from a morning's shopping, that she had booked her passage on the boat of the following week.

"I beg your pardon?" Jane asked, putting down her glass. "When did you do that?"

"This morning. Chun Chan has started packing."

"And—what about him?"

She shrugged her shoulders. "I've tried to get in touch with him but it's impossible." She lied; she had carefully avoided getting in touch with him. She even tried not to think of him, for there was only one danger that threatened her security: the thought of how desperate he would be, how upset. In his eyes it must be a flight, a treason, whatever he might have done to her with his mysterious disappearance and his silence. But she had to choose between him and her child, and this much she realized: she had chosen from an instinct that was older than her conscience. She was sacrificing her husband to save her child from the clutches of the jungle; the life she cherished, the mysterious bearer of life eternal in the warm darkness of her womb, must not grow into a tiger cub in the wilderness, but into a young white citizen of a civilized community, a Dutchman, not a colonial.

Occasionally, in moments that took her completely unawares, the realization of what she was doing overwhelmed her; as she laid the table in the Frenssen's home, or combed her hair in front of the mirror, or shut her purse with a sharp snap in the silence of their empty house. She could walk through the rooms without emotion, she could take his portrait off the mantelpiece and put it in a suitcase without a twinge in her heart, but when she put a chair straight, or poured water into the teapot, she was sometimes suddenly overcome with the full realization of their lost happiness. Anton, Anton! She had to control herself forcibly in order not to burst into tears, to cry out with grief: Anton, Anton, darling, my darling, my sweetheart, where are you, where are you? But then she pressed her fists in her eyes, clenched her jaws until the pain calmed her, and straightened up with the courage of loneliness. For Anton was lost forever, to her and perhaps to the world; Anton had gone back into the primeval chaos of the wilderness, with which he had once betrayed her. But her love for him would remain; it would grow and thrive like a tree; and his child, which she would have in her power from birth, would be made to conform to the image she had had herself, once upon a time, of its father.

And then, at the height of this certainty, at the very moment that she was about to commit the irrevocable, his last emissary came. She stood packing the last suitcase in the empty house, about to go on board, to Holland, and here was Chun Chan, announcing a strange officer.

"Where is he?" she asked.

"Outside, njonja dottel. He sitting on the velandah."

She closed the suitcase, hesitated; then she went out onto the verandah.

«« »»

It had been further than Willem expected; when he stood looking at the small bungalow with the white chickens in the yard and the orange table lamp behind the window, he was so tired that he sat down at the top of the steps leading to the verandah, after giving the Chinese boy his name. There she found him, resting his head on his hands.

"What can I do for you?"

He looked up and saw her standing behind him, a thin, blonde girl with light blue eyes, a child.

"Are you Mrs. Zorgdrager?"

"I am; who are you?"

"I am Bert Waterreus's father."

He saw her mouth harden and was glad he had come. There was something very touching about her, a great loneliness, a great courage. "May I come in?" he asked. "Or would you rather I went away?"

She stood looking at him for a moment before she answered; he realized that she had made a decision which she wanted to protect, and wondered what it was. "Do come in," she said.

His compassion for her grew as she led the way through the passage to the room with the orange lamp. Her shoulders were too frail to carry an independent life, let alone a marriage with an adolescent. He hoped that God would enable him to help her, for, of the three children, she needed it most.

She invited him to sit down in a low chair, but he said he would rather sit at the table as he was convalescent after an operation; this was his first outing. Her suspicion changed into a motherly concern. She asked whether he would like to drink something, or to eat something, or to put his legs up, or have a cushion at his back. He thanked her and said he did not need anything and then, suddenly, she asked him why he had come, with an abruptness that was revealing. He answered, "My daughter wrote to me that she had stopped writing to your husband at your request. I know my daughter and I know your husband; I wanted to meet you too. I hope I may be able to help you."

"It's very kind of you," she said, "but I don't need any help. Did my husband send you?"

"No. Isn't he in Batavia?"

"Sumatra, on a jungle expedition."

"Does he know you are leaving?"

"I would have loved to let him know, but I don't know exactly where he is, so . . ."

"I wouldn't decide too quickly. He is still very young."

She tried to smile, but her lips trembled. "I'm afraid I have no choice, I leave on doctor's orders."

"Ah. I hope you aren't ill?"

"No . . ." she said, with a moving mixture of nervousness and pride. "I'm expecting a baby."

"Congratulations," he said. "That is wonderful news."

Then she gave him a look that he would not forget for the rest of his life, and burst into tears.

He got to his feet carefully, for the floor was slippery, and sat down on the arm of her chair. It was an uncomfortable position for his wound, but he did not care. He put a hand on her shoulder and, as she fell with her head against him, racked with grief, he put his arm around her. She was so defenseless that he closed his eyes and thought a prayer for mercy; then he felt the force flow through his hand into her trembling body, and she became still under his shield.

It moved him deeply, the miracle of mercy that he was allowed to transmit once more; moments like these were worth a lifetime of diabolical terrors. And the greatest of all was that the mercy, granted to this girl on her child's crusade of small grief, had been won by Betsy in twenty-five years of inhuman suffering, just as Christ with his martyr's death had wrested mercy for all mankind from a terrible God. If Betsy had not died as a decomposing trunk in stench and darkness, he would not now have been able to lift this child out of her misery with nothing but a hand on her shoulder and a silent prayer.

"Come," he said, "tell me. I believe I can help you."

She stood up, her face wet and swollen, went to the table and handed him a letter that was propped up against the vase. On the envelope was written, *Anton*.

"You'll read it all in there," she said. He saw her trembling and said, "Come and sit here with me. We'll read it together."

She sat down beside him, he opened the letter, but she did not read it with him. She lit a cigarette and blew the smoke toward the ceiling. He could not help smiling, though he was worried by the defiance forced upon her in her short life.

It was a long letter but the gist of it was simple. After he had read it, he folded it and sat thinking. She looked up at him; the defiance in her eyes fled before the compassion of his look. "I am doing the right thing, aren't I?" she asked, and it sounded like the cry of an anguished heart.

"Let us ask," he said, took her hand and knelt by the chair. He stumbled with pain and stiffness and she fell on her knees beside him to help, thinking he had fallen; but he folded his hands over hers and closed his eyes and said, "God, give her the answer. Give her peace, for Christ's sake and for the sake of your martyrs." He felt the force flow through his head and heart into her. When, after a moment, he rose painfully to his feet, she did not help him but remained where she was, her hands in her lap. At last she looked up, with eyes that did not really see him. He asked, "Did you get the answer?"

She came back from far away, looked at him, and then she answered, "Yes."

"Good," he said. "Now, how can I help you?"

"Be here, when he comes back."

"I'll do that. May I see you onto the boat?"

She nodded; in her eyes there was still that wonder.

«« »»

Why she had started crying at the sight of the old man she could not understand. She had defended herself against him with all her common sense and her self-respect; to kneel on the carpet to pray just like that, like children before going to bed, was ridiculous, almost irreverent. She had not thought much about God during her lifetime, just as she had not thought much about the Queen. God existed. He had clergymen to remind mankind of that fact on Sundays, and it was a good civilized custom to close one's eyes for a moment before a meal, for to start drinking one's soup at once was unmannerly. During her months of loneliness, she had not given God a thought; and there came a white old man, who knelt on the floor, took her hands in his, and before she knew what he was doing a great peace came over her, white silence, and at the same time the knowledge that she must go. Her spiteful thoughts of teaching Anton a lesson by going were nothing but ripples on the surface of her consciousness; she must go, whatever she might wish or think, for something stronger than herself drove her, something as mysterious and irrevocable as the Force that made the tiny being grow within her.

Many friends went to see her off on the boat; she had never realized she had so many. But she was constantly aware of the presence of the old man in the background, a still white figure behind the laughter, the chatter and the restlessness of the others. He stayed with her until the boat left but they did not speak again. He just was there, looking like a porter in his badly fitting uniform and his white peaked cap.

She looked down at him from the promenade deck as the siren wailed its cry of departure. The hawsers splashed into the water, a tremor ran through the ship, a wave of farewell rose from the crowd on the quay. Everybody waved, cried, wept with laughing faces; she waved at the Frenssens, the friends, the quayside, Batavia. When she looked at the old man in the background again, he was watching her, and with a gesture that filled her with a sinking feeling of solemn irrevocability, he brought his hand to his cap for a salute.

It was ridiculous, ridiculous—but it was such an impressive gesture that it made her sink forward with her head on her arms on the rail. One of her fellow passengers comforted her, a motherly woman who smelled of perspiration and peardrops and had the jolly laugh of a farmer's wife. She said, "Come on, girlie, chin up. We're going home now." She sniffed and dried her eyes and smiled in embarrassment and went to drink a glass of lemonade with the farmer's wife, who babbled about the menu and the trembling of the engines and the best way of getting one's laundry back quickly, by taking it oneself to the linen room early in the morning instead of waiting for the Javanese stewards to collect it with the trolley.

When she came back on deck, Java was gone. The sea was blue, the sky was blue, and in the blue fluttered the Dutch flag. She gazed at the wake, the last trail that linked her with Anton. But his image was very vague, as if she had reached Holland already, as if the whole of the Far East, her marriage, her fears, despair, tears and pain had been left behind, teeming behind a white sentry of whom she could remember nothing but his salute.

That night, before going to bed, she knelt on the rubber mat on front of her bunk, folded her hands and felt at a loss as to what to do next. She could not find any words, nor think of a prayer; yet it was a mysteriously fortifying moment. It was as if, for one second, she felt that white Force come over her once more, and she rose hastily to her feet, alarmed.

It took her a long time to fall asleep. Her thoughts would not come to rest. Batavia, Anton, the wilderness . . . It seemed as if it had all been for nothing, one long mistake; as if she had been lost in an enchanted forest from which she had now escaped with empty hands. But in the dreamy hubbub of her drowsy thoughts, just before she fell asleep, she smiled with a childish feeling of pride and achievement.

For from that journey to the heart of darkness she brought back a treasure that she could not have found anywhere else in the world: a child, her child, hers alone. For she could not remember its father clearly any more; all she remembered, and would remember to the end of her days, was that moment of leaving the forest, and the old guide's salute of farewell.

«« »»

When Anton woke up in a golden green morning, from the deepest sleep he had ever known, he discovered a native girl kneeling by the side of his cot, and he took a long time before he recognized her. He lay staring at her intently and gravely, cautiously picking up the threads of reality and joining them once more. He gazed at her eyes, her smile of white teeth, the oily braid of her black hair, the sheen of sunlight on her bare shoulders, the rust-colored pattern of her sarong—only when she giggled nervously under his expressionless gaze did he open the letter she had been holding out to him.

Young man, I forgot to tell you that any prehistoric objects dug up during my absence should be buried at once and not mentioned in the log. If, on my return, I find another stack of pots and bones waiting for me, there will be hell to pay. Cordially yours, B. Jansen.

He stared at the letter with a frown, then turned the paper over. On the back, he read: *Please give the man who brings this ten cents and a kick in the pants;* then he looked up at the sound of shrill parrotlike quacking. In the triangle of sunlight at the entrance of the tent the girl and Brits-Jansen's pygmy were having a row, and it was such a hilarious spectacle that he felt he was still dreaming. The dwarf, dancing with rage on tiny bowlegs, wore, as a sole item of clothing, a string of beads from which dangled a purple ribbon with a silver pendant of two palm leaves; facing him, her arms akimbo like an angry mother, stood the girl in the rust-colored sarong, scolding him as if he were a monstrous child. The sight was so unreal that he finished it with a shout. The dwarf and the girl fell silent and turned to look at him simultaneously. When he made a move to get up the girl rushed toward him, pushed him back with surprising strength and babbled a story in obscure Malay from which he understood only the words, "ill," and "massage." She pulled off his shirt before he had recovered from his astonishment sufficiently to defend himself, climbed onto the bed, stood on his belly, steadying herself at the ribs of the tent, and started to massage his muscles with her toes. He tried to chase her out of his dream, to go hunting for that other hallucination: the dwarf with the *Palmes de l'Académie,* but she held him down on the bed with her weight and continued, giggling, to trample on him as if she were pressing grapes. Her toes kneaded and pinched and pressed and tickled; a drowsy laziness overcame him and he could not help closing his eyes and sagging back into a strange half sleep; after an undulating slumber that seemed to last for hours he woke up feeling fresh and vigorous.

He was waked up by the clatter of earthenware. When he opened his eyes he saw the dwarf and the girl laying the table in perfect unity, the pygmy eating a banana. He suddenly remembered his name, Stegomyia Fasciata, Brits-Jansen's batman. He felt like bursting into laughter and into tears at the same time. What a wonderful, crazy world; what a joy to watch those two creatures devotedly laying the table for him; what peace to hear the whistling, warbling, whispering jungle in the background, to smell that spicy smell of food and wood smoke, to taste that bitter-salty taste of sweat and sap as he licked his lips, the taste of the wilderness.

The dwarf was the first to notice he was awake. He took the banana out of his mouth, grinned with filed-off teeth, and asked, "Tea? Beer?" He answered "Tea," and smiled at the girl. She looked at him coyly; and he said, "Hello there." She came toward him as if she were approaching a dangerous animal that lay purring momentarily, stared at his eyes for a long time; then, with a movement quicker than that of a bird, she kissed him. It was so unexpected and so comical that he roared with laughter. He laughed until the tears ran down his face, and only calmed down when he saw the girl and the dwarf gazing at him in alarm, two heads peering over the table. He got up, stretched, yawned, pulled up his trousers and went outside into the sunlight. The clearing in the forest was cut in half by the shadow of the trees. In the shade, the coolies stirred around their wood fires, clattering pans, breaking kindling wood; the sounds were small and subdued in the colossal humming silence of noon. He called, "Mandur!" saw a native detach himself from the throng and run toward him. He felt a wave of shameful, delicious pride and self-importance as the man bowed into the dust in front of him and chanted, "Saja tuan?" Ah, this was the life he was born to live.

He ordered the mandur to bring him the plans of the road, the log books, the wage lists; then he went to wash in the sail-cloth washroom, where he found everything arranged for Brits-Jansen's bulk: a bucket like a tub, a towel like a rug, tooth mug like a bucket. Only as he was scrubbing his chest and shoulders did he discover a third tray with a brush a foot long, and he realized that he had been scrubbing himself with Brits-Jansen's toothbrush. He burst into song, a noisy senseless aria, "Formidablos, colossablos, Carmen jungle cigarillos!" He bellowed, trumpeted, splashed and gargled until his throat ached with the high notes and his skin tingled with vigor. Then he came out into the sunlight, Brits-Jansen's bath rug round his hips, and found all the coolies standing stock-still, gaping at him; the girl and the dwarf were peering out of the tent. They ducked back as they saw him coming; when he stooped into the darkness of the stifling hot interior, they were waiting for him with a shirt big enough for a baptism. He put it on because he had no change of clothes; it reached down to his calves and the sleeves hung over his hands. The girl started to laugh on a very high note, with a strange gackering jungle sound; life suddenly was so irresistibly happy and mad and delicious that he flung an arm around her waist, kissed her, and bellowed at the dwarf, "Stegomyia! Tea!"

The jungle, the jungle . . . It was like an awakening in the radiant reality of the blossoming earth, after months of stumbling through the mine shafts of a nightmare. He felt himself grow, expand in the wilderness; after his siesta he started by working himself to a standstill in the forest at the head of the road. He made stern jokes with the mandur, cursed the coolies but with such abundance of vitality that they grinned in recognition of his high spirits. The swinging of the gun against his hip, the whiplash of the creepers, the smarting of his heels in his jungle boots, the stinging of the sweat in his eyes delighted him; when suddenly a snake dangled from a tree, hissing with darting tongue, and the coolies fled screaming, dropping parangs and picks, he grabbed his gun, took aim, and at the crash of the report tears sprang into his eyes with pain and joy. The snake slithered down, flopped to the ground with a rustling thud, the coolies came back, and at the sight of their admiration his happiness became so overwhelming that he ran back to the tent as fast as he could, for he had to hug somebody, press somebody to his heart as a lightning conductor for his pent-up exultation.

He overpowered the girl just as, that gruesome morning, he had overpowered Els; but what had then been an explosion of despair and fury was now an explosion of joy; and instead of leaving the other wilting and bruised like a trampled flower, it was now he himself who, an hour later, sat with his head in his hands and the feeling as if he had nearly drowned. He was greeted with the flash of white teeth in the candlelight, and the triumph of two glistening eyes, and a bottle of tepid beer handed to him at bed level by the pygmy.

That night, after the meal that like all Brits-Jansen's meals in the jungle had been vegetarian, he ordered Stegomyia to make tea, packed the girl off to bed and sat down, his feet on the table, to read the log books by the light of the lamp. He finished reading within an hour. The making of this road was so easy that even a totok would have enjoyed doing it. It was a holiday for soul and mind. Physically it was murderously exhausting; he who did not emerge broken after a month was a superman. Brits-Jansen had been working on it for nine months and loved it. Weird creature, Brits-Jansen, mysterious creature. He suddenly felt like smoking a pipe, as always in the jungle; in town, he only smoked cigarettes. The pipe Brits-Jansen had left for him tasted bitter; he remembered that there used to be new pipes in his instrument case. He took the lantern with him into the corner where the tins were, and had to chase the dwarf out of his nest on the empty gin tins to get at the case behind them. This job had not asked for a doctor, but for a road builder's foreman; with his instrument case, Brits-Jansen had stored his profession for the duration. He did find the new pipes; he found something else as well: a springback cover filled with untidy sheets of paper, covered with Brits-Jansen's handwriting. On the title page he read *Notes Leprosy*. He took it with him to the table, lit the pipe that, even though the smallest of the lot, was as heavy as a horse's bit, poured himself a mug of tea, and started to read.

The pygmy snored, the girl breathed softly in the darkness, sometimes the bed creaked as she turned in her sleep. The wilderness was full of cries, quackings, tuneless flutes, furtive rustling, and the endless undulating zooming of the swarms of mosquitoes behind the curtain. At dead of night, elephants roamed round the camp, attracted by the watch fires, betraying their presence by the huge, mysterious rumbling of their insides and colossal sucking sounds as they dragged their feet out of the swamps. After a while they lumbered away, crashing, rumbling, roaming monsters in the darkness.

But he hardly heard them, for what he was reading was even more impressive than the jungle. On those few hundred dog-eared sheets of paper, covered with an almost illegible scrawl, smudged with coffee and swatted gnats, the giant had thrown down a masterpiece so brilliant and at the same time so full of elementary mistakes that it reminded him of a cave drawing of prehistoric times. Out of that tattered cover, those torn pages, rose, rather than a picture of leprosy, his own portrait like a vision, a great romantic, a knight out of a legend, wandering alone in a virgin wilderness, haunted by demons and an undying hope.

When he finished reading and closed the cover, he did so with reverence. He refilled his pipe, lit it at the candle because the lamp was empty, blew the smoke at the night, lost in thought. He sat there for more than an hour; when at last the candle had burnt down, he dropped on his bed with a headache and eyes smarting with exhaustion, to jump with a stifled cry as he felt something warm and alive; he had forgotten the girl. She snuggled up to him, murmuring in her sleep, and slept on, the soft warmth of her breath caressing his chest.

Only then did he realize that, since his arrival in the camp, he had not given Els a thought, even though it was the vision of her, lying on their bed unconscious and violated, that had haunted him all the way from Batavia without a moment of respite. Els. The memory of her should have filled him with shame, yet he realized, without guilt, that he had forgotten her the moment the jungle had gathered him to her once more. In the jungle she seemed as real as the National Anthem, his car, the lawn mowers of Batavia rattling in the dusk, an atom of Dutch coziness in the crater of the universe, a tea light in the forest.

"Hawaaw!" the dwarf cried in his dream, and kicked the tins of his bed with a hollow sound. The girl in his arm sighed, warm on his chest. He fell asleep with a boyish image of Brits-Jansen, fading in the darkness:

a knight in rusty armor, dented and splattered with blood, who staggered up to the foot of God's throne and reached up a spring-back cover toward the light, before collapsing with a clattering crash.

The crash was Stegomyia, falling out of bed; he awoke with a start. He only realized he was awake as he felt the coldness of the gun in his hand. The girl had thrown her arms around him and hid trembling behind his back. The dwarf coughed, muttered something, and climbed back onto the tins. He put down his gun and turned over to sleep; but she kissed him fiercely and passionately. He let himself sink once more into the swirling darkness of the jungle while outside, in the blue daybreak, the birds of dawning started to chirrup in the clouds of the morning mist.

«« »»

During his journey back through the jungle, Brits-Jansen rehearsed what he would tell the boy. He would say that his wife was expecting a baby and that, in his opinion, it might well be necessary for her to go back to Holland. He should proceed cautiously, and spring his news only when he knew how the totok had reacted to his therapy.

As far as the therapy was concerned, his first look told him. The sweating, yodeling highwayman that came running toward him the moment his coolies broke through the undergrowth was the reverse of the neurotic he had left behind six weeks ago. Stegomyia came leaping for him on his short legs like a frog and jumped up at him, squealing with joy. He went toward the tent, a hand in the nape of the dwarf's neck and an arm around the boy's shoulders. As they approached, a brown girl's face peeped out of the opening with such naughty eyes and such a disarming grin that he lifted her off the ground and rubbed her in his beard for a fatherly kiss. Then, at last, at last, he could sit down at his own table on his own bench, home.

It all looked neat and tidy and, as he had ascertained at a glance, the camp seemed active and orderly, so this part of his expedition was obviously a success. The mandur, grinning and bowing cringingly, came to present his compliments and he slapped the double-crossing bastard's shoulder; the boy obviously had not lacked authority and there were only three dead to report: one snakebite and two falling trees. What a joy, what a relief to be home again! He would have liked to take a bath now, eat himself into drowsiness and get six hours' sleep, but first he had to administer the boy's pill.

After lunch, as they sat picking their teeth, with their feet on the table, the boy suddenly put a new log book in front of him, and when he asked him, "What's that?" he put the cover with his notes on leprosy beside it. His first reaction was one of anger, because he had dared open his instrument case in his absence, but when he said, "While you were away, I copied out your notes for you," he opened the new log book and leafed through it. He saw to his amazement that, in those six weeks, the boy had indeed deciphered his notes from beginning to end, divided them into chapters and paragraphs, and copied them in a schoolboy's handwriting across the columns of an empty log book. It was a moving discovery, and he was about to say something sentimental when a paragraph caught his eye. *After this brilliant exposé by Dr. Jansen, certain footnotes are deemed necessary to clarify his conclusions. First of all, one should, while considering his analysis of capillary reactions, bear in mind that this is the work of a pioneer, venturing into uncharted territory, so . . .*

Then the bomb burst. That he had played with his camp, fine; that he had continued to dig his road, all right; that he had broken open his instrument case, taken out his private papers to copy them word for word, so be it; but that the megalomaniac, the clodhopper had violated the borders of the most elementary decency to the point of adding footnotes to *his* book as if, God blast him, he could understand one billionth of what he had been copying with his bloody tongue between his rotting teeth, into a new log book into the bargain, that was the limit, the death blow to all fatherly indulgence, that was . . .

The blowing-up he gave him was so colossal, the explosions of his curses, the lightning of his invective, the rolling thunder of his wrath were so obliterating in their fury and so ear-splitting in their volume, that the whole of the camp stood petrified and Anton, chalk white, stumbled out of the tent and ran erratically to the head of the road, where he could go no further. He looked round at the ring of coolies gaping at him with vacant faces, recovered his senses, cursed them back to work and started to march to and fro behind their backs, muttering, snottering, with shock and fury.

Brits-Jansen, after having hurled the log book at the head of the fleeing skunk, picked it up again, flung it on the floor and trampled on it like an infuriated elephant, slumped on the seat, decapitated a beer bottle and emptied it. He tried to light a pipe and flung it away. Finally, as his anger subsided and with it the chance of final gratification, he picked up the mauled log book once more to recapture his fleeing fury.

But, although he read on, he did not recapture it. He started by shrugging his shoulders, snorting, crying, "Phooey!" and hitting the defenseless page with his fist; but after his second bottle of beer he only grunted, waiting for the first chance to tear the damn thing apart, grind his heels in it, pick it up like a sod and fling it into the jungle, into oblivion. He searched, leafed, tore pages as he turned them, but his anger changed slowly into wonder, and, in the end, into shame. It was terrible, unimaginable, but the boy was right. "Footnotes," he called them, but they were corrections. Feigning modesty, full of nauseating flattery, the youngster hit him across the knuckles on practically every page. He might call him "genius" and "Cyclopean creator of this monumental masterpiece"; but he had to face it: the boy was right. It gave him a feeling of dull despondency, and yet a dawn of delight. Of course, the totok had made scores of mistakes in his turn, but that was only natural as he did not yet know the beginnings of leprosy. All he had done really was to try to cover up how "the brilliant scientist" contradicted himself every five minutes and ran into doors he had slammed shut himself a second before. Ah, if only he had given the book a little more thought, if only he had not just scribbled it down when he was drunk or lonely for want of a correspondent! Anyhow, it might not be "a revolutionary creation of gigantic scope" as the youngster called it; the footnotes, despite their amateurishness, were a brilliant piece of work. At last he knew for certain that he had found his true successor, and he had kicked him squarely out of the tent.

He sat waiting for him to come back, drinking beer first and tea later, to end with gin as darkness fell. When it was pitch dark and dinner was served and the boy had still not returned, he went to look for him. He found him sitting on a tree stump, staring at the coolie fires. The girl sat beside him on the ground, her head on his knee, pleading. At his approach, she leaped to her feet and stood in front of the boy, protectively; the boy stood up behind her. "Dr. Jansen," he said in too high a voice, "I hope you won't mind my saying . . ."

"Shut up!" he said. "It's my fault. What you did was shameless. I'm not sorry I gave you a piece of my mind, and I'll give you some more of it tomorrow, but your work is good. It is even"—and here he brought his beard so menacingly close to the boy's face that the latter almost fell backward into the undergrowth—"excellent!" After that shout of fatherly fury and pride, he grabbed the youngster by the scruff of his neck, dragged him back to the tent and plonked him down at the table. Only then did he realize what had been the weight on his other arm: the girl, who had tried to stop him murdering her young hero. It mellowed him. He slapped her buttocks, hung his hat on the pole and sat down with a sigh of contentment for a meal of celebration with his crown prince, forgetting all about honey lamb.

<<< >>>

Anton opened the door to the living room and stared in amazement. Underneath the orange table lamp, instead of Els, sat Bert's father, asleep. On the table, propped against an empty vase, stood a letter: *Anton*.

He read the letter while the old man, slumped in his chair, slept on.

Dearest Anton, I have fought, prayed, done everything to stay, but I couldn't. By the time you read this, I shall be at sea on my way to Holland and, however terrible this may be, it is for the sake of our child. I have tried to formulate for myself how and why all this has happened. . . .

By the time he finished the letter, he had, at last, realized it. He had walked into the trap that the wilderness had set for him, like an animal; now the trap had sprung. Like an animal; for by closing his eyes to the sin he had committed, he had robbed himself of the one thing that might have saved him: his power of identification with someone else. He had suppressed every thought of Els consciously, passionately during all those weeks in the jungle, to surrender himself to lust and pride, to gorge himself with self-importance. He had hazarded further than ever into the maze of the enchanted forest, confident of the thread in his hand, that would guide him back when the time came: Els. Now he stood in the heart of the forest, holding the end of the broken thread. Els had gone, forever.

He folded the letter, put it down on the table and lit a cigarette. He felt the whirlpool of panic slowly dragging him down, but before it took hold of him, there was a moment of icy clarity, in which he overlooked his life as from a great height. He had had a human life in his hands and broken it, he had begotten a child in a paroxysm of adolescent rage: now he stood eye to eye with the destiny he had conjured up himself. What was to become of him, now that the loose end of Ariadne's thread hung limp in his hands? At best, if he were one of the chosen few, he would become a Brits-Jansen; but he was no Brits-Jansen. He was Anton Zorgdrager, who had gorged himself with fornication, and imagined he was "strong" and "free" because the fornication had taken place in the jungle instead of in a hotel room. For such as he there was no mercy in the jungle; he had spotted them occasionally: the furtive slinking silhouettes of outcasts who had been unable to rid themselves of their native women and sold their souls for an eternal night of lascivious delight. That was his future: the kampong. He had been able to shake off the lung-plague girl because of Els; now Els was gone, he was defenseless against the jungle. A sob crept up in his throat; he tried to fight it down for one frantic second, then it burst out of him like a hoarse cry and he sank into a chair, staring in horror at the damnation that rose before him. Then the old man opened his eyes.

He had forgotten all about him; but when the white eyes opened, retribution stood still as before a shining sword. Sweat broke out on his forehead with the sting of needles, and the nausea of shock overcame him, but he realized: all the strength that had struck him with awe at the deathbed of Bert's mother was now concentrated in the eyes of the old man, and faced him.

«« »»

Willem saw the letter lying open on the table, the cigarette curling smoke on the ashtray beside it. The boy must have come in after he had fallen asleep, after a watch of more than four hours. Now, there he sat, white with shock, and stared at him.

Compassion rose in him at the sight of those eyes, wide with fear at their first glance at God's torture chamber, for it was as if he were faced by the young Willem of forty-three years ago. He got up and patted the boy on the shoulder, banishing that memory. Willem Waterreus had ceased to exist; he had now been called to the highest service, to be a tool in the hands of God.

"Where . . . where is she?" the boy asked, hoarsely. It was a heartbreaking question because he must know. He told him, gently, for it was not for him to punish. He was allowed to comfort, to bless, for behind him stood Jesus and His martyrs, who had wrenched a reprieve from a terrible God.

The boy listened to him motionlessly, hardly breathing; he made his story elaborate in order to give him a chance to take roots in his peace. When, at last, he gave him a chance to speak, the boy had indeed calmed down and was able, calmly, to put a few questions; he answered them mechanically, for his thoughts were searching for a solution. What counsel could he give that boy? What were the boy's possibilities? What means had God given him to disentangle himself from the nets of the devil? No soul is thrown into purgatory without a chance to save himself; every sinner carries within him, however deeply hidden, the seed of his own salvation. Then, unexpectedly, God provided the answer.

When he said, "Let us pray together," the boy suddenly stiffened. "Thank you very much," he replied, "but I would rather not, if you don't mind." When he asked, "Why not?" the boy began to talk. He talked in the same way he had written to Bertie, that night in the office: about the superstition of prayer, the intellectual cowardice of faith; and, then suddenly, the formula: "serum of conversion."

It was such a moving moment that he felt his eyes fill with tears. The boy, in his heartbreaking innocence, had provided the answer and shown by what trail he would find his way out of the maze of horror and pain that lay ahead of him. "Serum of conversion . . ."

He suddenly realized how tired he was, and he started to think about going home, for his work was done.

«« »»

Anton did not realize how exhausted the old man was, until he got up to get paper and pencil to make the first notes in his great experiment.

That Bert's father should have been sitting at the most important cross-roads of his life was a gift from Fate. He had been about to throw himself senselessly into a whirlpool of panic when, suddenly, he made his discovery. The moment the dear old soul wanted them to kneel on the floor together, he suddenly saw it: there was a way out from his irrevocable doom, a weapon against the colossal tidal pull of the wilderness. Instead of capsizing in a senseless maelstrom of emotion, he straightened up in grim sobriety. He had found the weapon, he was saved.

Els was in Holland, all right. He was in the Far East, fine. Another seven years and he would have finished his service; many other men were alone in the East with their wives in Holland; it was difficult, but possible. He would defend his marriage with all his might, and he would keep the jungle at arm's length by concentrating on his experiment, on the great plan he had seen in his grandiose vision that night in Man-Pu-Ko-Chu. He would search for the serum of conversion and, even if he did not find it, he would give the first thorough biological analysis of the Christian faith. He would examine every single case of conversion he could hunt down; he would not rest until he had traced the biological transformation behind the psychological phenomenon of conversion. And this time it was no longer a boy's dream, figment of an adolescent's imagination. This time it was his only weapon in a battle for life and death, a battle for his soul with the wilderness.

The future suddenly revealed itself once more as orderly and geometric, like a Dutch landscape, with the straight roads converging in the haze of the distant horizon. He would correspond with Els, apply for a post with the Inspection Circuit, and concentrate on his research. He would have to do so secretly, for if he told the Chief what it was, he would never get his permission. He would use leprosy as a camouflage; in reality he would be looking for the serum of conversion. He would not rest until he had pinned down God underneath his microscope, and he knew at that moment, with an utter certainty, that one day he would succeed.

As he told the old Salvationist about it, the other listened attentively but his face slowly wilted with exhaustion. "Well, brother," he said, "if you are looking for cases of conversion, you can begin with me." Only then did he realize that the poor old man was about to collapse.

He offered him Els's bed; after a weak protest, he accepted and shuffled into the bedroom after wishing him good night with an apologetic smile. The secret power in his eyes had vanished; when he pulled the door shut behind him he was just a tired old man in an ill-fitting uniform.

Alone in the sitting room, he wrote a long letter to Els, in which he put more love and sincerity than he had given her during all the months in Batavia. Then, dizzy with fatigue and too much smoking, he took a new exercise book out of the cupboard, broke it open and wrote on the fly leaf, *Hormones and Conversion—A Psychopathological Experiment.*

He blotted it, turned the page, leaned back in the low chair to formulate the opening in his mind, and fell asleep, while the wilderness whispered behind the mosquito curtain.

CHAPTER ELEVEN

THE case of the assistant controller of Kakoto was an amusing one. The boy—for that was all he was, fresh from home—had been ordered by the resident of Celebes and dependencies to make a report about the state and the mood of the Toradja population in the swamps beyond Kakoto. The resident had intended his order to be a trial of intelligence and tenacity, but in actual fact it was one of those notorious whims with which the aging official alarmed his superiors in Batavia.

In order to make it easier for the totok to establish his authority vis-à-vis the natives, he had been given the nominal double post of postmaster and harbor master of Kakoto, and he left full of boyish enthusiasm. A few weeks afterward, the old resident had died of a stroke at the telephone, during a row with the head of the Juridical Department over fifteen crates of beer. After the resident's death, his staff forgot that the appointment of postmaster and harbor master of Kakoto had only been a formality to test an apprentice; not only did they leave the poor totok sitting there utterly alone, the only white man in a district the size of Holland, they even forgot it was a double post. When the central office in Batavia received a request from the harbor master of Kakoto, Celebes, for a transfer because of his strained relations with the local postmaster, it struck nobody as strange.

This kind of request was received regularly in Batavia. In the distant outposts, where the heat seems more oppressive and the solitude becomes unbearable, white officials often fell out among themselves, in which case, sooner or later, one of them was sure to ask for a transfer. The request of the harbor master of Kakoto, Celebes, received the usual treatment. At first it was put, with its enclosures, in darkness for several months, like a hyacinth bulb, to see a glimpse of daylight only when a clerk opened the wrong drawer. After three and a half months, the bulb started to sprout: a telegram arrived from the resident of Celebes and dependencies urging

315

a decision regarding Kakoto, because of further complications between the two local officials. The request was brought to light, leafed through by many bored people; it was couched in a marble official style, ornate like a Victorian memorial. The harbor master seemed to be a humorless person, who had tried to keep the peace as long as possible with the postmaster, who was obviously a querulous alcoholic. They shared not only their living quarters but also their office; the agreement was that every morning the postmaster would use it, wearing a red peaked cap, and every afternoon the harbor master, wearing a yellow peaked cap; and the postmaster had not stuck to this amicable arrangement. At first the harbor master tried to talk to him in a friendly spirit, and when that had no effect, he left a polite letter in his office addressed to the postmaster only to find, the following afternoon, a most insulting reply. This was the beginning of a correspondence that was to last for months, copies of which the harbor master had enclosed with his request so as to enable his superiors to judge for themselves with what leniency, good humor and patience he had borne the postmaster's insults.

Of course, nobody ever read enclosures, so the request went quietly through all the stages of a growing hyacinth without anybody noticing that it was not an innocent flower, but a poisonous orchid. The eventual discovery was accidental.

The sixth official, who had put the request in the tray marked *Urgent* to ripen, mislaid his nail scissors. He looked everywhere, waxed impatient, turned out his desk, leafed angrily through all his papers and suddenly stood petrified when his eye was caught by a drawing so staggeringly obscene that only his own drawings, made as a schoolboy on the wall of the old women's home in his village, equaled it in his experience. He stared with incredulity at that memory of a Dutch boyhood in the tray marked *Urgent;* leafing through the folder of which the drawing formed part, he discovered many more and worse drawings, accompanied by words that made him put on his spectacles. On the cover, he found the information that these were copies of the correspondence between the postmaster of Kakoto, Celebes, and the harbor master, *ibid.*

Only after many colleagues had read through the collection, gaped, giggled and tut-tutted, only after the folder had been furnished with the stamp *Top Secret,* were the index cards of both correspondents called for from the archives, Division Staff Documentation. And then the mask fell: the answer from the archives, Section Staff Documentation, that arrived several weeks later, ran, *Harbor master postmaster Kakoto is a double post*. At this information, the folder, marked *Top Secret and Urgent,* was sent to the Head Office of the Government Health Service, for the correspondence that the gentlemen had relished so gleefully was the outburst of a madman.

Dr. Piet Kramer received the folder, glanced through it, wrote on the cover, *For the Attention of the Inspection Circuit,* crossed out the title, *Postmaster Kakoto Celebes versus harbor master ibid.,* and changed it into *Schizophrenic, Route 6.* Then he ascertained on the chart on the wall of his office how far the inspection doctor on Route No. 6 had proceeded on his circuit, found his drawing pin on Kolaka, Celebes, and decided to send the document by special messenger to Malili, the next station, to enable the doctor to deal with the case Kakoto on his way to Malangke.

It would have been just as expedient to send the folder by government mail, even quicker, but it was a good tradition to throw totoks into the boiling water at once, like lobsters; so Dr. Kramer inspected the list of new arrivals, and his finger stopped at the name *Schutters, Theodore* behind which was written the date of that day. He glanced at his watch, saw that the boat was due in half an hour, opened the time table of the Royal Steam Packet, found that the fortnightly steamer left Java that same night and wrote on an order form: *Schutters, Theodore, by military plane to Surabaya for steamer Makassar-Malili as assistant R. 6. Urgent (totok).* Then he rang for the mandur, to hand the order through to the transport office for the attention of Dr. Martens.

An hour later, a pale, intimidated young man stood in front of his desk, nervously turning his topee in his perspiring hands while the man in shirt sleeves at the bottom of the enormous chart of the archipelago went on writing as if he were not there. The fan whirred in a fearful silence, the totok breathed heavily through his nose, and his heartbeat was audible in his respiration. After a few minutes, the man in shirt sleeves put down his pen and said, "Well, Dr. Schutters, I'm pleased to see you, but I'm afraid time is rather short. Your plane will leave in about an hour's time. . . ."

And then there followed the usual little speech: it was a pity that this wouldn't give Dr. Schutters a chance to get acquainted with the service first, and he was aware that it was unusual to send a newcomer out on an expedition before he was acclimatized, but he was forced to improvise because the circumstances were unusual. An official of the Foreign Office had gone mad in East Celebes, so it was most urgent that someone go there at once, or grave consequences might ensue as the patient was sitting in a very dangerous region. It was impossible to get hold of the local inspection doctor within the time limit, so someone had to go and try to catch up with him on his circuit before he passed the madman's district, and that was where Dr. Schutters might fit in nicely. He could refuse, of course, because it was a tall order that would put him to a severe test, but on the other hand it was a fine chance to get to know the archipelago a bit, for the route . . .

He turned round and traced the route on the map behind him with a pointer. By Royal Air Force to Surabaya, from there by Royal Packet to Malili, where he would commandeer a prahu and a guide and hire four coolies, then two weeks along the edge of the jungle until—somewhere between Malili and Kolaka—he would catch up with Dr. Zorgdrager's prahu. Dr. Zorgdrager was one of the most brilliant doctors in the Service, a young man of tremendous experience and a well-known leprosy special-ist; a newcomer could not ask to be in better hands. It wasn't much of a trip really, things always looked worse on a map than in reality, and if Dr. Schutters managed to cope with it satisfactorily, it would of course be a splendid recommendation for someone new to the service. He would hear all the details from Dr. Martens, head of the transport office; just one other thing: he should not tell the coolies that they were on their way to a dangerous lunatic or they would beat it like bats out of hell; and that would not be funny, of course: to find oneself alone at sea somewhere on an uncharted coast with nothing to eat except a schizophrenic's case history. Well, so long, Dr. Schutters. Have a nice trip and all the best. Dr. Martens will help you on from here.

Dr. Martens: tall, thin, sickly, dandruff on his shoulders, bags under his eyes and a croaking voice: "Well, what a job to give a totok! Van Heuveln has already gone west on that coast; if you manage to catch Zorgdrager in that swamp, you may thank your lucky stars. How like the old man to . . . Well, let's get cracking—mandur, ambulance!"

There followed an unnervingly fast drive in an ambulance to a hospital like a barracks: swarms of native male nurses in white sarongs, the stench of closed-in heat and disinfectant, then a native doctor with a white skullcap: "Dr. Sardjono—Dr. Schutters." A handshake; "Your first job in the Service?"—"Yes . . ."—"Well, give Zorgdrager my love, will you, and if you get a chance in Malili, do me a favor and say hello for me to

Dr. Breszezinska-Jansen and tell him that the East Asiatic Association of
Archaeology has nominated him honorary secretary. He'll be delighted
to hear it. What was it you wanted, Martens, for the boy? Oh, yes, two
P.G. Mandur! . . ."

After a mad rush of collecting the expedition kit, sorting out instrument case, flea boots, netting, compass, maps, corned beef, sugar, field
glasses, Martens panted: "For God's sake, totok, let's nip across for a
quick one before we die." In the café across the road, he was greeted by
friends, "Hallo, Martens. You owe me a drink, remember? Who's that
you've got with you? A totok for Celebes? Ah, he goes to see Zorgdrager?
Well, well. Tell me, colleague: have you been converted?" And then a
burst of guffaws, incomprehensible and alarming.

At last, shivering in his sweat-drenched suit, he sat for the first time in
his life in an airplane. To be alone at last seemed a relief but it became
an oppression as the plane took off and he was choked with fear at the
colossal roar of the engines. Once the plane floated zooming toward the
hazy horizon, which was darkening quickly in the falling night, the loneliness suddenly turned into panic. God Almighty, there he was, only
three hours after his arrival, sitting in a plane, shivering with cold and
nerves, on his way to a madman, three weeks into a swampy jungle on
the coast of Celebes, and nobody had thought it worth while to tell him
how to hire coolies and how to commandeer a prahu and what language
to speak and how to know where he was, only: "Don't tell the coolies
you're on your way to a lunatic or they'll beat it," and "If you manage to
find Zorgdrager, you may thank your lucky stars." He rubbed his neck,
whimpering with hyterical fear; he peered through the mica window and
saw the mountains, the paddy fields, the coast and the sea aflame with
the setting sun as if they were flying across a colossal conflagration. Then,
with trembling hands, he took his wallet out of his pocket, found Moira's
photograph inside and, when she smiled at him as she had been smiling
all those nights, those mornings, those hot afternoons on board ship at the
foot of his bunk, he felt a faint alarm. It was still far away and hazy, yet
unmistakable, like the menace of a small cloud at the horizon of a radiant
sky. For suddenly he realized, as he gazed at her, that for the first time
something was happening to him which he would never be able to share
with her. This unreality, this feeling of teetering on the edge of a precipice
of despair he would never be able to transmit to her, whatever words he
might use.

The plane zoomed toward the night and, as they floated through the flaming clouds, he felt the first chill of the white man's fate in the Far East: loneliness.

«« »»

Up to Malili, he was still master of the situation. On board the steamer he met a planter on his way to East Celebes who told him a few things. About that doctor, Breszezinska-Jansen, for instance, whom he hoped to meet in Malili: he was the oldest doctor of the Government Health Service, and would certainly help him to hire coolies and commandeer a prahu.

During the endless blinding days at sea, while he felt faint with heat and could not write in his dairy for Moira because the pages stuck to his perspiring hands, he questioned the planter about the man he was bound for: Dr. Zorgdrager, inspector on Route No. 6. The planter was not able to tell him much; all he knew was that Zorgdrager had been Breszezinska-Jansen's assistant and that together they formed the Service leprosy team, and that the young man's wife had gone back to Holland a couple of months before to have a baby. He could not think of any explanation for the strange guffaws in the bar at Batavia after somebody had asked whether he had been converted; all those jungle doctors were a bit odd, the planter said; after spending more than a year in the forest, nobody could be expected to be quite normal. They would laugh at things that no one else thought funny, fly into a rage at a harmless joke and weep on hearing a child on the gramophone.

He knew that in Malili his trial would start. On the eve of their arrival, despite the heat and the headache after too many whiskies, he wrote a long letter to Moira in his cabin, her portrait trembling in front of him, propped up against the ashtray. *Moira, darling, I am scared. I confess it to you honestly, I am scared stiff about tomorrow and . . .* He tore the leaf off the writing pad, and started afresh. He should not tell her how scared he was. He should be witty and lighthearted, not only to prevent her worrying; there was another reason, secret and elusive, why he shouldn't write down his fear. By refusing to acknowledge it in writing, he could still banish it from his thoughts. He started a new letter, casual and lengthy, with a full report of his conversations with Jacob van Ees, the planter; but after half a page his fear slyly found its way into his phrases once more. It seemed, as he stared at her portrait in despair, as if her smile wilted, her eyes became more and more worried, until in the end he grabbed the photo and stuffed it back into his wallet.

That night he did not sleep. He tossed, sweating and panting, with shivers of fever and fear, until at last the sun rose and the gray disk of his porthole blushed with the dawn. The business of leaving brought him a couple of hours' respite; but once the ship had dropped anchor in the Oesoe Bay and he had been lowered into the prahu with his crate, his mailbag and his two tins of P.G., panic overwhelmed him. Only the knowledge that Jacob van Ees stood staring down at him prevented his bursting into tears. He waved bravely; the prahu swerved away from the ship and, rustling, the wind filled her sail. Wavelets started to babble against the bows, a triangle of sunlight began to glide from one gunwale to the other, lighting up the floorboards and the bare legs of the natives, and sparkling on and off on the corners of his tins monotonously with the swell. He looked ahead at the mountains, the coastline, the fuzzy fringe of the jungle, reaching from horizon to horizon, an impenetrable wall of blue forests, and he had only one hope, one fixed point in the future to which he could cling: Dr. Breszezinska-Jansen, the Nestor of the Service, who would help him. He closed his eyes unobtrusively after a furtive look at the natives, and tried to feign sleep, but in reality he prayed, God, dear God, he prayed, let him be there, let him not have left yet, let him be there, for God's sake, Amen. He saw huts, bungalows, the corrugated iron roofs of warehouses loom up in the blue of the coast, and an almost clairvoyant intuition told him that he would be there.

His intuition proved right. Dr. Breszezinska-Jansen, the world-famous archaeologist, was still in Malili. He sat in the passangrahan, at a table laid for ten, with a dwarf. He had a beard, and the small eyes of a pig. He looked up from a bone he was gnawing; grease glistened in his beard. When he heard that he had been nominated honorary secretary of the East Asiatic Association of Archaeology, he bellowed like a steer and hurled the bone at his head. And not only the bone: dishes, platters, mugs, stools, knives, legs of mutton, anything he could lay hands on he flung after him as he fled; when at last he stood, weeping and panting, in a dark corner of the deserted town, he could still hear the obscene roaring, the demented cursing of the monster with which his intuition had linked him so intimately.

A clerk of the steamship company—a godsent angel whom he addressed in despair after an hour of wandering, because he was white—helped him to commandeer a prahu, to hire coolies and to find a guide. But the next morning, as he sailed away from the last human outpost on six hundred miles of barren coast, he was haunted by a single phrase. When he had asked the clerk whether he knew anything about Dr. Zorgdrager, the jovial man had answered, "Not much." "Well," he had said, hearty but hoarse, "he can't be any worse than Dr. Jansen." The clerk had shrugged his shoulders and said, "I don't know. According to what I've heard, he is."

The guide asked ingratiatingly whether he would like him to put up a small awning for him to sit under, out of the sun, and he answered, "Yes— er, that is to say—er—an excellent idea."

Two weeks later he took it down, and what had happened to him in the meantime he would never write to Moira. For nothing had happened, nothing at all; all he had done was to sit underneath his little awning, a sliding square of shadow in the scorching sun, until in the end he took it down. Nothing in the wilderness of unchanging, eternal, rioting green retained a trace of what happened to him—only a dotted line of empty beer bottles, bobbing on the lonely sea, and a little awning that was washed ashore eventually in the Gulf of Boni, to rot away on the fringe of the jungle.

On the evening of the fifteenth day, a coolie in the bow of the prahu jumped up, pointed at a speck on the horizon and cried, "Lajar, tuan, lajar, lajar!"

A sail.

«‹‹ ›››

Later he would write to Moira. *And then, after what seemed hours our two prahus came alongside each other and we waved like boys.* He would omit to add that only the natives waved back at him.

In the stern of the other prahu that he had watched approach out of the sunset with a mixture of exultation and apprehension sat a man with a tropical helmet, sunglasses, and a pipe. He was reading something, and barely looked up as his coolies cheered their greeting and the sails of the prahus slammed, windless, with the waves.

Here he was, after two weeks in hell, with a mailbag, the case history of a madman and two mysterious tins of medicine; only God knew how hard the battle had been, what a miracle it was that he was there at all— and the man for whose benefit he had done all this did not wave, did not call a word of greeting, hardly looked up from what he was reading. He was a thin, hard man who did not look young at all when at last he stared at him with the vacant eyes of his sunglasses and asked, "Head office?"

"Yes," he said, "my name is Teddy Schutters. I have an urgent message for you, two tins of P.G. and your mail."

"Fine," said the man.

"I—I believe I am your assistant," he said, blushing because of his clumsiness after those weeks of grandiose manliness.

"Is that so?" said the man.

Then there was a silence which he would not forget for the rest of his life. The prahus reared alongside one another with slamming sails and ramming beams, and water splashed over their gunwales as they crashed together.

He bit his lip and clenched his fists to suppress a crazy impulse to fling the mail in the face of that bugger, kick his guide and snarl, "Back to Malili!" Luckily, the fact that his mandur began to hand over the mail and his luggage gave him the chance to look away. He saw the brown hands grab, heave up and reach over, he saw other brown hands grabbing the bag, then the first of the tins came up. The moment his mandur reached it out over the edge, the prahus crashed together. He cried out in anguish; the tin fell with a flash and a splash into the water.

Then it happened. All the despair, fury and pent-up fear of those terrible weeks burst to the surface; he jumped to his feet, screaming with rage, and began to lash out at the natives with both fists, flailing crazily, while tears of rage sprang out of his eyes.

Then a hand grabbed him by the scruff of his neck. For one split second, he stared into the black mirrors of the sunglasses, then a hand lashed across his face and he fell on the seat, sobbing, his head in his hands; defeated at the last moment, after he had for one half hour believed that he had really made it.

«« »»

The moment the boy burst into tears, Anton had the unnerving feeling that all this had happened before.

When his mandur had drawn his attention to the approaching prahu, he had assumed it to be a planter or a commercial traveler, eager for gossip, but when a boy had started to wave and shout, "Hullo!" and "Ahoy there!" he had buried himself in his book with irritation. The first hint of having experienced all this before came when the young man said, "My name is Schutters" and announced two tins of P.G. When the boy took a fit at seeing one of his tins go overboard, he jumped across and struck him, harder than he had intended. Then he realized whom he had struck: himself.

Yet it was not the memory of his own arrival in Rauwatta three years ago, when he had wept at the discovery that the tins contained gin; it was a memory much older, and during the hour that followed he tried to trace the origin of the association. For the moment he had seen that boyish face and heard the eager voice calling in the distance, twelve years had fallen out of his life.

He sat, one hot summer afternoon, cramming in his attic room in the old vicarage, stripped to the waist, wearing pajama trousers, a mug of black coffee half empty on the window sill, a wet towel round his head, four open books in front of him. For three months he had crammed twelve hours a day for his graduation, and he had gone through a complete transformation. He had become a man, he had said good-by to childhood forever, three long months he had lived in a bitter, humorless man's world, banishing all interests except his work. He could not remember now what he had been studying that afternoon; but he remembered the neighbor's radio and the women's choir that sang "Where the Shining Dunes Await Us" in a five-part arrangement of jubilant housewifery. Never, before or after, had he been so adult as that afternoon, so chaste, so stern with himself and the world; then, suddenly, a boy's voice had called from below, "Anton! Zorgdrager! Anton!" Had it not been for the curious neighbors, he would not have answered at all; he stuck his head out of the attic window irritably and saw, caught in the net of sunshine and shade thrown by the elms, the dappled moonface of Wim Pelt, the son of the lighthouse keeper. "Coming for a sail?" Wim called. He shook his head. Sail? He was finished with all that.

The main thing he remembered now was that he had gone for a sail after all. If he remembered rightly, Wim Pelt had come upstairs, had somehow managed to persuade him to go, and that one afternoon had grown into a mad week of stupid and loutish exuberance. They had deliberately collided with an old gentleman in a blue rubber canoe, they had damaged a little jetty because they wanted to frighten an angler who sat, dozing, balanced precariously on the edge; they had chased two girls in a dinghy and, once they had cornered them in the reeds, they had not known what to do with them. He had wiped out those three months of manliness with one week of pointless pranks, and passed his examination only by the skin of his teeth, because the algebra problem happened to be one he had done before. Now a boy's voice called out of the sunset, across the coppery swell of the Gulf of Boni; why should that old memory come to mind? That hot afternoon in Holland; the women's choir, the mug of cold coffee on the window sill?

The realization that he had struck the totok much too hard made him more kindly disposed than he had been for months. The boy looked ridiculously young with his red eyes, his flaxen hair and the fiery blush of the smack on his cupid's cheek. Good heavens, what a child; he could not have been that young when he arrived at Brits-Jansen's camp that morning in the Borneo jungle. This was almost indecent; to chase a fledgling like this into the wilderness was an outrage. He saw the totok's mandur ask his own crew for food, and could not help thinking that if they had not met when they did, the Toradjas in the boy's prahu might have succumbed to their age-old tradition of cannibalism.

He felt like smiling when the boy sniffed and wiped his nose with the back of a dirty hand, and it occurred to him that it was a long time since he had really laughed. Well, that was not surprising. He had spent all his waking hours alone in a prahu, with no other company than six silent sirih chewers, no other patients than whole tribes of incoherent Stone Age people, and no other thoughts than those written down in five exercise books full of reports of his experiments. Once a week there had been a letter to Els, and occasionally a hurried tribute to leprosy in the shape of a couple of pages added to a clinical treatise: *Elephantiasis Graecorum and Its Psychological Background*. No difference at all from the boy in the attic, a wet towel round his head.

He did not care for that idea; to divert his thoughts he unscrewed the cap of the surviving tin of P.G. to give the boy a pick-me-up. But, suddenly, the possibility struck him that this totok did not know either what the tins contained, and that that was the reason for his going berserk at seeing one of them fall overboard. Frowning, he tried to recall how Brits-Jansen had told him the truth. "Medicine? What do you mean? This is gin." It had been the last straw. He should go about it differently if he did not want to humiliate the chap beyond repair. He unobtrusively screwed the cap back onto the tin, put it down behind his back and looked inside the prahu to see whether there was any beer. He saw an empty crate and, in a corner hidden by a rib, a metal cap from a bottle. It was probably nonsense, but as he saw that little cap glint in the sunset, he was almost certain that the boy had tossed it up with his eyes closed, heads or tails, praying for a sign. He grinned, and sniggered at the thought; an unnatural sound that startled him. "Where are you from?" he asked, more gruffly than he intended.

"Ma—Malili," the boy replied.

"Is that so?" His voice tried to express admiration. "How long did it take you to get here?"

"Two weeks . . ."

"Well," he said, raising his eyebrows, "congratulations, my friend. This is the most dangerous coast in the Far East." That was nonsense, of course, but if his diagnosis were right, the boy would believe it for the rest of his days, even if later he were to paddle along the New Guinea jungle in a canoe with a dozen sharks in his wake.

"It was—it was pretty tricky," the boy said, uncertainly.

Now what was the question Brits-Jansen had asked that had put him so much at his ease? He couldn't remember, but it had something to do with Els. "Women will never understand," he said, and it sounded ludicrous in his own ears. "I tried it myself after my first expedition into the interior. I died a thousand deaths and made it by the skin of my teeth, but my fiancée never knew any better than that I had a very exciting time." After this little speech, only one reaction was possible: ugh; but the totok reacted with such humorless intensity that he had to cover his mouth, pretending to rub his chin.

"Yes," the boy said, "I can well believe it."

Then he remembered what Brits-Jansen had asked. It had been a low trick, but he could not resist it. "Show her to me," he said, putting out his hand.

The boy stared at him incredulously, then put his hand almost automatically into his shirt pocket and pulled out a pathetic snake-skin wallet. He opened it and produced a photograph. A fat, smiling girl with innocent eyes, blond hair and a sensual mouth.

"Charming," he said, and remembered in the nick of time not to turn the picture over to see what was written on the back, for Brits-Jansen had not done that either and he had been grateful at the time.

And then, suddenly, he had to shout loudly at his own prahu in the distance, "Mandur, datang di sini, ajo lekas!" to hide his irrepressible laughter when the boy said with a sigh, "Yes . . . but for her . . ."

His prahu came foaming toward them, and swung alongside. They stepped over and, for the sake of completeness, he made the tea himself.

«« »»

They drank their tea in the caravanlike hut of palm leaves on the poop of the biggest prahu. The lantern swung with the swell; the sea breeze had dropped, and in the eerie calm before the land wind rose the smoke of their pipes floated in thin flat layers underneath the ceiling. Teddy Schutters felt light-headed with exhaustion and relief. Whatever people might say about this Dr. Zorgdrager, he was a splendid chap. He could not be much more than thirty-two, thirty-three, but he possessed the knowledge of human nature of someone much older. His insight into one's secret thoughts was astounding, and his smile, forever stealthily twinkling in his gray eyes, would be unnerving if he were not so obviously endowed with a heart of gold. He divined, for instance, at once how the old archaeologist had received him; and he asked casually whether it had perhaps been Dr. Sardjono who had asked him to pass on the message about the East Asiatic Association. After he told him it was, he confessed that, years ago, when he was new to the service himself, the same Dr. Sardjono had asked him to say hello for him to a colleague in Borneo, with practically the same result. Some people could not resist ragging a newcomer and, strangely enough, they were often the nicest of the lot. Sardjono was a highly sensitive, intelligent chap with an inferiority complex about his color.

The story put him at his ease, and he told Zorgdrager all about the journey, his worries and his fears, to see whether their experiences had more in common. They had, obviously, because the older man was fascinated by the conversations he had had with Jacob van Ees, the nightmare of confusion of his one day in Batavia, the friends he had made on board the steamer on his way from Holland and in the end, when darkness fell, he listened to a description of Moira and their love with his eyes closed, in what was obviously a gesture of delicacy to enable him to talk more freely about something so private; then his pipe fell out of his mouth.

It would have been an unfortunate moment if Zorgdrager had not reassured him at once with a frank boyish grin and the confession that he had had an exhausting day. He felt almost guilty, and hastened to say, "I'm so sorry. I've forgotten to give you the urgent message," and told him about the schizophrenic in Kakoto. When he handed him the cover with the case history it was a solemn moment. "Poor beggar," he said, "and do you know what is, I think, the saddest thing of all? His name."

"So?" Dr. Zorgdrager said.

"He's called Frolick," he said, and laughed wholeheartedly for the first time since he had become a man.

«« »»

Frolick . . .

After he had wished the boy good night without betraying how his laughter had shocked him, he opened the folder labeled *Schizophrenic, Route 6,* and the past returned with agonizing clarity as he recognized, in the first enclosure, *To the Postmaster of Kakoto, Celebes,* the precise, clerical handwriting of old Harry Frolick.

Why the discovery should give him such a shock seemed obscure at first. After all, they had only known each other for a few weeks on board the boat and there was no other tie between them than the memory of a journey together, a warm bottle of beer in the Y.M.C.A. in Batavia and Bach's Toccata and Fugue, to which Frolick had listened with his finger tips joined in a small Gothic arch. As he turned the pages of incredibly obscene letters, written in that impeccable hand and correctly paragraphed, he remembered the blue silk underwear, the refined accent, the profile with the Adam's apple as he stood shaving in his cabin, and the joke about the old professor and the girl students which the schizophrenic of Route 6 had told that night in the little room in Batavia, on the eve of their baptism of fire in the wilderness.

It was difficult to believe that only three years had passed since then; it seemed like a previous existence. Witzenburg had gone back to Holland, under a cloud; Frolick had gone mad in the forest; Enters, who had dreamed about cultivating broccoli in Java, had disappeared to some tea plantation in the backwoods of Sumatra. A drunken planter had told him some time ago that a certain Enters lay buried in his back garden when he took over the mess; he had had the grave flattened and sown over for a tennis lawn. If it were indeed the Enters he had known, then he himself was the last of the Four Musketeers who had set out for the Far East so full of self-confidence, and he himself had not come through undamaged either. For although since Els's departure he had not looked at another woman and concentrated on his work like a maniac, within the jungle of his soul a tiger still prowled. When the totok had handed him the photograph of his fiancée, his first thought had been "sensuous mouth," and as he sat listening to the boy's endless confessions about their innocent romping in the reeds on the Loosdrecht Lakes, he had come to the grim conclusion: I have not changed at all. For, instead of smiling indulgently at his touching story, he had got lost in a dark daydream about what he would have done in the boy's place, to wake up only when the pipe fell out of his mouth.

With that folder on his knees, staring at the thin rapier of the prahu's mast vainly scything the stars, he realized that his decision of three months ago had been very adolescent indeed. It had been boyish to assume that he could change the tiger's stripes by volunteering for the most barren circuit in the Service, sailing the moment temptation beckoned, concentrating on missionaries and converts and his Bible. Here was the tiger, prowling by the light of the stars, his steady luminous gaze staring at the girl with the sensuous mouth, giggling in the reeds of a Dutch lake.

He put out the lamp and lay down on his mat, but the waving cornfields, the image which so far had always sent him to sleep, turned into reeds. He lit the lamp once more, opened his Bible at the Epistle of St. James. *What doth it profit, my brethren, though a man say he hath faith, and have not works? Can faith save him? ... Thou believest that there is one God; thou doest well: the devils also believe, and tremble. But wilt thou know, O vain man, that faith without works is dead?*

Postmaster! the harbor master of Kakoto wrote, *if I receive one more of those shocking letters full of sin and filth, I shall call in the Government!* The government. It was the cry for help to God of a drowning soul, the suicide of an intellect. One thing was certain: had Frolick been a Christian, a true one, it would not have happened. But how could he have become a true Christian, guided as he was by pompous bores like his own father, jolly padres like Witzenburg, or iron-clad old conservatives like Professor van Goor? It was those pharisees, those highwaymen of the Narrow Road, that had robbed the Dutch middle-class boy in Kakoto, Celebes, of the God that could have saved him. They had forced him to write that request to the government by corrupting the teachings of Christ into an intellectual parlor game, His church into a party headquarters, His martyrdom into a dear old tradition. They should have shown him by the example of their love that to become a true Christian was to enter a higher plane of humanity, where the works radiated the faith. But one thing he had discovered during his analyses of cases of conversion: to attain that plane, truly attain it, each man had to climb, all over again, the winding road to Golgotha.

The inspection prahu *R. 6* slowly sailed on through the night, rolling and swaying with rustling sail and creaking mast, the Gulf of Boni babbling under her bows. Underneath the mosquito tent lay the boy, the messenger who had brought him all this: the memories, the doubts, and the terrifying letters of a lunatic.

The sun rose and he gave up trying to sleep. He looked up Kakoto on the chart, gave the mandur the course and ate a frugal breakfast in the blue dawn. The boy slept on, his mouth open, his head on his rolled-up clothes, under which the girl's photo must be hidden.

The difference between himself now and three years ago seemed frightening. Given the opportunity, would he go back to that innocence, that boyishness? Wake up on the Kali-Woga instead of in the Gulf of Boni, and arrive in the heart of the wilderness once more to meet Brits-Jansen?

He searched for the truthful answer, but in vain.

«‹‹ ›»›

Kakoto, hidden at the far end of a narrow winding creek, halfway between Malili and Cape Kanakea, was a far-flung outpost indeed.

The *R. 6* crept slowly up the narrowing tunnel of foliage, paddled by four intimidated Toradjas, cursed in whispers by a hoarse mandur whose alert little eyes darted snakelike to and fro, without his stopping the stream of abuse that poured mechanically from his lips, nor the waving of the palm leaf with which he fanned himself. The stench of salty refuse that hung like an invisible fog over the water seemed to intensify the heat; the sun-bleached knuckles of uprooted trees lay in stacks along the banks of the creek like skeletons of prehistoric animals washed ashore by the Great Flood. Yellow mud, stirred up by the surging waves groping blindly up the creek, eddied in the limpid water like smoke from subterranean fires. It looked like an entrance to hell.

At the far end of the creek stood a jetty, on thin legs hairy with seaweed, and behind it the roofs of a score of huts could be seen above a man-high wilderness. There was no path, no clearing, not even a flagpole to indicate any effort of defense against the jungle; it seemed like a deserted lair of witches, a nest of evil from which the buzzard had flown. Nobody appeared when the prahu, with silent strokes of the paddles, crept toward the jetty; no eyes spied through the alang-alang; no smell of cooking or smoke indicated a human presence. It might be the hour of the day, it was possible that the inhabitants of Kakoto slept in the heat of the afternoon; but when the prahu moored to the hairy poles and still nobody showed himself, it was obvious that the village was deserted.

Anton had deliberately chosen the afternoon for his arrival, even though it was the hottest time of the day. He had read Frolick's letters attentively and discovered that the harbor master had the afternoon watch; he wanted to meet the poor chap in his role of Dr. Jekyll, in the hope that Mr. Hyde had not yet won the battle. The desolation of the village was an ominous sign; the fact that the inhabitants had fled indicated danger. His Toradjas could not be made to leave the prahu; they looked at him in dumb hostility, clutching their paddles. The totok looked up at him with eager boyish eyes; during the past few days, he had told him so much about Moira and made such interminable confessions about his true opinions of religion, capitalism and birth control that it had become obvious that he considered his chief as a great friend, for whom he would, if needs be, strike out into the wilderness to look for a lunatic.

Anton had told him that he knew Frolick, to give himself an excuse to leave the totok behind. Now the moment had come, and he said, "Take the prahu back into the open, and wait there till I call." But the boy had no ears for that; he looked pale and sweated profusely but his voice was determined when he answered, "No, sir. I won't let you face him alone in that jungle."

"Believe me," Anton said, "it is much better that you stay in the prahu. I know him and the sight of someone else may make him aggressive. Apart from that, we run the risk that the Toradjas may make off with the boat unless one of us stays with them."

But the totok must have decided days before to accompany him; it needed a snarl and a curt command to make him obey, with hurt blue eyes. The snarl came when, in the menacing, lisping silence of the wilderness, a children's choir started to sing.

"As pants the hart for cooling streams," they sang, with parrotlike mechanical voices. *"When heated in the chase . . ."*

Anton put his revolver in his hip pocket and hoisted himself onto the jetty. It creaked and swayed; a swarm of moths burst forth from under him like the smoke from a silent explosion. There was a nauseating stench of rotting plants and shellfish.

"So longs my soul, O God, for Thee and Thy refreshing grace."

As he stood listening, his hand on his hip pocket, trying to make out the direction of the sound, he noticed his mouth was dry. It was the only sign of fear. He slowly walked along the jetty with cautious steps, inaudible on the moss.

"For Thee, my God, the living God, my thirsty soul does pine . . ."

He stopped at the edge of the jungle, still uncertain of where the sound came from. Somewhere, something lay decomposing; that was the terrible stench.

"Oh, when shall I behold Thy face, Thou Majesty divine? . . ."

He went into the alang-alang, toward the stench.

"Why restless, why cast down my soul? Hope still and thou shalt sing. . . ."

His foot hit something soft; a swarm of golden flies rose buzzing, a shower of sparks in the sunlight.

"The praise of Him who is thy God, thy health's eternal spring."

It was the corpse of a child.

The choir jubilated with metallic voices; he felt sick as he bent over the body. It lay spread-eagled in the grass as in a green basket, mutilated and raped. It could not have happened more than twenty-four hours ago.

"To Father, Son and Holy Ghost, to the God whom we adore, be glory as it was, is now, and shall be evermore."

He stood up when the choir stopped, and listened. The flies had come back and he felt dizzy with the stench and the heat. The children's voices started to screech once more: *"As pants the hart for cooling streams . . ."* He went cautiously forward into the wilderness.

"When heated in the chase . . ."

The stench lessened, then it grew once more.

"So longs my soul, O God, for Thee . . ."

In a hut from which rats fled rustling lay another corpse of a child, almost a skeleton.

"And Thy refreshing grace. For Thee, my God, the living God, my thirsty soul doth pine. . . ."

The hut was full of deserted tools and crockery, as if its inhabitants had suddenly taken flight.

"Oh, when shall I behold Thy face, Thou Majesty divine?"

Only after the children's choir had started its monotonous chant for the third time did he find the hut with the gramophone. He saw its horn through a window; he also saw, as he approached cautiously, a desk with a mess of molding papers on it, an empty rattan chair. He felt someone watching him from the jungle and looked round, turning his head slowly. In the alang-alang he spotted a yellow patch.

"*To Father, Son and Holy Ghost, to the God whom we adore . . .*"

He waited until the record was finished; when nobody stopped the gramophone and the needle went on senselessly scratching, he said, "Well, Frolick? Remember me?"

Nobody answered. There was no sound but the scratching of the needle on the gramophone record.

"I am Anton," he said, "Anton Zorgdrager. I've come to take the postmaster with me."

The sweat turned cold on his forehead in the stillness. The needle scratched, scratched, scratched.

"Where is the postmaster?" he asked. "Can you show me his hut?"

Scratch, scratch, scratch, scratch, scratched the needle, slowing down.

"Come on, Frolick, don't be childish," he said, startled by the hoarseness of his own voice. "Show yourself, old boy. We know one another well enough, don't we?"

Then the yellow patch in the alang-alang moved. The scratching of the needle became a slow scraping. He saw with relief that the patch was a cap; yellow was the color for the harbor master. But when he saw him, he was horror-stricken. The skeleton that stood facing him, peering from underneath the tatters of a yellow peaked cap, half hidden still in the wilderness, was naked. His skin hung in leathery folds from the joints of his shoulders, the washboard of his ribs was caked with dirt, and sores and scratches showed among the hair. He was overgrown with hair like a fungus; a matted beard hung down to his breastbone, his pubic hair went up to his navel, his arms were fuzzy up to his elbows, but most horrifying of all was his face. It was the muzzle of an ape man, with bared fangs and vicious small eyes without a soul. Two years of wilderness had undone two hundred thousand years of evolution; he stood eye to eye with the Homo heidelbergensis.

"Hello, Frolick," he said.

The ape man grimaced, swallowed, filled his cheeks with air, and made a sound that was no more than a toneless exhalation. Then he licked his lips, swallowed again, blew up his cheeks once more and said, "Ba . . ."

He tried to laugh and said, "Well, old boy, it's a long . . ."

But the eyes of the ape man flashed dangerously. A claw flew up and silenced him. The beard moved as he swallowed once more, blew out his cheeks and, after a great effort, forced out at last, "Bach."

"Yes, of course," Anton said, his cheeks taut with self-control. "Toccata and Fugue, remember?"

The ape man nodded, five, six, ten times, with a violent motion, and laughed, a wailing animal sound. But when the small eyes peered at him once more, Anton felt his mouth go sour with revulsion and pity, for the eyes were full of tears that rolled, glistening, down into the beard.

He did not know what to do: whether to go toward him, hold out his hand, try to make him talk, or to shoot him down where he stood. He was beyond helping. The only thing a friend could do was to kill him. As he stood in awe of the responsibility thrust at him, the ape man came out of the jungle. He took his hand with a claw and, jabbering, dragged him toward the entrance of the hut with a bestial strength.

The hut stank like a tiger's lair. Nothing was left of the office it had once been but the desk with the mess on it, lopsided, its legs gnawed away by ants, a rusty clock, the chain of which was grown over with creepers, a moldy frame on the wall with a smudge behind cracked glass: the remains of a portrait of the Queen. The seat of the rattan chair was broken, the arms loose; the gramophone was the one piece of furniture that had not fallen into ruin. On a hook by the door hung the rag of a red cap.

The ape man saw him look at the rag, and growled. He hurriedly smiled and opened his mouth to speak, but was pushed down into the rattan chair, that sagged with a screech. Then the ape man put a finger to his lips, wound up the gramophone, put the needle on the record, and the children's voices caroled, *"As pants the hart for cooling streams when heated in the chase . . ."*

As he sat, motionless, he stared at the ape man, who stood with his ear close to the horn, his mouth open, his arms dangling, his emaciated chest heaving with emotion. It was a spectacle so grotesque that he had to force himself to look, to smile, not to betray his thoughts with a single movement. They were not really thoughts, but a rapid incoherent succession of pity, suspicion, memory, anger. The anger remained; it urged him to jump up and grab that gramophone with its screeching parrots' voices and hurl it into the jungle, to shoot down the monster facing him, to wake up from the nightmare into which it had lured him.

But when the record had played itself out, the ape man did not move, nor did he stop the gramophone. The needle scratched again, scratched, scratched, scratched, scratched; the ape man seemed to be listening to something that rustled in the jungle. Then he looked round, slowly, and his small eyes changed. They seemed to go muddy with a dull lust for blood, a viciousness that was no longer tragic because it was devoid of the last spark of humanity. The beard moved again, the fangs bared as, chewing, he mouthed a word. "Ga . . ." he breathed. "Ga . . . goh . . . go, go, go, go . . ." and his claw motioned him to go away.

Anton got up, and his anger sank away before a great compassion. He stretched out his hand, wanted to say, "Good-by, Frolick, my friend . . ." But the ape man recoiled and growled. They stood facing each other for a moment; the scratching of the needle slowed down to scraping. Then he said, "So long, Harry," and went outside. He only discovered that the hut had a door when it slammed behind him. He whipped round with the gun in his fist; but there was nobody behind him, the door of the hut was shut. When the children started to sing once more, he discovered that the catch of his revolver was still secured.

"As pants the hart for cooling streams when heated in the chase . . ."
He slipped the catch.

«‹‹ ›››»

When Teddy Schutters, after waiting breathlessly for a sign of life from the wilderness, suddenly heard a shot, he could stand it no longer. He ordered the Toradjas, who had frozen with fear, to paddle him back to the jetty. They hesitated, he repeated his command with an authority that astonished himself, and they obeyed.

But they refused to follow him ashore. He knew there was a chance that they would make off with the prahu the moment he turned his back on them, but he could not leave Dr. Zorgdrager alone in the jungle now he had heard that shot. He took his gun off his shoulder with shaking hands and went into the wilderness.

He came across the little corpse, but he did not stoop to look at it. He fled into the alang-alang, overcome with a violent fear. When suddenly he broke out of the undergrowth, he found himself in a small clearing opposite a hut, the door of which hung open. In front of the hut sprawled a naked body, its head back, a pointed Adam's apple protruding from its hairy throat. Beside the body lay a red cap.

He approached on tiptoe, his gun at the ready, glanced through the open door and saw Dr. Zorgdrager sitting behind a desk, beside an old-fashioned gramophone. "What's this, Schutters?" he asked. "I thought we agreed that you were to stay on board."

"I heard the shot," he said. "I couldn't stick it any longer. Is that—him?"

"Yes."

He looked at the body from where he stood. It was a dirty emaciated corpse. He could not even see that it had been a white man. "Did you—kill him?" he asked.

Zorgdrager looked up calmly and replied, "No. He crept up on me from behind and snatched my gun away. Before I could grab it he had shot himself."

Teddy said, "Oh."

"Go back to the prahu and get two spades," the doctor said. "Keep the Toradjas where they are. You and I will bury them together, him and the other two."

He had not known about a third one, and took a long time coming back with the spades. When he arrived, he found Zorgdrager busy in the hut; the bureau lay on its side, its drawers had been taken out, even the floorboards had been ripped up. When the doctor saw him in the doorway, he said, "Can't find a thing. He must have burnt the lot."

"What are you looking for?" he asked.

Zorgdrager shrugged his shoulders and looked about him wearily. "I don't know," he said. "Anything." Then the silence seemed to strike him. "All right," he said. "Let's get on with it."

They dug one grave beside each body. It was exhausting work in the heat; after the first grave was filled and smoothed down he felt quite dizzy and in need of a rest. But Zorgdrager spurred him on, saying, "Come on, boy, we must be out of here before nightfall." He tried to play for time and asked, "No cross, no name?" but the doctor said, "No."

When at last they had buried the third body, he felt himself that it was high time they left. An eerie feeling had crept up on him as he stood digging with his back to the wilderness, as if they were being watched by many eyes; yet there was not a sound to be heard, not a twig snapped, not a leaf rustled. When Zorgdrager stood wiping his forehead with his sleeve, his helmet on the back of his head, he could not keep it to himself any longer. "I believe there are people about. . . ." he said.

Zorgdrager lit his pipe. "Of course," he said, puffing. "The moment we're gone, they'll be back."

When they left for the jetty, they passed several huts into which the doctor cast a glance. They were empty, he assumed; all he noticed was the smell that came out of them. It resembled the smell he had noticed occasionally at night at sea, in his prahu, when the Toradjas lay asleep, only it was stronger. As they entered the alang-alang at the far end of the clearing, the feeling of being watched became so oppressive that he trod on the doctor's heels. The doctor looked round, he muttered, "I'm so sorry," and the doctor said, "That's all right."

The prahu lay waiting where he had left it, and he heaved a sigh of relief. The Toradjas looked up at them silently when they appeared. "Go ahead," the doctor said, and Teddy lowered himself into the prahu. The doctor followed, after a last look round, as if hesitating. He blurted out, "If we have to be out of here before sunset, I think we'd better go, sir."

Zorgdrager grunted, tapped out his pipe, lowered himself into the boat and gave an order to the mandur, almost casually. The Toradjas cast off, the mandur chanted "Ah-ee . . . ! Ah-ee . . . !" The paddles dipped and thrust and the prahu slid silently down the dark green tunnel of foliage, past the ghostly stacks of giant bones twisted in agony, toward the far end, where, like the heart of a gigantic flower, the orange sunset beckoned with a nostalgic beauty. Teddy suddenly felt strangely fond of the earth, of life, of nature, all sensuous things. He turned to the doctor to tell him how he felt, but he was not given the chance. The doctor told him to take off his clothes, as he was doing himself; then they threw them overboard. He had to wash from head to foot in the penetrating stench of Lysol. When at last they lay naked, side by side, underneath the palm-leaf awning with the narrow table between them, the doctor said, looking at the ceiling, "How stupid of me to take my revolver. I should have foreseen that he would shoot himself."

Teddy said, "Of course," hoping his disbelief was not obvious.

"I could have known he would," the doctor said, sitting up and opening his chest to take out a clean shirt. "It is the classic ending to all cases of schizophrenia. The good exterminates the evil, or the other way round, whatever the case may be."

"Yes," he said.

"In this case," the doctor concluded, "the harbor master has killed the postmaster."

He was about to say, "Come, sir, you need not have any secrets from me, I won't tell anybody. I respect your motives." But before he had formulated all this in his mind, the doctor went on, "You must have noticed something when you saw that man lying there."

It took him unawares. "N-no . . ." he stammered.

"You were looking," the doctor continued, "at the corpse of a Homo heidelbergensis, a prehistoric man. Even the growth of his hair had degenerated and his thigh muscles were abnormally developed. He must have swung himself with apelike speed from branch to branch on his manhunt."

"You mean—he killed those children?" he asked.

"Of course," the doctor said. "The harbor master listened to children singing a hymn with tears in his eyes; the postmaster raped and strangled them."

He suddenly felt sick. Then the doctor said, before pulling the shirt over his head, "One of these nights, I'd like to talk to you about Moira's mouth."

«« »»

As he stooped out of the hut, Anton was angry with himself for having said such an idiotic thing. Not only was the boy's fiancée none of his business, but he had to be careful not to antagonize the totok, for he would have to witness the report of Frolick's death and he should not suspect the truth.

The truth . . . When night fell, a dark velvet night hung with stars, each one reflected like a quivering candle flame in the oily waves of the Gulf of Boni, he tried to put the truth into words. He tried it first by lecturing the totok about the case of the schizophrenic, Route No. 6. He began by expounding his ancient theory about the jungle being a hothouse in which all the latent passions, et cetera, and the boy sat reverently listening as if he were being initiated into a secret brotherhood, Rosicrucians of the jungle. And perhaps that was true; perhaps the occult lore of that distant past came closer to solving the riddle of Frolick's Calvary than modern psychiatry. One thing was certain: in the forest, in that lisping loneliness, that hot darkness full of devils, the individual became a battlefield. In that nidus of all life, isolated man was silently watched by millions of spying eyes, beset by the jealousy of those left behind on the spiral road of evolution. Perhaps Frolick was not a victim of a disease of the soul; perhaps he had been captured and tortured, prisoner of a million years' war, by the hordes left behind on that pilgrimage toward God: the evolution of matter into spirit. But although he managed to impress the boy, he could not convince himself. For the point was not whether Frolick was a lunatic or a mystic martyr of mankind, the point was that he had shot him.

Alone, later that night, with his pipe underneath the stars, he had to admit it. He would give anything, anything at all not to have done what he had done. For, at that shot in the jungle, he had crossed a border-line. His sins and the feeling of guilt they engendered had suddenly stopped being his private preoccupation. They had resulted in the death of a man.

That was the gist of it: never mind whether he had been right or wrong to shoot Frolick: why had he done it? The man who shot Frolick was not the product of one isolated act of God, but the outcome of a long process of causes and effects. If he had not left Els, if he had not hidden his guilt behind lofty musings about conversion, he would have been a different kind of man, a man who might not have fired that shot. So his betrayal of Els and Frolick's death were irrevocably linked together. He did not like that conclusion; he scrambled to his feet, went back once more into the hut, taking the lantern with him. He took a sheet of paper, to write out his report, but as he sat staring at the blank page and at the back of the totok turned away from the light he could not form a coherent sentence in his mind. He tried to identify himself with Frolick, tried to find the medical interpretation of his case. For, whatever his own doubts, he would have to convince Dr. Kramer now. And Dr. Kramer was a wise man.

He closed his eyes, and arrived in his mind in Kakoto: a little village, peopled with Stone Age creatures who were still beset by primeval fears. There he was, young white knight in shining armor, infinitely superior to his subjects; then the slow realization that he was not, that he was a victim of the natives, their slyness, their familiarity with the jungle; then the disintegration, the sowing of the seed of death in the thought: if I were a beast of prey, they would fear me all right.

He was sure that this interpretation was right. As a man, Frolick had been defenseless against the wilderness; as an animal, he became king. No other animal, not even a tiger, could hold out against a kampong full of humans who would not rest until they had trapped the marauder and killed him. But from the ape man they had fled. What had the ape man lived on? How had he managed to snatch those children, protected as they must have been by at least thirty armed adults? Like a monkey he must have swung, from branch to branch, through the treetops of the forest; silently like a snake he must have slithered down the trunks; like a tiger he must have spied from the undergrowth, pounced, grabbed; strong as a gorilla he must have been to climb back up that tree carrying his struggling prey, to vanish in the foliage before the humans below had had a chance to shoot at him with their arrows, or throw their nets. The hairy corpse that had lain in front of the hut had had nothing in common with Frolick any more; Frolick had died when he signed his last request to the government. The body in the jungle had been the spoils of that most dangerous monster of creation: degenerated man, the devil of the Holy Scriptures.

The devil . . . Ludicrously, the word had flashed through his mind as he stood, his revolver in his fist, facing the closed door. Then, when the children's choir finished its song for the last time and the needle panted on the record, the door had slowly opened. For one second he had seen the crouching ape man, wearing the rags of the red cap, his muscles tensed for a tremendous leap; his gun had barked at the very moment of the leap. He had crashed down, somersaulted, and lain there, writhing in a gruesome agony. When at last he had lain still, he approached cautiously, hoping that death would have brought back some peace, some humanity to that face. But the muzzle that had stared past him at the sky with broken eyes was one of frozen bestiality. As he had stood looking down at him, the whole wilderness had seemed to hold its breath. In that second of stillness, he had known for certain that he had indeed slain something devilish, something infinitely evil. But now, alone at sea, caught in a net of stars, the ship under his feet rolling and heaving, he grabbed his head in a whirl of doubt. As he sat there, his head in his hands, listening to the soft creaking of the beams, the splash of the waves, he was overcome by an overpowering sadness. Bach, *Passion of St. Matthew, "Wer hat mein Heiland so geschlagen?"* He heard that choir of angels lament in his memory and was hit once more by the full impact of what he had done. Frolick—God! Frolick . . . The angels sang, and it was as if a pale earnest boy listened with him, his finger tips joined in a small Gothic arch, a timid prayer.

He seized the tin the totok had brought, unscrewed the cap and took a double ration. The gin, as it seared his gullet, hurt at first, then it sent capillaries of warmth radiating from his stomach. He was suddenly beset by a primeval terror that took him completely by surprise, and he hurried out, back onto the deck once more. He sat alone in the night, clutching a tin of gin, haunted by a part song of Bach's angels, and a tinny children's choir. He drank with a vengeance, with a destructive purposefulness. By the time he had finished the tin, the gin had started its magic.

He sat, smiling, in a dark velvet universe, hung with the flashing diamonds of stars, and caressed by the cradling glow of a golden lamp. He loved Frolick, the Toradjas, the totok, Els, he loved everybody, he even loved himself. He was full of wisdom, patience, understanding and forgiveness. The world seemed one colossal, splendid, heart-rending joke; he could not help smiling in the heart of his web, drunken spider winking at the moon. He smiled before he quite knew why, but he felt the discovery slowly slide toward him as he half closed his eyes, slide toward him along a moonbeam. It was the most important discovery of his life, it was the funniest joke since his arrival in the Far East, it was capital and glorious, and he sat there, tears streaming down his face, slapping the deck, swaying back and forth in celestial mirth. The totok, a swimmer emerging from the pool of the night with tousled head, resting on golden arms on the edge of the pool, gazed at the empty tin of P.G. and asked, "What is it?"

And then he told him. In one sentence, he told him, the whole story of his childhood, his youth, Els and Bert, his hopes and fears, his dreams and sins, and his great, great delusion. "This," he said, lifting the tin off the deck, "this is, or rather was, the serum of conversion." Then he sent the tin sailing into the night, covered his face with his hands, tried to discover what had gone wrong with his joy, and was sick over the edge.

Teddy Schutters took it like a man.

CHAPTER TWELVE

D URING the following weeks, Anton found himself absent-mindedly humming the tune of the panting hart at some time or other every day. The more determinedly he suppressed the memory during the daytime, the more hauntingly it returned at night.

He had never dreamed much and nightmares had rarely bothered him; now the dead Frolick stalked him nightly through the swaying ferns of sleep, bent over him, blew out his cheeks, swallowed as if trying to say something, to flee rustling in the dream weeds when the sleeper woke up, drenched in sweat. A nonsensical thought forced itself upon him: it seemed as if the ghost of the Homo heidelbergensis hovered in the atmosphere of the planet, because it had a message for him—a message from the other side, a warning.

His first reaction was quinine; those dreams must be the symptoms of an approaching bout of malaria. But instead of exorcising it, quinine seemed to sharpen the nightly image, to give it a supernatural vividness. He came to the conclusion that he must be overworked; the circuit had been exhausting.

The best remedy would be a couple of weeks' leave, a good old bachelor's binge in Surabaya or Singapore, but he had three more weeks to go. Three more weeks of improvised operations in the jungle, of hundreds of injections to be given to hordes of pathetic skeletons carried out of the jungle; of endless snifters and endless boring conversations with the doctors in the outposts, whose only recreation was the three-monthly visit of the colleague on inspection and who expected him to make good, in one night, a three months' lack of newspapers. And, God help him, three more weeks of the totok's monologues.

Schutters, Theodore, had turned out to be a good-natured Boy Scout, full of good will, but such a revolting sentimentalist that the nightmares almost came as a relief after his nightly barcarole; at the setting of the sun, he invariably set out for a sentimental journey across a lake of treacle toward the shrine of his beloved. Moira became such an emetic that Anton felt his mouth contract at the very mention of her name. He tried to fend her off with nervous harangues about leprosy, the Government Health Service, the humane element in same, and the nuptial customs of the Papuans; the trouble was, however, that the only subject capable of banishing Moira from the boy's mind was the very one that attracted Frolick's ghost. The boy would really listen only when he analyzed the attraction of the jungle, the dangers of isolation, the moral decay of loneliness. For "sin" was, when all was said and done, a thing that had to do with man's life in a community; it was difficult for a lonely sailor marooned on an uninhabited isle to sin. So that mysterious, compelling urge to strike out toward the heart of the virgin wilderness was, in reality, a flight from one's own conscience, whatever the romantics might say.

The boy listened to all this with fascination, although it seemed as if his helmet slowly rose, pushed up by a couple of growing asses' ears, for his understanding was nil. What he adored was evocations of the jungle, the hot darkness, the ripple of distant laughter, the flute-like warbling of unseen birds, the hiss of the snake, the midnight rumble of the elephants' digestion—he adored it as if he were watching the film *Trader Horn,* and, at least, it kept Moira's ghost away. But the result was, inevitably, that the ape man's ghost came closer than usual that night, mouthing its wordless message. As the weeks passed, the nightmares grew worse. He woke up earlier and earlier, sat watching the sunrise in dumb anguish, all thoughts silenced with nothing but the bare despair of his soul. A shot in the jungle, a drunken night, and all he had ever possessed was gone.

When, at last, they put into Makassar, he found in the post office three letters from Els, a note from Brits-Jansen and two issues of *The Lancet.* Els's letters were addressed to someone who had little in common now with the perspiring scarecrow in the little post office. He read them while, behind him, Theodore Schutters selected picture postcards for Moira, turning the squeaking stand until the shrieks made the hairs on the nape of his neck tingle.

Darling Anton, our little one is getting so impatient now in its secret hiding place that it wakes me up at night by kicking . . .

He stuffed the letters back into their envelopes to read later and cried, "Stop turning that damn thing! You are setting my teeth on edge."

Schutters, Theodore, stopped at once in abject obedience, and showed him a luridly colored picture of the jungle. "What about this?" he asked. "Don't you think she'll love it?"

He looked from the postcard to the plump boyish face glistening with perspiration, and said, "Hm." Then he opened Brits-Jansen's note. It was practically illegible and ended with the words *Excuse pencil*. It seemed he wanted some information about tertiary frambesia and thought it a happy coincidence that his young associate had been transferred to Route No. 9, the northern coast of New Guinea, where he would find a plethora of material by interviewing the doctors of the Salvarsan campaign. It was the first intimation the young associate had had about a transfer; when Teddy Schutters asked, "Bad news, doctor?" he looked at him vacantly. In the district doctor's office, the familiar yellow envelope from headquarters was waiting for him and inside a letter that confirmed Brits-Jansen's gossip. As from the 15th of the current month, Doctor A. Zorgdrager was transferred to Circuit No. 9 in order to relieve Dr. Bevers, who was going on leave, and he was ordered to contact with all speed Dr. Annema in Manokwari, who would give him detailed instructions. Dr. Havermans would replace him on Circuit No. 6.

Dr. Havermans proved to be a tall, humorless nose-picker who was more like a sleepy bank clerk than a pioneer of science. But after a score of cocktails in the club, he proved to be a man of iron whom the wilderness would not easily daunt; he was still staring sleepily ahead of him and calmly picking his nose when Dr. A. Zorgdrager and his assistant sat pushing each other playfully, helpless with laughter. When at last they made their way to their boardinghouse they sang the "Skaters' Waltz," and they arrived arm in arm, closely united in manly comradeship. The district doctor had told them the boardinghouse was excellent; it was run by a young widow whose husband had been an oil prospector for the Royal Shell and vanished in the New Guinea jungle, together with some geologists, on a prospecting trip. The young widow opened the door herself and was quite pretty; when Anton gazed drunkenly round the parlor, his eyes fell on the portrait of a man on the mantelpiece. He had seen him before, but he could not remember where; in any case, it was a shame that this pretty little creature should have had anything to do with such a fat slob.

The pretty little creature gave them still more to drink; when they were shown to their rooms they bade her an elaborate good night, ignoring the dawn. Schutters drawled, "I bid you a very, very pleasant night indeed, Mrs.—er—" and the pretty little creature said, "Flabbinga."

"Flabbinga?" Anton cried. "Wait a moment! I know him. We traveled together to Banjermasin, years ago."

"Ah?" said the girl. "You know my husband?"

"Do I!" said Anton. "He could be my brother."

He did not bother to undress, but fell asleep on the top of his bed with his helmet on his chest, forgetting all about the ape man until it started to rain in the early morning.

He woke up with a strangled cry and lay squinting at *The Lancet* and Els's letters for hours, not daring to fall asleep. At last there was a knock at the door, and the young widow came in. She was profuse in her apologies for bothering him so early, but she could not help herself; he was the first person she had met who could tell her anything about her husband, and she asked him to tell her everything, anything he could remember, to repeat word for word what Henk had said to him.

He did his best, in spite of his headache; in the end she insisted that he should bolster her certain knowledge, her absolute positiveness that Henk was still alive by assuring her that lots of people got lost in the jungle of New Guinea and came out again months later quite normal. He obliged, although to his knowledge anyone who had the misfortune to get lost in that darkest of all dark continents so far had vanished forever in the foggy swamps and the impenetrable forest. Flabbinga had been missing for four months now, so he had probably been dead for three, yet he told her kindly that he would not be a bit surprised if Henk were to turn up, his usual beaming self, any day now.

Henk. He had never known that the jolly fat man who had hired his coolies for him and sung *"Je crois en toi, O maître de la nature"* while shaving, was anything but "Flabbinga" to anybody. In his memory the pale blue eyes, pendulous cheeks and asinine laughter of the distant friend had vanished almost completely. The priest on board the Henny, for instance, was much clearer in his mind, and so was Captain Krasser; old van der Waard on the other hand had yellowed beyond recognition. Life went fast in the tropics. It had only been three years ago.

During the rest of the day, after he had tentatively looked at Makassar and turned away with some distaste, the young woman insisted on staying with him for tiffin and tea, talking about dear Henk all the time. He invented a character called "dear old Flab" and began to experience the joys of creation, so it was his own fault that when dusk fell she suddenly clasped his hand and kissed it. It startled him for a moment, for he mistook it for a theatrical gesture of gratitude. When he saw her eyes, however, he realized his mistake. She looked up at him from the pouf on which she was sitting with half-closed eyes and parted lips, and he bent over and kissed her before he quite realized what he was doing. "I know he's dead, I know it," she whispered. "Help me, for God's sake, help me to forget him." It seemed a far-fetched pretext, but the kiss made him accept it with alacrity. His vision in the prahu at the totok's arrival had been accurate, all right; this was Wim Pelt all over again, the loutish pranks, the giggling girls cornered in the reeds. The only difference was that then they had not known what to do with them.

The next morning Schutters, Theodore, asked, "Where were you? I sat waiting in your room until half past one," and he answered lamely, "I went to see an ex-patient." The totok said, "Oh," and the asses' ears began to grow once more, but before he had a chance to tunnel any further, the young widow came tra-la-la-ing into the parlor, full of gaiety and girlish chit-chat. During breakfast, Henk was dragged into the conversation every minute or so, making Anton feel vaguely inadequate.

By the end of three days, Henk was no longer mentioned and Schutters, Theodore, had become steeped in adolescent gloom, from which he gazed at his chief in mute reproach. He might be a sentimental idiot but he was not blind; after he had waited once more until the small hours for Dr. Zorgdrager to come back, he had begun to suspect the identity of the ex-patient. Dr. Zorgdrager himself, frantically postponing feelings of shame, imagined himself in Love; in Annie he had met his Great Passion. She was a Revelation.

She was indeed a revelation; he had never had a proper notion of female logic until she convinced him that their love made the memory of Henk more beautiful. Henk was now in Another World, a Better Reality, he could only rejoice in their Happiness. She managed to convince him that Henk's greatest act of love toward her had been to help him find those coolies in Banjermasin, for by doing so, he had sown the seed of this miracle of tenderness that now united the sweetest strongest gentlest man in the world with the devotedest loneliest faithfulest and boofulest girl of the archipelago. After three days of this, at five o'clock in the morning, they pledged one another eternal love; he would write to Els that he had found his life's companion and she would keep a diary for him. "Oh bunny, bunny, bunny, why must you go away? Why can't we stay together forever? Why is Fate so . . ." The djongos knocked on the door disrespectfully and shouted, "Njonja, muggie tea!"

For a man who had been somberly dissecting his soul for four months, this development would have been surprising if Wim Pelt had not shouted up at him that morning in the sunny street of a Dutch provincial town, twelve years ago. When the Royal Packet steamer put Dr. Zorgdrager ashore in Manokwari, New Guinea, the journey along the loneliest coast of the Far East attracted him for more than one reason.

»«« »»»

Manokwari was a typical border settlement on the edge of an uncharted wilderness. It clung precariously to the edge of a continent of virgin forests, mysterious lakes, lost mountains and thundering cataracts of rivers unexplored by man. The sea was very blue; when they arrived the little town looked like a toy village, built by schoolchildren under the guidance of a young teacher, on a glass plate painted cobalt blue. When Anton and Teddy stood on the jetty with their cases, and peered at Manokwari, their helmets tilted forward against the blinding sun, the totok said, "What a hole," incredulous that this could be the capital of a district the size of France.

It was hot, silent, and windless; the flag on the tinfoil palace of the resident hung limply in the breathless heat. The district doctor had sent a sado the size of a goat cart, pulled by a tiny pony; when, after a tripping little ride, they were delivered at the front porch of the doctor's house, they felt like a couple of Gullivers in Lilliput. Not only was the bungalow minute, Dr. Annema himself turned out to be a Friesian dwarf with a passion for collecting Papuan penis sheaths and Kalebas pipes. Of both articles he had a collection that filled the three rooms of his house to capacity; he ate among the penis sheaths, and slept among the Kalebas pipes, one of which he was smoking as he welcomed them. It was so big that he had to prop up his elbow while puffing at it, and he talked incessantly in a strong Friesian accent amid blue clouds of acrid smoke. Teddy Schutters, who had had difficulty in accepting Manokwari as the important town of his imagination, was at a total loss when faced by Dr. Annema, for Dr. Annema was the commander in chief of one of the most romantic crusades of medical history: the Operation Salvarsan.

Operation Salvarsan was a challenge to every young doctor's imagination. For more than three centuries the dark continent of New Guinea had repulsed the white intruders with remarkable success. Scores of self-confident captains, generals and marshals had recoiled from that island, cursing and dying; hundreds of expeditions had been drowned or annihilated by the swamps, the mosquitoes, the jungle and the Papuans. In the end, the soldiers had turned the island over to the doctors: the Chief of Staff in Batavia declared New Guinea the exclusive territory of the Government Health Service, with the Head of Service as its commanding officer, to let them try to subjugate the hellish wilderness and turn the naked aborigines into loyal subjects of Her Majesty. The Government Health Service had undertaken the pacification of New Guinea after the expected losses had been closely calculated by a number of heads cooler than the snow-capped spires of the Nassau mountains among which was hidden the source of the Idenburg River which ended in the poisonous swamps around Cap d'Urville, breeding ground of the mosquitoes for the hell of the north coast. The losses were considerable; of all the doctors who entered the jungle with their syringes to inject Neo-Salvarsan into thousands of syphilitic Papuans and hundreds of thousands of frambesia sufferers, more than half turned tail after only a few miles, and the majority of those that did not come back within a fortnight never came back at all. Yet the Government Health Service managed to establish a bridgehead, despite the crushing superiority of the enemy. The natives, after having been terrorized for thousands of years by their witch doctors and incited to slay every intruder, put down their klewangs and blowpipes at the feet of the white magicians, for what hundreds of generations of tyrannical witch doctors had been incapable of doing, the white magicians did: they cured the scourge of New Guinea, the frambesia. After one single injection the swellings subsided, the gruesome wounds closed up; the island that had managed to repulse the Dutch from the very first arrival of the East India Company fell for Doctor Ehrlich's Magic Bullet, the Salvarsan. The pacification of New Guinea by the jungle doctors was an epic which had fired the imagination of all medical students in Europe, and given many a tenderfoot his favorite daydream; Teddy Schutters was one of them. And now he sat facing the supreme commander of that impressive crusade of peace: a Friesian midget, with three rooms full of penis sheaths and a sado like a goat cart, coughing in the pungent stench of his Kalebas pipe.

Everything to do with Dr. Annema looked like a toy; the map of the north coast pinned, among his collection, over his little steel desk looked as if it should have Cupids blowing the winds from the corners, and two Tritons holding up a scroll with the inscription, *Ye Olde New Guinea*. The map showed some sparsely sown little flags in different colors spread out along the coast, and the route of the inspection prahu was indicated by a red line that linked the flags with playful bows and loops. The whole thing looked like an exciting parlor game, to be played with dice and counters, like Snakes and Ladders.

"This little outpost has me worried." Dr. Annema said in his North Country singsong, pointing at one of the little flags with the stem of his pipe. "Dr. Ganwitz is still missing."

"Is that so?" Anton said, almost amused, so strong was the suggestion of a parlor game. Dr. Ganwitz was probably down a snake.

"He left three months ago on an expedition into the interior," Dr. Annema went on, "to look for a couple of prospectors lost in the jungle."

Anton was acutely conscious of the totok's glance. "If you like, we'll go and have a look for him," he said.

Dr. Annema threw up his short arms, as if threatened by a gun. "No, no," he cried. "The military have organized two expeditions already to look for him and those other fools, and that is quite enough. All we want in this part of the world is peace. You might go and have a look at the post itself, if you like, just to see if by any chance he is back, but that shall be all."

The totok had been bitten by the bug of Rider Haggard. "But surely, Dr. Annema," he said, "you do not want us to rest until we have found our colleague, dead or alive?"

Dr. Annema laughed, showing black little teeth, and he said good-naturedly to Anton, "This boy seems to think we're rolling in money. Economy, my friend, is the key to success. Even in matters of the spirit. That reminds me: a drink, you two?"

As they sat sipping their drinks, Schutters, Theodore, remained pensive. "What's the name of that outpost?" he asked, in the middle of a story.

Dr. Annema frowned and said, "Mamawi," in a cloud of smoke.

《《《　》》》

The moment they rounded the cape, and sailed up the creek leading to Mamawi, the resemblance was striking. The approaches to Mamawi looked so much like those to Kakoto that it seemed a hallucination. Anton, in the bow of his prahu, a gun across his knees, frowned.

At first, the rumors circulating in the service about Route No. 9 had seemed a romantic exaggeration. He had, by now, made so many voyages along barren coasts that he suspected that those who singled out Route No. 9 as something especially gruesome just wanted to sound important. But after three weeks on the route he had to admit that New Guinea was by far the worst.

It was not so much because of the jungle itself; the jungle was pretty much the same anywhere, and the coast was no less hospitable than Celebes or Borneo, although the distances between the settlements were much greater. It was a mysterious presence in the jungle that gave the constant exhausting feeling of being watched from that dark forest on starboard. Occasionally the feeling became so oppressive that it seemed as if the wall of the wilderness were only a hedge, behind which men crept surreptitiously, spying, waiting for a chance to pounce upon them at dead of night. Occasionally, out of the twittering silence of the jungle, a sound of muffled thudding was carried across to them by the land breeze, a soft, pulsating hum.

And such was the case; the commander of the military police in Manokwari had warned them that they would be watched all along the coast by the vermin that lived in the jungle. Every movement, every maneuver, every anchoring would be seen and drummed along the coast. For that reason they had eight Madurese soldiers with them as an escort, armed with guns, revolvers and a machine gun, under the command of a corporal.

At first, Anton had protested against the escort. The prahu R. 9 was bigger than the R. 6, but they would need the extra space for their food and the Salvarsan supplies for the outposts along the coast. But Dr. Annema had ordered him to take the escort, as it was better that the isolated settlements received a small ration than that the prahu should be ambushed by a fleet of pirates in hollowed-out tree trunks somewhere along the coast. And after the first few nights, Anton was grateful for the presence of the Madurese and their weapons. For at night the hostility, dormant though noticeable during the day, became virulent and unnerving. Surreptitious splashings circled the ship; the muffled knocking of paddles against wooden hulls sounded in the darkness; occasionally there was a stifled cry of excitement or a cough. Once a whizzing sound had whirred over the ship and was instantly answered by a salvo of the guns of the Madurese, who had the sharp ears and the instant reaction of bats. Even before Anton or Teddy heard either a rustle or a splash, the corporal hissed a warning, the dark shapes rose from their mats as if they had been lying wide awake, the barrels of the guns glinted dully in the darkness by the light of the stars, motionless and silent until another hiss made them belch a six-pronged flash of lightning, which was followed by the long rolling thunder of its echo, fading in waves along the coastline.

During those hot, ghostly nights they began to feel united with the explorers of the past, who had written about this last bastion of the Stone Age in old-fashioned, stilted sentences. Through the quaintness of their language their fears emerged with surprising reality; two centuries seemed as nothing at the foot of this dark millennium. This was not a battle of man against man, not a raid of well-armed desperadoes on an island full of dancing blackamoors with boomerangs and knobkerries; this was a groping voyage along the very edge of the world. Here the White Savior with his Glad Tidings was confronted by the interstellar darkness of unwritten history, in which the Light of the World was but a will-o'-the-wisp among the nebulae. However infantile, helpless and pitiful the Papuans might be when they came as cowed individuals to get their injections from the white magician, their invisible presence as a tribe behind the ramparts of the wilderness was terrifying, and had a supernatural tinge that unnerved even the most experienced jungle trotter. It was difficult to define the terror they inspired, for it was not the fear of something tangible. It was a deeper, more primitive fear, which felt like something darkly remembered from the aeons before the Great Flood. When the prahu rounded the cape and sailed up the creek toward Mamawi, the resemblance with the approaches to Kakoto suddenly provided Anton with a key to that fear. It was as if the New Guinea forest were peopled not with one, but with veritable hordes of Homines heidelbergenses. The fear that had assailed them along the coast was the fear of that old devil of the Scriptures again: degenerated man.

The creek of Mamawi ended in a mass of rotting plants, in which the prahu slowed down to a standstill as if caught in a morass. But it was not a morass; it was a thick gelatinous layer floating on the surface of the water in front of the jetty, driven there by the wind and the tides.

The Madurese tried to clear a channel for the boat with their paddles, and disturbed a swarm of flies which billowed so thickly around them that it obscured the view. Only when the flies attacked them did Anton realize that they were hornets.

The Madurese panicked, and it took almost half an hour before they could paddle on, hands and heads wrapped round with scraps of mosquito netting, like beekeepers. The distance between the prahu and the jetty was about a hundred yards, but it took them three hours before they could reach one of the mooring poles with a boat hook and draw the boat ashore. The eight Madurese pulled together at the hissed command of their corporal, and toppled backward when the jetty collapsed with a muffled creaking in a cloud of ant powder. The crash seemed to rouse the surrounding jungle as if it were one gigantic living organism, which had been motionlessly watching them all those hours; swarms of birds swooped out of the trees and the undergrowth, squawking and chattering, clouds of fiery butterflies whirled out of the reeds, in the darkness of the jungle hordes of creatures rustled and ran, a squall of running, stumbling, scurrying life.

The tremendous upheaval caused by the collapse of the jetty was so unexpected and startling that the Madurese lay for some moments in the bottom of the prahu, as they had fallen, like the transfixed image of a motion picture. Then the corporal hissed; they scrambled to their feet, grabbing their guns; two of them lassoed the last remaining pole of the jetty and pulled the prahu toward it, while the others, their guns at the ready, watched the jungle with restlessly roving eyes.

When the first Madurese swung himself onto the remains of the jetty, he seemed to chase the last rear guard of life away into the jungle. As they climbed ashore, obeying the hissed commands of the corporal, the wilderness twittered, chirped, creaked, rustled and palpitated with invisible wing beats, until, abruptly, it fell silent. The sudden silence seemed as ghostly as the noise had been; and for the first time Anton smelled the odor of which so many explorers had spoken as being unique, and typical of the New Guinea jungle: a cloying, sweet smell, like the smell of freshly baked bread.

He wanted to follow the Madurese ashore, but the corporal held him back. First they had to reconnoiter the wilderness before tuan doctor was allowed to leave the security of the prahu. The eight soldiers moved cautiously through the tangle of the undergrowth, with only the tips of their guns visible occasionally among the waving reeds, that gently sowed clouds of pollen onto the water. One stumbled with a muffled cry and crashed into the brittle reeds, causing an explosion of furious flies. At last, after twenty minutes of waiting, the corporal came out of the jungle and beckoned Anton.

When Anton and Teddy had hoisted themselves onto the jetty, about to enter the jungle, the smell of newly baked bread was so strong that it was nauseating. It was not quite like bread; it reminded Anton of his childhood in Holland when he had gone to look for the sweet roots of sedge on the river's bank with the neighbor's children. It was the same sickly smell of muddy sweets, intensified a thousand times. The corporal beckoned, and they followed him cautiously as he moved forward, his gun across his chest, through the man-high reeds that showered them with pollen as they passed.

Mamawi settlement lay hidden behind the reeds, so close that it was difficult to understand why the Madurese had taken so long to find it. All it consisted of was a small clearing with a broken flagpole, behind which stood an old rusty railway carriage without wheels, entirely overgrown by the wilderness. The Madurese had forced open one of the doors and were now clearing away the tangle of pale wet creepers in the dark iron cave of the interior. The stench of decay and putrefaction was stifling inside, and the floor so slippery that it was difficult to remain upright. It was a mystery how the crazy thing had ended up in the wilds of New Guinea. On the doors were still the brass numbers 3, and, inside, enameled notices saying, *Do Not Spit* and *Do Not Open Before the Train Stops* in Dutch and Malayan. The railway carriage at Mamawi was one of those mysteries peculiar to the Far East, like Sultan Rahula Rattan Rauwari's billiard table.

The carriage, after the tangle of roots and creepers had been cleared, proved to be almost empty. In one corner, an iron table stood bolted to the floor, with underneath it an instrument case that no one could open and, on top of it, a bottle. In another corner were found two lumps of green mold that turned out to be a pair of shoes, and from the communication cord dangled the rusty skeleton of a tropical helmet. It seemed as if the settlement had been deserted years ago; but Anton knew the jungle well enough to realize that a couple of months was all that was needed to arrive at this result. Together with the Madurese he searched the carriage; but after an hour, all they had found was a couple of rusty forks and spoons, a little gluey stick ending in a lump of rust which must have been a fountain pen, and a parang, the handle of which had been eaten by ants. The only thing left behind by Dr. Ganwitz was his instrument case, but when they tried to dislodge it, they found that it was either bolted or rusted solid to the iron floor. There seemed to be nothing left to do but to shut the doors of the carriage and go back to the prahu. They were about to do so, when Anton's eye was caught by the bottle on the table. It looked strangely clean and new: a brown whisky bottle. He took it outside, inspected it in the sunlight, and saw that something was hidden inside, a rolled-up piece of paper.

He opened it, shook out the paper and found, written on it in fat red letters, *138:14:1 East, 2:47:18 South, very ill, for God's sake send help Vollenhove Bergmans dead Ringers dying for God's sake Flabbinga.* At first he thought it had been written in red pencil, but the letters were greasy. He rubbed them, smelled his finger, and noticed a faint scented smell. It was the smell of kisses in the dusk, of whispered words of love and cries of delight, of disgust and desire and humiliation and cowardice. The message had been written with Annie's lipstick.

«« »»

When Teddy, at last, asked Zorgdrager, "Are you—are we going to look for them?" his voice quavered. The doctor had been gazing at the chart, rubbing his chin, for minutes on end and even now he did not answer. Then, suddenly, he stood up, called, "Corporal!" and told the Madurese to make preparations for an expedition that might last a fortnight. At that moment, Teddy could not curb his enthusiasm any longer, slapped the doctor's shoulder and cried, "Wizard show!"

The look Zorgdrager gave him was so mortifying that he mumbled, "Sorry," and hastily busied himself with the sorting out of his luggage in the cabin on the aft deck. Zorgdrager could not know why that decision had delighted him so; he had no means of knowing that by that one word, "Corporal!" he had completely reinstated himself in the esteem of his assistant.

When they had left Kakoto, Teddy had felt that he had found a wonderful, adult friend. From whatever angle he had considered Dr. Zorgdrager, he was an inspiring example. Never before had he met a man of such authority, sense of humor and honesty. At first, during their nightly conversations, he had been shocked by Zorgdrager's almost ex-

hibitionist frankness about himself and his foibles, but when he realized
that the man mentioned his foibles only to illustrate his highly original
and fascinating philosophy, his shocked amazement had turned into
admiration. What inner certainty, what strength the man must possess, to
be able to analyze himself so mercilessly and not to bother for a second
about his prestige. During those nights, Teddy had managed, bit by bit, to
piece together Zorgdrager's life history and he had been surprised not to
find a single sin in the man's past that would justify the bitter opinion he
had of himself. His marriage had gone wrong; but was that only his fault?
The woman sounded a bit of a prig, quite different from Moira. Of course,
one should not analyze those confessions in one's mind, for that seemed
somehow disloyal, but Moira was certainly much more warm-blooded
than Mrs. Zorgdrager seemed to have been. Perhaps the day might come
when he would change his opinion but, for the time being, he maintained
that if a husband described his wife as "a pale-bellied sow," the wife was
at least partly to blame. Then, like a blow, he had made the discovery in
Makassar that Zorgdrager was having an affair with the landlady. It had
sobered him cruelly, for it changed Zorgdrager's imposing theories about
sublimation, asceticism, conscience and human responsibility into hot air,
a game of words with which to pass the evening, and made his intimate
confessions seem sordid in retrospect.

After Makassar, Zorgdrager's glory had waned; by the time they
arrived in Manokwari the whole of the Far East, Government Health
Service included, had lost its aura of romance and mystery. The toy
village, the dwarflike Dr. Annema, the callousness with which they discussed their vocation and the glorious dead of Operation Salvarsan had
given a sour taste even to the epic of the pacification. The voyage along
the coast of New Guinea to Mamawi had been a disappointment as well;
not a single adventure, no interesting people, no more exciting conversations by the light of the stars; every day was the same as the other, visiting, in their settlements, doctors that all seemed to be like Zorgdrager:
tall, thin, without enthusiasm, faith or compassion, and all of them
indulging in the same bitter humor that had once seemed a masculine
armor to protect a compassionate soul. Egotists as hard as nails, the whole
lot of them, and he would be damned if he would let himself become
like one of those. A growing homesickness for Moira had crept over him
during the journey; during those three weeks he had nurtured a vision: a
winding lane with a hedge of brambles, hawthorn and honeysuckle, the

crunching of their bicycle tires on the gravel, the humming of the wind in the telephone wires, the smell of hay and pigs' manure. He would have gladly exchanged one Sunday afternoon in the countryside with Moira for a whole year of pioneering with Dr. Zorgdrager, and it was a sad reflection that only a month ago, in the Gulf of Boni, Moira's main function had seemed to be that of receiving glowing letters about Dr. Zorgdrager.

And now, suddenly, all this had changed. Whatever people might say about Zorgdrager, whatever he may have thought himself, he was a wonderful chap. As he hastily grabbed some things for a jungle pack, he saw, in his mind's eye, as if in a thrilling movie, Zorgdrager finding Flabbinga after a superhuman march of days. He saw them operating on the emaciated Flabbinga, nursing him until at last he could be moved, and in the end he heard Zorgdrager say, with that gruffness of his which hid such vulnerable gentleness, "I must tell you the truth, Flab. I'd never have gone to pick you out of hell if I hadn't trifled with your woman. I am sorry she and I betrayed you, but remember that, by doing so, she saved your life." What the smiling convalescent would reply to this was not quite clear in his mind, but he would cross that bridge when he got to it. For the moment, the whole thing was a wonderful, heroic adventure: a note in a bottle with nothing but a few cryptic words and numbers, an exciting march through the mysterious jungle, a grandiose operation by torchlight in the midst of dancing natives and a triumphant return to the coast with the white man saved from the jaws of death. "When do you think that note was written?" he asked.

Zorgdrager shrugged. "I don't much care how old it is," he said. "What I should like to know is: who put that bottle on the table?"

"Somebody . . . somebody must have taken it for him."

"Who? How did he know we were coming? Why did he leave it here rather than take it to one of the settlements?"

"I see," Teddy lied.

"If you ask me," Zorgdrager said, rolling up the chart, "the whole business is a trap."

"Whose?"

"Oh, somebody fairly intelligent. As long as we were hugging the coast, the Papuans didn't dare attack us. They only feel sure of themselves in the wilderness. I wouldn't be surprised if they had enticed Ganwitz into the jungle with the same trick, the same little note even. Who knows?"

"You mean . . . that note is a fraud?"

"No," said Zorgdrager. "That note is genuine, I'm afraid, so we had better go and have a look all the same."

"Even though you're practically certain it's a trap?" Teddy asked intensely.

"Yes, worse luck," Zorgdrager said. "It's just one of those things."

"Doctor," Teddy said with a quiver in his voice, "I am with you all the way."

Zorgdrager shot him a wary glance, hitched up his trousers and mumbled, "Fine," before he swung himself onto the jetty, calling the corporal.

«« »»

When Anton straightened up, considered the winding line of the route he had drawn on the chart, and lit his pipe, he frowned at the madness of the undertaking. Flabbinga, even if he had written that note recently, would certainly be dead by the time they found him. If he went, he would do so against the adamant instructions of Dr. Annema and his own common sense. Then why did he go?

He picked up the note once more and saw, in his mind's eye, a skeleton, bared to the bone by ants, and by its side a little brass tube. What in heaven's name had induced the man to take her lipstick with him into the jungle? Fetishism? Well, whatever it was, there was no doubt that the impulse had been a lucky one.

The corporal, when he learned of the expedition, looked worried. He must have received similar instruction not to venture into the interior. He was not impressed by the humane side of their expedition; it was the bottle that lured him from the path of duty when he realized that it had been put down there as a trap. He could not resist the challenge; like all Madurese, he was a manhunter at heart. The idea that a grinning Papuan imagined that he only need entice him a mile or so away from the coast to kill him at his ease was too much for him.

So, within the hour, the column was ready. Three soldiers carried the medicine chest, the P.G. and stores; three others were to cut the trail, two to remain behind in the prahu. These were ordered to sail back into the open again and anchor a mile out to sea.

When the corporal hissed, "Awas—awas!" the soldiers shouldered their loads, the parangs of the cutters smashed into the living wood and juice spurted into their faces. Anton shouldered his gun, and the totok looked up at him with radiant eyes.

"Good luck, doctor," he said, and adjusted his topee, then, clasping his gun, he set forth into the jungle.

«« »»

From their long nightly conversations on the deck of the *R. 6,* Teddy best remembered Zorgdrager's remarkable theory that the wilderness brought about an intensification of all latent passions. It not only applied, so Zorgdrager had said, to one's dormant negative characteristics, but also to those that were positive. At the time, he had listened to it with reverence and enthusiasm; in his imagination, he had seen himself in the heart of the forest, a Dutch Albert Schweitzer, a Hopalong Cassidy of philanthropy.

But reality was different. The first unexpected thing was the darkness: no patches of sunlight on the trunks of age-old trees, no beams of light like golden sheaves through the soft green dusk, but a dank, chilly darkness to which his eyes accustomed themselves with difficulty. Instead of a bouncing march through golden grass, it was an endless stumbling through an echoing grotto full of toadstools, mildew and slippery refuse. The crowns of the trees were an impenetrable dripping ceiling, from which the wet trunks hung down like black stalactites, a subterranean world of horrors. The feeling of being watched, which he had occasionally during the trip along the coast, now became a haunting certainty: the cavern was full of rustlings, knocking, thuds, hundreds of stealthy footfalls; the darkness was charged with evil. Instead of gaining in stature on the journey into the heart of darkness he felt as if he were getting smaller and smaller, until in the end he seemed to be wearing a little pointed hood and tiny boots with curling toes: a lawn dwarf in the wilderness. Instead of the iron rations, the disgusting jungle food and the dank echoing vaults of the forest clearing his spirit, sublimating his impulses and sharpening his intuition, he was gradually reduced to a panting domestic animal with palpitations, without a more grandiose vision than that of a nice dish of meaty food and a warm basket, and no other daydream than to take a bath with Moira and fall asleep together without an alarm clock, a box of marshmallows on the night table. The radio would play dance music, "I Cover the Waterfront" or "Stormy Weather," the gas fire would hiss softly, and he would not have to get up again to turn it off for, after a quarter of an hour, the coin would fall and the gas would shut off automatically. The pillow would smell of the laundry and Moira's hair of attar of roses; his hand would caress the soft skin on her bare back and she would kiss him with a sigh of marshmallows and the whispered words, "You're driving me crazy." Perhaps they would have even bought one of those lovely maraschino cakes—what was their name? Abdullah's Delight—they would eat big chunks of it in bed; she would say, "Of course, darling, let's finish it. When it's done, it's done," and he would spill soft crumbs on his chest which she would pick up with kisses. He saw that scene of sensual coziness so clearly in his mind's eye after the second day that, while chewing the ghastly kladdi or rebong or whatever the name of the boiled pig forage might be that the soldiers harvested from the undergrowth, he tasted the sweet alcoholic creaminess of Abdullah's Delight and fell asleep on his camp bed with one leg across his kit bag: home at last, after another endless day of stumbling, sweating, panting, listening, picking off leeches, swatting ants and crashing on his elbows with cries of pain as, once again, he was tripped up by a root or the loop of a creeper.

Yet Zorgdrager had been right, for although he himself might shrivel in the jungle, the maniac behind whom he trotted like a winded pug went through the opposite of his own metamorphosis. On the evening of the first day, he had still nursed the boyish hope that sometime in the future he might be like his chief; on the evening of the second day he knew better. Zorgdrager had turned into a creature from another world, a spirit of the forest, a bodyless faun. Every hour he seemed to recede further and further from the thin, nervous pipe sucker with the sunglasses and the dirty sun helmet he had known before, as if that familiar character had been a disguise which he was now shedding. He led their small caravan through the trackless forest with unnerving sureness. His alertness never faltered, his senses never flagged; he heard mouse-small rustlings in the undergrowth before anyone else; he saw trails in the wilderness and spotted winding game paths which the soldiers overlooked; he also spotted the Papuans in the darkness, and challenged them occasionally with a reckless wave that nearly made Teddy weep with sickly fear. At night, in the flat lamplight underneath the bat's wing of their bivouac sheet, he talked for hours. His eyes, that seemed to grow lighter as the forest grew darker, looked straight through the child's skull of his assistant, reading his thoughts, listening to his babble of love, watching the vision of Moira's smooth legs in the glow of the gas fire with an amused yet disinterested smile.

On the evening of the third day, he knew for certain that he would never be a jungle doctor, no pioneer in the terra incognita of this steaming, hostile wilderness. The companionship he had felt with Zorgdrager when they had been about to strike out in search of a dying man had turned into dejection. Whatever Zorgdrager might be searching for in the jungle, he would have to leave Schutters, Theodore, behind at the border of civilization and continue alone, errant soul shedding its body, leprechaun of the virgin forest.

"I'm sorry, doctor," he said, staring at the drops that jiggled down the bivouac sheet, like tears.

"Hm?" Zorgdrager's voice asked. He was scraping out a pipe.

"I'm no good to you whatever," he said.

The pipe knocked on the table and Zorgdrager's voice said, "Nonsense. Apart from being company, I may need you desperately if the chap is still alive."

It was a lie, a lie, even if Flabbinga were still alive. "Thank you," he said lamely.

The pipe hissed as Zorgdrager blew it clean. "I'm beginning to suspect that he is still alive," his voice said. "The trail we are following seems to lead directly toward the spot. And it is too clear by half. I won't be surprised if the cunning beggar who planted that bottle has kept the bait alive."

"Why would he?" Teddy asked, seeing the other in his imagination: a gigantic savage, an ivory needle through his nose, tattooed with magic symbols, an ornate penis sheath as thick as an arm, with a tuft of feathers from a bird of paradise.

"I don't know," the voice said, "but it seems to me as if there is a plan behind all this. Perhaps he wants Mamawi occupied once more, now that Ganwitz has gone."

"Do you think Ganwitz is dead?"

A match scraped and spluttered before the voice answered, puffing, "Suppose so."

"Murdered?"

"No. Driven to suicide, maybe."

Teddy's eyelids dropped. "But—but why?" he asked.

"Ah ha," the voice began, "you see, this whole situation is a battle, really. A battle between the Homo sapiens and Homo heidelbergensis. The pacification of New Guinea is more than just a skirmish between natives and intruders; it is a duel between degeneration and sublimation, between the Stone Age and Christianity, between . . ."

Moira sighed and whispered, "Hmmm, delicious." He chewed slowly, sensuously savoring the Delight of Abdullah as he spiraled gently down into warm, downy sleep.

«« »»

On the afternoon of the sixth day, the parangs of the soldiers clearing the trail slashed into the open of a sunny, summery meadow.

It looked like a mirage: in the heart of the forest, a green succulent plain full of white and orange flowers, and in the center of this prairie, that was caressed into waves by the wind, a hut made of palm leaves, like a duckblind in the middle of a lake.

When Anton saw the hut, his suspicion deepened into certainty. On the very day, almost the very hour he had calculated, the expedition had reached its goal. It looked like a feat of jungle navigation of which he could be justly proud; everything had gone according to plan. The only trouble was: the plan was not his.

The totok stood staring at the prairie and the hut, his mouth open, his sun helmet on the back of his head. He had been wearing that helmet all the time, stubbornly, although they had not seen a ray of sunlight for six days. Perhaps it was a talisman. "Is—is this it?" he asked in a hushed voice.

"Yes," said Anton, and he called the soldiers to life. "Awas—awas!" The column slogged swishing through the grass, the soldiers in front with their guns ready, those behind peering from under their loads. Teddy had eyes only for the hut; Anton and the corporal never lost the edge of the forest from sight. But nothing moved in the shade of the trees. The rippling grass was soft and shiny, perpetuum mobile under the ghostly caress of the wind. It seemed as if no human being had ever before beached on this island lost in the forest, as if the prairie had lain there untrodden for aeons: blossoming, sowing, dying and blossoming again, ever since the beginning of time. The hut, as they approached, looked more like an angular shrub than a structure built by man; grass was growing between the dead palm leaves, that rubbed together with a creaking noise, stirred by the wind. The soldiers, at a hissed command, formed a ring round the hut. The corporal's eyes continued to rove along the edge of the forest. When the ring was closed and the soldiers dropped their loads with rustling thuds into the grass, Anton walked toward the hut with his revolver in his hand and Teddy followed him, his gun wavering.

The entrance to the hut was low, hidden behind a screen of palm branches. Anton kicked it aside; a gust of stale air burst from inside. It was a sour, stablelike stench of wet straw and excrement. In the entrance lay a bottle.

It was a replica of the one they had found on the table in the railway carriage at Mamawi. An angular brown whisky bottle with a moldy label. As Anton stooped and peered inside the hut, he saw, in the semicircle of light behind the doorway, a number of similar bottles. Then he saw something stir behind them.

It stirred slowly, jerkily; it looked like an animal, cowering under the stare of the silhouettes outside, waiting for a chance to slip out, back into the jungle.

"Flabbinga?" Anton asked, softly.

The thing moved, jerked; straw rustled as it fell into the light with a thud. It looked like a small skull, the bald skull of an animal, in the darkness. Then Anton saw what it was. It was a knee.

He crawled inside. Teddy did not follow him but squatted outside, staring at the knee. He heard Zorgdrager rustle; a moaning; then a deep sigh, like a cow. The knee moved in the straw, as if it had a life of its own. It got up, and fell sideways into the darkness. The sunlight glinted on the bottle in the entrance. Teddy looked at the label underneath the mildew and distinguished letters. "G-l-d-S-l-k." He stared at the letters, trying to make out what they meant, while listening to the rustling, the panting, the muffled groans inside the hut. He had just made out the words "Golden Silk" when Zorgdrager's voice called, close by, "Stretcher!" He jumped up and called the corporal. "Stretcher, ajo lekas!"

Two soldiers pulled the stretcher out of the luggage pack, rigged it up, and entered the hut with it. The corporal followed them.

It was a long time before they came out again. The corporal came first, then a soldier, crawling backward, dragging the stretcher. As it was pulled jerkily out of the hut, Teddy gazed at the thing on it.

It seemed to consist of three objects: a skinny head with leaden eyeballs underneath swollen lids; an emaciated thorax with two bony arms, the hands of which were monstrously swollen; and a distended swaying belly. The legs were covered by the rags of a flannel blanket, alive with vermin and full of glistening straw. The body was festooned with blue clusters of leeches; in the beard, around the crack of the mouth, a small red beetle was frantically fleeing before the sunlight.

As Teddy stood motionlessly looking down on the body, Zorgdrager came crawling out of the hut, blinded by the sun. "Anti-shock," he cried, and as Teddy ran toward the instrument chest, it started.

It broke loose like a thunderstorm out of the jungle; it rolled, reverberated, crashed and banged all around them, in triumphant echoing volleys: the drums of the Papuans. They must have been watched from the first step they had set on the trail into the jungle, and now that they had reached the bait that had drawn them into the heart of the wilderness, the drums thundered the triumphant message in their hundreds, from horizon to horizon, one long, rollicking roll of drunken revelry. It was such an unnerving change from the silence of the windswept prairie to this deafening outburst of hatred that, but for the body on the stretcher, Teddy would have panicked.

The body had changed everything. It had turned them from intruders into doctors; it seemed as if the thunder of the drums, the advancing bloodthirstiness of the jungle, took them outside themselves and replaced their own puny personal pasts with the past of the Service, of all the grim, lonely doctors who had ever fought death in the wilderness against overwhelming odds. Teddy realized that if either of them were to betray a hint of uneasiness now, the soldiers would throw away their guns and their luggage and flee for their lives into the forest, into the arms of death. He was amazed at the calm that had come over him; when he bent over the body he felt completely secure. Yet the battle with death was without hope as far as the man on the stretcher was concerned. Even Teddy, who knew himself that he was a poor diagnostician, saw at a glance that his condition was practically hopeless. Crouching close together in the scorching sun, they gave him the anti-shock infusion even though they both knew that, if they were to start operating, they would probably kill him.

Yet an operation was essential. Teddy diagnosed, with surprising awareness, what ailed him. When Zorgdrager said, "Stop," he cut off the flow; and while Zorgdrager retracted the needle cautiously from the vein, he asked: "Liver abscess?"

"Indeed," Zorgdrager said. "Prepare him for an operation. That, by the way, was a good diagnosis, my friend."

Teddy shrugged his shoulders, for he felt no pride. All he felt was that awareness. He started work.

«« »»

Night fell swiftly. The Madurese set up camp while Teddy and the corporal put up an operation tent and improvised a table. Teddy watched by the patient while Zorgdrager, a little image of another world in the heart of the wilderness, sat bent over a microscope at a small steel table, examining a blood sample of the dying man.

They worked swiftly and with concentration for it was obvious that every minute counted. No one betrayed any reaction to the surrounding fiesta. The drums rolled, frolicked and thundered incessantly. They seemed to transmit a minute description of every move made by the men in the meadow to listening multitudes in the darkness of the continent. The fear they had caused at first had changed into an almost exhilarating tension, as if the men, now working to save a life, were helped by the knowledge that they were watched by thousands of invisible spectators.

At nightfall, a ring of fires was lit around the tents. The Madurese had not piled their guns, nor changed into sarong and kabaya as was their habit at night. They squatted between the fires, facing the forest, their guns across their knees. In the center of the bivouac, a spidery watchtower had been erected, on which the corporal squatted behind the machine gun. No lanterns flickered at the tops of the tents; they had all been assembled underneath the transparent cloth of the operation shelter, an island of tranquil yellow light in the unquiet shadows.

Inside the tent, the body lay on a white sheet on the table. The lanterns illuminated him with a soft, trembling light. It looked like a primitive painting of the Descent from the Cross: Henk Flabbinga, dying on the white slab, seemed to have expiated all the sins of mankind. His waxlike face with the half-closed eyes and matted beard looked like the mask of all human suffering; the swollen hands on the bony arms lay open by the sides of the mount of his belly in a gesture of surrender. He lay, naked and alone, before God; on the little table by his side sparkled the scalpels, the clips and the trocar: the spear of the Roman soldier.

Yet, despite this impressive situation, with the drums of the jungle thundering relentlessly around them, the operation itself lacked all vestiges of romanticism. On previous occasions, Teddy had never been able to forget that the human being stretched out on the operation table was a personality, a neighbor. As he approached the table together with Zorgdrager, stark naked, he had a deep feeling of symbolical meaning. The man had to die, it was unimaginable that his life should not volatilize under their hands, though they had done what they could to give him as much strength as possible. He did not need anesthetics, and the infusion went on dripping regularly; his heart was weak and exhausted like a bird that had beaten its wings until it was spent against the bars of its cage. When Zorgdrager made his first incision, Teddy came to the same tacit decision as he obviously had: even if he is certain to die under the knife, we will give him all we have.

When he spotted the trocar, he concluded that Zorgdrager would perform the Manson operation, bringing in the drain from the outside after the abscess had been pinpointed by punctures. It was a simple but a hazardous operation. The liver was full of big blood vessels; if one of them was damaged by a puncture, it would be fatal in this case, for the abscess was not easily accessible, but deeply situated in the upper part of the right lobe of the liver. They had not been able to ascertain whether it was a solitary abscess; chances were that there were others, still deeper. Only at the first incision did he realize that Zorgdrager was performing the transperitoneal operation, a tremendously complicated and very delicate affair which meant he must be very sure of himself despite the circumstances.

As soon as he realized what Zorgdrager was about, the body ceased to be Flabbinga, the wilderness ceased to menace them with its rolling drums of triumph, they ceased to be centurions at the foot of the Cross. They were transported out of the wilderness, back through time, to the other side of the planet: two attentive, tense boys bent over an old radio set on the work bench in the attic; the stench of the lanterns smelled like the airless heat of a paraffin stove, the distant drums sounded like rain on the roof tiles, and the voice of the corporal, and the answers of the sentries, like the cries of vendors in the street below.

During the long hours of that night, Teddy formed a complete unity with Zorgdrager. They were like one body, controlled by the same center of thought and will. When Zorgdrager put out his hand, he was given the instrument he required without asking; Teddy wiped the sweat off his forehead and his chest, reached him the needle for the stitching of the peritoneum onto the skin, clipped back the arteries and changed the swabs without a moment's hesitation. Zorgdrager looked ridiculously young, standing naked in that light, pottering with the human engine; he muttered and talked incessantly, saying absent-minded, childish things —"Fine, that's that"; "Now we get this little gent here"; "Easy does it, easy does it"; "Oops-a-daisy"—but the work his hands were doing was completely controlled. He took no risks, never hurried, his movements were precise and cautious, despite the alarming flutter of Flabbinga's heart and the soft snoring that sounded ominously like the death rattle. The pounding, exulting drums in the background, that occasionally swelled to a roll that made the delicate lancets tremble on the table, left him unmoved.

After he had opened the abdominal cavity and attached the peritoneum to the skin, he probed his way with infinite caution between stomach, duodenum and colon and, when at last he had bared the underside of the liver, he took hours feeling, pressing and gently probing before he finally said, childishly, "Hurray, hurray, goody goody, there's only one. It's a solitary abscess, my friend; Flabby is lucky. Okay, let's puncture. Swabs."

He plugged the wound carefully, despite the obvious fact that life was sinking rapidly in the motionless chilled body; and the puncture itself, which he at last performed after endless pernickety probing, staring at the lamps, was done calmly and with apparent ease, as if he were putting a new lead in a pencil. As it turned out, it was fortunate he had plugged the wound so carefully, for the pus spurted from the hollow needle with great force. He had been right, it must be one big solitary abscess.

Inserting the drain was almost a relaxed job; he opened the abscess with the forceps, carefully put in the end of the rubber tube and, as they started to close the wound, he hummed with boyish satisfaction as if the radio were playing. The stuffiness of the paraffin stove became overpowering, the rain beat on the attic window and the vendors yodeled their monotonous chants, while the boys hummed in unison. But outside, behind the horizon of fires, the drums of the Papuans thundered, while the two men, after closing the wound, stood staring motionlessly at the dripping of the drain. The unconscious Flabbinga inhaled the stench of the paraffin with halting gasps, bobbing precariously on the black lake of death; and then, suddenly, the drums fell silent. The two men looked at one another; Teddy, at a tacit command, went outside to investigate. The corporal was waiting outside the tent.

"What's happened?" Teddy asked.

The corporal shrugged his shoulders and looked across the flickering ring of fires at the darkness beyond.

Nothing had happened, nothing at all. When they stood side by side once more, watching the sick man, they both had the same crazy thought: it seemed as if the Papuans had had a spy inside the tent, and stopped their eye-witness account of the operation the moment it was over.

Anton decided he must be light-headed with exhaustion, left Teddy to watch over Flabbinga, and went to bed.

«« »»»

For twenty-four hours, Flabbinga's life hung by a thread, then he started to recover. The swelling of his hands and feet went down, and on the second morning after the operation, consciousness began to return. The eyes lost their fixed stare, changed from lead gray to blue, started to move and to look round with the wandering, half-blind gaze of the newly-born child. The mouth began to twitch, to tremble; the sweat of death on his waxy forehead evaporated and did not return; the drain in his side dripped no longer; he even began to move his arms and legs. It was a strange, impressive sight; the return of life into that body seemed more mysterious than a birth. In a matter of hours Flabbinga retraced the same road he had traveled as an infant; as the blue in his eyes intensified, it seemed as if his memories of the other side faded.

They fed him at first with infusions, then with teaspoonfuls of soup that dribbled down his chin; but life, once it had gained a foothold, recaptured his body with the voracity of the jungle. On the morning of the fifth day he was strong enough to be moved, the bivouac was struck and the voyage back to the coast begun. Henk Flabbinga was returning home from eternity: a swaying body on a stretcher, floating through the dark caverns of the jungle on the shoulders of four soldiers, surrounded by an escort, their guns in readiness. Over the stretcher an awning had been improvised on four sticks, which scraped along under the low branches; it was intended to protect the patient not only against leeches and ticks that could fall on him from the foliage, but also against the arrows of the Papuans. Anton had instructed the soldiers not to take that awning away under any circumstances, and to be prepared at any moment of night or day for an ambush or an attack from above; but nothing happened. They labored on through the eternal twilight, set up camp by small springs in the jungle, and watched by their fires and lanterns until the chirruping of the birds of dawning in the treetops announced the beginning of a new day. There came no ambush, no drums, not even the snap of a twig or the rustle of leaves in the forest. As they drew closer to the coast Flabbinga began to babble and to grin, and although his noises were still unintelligible and it was obvious that he had no notion as yet of what was taking place, he began to radiate a weird, drunkard's gaiety. He seemed to take an elementary pleasure in the swinging of the stretcher, the swaying and scraping of the awning above him, and in the flickering of the watch fires, at which he lay staring with fascination and mysterious mirth, the reflection of the flames sparkling in his vacant eyes. He still bore no resemblance to the portrait in Makassar, but the soft skin bag of his face, in which the skull had been contained like an irregular ball, began to fill out slowly, first with humanity, then with age, and at last with character. His beard, which at first had seemed a parasitic weed, began to acquire an apostolic dignity; when they struck their last camp, hoping to arrive in Mamawi that night, Flabbinga began to sing. At first they thought he was moaning with pain, or crying out with fear; but when they looked at him in alarm, he grinned a them with a grotesque, almost sinister amusement and they realized he was singing with joy.

They carried the singing Lazarus silently through the forest, and Teddy began to feel like joining him in his wordless song. Back to the coast! The nightmare was over; only a few more miles and they would escape from the spell of the haunted wilderness. He too had a feeling of being reborn, of returning from a nightmare journey into the gardens of death. He seemed to grow, once more, out of the lawn dwarf's boots and the rabbit's fear into what he had once hoped he would be: a jungle doctor. What had seemed a boy's dream had become reality: a letter in a bottle, a heroic expedition into the interior, the rescue of a human life in the nick of time, a triumphant return to the coast with, on a stretcher, the white man wrenched from the jaws of death. Moira rose, pink, radiant and proud, out of the glinting shell of the ocean that seemed incredibly clean and cool as they spotted it at the end of the trail.

When the soldiers made a fire and gave smoke signals, he wrote in his mind, *When we had reached the rusty railway carriage of Mamawi once more, the Madurese gave the arranged smoke signal and, within the hour, the R. 9 came foaming up the creek, with the soldiers waving and cheering underneath the triangular sail.*

It was an hour he would revive many times in his memory, an hour of masculine triumph. Compared to him, Zorgdrager seemed oddly nervous, almost pitifully so. He had lost the sureness that had made him so impressive in the jungle; he fussed like an old woman around the soldiers and the stretcher on which Flabbinga lay snoring blissfully, his head on one side, his eyes half-open. No wonder Zorgdrager felt nervous, for now those eyes could become conscious any time, and stare at the man who had seduced his wife.

The prahu struggled through the refuse toward the jetty. The hornets swarmed again in the clouds, the paddles splashed; another half hour, a quarter of an hour perhaps, and they would leave the jungle of New Guinea behind them.

"Stay with him," Zorgdrager snarled, as Teddy wanted to go to meet the prahu. "Keep that awning upright, and stay where you are."

"All right," Teddy muttered, and anger twitched in his fists. Soon he would have to have a heart-to-heart talk with Dr. Zorgdrager, for his totok days were over. If he wanted to snarl, he should do so to the Madurese or the Papuans. The Papuans! He had frightened the daylight out of him by peering and listening in that forest; now Teddy began to suspect him to be a fussing alarmist. He sat rolling a cigarette, calm and entirely free of the trembling in his thighs that had become so familiar in the wilderness. If he compared himself now with the boy who had set out into the jungle . . .

He looked up, his hands suddenly motionless, at the rustling thud in the undergrowth. It seemed to come from behind the railway carriage. He looked round; there was no one in the clearing except himself and the sleeping Flabbinga on his stretcher; the soldiers were gone, to carry the luggage into the prahu. A twig snapped overhead, and he looked up swiftly, but there was nothing to be seen. He licked his lips, jerked his head round as something rustled again in the undergrowth beside the railway carriage; the little muscle of fear in his thigh began to tremble once more. He jumped up, cried, "Zorgdrager! Hey! Zorgdrager!" and ran toward the jetty. "Zorgdrager, hal . . ." Then he stood still, petrified, as he heard a long wailing cry behind him, that died down in a wet gurgle. He turned round and ran back to the stretcher.

Flabbinga lay as he had been lying all the time, his head on one side, his eyes half open, but his body was full of little black sticks. As he came closer, he saw they were arrows. One had perforated his neck. When steps came running up behind him, he did not turn round; he could not tear his eyes away from those arrows. Then he heard panting beside him, and Zorgdrager's voice, saying, "You goddamned idiot . . ."

Flabbinga was dead.

«« »»

They buried him at the edge of the forest, a few paces from the spot where he had died.

Anton made a last round through the reeds and the alang-alang that covered the clearing in front of the rusty railway carriage. He thought about the letter he had to write to Annie, and that all he could send to her as a keepsake from her dead husband was a leaf torn off a writing pad with a message written in lipstick. When he entered the carriage he saw, on the table where the bottle had been, a stack of clothes, two pairs of boots, a haversack with compass, sextant, a revolver, a toilet case, a sun helmet and, leaning against the table, a double-barreled gun. The bottle was gone.

He whistled to the corporal, had the stuff on the table collected and carried on board the prahu; then they sailed. No one looked ahead, at the sea; the guns were aimed at the forest, ready to fire, until they rounded the cape. After the swell of the open had taken them over and they were cradled toward the setting sun, Anton opened the toilet case. He found shaving utensils, toothbrush, comb, soap, but no lipstick. The clothes looked clean, the boots were not moldy, the revolver and the gun were greased. The expedition had proceeded according to plan—the other's plan.

As he sat filling in the log, he thought of the mysterious intelligence behind it. He remembered how Teddy and he had stood watching the dripping of the drain after the operation, and how the drums had fallen silent. He wondered what was behind all this; what purpose. He sighed and started to write. Perhaps he would know one day.

Before he had written two lines, the thought struck him. This is the fifth one. One by one, the roots have been cut that connected me with the boy who came sailing up the Kali-Woga; all the people who meant something to me before I fired that shot over the corpse in those rapids, they have all fallen one after the other. Witzenburg, Bert, Els, Frolick, now Flabbinga. I am being slowly dismantled by the wilderness, until there will be no one left who knows me for what I really am. Then the net of the jungle will be flung over me.

It was a nonsensical thought, only a tired man exhausted by a forced march and dispirited by a defeat would arrive at such a conclusion. But although, after shrugging his shoulders, he wrote on, although he smoked his last pipe on the aft deck underneath the stars as usual, although he rolled himself in his blanket in the hut to fall asleep at once, as usual, he could not banish the thought from his mind. There went a straight line from the Kali-Woga to Mamawi; he was being cut off from the last roots that still kept him from being drawn into the wilderness. Anton Zorgdrager, my boy: you may struggle and you may try to fool yourself, but you are slowly drifting toward your Last Judgment in the wilderness.

Nonsense, nonsense. Leave, that's what he needed: drink, dance, blaring music. The music blared, and dissolved into the creaking of the beams, the slamming of the waves against the bows until it slowed down to a green silence full of waving ferns that were slowly moved aside.

The dead Frolick, of whom he had not dreamed since the beginning of the expedition, was back with his message. His wordless message from God.

«‹‹ ›››»

Dr. Annema's tiny face lost none of its jollity when he said, puffing at his Kalebas pipe, "They popped him off with blowpipes."

It would seem that white patients were often popped off with blow-pipes, to judge by Dr. Annema's reaction. He was much more irritated by the fact that Zorgdrager, despite his explicit instructions, had ventured into the jungle to look for the bloke. Just think of the things that could have happened: he could have lost his Salvarsan rations for all the settlements along the coast, to say nothing of the P.G., and what was the net result of his insubordination? Two weeks' delay and a corpse. Orders were not given to keep district chiefs occupied; they were the result of experience, young man. That kind of expedition should be left to the military.

After this Dr. Annema became quite interested in the expedition. He asked Anton how the Papuans had reacted, and when he was told about the drums he nodded knowingly. So that medicine man or witch doctor or whatever one wanted to call him was still about, despite the fact that the military police had reported his execution by hanging in the jungle. It must be him, for it was unlikely that he would have a successor as cunning as himself.

When Anton pressed him for information, the doctor said that all he knew was that the medicine man was called Hoomabbi, or Boobabbi, and that Hugenholtz and Ganwitz had both written extensively about him in their reports, before dying in the jungle. Ganwitz had been an excellent doctor, a man of great experience, one of the oldest members of the Government Health Service; he had sat twiddling his thumbs in Mamawi for six months without giving a single injection; the Papuans just did not turn up, on orders from Booboomi. Six months wasted, and not a shadow to be seen of that Boobibbi, only those bottles. Yes, of course, Dr. Annema knew all about the bottles; a couple of years ago, an English freighter had been shipwrecked near Cape d'Urville. In its cargo had been several hundred crates of bottles of whisky and the Papuans had filched them. That Booboomi must be a jolly chap to go and spend a weekend with. The current rate in the jungle was two buffaloes and a woman for one bottle of whisky, so rumor had it. If that were true, Dr. Annema would be able to buy a ton of penis sheaths for a tin of P.G. For compared to good old P.G., that sour hooch wasn't worth a thimble. True or false? Ha ha! Dr. Annema shook with toddler's laughter in his high chair, and cried, "Have another, boys, I've got a warehouseful."

Anton and Teddy had another, while the Papuan djongos in the kitchen smashed the crockery, bellowing, like a monster of Frankenstein. It was a miracle that Dr. Annema was still alive with a cook like that, but then he lived mainly on mince pies and P.G. Ha ha! A good diet, what? Once upon a time, the monster of Frankenstein had served a rabbit which looked tasty, only its hind legs had been rather long and its knees back to front, so Dr. Annema had asked, "What is that?" and the Papuan had answered, "Kera," a monkey. Ha ha! A good one, what? A monkey. Yes, and to think there were people who thought that life must be boring in Manokwari. Have another, boys, a warehouseful.

The meal was gay but the food terrible. As they sat sipping their coffee behind the mosquito curtain on the tiny front porch, like patients on a balcony of a sanatorium, they chatted about Salvarsan, frambesia, women and outpost Mamawi. When Anton said that he wouldn't mind having a try at reopening the post, Dr. Annema gave him a sharp look and said, "I see. You're one of those."

"What do you mean?" Anton asked laughingly. "I'm serious. For a long time now, I've been looking for an opportunity to study frambesia in connection with Brits-Jansen's research, and I thought that in Mamawi . . ."

"In Mamawi," Dr. Annema said, with discordant grimness in the midst of that gay evening, "there is no frambesia, no syphilis, no leprosy, no dysentery, not even a corn for you to study. In Mamawi there is nothing but a railway carriage, that should have been blown up long ago, and the wilderness."

"You're forgetting Sukabumi, or whatever his name is," Anton said.

Dr. Annema rubbed his eyes, sighed and asked, "Tell me, just as a matter of interest, what is it about this witch doctor that fascinates you so? I mean, I'm fascinated by him too, but I wouldn't dream of going to meet him on his own ground."

"Neither would I. All I am suggesting is that I should occupy the outpost for you."

"All right. I'll keep you in mind."

"I'd hate you to think that I was after a duel in the jungle, or something. Ganwitz wasn't either, I assume?"

"Ganwitz," Dr. Annema said, darkly, "was a Turk."

The rest of the evening was spent drinking and listening to Dr. Annema's memoirs of student days. Mamawi was not mentioned again, but when he went to bed Anton remembered the look the little man had given him, which was the only time that Dr. Annema had disclosed his true character. For to assume that this dwarfish caricature had become chief of the most daring medical project in Asia by accident was nonsense. There was more to the little man than a collector of penis sheaths. He decided to have a word with him, and knocked on the door of his room. A sibilant voice called, "Yess?" and he found the doctor sitting upright in what seemed to be a very big bed, with two pillows propped behind him and a pair of spectacles on the tip of his nose, smoking a pipe, a file of papers on his lap.

"Sorry to disturb you," Anton said, "but I'd like to have another word with you about this Mamawi business."

"That's funny," Annema said, revealing two gaps in his teeth. "I was just looking through Ganwitz's file."

"I really came to explain why I made that suggestion. I have the impression . . ."

"Wait a minute," Annema said. "Before you give me your reasons, see if they run something like this. *'On my last visit, I had the distinct impression of facing not just a jungle but a human intelligence inside it. If I understand the project rightly, it is not the intention of the Government Health Service that its doctors on Salvarsan operation shall act as planters, surveyors or prospectors. It is the intention that black magic and obscurantism shall be opposed by the forces of enlightenment and civilization, so I maintain that, by going to Mamawi and giving battle to whoever the man in the jungle may be, I am executing the spirit of the project Salvarsan, although you yourself may react with a grocer's reservations.'* The grocer," Annema said with a grin of gaps, "was I."

"I see," Anton said.

"I am still a grocer," the little man said. "I am still alive."

"What makes you so sure that he is dead?"

"You'll see," the little man said cheerfully, "you'll see."

It was not quite the conversation Anton had envisaged, so he concluded lamely, "I'd just like to repeat my offer, sir, and I think that Ganwitz really put it very well."

"Oh yes," Annema said, "he did. But he is dead. And it is not our intention that you shall die. That's all."

"For economic reasons?" Anton asked.

The grin vanished from Dr. Annema's face and he said, "You go and talk to Dr. Kramer, my young friend. It's his job to answer that kind of question. Good night."

"I'm sorry. I didn't quite mean it that way."

"Whatever way you meant it," Dr. Annema said, no longer looking at him, "I should like you to remember that we are doing serious work here, by which I mean that we are interested in the natives' salvation, rather than in our own. Good night."

Anton shrugged his shoulders and left it at that. His room was narrow and bare, and resembled the one in the Y.M.C.A. in Batavia where he had spent his first night in the Far East. On the wall was a photograph of some Friesian town: a row of identical houses with, on their roofs, an enormous placard that advertised *Pimentel's Hunting Water for Live Head Impurities* with the floor-high image of a mother dousing the head of a child with Pimentel's Hunting Water, thus chasing out a horde of little devils with six legs. The mother's mouth was connected with a balloon which read *There they go, son!* It was an unusual picture to hang in a guest room; perhaps Annema was born underneath those live head impurities, or else a calendar had once been attached to it. He undressed, blew out the candle and lay down to sleep, thinking about Ganwitz. Annema had been reticent about the man; he had given the impression that he might still be alive. And then, suddenly, a thought struck him.

Staring into the darkness, he considered for the first time the possibility that the intelligence in the jungle might not be a Papuan. The plan was too refined, too well conceived; for the first time the thought struck him that it might be a degenerated white man, a Homo sapiens deteriorated into a Homo heidelbergensis. Ganwitz? Could it be that the lonely doctor in that Godforsaken outpost had gone through the same degeneration as Frolick had in Kakoto? Could it be possible that this unobtrusive stranger whom nobody knew, about whom no one talked, had fallen victim to that fatal schism in his personality, and split slowly but irrevocably into a good spirit and an evil one, an angel and a demon, as Frolick had? Something about the whole setup made him consider that possibility, mainly its pointlessness. What was the point of enticing a platoon of soldiers into the jungle by keeping alive a desperately sick man, and yet not attacking that platoon? What was the point of killing Flabbinga at the very last moment and letting the others escape? When he came to the conclusion that the whole thing had been a bait, put out to make Dr. Anton Zorgdrager volunteer for Outpost Mamawi, he shrugged his shoulders, turned over and fell asleep.

The green silence was full of swaying ferns, that were slowly moved aside.

«« »»

Dr. Annema stood waving on the jetty against the backdrop of his toy village, until the steamer had turned the cape and headed out to sea. Then Anton and Teddy made for the bar to have a quick one before dinner.

The hot room was jammed full of passengers, and familiar faces grinned everywhere. Everyone knew everyone else by sight; the bars of the Royal Steam Packet were like the foyer of a provincial theater. As he put down his glass, Anton saw the reflection of the totok in the mirror behind the bottles, staring dreamily ahead of him. He remembered his own daydreams on the way back to Batavia after his first expedition into the jungle: a medal, a dinner with the Governor General. It had ended with rijst-tafel with Brits-Jansen in Des Indes. "One portion is for the gentleman, the three others are for me."

How did the boy see him? In the same way as he had seen Brits-Jansen: Whichever way he saw him, Dr. Zorgdrager and Dr. Jansen had only one thing in common: both of them were slaves of the wilderness; they had sold their souls to be rid of the mirrors of their neighbors' eyes. The mirror behind the bottles was the first he had seen for months; two months to be exact. The first mirror since the one with Annie's white arms, pinning up her hair, hairpins in her mouth, shiny pink brassière, little nests in her armpits. Hm. *Our little toddler in his tiny nest is about to enter the wide, wide world,* Els wrote. *Isn't it wonderful that we can work out exactly when he will be born?* "Wonderful," she called it: that gruesome morning, that beating, kicking, screaming, that flight as from the devil. Wonderful. Women forgot remarkably quickly; or did they? No. They forgot nothing, but they changed reality in their memory to suit their current mood. Her letters were getting more and more embarrassing, almost painfully so. *My sweet, sweet angel*—who has sold me, betrayed me, raped me? Nothing of the kind: *My dear, only Fatty.* "Fatty." Whatever he might have been in the past, he had never been fat. He looked at himself among the bottles, a thin, weatherbeaten face with light blue eyes, rather bitter, rather nervous, rather like all the other faces in the bar. They were all middle-class boys in the haunted hothouse, with their signet rings and their wrist watches and their "Djongos! Sama djoega!" Fatty. It had nothing to do with distance; Annie had talked about Flabbinga in exactly the same way: *"Henk is such a bully,"* and there lay the emaciated body, descended from the Cross, on the white slab in the wilderness. *"Wer hat mein Heiland so geschlagen?"* The choir of angels made him hurriedly slap Teddy Schutters' shoulder and cry, "Hey! Mind if I share the daydream?"

The totok jumped guiltily and spilled his drink. "Oh . . . er . . . yes?" he stammered. He must have been dining with the Governor General after His Excellency had been honored and pleased to pin this distinction personally on your chest, Dr. Schutters. "If you think you'll ever hear another word about that expedition," Anton said, "you're mistaken."

The totok looked at him in bewilderment. "Expedition?" he asked.

"Yes. Weren't you dreaming about a medal?"

"No . . . I was thinking about furniture."

"Furniture?"

"For our bungalow, when Moira comes over. Do you remember that little mocca table with the red top, in Makassar?"

Somewhere a drunk began to pound an upright piano, hoarse voices sang "Wedding March of the Teddy Bears; They come prancing down in pairs."

Someone tapped his shoulder. In the mirror he spotted a stranger's face and a peaked cap among the bottles.

"You Doctor Zorgdrager?" a voice asked.

He turned round and said reluctantly, "Yes . . ."

"Cable for you," said the peaked cap. "Congratulations."

He opened the telegram with a feeling of fatality.

"They give hairy, beary kisses," the drunks sang. "And they tickle the bear missus. . . ."

Wednesday night two hours summertime son Jacob blue eyes fair hair seven pounds four ounces mother child flourishing congratulations Dadmums.

He muttered "Thanks" to the wireless operator, hoping the man would forget about it. But within five minutes, the whole ship knew. He had to stand round after round, shake hands, let his shoulders be pounded, receive punches in the kidneys and laugh with the lot of them when a wit suggested the child should be christened, "Jacob P. G. Zorgdrager."

When at last he had a moment to himself, he wrote two telegrams. One to Els, *Am with you in thought dearest chin up* and one to Dr. Piet Kramer, *Request transfer to Post Mamawi Zorgdrager.*

As the telegrams went via the wireless operator, Teddy Schutters knew about it within a quarter of an hour. "Why?" the boy asked. "What on earth do you want to bury yourself in that impossible hole for?"

"Various reasons," he answered. "Frambesia, among other things."

The boy looked at him warily; then he asked, "Do you think they'll give you an assistant?"

He grinned and said, "No. Mamawi is a one-man post. I'm sorry, old boy, you'll have to look for another boss."

The totok breathed, "Oh, rot," but it sounded strikingly like, "Thank God."

That night, he tried to formulate a valid reason for his application in a letter to Els, but he gave up after two lines, for he could never tell her the truth. It had to do with Flabbinga's eyes as he returned from death, the eyes of a newborn child, still full of mysterious knowledge of the other side. If, with a troubled conscience, he bent over a young baby, it was afraid of him, whereas it grinned toothlessly at Brits-Jansen's monstrous looming shadow when he tickled it clumsily and made noises in his beard that would have made a watchdog flee. During the first six months of its life, the human child knew more about people than it would ever know again, if it lived to be eighty; and now there lay one of those, staring around him with wandering eyes, somewhere in Holland. His son. Years later, he would sit opposite a young man with a pipe, for whose life he was responsible. Interesting set of questions that young man would put to him. Why was I born? What did you do for me? What example have you left for me to follow? What gave you the right to desert my mother, to imbue me from birth with the image of a coward whose only answer to any of the great conflicts of life was flight?

When he opened that telegram, one thing had crystallized in his mind from all the months in which he had tried to suppress the thought of his imminent fatherhood: his son would have a father worthy of the name, or no father at all. Rather than burden him with the presence of a weak failure, he would leave him the legend of a brave man lost in the jungle on a crusade to cure the Papuans of that terrible scourge. Rather than the pale, apologetic hands of an unsuccessful village doctor, smelling of soap and Lysol, his mother's work-worn hands, turning the leaves of an old album with photographs of a young man in a badly fitting tropical suit, and her voice, saying, "That is your father, the last picture taken of him before he went into the jungle, never to return." The child would ask, "Why not?" and then the mother would gently close the album, and answer . . . Yes—what? "Because he was a hero?" or—"Because he was a coward?"

Father Zorgdrager went to bed, while the planters sang the unspeakable details of the "Teddy Bears' Wedding March" with distant Christmas voices in the starry night.

CHAPTER THIRTEEN

I<small>N</small> B<small>ATAVIA</small> a letter waited, addressed to him in unfamiliar handwriting. When he opened it and looked at the signature, he could not think who "A" was, until he read the letter.

Ugh—what a mean, beastly trick to send me those rags! If you had written to me like a man go to hell I would not have minded so much for I have come to myself too since those days and I certainly dont want to set eyes on you any more. Ugh—how dirty, how mean, to send me that stack of man's clothes and boots and that dirty box with someone else's things and to write me that mean letter full of dirty hipocrysy. You dont think that I deceived Henk so deeply that I forgot what size boots he wore and what make woollies and those shirts he could never bear on his body because they were too tight under his arms. It is not sufficient to know that Henk is dead? Must you pester me on top of it all by sending me a bag of rags and then to act as if you had found it and operated him? I did not know that a human being could be so mean, I hate myself at the thought that you and I—but I wont even write it, it is so dirty. God will punish you, you can be sure of that, and if ever you should come back in the neighborhood, I'll tell you something that I am too ladylike and indignant to write down. You belong in hell. A.

P.S. I have protested to the Head of Health of the Government Service in Batavia.

P.P.S. I have been so punished with that note in lipstick until I realized that you must of course have written it yourself because I must have told you that poor Henk always took something of mine with him if he went into the woods, e.g., comb, garter, etc. You have remembered that very well from when you were seducing me and I did not know what I was saying. How was I ever able to betray such a dear good man with such a mean, skinny beast.

P.S. If I (P.T.O.)

don't get satisfaction from the head of (P.T.O.)
Health, I shall go to the police because I know the new (P.T.O.)
Superintendent VERY well.
P.P.S. . . ."

He tore up the letter before he had found the last P.S. in the maze of crossed lines, threw the scraps into the wastepaper basket in his hotel room, lit a cigarette, sat a moment drumming with his fingers on the top of his desk, then he went back to the wastepaper basket and fished out the scraps. He spent half an hour piecing them together; during that time, his anger and his injured vanity calmed down and he reread the letter with a feeling of shame.

Only when he was on his way to the Head Office did the thought strike him that the man they had found might not have been Flabbinga at all. What had made him so sure he was? He had not recognized him; the general build had been the same, and he had just taken for granted it was he. But Flabbinga had been lost for more than four months when he found that note; Ganwitz had probably left on his own expedition after receiving the very same message written in lipstick. Ganwitz had left Mamawi three months ago; if Flabbinga had been desperately ill three months before they found him, he could never have been the dying man in the hut of palm leaves. Or could he? A solitary abscess could take months . . .

The same ghost in gray that had welcomed him on his arrival from Holland opened the door of the Head Office for him, and led him silently along the twilit corridors to the door on which he knocked with a bony hand. The man in shirt sleeves sat behind his desk full of papers, underneath the purring fan, in front of the map of the archipelago, as he had been sitting for years. "Morning," he said. "Sit down. Just a moment," and he went on writing.

While Anton waited for him to finish his little ritual, he looked at the map behind him. On Post Mamawi, New Guinea, he saw a little flag, so his request had obviously been granted.

Dr. Kramer blotted the paper, put down his pen and said, "To tell you the truth, I expected you to ask for European leave after I had sent on that telegram to you."

"Why?" Anton asked, with a sinking feeling in his stomach.

"Just like that," Kramer replied. "A hunch."

"But my time isn't up yet. I've got another year to go."

Dr. Kramer took a cigar out of the box on his desk. "I would have given you that leave," he said, biting off the tip, "and been glad to see you go at that."

"Thank you," said Anton.

"No reason to take umbrage, let's be frank about it. Up to now your work has given me the impression that you are, how shall I say, an emotional person. And for emotional people I have, in my function as Head of this Service, little patience indeed. The G.H.S. is not a philanthropic organization. It does not serve the suffering natives of this archipelago out of romantic considerations. It does a tough job, to support a tough policy."

"Interesting," Anton said. "Would you mind telling me what this has to do with me?"

"Certainly," Kramer replied, calmly. "That is the idea. And I'd like to remind you that you're not here for a student's debate, but to receive my orders. If ever the time should come that you have to sit behind this desk, you'll understand how a man in my position reacts to cheeky muddle-heads."

"Thank you."

"You're welcome. I mentioned it to make clear to you the basis of this conversation. As a human being, I could be interested in your case, but as it happens I occupy a commercial and a political post, not a humane one."

"That is obvious."

"Have a cigar," said Kramer, "and try for a couple of minutes to forget about yourself, just as I am forced to do ten hours a day. I wouldn't bother with all this if I weren't interested in you."

"As a case?" Anton asked, accepting the cigar.

"As the doctor of Post Mamawi, New Guinea," Kramer replied, and held out a match for him.

"Thank you."

Kramer shook the match out. "To start with," he continued, "you must be conscious of one thing, always and everywhere: we Dutch in Indonesia are living on a volcano. We are the rearguard of a raiding party, and whatever we may do and whatever we may tell them, we remain the rearguard of a raiding party. The first Dutch admiral to raid Java with a couple of ships full of jailbirds and six hundred cannon did not do so in order to found the Government Health Service. So whatever the newspapers, the Cabinet Ministers and the Governor General want to tell the people of these islands is their affair; you, as a doctor of this Service, must be constantly aware of the fact that your main function is a *political* one: pacification. You in your case must be doubly conscious of it, because you are an emotional person and because you have volunteered for the worst outpost in my collection. The moment you should imagine yourself to be a pure personification of Christian charity, you'll commit an error that will cost you your neck."

"Why?" Anton asked. "I would have said that that is the only conception possible, unless I want to be disgusted with myself."

"To be disgusted with oneself," Kramer said dispassionately, "is the privilege of emotional people. As long as you consider yourself the center of the universe, you will remain disgusted. But as the doctor of Post Mamawi you are not the center of the universe; you are a representative of the East Indian Company that trades in coconuts, sugar and coffee. Don't try to see yourself as something different, or else you'll go the same road as Mr. Ganwitz."

"Which is?"

"Suicide."

"I didn't know that. I thought he'd gone into the jungle to look for a patient."

"Mr. Ganwitz ventured, alone, into a wilderness full of hostile Papuans. If you know a better name for such an action, I'll be interested to hear it."

"Self-sacrifice. Charity."

"Crap. Mr. Ganwitz did not sacrifice himself, but the prestige of the East Indian Company. No need to tell me that the East Indian Company no longer exists and that its commercial aims have been replaced by the humanitarian and social ones of the state of the Netherlands, for I am not a native, nor a newspaper reader in Holland. I am a head official of that company, and although I could spend a night proving to you that the natives benefit by our work, I remain a head official of the company. I must constantly realize that if this archipelago starts to cost us money instead of the other way round, we will be bankrupt; and whatever we may be—traders in oil, rubber and cotton, or apostles of Christ—bankrupt is bankrupt. That is why Mr. Ganwitz should have stayed at his post, with or without patients, instead of striking out into the jungle, looking for a sick man, the philosopher's stone, his soul, or God. Do I make myself clear?"

"Indeed."

"So if you want to succeed Mr. Ganwitz you'll have to convince me that you fully realize the limitations of your function. In the first place, you'll be one, isolated man in hostile territory. You are armed with one of the most effective means of pacification at the disposal of the Colonial Office: Salvarsan. You are armed, Mr. Zorgdrager; Salvarsan replaces the saber and the machine gun, not the crucifix or the holy-water sprinkler. You must be constantly conscious of being alone in a jungle full of enemies; you have in New Guinea exactly the same task and exactly the same function as that first Dutch admiral had in Java, and if you should come to consider yourself as the first missionary who has come to convert the cannibals, it will cost you the same as it cost the real first missionary in this archipelago: your head. Now you'll say: what I do with my head is my affair; but then you forget that it is not your head, for it belongs to the state of the Netherlands until such time as it is returned to you, when your contract expires. You have no right to let yourself be beheaded, for whatever reason, without permission of the state of the Netherlands, represented by me. Understood? So next time you receive the invitation to set out alone into the jungle for the sake of an oil prospector of the Royal Shell, you shall inform me of the circumstances and wait until I have contacted the Royal Shell and we have decided which head is more expendable, the Salvarsan or the Oil head. And now, I'll thank you to tell me the reasons for your request to be transferred to Mamawi."

"To collect material for Dr. Breszezinska-Jansen, in connection with his research into frambesia."

"It sounds as if you've learned that by heart. You'll have to think of a better one if you want to convince me that you have not volunteered for Mamawi in order to escape from a son of seven pounds, a flourishing mother and a congratulating Dadmums."

"It sounds as if you have learned that telegram by heart," Anton said, shaking with anger.

"I have a good memory," Kramer said. "I remember, for instance, your saying, 'In the jungle my diagnosis is better,' some time ago, and 'Only in the wilderness do I feel at home.' The jungle and the wilderness, mark you, not a word about leprosy or frambesia. By which I mean to say that anyone trying to escape from himself and his responsibilities should not go into the forest, but to the cinema. You must not think that you are an exception, or that your case is unusual. These colonies are full of young white men terrified of themselves; but because you are an emotional person, this circumstance might prejudice your work. That's why I said: if you had asked me for European leave, I would have granted it, for if I have the choice between letting you fight with your own shadow in an outpost of our pacification brigade, or letting you pinch a maid's bottom in a scullery in Holland, I choose the latter alternative on the consideration that the state of the Netherlands has to foot the bill. If you make a mess of things in Mamawi, you'll do thousands of guilders' worth of damage; if you make a mess of your own life in Holland, it won't cost us a penny. You have paid for your initial expense after three years of service, the rest is profit. Your cigar's gone out."

Kramer struck a new match and held the flame out to him. As Anton bent forward to light his cigar, his helmet slid off his lap and fell to the ground with a hollow thud; as he stooped to pick it up he bruised the cigar on the edge of the desk in a shower of sparks. The cold sweat of anger and embarrassment broke out on his forehead. He wished that the bastard on the other side of the desk would stop pulling him apart on his little slab.

"So, if I understand you rightly," he said hoarsely and, he realized, loutishly, "you consider me as a worthless wreck that you really want to get rid off, but that might do for a couple of months to plug the hole of Mamawi."

Kramer looked at him for a moment, then he said, "I consider you to be someone with possibilities and qualities, who made a mess of his marriage and now tries to get even with his conscience. If you want to try that in Mamawi, I won't stop you as long as you don't make a mess of things. But I can tell you, here and now, that the last place to hide with a bad conscience is Mamawi."

"Would you know of a better one?"

"Certainly. The church. Or the living room, with your wife underneath the lamp, knitting."

"I'm afraid that neither of these alternatives is at my disposal, at the moment," Anton replied, his throat getting drier all the time.

"They are easier to get at than Mamawi," Kramer said, "but both of them force you to get off that chair in the center of the universe, and you've got something against that because you are an emotional person. You want Our Lord to come for you, and take you across His knee and break you in pieces. Well, Mr. Zorgdrager . . ." and he bent sideways in his chair to open a drawer, "in Mamawi that may well happen. But don't expect us to send an expedition to collect what's left of you—that is all. Now I've got a small item here that I'd like some light on." He took a folder out of the drawer and put it on the table. "That oil prospector's wife has written to me to say that the clothes you sent her did not belong to her husband. How did you identify the patient?"

Anton told him. He told of the note in the bottle, the geographical indications that turned out to be accurate, and how he had not considered for a moment that it could be anybody else.

Kramer listened with half an ear, leafing through the papers in the folder, among which Anton spotted his own report. "I have a letter here from Dr. Annema," he said, "saying that the double-barreled gun belonged to Dr. Ganwitz; and a declaration from the commander of the military police in Manokwari that the revolver is a service revolver, the number of which is booked to a certain Sergeant Fluters, or Suters, who was reported missing on the first expedition sent out after those oil people, so it looks like one hell of a mess."

"What would you like me to do? Shall I have the body exhumed?"

"Too late. I asked that woman for a chart of his teeth and possible bone scars; she replied via the police commissioner in Makassar that all she knew about his teeth was that they were 'normal,' and she did not mention bone scars at all. That sergeant had no tooth chart either, at least I didn't receive one."

"And Ganwitz?"

"I hardly knew him, neither did anyone else on the coast. At least, nobody ever looked at his teeth. Dr. Jansen may perhaps know something about him; they entered the Service at about the same time. He had no next-of-kin, left no testament, not even a passport. At the time he came over, they did not ask for one."

"What shall I do with the grave? Leave Flabbinga's name on it?"

"What kind of a grave is it? Wooden cross?"

"Yes—with the name painted on it."

"In case that cross is still there when you arrive," Kramer said, "I'd put on it 'Unknown European' until further notice. The military police will probably ask you for a full description and a dozen sworn statements, but as far as the Service is concerned, your part of it is completed herewith. Is that understood?"

"Yes, sir," Anton said.

«<< >»»

When the launch of the Royal Packet steamer approached the jetty, Anton saw Dr. Annema standing at its far end with a Kalebas pipe. When he climbed ashore, the little man virtually embraced him. He had a lot of stories to tell; it was fantastic, all the things that had happened in Manokwari since he left.

As they sat on the tiny porch, sipping P.G. while the monster of Frankenstein lowed and smashed in the kitchen, Dr. Annema told the exciting news: the corpse that lay buried in Mamawi wasn't Flabbinga at all, but someone else, one of six other people; the gun they had found in Mamawi belonged to Ganwitz; his cook had put a delicious rabbit in front of him, only a bit long in the hind legs and its knees back to front, and when he had asked, "What is that?" the Papuan had answered, "Kera," a monkey. Ha ha, a good one, what? Yes, and then to think that there were people who thought that life must be boring in Manokwari. Oh yes, and the commander of the military police wanted to see him about the body.

The commander of the military police came to pay them a visit after the gruesome meal, and Anton recognized him with uneasy suprise as the major from Labuan Redjo. The major seemed as little delighted as he by their meeting; he directed the mortar fire of his conversation at Dr. Annema, with his chin stuck out and a hacking cough that made the fat little doctor cover his glass with his hand. When the major heard that Zorgdrager was to be the new doctor for Outpost Mamawi, he said, staring at the penis sheaths with bloodshot eyes, "Hellhole. Pocket of resistance. If I had my way, Mooroobi would be dangling from the yardarm within a week."

"I thought you had killed Booboobi," said Dr. Annema.

"When?"

"Well, on your last expedition. Wasn't that Booboobi?"

"No," the major said, crossly. "That was some other swine. The name, by the way, is Mooroobi."

"Booboobi," said Dr. Annema.

"Mooroobi," the major insisted. "I've got his name in my reports."

"So have I," said Dr. Annema, "Ganwitz never wrote about anybody else."

After having tried to sell one another Mooroobi and Booboobi for some time, the major and the doctor went into the study to look up the name in the files. They came back with "Burubi" and a new tin of P.G.

"To Mamawi," said Dr. Annema, lifting his glass; the major said, "Hm." They drank. The major choked, and sat convulsed with coughing in his squeaky rattan chair until the veins on his temples had turned into cords and his eyes looked as if he had been strangled. At last he swallowed, sighed with an acrid stench and said, "Well, chaps, time for 'lights out.'" After he had left, Annema said, "Excellent man. Excellent for his job," and lit his pipe. Anton said nothing. Fortunately, he would have nothing more to do with the major.

But he was mistaken. The major sent for him the following morning and he went to see him in his office: a stiflingly hot shack of corrugated iron, smelling of paint, gun grease and old paper. The major, sweating profusely behind his empty desk, gave him instructions. He was not to go into the jungle, he was not to use his firearms unless provoked, in which case he should shoot to kill. He would be given Ganwitz's gun, which was old-fashioned but serviceable. The major demonstrated it in the yard, outside the latrine. He put a stick in the ground with an upturned bottle on top of it, broke the gun on his knee, stuck two fat cartridges into the barrels, pulled five or six triggers, took aim, held his breath; then the gun went off with a double bang, as if a door were slammed shut in a marble hall, and the bottle exploded; from then on the major walked lop-sidedly. Anyhow, that was his gun and he would also get a service revolver which the major thought unnecessary to demonstrate, enough cartridges for a month of civil war and a tiger trap. After that, the major had to talk seriously with him about the case of that body. Who the devil was it they had picked up in the jungle? Ganwitz? Sluiters? Vollenhove? Bergmans? Ringers? Flabbinga? After an hour and a half of cross-questioning and endless notes, only one thing had become apparent: the major had been exiled to New Guinea, since their meeting in Labuan Redjo.

On the eve of his departure, Anton wrote three letters. They were strange letters, as if he were saying farewell: to Els, to Bert and to Brits-Jansen. He wrote them in the guest room of Annema's house, staring at the photograph with the mother and the child demonstrating Pimentel's Hunting Water on the rooftops of the Dutch provincial town.

Dear Bert, he wrote, *I am about to venture into the jungle alone. Maybe it doesn't interest you very much, but I wanted you to know all the same. In a couple of months' time, I may know more . . .* He stared at the little devils, fleeing from the child's head. During the past months, he had thought little about Bert, as if he had pitched the memory of her overboard together with the empty tin of the serum of conversion. Ah, non-sense. *There they go, son!*

Dearest Els, Since my last letter from Batavia, a lot has happened. I have been transferred to a permanent jungle post and this means, I'm afraid, that you will not be hearing from me so often. . . .

A pity that he could no longer see Els in his thoughts as he had done when sailing up the Kali-Woga. To her, he obviously had turned back into that old Anton; to him . . . Nonsense. No sentiment, now. There they go, son.

He wrote for over an hour. By then he had also finished his note to Brits-Jansen, and went to have a nightcap with Annema on the porch, which the mosquito curtain turned into a four-posted bed. Annema was a little sad to see him go; not that nothing ever happened in Manokwari, but it was nice to have a colleague to talk to, for once. He talked about the monsoon that was due any day now, and the price of penis sheaths that had doubled since his arrival; then he said, "I have some experience myself of sitting about in the jungle without much to do; I advise you to keep a diary. And in case you have any trouble with Burubi, fight him with his own weapons. If he starts any hocus-pocus, you hocus-pocus right back."

"Hocus-pocus?"

"That's right."

Anton smiled. He began to like the little man. "You hocus-pocus right back"—how funny it would be, if that advice were to save his life. The only pity was that he hadn't the faintest idea what the man meant. It sounded like a sort of home remedy: *Dr. Annema's Hocus-Pocus Water for Live Forest Impurities,* and a picture on the bottle of a horde of little devils that . . .

"Have another," said Annema. "I've got a warehouseful."

«« »»

All the days and all the nights that the prahu sailed along the coast, the drums of the Papuans rolled behind the wall of the jungle. It was the same sound that had accompanied Teddy and him when they sailed along the same coast with the *R. 9,* but this time it sounded different. It seemed to him as if he began to understand the syncopated message of the distant thunder of the drums: "Ma-ma-wi—Ma-ma-wi—Ma-ma-wi."

Of course, it was nonsense. It was he himself who was different, not the drums. At the time he had been just a sightseer, the coast had been a spectacle and the jungle a romantic background. Now he was to live in that jungle all alone, for three months at a stretch, until the prahu of the inspection doctor called with his rations.

They rounded the cape once more and sailed up the creek until they got stuck in the gluey layer of refuse in front of the jetty. They were attacked once more by a cloud of bloodthirsty hornets and once more they roused hordes of invisible animals that rustled and ran in the wilderness as they pulled themselves toward the creaking jetty. When, at last, he swung himself ashore, and looked around, he realized that time was at a stop in Outpost Mamawi. The reeds sowed downy seeds over the water; the smell of freshly baked bread turned into the stench of rotting roots; the alang-alang had overgrown the clearing, and the railway carriage had vanished under the vines and the creepers once more. All traces of their visit had been wiped out by the wilderness. Only after long searching did he find the grave. The wooden cross was lying face downward, gnawed through by ants.

Inside the carriage, a new tangle of pale roots had penetrated the broken windows. Once more the soldiers of his escort had to spend hours cutting them with their parangs and carrying them outside by the armful. When at last the interior was cleared, he saw that nothing had changed there either. The moldy shoes still stood in the corner, the rusty skeleton of the sun helmet still hung from the communication cord, the iron table and the rusty chest still stood in the same spot, the enamel plates still warned him not to spit, or to get out before the train stopped. As he started to clear out the last of the rubbish and lifted the remains of the sun helmet off the communication cord, he found a third plate: *Pull Only in Case of Danger.*

The reoccupation of outpost Mamawi took three days. During that time, the soldiers cleared away the undergrowth round the carriage, cut the reeds and the weeds that had overgrown the clearing and burned them in a huge bonfire. The path to the jetty was widened and hardened with turf, the jetty itself was demolished and a new one constructed with hardwood from the jungle. The layer of refuse in the dead end of the creek was raked ashore, where it lay stinking horribly for a day, after which it solidified into a stone-hard gray mass. The instruments, the furniture and the stores of medicines and provisions were carried in and neatly arranged. After three days, the railway carriage looked almost homey, with a camp bed, a dining corner, three cupboards, two canvas chairs and a low table. A sturdy table had been put up outside, underneath a shelter of palm leaves that would serve as a laboratory. It communicated with the living quarters via the door at the end, which had once enabled the conductor to step from carriage to carriage. All but one door in the side facing the clearing were removed, and their openings were sealed with galvanized mosquito screens. A platform was built in front along the whole length of the carriage, with an awning of palm leaves and a balustrade of bamboo. The result was a most inviting verandah; Anton carried out the two deck-chairs and the low table to try it. Then he saw the corporal grin, and carried the second chair back inside. Finally, shutters were made for the open doorways; they would not offer any protection against bullets but were arrowproof.

During those three days of preparation Anton came to enjoy the prospect of remaining there alone. Every hour the wilderness gave him back greater resilience, vigor and self-confidence; when, at last, on the afternoon of the fourth day, the prahu with the coolies and the soldiers sailed away, he had once more attained that state of superiority and lucidity for which he always longed with nostalgia outside the magic circle of the jungle. The moment the prahu rounded the cape, the drums of the Papuans, that had been silent since their arrival in Mamawi, began to roll once more in the distance; but they did not roll for long. When evening fell, it was silent in the jungle for a while: the chirping, zooming, twilight silence of cicadas and mosquitoes, that would soon give way to the warbling, quacking, fluting and rustling of the feverish night. He lit the lamp, sat down at his desk and arranged his papers. He prepared a card index for patients, started his log book and his personal diary. When at last he went to bed and turned down the lamp, it was night.

He lay in the darkness listening to the night sounds of the wilderness, and it penetrated to him that something had changed since the prahu went away. Something was lacking, something that had at the same time irked and stimulated him, and it left an odd, depressing void. A feeling had vanished: a feeling of alertness, of wanting to turn round quickly and unexpectedly, a feeling of tension in the nape of his neck. Then he realized that since the prahu had sailed away and the drums had stopped, nobody had watched him. The jungle was empty. The eyes that he had felt on him all the time, that had peered at him and accompanied him for all those weeks during his trek through the forest with Teddy and the soldiers, had turned away from him, to accompany the prahu that was now sailing slowly along the coast. It was as if the mysterious intelligence in the forest had lost interest in him, now that he was imprisoned in that railway carriage at the edge of the wilderness, from which he could not possibly escape.

At first he tried to tell himself that it was a relief, but he could not sleep, for in the darkness he began to see something clearly: the reason why he had come to Mamawi. He had come, like Ganwitz, to challenge the unknown man in the wilderness to a duel for its possession. Alone in the jungle, as he had been when he had gone to see Brits-Jansen in Atjeh, he was afraid, but the moment he felt another human presence, he was invincible. It was an alarming conclusion, and it filled him with a sudden sickening fear. For if it was true, if he had indeed been forgotten by all the men in this jungle, even by his enemies, then Burubi, the magician, had uncovered his one vulnerable spot without hesitation. Then he was left to the loneliness and his conscience; the Papuans had left it to God to finish him off.

He lay staring with wide-open eyes into the darkness, listening to the noises in the jungle. It was full of noises, yet it was empty. The sixth sense that had awakened in him once more under the spell of the wilderness groped vainly in the emptiness. There were no more people around Outpost Mamawi. He was alone.

He jumped up off his bed and stumbled in the darkness, groping along his cupboards, the chair, the table; his trembling fingers felt the lamp, took off the glass, struck a match, and lit it. He slumped in his chair and stared at the growing flame in the lamp, at his files, his card index, his log book, his diary. Only then did he realize that, again, he had conformed to a plan. Sweating motionless, alone in the chirping night, he felt as if everything he had done since first setting foot in Mamawi had conformed to that plan. The finding of the dying man, the digging of the grave, the somber listening to the "Wedding March of the Teddy Bears," the birth of Jacob, his talk with Kramer in the white office, everything that had happened to him since he had first discerned the sweet sickly smell of rotting roots had been arranged beforehand, in a master scheme, with as its goal: this. Loneliness, silence, and a slow, crazy fear.

It was a fear more chilling than the one that had lashed him on through the jungle of Atjeh toward Camp Lung Plague. Then he had known this same sensation of being alone in the wilderness, utterly alone, a stumbling, lonely manikin in a colossal world of dark giant trees, a feverish second in eternity; but then he had been able to turn that fear into activity; then he had run faster and faster along the swampy winding trail, through rustling tunnels of foliage; he had crashed through the undergrowth, galloped over soft mossy ground, splashed through murmuring brooks, scrambled up and down slippery rocks; then he had had a goal, a hope: people. Four more days, three more, two, and he would see the first of the telephone poles with the beer bottles, would rush along the widening trail, jumping, stumbling, panting, to collapse at the sight of that ultimate security: a fellow man.

Now he felt the same fear, and although it was still faint and innocent, it would grow, slowly groping like a poisonous creeper; it would overgrow his sense of proportion, until he was changed once more into that second in eternity, that helpless ant, scrambling in a forest as vast as the world, that damned soul, banished to an uninhabited, ghostly planet. But this time, all he could do was to remain seated where he was: motionless, staring, sweating. For wherever he might go this time, wherever he might stumble, run, call, scream, there would be no answer. Human life would retract beyond the reach of his senses, recoil from his groping hands, back away from his wailing cries, but it would close in on him from behind, soundless, imperceptible. It would let him stumble on, center of a circle of loneliness, until, at last, he would collapse and die of hunger, exhaustion and fear. Only on the threshold of death, in that very last moment of irrevocable dissolution, would he see black shadows creep nearer, watching him. Then, as he lay in his last coma, they would turn him on his back and prod him, as they had prodded the dying man in that hut of palm leaves, lonely in that lake of grass. He knew, suddenly, who had been the man descended from the Cross, lying on that slab with broken eyes, a beetle scurrying in the weeds of his beard, and whom, naïvely, he had tried to nurse back to life. The Unknown European in the grave outside was Doctor Ganwitz, his predecessor.

During that first night of solitude, in the railway carriage of Mamawi, he saw, as if it were enacted in front of his staring eyes, what must have destroyed Ganwitz in this wilderness; he saw how loneliness had bewitched him, turned him into a chattering madman; how he had burst into tears at the hand stretched out to him from the jungle: the bottle with the cry for help from a fellow human being; how he had ventured into the forest with his gun and his haversack with instruments, and how he had been worn down, emaciated, driven to death in the center of that circle of loneliness. It was the same process that Frolick must have gone through in Kakoto, the age-old formula of the native against the isolated pirates of the East Indian Company. This was what he had been longing for in his folly, his egotism; here he sat, free of past and future, free of Els and the child, of Holland and Batavia, of all responsibility for what he had done. It had seemed a place of retreat, he had seen that rusty railway carriage in the jungle in his mind's eye as the bare, chaste cell of a monk, where he would be alone with a compassionate and understanding God. Only now, now the door had been slammed shut behind him and bolted, did it turn out to be a condemned cell, where he sat waiting for torture and the scaffold.

As he sat staring motionlessly at the lamp flame in the mindless mirth of the jungle night, the fear became so choking that he forced himself to get up and fuss about the hut, dragging chairs and tables from one spot to the other, emptying cupboards and arranging them anew; until at last the steam clouds of the blue daybreak began to float slowly up the trunks of the trees, and the birds in the foliage and the little animals in the under-growth started the same clear noises of the morning.

It seemed as if, together with the sunlight, reason flowed back into the vortex of his terror. During the first day, he managed to busy himself with little jobs which, for a number of hours, brought him a feeling of security. But when the sun set behind the ramparts of the forest, the fear returned. This time he resisted, grimly. He began by formulating exactly what was happening to him. He knew that by sitting there, sleepless, staring, he surrendered to his most exaggerated thoughts. He knew that he should sleep at all costs. He knew that he should cling to the arrival of the inspection prahu, three months away. But three months in the jungle were longer than three years in civilization. Within three months, the reeds and the alang-alang would be back in the clearing. The creepers would have encircled and overgrown his hut once more, the white roots would have groped and curled their way inside the hot iron greenhouse, to smother and choke with a tangle of wet webs everything he had put up so self-confidently, and recklessly.

He started a letter to Bert. He wrote for hours, reread the beginning of the letter after refilling the lamp. It seemed as if, during those few hours, he had drifted so far away from the man that had begun to formulate his thoughts when the lamp was full that the letter almost read like one from a stranger. Yet he would finish it. He would note down hour after hour, day by day, what was happening to him. At last, he slumped onto his bed with a hammering headache and burning eyes. He got up again in his half sleep to write on a piece of paper, *Rubbish dump—latrine*. When, the next morning, he woke up in the blue dawn, he found the paper and could not remember having written it. It looked like a message left behind by someone whose watch he was taking over. A message from the postmaster to the harbor master of Mamawi.

This was nonsense. This was despicable, spineless cowardice. Frolick, for God's sake, had been sitting in that jungle for over a year before his personality split. He hadn't been alone for two days yet. The realization of how easy it was to split into a postmaster and a harbor master, an angel and a devil, even after a couple of nights, made him shake off the spell of the wilderness with determination. He managed to keep himself under control, to fall asleep at night before the fear began to whisper. In the daytime he dug, chopped wood, raked the clearing, worked himself to a standstill, to slump on his bed at sunset like an insensitive body and sink into the unconsciousness of a leaden sleep. He labored, dragged, carted, for a whole week, until in the morning he could hardly move his limbs for stiffness and pain; on the eighth day, it started to rain.

At first, it came as a relief: the distant lightning, the growling thunder, the wind foaming through the trees; the shuddering, swelling tremors of the approaching thunder claps, the tremendous twitching ferns of lightning; and then, at last, with a clatter and a roar that crushed all other sounds, the cataract of an endless cloudburst. Endless, endless. When it started it seemed that this violence of falling water could only last an hour at the utmost; but after the cloudburst had continued the whole afternoon and changed the world into a steaming, boiling chaos, night fell without bringing any change in the violence. He was suddenly overcome once more by the fear of loneliness. Now that he sat there defenseless, immobilized by that incredible rain, it threw itself upon him once more. Everything he had achieved during that week of Herculean labor was washed away within a few hours. The paths, the flower bed, the rubbish dump, the latrine, the dike along the edge of the creek, all of it dissolved under the onslaught of thundering water, until he himself seemed to be cast adrift in his iron coffin and torn along by a colossal flood, last spark of life in the destruction of his creation by a wrathful god.

That first night of the rains was the worst; after that came, under the uninterrupted, monotonous drumming of the rain on the iron roof, the slow anesthesia of putrefaction. Everything grew moist, clammy, wet, everything began to soften, to warp, to swell, to grow moldy in that stifling hothouse. Books fell out of their covers; his letter to Bert became unreadable because the pages started to print the writing upon one another. In the end, the pages glued together into one solid mass. The wood began to warp, to crack, the leather began to swell up until it was covered with a green fur, the metal began to rust, the bedclothes to smell. On the morning of the fourth day of rain, he found fungi everywhere in the hut: soft yellow ears growing out of cracks, joints, food scraps, the sink, the pen tray. The dust of the dry months sprang to life under the rain; life became a battle with the invading jungle.

But with the fungi, the mildew, the sweet smell of freshly baked bread, came the anesthesia: the indifference, the sleepiness, less and less illuminated by flashes of consciousness, dimly, like the flashes of lightning in the steaming chaos outside. After a couple of days, he let the fungi grow, watched with an impersonal, almost fascinated interest the first white feelers creep through the cracks of the door and the shutters. He became lighthearted, and walked, humming, to and fro in the little iron tunnel, sometimes grinning, sometimes singing, sometimes leaning against the wall, staring dumbly at the pigsty that the jungle had made of the hut, sometimes banging on the iron wall with his fists, calling at the rain, "Hey! Stop! Hey! Have you finished? Hey! Stop that goddamned noise!" He lost the notion of day and night, of time and date; it might be the tenth, it might be the thirtieth day when, with a mixture of drunken giggles and a last desperate notion of disaster, he began to play at trains. "Tickets, please." "Don't lean out of the window." "Hey! don't open before the train stops!" He pointed at the notice, *Pull only in Case of Danger,* leaned against the wall, weak with laughter, and pulled. In the corner of the hut, something fell on the floor with a clatter.

He shuffled toward it, knelt down, peered and groped, and found a rusty key. Key? There was nothing here that could be opened or shut with a key. He took it to the wastepaper basket, a cretinous action, and dropped it. It fell on the floor. He stooped to pick it up and saw, under the table, the iron chest that no one had managed to dislodge. He crawled toward it, scraped and hacked at the rust and uncovered a little hole, a keyhole.

He tried to put the key into the hole. He had to hammer it in with the heel of his shoe because of the rust. He tried to turn the key, but it would not budge. He got a pair of pliers and wrenched the key round. It turned with a screech and a click. He tried to open the lid of the chest, but it was rusted solid. He fetched his parang, hammered the blade into the crack and heaved. The lid screeched, the crack widened; he heaved once more with all his might, the lid squeaked open, and broke its hinges. Inside the chest, he found a second chest, made of tin. He hacked at it with his parang. It was full of instruments, books, and cardboard boxes. He took one of the books out. It was closed with a small lock. He tore the lock off with the pliers, opened the book, and found it was filled with handwriting. He turned the pages; they were full of photographs, railway tickets, picture postcards, hotel bills, menus. He leafed back to the title page: *Diary, March '21—January '22.* He counted thirteen of those books. On the flyleaf of the last one was written, *Diary Mamawi.* It was only half full, and nothing was pasted onto the pages. He took one of the cardboard boxes out of the chest and opened it. It was filled with oblong packets wrapped in tissue paper. He tore the paper, and found a lock of hair. The hair was fair and glossy, and held together with a thin blue ribbon. From the ribbon dangled a label: *Mitzi, Budapest. May-August, 1919. Many long enchanted nights, My head did slumber on your breast,—But, my heart, O dearest mousey, Did not find its peace, its rest.* . . . He opened other packets, found more locks of hair, all of them labeled with names and poems. He took a second box out of the chest, and found that one to be full of hair locks too. He put it back, recovered the last book from the confusion he had made of the contents, and opened it at the first page.

Friday, January 19. A moment ago, I watched the prahu with the soldiers vanish around the cape and now I am alone in Mamawi. The crazy carriage looks almost cozy now, with its verandah and the shutters in front of the doorways. . . . .

The roar of the rain faded before a voice that, whispering, enticed him back to consciousness. As he sat reading the thoughts of someone else who had traveled the same road, he slowly found his way back, out of the spell of the jungle. It was as if he were reading his own history, observed and related by a wise and experienced man. When the man had reached the point where he was now: sitting dazed in an iron coffin under the lashing rain, with the invading wilderness feeling its way through the cracks, degenerated in his own filth and the mildewed remains of his humanity, he stopped reading. He looked around, and saw. He saw the fungi, the filth, the confusion, the warped wrecks of his cupboards, the shapeless lumps of his log and his diary, the animal's lair that was his bed. He put the book aside, cautiously, as if it were alive, and cleaned his stable.

He opened the door and flung the refuse out. He filled a bucket with the rain water that clattered down from the roof of the verandah, and scrubbed the floor with soap and disinfectant. He scraped off the fungi, cut off the tangled creepers, scrubbed until the last vestige of mildew had vanished. Later, when the hut was empty and clean, he cut his beard, heated water, cleaned the sink and shaved. The rain clattered, splashed, the wind lashed the roof with the whips of wet branches and furious gusts of water, but, for the first time, he heard those sounds for what they really were: rain and wind. After he had shaved, he made tea, cooked a meal, ate it and washed up. Then he filled a pipe, lit the lamp and sat down to read on.

Now, at last, the rains have stopped, the dance of death is starting in earnest. Something I had never expected has happened; the Papuans have come back. I can't see them, I don't hear them, but I know: they are there. . . .

Doctor Ganwitz of Mamawi, rotting in the rain, had come to the aid of the young colleague who, once upon a time, had almost saved his life.

«« »»»

It took him days to read the thirteen diaries. He read continuously, as long as daylight lasted, while the rain grew in volume and fury, until in the end it seemed to pound on the roof with clattering claws, an enraged monster that saw its prey escape. The moment he caught himself thinking in that vein, he said aloud, "Stop it. Whatever happens, don't give the jungle a personality. It is rain, ordinary, straightforward rain." It might be, but it was very heavy, and it never stopped. It prevented him from going outside, it kept him prisoner in his iron cell, and would do so for weeks to come. As he sat reading Ganwitz's daily report of that same rain, he realized how he had been saved in the nick of time. For Ganwitz was a giant compared to him; Ganwitz knew the wilderness as intimately as Brits-Jansen did, and Ganwitz confessed the rain got on his nerves in the end. If it had got on Ganwitz's nerves, it would have driven him out of his mind. He smiled, a bit wanly, at the thought that he was, despite everything, still a totok compared to those men. He had crawled through the needle's eye. "Camel through the needle's eye . . ." The image of his father, dream penguin, floated in the darkness of the far corner, and he thought he heard the ticking of the grandfather clock. It suddenly seemed incredible that the vicar's child who had sat listening to his father's pious monologues during those long winter evenings was the same person as the man now caught in a railway carriage in the jungle. He hastily read on.

The moment he read on, he felt certain once more that he would make it. Here was a man, twenty times as strong as he, who had gone through it all and left behind a minute report of what would happen. He felt as if he were protected by a super Brits-Jansen; for the more he read, the more impressed he was by the personality that rose out of those pages. At first he was horrified, as he found out what was still in store for him if Burubi were to give him the same treatment that he had given his previous prisoner, but soon it was Ganwitz's personality that impressed him more.

Never before had he identified himself so passionately with another human being. Never before had he come to know a neighbor so intimately, eavesdropping on his innermost thoughts, following all his moods, watching all his up-and-downs of despair and exultation. It was a long story, a story of loneliness. Youth in Budapest, Heidelberg, Vienna; medical officer in the 1914-1918 war, prisoner of war in England, ship's doctor on a hadji ship; in the end: jungle doctor of the Dutch Government Health Service. And all that time he yearned pathetically for some affection, for someone to share his life; at the same time this longing was dissected and ridiculed by a second ego, watching over his shoulder, smiling contemptuously at his homesickness for love. Countless theories about the meaning of life, God, survival after death, good and evil, guilt and conscience, came and went in the course of the years, surprising in their originality and brilliance, only to be defeated by the originality and the brilliance of their counter-arguments. When the wanderer arrived at last in Mamawi, he had come back to his point of departure: a lonely soul, longing for some affection; the only difference was that by then he had lost hope. He would never share his life with someone else, for he would never rid himself of that ghostly companion within his own soul, the contemptuous analyst of his lonely heart. Imprisoned in the lonely railway carriage in the tropical rains, he had written his own verdict on the pages of his diary. It was a negative credo, that ended in the complete acceptance of the senselessness of life.

When the rains had stopped, he had hoped that the purgatory was ended, that at last he would be able to forget himself by succoring the sick, the hordes of patients that would come out of the jungle. But no patients came. He waited, day after day sitting at his table in the clearing in front of the hut; every evening, he carefully packed the instruments, the syringes, the ampoules, the cotton wool, the bandages that he had unpacked and arrayed on his table that morning. Then something arrived at last: bottles. Flat, brown bottles, that he found on his table, a new one every morning. Bottles of whisky, arriving out of nowhere on the table in his hut, at dead of night. He analyzed the whisky; it was not poison. It was just whisky. He tasted the whisky; it was good. *Golden Silk* the label said, *Distilled by John MacLaren & Sons, Pitlochry, Scotland,* with, as a trademark, a little dog walking on its hind legs, blowing bagpipes. He drank a glass of it. It was excellent whisky, and he was given a full bottle every day. He realized of course that there was a trick in it somewhere, that the witch doctor of the Papuans not only wanted to terrify him with the mysterious arrival of those bottles, but also hoped that he would drink himself senseless.

He started by stating that, of course, he was not that much of a simpleton. He would deal with that black juggler all right. After all, he had thirty years' experience of dealing with black jugglers and he enjoyed the prospect. He did not drink the whisky; he kept watch day and night, to find out who put those bottles down. He concealed himself, under the table, in the cupboard, under his bed. He sat watching the door for hours from his hiding place, but nothing happened. But if he turned round, or shut his eyes for no more than a second, there was a bottle on the table. He barricaded the door, he sat upright in his bed, his gun across his knees, staring at the table; but no one could stare at a table for twenty-four hours at a stretch. When he dozed off for a minute and came to with a start, there was a bottle on the table. In the end he thought, what does it matter? In the corner of the carriage the stack of bottles grew daily. He opened one and drank.

The drink clarified his thoughts: he suddenly saw through the whole setup. He divined all the ruses and the subterfuges of that sly primitive brain. He took another gulp and his thoughts cleared even more; he lost interest in the brain. He was fascinated by a new theory of the meaning of life and death that he had been thinking about for days and to which those two drinks had suddenly provided the missing fragment, as of a jigsaw puzzle. He wrote a long dissertation in his diary, pages and pages of it, drinking all the time, until it ended in gibberish. The following day, he started afresh, to end in gibberish once more. Every day now he emptied the bottle that he found on his table in the morning. Every day he assailed the mystery of life and death in his diary, on the principle that it was not his personality or his life that mattered. He was a dead loss anyhow. The only thing he could do to make his life worth while was to write down that theory, the pellets of gold washed out of the loose sand of his existence.

But every day his writing became less legible, his reasoning less coherent. He started to write in German, in Hungarian; in the end he mixed three languages in the same sentence. Then followed a note: *No bottle today.* Another one: *Today again no bottle.* Then followed a series of days without bottles, and in that sobriety, suddenly the realization: *But I cannot surrender like this! It is impossible that this creature should overpower me. I know what he wants. I know that he wants to turn me into a drunken sot. Why did I drink? It is not only the loneliness or the exhaustion. There is another reason for this defeat. Could it be that I am bewitched? Guna-guna tricks about. Quite possible. I'll go and investigate at once. Later. Have unearthed an egg, buried underneath the steps to the verandah. An egg about three inches long. I found on it inscriptions made by a human hand. Guna-guna tricks all right.*

After that followed the most remarkable page of the thirteen books. The page that Anton read and reread until he knew it by heart. It was a brilliant analysis of guna-guna, the black magic of the wilderness, and most remarkable of all was the conclusion at which Ganwitz arrived. According to him, there was only one antidote against the guna-guna of the native witch doctors and that was the white magic of Christianity. He wrote about patients that he had seen wither away with inexplicable ailments, and who revived when a nun came to them as a nurse, to succor them in their last hours. He told of a dying man who had suddenly and inexplicably got up from his deathbed and staggered out onto the verandah; he had found out later that, at that very moment, a stranger had come into the house: an old schoolteacher, whom everyone took to be an eccentric but who turned out to be one of the purest Christians he had ever met. It sounded like a fantastic theory but, according to Ganwitz, it was white magic and white magic alone that could counteract the effects of guna-guna. Conditions for the achievement of the power of white magic were: absolute abstinence in all sensual matters, an entirely chaste and unselfish life, a complete effacement of the ego for the sake of the other or others; and this not just for a couple of months or so, but for years; Ganwitz's estimate of the minimum was twelve years. He knew full well that he himself had no powers of white magic, and that made him powerless in the face of the guna-guna of the witch doctor from the wilderness. His last entry ran, *Today, suddenly, another bottle. Opened it with shaking hands, simpering with relief. Inside was a note written with red pencil: "138:14:1 East, 2:47:18 South, very ill, for God's sake send help Vollenhove Bergmans dead Ringers dying for God's sake Flabbinga." No whisky.* That was the end of the diary.

The theory about black and white magic urged Anton to write down his thoughts. He remembered the conversation he had had with Brits-Jansen, that afternoon in his laboratory in Man-Pu-Ko-Chu. "Black and white magic," Brits-Jansen had said, "are not two different faculties. They use the same power destructively or creatively. The important thing is: it is the same power." Now, after Ganwitz's diagnosis of guna-guna, he wanted to write himself, impelled by a great feeling of urgency, as if the plan that had formed in his mind would escape him if he did not formulate it at once; but there was no paper left except for the blank pages in Ganwitz's last diary. The paper he had brought from Manokwari had been spoiled by moisture. Then his feeling of urgency became more compelling, and he realized something had changed. He looked round, suddenly tense and alert, but everything looked the same. Then he heard it: the rain had stopped. It was silent. If he were indeed being submitted to the same treatment as Ganwitz before him, the duel with the witch doctor was about to begin.

It was a dangerous moment. Everything depended on what he did now. He should defeat that Papuan as from their first meeting. One thing was certain: it would be a battle of life and death; it would end only with the extermination of one of them. Everything he did should converge on that one aim: to entice the witch doctor into the open and shoot him like a beast of prey. To defeat Burubi in the jungle was impossible; he should entice Burubi to come to him, to hazard within reach of his gun.

He cleaned the gun and loaded it. Then he went outside for the first time since the rains had started. The forest lay steaming in misty sunlight; the birds and the small animals chirruped and palpitated in the dripping shrubs and the steaming foliage as if it were the first morning after the Great Flood. The clearing had turned into wilderness once more, and the jungle leaned on the roof of the railway carriage. He would have to start all over again.

When he came back inside, he found a bottle on the table.

<<< >>>

He stood looking at the bottle for a long time. It was a bottle like the one that had contained Flabbinga's message, of which he had seen dozens strewn on the floor of the hut of palm leaves. *Golden Silk—Distilled by John MacLaren & Sons, Pitlochry, Scotland,* and the little dog with the bagpipes.

He felt a trembling in his knees, but it was not fear. It could not be fear, for the bottle meant that battle had started. All the time he had sat reading, he had longed for that bottle; well, here it was. He tried to imagine what would have happened if the dead Ganwitz had not come to his aid in the nick of time. He understood now why the Papuans had killed him when he was about to escape from the jungle. They must have believed that, with him, they destroyed the secret of their black magic, their patent for the extermination of the white devils. He laughed, nervously, when he thought of Doctor Annema's hunting water. Burubi obviously had his own. There they go, son.

But he was one step ahead of them. They must be convinced that he did now know how all this would end, that he would sit staring at that bottle in unbelief, wondering whether he had gone mad. He was certain that if he were to dig underneath the steps to the verandah, he would find an egg with magic symbols on it. He must be careful now, never hurry, never lose that goal from sight: to entice Burubi out of his hiding place and shoot him down with Ganwitz's gun. He felt as if Ganwitz were with him, as if during those days of reading he had absorbed more than just his thoughts: some of his personality, his soul. It was a silly thought, but he did not suppress it. Against Burubi's hocus-pocus he needed . . .

And then he knew. He heard Annema's voice again, "In case you have any trouble with Burubi, fight him with his own weapons. If he starts any hocus-pocus, you hocus-pocus right back." He remembered his thought at the time: how funny it would be if that advice were one day to save his life, but how, he had no idea. Now he knew. Dr. Annema had, with that advice, indeed saved his life. He suddenly saw what Dr. Annema's hunting water was. There they go, son! God bless Doctor Annema, with his penis sheaths and his Kalebas pipes. God bless Friesia in the wilderness.

He saw, at once, his whole plan complete. It was very simple, but it should be executed with great care, and with a great sense of detail. Kramer had been right: he did not stand here as the first missionary, but as the first raider. Ganwitz had had himself beheaded in the jungle; he would keep his head, to the undying glory of the East Indian Company. He would teach that murderer of Mamawi the lesson of his life; he would revenge the thousands of middle-class boys slaughtered in this hot wilderness, ever since that morning long ago when the first plump ship with bulky sails and pot-bellied cannons came tacking up the creek, flying a Dutch flag as big as a house.

The bottles had always been put down in the same spot: on the table. The table still stood where it had been when Ganwitz was here. It was unlikely that the Papuans sneaked in via the door; Ganwitz had barricaded it and the bottle had arrived all the same. Hocus-pocus was nonsense; here he stood, freshly washed, shaved, and with his peasant's cunning unimpaired by the water torture. Whoever wanted to tell him that those bottles ended up on the table by supernatural means could tell him another. Over the table was a ventilator with an iron cap outside. He had had his eye on the hole of the ventilator, from the first mention by Ganwitz of the mysterious arrival of a bottle on that table. Probably the cap was loose; a Papuan crawling over the roof on all fours would hardly be audible above the sound of the wind in the trees. Those creatures were as silent as cats.

Of course, that must be it: they spied on him through the cracks of the shutters or through the slits in the hood of the ventilator, until he turned round. Then, quick as lightning, they lifted off the cap, lowered the bottle and put back the cap.

How did they lower it? With a rope? Or a loop of rattan? It would take them too long. Probably they put their arm through the hole, perhaps with a short length of rope to put the bottle down inaudibly. Would the witch doctor do it himself? Probably not. He must have stooges to do that.

Now, how could he bring that witch doctor to climb onto that roof himself? Only by applying Dr. Annema's hunting water. By terrifying the stooges to such an extent that they could not be forced to hazard onto that roof themselves, not even by the most gruesome threats. He must give a performance of hocus-pocus that would keep them awake nights with chattering teeth, and he must do so in the open, visible to all the spying eyes in the trees and shrubs around the railway carriage of Mamawi.

But at first, he must be certain that those bottles were indeed lowered through the hole of the ventilator; otherwise his whole plan would come to naught. He opened one of the boxes containing Ganwitz's souvenirs of love, took out one lock of hair. *Many long and tender nights . . .* He pulled out six long blond hairs, waited until dusk so that the spies outside could not see what he was doing, then pasted them crosswise across the opening of the ventilator against the ceiling. It was a devil of a job in the heat, fiddling with his hands above his head, in almost pitch darkness. When at last he lit the lamp, he started to hunt mosquitoes with the swatter so as to look at the ceiling without betraying the fact that he was inspecting his work. He saw they were perfectly fixed; if someone were to put his hand through the hole from above, he would break the hairs without fail.

He prepared a meal and ate it standing at the sink, for he did not want to use the table. He wanted to leave the bottle where it was. He spent the rest of the evening cleaning the tiger trap the major in Manokwari had forced upon him. Now he was grateful for it; without that trap, his plan would have become much more complicated.

When he had finished, he smoked a last pipe and leafed through Ganwitz's diaries once more. Instead of its being his last pipe, it became the first of many, for he read on until the dawn. He read and reread at least twenty times the minute description Ganwitz had given of the rites and the magic dances of the Papuans, written when he was stationed in Hollandia. At last he fell asleep on his bed without undressing.

He was waked up by the sunlight and the birds. He was wide awake at once and looked at the table. A second bottle stood beside the first. He got up and inspected the hairs across the hole: they were broken.

To see that he had been right made him decide to risk it. He went outside with a spade, put the steps to the verandah aside and started to dig. After three spadefuls, he found the egg. He did not look at it; he went inside, got the two bottles and walked to the center of the clearing. There he cried, loudly and clearly, "Nuts, Burubi! Nuts to you and your monkey tricks!" And he flung the bottles and the egg one after the other into the forest.

It seemed as if a shiver went through the wilderness; but watch out, my friend! That was childish imagination: the wilderness was a collection of trees and shrubs, and these did not shiver unless there was a wind blowing. There was no wind. It was still. The birds twittered gaily in the trees. He went back into the carriage, closed the door, and made a scarecrow out of two sticks and a set of soiled clothes, which he filled with straw from his mattress. As he cut open the mattress, he was stifled by the stench of moisture and mildew, but he did not open the shutters or the door. He worked on, with quick concentration, until the scarecrow was finished. Then he slumped in his chair, sweating, and waited for night to fall.

At dusk he put everything ready. He emptied Ganwitz's boxes, and arrayed the locks of hair in rows on the table. He loaded his gun, put it with his parang against the table. When it was too dark for those outside to see what he was doing, he fixed the tiger trap at the ceiling, in the way he had rehearsed countless times in his mind that day, staring at the ventilator. He fitted the murderous instrument, its toothed jaws spread wide, underneath the hole in such a fashion that it could not be seen from above. Then, with great caution, he wedged a thin strip of bamboo between the side of the hole in the ceiling and the trigger of the trap. The trap smashed three strips before at last its jaws remained gaping, precariously. The little bamboo strip was the one weak point; the Papuan might see it. But he would probably not look, and, even if he did, those bottles were obviously lowered in darkness or at the first flush of daybreak, when it was still too dark for him to see clearly.

When everything was ready, he removed all his clothes except his shoes. He put his belt round his bare waist and attached to it all the locks of hair, one by one, until he wore a little skirt. There were plenty of them; Mitzi, Liesl, Yolan, Eva—all those mementos of the blissful hours of the lonely man in the jungle were dangling, poems and all, around his waist. It seemed sacrilege, yet he knew that the dead Ganwitz would delight in the sight. He must look ludicrous with his white legs and plump shoes, stark naked but for a skirt of hair locks that was far too short. When he put on his helmet, he burst out laughing; but he took a grip on himself at once, for the laughter seemed to release his nerves.

He drenched the scarecrow with paraffin, lit all five storm lanterns, took them like a bunch of light in his left hand, in his right hand he took his gun and his parang, then he put one arm round the smelly scarecrow and staggered outside, pushing open the door with his knee.

Before going down the steps to the clearing, he had a moment of fear, a sort of stage fright, for he felt that hundreds of eyes were staring at him from the darkness. He suddenly felt like a crazy milkman, carrying all those tools; why a milkman, for God's sake, he didn't know. Then it seemed as if the ghosts of his murdered predecessors closed their ranks behind him, a phalanx of revenge, many, many more than he had thought, and he marched toward the center of the clearing, singing:

> *Wedding march of the Teddy Bears,*
> *They come prancing down in pairs,*
> *They give hairy, beary kisses,*
> *And they tickle the bear missus. . . .*

He stuck the scarecrow upright in the ground.

> *Lots of luck and happiness . . .*

He put the lanterns in a five-pointed star around the scarecrow.

> *To the Teddies of Loch Ness . . .*

Christ Almighty! He had forgotten the matches.
For one second, he stood petrified. If he went back now, the whole performance would flounder.

> *Wedding march of the Teddy Bears!*

he crowed, with a prayer in his thoughts, while he pressed the muzzle of his gun into the chest of the scarecrow.

> *They come prancing down in pairs . . .*

With a double thunderclap and a flash that blinded him, the gun went off. He stood for a few seconds, cringing with pain, with a horrible feeling of utter failure in a darkness full of whirling stars, pressing his hands in his stomach. Then the miracle happened: with a soft crackling and a stifling stench, the straw began to burn. What had seemed a miserable failure turned into a triumph: this exploding into fire after the lightning of the shot was even better than if he had lit the damned thing with matches.

> *Wedding march of the Teddy Bears—*
> *Burubi!*
> *They come prancing down in pairs—*
> *Burubi!*

He danced, with wild, crazy jumps, around the torch of the scarecrow that started to flare up fiercely with greasy billowing smoke.

They give hairy, beary kisses—
Burubi!
And they tickle the bear. . . .

In the jungle, like an explosion, the thunder of hundreds of drums began to roll, closer and more horrifying than he had ever heard them. He wavered for one moment, then he danced on.

And they tickle the bear missus—
Burubi!
Lots of luck and happiness—
Burubi!

The drums thundered, pounded, until the earth shook; their booming rhythm seemed to call forth an echo in his body, an undulating, throbbing daze, and he found himself obeying the air-splitting rhythm from the darkness:

To—the—Teddies of—Loch—Ness;
Bu-ru-bi!
Wedding march—of the—Teddy—Bears,
Bu-ru-bi!

The pulsating throb of the drums awoke a ghost inside him, the ghost of a forefather that had danced thousands of years ago around the fires of the Stone Age, and it seemed as if that slowly awakening ghost possessed him more and more. A dark longing pulled him away slowly from that fire, transfiguring the words he screamed into senseless mouthings; his stamping, swinging, swaying limbs slowly slipped from the grip of his will. He realized with a feeling of panic that he was losing the battle, that the drums had exploded in their thundering jungle syncopation at a sign from the witch doctor, that he was busy dancing around and into the grave he had dug for the other one. Yet he was losing the power over his body more and more, his boyish plan of campaign was mercilessly hammered into a degeneration, a dizzying fall of man; his feet stamped with thousands of other black dusty feet; he thrust out his pelvis and thrust back his buttocks in a grotesque dance of fertility; he . . .

A whiplash made him scream and leap and wake up from the spell of the drums with the burning pain of hundreds of needle-sharp, vicious stabs. He thought, as he still staggered under the spell of that thundering daze, that they were arrows, that they were shooting at him with blowpipes from the wilderness, that he would collapse and bleed to death at the feet of the burning Burubi; then he realized that they were the hornets, attracted by the light. His naked body, jigging round the burning torch, was obscured by a cloud of snarling insects. They seemed to throw themselves on his defenseless skin in thousands, to tear him to shreds with lashes of hellish pain, but they saved him. He knew, while he staggered, screeching, round that fluttering torch, crazy with pain and fury, that he would fall ill, that he would not be able to move a finger the next day, that he would be swollen and raw all over; but the hornets saved him, for now he jumped so wildly, so fitfully, under the lashes of their torture, that he escaped from the deadly rhythm of the drums. The forefather fled back into his cave, the spell of the jungle released his limbs, and he turned once more into Anton, Anton Zorgdrager, doctor of the Government Health Service, middle-class boy in the haunted hothouse, who would teach those goddamned niggers the lesson of their lives. The fact that the hornets had attacked him meant that there must be hundreds of Papuans about, that they must be lying in the creek in their hollowed-out tree trunks, or the insects would not have been disturbed.

> *Wedding march of the Teddy bears!*
>
> > *—Burubi!*
>
> *They come prancing down in pairs—*
> > *Nuts, Burubi, nuts to you!*
> *They give hairy, beary kisses—*
> > *Your guts, Burubi! I'll spill your guts!*
> *And they tickle the bear missus—*
> > *A bloody mess you'll be, Burubi! I'll trample you into one bloody mess!*
> *Lots of luck and happiness!*
> > *Ha ha! Ha ha! I'm winning!*
> *Long live, long live, long live—the Teddies, the Teddies of . . .*

The scarecrow fell in a whirl of sparks. The drums fell silent.

He stood still, his heart hammering in his chest, his temples bursting. He ripped a lock of hair off his belt, held it out over the fire, cried "Mitzi —Budapest!" and dropped the lock into the flames. It caught fire with a flash, a hissing splutter, and was gone.

He ripped off a second lock. "Lotte—Vienna!" It fell, spurted fire, and went out.

"Gretchen—Heidelberg!"

He burned all the locks, one by one; the names of Ganwitz's loves echoed in the forest and vanished with blue hissing flashes in the smoldering embers of the fire. He called the names in a deep silence.

When he had burned the last lock, he stood naked in the circle of the lamps, giddy with pain and the poison of thousands of insect bites, but triumphant in his grotesque nakedness. They had not got him. He had made it. He picked up the lanterns in one hand into a bunch of light, shouldered his gun, grabbed his parang and strode back to his hut. At the top of the steps, on the verandah, he faced the wilderness once more.

"NUTS—BURUBI!" he roared. "NUTS TO YOU!"

He waited for the answer. The echo resounded and died in the caverns of the forest. Burubi was silent.

He turned round, struck his parang in the wood of the verandah in front of the door; then the door of the railway carriage slammed shut and he fell on his bed, leaving the lamps burning.

≪≪≪ ≫≫≫

When he awoke, it was daylight but there was no bottle on the table. When he tried to get up, he groaned and slumped back on his bed.

It took him over an hour to paint himself with iodine; he tried to dress but he could hardly move. He dizzied through the day in a daze; he did not eat, he did not drink, he wept with regret that he had thrown those bottles into the forest; at that moment he would have sold his soul for a glass of Golden Silk. But there was no bottle; the tiger trap was undisturbed.

That could only mean one thing: the subjects of the witch doctor refused to climb onto the roof of the white magician who had challenged Burubi and cursed him. If his plan worked, if, with Ganwitz's help, he had really fathomed the mentality of the Stone Age people in the wilderness, then Burubi would be forced to come himself. If he did not come, the battle was lost.

Toward evening the fever started; so did the drums. They rolled, rolled, they filled the jungle with the endless, monotonous rumble of their thunder. He lay, his teeth chattering, on his bed in the scalding and chilling waves of fever. He loaded his gun and put it beside his bed; that was all he could do. If they came now, they would slaughter him before he could lift an arm or stretch out his hand toward his gun. The night was a whirlpool of fiery weeds, incandescent green and violet soapsuds, floating toward him and exploding silently in the darkness, faces bobbing to and fro in red billowing smoke. He must have fallen asleep at a given moment, for something dragged him upright in a blue twilight. A loud snap, a thud, a clatter of shattering glass.

He grabbed his gun, staggered to his feet, stumbled toward the table. His shoes crunched glass under his feet; he smelled whisky. Then he looked up and saw a clawlike hand, a lower arm smashed between the jaws of the tiger trap. Blood dripped down the arm, down the hand, drops dangled from the fingertips; then something pulled at the arm, the drops fell, the trap scraped against the iron of the ceiling. He stuck his gun through the hole, pushed it up until it touched something resilient, and pulled the triggers. The explosion struck him in the face; he recoiled, stumbled, crashed to the floor and sank into oblivion.

«« »»

The flies woke him up. They flitted, golden sparks, through the red dusk of the sunset. They teemed over a dark patch on the floor, swarmed around the hand that hung from the ceiling, clustered on a dark pool on the table underneath the hand. He smelled whisky.

He got up with difficulty, but the pain was less and his head much clearer. He dragged himself to the door and opened it. As he did so, a great rustling fled into the wilderness. The sound brought back the full realization of what he had done.

He climbed onto the roof, slowly, halting with tiredness and pain after each movement. On the roof lay a black body in the sunset; an old, dirty body alive with lice and flies, a chain of teeth and beads round its neck, a dirty skirt of feathers round its hips. When he approached, his footsteps hollow on the roof, the flies swarmed up and the lice scurried aimlessly, trying to flee. The chest of the body was mutilated horribly by the double shot; when he pulled at its legs, something fell with a thud and a clatter inside the hut. He swallowed, and pulled again.

He dragged the body by its legs to the edge of the roof and pushed it over; it landed in the undergrowth with a rustling thud. He climbed down, fetched a spade, went inside and shoved the spade underneath the arm with the trap, then he carried it out. He carried it to the spot where the cross lay face downward in the weeds, and went back to get his parang.

He cut the weeds and the rattan on the hillock and dug a grave, until he hit a bone; then he stuck the spade in the ground and went back toward the hut. It was dark now. He lit a lantern and took it with him to look for the body. He dragged it out of the shrubs, across the clearing, to the grave, and pushed it in. He put the arm and trap with it. Before closing the grave, he took off the necklace and put it in his pocket.

After pressing down the earth and flattening it with his spade, he put the cross on his shoulder and went back to the hut in a cloud of mosquitoes, the shadows of his legs gigantic on the wall of the forest. He laid the cross on the verandah beside the doorway, boiled some water and scrubbed the hut with soap and disinfectant. That done, he climbed onto the roof, scrubbed the place around the ventilator, and put back the iron cap. He climbed down, took a hammer and a nail out of the toolbox, hammered the nail into the post beside the steps to the verandah and hung the necklace from it. Then he went indoors, washed himself from head to foot, and took a pot of paint and a thin brush out of the stores.

The inscription on the cross had almost disappeared. He sandpapered the wood, made himself some tea and lit a pipe. Then, like a contented handyman in his workshop, he carefully drew the letters before painting them in. He drew them between four horizontal lines drawn along the barrel of his gun: *Unknown European,* on the first line, *Unknown Papuan* on the second. When he had finished he cleared away his tools, put the cross in the corner to dry, blew out the lamp and went to bed.

Before falling asleep, he lay listening to the cacophony of the jungle night. It no longer terrified him, for the forest was full of people. The atmosphere was charged with fear, but it was no longer his own; it was the fear of the Papuans for the white magician. Tomorrow he would begin work.

He began at sunrise by dragging the table out of the shelter. He put it in front of the verandah and covered it with a sheet. On it he arranged the Salvarsan ampoules, the cotton wool, the iodine, the syringes. He picked a handful of flowers from the water's edge, put his gun and his parang crosswise on top of the blackened remains of the burnt scarecrow, and sprinkled them with flowers. Then he went back to his table, sat down behind it with Ganwitz's last diary in front of him, opened at its first clean page.

Ganwitz had ben sitting like this for days on end, in the burning sun, but no one had appeared. Only when he saw the first patient come out of the forest would he know for certain that the battle was won.

He lit a pipe, and had not even finished it when something stirred in the undergrowth on the fringe of the forest. He did not look up, he went on smoking, pretending to read. He heard the alang-alang rustle, and the dry reeds snap, as slow, cautious footsteps approached across the clearing. He kept his head down, but he looked as far ahead of him as he could under the brim of his helmet. He saw black legs come toward him, hesitating, timid; he saw the gruesome wounds of frambesia. Then he looked up.

An old Papuan stood in front of the table, emaciated and dirty. He gazed at the white magician with sad black eyes, then he licked his lips with a pink tongue and said, "Damai, tuan besar . . ."

"Damai, saudara," he replied. He stood up, went round the table, pulled a plug of cotton wool off the roll, drenched it in iodine and, after he had cleaned the spot on a trembling black arm, gave his first Salvarsan injection with a trembling hand.

The pacification of District Mamawi was accomplished.

CHAPTER FOURTEEN

WITHIN a month, Outpost Mamawi had become a model settlement. After the first day, when only two patients had dared appear, their number increased gradually, until after a week the maximum of six per day was reached. It was less than in other settlements, but it was a beginning.

In the forest, the Papuans had seemed to be prehistoric monsters; once they appeared in the filtered sunlight of the clearing in front of the railway carriage of Mamawi, they proved to be plaintive, humorless and sentimental health scheme patients, full of self-pity and spiteful gossip about their neighbors. After the first few days of bashful silence they started to chatter, and it seemed as if they came to get their injection only in order to unburden their minds. At first, Anton did not understand a word of what they were saying and tried earnestly to discover the portent of their endless jeremiads; but soon he discovered that he only needed to change the color of their skins in his mind to understand every word: "And then I said to Mrs. Smith, Mrs. Smith I said, if you throw your dirty water once more over my clean steps, I said, then I swear, I said . . ." and at the pain of the injection, they cast squinting eyes heavenward, clawed a hand in their cheek and groaned, "Oh, God, what have I done to deserve this—ouch, OUCH!—oh, God—thank you, doctor."

There was a fat old woman who came every day, waddling on swollen legs, with swinging breasts like a gorilla mother; all she did was to sit down on the other deckchair by his side and chatter, during which she ate some sort of berries from a basket on her lap. She gossiped more to the berries than to him; occasionally she offered him one by putting it down on the white sheet of the table; after a couple of days the corner of the sheet was full of purple patches. There were two gangling adolescent louts who chewed sirih manfully and spat around them like llamas, but who trembled fearfully when they were given their injection; he recruited them as aids. At first it seemed as if they preferred to live on the dole, but in the end the glory of taking part in the rituals of the white magician proved more alluring. After their wounds had been healed by the injections they began to do small jobs, which he explained to them in sign language. They dug a small vegetable garden, scrubbed the floor of the hut, stole everything they could lay their hands on, and passively let it be pulled out of their shaggy wigs every evening, before going back into the forest. The melancholy old man he had treated first, and whose name was Mutiara, spoke a few words of Malay and helped him occasionally as an interpreter.

After a few days, it became obvious that the only way to make the Papuan yokels work was to give them new names, preferably double-barreled ones. He christened the tallest of the two "Burung-Sopan," Bird of Paradise, and the other one "Kubis-Telor," Red Cabbage; the result was that they built a new shelter beside the laboratory and remained there at night instead of going back into the forest. The fat woman with the pendulous breasts moved in as well, was christened "Tunangan-Bersih," Pure Fiancée; she mumbled, sighed, and scratched her shins with her feet for hours on end before she fell asleep in her lean-to on the other side of the railway carriage. She cooked two meals a day for tuan doctor and for the two good-for-nothings he called his aides; after she had twice started a fire with the Primus and staged an elaborate faint on the verandah, Burung-Sopan and Kubis-Telor built a kitchen for her on the other side of the clearing, where she could sing and dance during her cooking, beating time with her big wooden spoons on her thighs, stopping occasionally to stir the soup with them. When Anton saw this for the first time, his stomach turned over; but on the consideration that these people had survived the Great Floods with the same hygienic methods he shrugged his shoulders and sat down at table. Although the number of patients did not increase and left him plenty of time, he was tired of cleaning his hut himself and cooking his own food; if this meant that he would be swindled by the two magpies and be fed soup by Pure Fiancée flagellating herself with her ladles, he would have to take it in his stride.

In the evenings, while smoking the last pipe of the day, he continued Ganwitz's diary in as small a writing as possible, to save space; but what he gained by scribbling microscopically he lost by an inveterate loquaciousness. He noted everything: the grimaces of the patients as he gave them their injections, the menus Tunangan-Bersih put in front of him, the odd jobs Burung-Sopan and Kubis-Telor had done; he wrote about the state his clothes were in, how many shoelaces he had left, when his parang needed sharpening; it seemed as if in this dream of self-confidence and happiness he could no longer quite see things in proportion. It was a rather odd development: now that he was sitting in the wilderness as the great white god, surrounded by childish chatterboxes who had no notion of good and evil, who reacted to sunshine with extravagant joy and to rain with the most depressing melancholia he had ever witnessed in a mammal, it seemed as if he had lost, together with his inferiority complex, his sense of values. He noticed it but it did not alarm him; he was safe as long as he kept his goal in sight: pacification.

The adoration and the attachment of the Papuans filled him with a slightly giddy pride. He was the Great One who had broken the tyranny of the black witch doctor; now he could do with these creatures whatever he liked. If he wanted war, they would fight for him, if he commanded them to go with him into the forest, they would follow him blindly; within the space of forty-eight hours he had changed from a neurasthenic on the verge of schizophrenia, a trembling white creature in a rusty railway carriage listening breathlessly to the wilderness, into a monarch as absolute as the Middle Ages had ever produced. All the conflicts, problems, and feelings of guilt he had dragged with him into the jungle withered and went within the week; after a fortnight of his rule he smiled indulgently at the memory of his soul searchings about Els, Jacob, Annie, God—they seemed ridiculous and futile preoccupations. For the first time in his life he had a feeling of being home, secure, fully conscious; and in this new reality there were only two conceptions that had any value: Salvarsan and tobacco.

Salvarsan and tobacco were the foundations of his power over the Papuans. Salvarsan caused the gruesome symptoms of frambesia to vanish within a matter of days, but one injection was not sufficient. If the cure was to be permanent, the patient had to submit himself to three injections, spread over three weeks, otherwise the disease would erupt once more within a month and with doubled intensity. Yet, he could not bring the Papuans to submit themselves to a second, let alone a third injection; the first had hurt, they were cured, why should they let themselves be hurt again? They also had no notion of time: three weeks or three years, it was too abstract for them to grasp. The only way to make them come back for another injection was by promising them a pack of tobacco on their return. For a pack of tobacco, they would have let themselves be mutilated and tortured. Without tobacco, Salvarsan was useless.

He had, among the provisions, the usual crate of shag; in the jungle he only smoked a pipe with his own tobacco, and he was glad of it when he discovered that the shag was as important as the Salvarsan. To increase the number of patients he had to distribute shag: half a pack for the second injection, a whole one for the third. The result was that his supply quickly ran out; ten days before the inspection prahu was due, he found himself without tobacco. He wrote a long report to Annema, explained that the supply of Salvarsan, although sufficient for single injections, was useless because a single injection was not enough, so he needed not only more Salvarsan but a prahu-ful of shag if he were to do his job properly. So far, he had not had many patients but, on those conditions, he expected an ever-increasing attendance.

When the inspection prahu arrived, Post Mamawi looked exemplary. The railway carriage had been freshly painted, the clearing neatly outlined, leveled and hardened; in its center, in a round bed with orange flowers, stood a bamboo pole with the Dutch flag at the top. He had planned to have the prahu welcomed by a guard of a dozen Papuans; but the moment the triangular sail appeared round the cape, the drums rolled in the jungle for the first time since the night of the fire dance, and within a minute Post Mamawi was deserted. The change was so instantaneous and uncanny that it seemed for a moment as if all that had happened in the past weeks had been hallucination; but Tunangan-Bersih's fire still smoked underneath the shelter of the kitchen, Burung-Sopan's rake leaned against the balustrade of the verandah, Kubis-Telor's prehistoric wheelbarrow stood peacefully in the shade of the coconut palm. After that one moment of alarm, their uncanny flight made him feel satisfied and proud. He was the only one they trusted, he was the great White Magician; the creatures who now came sailing up the creek were the age-old enemies, the East Indian Company. If ever he, Anton Zorgdrager, were to leave Mamawi, all his work would turn to nothing. When a heavy man in a sweat-stained suit, a jersey of body hair and a dirty sun helmet hoisted himself groaning onto the jetty, he was welcomed by a kind but distant ruler.

The man was Dr. Bevers, the inspection doctor, who had five years of New Guinea behind him and who had heard it all before. He knew this bloody country as if it were his own back garden and the mischievous urchins could no longer fool him by blackening themselves and calling "Boo!" He was too fat to chase them, but he saw them coming even before they had swung their bowlegs out of bed for a new day of pranks. He looked at Zorgdrager, A., the totok of Post Mamawi, with a casual glance of his small narrowed eyes and said, "Hello there."

"Welcome to Mamawi," Anton said, and as he shook the clammy hand, he recognized the man: he was the hairy poet who, together with Brits-Jansen, had composed the obscene dirge for some colleague's nuptials, that night long ago after their return from Borneo. He wiped his hand surreptitiously on his trousers as he accompanied Dr. Bevers to the verandah. Dr. Bevers barely glanced at the clearing, the flag and the flower bed; all he did was to wipe his forehead with a sodden handkerchief and fan his armpits with his helmet. On the verandah, he let himself down, groaning, into one of the deckchairs and crashed through it at once with the report of tearing canvas, said, "Sorry," and lowered himself into the other one, which held. He looked around without a trace of interest, let alone pleasure or admiration; he looked as if he were assessing the value of the furniture for income-tax purposes. Then he said, with a sigh, "Well, what's new?" and started to wipe his left armpit, one arm in the air and a hand inside his shirt.

Anton told him, as dispassionately and concisely as he could, that the pacification of District Mamawi had been accomplished by his killing Burubi and that . . .

"Who says so?" Bevers asked.

"Who says what?"

"Who says it was Burubi? Did he leave his card?"

That was too much. "Dr. Bevers," Anton said, with trembling fists, "I'll thank you to unload my rations and my provisions at once and to get the hell out of here."

"Keep your shirt on, colleague," Bevers said, unmoved, and he stuck up his other arm to wipe the right armpit. "I'm not sitting here to sell you something, but to let you benefit from my experience. I'm not doing it for pleasure."

"That is obvious," said Anton.

"But you aren't sitting here for your pleasure either," Bevers continued.

"It's very nice to tell yourself that you have exterminated Burubi and to let yourself be fooled by those black buggers, but I don't believe a word of it. Burubi, my young friend, is the most cunning bastard on the island. That man has been shot, hung, beheaded and garroted so often that I'm getting tired of it."

"I'm sorry I mentioned it," said Anton. "What I wanted to ask you for is a double ration of Salvarsan and a triple ration of shag."

"Oh yeah?" said Bevers. "Can I interest you in a grand piano?"

Anton eyed him stonily for a moment, then he started to talk. He talked calmly and precisely, but occasionally his voice skidded on the ice of his self-control and squawked, after which he needed a moment to recover before he continued, calmly and carefully. But while he sat talking, a strange dizziness overcame him, the slowly rising realization that a hysterical fury was pent up inside him. During the past weeks he had imagined himself as being calm and composed; now, as he sat talking on the verandah, he realized that he had fooled himself. It was as if the fury were rooted too deeply, were too entangled with his self-esteem to be released by merely blowing his top. If he let the fury over-power him, he would kick that fat bastard with his derisive sneer off the jetty, set the Papuans onto him.

"That is why I consider myself justified in applying for those increased rations," he ended, carefully.

During his long monologue, Bevers had observed him, not intently, not even with interest, but almost absent-mindedly. When at last he fell silent, he said, "Want to know something, boy? And don't get sore now, will you? What you've done here in Mamawi is fine, but it's high time you made your getaway."

"Is that so?" said Anton. "I flatter myself that I've got everything perfectly under control, and I see no reason why that should change as long as the gentlemen in Batavia and Manokwari allow me to do my work, instead of forcing me to waste Salvarsan on half cures."

"I'm not talking about Salvarsan," said Bevers. "I'm talking about you. You think you have broken the back of the resistance; you are amazed that the half-wits that came out of the forest could ever have terrified you the way they did. The explanation is simple: they are half-wits, indeed. Those who came to you out of the forest weren't the men of the drums, but their village idiots. Do you begin to see now why I am sick of those claims of 'I shot Burubi through his stomach!' 'I pulled the legs out of Burubi and stuck him six feet under the ground!' Believe me, boy, I really do know this coast by now. After the years I've been hanging around here, I've got a fair notion of the mentality of this race. I've now reached a point where I don't have to set eyes on a Papuan to know whether I've really got him under my thumb or not. Believe me, what is happening to you at this moment is a hoax. What you are injecting and pacifying are headless chickens, shooed toward you by the fighting cocks. You feel like a little Napoleon right now, and that's what you are: of a village full of idiots. I heard those drums when I rounded the cape; those weren't the drums of shy subjects, too bashful to appear in front of the visiting official and sing the anthem. Those were the drums of an enemy. That's why I say: instead of asking for more Salvarsan and wasting tobacco on a lot of feeble-minded decoys, be satisfied with what you've done and beat it. You can put a report in front of Kramer that will take his breath away. You're sure to be promoted. So have yourself photographed by me, beside that flower bed and that flagpole, as a keepsake for your children, and leave Mamawi to someone else."

"Who, for instance?" Anton asked calmly.

"If I have my way," said Bevers, "if Batavia will at last listen to a man who knows this country: to Burubi. Let that bugger die a natural death, and let his rabble perish of syphilis and frambesia to their hearts' content, instead of squandering Salvarsan and doctors in a guerrilla war that we must lose, for the simple reason that it is his country and not ours. Ten yards deep inside that jungle we are as blind as owls by day, but that's where he only begins to see. It's a damn shame the way they let first-class people like Hugenholtz and Ganwitz and yourself go to this hellhole, when I could have told them beforehand that it is suicide. I did tell them, for Chrissake, and I'll tell them again. But they won't believe me; that's why I advise you, for your own good: beat it. I'll write a report about you that'll make them sit up, and I'll diagnose you as a case of malaria. I'll tell them that you have resisted to the utmost, that you didn't want to leave your work after just getting started, but that I considered the state of your health to be such that I had to force you to leave your post, and I wouldn't be far wrong either. If you haven't had an attack of malaria yet, you've got one coming."

"Thank you," said Anton. "In other words, you would give up the

pacification of New Guinea by the Government Health Service altogether?"

"I didn't say that," Bevers replied, tiredly. "The rest of the settlements
are sound. The Papuans who have themselves treated there are rabble,
but they are the genuine article. It is only here in Mamawi that those
village idiots pop up every time. Hugenholtz had exactly the same setup
as you have: nice little garden, flagpole, childish patients, two boys, a fat
old cook—only he had an old djongos as well. A jewel of a settlement;
a showpiece of pacification. Three months later, his carcass full of
arrows lay rotting in the reeds and the only thing left of his love nest
was that bastard of a railway carriage, rusting in a scorched wilderness.
If you ask me, it's the railway carriage that has turned this hole into
such a slaughterhouse. I don't know for certain how the thing got here
but I believe the oil boys had it brought over as a canteen when they
were drilling around here. If only that hut had been made of wood, it
would have burned down with the rest and everyone would have
forgotten Outpost Mamawi long ago. But because the bloody thing is
made of iron and remains upright whatever happens, there are always
new hotheads who want to try it once more. And that's the argument
of the Head Office: it's a voluntary post. If they want to leave it
unoccupied, they'll have to scrap it altogether, and they won't do that,
the bloody bureaucrats. Live and let live, who knows, some idiot may
succeed in sticking it one day. If I had my way, I'd come here once more,
only once: with a load of dynamite to blow that rat trap sky high. It
would be the greatest service I could render my colleagues, greater than
five years of tramming Salvarsan and gin up and down this coast."

"I'll consider your advice," said Anton, "but in the meantime, I'd be
grateful if you could ask Doctor Annema to send me, next time you come,
three . . ."

Bevers looked at him with an odd expression in his eyes. "It's like hearing
Hugenholtz," he said. "You give me the shivers. What is it, in God's
name, that makes you boys go crazy like this? If you don't come with me
now, you're lost."

"I prefer to postpone my decision until your next visit," said Anton carefully, "when I shall expect a double ration of Salvarsan and a triple ration
of shag."

Bevers's eyes changed, and he looked at him as he had done before,
absent-mindedly, without interest. "Please yourself," he said. "Corporal!"

The corporal of his escort came trotting up from the reeds. He gave the order to unload the rations.

Before nightfall, he was gone.

«‹‹ ›››

The moment the prahu vanished from sight, they came back: the chattering Tunangan-Bersih, the spitting Burung-Sopan and Kubis-Telor. Within five minutes, the kitchen fire smoked underneath the soup kettle once more and the singing fat woman beat time on her thighs with her wooden ladles. The yokels raked and wheelbarrowed again—everything was as it had been: orderly, pleasant, peaceful; yet it was no longer an idyll. How could he have been so blind during all those weeks, let himself be fooled to that extent by his own megalomania? Of course, Bevers had been right. However strange and childlike the Papuans might be in their stage of instinctive prehistoric creatures, these Papuans were different. They were mad.

For a few moments, he wavered. They were the most important moments of his life, and he knew it. If he ran to his hut now, ripped his gun off the hook and fired a shot in the air, the prahu would turn round and come to his assistance; he would go on board and escape out of this dream of triumph and happiness that had turned into a nightmare. It would save his life. . . . Would it? Who said all this was planned? Who said so, even though so far only half-wits had turned up as patients? . . . He knew, at that moment, that if he turned tail and fled now, he would convince himself within half an hour that it was all nonsense, that his victory had been real; he would lose his self-respect, his feeling of at last, at long last, having accomplished something completely. It would add one more conflict to the many that he had solved by flight. No; this time he would stand firm. Even if it was a choice between life and death: he would stand firm! But after standing there for a minute in the wilderness, he no longer knew what to do. If he fled, he would abandon everything that had made life worth living; if he stayed on, he might never emerge from the jungle again, yet he would have saved something that was more important than the mere biological fact of being alive. Even if, in three months' time, he were to lie rotting in those reeds, pierced with arrows, like Hugenholtz, like Ganwitz, it would somehow be a victory, whereas . . .

He felt that eerie, giddy faintness come over him once more, clouding his thoughts, making him sway unsteadily, forcing him to sit down on the steps of the verandah. It was the same faintness of fury, that same urge to murder, that had overpowered him as he sat listening to that contemptuous bastard. Perhaps the man was right, perhaps he was in for an attack of malaria. Perhaps that was the cause of those extremes of self-confidence and despair, between which he was torn until cold sweat broke out on his forehead and his clothes seemed to choke him. It was impossible, simply impossible that those grandiose weeks should have been a chimera. It was impossible that he should have suffered such a grotesque defeat after all those months in the rain, that resurrection with the aid of his fire dance, that battle for life and death with the black magic of the wilderness. The stakes had been too high for that, he had fought too desperately to achieve it, his ruses had been too cunning, his hatred too vicious. It was impossible. Impossible. No human being alive could do such superhuman things and concede afterward that he had been living in a fool's paradise. It was unimaginable that all this—the camp, the little garden, the flower bed, the patients, the laboratory, the wheelbarrow, the kitchen, the whole idyllic lot—had developed according to plan, the plan of that intelligence in the forest. His own actions had been too spontaneous for that, too unexpected, even to himself. It suggested a knowledge of human nature and a wisdom in that prehistoric creature in the jungle that would turn all generals, psychologists and politicians in the civilized world into incompetent amateurs. *"Don't forget this is Burubi's country. . . ."* But it was not Burubi's uniquely. He himself had the wilderness just as much in his power as any Papuan had. He had traveled three days through the jungle to a pinpoint on a trackless chart, and he had arrived, according to plan. . . .

He groaned, his head in his hands; he listened to the tuneless singing of Tunangan-Bersih. Tuneless, senseless. Impossible! It was a lie, the cynical denial of triumphant reality! The swine had been jealous, embittered by the tropics, too small for a napkin, too big for a bib! If indeed he were such a genius, if indeed he knew the Papuans and the jungle so much better than anyone else, why the hell wasn't *he* sitting in Manokwari as head of Operation Salvarsan? What kind of a Service was this, that made brilliant psychologists tram gin up and down the coast, like grocers, and delivered the fate of a continent into the hands of cretinous collectors of penis sheaths? Of course, that was the explanation: spite, bitterness, a destructive urge resulting from disillusionment. Bevers was a scoundrel, a dangerous alarmist, and he wouldn't hesitate, if need be . . .

A shiver shook him and he lost his balance. He had to hold on to the posts of the balustrade. Whatever Bevers might be, his diagnostics weren't bad. This was the first gust of a squall of malaria. But the shiver passed; the tenseness eased off. He let go of the post of the balustrade; it was nonsense. He had danced round a fire stark naked, he had been stung so viciously that he had hardly been able to move the following day, and he had not caught malaria. Or had he? Sometimes, the incubation period seemed to take an uncanny length of time. . . .

Rubbish! He must shake off that doubt, scorch that hysteria from his soul with action, self-control, virility. He would be damned if he had malaria, and he would be double damned if he would let the pants be frightened off him by a jealous alarmist. His patients were sane! If Burubi, or whatever the sonafabitch called himself, were indeed still alive, why had he not killed him off before now? Why had he murdered Ganwitz the moment he threatened to escape from the jungle with his secret, but let him sit there quietly talking to Bevers for an hour without intervention? During that hour, he had told Bevers everything that Ganwitz could possibly have told anyone. Why had he not been killed? Why should that supernatural demigod in the wilderness admit one little white man after the other into his domain, if it were only to play an endless, involved, deadly-tiresome game of cat and mouse with them?

It was begging the question. Why did a cat play with a mouse, instead of biting its head off at once? In the wilderness, all man-made logic turned to claptrap. Only brute vitality, Brits-Jansen had taught him, ruled supreme. "*Whatever happens, stay on top.*" He would stay on top whatever happened, even if he were served by lunatics, pounced upon by malaria, inflated by vanity into a delirious King of the Village Idiots: he would stay on top. All Bevers had to do was to bring him a double Salvarsan ration and a triple ration of shag in three months' time; for the rest, he could drop dead.

He went to get up and enter the hut but a new tremor shook him with such violence that he missed the post of the balustrade and fell on his knees. For a few minutes he lay struggling for breath, trying to loosen the muscles of his jaw with hammered commands of his will; then the cramp eased, and he dragged himself inside. He stripped off his clothes;

they were sodden with sweat. He staggered to the table, opened the drawer, and took out his revolver. No matter who was right, Bevers or he, they would not get him alive. If it were indeed malaria, if he were to lie helpless on his bed for days, delirious with fever, nobody would sneak up on him and find him defenseless. He would . . .

He slumped on his bed as his knees gave way, and he felt a new tremor creep up from his calves. He tensed his muscles, realized too late that it was a mistake; when he tried to relax he could not. The fever came rolling toward him, luminous in the teeming night, a wave with an incandescent, hissing crest, full of scurrying little animals, radiating heat as it curled over him, toppling. He prepared himself for a boiling cascade when the fiery crest crashed over him, but a scalding coldness hit him; it was a wave of ice. While he lay staring, frozen, through the dark green glass of the petrified wave, a drowned man under the ice, he prayed: "God, God, wherever You may be, whatever I may have done: mercy, mercy, let me breathe once more, come back to life once more and I'll fire that shot, I'll call Bevers back, I'll go back to Els, I won't try to run away any more from what I've done, I'll love my neighbor, I'll let myself be converted by Bert's father, mercy, mercy, and I'll fire that shot, let me go, let me go. . . ." But God prized open his fingers, gently, yet remorselessly, and took hold of the revolver. God said, *"Lepas, tuan, lepas,"* and after a last, desperate resistance he surrendered with a sigh and let the revolver be taken away from him. God had black, sad eyes, deep black, almost blue, a bluish glow, with gold, a little golden light. For one breathless second, he realized that the little golden light was a reflection in a black eye. He recognized Mutiara, the old melancholy Papuan, his first patient; he realized that he was lying on his bed, that the Papuan had lit the lamp and taken the revolver out of his hand. He realized that the Papuan was afraid the revolver would go off in his seizure, he realized . . .

Somewhere, a gong was struck, a bronze, booming sound that rippled out in widening, concentric rings of sound until the first of the rings touched a bell, the bell of a bicycle that trilled persistently, *rrring-krring—rrring-krring—*"Don't, Els!" he said. "Don't wake those people up." But she went on stubbornly, ringing the bell of her bicycle, the nail of her thumb white with pressure. *Rrring-krring—*until at last a bolt scraped and a latch clicked, and the upper half of the door was opened by a sleepy farmer without any teeth. "What is it?" the farmer asked.

"Have you any buttermilk?" she asked with an unbearably affected voice.

"No," said the farmer. "It is Sunday," and the door slammed shut, the bolt scraped.

Rrring-krring . . . He yanked the handlebars out of her hands. "Stop that!" he said. "I told you before . . ." But his voice stuck in his throat, for he saw her eyes widen, her mouth open, her teeth get longer and longer; then her eyes rolled upward, and the upper jaw of a set of dentures fell out of her mouth. She gurgled, and slowly pitched forward, her body pierced with black arrows. But it was not she, it was Bevers, whose knees sagged slowly until he fell, like a sack of flour, on the floor of the prahu. The soldiers, who had been staring at him frozen with fear, suddenly sprang to life and their guns slid off their shoulders, as behind him a tremendous wave of shouting, screaming, cheering came rolling nearer, nearer, lashed on by the rolling thunder of hundreds of drums. The guns crashed, the machine gun rattled, the prahu recoiled from the jetty, he screamed, "Stop! Stop!" wanted to throw himself into the water, swim after the prahu; but a calm hand like a vise of steel held him back, and a soft voice said, soothingly, "Senang, tuan, senang." He struggled, kicked, his nails slithered down a wet arm until they hooked in flesh, and he felt blood dripping down his fingers; but the hand did not weaken its grip, and the voice sang, soothingly, "Senang, tuan, senang." He knew, as he reached the surface of his consciousness for a second, whose were the black-blue eyes, with the golden lights, that seemed to soothe him into a weary, sad lethargy, a dark sleep of nostalgia and sadness. He sank, wailing, into what seemed a dark security, but was sucked under once more by a whirlpool of fever.

He did not know how long he lay there, writhing on his drenched bed, haunted by the vision of Bevers pierced by black arrows, his drooling dentures falling out of his mouth. The vision came back again and again; every time, he tried to jump into the water and swim after the prahu; every time, the hand held him back. In the end, his periods of respite grew longer. Every time he breathed more and more freely at the surface of consciousness, after his escape from drowning in that vortex of fear. During those intervals, something seemed to bring relief, something warm, hazy, misty, pungent. Finally, after countless returns to reality, he began to register what it was. The old Papuan was smoking a pipe, and blowing the smoke in his face. The smoke gave him relief, a spicy, drugging aroma that penetrated his nose, his throat, his lungs, where it induced that lethargy, that dark, sad sleep.

At long last, the Papuan no longer blew smoke into his nostrils and it was from that fact that he gathered that the fever was receding, rather than from the peace that returned to his tortured body. He lay, weakly panting, on his bed, too limp to move, too exhausted to think. He felt a deep gratitude toward old Mutiara with his dark, sad eyes; the Papuan's presence brought a feeling of security. He must have been sitting there for days on end, soothing, calming, letting himself be scratched and bitten, watching over his master with unwavering loyalty until, at last, the demons of the wilderness had let him go. "Village idiots," Bevers had called them. Whatever the others might be, this was no village idiot. This was one of the strongest, calmest human beings he had ever met. The black eyes had a weird, sad power that reminded him of something, of somebody, long ago. He tried to remember whom and where; he gazed into the black eyes for hours, while his spirit slowly disentangled itself from the jungle of his fever, and the growing feelers of his thoughts began to grope feebly into reality.

Mutiara remained at his post. His eyes were either violet, a strange purple glow, or dark blue velvet, with golden sparks. He realized after a while that it was the changing from daylight to lamplight; it was his first notion of time. The eyes seemed to watch him all the time; and the peace that radiated from them brought sadness, lassitude, resignation, passivity. The vision of Bevers dying came back sometimes, but no longer as a nightmare; it came back in an odd, disembodied light as if it were more a premonition than a memory. He tried to discover an explanation for the vision, but he could not arrive at it by thoughts alone. He arrived at it by gazing into those sad eyes; as he did so, it seemed as if the premonition slowly took root in his thoughts. At first he saw the prahu more clearly: the soldiers, their guns, the machine gun. Then he discerned the crates of the cargo: Salvarsan and tobacco, the rations for the other outposts further along the coast. There was enough of both in that prahu to last him a year, and he thought about Bevers. "Village idiots! Can I interest you in a grand piano?" Bevers would never bring a double Salvarsan ration and a triple ration of shag. He would lecture him again. . . .

And then, suddenly, he knew the meaning of that vision. It must have symbolized a decision that had shaped itself in his subconscious long before

it penetrated his brain. The way in which Mutiara had nursed and comforted him proved that Bevers had been wrong. His victory over Burubi
had been genuine. The Papuans expected the White Magician to cure
them. They would turn up in ever-increasing numbers. They would find
him without Salvarsan, without shag. If Bevers returned without the
rations he had asked for, he would have to confiscate the rest of his cargo.

It was a momentous realization. He would declare war! A holy war of
humanity against the selfishness, stupidity and avarice of the bureaucrats
and the colonials. If Bevers did not bring those rations, he would force
him at the point of a gun to unload his cargo, and if Bevers ordered his
soldiers to resist, the Papuans would finish them off. It would be a revolution of the wilderness against the invaders, and he would be justified before God and mankind. He had done what he could; if he had to use
force to make Bevers unload that prahu, it was not his fault, it was the
fault of the East Indian Company. His task in this jungle was not a
political one, but a humane one; the old Papuan by his bedside had unmasked the man in shirt sleeves behind his desk in Batavia as a cynical
opportunist, and revealed his callous denial of the very soul of his mission.
After Mutiara's silent proof of Christian charity, he was on the side of
the Papuans. In the wilderness he had found his spiritual home.

When he came to that conclusion, a deep peace pervaded him. Even
Mutiara seemed to notice it; for the first time after all those days and
nights, his eyelids drooped, and his face became impressive to behold. It
looked like a prophet's head carved in ebony, a black mask of superhuman
power and infinite sadness. He wished that he could console the old
Papuan, give him a token of his gratitude, his friendship. He wished he
could educate him and keep him with him as an assistant, a helper in the
wilderness. He thought, with hostile contempt, of that innocent idiot,
Teddy Schutters. What a difference in those two faces, what difference of
humanity, wisdom, sorrow. . . .

And then, as if a flash of lightning illuminated for a second the smoky
recesses of his lethargic mind, he recognized the expression on the Papuan's
face: it was the same expression as the one he had observed on the face of
Captain Willem Waterreus, during that first prayer in the dining hall of
Man-Pu-Ko-Chu, when he had diagnosed his erotomania. He recognized
the power those black eyes had radiated, the spell of that tremendous will,
to which he had surrendered helplessly. In that last second of independence,
while the ebony face was unguarded by those eyes, he heard Brits-Jansen's

voice, saying, "*Black and white magic are not two different faculties, they use the same power destructively or creatively. The important thing is: it is the same power.*"

The world stopped for one breathless, trembling second. In that second, like a silver fish from the bottom of a black lake, the knowledge came flashing to the surface: the name of this man is not Mutiara. It is Burubi.

Then the eyes opened once more in the ebony face; and their black, deep violet glow overpowered him with the speed of thought. He sighed, and sank back on his pillow. It was nonsense, nonsense. He was safe. He had a great future. He would attack Bevers's prahu when it came back, confiscate its cargo, unleash hell, but at last, at last, he would perform a great and unselfish deed. Even if it were to cost him his life, and that of Bevers, and that of all the doctors of the settlements along the coast, it would be a grandiose deed of self-denial and courage. It would give his life a meaning, before the fall of the axe of death.

He fell asleep with the vision of the drooling dentures falling from that gaping mouth as a goal, a haven at the far end of the dark tunnel of his dreaming thoughts.

«« »»

He recovered. He began to sit up, to stand up, to grope from bed to table, to shuffle from table to door. But the sadness, the numbness remained: he would have let himself sink with relief, almost with sensuousness, into that tunnel of thoughts and let himself be carried away, cradled by the dark river of destiny, with a deeply satisfying feeling of fatalism, if there had not twinkled, somewhere in the twilight, a small core of hope, a diamond on the river bed, the reflection of a star. He paid little attention to the star; he turned away from it in bored indifference; but it went on twinkling, signaling in the darkness, wherever he went. It had to do with a memory, another river, long ago; but he could not be bothered.

Only when he ventured outside, and made the few steps into the jungle to the latrine, did the star penetrate the haze of his lethargy with an unexpected light. It was a blinding light, approaching; before it dazzled him, he recognized it. It was the metal cap of a beer bottle.

For the first time since his illness a tremor shook him again like a new gust of fever, and he was stricken by a terrible feeling of insecurity, an urge to flee, to stumble back into the sunlight, the clearing, the hut, back into the still presence of Mutiara, his friend, his helper, his comforter. But, at his first step back, groping for support in the shrubs, he realized that he was returning to the goal at the far end of the dark tunnel: gaping mouth, drooling dentures, the ambush of the prahu, Bevers's death. Frowning, he forced himself to remember where he had seen that beer-bottle cap before. Where? Where? As he sat frowning, trying to pierce the fog of the past, he began to discern a shimmer of the truth in the darkness. The decision to confiscate the cargo of the prahu by force was not his own. It had been suggested to him by Burubi, the magician. While this realization penetrated his lethargy like a wedge, and the light of the truth streamed in, he knew which beer-bottle cap it was. He had tossed it up, after praying in despair on the River Kali-Woga. He had prayed.

Prayed . . . ? Ganwitz. Holiness. His only hope in this dark tunnel of black magic was the white magic of Christianity, as Ganwitz had written. Not the Christianity of his father and the Pharisees, but the Christianity of the Epistle of Saint James: the works, not the faith. Complete chastity, utter humility, self-denying love, a pure adoration of God instead of prayers like mumbled petitions to a vain millionaire in the clouds, this Christianity alone could save his soul from that satanical power; but he was as far removed from that state of grace as an ape. He was a damned soul in the wilderness, fallen man in the jungle of a lost paradise; wherever he groped, wherever he went, wherever he looked, stood the archangel with the burning sword, barring his path.

But he should not waste time on self-pity. He should accept the inevitable punishment, yet attack the spell of the magician at the roots, tear out that poisonous weed, the vision of Bevers pierced by black arrows, the dentures falling from the gaping mouth. If he could purify himself that far, if he could scrape together enough vestiges of a Christian upbringing to remain conscious of the sinfulness of that vision, he might perhaps prevent its turning into reality. And, if God had mercy on him, he had one chance left to achieve that: flight. This time it would not be a flight to save his own life, but that of someone else: Bevers, the sweating bastard, the . . .

The moment his hatred for Bevers returned, the peace, the nostalgic resignation returned also, and he shuffled back toward the hut with a feeling of great relief. It was imagination, aftermath of malaria. He must suppress those flashes of hysteria, he must recover and take up his work again, eke out the provisions he had; once the inspection prahu returned, he would see. There was every chance that his request had been granted, that he would get his extra ration. A few more days of rest and sleep and he would laugh at those demons of his feverish imagination. Mutiara is Burubi! It was too silly for words. Burubi lay buried underneath the wooden cross, together with Ganwitz. Both of them were asleep forever, in the same grave.

As he entered the hut, the old Papuan was making his bed, silently, with moving devotion. How could he think such crazy thoughts about that loyal soul? Mutiara was a gem, the best djongos . . . Then Bevers' voice came back to him, saying: *"Only Hugenholtz had an old djongos as well."*

"Senang, tuan, senang," the old man said, with patient, soothing calm. "Tempat tidur, tuan; tidur."

He obeyed, went to bed, and fell asleep with a sigh, at the command of two sad, black eyes.

«‹‹ ›››

But the moments of clarity returned. At first, he thought that the change took place when the Papuan was asleep; then he realized that it had something to do with distance. Every time he left the clearing to go to the latrine, he saw the dark tunnel of destiny again that led irrevocably toward the death of Bevers and the revolution of the Papuans; back in the clearing, he relaxed again in his indolent fatalism. He started to experiment to see how far he could retain his independence, as he returned inside the action radius of the Papuan; he discovered that the distance varied in proportion to the time he had spent in the forest, praying.

It was not quite praying. His thoughts did not direct themselves at Somebody, or Something, not even himself; his prayer consisted of kneeling in the forest at the foot of a tree, closing his eyes and folding his hands and letting himself be drawn away from the center of his universe.

Doctor Kramer had been right: he sat on a chair in the center of his universe. Only during those hours of purification in the wilderness could he think about Els without self-defense, explain Annie's letter by identifying himself with her. He did so without a feeling of holiness or expiation, but with an almost clinical detachment. After he had identified himself in his mind with others for some time, instead of considering them as planets revolving around the sun of his ego, he attained an independence that he could carry further and further into the magic circle.

At first, he had to force himself to stay outside that circle of security and fatalism. A tremendous tidal pull drew him back toward those eyes, that soft singsong voice, that peace, that lovely lack of responsibility. Yet, although the tidal pull increased, he became more and more independent, and the conflict between the two tendencies within him became more violent every day. He knew that he would be saved if only he could take that independence, that white armor of purity right inside the hut, if only for five minutes, for it would enable him to pack his haversack with a few essentials without which flight would mean instant suicide: a compass, his revolver, a chart, iron rations, waterproof matches. The journey he would have to make was murderous: right across the island, via the Carstensz Mountains, to Merauke. He would have to head southwest through the wilderness behind Mamawi, until he reached the Idenburg River; he would have to follow the river upstream to the fork where two small streams converged; he would have to follow the westerly one as far as its source, and then head due south until he reached the coast. He would probably not make it; it was unlikely that he would even reach the big river; yet he had no choice if he wanted to save Bevers and the others, the whole Operation Salvarsan. It gave his flight a purpose that was more than mere self-elimination; it gave him the strength to continue his planning, despite the probable outcome.

As the days went by he managed to carry his independence further and further toward the hut, but he sank back more and more deeply into the fury, the hatred, and the megalomania. In the end, he was longing for the arrival of the prahu, in the hot darkness of his vicious fatalism. Only after he had killed Bevers and stolen the rations could he start his own life; only then would the patients come out of the forest in droves and he would in truth be the White God he had imagined himself to be during those few weeks before Bevers came. To tear himself away from the center of the hut became an ever-increasing effort; one day, when he had succeeded and fallen on his knees once more in that grotto of loneliness underneath the giant trees and changed into that other Anton, that disembodied spirit of selflessness, he heard, behind his prayers, a small voice, whispering in the stillness. "It is happening," the voice whispered. "Anton, it is happening. You are splitting up into an angel and a devil, postmaster and harbor master of Mamawi."

The whispering voice gave him the last ounce of strength he needed to carry his white armor of purity into the heart of the hut. Luck was with him: Mutiara was asleep. Silently he took his revolver, haversack, parang, compass, lighter, chart and six tins of rations, tore out the blank pages of his diary; then, fighting against a rising tide of fear like a drowning man, he tiptoed out of the door, crept down the steps to the verandah, ran across the clearing, and vanished in the wilderness.

The moment the darkness of the jungle closed over him, he wavered. A faint, distant voice called "Postmaster . . . Postmaster . . ." across the lake of death. Only then did he realize that he had his revolver in his hand.

He looked down at the dull, glinting barrel. He knew what lay waiting for him, that he had jumped now, and was falling, falling into the abyss, the vortex of the spiral road of evolution. One day, two days, a week, and he would have changed from Homo sapiens into Homo heidelbergensis.

He clenched the revolver so tightly that his hand trembled. One quick move, and all would be over—before someone else would have to do it, before he had changed into an ape man, the most terrifying beast of prey of the jungle, that either would be shot as he had shot Frolick, or would die a loathsome death in a sodden grave of ferns, somewhere in a swamp in the forest. He stood at the beginning of a road that led to the very heart of hell, and there was no light to guide him—only a pathetic little image: a baby, staring at the world with half-blind eyes, still full of memories of the other side.

That image made him throw away the revolver. It vanished with a rustle in the undergrowth. Even if he were to spend a year looking for it, he would never find it again. He had made his decision; there was nothing left but to lift his parang and make the first stroke of his pilgrimage through hell, toward the other side.

God, give me a chance, he thought before his blade flashed; then it smote the wood and drops spurted in his face, blood of the wilderness.

<<< >>>

The change that came over him, after two days in the jungle, was unexpected. After dark, as he lay underneath his shelter of branches and palm leaves, listening to the sounds of the night, he felt no fear. Instead of being beset by the panic that he remembered so clearly from his journey through the Atjeh jungle, he became more and more composed and clear-headed. He had left something behind in Post Mamawi, something malignant, that began to putrefy as he drew away from it. He felt as if he were a ghost, floating effortlessly over the smoking abyss of death, while his body remained behind, decomposing.

The body belonged to Dr. Zorgdrager, G.H.S., who was born at that

shot by the rapids of the Kali-Woga in Borneo, and whom he had taken
to represent the best in himself ever since. Now, the further he penetrated
into the jungle, the less attractive the image of that doctor became; in the
end, it was loathsome. It was an odd undoing of part of himself, and it
seemed, as the distance between him and that other part widened, that he
was following a thread, the same thread between body and phantom that
he had felt tugging at him on the Kali-Woga, when it had stretched between him in the prahu and the beer bottle floating back to sea, home. It
was as if he had picked up that thread now, and were following it, as if,
slowly but with ever-growing confidence, he were finding the way back
to the purity of his childhood. He wished he had brought a lamp with him
to write by, for the moment the sun rose he had to get on his way. At the
first light of dawn he rose, effaced the traces of his bivouac, and hacked
himself deeper into the jungle, south-southwest. Every morning a feeling
of urgency overcame him that gave him no chance to write anything down.

Yet there was a lot to write. Every thought that occurred to him as he
rustled on through the jungle seemed worth recording. The thoughts grew
clearer and clearer, simpler. He discovered that everything could be
brought down to simple combinations of causes and effects; these conclusions delighted him so much with their lucidity that he regretted more
and more not being able to write them down. For that was the strange
thing: once he had arrived at a conclusion, he instantly forgot it. It seemed
as if he were turning out his brains; the moment he arrived at a conclusion that delighted him in its simplicity, it vanished forever from his
memory: cleared away, gone. It made him lighter, purer; yet it left behind
a small feeling of regret like a farewell. He hacked on with regular strokes,
untiringly, forging ahead through that tangle of memories, emotions and
desires, solving everything: his relationship with others, his relationship
with God, the secret of good and evil, of sickness and sin, of life and death,
love and forgiveness. If only he could have taken the time to write down
his conclusions the moment he reached them, he would, after six days in
the wilderness, have solved the Gordian knot of all the riddles of a
lifetime.

But, although he occasionally hesitated as to whether he should sit
down and take out his writing pad, something spurred him on: that feeling of urgency, the thought of the body of Dr. Zorgdrager, rotting in the
reeds of Mamawi. For, although the body was dead, it moved. It started
to crawl; after six days it got up, swaying, blind, dripping mud, and

began to follow him into the wilderness. It was a foolish obsession, even amusing; he could smile at it, as long as he continued to hack his way south-southwest through the unchanging, pathless jungle. Yet he underestimated the obsession; for though he could laugh at it by day, it spoiled his nights.

Instead of lying fearlessly in the darkness and sleeping dreamlessly, to get up the next morning with a feeling of peace and relaxation, he now began to be troubled by the body in his dreams. It seemed as if, in its gruesome blindness, it did not notice the difference between night and day, but stumbled on, while he lay still in the darkness, losing time. He saw it clearly when, in his troubled dreams, a disembodied spirit, he climbed up the giant trees, spread gauzy wings and soared into the sky, higher, higher, until he could survey the forest between his bivouac and the sea. Then he saw the body, far away, as through a telescope, struggling onward in the moonlight: swaying, stumbling, falling, but crashing on, unerringly following the trail that linked them. He awoke from those dreams more and more tired every day; the thought of that body overtaking him at night made him hack faster through the wilderness, until he began to fall on his face occasionally, into the springy net of creepers, to lie there, panting, for minutes, hours sometimes, before he could gather enough strength to get to his feet again and push on through the jungle.

Yet the clarity remained with him, and the elation of purification; at the daily summit of that clarity he realized that he must sit down and write, even if it were to cost him half a day. He would be haunted by a feeling of guilt and dissatisfaction until he had written down those conclusions, even though, in the time that he would lose, the blind, swaying body would gain on him. For if the body should overtake him, if one day he should be joined by the rotting carcass that had tracked him down through the maze of the wilderness, he would have only one weapon against the monster: his conclusions, the ultimate truth that purification had brought him.

One morning, on waking up, he discovered that he had made camp underneath on old low tree, with heavy branches close to the ground. He hoisted himself onto the lowest branch, climbed higher, as high as he could, and there, in the green twilight, in a small nest of security and stillness, he began to write. He had been afraid that he would have forgotten all those conclusions and associations, but he discovered with a feeling of happiness and gratitude that they came back the moment he started to write. He had planned to divide the conclusions into chapters, but his thoughts were too swift for any editing. He wrote without paragraphs, without punctuation, at breakneck speed; never before in his life had he known such happiness, such joy, such complete fulfillment as on that day in the tree. All the answers and conclusions, all the magnificently simple solutions to all the mysteries of life that had flitted past him in the wilderness to vanish, like butterflies, in the dark tangle ahead came back to him that day; only by writing with a speed that left him breathless could he keep up with them.

When the sun went down and he could no longer read what he was writing, he finished the last page with a flourish, and climbed down. At the foot of the tree, he counted the pages in the darkness. There were sixty-seven. He planned to read them through the next morning, but during the night the fear of the approaching body began to oppress him once more, and the next morning he thought better of it. He folded the sheets and stuck them inside his shirt; he would forget about them until such time as the body should overtake him; then he would pull them out, and they would deliver him from his ultimate fear. But perhaps that would never happen, perhaps he would reach the other side with his conclusions unread. In that case he would copy them and edit them in Merauke, and keep them for Jacob. Whatever happened, whatever the boy might think of his father, no other son had ever received such a treasure at the start of his life as his son would, with the sixty-seven pages of pencil writing he now carried inside his shirt. They contained the answers to all the questions, all the problems, all the fears a man might ever experience; they contained the secret of life, wrenched from the wilderness.

But the body came closer every night. He saw it more and more clearly through the telescope of his dreams. He could not see its face, it was still too far away; but he knew from the way it stumbled, fell, scrambled back to its feet and threw itself crashing into the undergrowth once more, that it was blind. It also seemed, now that he no longer smoked, that he could smell it: a repulsive stench of putrefaction, of sweat and filth and decomposing flesh.

Every day he hacked faster, more urgently, into the wilderness; but every day the body came closer. He no longer needed to be asleep to see it: he began to smell it by day as well. He began to hear it even: panting, growling, thrashing in the undergrowth behind him. The obsession of being pursued by a monster became so vivid, so terrifying, that in the end he went on hacking, hacking without rest, the whole day long, until toward nightfall he crossed a trail that looked as if it were freshly cut. He stood at the crossroads of his own trail and that mysterious other one, panting, coughing, his parang trembling in his hand; then he heard a crashing behind him in the jungle and he hacked on, possessed by a panic. He must hack, hack on, hack on, night and day, he must not rest, for the monster did not rest either. It crashed on through the undergrowth untiringly, unhampered by the night in its blindness, and it would overtake him before sunrise unless he hacked on. And if that should happen, if it were to catch up with him before dawn, he would be lost. For in the darkness he would not be able to read his conclusions; the only weapon with which to free himself from the embrace of that rotting body, groping for his throat, would be powerless in the dark. So he must hack on until daylight, even if it were to cost him his life.

He hacked on throughout the night, and it was a night of nameless horror. The monster crashed, mumbled, snorted, closer and closer behind him. He stumbled, flailed with his parang in space, hacked away at yard-thick trees with the fury of a crazed woodpecker. At dead of night the stench, the snorting, the crashing of the monster in the undergrowth seemed to come from all sides at once, to close in on him in narrowing rings, a spiral of horror; then dawn broke. He hacked on for another hour, obsessed by a crazy fear of death, yet knowing that he was committing suicide by squandering his last remaining strength; then, unexpectedly, he broke through the undergrowth into a clearing, a pool underneath the trees.

At first he thought it was a crater, for red clouds of smoke rose, rolling slowly between the trunks of the trees; then he realized it was the morning mist. He heard the monster break, snorting, through the shrubs, a few paces behind him. He staggered to the pool, threw himself down, but as he lowered his head to drink he saw he had fallen on top of the monster. It stared up at him from the pool with bloodshot eyes, leering from the stinking tangle of a beard. He saw scratches in the beard, and lice around the eyes; only then did he discover who had persecuted him all those nights and all those days. It was Frolick, the ape man of Kakoto.

He was dazed by fear and the stench, but, lying on the panting belly of the monster, its hot stinking breath scorching his face, he pulled the papers out of his shirt, the ultimate weapon, the sixty-seven pages with the answers to all the questions of man lost in the universe.

"*Anton Zorgdrager,*" he read; "*Anton Zorgdrager Anton Zorgdrager Anton Zorgdrager.*"

His breath stopped. He turned the page.

"*Anton Zorgdrager Anton Zorgdrager Anton Zorgdrager.*"

Four, six, eight pages.

"*Anton Zorgdrager Anton Zorgdrager Anton Zorgdrager.*"

During that radiant, glorious, unforgettable day of purity, wisdom and compassion, he had filled sixty-seven pages with his own name, repeated thousands of times.

The claws of the monster tightened around his neck. He tried to breathe, to struggle, but he was exhausted. He retched, felt he was losing consciousness, then a bitter wave welled up in his body and he vomited in the face of the demon. The vomit destroyed its face; it disappeared in a glistening ripple of widening rings. The rings widened, widened, then faded, and the face started to form once more. Just before the face became still, he experienced a last notion of reality.

He realized that he lay staring at his own reflection, that the stench that had pursued him was his own, that, for the last time in his life, he lay eye to eye with himself.

In that ultimate moment, before the last spark of humanity was extinguished within him, he thought of Frolick. Frolick was the last human being to accompany him into hell. Why? It was a sign, a message. He realized, as sleep numbed him like slowly rising water, that the crux of his life lay in Frolick. But why? Why?

He tried, desperately, to understand, but he could not. He went under in that slowly rising black water, and fell asleep.

<<< >>>

The thing that got to its feet, swaying, grunting, at the edge of the pool was no longer Anton Zorgdrager. It was the ape man of Mamawi, a stinking body without mind, without conscience, but with a vague, instinctive cunning. It drowned the remnants of the skin it had shed: the haversack, the tins, the compass, the instruments, the parang, the sheets of paper. It wiped out all traces on the water's edge; then it slunk into the wilderness, soundlessly, leering, sniffing for a scent. There was no scent, only its own stench. All life had vanished from the forest before it.

The ape man did not creak and rustle in the undergrowth, as the clumsy human animals did that crashed through the jungle like a herd of elephants. It climbed into the trees and swung soundlessly from branch to branch, with only occasionally the crack of a snapping twig, or the whisper of a falling leaf. The wilderness had changed from a dark tangle of creepers and impenetrable shrubs into a twilit hunting field, hiding place of countless living creatures. In the trees there were fruits with bitter juice that paralyzed the tongue and numbed the inside of the cheeks, but although the fruit satisfied hunger for a short while, there was another hunger, a deeper one, a yearning for something warm and soft, something alive.

Life was everywhere: it rustled in the shrubs, it palpitated in the foliage, it barked and grunted at the foot of the tree in the darkness. It snorted, grunted; snorted, grunted; closer and closer; then it fell silent. There was a duel between two silences, two motionless, breathless silences; then the ape man let go of the branch and fell. He fell on top of something warm and soft and squealing, squealing, until the echoes of its squealing filled the wilderness with terrified shrieks that made all life flee, rattling, quacking, flapping and rustling from the shrubs and the foliage. The ape man tightened his grip, tightened it, tighter; the soft warm body struggled and kicked and squawked; the ape man tightened, tightened his grip with merciless ferocity. The squealing sharpened to a shrill, desperate screeching; then it died down to choking, rattling, coughing, until it ended when the body went limp and still with a soft sob.

A flash of consciousness scythed through his darkness, a lighthouse beam of despair. There he lay, on the swampy ground, with a dead pig; what . . . He bit, groaning, hissing, till he tasted something warm and sweet; then he gnawed, tore off a lump of life with his teeth and chewed it. It was soft; it gave a lovely, sleepy satisfaction; but it remained whole. He chewed on it, chewed, but it stayed in a soft, entire lump. He took it out of his mouth and tore it into fragments, which he could swallow. He ate until he could eat no more; then he climbed sleepily back into the tree, found a lair and slept.

He did not wake up to reality again, although he was awakened together with the other animals of the wilderness by the steaming dawn. Life was a green whirl of leaves, branches, shrubs, occasionally a flash of sunlight. Life was an endless, uniform continuity of swinging, falling, struggling, with ringing, piercing screeches, and long red stillnesses of chewing, swallowing, sighing, dozing.

Yet there was something else in life that yearned for gratification, a dark urge, that wandered among the trees sometimes: the longing for a friend, a companion, another life that was not hostile. A warm, soft wriggling that would not end in screeches and swallowing; a body, not to be devoured but caressed. Life was a timeless, swinging journey that seemed aimless, but was urged on by that yearning for a friend, a companion, a gay, gentle game, a scent. A scent in the dusk. The scent of blossoms in blue-black hair. He searched—swinging, falling, killing, dozing, timelessly —for that scent, that tender look of laughing eyes, that welcoming softness, that surrender, that ultimate rest. Sometimes behind that urge something shimmered; a vague consciousness of a reality other than this one, other than this timeless swinging through patches of green light and shade. But it was vague, and sad: a dream remembered; it vanished in the heat of the chase, the searching for the beckoning, fleeing, hiding happiness, for the kiss instead of the bite, the embrace instead of the strangulation, the sleep with a trusting body warmly in the arms, instead of the sighing, the scratching, the stretching and the yawning, the slow smacking of the lips and the sad, wandering look of loneliness.

Then, suddenly one day, a great rustling approached in the forest. It interrupted the tearing of soft warm flesh on the swampy ground; it chased him into the tree; it disturbed the regularity, the security, the familiar half sleep of ages. It hacked and crashed, rustled and coughed; it tunneled, nibbling, through the restless green.

Then it broke through the shrubs and stood still under the tree. It sniffed, it peered, it listened; it saw the carcass of the boar in the ferns and waddled toward it on little bowlegs. It bent over the boar and looked up into the tree. It was a naked brown child with a sparkling bangle between its thighs.

The sight of the child unleashed a wild viciousness, a fearful hatred. The hatred made the hands claw slowly round the sleek roundness of a branch; it made the body swing soundlessly in emptiness; it made the muscles tense and slacken for the fall.

It was the fall that always ended in the squealing struggle, the rolling and crashing down and rolling again, with the shrieks turning into screeches, to end with the bite, the gnaw, the tear, the chewing. Now it ended with a crash on the empty ground; the sparkle between the thighs of the child flitted aside; and a terrible, paralyzing pain bit into the grip that had never missed. Then something rustled, creaked, crackled in the wilderness, a voice cried a sound that suddenly disturbed the sad dream beyond the horizon of consciousness.

"Tuan!" the voice cried, "Tuan! Tuan!"

He tried, snarling, to lift himself out of the ferns; but the pain paralyzed his arm, and blood ran warm down his skin, down his elbow. Then he saw something sparkle in the ferns: the bangle between the thighs of the child. He stared at it, and out of the dream beyond the horizon rose sounds. Mysterious sounds. Words. *Palmes de l'Académie.*

While he lay staring at the silver medal, giddy with pain and awakening, the undergrowth swayed and shook. He looked up and saw a gigantic white shape wade toward him through the twilight, a white giant with a beard, a gun in his fist.

The sight of the giant brought back a vague memory of paradise before the fall of man. The sad dream became, for one second, reality once more.

The child was not a child, it was a dwarf. The giant in the twilight was Brits-Jansen. Now it would happen; now would happen to him what had happened to Frolick: he would be shot down as a last deed of friendship by an old companion. He stood up to his full height, laughing, yet with tears hot in his eyes, and said, as a powerless joke of courage to God, "*Bach.*"

The giant approached a few crackling steps, but, instead of raising his gun, the giant's fist swung up and hit him, like a sledge-hammer, under his jaw.

As the world exploded in a cloud of destruction, he realized the mistake, the great sin of his life.

I should have knocked Frolick down. I am a murderer.

Then he collapsed, and fell into eternal damnation.

CHAPTER FIFTEEN

WHEN Brits-Jansen saw the boy get up and go into the hut with the old Salvationist, he lowered himself incredulously into the deck-chair on the verandah and crashed through it with a tearing noise and a curse of alarm.

He scrambled to his feet and flung the wreckage of the chair over the balustrade into the clearing; then he sat down on the steps and stared at the butterflies that danced over the flower bed. The smoke of the kitchen fire, still glowing from the night before, floated in a long flat wraith over the clearing and the flowers; the butterflies fluttered searching above the smoke, lowered themselves cautiously, swirled upward in alarm once more and disconsolately danced off to the edge of the forest. He shook his head violently, as if to wake himself up, and muttered, "I'll be damned!" For old Ganwitz had been right.

He hardly remembered Ganwitz: a shy, humorless sourpuss who had never joined in the wild parties of those first years of the Service. After those first twilit years, they had never met again, but he had come across his name occasionally in reports later. When Annema told him in Manokwari about the boy's predecessor in Mamawi, the name of Ganwitz had provoked no image, only a thought: another one dead.

Years ago, Annema had been his assistant for a while, like almost every doctor in the service by now. When they met again on his visit to Manokwari, they fell back into their old relationship, despite the fact that, in the meantime, the little man had been promoted and was now officially his chief. Had Annema not become his assistant again at the first sight of his beard, he would never have been able to make off with a prahu and escort for a joy ride to Mamawi. But Dr. Annema had not uttered a squeak of protest; he had fallen over himself to provide a prahu, rations, an escort and even gave him his own bed for the four days he lived under his roof. He also allowed him, acme of hospitality, to chase that toad of the military police off his verandah with the thundering question, "Well, major? Waiting for another minister?" The major, with haunted eyes, recoiled into the night from which he had sprung thirstily, and he did not set eyes on the windbag again until the latter appeared on the jetty with six maggoty Madurese, when his prahu was about to sail. The Madurese seemed to be intended as an escort to protect him from the Papuans and that made him laugh so much that the major took shelter behind the ranks. "Regulations are . . ." the red face quacked, safe behind the hats; and he climbed back onto the jetty, unable to resist the temptation. "If you come out from behind there," he said, "I'll show you where to put the regulations."

The major did not budge, but let himself be soothed by Annema who, standing on tiptoe, whispered in his ear. "As you like," he said in the end, grudgingly. "I'm only doing my duty."

Later, of course, he regretted it. For, when he arrived off Poelau Japen, he met Bevers in his prahu, listened, frowning, to the story of Outpost Mamawi and the boy's condition, and wished he had taken those Madurese. Now he was forced to swindle Bevers out of his own escort and that was no easy matter, for Bevers was an old hand, as hard as nails, one of those who did not care how many totoks were about to be slaughtered by the Papuans in the forest. He had warned the totok and suggested he come back with him, the totok had told him to go to hell, so he saw no reason why he should strip himself of his escort just to . . .

The fact that he let him sail away with his escort in the end with no more than a curse, proved that Bevers had a bad conscience. He knew very well that he should have used his authority and dragged the boy on board his prahu by his ears. But Bevers was a fat, lazy bastard and had taken the easy way out, like Pontius Pilate; now he let him go without protest and even waved good-by before he vanished in the sunset.

Bevers's information had been alarming. If it was indeed true that the boy had walked into a trap baited with village idiots and was about to get an attack of malaria, then things did not look bright. The village idiots were not so serious; he himself had been met several times by a bevy of half-wits set onto him by some philosopher in the forest; they were easy enough to deal with for a man with a sense of humor. The malaria was more serious; even without fever a totok would have enough trouble to remain on his feet once the natives started to play at ghosts in bed sheets, and wound up their bump-and-tinkle sets. With

a fever, the boy would have a hard time of it in the wilderness, surrounded by dancing demons, grimacing bogymen and caroling yodelers
in the forest. He might go mataglap, and once a white man started to
run amok it was a hundred times worse than when a native did so. If
that white man happened to be your own adopted son, whom you had
chased into that jungle yourself, then the idea became even grimmer.
It was his doing that had sent the boy there, to collect material on
frambesia. When he had first heard of it he was delighted, as it proved
that the boy had fallen in love with leprosy; now he could pull the
hairs out of his head.

While the prahu foamed along the coast, his brooding visions of the
boy in that outpost became more and more sinister. He saw him rape
Papuan wenches, saber down half-wits and put an end to himself in a
delirium; he saw him stand ready with hordes of armed natives, gun
in his fist, waiting for the prahu, to receive it with murder and rebellion.

That last vision was not so silly. The charade with the village idiots
was usually the beginning of a process of assimilation, during which
the natives incited their victims to insubordination, mutiny, and finally
fratricide, a sort of romantic holy war. Should they succeed, the whole
coast from Hollandia to Cape d'Urville might burst into flames. When
the prahu approached Mamawi, he hid his escort underneath sails and
mats, their guns held in readiness; if the boy had indeed gone mataglap, he
would react unfavorably at the sight of a platoon of armed Madurese.

As they rounded the cape and sailed up the creek his fears seemed
justified, for there was no sound of drums. The forest was as still as death.
That was uncanny. Either the post had indeed been pacified, or else they
stood ready in their hundreds to beat the bejesus out of him. But when
he caught sight of the settlement at the far end of the creek, the first thing
he noticed was a flag. And when he moored at the jetty and heaved
himself ashore, he saw, behind the clearing with the flagpole, a neatly
kept railway carriage with a couple of tidy outbuildings; in the corner of
the clearing was a kitchen and at the foot of the flagpole a flower bed
with gay colors. But the settlement was deserted.

That suggested another explanation for the silence of the drums: the
boy, crazed by fever and hocus-pocus, might have wandered into the
jungle; in that case the black vermin would, of course, have sneaked
after him. There was a malignant atmosphere about the deserted settlement, something purringly vicious; the only one that crowed with

delight as he gamboled ashore was that sonofabitch, Stegomyia. During their journey along the coast of his native land, the dwarf had waxed more and more sentimental; now that he could at last kiss his mother earth he did so, leaping like a frog, turning somersaults, rolling on the ground as if stung by a hornet. The irritating thing about this performance was that it was pure make-believe; a pygmy did not react to his motherland like a German in leather shorts. He had got the idea of this ritual from a film they had seen together in Surabaya, *Mutter Deutschland* starring Harry Piel.

He entered the railway carriage, revolver in hand, while Stegomyia carried on behind him, picking flowers from the bed, prancing on his little bowlegs and throwing kisses at the forest, as Harry Piel had done at the stepped gables of Peenemünde. Inside the hut, everything was neat and tidy; but the bed had not been slept in recently, for an animal had nested in it, and animals did not nest in beds while the human scent remained. On the table lay an open book.

So I decided to apply for 2 X Salv., and 3 X shag; the inspection prahu ...
He leafed through the book, and found the first part was written in a different hand.

Friday, January 19. A moment ago, I watched the prahu with the soldiers vanish around the cape and now I am alone in Mamawi. The crazy carriage looks almost cozy now. . . .

"Heimat! Heimat!" a tame crow's voice squawked on the verandah. He bellowed, "Shut up! Tea!" and started to read.

He read until darkness fell. By then, the dwarf had made tea, cooked a meal, washed up, poured out beer and finally forgotten his Heimat for his fleas. He lit the lamp and read on; when at last he sat smoking a pipe behind the mosquito curtain, he was certain of it. The boy had vanished in the wilderness. That was not so good. To find him would be one hell of a job. There was no guide, nobody who knew the district; Stegomyia, despite his antics, knew as much about this jungle as Harry Piel. Yet Stegomyia had useful canine qualities: he smelled a white man a mile away, and could follow a trail with his nose and his little black beady eyes close to the ground; he smelled and saw many more things in the wilderness than his master did with his pipe and his steel-rimmed spectacles. He asked, "How long ago did the tuan leave this hut?" and Stegomyia, catching fleas, answered, "Sepulu."

"How do you know it's ten days and not a fortnight or three weeks?"

"Poros. Dapur."

Well, well, the ashes in the kitchen. That dachshund stuck his nose into everything, got to know everything, and stayed stupid. "Why didn't you say so before?" he asked, unreasonably.

"Guna-guna," said Stegomyia.

That was unexpected. The pygmy had never used that word before. It did not seem to terrify him unduly, for he went on flea hunting without looking up; for all the emotion he showed he might as well have replied, "the grocer." Ganwitz too had used that word in his diary, and infected the boy with it. The boy had dug up an egg underneath the steps to the verandah and thrown it into the jungle with two bottles of perfectly good whisky, before he had started to leap around a fire in his bare bottom and catch malaria. Guna-guna was one of those things with which he had no patience as a man of science; but as a fat frightened body in the darkness it terrified the wits out of him. During his years in the Far East he had not given it much attention but often felt its fear; P.G. had always taken care of it. Now here sat a dwarf who calmly said, "Guna-guna," while inspecting his armpits.

The following morning, he told Stegomyia to furnish proofs of his statement, and the pygmy took him round the camp. True enough: on the trees, the posts of the balustrade, on the cross of the double grave even, small hieroglyphics had been carved, senseless squiggles like the doodlings of a child. If that was guna-guna he would not worry unduly. Ganwitz had written, *Only holiness will work against this black plague;* before trying holiness, he would have a go with rat poison. For the time being, however, his first task was to find the boy in the wilderness.

The next day they set out, with four soldiers. The rest of the escort stayed behind in Mamawi to guard the prahu. They had advanced only half a day into the jungle when Stegomyia said, "Dekat"—near. That was odd; the dwarf himself had said that the boy had left ten days before. From then on they came across odd traces: carcasses of wild boar, golden with flies, at the foot of trees; the wounds of a parang on the green wood of the undergrowth, the remains of a hacked trail. It was a crazy trail: it circled round in narrowing rings, crossed itself, and led in an arc to a pool in the forest, at a shot's distance from the camp. In the pool floated something white: a sheet of paper. He sent Stegomyia to fetch it; when it was handed to him he found it had been covered with writing in pencil, which was now illegible. The carcasses of wild boar lay in a ring round the pool, they must have been attacked at dusk when they came out of the jungle to drink. But when he looked at one closely he saw the remains of a rattan rope round one of the legs; the boars had been attached to those trees as bait. Then Stegomyia suddenly cried, "Tuan, tuan," in the jungle. He broke through the undergrowth and heard a panting struggle; then he found a native lying among the ferns.

It took a moment before he recognized the boy. He was naked, except for the remains of a pair of boots and the rags of a pair of trousers. His eyes were those of a lunatic, animal's eyes leering from a matted beard. His skin was caked with dirt and the sores of scratches showed among the hair; his arm was bleeding from a wound where the dwarf had struck him with his parang. The boy rose, swaying, to his feet, a shimmer of consciousness flickered in his eyes, then he grimaced, swallowed, blew out his cheeks and said, "Ba . . ." But the fleeting consciousness vanished, and was replaced once more by the panic of the cornered animal. He saw him tense his muscles to leap at his throat, and he knocked him down with a right hook, harder than he intended. It was as if the colossal punch turned the boy back into a human being for one second; his moronic grin faded before a dumb amazement, then a deep human horror dawned in those eyes, a terrible childish sorrow, before he collapsed among the ferns with a rustling thud. He would not forget that moment as long as he lived.

He had the poor chap carried to the hut, unconscious—an unconsciousness that seemed healthy in the morning, rather long by the afternoon and alarming at night. He gave him an injection, tried to feed him P.G., tried everything to bring him round, but in vain. The boy had vanished in an impenetrable night.

He watched by the side of his cot in the railway carriage all through the night; throughout the next day and the night that followed. By then, the boy's pulse felt as weak as a bird's heart through the callous of his finger. Then Stegomyia said, "Guna-guna," with grinning satisfaction, and he started to read those diaries again.

Only holiness, wrote Ganwitz, *will work against this black plague.* He had tried everything in his portable medicine box and, bar holiness, there seemed to be only one solution left: back to civilization, with the unconscious boy on a stretcher, and deliver him into the hands of the psychiatrists in Batavia. That prospect decided him. He would override prejudice, and follow Ganwitz's advice. He sent the prahu with the corporal and four soldiers to Wareni, the nearest settlement, with two telegrams: one for

Willem: *Zorgdrager dying, you only hope, come soonest via Head of Service Batavia,* and one for the little runt Kramer, *Zorgdrager mataglap permanent coma diagnosis gunaguna know it is bullshit but give Waterreus Salvation Army facilities for coming Wareni planewise if costs prohibitive rob my pension regards.*

The prahu left, and it seemed a relief that a decision had been made; yet then and there began the most lugubrious week of his life—alone with four terrified Madurese and a pygmy in a haunted railway carriage in the wilderness; a ghostly hut full of secret rustlings, soft knockings, lispings, hummings and the heartbeat of distant drums, with an unconscious boy dying in trembling lamplight. Never before had he felt such enmity in the jungle; every sound seemed an explosion of hatred, every rustle, crack, squawk or snap in that stillness seemed to emanate from one gigantic living being, watching them, holding its breath, restraining itself from betraying its presence in the mounting fury of its hatred, while it circled slowly and noiselessly around the defenseless railway carriage that cowered in the shrubs. In the end even the barely breathing, unconscious boy seemed to be listening to the silent waiting enemy. It might be loneliness, boredom, anxiety about the boy; whatever it might be, he began to understand how the boy had gone mataglap. The tension became so unbearable that, in the end, he felt like drawing that circle in the sand, slowly, slowly, as he had watched so many natives do before leaping up, shrieking, to throw themselves upon their imaginary enemy, the jungle.

After a couple of days even the pygmy began to droop. At first, he had made tea and cooked the meal in the kitchen on the edge of the clearing with apelike indifference to all supernatural goings-on. But on the second day he used the Primus in the hut; on the third he refused to leave the hut altogether, even to go to the latrine, so he found himself forced to throw him out onto the verandah like a puppy, the moment he noticed him squatting in a corner with sanctimonious eyes. The first night the Madurese slept underneath their own bivouac shelter on the edge of the creek; the second they carried their mats to the verandah; the third they joined him in the hut. The result was unexpected, as he had never believed in familiarity with the dark brother of the Equator: the concentration of their collective human intelligence in that iron box seemed to give him a sort of protection against the panting hatred of the night. They forgot the difference in their worlds and discovered their common humanity in the face of the supernatural menace of the wilderness. For had the Papuans wandered near the camp, had their drums rolled in the caverns of the forest, they would have prepared themselves with a sigh of relief for a fight between men. But the drums hummed only rarely, and so far away that their rolling seemed a sound of the wilderness itself, a grunting stripped of humanity, part of the slow encirclement of that paralyzing, venomous hatred.

The fourth night they did not sleep. Without betraying that they were consciously doing so, they helped one another to remain awake. For all shared a prehistoric fear: that the demons of the wilderness would pounce upon them and garrote them the moment they let the light of their humanity be hooded by their closed eyelids. They started by sighing on their mats, scratching, coughing, smacking their lips, tossing and turning, slapping the bare skin of their thighs and their arms, as if to swat a mosquito. They had left the lamp burning low, a blue twilight in the night; in the heart of darkness he turned it up and let it blaze, shrill and yellow. They rolled up their mats and started to throw dice while he sat leafing through the diaries once more at the table. After half an hour, he joined them in their game; and at first he won because he cheated. Then he lost because, as his fear deepened, he became concerned that God should feel kindly disposed toward him. But the game soon lost its attraction, for every time the dice clattered and rolled the wilderness seemed to profit from those small noises by creeping a step nearer outside. In the end, they just sat, leaning against the wall and the table, listening with their eyes glistening in the lamplight. The harder they listened and the more silent they became, the more they heard: strange flutelike warblings wandered through the night, a huge, panting breath seemed to heave close by, as if a colossal body lay just behind the carriage, its ear to the wall. The distant drums pulsated so regularly in that silence that, at last, he realized it was his own heart. The panting behind the thin partition might be that of the dying boy, whose breath came almost inaudibly, but seemed to reverberate in the stillness of their listening.

The fifth night, this strange unison into one silent family round the boy's deathbed became so strong that it brought him closer to the natives and the pygmy than he had ever felt since his arrival in the Far East. Never had he been so conscious of their common humanity as during that night. The creatures whom for thirty-five years he had submitted to auscultation and percussion, into whose gullets and recta he had peered, whom he had operated on and inspected, suddenly revealed themselves as his brothers that night, without their exchanging a word. He felt closer to them than he had ever felt to anyone; for, with everyone else, he had always remained I, Brits-Jansen; whereas with those silent Madurese and that whimpering pygmy in the railway carriage of Mamawi he suddenly found himself thinking We. He shared his cigarettes with them, and from the tacit way in which they accepted them and handed round the match with the flame, he realized that they felt the same way. The abyss of three centuries vanished during that night watch; he realized how pathetically superior he had felt to these brothers for thirty-five years, and that he was the poorer for it.

But even that feeling of unity, security and brotherhood in the face of the menace of prehistoric evils evaporated on the sixth night as the fear grew fiercer. It grew every hour; in the end he knew: one more night like this and someone will run amok. He expected it to be the corporal, for he had stopped blinking his eyes as he sat staring at the lamp as if hypnotized. That glassy stare in a marble face was the beginning.

The seventh night he put everything ready in case of trouble: a rattan rope, a syringe with scopolamine. At four o'clock in the morning, the corporal got up, quietly, but with an odd, jerky stiffness. At the very moment that he stretched out his hand toward his kris, they all leaped on him. The pygmy rammed himself between his calves like a pig and tripped him over, the others pinioned arms and legs; within three seconds, his thumb slowly pressed home the piston of the syringe. They dragged the panting madman to the verandah, where he lay vomiting in the darkness, retching and groaning, for twenty minutes; then they dragged him back into the hut, where he lay, limp, on his mat, moaning softly. That night he knew: I have lost. Of course those telegrams were nonsense, of course Willem won't come and, if he does come, it will be even worse nonsense. There is nothing for it but to sail back to Manokwari tomorrow, and let the psychiatrists in Batavia take over. At sunrise, he said, calmly, "Muatkan"—load the boat, and discovered how intensely the Madurese had been waiting for that order. Within fifteen minutes, the prahu was loaded, the hut emptied; they lifted the stretcher with the boy— and at that moment, something rustled in the forest, and something black slunk through the green shadows in the crown of a tree. If the boy should ever be carried out of the hut, he would die as Ganwitz and Hugenholtz had died: his body pierced by black arrows. He gave the order to unload again. The pygmy cooked a very bad meal, and they sat down in a circle around the stretcher with the boy, waiting for the night.

But no one spoke a word, and he was overcome by a bleak loneliness, for the brothers had become enemies. He knew that they were waiting for a chance to flee and leave him alone under the spell of the guna-guna, alone and lost beyond hope in the haunted wilderness. Before night fell, he made them pull the prahu ashore, right into the center of the clearing, and after the lamp was lit and they were all gathered together in the railway carriage once more, he sat looking around innocently, but without relaxing for a second. His hands were in his pockets, and in his right-hand pocket was his gun. The boy breathed very weakly, irregularly; they were waiting for his death, and if he did not die within the next twelve hours, there would be fighting in Outpost Mamawi, a crazed outbreak of senseless slaughter, a whole community running amok.

The only one who was with him during those darkest hours, that eternity of listening and waiting, giddy with tension and thirst, was the pygmy. Stegomyia did not long for the security of the open sea, alone in a prahu with four mad Madurese; Stegomyia longed for the nearness of his giant friend, for the reassuring radiation of his body warmth, for the sturdy thumping of his fatherly heart underneath the triple layer of singlet, fat and ribs. Stegomyia crept, during that worst night, closer and closer to him, and for the first time he sniffed the smell of the pygmy with a sentimental nostalgia. He began to get weird thoughts, as he sat listening and waiting in the deepening night. He saw himself bargain with Saint Peter for admission of the pygmy into the hereafter. He saw them pass together through gates of gilded marzipan, with in the distance Christmas mangers full of sugar animals on cotton-wool clouds. He saw himself and Stegomyia enter the Colonial Club in The Hague, the dwarf in a miniature dinner jacket and top hat, like Coba the Chimpanzee in the children's zoo in Amsterdam. He saw himself on a raft in the Pacific with an oar for a mast and his singlet for a flag of distress, and Stegomyia fishing, with fleas as bait. He thought for the first time about the pygmy's mother, and saw her hug the mouse-small infant and feed it with a fountain-pen filler. He got so dizzy with the effort of keeping his eyes open, holding his breath to listen, feeling his buttocks go numb, sweating almost audibly in the hot teeming night, that he felt with tears of relief the bites of the first fleas received from Stegomyia in his trembling intimacy. He motioned to the pygmy to catch them; during the next half hour, he sat, his burning eyes wide open, frowning, grinning and giggling while tiny hands crawled and scurried up and down his back, round his waist and sharp little nails bit here and there like a bird's beak. But in the end even that no longer helped to keep the sleep at bay. A couple more hours, one more hour, and he would sag aside, turn turtle in sleep, snoring, to wake up and find the Madurese gone.

As Stegomyia's flea hunting no longer had any effect, he fought his battle with sleep by standing up. He stood for hours, swaying, snorting, his head bent under the low ceiling, while the Madurese sat motionlessly waiting. When at long last the sun rose, he staggered outside, the pygmy at his heels, shuffled across the clearing toward the jetty, sat down at the end with his legs dangling over the edge and then, with the sigh of a dying bullock, he slumped on his back, asleep. He was awakened by splashing, leaped to his feet, bellowing, "Brenti, brenti, kembali traperduli!" and the prahu came sailing back obediently, its sail hanging limp in the windless air. He was trying to work out in his mind how the double-crossing bastards had managed to drag the boat into the water without waking him up, when he saw a hand wave at him. A white hand. Then a face smiled and nodded; a white face. Willem.

The arrival of the old Salvationist in Post Mamawi was unforgettable in its normalcy. He climbed ashore, said, "How are you, brother?" and shook his hand, then he looked around at the railway carriage, the flower bed, the flag and the pygmy with cheerful kindness and said, "What a charming spot."

A charming spot. It almost made him burst into tears with relief, tenderness and nerves. Then the old man asked, "What can I do for you?"

"Nothing," he said, stupidly. "Only, I thought perhaps you could pray a bit for the boy or something. I believe he is—well—bewitched."

Willem looked at him in surprise with his white old man's eyes and said, "Fancy."

He led the way toward the hut. The Madurese, asleep on the floor, woke up with a start and the old man wished them a good morning. Then he bent over the stretcher with the boy, put his hand on his forehead and the boy moved.

That movement, at that moment, was so uncanny, after all those days and nights of still unconsciousness on that stretcher, that everyone stood gaping at the boy as if they could not believe their eyes. The pygmy, the corporal, the soldiers, he himself, they gaped at the sleeping boy as at a miracle; Willem looked round, puzzled, and asked, "What would you like me to do?"

He put his hands on those thin shoulders and said, "That boy, Willem, has been lying in a coma for a week. I have done everything I could, but I could not bring him back to life. Yet the moment you put your hand on his forehead, he moves!"

"Oh," Willem said, "but what . . ."

"That boy, Willem," he said, urgently, "is possessed by a devil. I have asked you to come because—because I wanted to try everything to save him, even nonsense. But now I know it is not nonsense, now I believe, I am certain that if you stay and pray for that boy, he has a chance."

"But I am not a faith healer; I . . ."

"Willem," he said, "for thirty years I tried to save Betsy, and I did not succeed. Try to save that boy for me, try for just one night, and . . ." And then he stopped in embarrassment.

Willem knelt by the side of the stretcher. He took the hands of the boy in his, and looked at him. A dead silence fell in the hut, and everyone held his breath, waiting for the magic word. It was a long time before the word came; the old man held the hands of the boy in his and looked at the gray, cavernous face without speaking. No one moved, for he was about to speak the magic word against the guna-guna. But he said nothing; he only held the hands of the boy in his, and looked at him.

When the sun stood in its zenith over Mamawi, he had still said nothing.

When the shadow of the flag had crept up to the verandah, he still held those hands in his, and he had still said nothing.

When the evening mist crept out of the creek toward the hut, and the darkness came out of the forest, he still knelt beside the stretcher, the boy's hand in his, looking at the lifeless face, but the magic word had not been spoken.

When night fell and the dwarf lit the lamp, he still had not moved. He seemed to sleep, staring at the boy's face, but there was a stillness around him that burned with strength.

The Madurese were squatting around him in a circle, waiting for the word, but it did not come. It did not come when the noises of the night began to rustle in the wilderness. It did not come when the flame of the lamp began to twitch, to die. It had not come when all of them, one by one, had fallen asleep. He wanted to remain awake, to go on staring at the white old man, kneeling by that sleeping boy on the stretcher, but, like Peter, he dozed off into a strange, silver sleep and woke up in the blue of the dawn.

The first thing he saw was the empty stretcher, and he closed his eyes again with a feeling of relief; then suddenly, it penetrated to him: the stretcher was empty!

He scrambled to his feet, wide awake, ran outside; on the verandah he had to stop in his tracks so abruptly that he nearly dived down the steps. For there sat the boy, on the steps, his head in his hands, the arm of the old man round his shoulders.

The Madurese, awakened by his exit, gathered silently behind him, peering over his shoulder. He felt Stegomyia press against his knee, until he too stood still and watched. The old man seemed to whisper to the boy, while the sun broke slowly through the rolling clouds of the morning mist. Then Willem stood up, and with him the boy, who staggered away a few steps; then Willem led him back toward the verandah. The Madurese retreated, Stegomyia scurried away, he himself stepped aside with a feeling of awe and took off his helmet as they passed.

When they had vanished inside the hut he slumped in the chair, and though it collapsed with a tearing crash, though he hurled the wreckage over the balustrade, though he stared at the butterflies dancing above the thin flat smoke until his eyes smarted, he did not wake up from his dream. He had seen the truth; old Ganwitz had been right.

«« »»

When Willem Waterreus received the telegram, he went to Batavia at once although he did not understand a word of it. How could he be "the only hope" at a young doctor's deathbed in the wilderness? Only in Batavia, in the office of the Head of the Government Health Service, did he begin to get a notion of what it was all about. A man in shirt sleeves sat behind a table full of telephones at the foot of a chart of the archipelago, and rose to greet him as he came in. "Sorry to have bothered you, Captain," the man said, "but this is really Brits-Jansen's idea. Would you mind going to New Guinea?"

"Why?" he asked.

"Young Zorgdrager has gone mataglap, and I gather that Brits-Jansen hopes your influence may do him good. Cigar? Oh, I'm sorry, of course not. Mind if I light one?"

"No, not at all. Please go ahead. . . ."

He watched the man strike a match, blow the first smoke of his cigar at the fan that whirred overhead, and then the man said, "If I may give you some advice, without knowing the finer points of the case: I would not let myself be influenced by—how shall I say?—atmospheric conditions. Do you believe in black magic?"

He smiled, despite his uneasiness. "No," he answered, "I don't believe in black magic."

"That's what I thought," said the man, "hence my advice. The trouble with that boy is a bad conscience. If you ask me, he has collapsed in solitude under an exaggerated feeling of guilt. You believe that any sin, however grave it may be, can be forgiven, don't you?"

"Indeed," he replied, "but that doesn't exclude punishment."

"Of course. But, if you ask me, the punishment has been meted out in this case. If I were you, I'd tell that boy that this'll do—I mean: that he has sinned, been punished and mustn't try to be any wiser than Our Lord. A feeling of guilt can also be a form of spiritual pride." He must have looked astonished, for the man smiled and continued, "I don't want to poach on your preserves, sir. You are, after all, a specialist in your own field as I am in mine. But, you see, I've had this boy in front of this table several times, and during my ten years in this office I've known several like him. Son of pious parents, adolescent hatred against everything connected with Christianity, anti-conventional in sexual relationships, emotional crisis with spouse, and then: into the jungle, tail between the legs. The difficulty with those boys is that they will think of their own salvation exclusively, never forget their own souls for anyone else's. Here in the Far East, and certainly in our profession, they all reach crossroads sooner or later, where either they leave their souls to the Almighty and get on with the job, or else distintegrate morally as well as physically into jetsam of the jungle. In the case of this boy Zorgdrager, I would appreciate it if you could help him a bit for he has a good head and might become a really good doctor. Do you follow me?"

"Not quite," he answered, apologetically. "How do you think I can help him?"

"I'm sure, Captain," the man said with a hint of a smile, "that you'll

discover that for yourself the moment you set eyes on your patient. I have
a plane for you to Wareni. You leave in an hour's time."

He was driven to the airport, to arrive that same night in Wareni. A
prahu took him along the coast and, during the voyage, he prayed that
God would give him one, if only one, indication of what was expected of
him. But what God gave him was peace and confidence, and He charged
him with His power, but He did not give him the knowledge of how to
use it.

At last, after a very hot journey, he arrived in a neat little settlement
in the jungle where Brits-Jansen lay asleep on a jetty. He was taken into
a railway carriage transformed into a dwelling and there, on a stretcher,
lay the boy, unconscious, dirty and emaciated, like the prodigal son on the
threshold of his father's house. A deep compassion welled up in him for
that tortured body, that cavernous face, those eyes closed in torment. It
was terribly hot and stifling in the room; it made him dizzy and he did not
understand exactly what Brits-Jansen told him. "Bewitched," he said excitedly. "Moved only when you touched him." For the first time since
Betsy's death, he felt himself overcome by a feeling of insecurity, not
doubt, not fear, but a growing unsureness, as if God had overestimated
him. For he did not understand a word of it, nothing at all; Brits-Jansen
said, "Pray," as if it were a kind of massage, and that made him almost
angry with helplessness. In his bewilderment and his increasing feeling of
insecurity, he knelt by the side of the boy and took his hands in his and
asked God, "Give me an answer," but it was as if he were kneeling alone
with that boy in a dark emptiness, waiting.

The boy was unconscious, and only now as he knelt beside him did
he see how deeply he had sunk. He was almost unrecognizable as the
frightened, perky young sinner he had left behind in that bungalow in
Batavia; this was the prodigal son at his journey's end. The face was
so moving in its utter loneliness that a small warmth of love and comfort
seemed to radiate through his arms into that emaciated body, and then
it was as if God gave the answer. "Child," said God, "I have filled you
with the bounty of my love for more than sixty years. Now give me back
my talent."

It was a strange answer, and he searched the boy's face to see if perhaps
he could find an elucidation of the answer there. And then, perhaps
because it grew cooler in the room and because his thoughts slowly came

to rest, he realized that the boy was slowly sinking backward into the darkness of death; but it seemed as if the compassion penetrating to him through that darkness caused him to hesitate, as if he were groping blindly around him for the thin thread of hope that was being lowered into the mine shaft of his desolation. A prayer formed in his thoughts: "God, let him live." And with that prayer, it was as if a few drops of his own life drained out of him into that tortured body. It frightened him, for it gave him a sensation that he had not known for a long time: fear of death; as if, in exchange for those few drops of hope and life, a few drops of fear of death had flowed back into him. He sat a few moments in doubt and felt an odd animal urge to let go of the boy's hands and retire within his own prayer; but the thought that God had planted in him came back again: *"For sixty years I have filled you with the bounty of my love. Now give me back my talent."* Then he began to understand.

Instead of his receiving an answer for the hundred thousandth time, he must at last provide the answer himself, the answer that God had demanded of His own Son: Here is a human being, one of the countless that are dying at this moment on earth. Are you ready to exchange your life for his? There he lies, a sinner, a weakling, a heathen. I have given you, in my loving-kindness, all the strength, all the love, and all the faith that Betsy attained after a lifetime of dreadful suffering. Now, at the summit of your state of grace, now, when you are about to eke out all you possess to as many human beings as possible for years to come; now I force you to your knees at the side of one worthless human being, and I ask: Are you ready to give it all back to me for the sake of this one? Or is the only answer that you can give to my boundless mercy an abacus, on which you calculate where you can be most useful? Answer, Willem, my child: can it be that the only thing my love has wrought within you is a feeling of being chosen, a human pride? "I have fought for that grace for forty years, I won't sacrifice myself for one black soul, I am worth more than he?" Or do you say: "Father, I understand none of it, but Thy will be done"?

He answered: how do I know that it is Thy will? and it seemed as if a wave of his life gushed from his body into the boy, to pull back a wave of the blackest, deepest despair in its stead.

He wanted to get up, to go outside and come to himself, for this was folly. He was giddy with heat, he was an old man, he was not well in the closeness of this hut, his life was oozing away through his arms. Why had these idiots brought him out of his colony, where hundreds were waiting for his help and his comfort, to throw him on his knees after an exhausting journey at the side of a deathbed, saying, *"Pray!"* as if he were a sort of juggler? But he did not get up; he remained motionless with the boy's hands in his, for somewhere a Voice whispered, "Don't ask, Willem. Answer. No sparrow falls to earth without being called by me; would an old, tired man be kneeling by the deathbed of a boy in the wilderness without being called by me?"

It was the beginning of an interminable, relentless battle between the remnants of his self-love and that Voice from eternity. For it was not a decision, it was a battle, an endless struggle between his fading life force and a mounting fear of death. It seemed as if, in those first hours of indecision, his hands were riveted to the boy's, for when night fell and he battled to get up, he remained nailed to that place of judgment beside the stretcher, by a force that overpowered him.

He became so weak and so terribly afraid at the dripping, dripping, dripping of that mysterious life force from his trembling arms into the panting body in the darkness that he prayed, moaned, implored for help, to Betsy, to all the comrades who had gone before through that dark gate of fear toward their promotion to glory. It seemed as if all the peace, all the equilibrium, all the faith and trust that he had won during his nights of nightmares in the past were taken away from him once more in a new nightmare of teeming hallucinations. All the time, two voices hammered in the background, one calling, "It's folly, imagination, you are working yourself into a frenzy for nothing, nothing at all; it is tiredness, it is the heat, it is ridiculous to squat there with still knees and numbed thighs, smarting eyes and cramped hands; get up! Go away! Put an end to that unworthy performance! Let the boy die, if die he must, pray for his soul, if you have to do something, but get up, get up, don't lower yourself any deeper into that pit full of the demons of your imagination, get up, get up, you are a Christian, not a quack, polluter of God's pure teachings, get up, get up, stop that sentimental adulteration, that vain play-acting as if you were imitating Jesus on the Cross, shame, shame on you, this is not Christianity, this is not written in the Bible, stop desecrating God's Holy Commandments in a stage performance! Get out of here; you idolator, counterfeiter of the truth! God will punish you for this betrayal, for this degradation of all that is holy, get out, you hypocrite, into the darkness, go, go!" But that other voice went on repeating: "Even if everything you can think of to justify your going away were true, *for sixty years I have filled you with the bounty of my love; now give me back my talent."*

Then, toward the end of the night in which he gave away everything that he had ever received, a human shape appeared in the doorway, a silhouette with tangled hair, black against the blue of the dawn. He took it to be one of the soldiers asleep in the hut, who had gone out without his having been aware of it. But, suddenly, the boy started to move. The hands he had held in his, throughout the night, suddenly began to live, tried to free themselves, and the fear that radiated from them was so terrifying that he felt he would faint if he did not get up now. He got up, the boy's hands in his; the boy rose from his stretcher, tried to tear himself away, to flee, but he pulled him gently toward the doorway, and saw that the silhouette was an old native. He said, dizzy with exhaustion, "Excuse me, please." The native drew back and he helped the boy outside, stumbling on the threshold. The native drew back, slowly, as they sat down at the edge of the verandah on the steps and stood staring at them while the boy pressed himself against him, trembling. Then the native drew slowly back, until he vanished in the darkness. There was an almost invisible blueness around them, the very first color of the dawn.

The fresh air revived him for, after sitting on those steps for a while, beside the boy, a lightness overcame him with the dawn, a lighthearted peace, a lightheaded clarity, in which there was one floating, humming thought: God is Love. Whatever might happen, however helpless he might be sitting there now, on those steps, with all his certainties scattered: God is Love. If he had sinned, God is Love. If he had obeyed, God is Love. He said it, a radiant prayer: "God is love, God is love."

The boy started to mumble, incoherently. The man in shirt sleeves in Batavia had told him that he should speak to him; that was why he had come. He should talk with the boy about sin and forgiveness, and the pride of the feeling of guilt. It seemed all rather confused and difficult, but he would do his best. He had never been a good talker, but he would try. He said to the boy, "Come. I believe I can help you," but it did not sound very convincing. He could not help, he was the last person to help; that night he had been punished for the seed of pride that surreptitiously had started to sprout within him. After all those years of hammering and forging and putting him into the fire and taking him out again and hammering him once more, God had at last turned him into the tool He wanted: a good male nurse, an obedient servant, who no longer turned away with revulsion and fright from gruesome wounds. But that was all he was: a male nurse with patience. He would never be a prophet, or a father confessor, or a visionary, or a sage, and if he should ever imagine again that he might be any of those things, he would be punished as he had been that night.

After a while he cautiously helped the boy back into the hut and onto his bed; then he fetched water and a towel and washed him. After he had washed him and settled him down to sleep, he prayed. He folded his hands, drunk with tiredness, and thought: "Forgive me, dear God. I have understood the lesson. I have come to myself and I see now the truth I had lost. I have journeyed three thousand miles to wash a patient, for that is my task until my promotion. I shall wash them, my God, to the glory of Thy name, and in it I shall find my fulfillment."

He fell asleep on a mat in a corner of the hut, a grain on the beach, a drop in the ocean, a star in the sky, one of those he had overheard, in that moment of grace, humming His name.

«‹‹ ›››

At first, Brits-Jansen still doubted that the boy's recovery was genuine; after two days he had to admit it; and after everything he had done to save him this was almost as if he had risen from the dead.

That old Willem was a funny chap: he still had not the faintest notion of what he had done. He was as fussy, kind and guileless as a district nurse; he washed, fed and changed the boy, went for a little stroll round the flagpole with him twice a day, and he would have gone for a nature ramble into the forest if he had not been held back. It had come as a surprise to him to discover that the dear old soul had no idea of what the jungle meant; he had been sitting in his leper colony on that mountain for twenty-five years, and he had as little notion of the jungle as if he had been in a monastery in Holland. But he was very good with patients; the way he looked after that boy was professional. It was as if he considered it a pleasure to wash and rub and slave and mother, and it might well be. Not many patients recovered in Man-Pu-Ko-Chu; it must be quite a satisfaction to him to see one return to life, instead of having to prepare him for the grave.

Not that the boy seemed eager to return to life. He began to stand up, to walk, to eat and to look around him, but he did not speak and his eyes were joyless. It could not be fear of the jungle that haunted him, for he did not even glance at it. It must be a memory, something of which he could not rid himself; his eyes, although they cleared and began to react to the world around him, seemed to be forever gazing at something beyond the horizon of reality. It was high time the creature returned to Java to a sturdy round of the clubs, a rijst-tafel that would put beef into him, and after that a game of billiards, with a flat-footed waiter to keep them supplied with beer. But the tricky part of it was to smuggle him out of here.

For, after that first attempt when he had heard the rustling in the foliage, he was convinced that the old witch doctor would not let his prey escape. A ruse was needed, and he spent two days thinking one out.

On the morning of the third day, he called everyone into the hut and made a whispered speech. The young tuan, he said, was now healthy enough to sail; but the Papuans would certainly try to kill him. Not that they would not get the better of the Papuans in a straight fight, but it was bad for the young tuan's health to make him the prize of a tug-of-war. So they had to be slyer than the Papuans, and he had decided that the slyest thing would be to behave as if the young tuan had died. Presently, when they left the hut, they should put on an act: make a show of sadness and despondency, within reason of course, and take down the flag. Then they should dig a grave by the side of that other one under the trees. In the meantime, the pygmy and he would make a doll out of rags and any stuff they could find, put it on the stretcher covered with the flag, and bury it with full military honors. The young tuan, with blackened face, would form part of the guard of honor in the uniform of one of the soldiers. After the burial, they would go on board the prahus and leave for Manokwari. The Papuans were sure to fall for it as they could not count any further than ten, and they would be out of the creek and into the open sea before the witch doctor had worked it out on his fingers.

The Madurese, who had been on their way for four weeks longer than the normal circuit by now, were game. Stegomyia threw himself onto the verandah, down the steps and into the clearing like Harry Piel after his mother's death, and gave vent to a number of screams that made him call back the little ham, hissing with anger. The only ones who were doubtful about it were the boy and old Willem.

The boy had sat listening to him with a gloomy face, and, when he finished his explanations, looked at him with such morose eyes that he said, "Chin up, young man, or you'll run the risk of being mixed up with the dummy." But the joke fell flat, and old Willem did not understand it at all. Bury a doll? Why? But who would shoot? In this quiet forest? But at least he did not protest; only when he was asked to say a prayer at the graveside for the sake of realism did he get angry. When the whole thing was explained to him once more, he was even more angered by the suggestion that, if he would rather not pray, he might perhaps take off his cap, fold his hands and sing the National Anthem; those Papuans didn't know God from the Queen.

He tried to calm the old man down, as he got really worked up about this innocent stratagem. He was sorry he had brought the subject up, for not only did Willem refuse to pray for a doll or sing the National Anthem with his hands folded, he even began to protest against blackening the boy's face. The boy was ill, the boy should be left alone, the boy . . . And so he saw himself forced, with a feeling of sadness and regret, to ask with a stentorian voice, "Who the hell is the physician here? You or I?" After all, saint or no saint, since the boy had got up Willem had cast himself in the role of nurse and he had never stood for any interference from nurses. Willem fell silent, and devoted himself in a protective, auntlike fashion to the boy; he himself went slowly down to the steps and strode sadly toward the flagpole, his head bent, his helmet in his hands, to haul down the flag. That bugger of a Stegomyia came out of the kitchen with ashes on his head and a sack around his loins; he had changed over from *Mutter Deutschland* to *The Sign of the Cross,* the second feature of that afternoon in the cinema in Surabaya; never had he been rendered a squandered guilder with so much interest.

The Madurese were digging furiously, as if looking for buried treasure. One of them had started making a cross. He returned, grief-stricken, to the hut to roll the rags of the boy's bed into a human shape. There was no mattress, he had used that for Burubi's effigy, poor chap.

The burial took place an hour later. The corporal had a spare uniform with him, and felt guilty enough after his fit of amok to lend it to him. It was a bit short in the sleeves and tight in the crotch, but as long as the boy did not stand in the front rank, he would pass muster. The doll on the stretcher was covered with the flag, and a wreath of flowers produced by Stegomyia; the platoon stood to attention in front of the hut; when the bier was carried out, the corporal hissed a command and they presented arms.

The procession marched, slowly and solemnly, toward the open grave without Willem, who had gone ahead to the prahu. The boy walked out of step and a couple of times he looked as if he would fall on his face with his gun, but at least he got to the grave on his feet instead of on all fours. In the trees, all around them, were furtive rustlings and cracklings; the bastards were waiting up there with their blowpipes and their arrows. He hoped they would take the trouble to dig up the corpse after the prahus had sailed. But when the stretcher was about to be lowered into the grave, he forgot about the Papuans as he spotted the cross. Some realist had painted upon it, with clumsy letters, *Tuan Zorgdrager, R.I.P.*

He looked at the boy, alarmed, for it might well be that he was not well enough yet to appreciate the joke. But the boy stood unmoved among the soldiers, and stared at the cross with stony eyes, his finger on the trigger for the last volley of farewell.

When the doll had been lowered, he took off his helmet and intoned mournfully, "Chin up, young man, a couple more minutes and we'll all be sitting in the prahus making a nice cup of tea. Don't wave that gun about, stand still. Well, I suppose this is about the size of a decent memorial speech. If they want to hear some more, they'll have to wait until some other goddamned idiot turns up to save their goddamned souls. And if you don't stay right where you are, Stegomyia, if you dare make as much as one step toward that grave and start a performance, I'll kick you in. After the volley: close the grave, right about face, and into the prahus like blazes. All set? Well, sleep well, dear friend. Amen."

He signaled to the corporal; a hissed command; the guns took aim at the sky, the parang flashed, and the volley crashed flashing in the stillness, trailing rows of echoes, rolling away in the wilderness. When the soldiers had filled in the grave with enough black earth to make it safe, Stegomyia fell on his knees, sobbing.

The grave was closed and flattened, and the corporal hissed once more. The soldiers formed ranks, turned round smartly and marched toward the jetty. They were minutes full of suspense, for if the Papuans had seen through the ruse, they would show it now. But nothing happened. Minutes later, the prahus sailed down the creek, toward the open sea, and Post Mamawi lay deserted once more behind the reeds, ready for the alang-alang, the ants, the creepers and the snakes.

The last to be seen was the little white jetty, bleached by the sun; then that too vanished in the green and the blue of the jungle and the sky, as the wilderness closed over it.

«« »»

Never before had Willem Waterreus felt so strongly that he was a spectator, witnessing the shaping of a human destiny by God's hand, as during the funeral.

The very first day after the boy had got up, the thought had occurred to him: here all men should stand back in deference, for this is a soul in the grip of God. The boy's eyes were not those of a sick man or of a lunatic or of an exhausted warrior back from the wilderness; these were the eyes with which Moses must have gazed at the first man he encountered on his return from the burning bush.

He had washed him, nursed him, fed him, but he had not said a word to him. He had not tried to comfort him or to soothe him; he had tried to fathom what was happening behind the opaque shields of those gray eyes, that looked almost blind sometimes, blinded by the bush, by the white flame that had hurled Saul from his horse on the road to Damascus. During the following days, the notion had dawned on him that everything happening around the boy was the catharsis of something, as if he had entered a theater just before the final curtain of a tragedy; and that feeling of witnessing the end of a drama was strongest during the burial of that doll.

He watched the boy come back from it and climb on board the prahu, with his blackened carnival face and his stage clothes, stumbling under his gun like Jesus under His cross. When they had sailed, he helped him pull off the clothes, washed him, gave him something to drink and made a bed for him underneath the shelter of palm leaves in the back of the ship, and he did so with a deference and a compassion that a human fate had rarely inspired in him. The boy sat staring back at the creek and the jungle; when the prahus reached the open and started to roll with the swell, he turned away and stretched out on the bed under the shelter, but his eyes were unchanged. It made no difference that he had left the stage of the tragedy now; he was still in the grip of God, blind Saul by the side of the caravan road, Jacob broken in the desert.

He asked himself whether he should intervene now that the final curtain had fallen; whether he might now put a hand on his shoulder in solace, call him back to life, to the future for which he was now inexorably heading, cradled on that bed underneath the palm leaves. But the boy's eyes deterred him.

At sunset, he called the natives together at the foot of the mast as was his custom in the colony. He chose the mast, because there the boy would be able to see him from his bed. The bow of the prahu rose and fell in the glow of the setting sun shimmering on the waves; they seemed to be fleeing from the night across a sea of flames. He had chosen a hymn with which to begin the service, and hoped that it might call forth an echo in that motionless body, that soul shut off from the world.

He started to sing with a steady voice: "*As pants the hart for cooling streams, When heated in the chase . . .*" and, suddenly, he saw the boy raise himself onto his elbows and gaze at him with such horror in his eyes that it chilled him. He sang on, his thin old man's voice quavering between sea and sky, and he realized that God's hand had not let go of the boy yet, that he himself was not a spectator in the drama but an actor, a chessman in a dark and fateful game. The boy lay down again, his head back, as if in unbearable pain; as he sang on, he tried to catch Brits-Jansen's eye, to warn him to go to the boy. But Brits-Jansen did not see him; he sat, his head bent and his beard spread on his chest, leaning against the seat beside his dwarf, and when his head rolled with the swell he understood that he had fallen asleep.

When the first verse of the psalm was at last sung to its end, he opened his Bible. Before he read he closed his eyes for a prayer, in doubt and confusion, but God silenced him; and he read.

"*All this came upon the king Nebuchadnezzar. He walked in the palace of the kingdom of Babylon, spake, and said, Is not this the great Babylon, that I have built for the house of the kingdom by the might of my power, and for the honour of my majesty? While the word was in the king's mouth, there fell a voice from heaven, saying, O king Nebuchadnezzar, to thee it is spoken; The kingdom is departed from thee. And they shall drive thee from men, and thy dwelling shall be with the beasts of the field: they shall make thee to eat grass as oxen, and seven times shall pass over thee, until thou know that the most High ruleth in the kingdom of men, and giveth it to whomsoever he will. The same hour was the thing fulfilled upon Nebuchadnezzar: and he was driven from men and did eat grass as oxen, and his body was wet with the dew of heaven, till his hairs were grown like eagle's feathers, and his nails like birds' claws.*

"And at the end of the days I Nebuchadnezzar lifted up mine eyes unto heaven, and mine understanding returned unto me, and I blessed the most High, and I praised and honoured him that liveth for ever, whose dominion is an everlasting dominion, and his kingdom is from generation to generation. . . . At the same time my reason returned unto me; and for the glory of my kingdom, mine honour and brightness returned unto me; and my counsellors and my lords sought unto me; and I was established in my kingdom, and excellent majesty was added unto me.

"Now I Nebuchadnezzar praise and extol and honour the King of heaven, all whose works are truth, and his ways judgment: and those that walk in pride he is able to abase."

He closed his Bible and looked. The boy had risen to his knees and hidden his face in his hands, and there was something about the still, kneeling figure that made him remember that night in the Salvation Army post, long ago, when he himself had knelt for the first time between the benches.

Overcome with awe and jubilation, he lifted his head and looked up at the sky. The sun sank behind the horizon; the prahu sailed on across a sea of blood, while high above them, in the dome of the sky, the first star broke through the fire of the sunset.

THE END

Set in Linotype Granjon
Format by Robert Cheney
Manufactured by The Haddon Craftsmen, Inc.
Published by HARPER & BROTHERS, *New York*